THE ALBANY CYCLE
Book II

THE ALBANY CYCLE
Book II

Quinn's Book
The Flaming Corsage
Legs

William Kennedy

Scribner

First published in Great Britain by Scribner, 2002
An imprint of Simon & Schuster UK Ltd
A Viacom Company

A portion of *Quinn's Book* first appeared in *Esquire*.
Quotation by Albert Camus on page 5 is used by permission of Alfred A. Knopf, Inc.

*

The author would like to acknowledge with gratitude the support of the MacArthur
Foundation during the years that *Quinn's Book* was being written.

*

'My Mother's Rosary' copyright 1915 by Mills Music, Inc.,
copyright renewed 1942. 'Arrah,-Go-On,
I'm Gonna Go Back to Oregon', copyright 1916 by Mills Music, Inc.,
copyright renewed 1943. Used
by permission. All rights reserved.

1 3 5 7 9 10 8 6 4 2

Simon & Schuster UK Ltd
Africa House
64–78 Kingsway
London WC2B 6AH

Simon & Schuster Australia
Sydney

A CIP catalogue record for this book is available from the British Library

ISBN 0–7432–2103–6

Typeset by Palimpsest Book Production Limited,
Polmont, Stirlingshire
Printed and bound in Great Britain
by The Bath Press, Bath

Contents

Author's Preface

All my novels can be seen as a quest for antecedents – of myself, my family, my world, a quest always personified in one or two individuals who move through columns of time, are shaped or misshapen by social forces of their day, who survive, or not, according to their own capacities for struggle and defiance. Their existence illuminates a world that was, without which I would not, in the same way, inhabit the world that is.

Legs (written before there was any conscious thought of developing a cycle of related novels) was the first manifestation of that ambition just beginning to define itself: a search for something lost, or forgotten, or never known, but which I knew existed. In the case of Jack (Legs) Diamond it was the survival long after his death of the legend of this Prohibition gangster – an odd triumph for a career bootlegger, thief, and killer – through the medium of the American imagination. He was murdered in bed in my city and I worked among men who knew him, who saw him dead, who wrote of his trials and tribulations for the Albany newspapers.

In the late 1960s I began to write a political novel with Diamond as a secondary character, but the discovery of his gaudy infamy demanded he have a book of his own; for that discovery suggested America's need to renew its myths of magnetic evil. Jesse James, Billy the Kid and other wild west outlaws had faded through overexposure in pulp magazines and as movie villains; the cowboy myth shelved; and here in the late 1920s emerged the mythic gangster, who has survived lawless Prohibition, the Mafia's spawn and necrosis, and who now propagates the narco plague. 'Honest to god, Marcus,' Jack Diamond tells his lawyer as he falls through death into myth, 'I really don't think I'm dead.'

Legs was followed by *Billy Phelan's Greatest Game* which has proven to be the crucible for all subsequent novels in the Albany Cycle to date. Katrina Daugherty, an aristocratic beauty who has a love affair with death, and her husband, Edward Daugherty, a successful but ill-starred playwright, have a passionate but disastrous marriage that engenders scandal, tragedy, and violent mystery, all of which were hinted at in *Billy Phelan*; and this marriage beckoned me toward a new work I called *The Flaming Corsage*, which was to include a four-act play of the same name by Edward as part of this turn-of-the-century novel. But I was ready for neither the turn of the century, nor a four-act play, and so I put the project aside for sixteen years until I had written plays of my own and become comfortable with life in Albany as the 19th and 20th centuries blended.

In subsequent years I wrote *Quinn's Book*, which focused on Daniel Quinn, who was ten years old in 1938 in *Billy Phelan*. That was my own age, and I wanted Quinn's odyssey into maturity to illuminate what my generation had experienced. This was almost fatal. I came to resent, then loathe, Quinn's 20th century, and so sent him traveling imaginatively backward to the 19th, thus giving me leeway to tell a story through scenes in alternating centuries, but always with the same Quinn: the antecedent Quinn fusing with and transforming the Quinn of now, and vice-versa. The two Quinns would find themselves enmeshed in ethnic and race wars, in political conspiracies, practicing a new style of journalism, witnessing a new and stridently lustful theater, confronting strife over money, labor, immigrants – forces common to both centuries.

But the method of dual centuries began to override my story with its cleverness and I really had no Quinn in either century, only forces; and so I abandoned the 20th century, turned Quinn into the narrator, and gave him the language that now opens the novel. This proved magical, the flashpoint of a creative act, and for the first time I saw Quinn and his old city, heard him in maturity telling his story as if it were happening for the first time; and so the book could begin.

The order in which the novels in this volume were written was *Legs* first, *Quinn* twelve years later, and the *Corsage* nine years after that. In all I prevailed as judge and jury of time gone, which I always hoped would be the vital principle of time present. This flirtation with time I love, and am bored writing anything that is not this. The links between these individual columns of time have riveted my mind on recognizable change, not only in the people of my stories: their maturing, their triumphs, their failures, as they struggle in ignorance with the forces that shape their acts; but also on the change in time itself, how it lived and died as the people did. Men and women moved through their days believing their folly was high wisdom, unaware their wisdom was high nonsense. Yet in tracking the history of those dead faiths and dead eras, I came to see that the way people clung to their ignorant beliefs was what shaped the conscience of their age. However dead those beliefs are now, they had once elevated men to heroism and bliss, reduced them to cowardice and sorrow.

I see these works as tragicomedies, and I access their history not in order to replay it or revise it, but to inhabit it. The books are meant to be independent works, as different from one another as Jack Diamond was from Daniel Quinn, as Quinn was from Edward Daugherty. And yet they also are, I hope, as kindred as blood, a mosaic of space, a collage of time that will stop only when the man who is writing them stops.

William Kennedy, Albany
April 2002

QUINN'S BOOK

This book is for Dana,
By Herself

Book One

... a man's work is nothing but this slow trek to rediscover, through the detours of art, those two or three great and simple images in whose presence his heart first opened.

— ALBERT CAMUS

A Cataclysm of Love

Albany

Winter & Spring

1849–1850

I, Daniel Quinn, neither the first nor the last of a line of such Quinns, set eyes on Maud the wondrous on a late December day in 1849 on the banks of the river of aristocrats and paupers, just as the great courtesan, Magdalena Colón, also known as La Última, a woman whose presence turned men into spittling, masturbating pigs, boarded a skiff to carry her across the river's icy water from Albany to Greenbush, her first stop en route to the city of Troy, a community of iron, where later that evening she was scheduled to enact, yet again, her role as the lascivious Lais, that fabled prostitute who spurned Demosthenes' gold and yielded without fee to Diogenes, the virtuous, impecunious tub-dweller.

This crossing was vexatious to all logic, for earlier in the day, before the wildness came, she might have crossed far more safely farther north via the dependable, strong-hulled ferry that would have carried her over a narrower and calmer band of the Hudson without incident and deposited her upon the steps of the Troy wharf. But recklessness was far likelier to send the shiver of lust through the spines of men, fire envy in the livers of their wives and daughters, and set tongues to gossipaceous clacking that would pack the hall for La Última's next performance; and so she had advertised in the *Albany Chronicle* that she would pay one hundred dollars, a bloody fortune, to any boatman who would, at four in the afternoon, take her, her luggage, her serving maid, and the child who traveled with her across the river from Albany to Greenbush, where she would board a carriage bound overland to Troy.

Her advertisement appeared at the end of a week's spell of
unseasonably balmy weather. She'd been in Albany five days,
enthralling theatergoers with her acting and dancing, her beauty
and sensual aggression. (Indeed there were some in the city who
blamed her not only for the warm spell but even for the evil and
grief that would befall us all on the day of her leave-taking.) The
balminess had brought on the partial melting of the river's heavy
ice, and had also halted all crossings by sleigh. A sizable channel
opened in the river's center and a few sloops went straightaway
downriver with little trouble. But cutting crosswise into that current
and its ice floes with a skiff was another matter.

The skiffmen had come out in number at the hour specified in
La Última's advertisement and clustered under the Great Albany
Pier with their craft, at rest on the shoreline's ice. But as the
warmth of the day deepened, those wary Albany water rats (I
include my master) were in agreement that the floes' growth in
size and frequency, indeed the whole river's present nature, which
was one of mild flood, argued that skiffs had no function on water
such as this; all agreed, I say, except Carrick, the rotten Scottish
hunchback of syphilitic mien, no longer welcome in the brothels
of Albany, who had reached no such decision and was firm in his
life's role as Albany's undauntable ferryman, ready to carry the
urgent mail, the woeful news, or the intrepid passenger across the
waters during storm or flood, and now the only soul at the pier
willing to transport this plumed cargo to the far shore.

La Última's crossing had attracted such crowds that the bridge
from the Quay Street shore out to the Great Pier (which paralleled
the quay thirty yards from the shore) creaked with the weight of
hundreds as La Última, her maid, and the child arrived in their
carriage. A dozen men on the quay shoved aside the mob of ill-clad
urchins who were vying for the right to carry La Última's trunk
and to escort, hand-by-glove, the grand señora (for she had lived
through three legitimate husbands, plus several hundred lovers).
As she dismounted from the carriage she took command of the
raffish disorder, singled out two muscular men, and gave them
five dollars each (thus ensuring the security of two families, or at

least the slaking of two thirsts, for the ensuing fortnight) to carry
her trunk and hand luggage. She strode ahead of her entourage
straight into the crowd, which parted at her advent to allow her
entry to the steps leading down to the boats. There, standing on the
ice in front of his skiff, Carrick greeted her, scraping obsequiously
and explaining that only he was willing to cross these waters with
her valuable self, prompting La Última to sniff in the direction of
the other boatmen and give us all the flick of her chin in contempt
for our lack of courage.

'It eees a pleasure to meet a rrreal mon,' she said in her
fraudulent, Hispanicized English (she was of Hibernian stock and
spoke the language perfectly). She lifted Carrick's woolen hat and
kissed him on his lumpy forehead as she might a pet piglet, then
handed him, most ostentatiously, the promised one-hundred-dollar
bill. The crowd cheered the hunchback, who flashed his toothless
smile, pocketed the bill, and then gave La Última his hand to help
her into his craft. The child and the maid followed (the maid
in height, facial contours, and hair color being very close to a
duplicate of the actress, it being commonly known that for special
suitors the women dressed like twins). Carrick and his helper then
lifted the skiff's line from its mooring post and pushed off from
the shoreline's ice out onto the water. The boatmen stood up in
the skiff and poled like gondoliers past the end of the Great Pier,
Carrick poking the water ahead of the bow, seeking the floes,
guiding them out of the way with the poling oar. And thus did
the crossing begin and the skiff move out into open water on this
dusky afternoon of high tragedy.

The skiff had reached the center of the river when we saw it
wedge into a floe that would not yield to the prickings of the
poles, saw it go crooked in the current and move slowly downriver
backward, out of the hunchback's control. I could see La Última
tightly gripping the side of the skiff with one hand, holding her hat
with the other. The great, unseasonal feathered and amber plume
in that hat, a match to her amber coat with the beaver collar, is
as indelible in my memory as is the vision of her maid holding
tightly to the child, and of Carrick and his helper poking the ice

with their long sticks, a pair of needles attacking an iceberg, as the boat floundered like a toy.

My master and another boatman, named Duff, immediately shoved off into the water – I was sitting in our craft but not consulted – and we headed out for the rescue, proving, I thought, that virtue needs only a challenge to be awakened from dormancy. But my master was moved for quite another reason, and we were halfway to the trapped boat because of that reason when we saw a large hillock of ice smash into Carrick's craft and stove in its side, causing it to instantly list and take in water. We reached it too late to save Carrick, his helper, or the maid, who were knocked out of the boat when the hillock struck. It was I, however, who reached the child about to go under and hoisted her into our own skiff, while Duff behind me held off the flowing ice to guard my flank in the racy waters. And then my master, John the Brawn, caught the beaver collar of La Última's coat with his boat hook, and with one mighty lift, hauled her and her sodden plume up from the current, alas beyond our help.

'One dead slut,' said my master as he also hooked La Última's floating trunk and lifted that aboard, too, that being the true focus of his concern. The child's countenance was as frigid in the face of death, loss, fright, and strangers as were the river's wicked waters, which were just beginning their avaricious devouring of human life. Not until springtime would the maid and Carrick turn up, sixty miles downriver, locked in grotesque, inverted embrace on the eastern shore (Carrick's pockets turned out), as if they had been out for an orgiastic swim and had died submerged in perversion.

We made our way back to the pier, I full of such fears as might have paralyzed me had I not been in thrall to the vivid young girl who held my hand with the same tenacity a starving wolf might grip with peerless jaws the flank of a vagrant deer. In truth, her grip was more memorable by double than the frigid bite of the river, which would leave me forever with fingers that only the summer sun could ever truly warm.

The crowd had grown ever larger on the bridge as word spread of our rescue effort, and as we moved onto the shore ice with our boat and our salvage, those crescive masses began struggling for greater vantage, shoving rudely among themselves, when suddenly, with a flagitious roar and an agonized whine, the old wooden span collapsed in twain, plunging a hundred or more of our citizens onto and through the fragile ice and into the deadly bath, while another hundred saved themselves with desperation leaps and wild clutchings to the fractured boards and railings; and there ensued then a mad scrambling upward and sideward by that doomed and threatened clot.

Their shrieks were the saddest sounds of my young days and instantly we all moved in our boats to help those we could. We saved about forty and lost we'll never know how many in those first few minutes before the onset of the even greater cataclysm, which, when we perceived it (I say we by way of collecting the common perspective we arrived at in a later and calmer moment), generated in us such fear of the Lord, of nature gone wild, of cosmic, mythic rage against our vulnerable puniness that we were negated as individuals and became as grains of sand, as desiccated leaves. We survived only because we survived. There is no other ascribable reason or logic behind who was saved and who wasn't, any more than there was logic in the way I alone of my family had come through the cholera unscathed.

The torrent came while we were frantically rescuing the drowning hordes from the bridge, roared down upon us from the northern river — a rush of ice like none in Albany had ever seen, even the eldest. It came, they later said, from the Mohawk River, careening with tumbling, tumultuous dudgeon into the Hudson, dislodging more and more of both rivers' heat-weakened blankets of ice, crunching and cracking and pushing more and more of its own fractured surface until, reaching Albany, the glut bedammed itself, clotted the whole transverse of the river's channel with chunks and prisms of ice in a sudden upthrust, a jagged wall built so quickly and with such superb natural engineering that had we not been hauling in the wet and the dead we would have given it the same attention we give an eclipse of the sun, for it was equivalently awesome.

The wall of ice grew from a relatively small, fencelike structure, say five feet high, across the thawed center of the river, continued building upon that fence a pyramid, a mountain, an instant Albany iceberg that never was before and probably never will be again. It rose to what some calculated as the height of ten men. Others said twenty. It grew swiftly upward with boundless force, brilliant chaos, and just as we thought it would never cease to grow, it was struck from within and below by some central power we could neither see nor understand, even now, but which exploded that mountain into a Vesuvius of crystal, showering the shores of both Albany and Greenbush with fragments, wounding an unsuspecting half-dozen people, killing two horses and a pregnant cat on the quay, and loosing a tidal wave that swept every object storehoused on the Great Pier, including barrels of coffee, piles of lumber and staves, and another dozen men, tumbling them into the torrent as if they were the river's own algae, which they would very soon become.

That wave would raise us all, the drowning masses, the handful of salvationists, to its stunning crest, then settle us back into a trough, rocking us on a slowly rising flood tide that would, half an hour after our departure, spill over the quay and crawl into storehouses, and, worse, into the plaster works and lime kiln, there mixing with and slacking the lime into chemical combustion that would set fire to a block of stores along the quay frontage: fire rising out of flood – the gods gone mad.

Because there was such panic, such fear, I focused finally on what was possible for us alone to do: save the child, this orphan of the river, who was shivering and unable to walk when I lifted her out of our skiff onto the shore and led her up the steps to dry ground, knowing, as we threaded our way through clusters of desperation, that this frail creature would die of frozen blood if I did not soon warm her. My master, meanwhile, lifted the corpse of La Última from the skiff and plopped it down on the shore ice, far more concerned with the contents of her trunk than with the disposition of her person. Even as the child and I were saving ourselves from water, John the Brawn, under the eyes of heaven and all the bereft, was hammering at the latch of the trunk with the end of his oar: a vision of how the fear of death easily yields to the power of greed. But the trunk would not yield, and so John turned again to the dead Magdalena Colón, clutched her under his left arm, and, gripping the trunk handle with his right hand, ascended the quay's steps, bumping both the actress's toes and trunk on every step as he came, but rising willfully up from the water to dry turf, a Palaemonic figure bereft of sanity.

On the quay the kin and kith of the lost were loud in their lamentations, while at least twoscore people were still clinging to the far segment of the fractured bridge, some of them failing of purchase and falling through the broken ice, either emerging by splash of will and main strength or vanishing in frozen weakness beneath the rising tide of ice and blood.

John stood the trunk on its end and gave both his hands to the dead Magdalena, lifting her into a semblance of womanly order, however dead, and laying her down again so as to catch his breath and consider the immediate future. He turned his gaze to the child we would soon know to be Maud, and he asked her, 'Have ye family?' Maud only stared at him as an answer, and then he cast an eye at Magdalena.

'Is that one your ma?' he asked, and that roused Maud.

'She was my aunt,' said Maud, 'and vastly superior to Mother as a human being.'

'Where is your dastardly mother?'

'She is with the King.'

'Ah, the King,' said John. 'She's a queen, is she?'

'She's the King's companion,' said Maud.

'And which king might it be that's keen on your ma?'

'The King of Bavaria.'

'Bavaria, a grand little place, so they say. And is the King, like yourself, stopping here in Albany for a bit of a visit?'

'They are both in Bavaria. The King has gone into exile,' said Maud, whose want of childish speech was giving me the image of myself as a tongue-tie, and I being almost fifteen, two years and three months older than she.

'Your auntie's fair croaked and your ma's in bloody exile. So where might your da be, then?'

'My mother always said she didn't know for certain where he was. But she's a liar.'

Just then, with those poor souls who were clutching the bridge's far segment sending up their continuing chorale of dangling doom, and with the living onshore throwing themselves into furies of grief over the dead and the missing, a woman whose husband, or perhaps brother, lay inert on the quay looked at us and recognized the corpse of Magdalena, her amber plume, sodden and bedraggled (but a swatch of autumn nevertheless), still jutting markedly from that dead skull. And that woman then rose up from beside her inert man, let seethe through her teeth a single word – 'Herrrr' – and, following upon this with the maddened and throaty growl of a jungle feline, flew across the space that separated us, pounced upon the courtesan's lifeless body, sank her teeth into that pallid cheek, and came away with a blooded wad of flesh in her mouth, which she savored with a bulging smile and then spat onto the dead actress's chest. Stiffened with loyalty to our corpse, I leaped into the tableau and yanked the toothy bitch by the arm, flinging her aside so that John the Brawn might lift our dead lady out of more harm's way.

John carried her to where a policeman stood guard over the lengthening row of the congealing dead, while other police pressed cabmen and private carriages into hauling the freezing victims to the city's clinic. My master lay the dead woman down, straightened her dress over her legs with a show of modesty I would not have predicted, and gently stroked her hair out of her face with two fingers.

'They mean to eat her like wolves,' said my master to the police officer.

'Move along, don't handle the dead,' the policeman told him.

John tipped his hat and smiled through his light-brown teeth, not one to argue with the law; for indeed John was fugitive from trouble in a dozen towns along the canal, his last excursion with the bottle ending in the destitution of Watervliet's Black Rag saloon, even to the felling of the four pillars that supported the tavern's second-story porch.

We went back for the wardrobe trunk, and only when my hands were full did Maud release her grip on me. She had watched the cannibalizing of her aunt without a word and offered nothing but a mute stare at that supine form, one among many. But as we walked from the edge of the quay with the trunk (I knowing nothing of John's next intentions), Maud halted and said, 'We can't leave my aunt lying there in the cold. It isn't civilized behavior.'

'We'll not leave her,' said John, who hailed a close carriage that was moving toward us. As the driver slowed, John grabbed the reins of the horse. 'We're sore in need of your service,' he told the driver.

'I've orders to do what the police want, them and none other,' retorted the driver.

'You'll succor us or I'll maim your horse and splinter your back-bone,' said my master, and the driver grumbled his comprehension of the priorities. With the cabman's help I put the trunk on his luggage rack and helped Maud into the cab, thinking John would enter with us. But he called to the driver to wait and went back to the quay's edge, returning with the limp form of Magdalena Colón across his outstretched arms. I had a sudden vision of my sister being so carried in from the street by my father, she then dying from the same cholera that would strike both him and my mother within a week, thus setting me on the road toward my rendezvous with John the Brawn. John was a man I thought I knew after my time on the canal under his heavy hand. I even once thought I was rid of him when his rotted canalboat sank in a storm near Utica, and glad I was of it. But I was not rid of him, and as he walked toward me now with the dead woman in his arms, I realized how little I really knew about him, or about any man. I especially could not find a place for the tenderness he displayed in stroking the hair out of La Última's eyes with his two callused fingers.

'Is she dead?' the driver asked him.

'Dead as dead ever gets,' said John. 'A dead slut with a hole in her face.'

And he thrust La Última into the carriage with us, sat her across from Maud, and flopped into the seat opposite mine, holding the corpse upright with his arm around her shoulder. Had she not been so wet they might have been taken for lovers bound for an escapade. Maud had taken my hand as soon as we sat beside each other, and I'd smiled at her. But she had only fired her eyes and turned her head, keeping hold, nevertheless, of my hand.

'Well, Miss, what shall we do with her? Take her up to Congress Hall and auction her off to the politicians? Put her on view at The Museum? Or is hers a Christian body crying for six feet of holy dirt?'

'Mrs Staats will know what to do,' Maud said. 'My aunt was fond of her.'

Maud looked intently at La Última's face, then reached over and touched the dead woman's cheek near where it had been bitten. 'It's so sad,' she said. 'She cared about her face above everything.'

'She had a pretty little face,' said John. 'We couldn't let them have it all.' He stroked around the raw wound with a single finger.

'Did you know her?' asked Maud. 'I never saw you with her.'

'I knew her,' said John. 'Saw her in New York, months ago. She acted, danced, sang. I saw her do her Spider Dance. Now there was a picture. A woman to remember, she was.'

'You would probably want to kiss her. Men always wanted to kiss her.'

'You're a bright-spoken, savvy child,' said John, and he turned his face to La Última, gripped her jaw between the thumb and first finger of his right hand, and kissed the dead woman long and vigorously on the mouth.

'You're a wicked man,' said Maud.

'They've told me that,' said my master, smiling and settling back into his seat. 'But have ye never seen anyone kiss the dead? They all do it.'

16

We'd ridden two blocks off the quay when the carriage driver stopped and called down to us, 'Where do we be goin'?'

We all then looked to Maud, who said staunchly, 'To the home of Mrs Hillegond Staats.'

'Do ye know that place?' John asked the driver.

'There's none in Albany doesn't,' came the ready answer, and the driver sped away toward the Staats mansion, a dwelling place of exalted lives, and a safe harbor as well for certain desperate souls who'd been chilled, like ourselves, by the world's bitter ice.

As we rode, Maud fixed silently on the face of her aunt, occasionally looking to me for solace, or perhaps wisdom of the instant, as if I and not my master were the source of power in this quartet of misfits. Maud took my free hand in her own (we now holding both each other's hands) and whispered to me, 'We must patch her cheek before we bury her, for she'll have no luck in the next world with her face like that.' And then she added after a pause, 'And we must bury her beneath a tree, for she loved trees almost as much as she loved men.'

I nodded my agreement and Maud smiled, the first smile of hers I had ever seen, and I have remembered it all my days. But I knew nothing of patching flesh. With what did you patch it? As to burial, it had not crossed my mind that any portion of the task would ever fall to me. But I had already twice assented to Maud's will, which, I would come to know, was an element very like Roman cement once it had assumed a shape.

Our driver turned onto the carriageway that led to the Staats mansion and called to us that we'd arrived. Maud and I held silence. John the Brawn grumphed and let Magdalena fall sideways, her head striking the carriage wall with a memorable thump; and he said he'd see who was at home.

'You're sure she knew this Staats woman?' he asked Maud.

'We were her guests for two evenings,' said Maud.

John opened the carriage door and the encroaching night reached in for us with a profound chill, a blast of northern air that had dropped the temperature perhaps twenty degrees in as many minutes. As John walked off in the half-darkness our eyes played the night's game and we saw that a half-moon was sending a straying gleam into one of La Última's eyes, now fully open and staring at us.

'Close her eye,' said Maud, gripping my hand as if she felt herself still in the wild river. 'You must never let the dead look at you.'

I dutifully moved the eyelid down over the eye, feeling the flesh soft, pliable, and without warmth, but not yet chilled, somewhat like the loose skin of a chicken dead thirty minutes.

'What can the dead see?' I asked Maud when I'd done her bidding.

'If you look in their eyes you see your fate. And one must never know one's fate if one is to keep sane.'

'I wouldn't mind seeing my fate,' I said, 'for then I'd know how to avoid it.'

'You can't avoid your fate, you goose. That's why they call it your fate.'

I let her have the argument, for I noted that Magdalena's eye was quavering, and I grew fearful. Slowly that same eyelid slid open, back to the point from which I had closed it, and the eye again fixed upon Maud and me. I leaned forward for a look but Maud tugged me back with her urgent bulldog grip. I broke her hold and looked squarely into La Última's eye by the light of the brilliant half-moon, at first seeing the conventional human orb: the maroon iris, the deep-brown pupil, the soft white transparency of the conjunctival membrane striped with the faintest of frigid purple rivers and tributaries. And then in the center of the suddenly luminous pupil I saw a procession of solemn pilgrims moving through a coppice: night it was, but snowing, and as fully bright as this true night that surrounded us. And there was Maud, her hand held by an old woman. There, too, moved John the Brawn, ahead of a figure wrapped in furs. I myself trudged forward alongside a black dog and I sensed that this was the funeral procession of Magdalena, made visible for us by her own dead eye. Her body, however, was not in portage, nor was it anywhere to be seen.

I intended to say nothing of this to Maud, having no wish to confirm the superiority of her mystical knowledge to my own.

But she knew from my steady gaze into that dead eye that I had indeed seen something queer, and so at her earnest tugging of my sleeve I reported the scene to her, was narrating the cortege's route, when the vision abruptly changed to an even darker night, with a ragtag troop of men swarming down a city street and smashing the windows of a newspaper office with stones and clubs. It changed a second time and a young man, his face familiar but to which I could attach no name, emerged from the same building in bright daylight, talking soundlessly but volubly to two men who held him by the arms as they walked. Suddenly he was thrown into a carriage, which swiftly wheeled off behind a matched pair.

I had no time to speak of this to Maud, for John the Brawn opened our own carriage door with a bravissimo shout: 'Out and down with you both. We are welcome guests of the mistress of this grand place.' And when he hauled both of us out, he lifted the trunk off the luggage rack, plucked Magdalena out of the cab, and threw her over his shoulder like a sack of barley. Then, with a dismissing wave to the carriage driver in lieu of a gratuity, he led us up the gravel pathway to the house, dragging the trunk. Maud held me back a few paces and whispered to me in a desperate tone of voice, saying I must always remember she was never going to marry anyone, was never going to grow up to be like her hated mother, or even like her saintly whore of an aunt, and that I must promise to steal her away from this house if it should come to pass that the Staats woman, or some other hateful adult, should try to take charge of her life.

'It's you who have first right to my life,' she told me, 'for it was you who kept me from sliding to the bottom of the river. Will you promise me – promise on your heart's blood – that you'll steal me, whatever the cost?'

Her vehemence took me over, and I swiftly and foolishly promised: I will steal you, if need be, no matter what the cost, no matter how long it takes.

'Now kiss me,' she said, and I kissed her on the cheek, the first female flesh other than my mother's and sister's to ever brush my lips. I also tasted a wisp of her hair and found the whole sensation surprisingly exciting to my mouth and lower intestines.

'Hurry along,' John said to us, and we mounted the steps of the canopied porch to see him with Magdalena slung over his shoulder, standing now beside a strapping woman whose stature seemed not to pair with the wrinkles of her skin: as if she had not shrunk with age but had grown muscular. Her cheeks were rosy coins of paint and from her naked ears dangled earrings that looked very like church bells. She was still formidably handsome despite the wrinkles and the grotesque nature of her adornments, and as we stepped into the first warmth any of us had known in what seemed like an age of icy blasts, she squatted to greet us. This hothouse crone – Hillegond Staats was her name – embraced both Maud and me together with those powerful arms, pulled us to her wrinkled, half-draped, and formidable bosom, which smelled of corn powder and myrrh, and wept rhinoceros tears of gratitude that an adventure of the heart was entering into her life. She said as much in words I cannot precisely recall, for the degree of their welcomeness crowds out their sound and shape in my memory. This giant creature, Hillegond, had us in her power, which was very old power and reeked of money and leisure and exploitation and looked for its deeper meaning in the eyes of madmen, dead whores, and children of the wild river.

'Come in, come in, my frozen dears,' the great crone said to us. John the Brawn shoved the door closed behind us and we stood in that grand entrance hall, dwarfed by the unknown, which billowed crazily through that mansion like the lovely heat that was already warming our souls.

When Hillegond ceased to squeeze the frigidity and the breath out of Maud and me, she shooed us into the care of a black man named Capricorn and a black woman named Matty, both of them slaves in their youth. Capricorn wrapped me in a blanket, took me to the kitchen, sat me in front of the huge gray brick kitchen fireplace, and fed me Dutch soup with apples, potatoes, carrots, and the livers of certain undesignated creatures, unarguably the most important meal of my life, while Matty took Maud elsewhere for a change into dry clothing. Capricorn, who as a freed slave thirty years earlier had been a man of social eminence among Negroes, was kindly toward me without undue deference. Meanwhile, Hillegond, my master, and the residual elements of Magdalena found themselves together in the *Dood Kamer*, or dead chamber, the room set aside in substantial homes of the old Dutch to accommodate death.

Hillegond's house was indeed old Dutch, and substantial. She was born Hillegond Roseboom, daughter of an Albany tavern-keeper of bibulous repute; and it is known that she said farewell to maidenhood at age sixteen (some insist she voyaged out years earlier) by marrying Petrus Staats, son of Volckert Staats, grandson of Jacobus Staats, great-grandson of Dolph Staats, great-great-grandson of Johannes Staats, great-great-great-grandson of Wouter Staats – all of these descended from a pre-Christian or perhaps even a primal Staatsman, though the voluminous family records (initiated by Volckert, preserved by Petrus) trace the family only to the sixteenth century, about the time Holland was declaring itself independent of Spaniards and preparing to shape the New World in the image of Dutch coin.

The first to reach the New World was Wouter Staats, who gained renown as a trader by perfecting counterfeit wampum (polished mussel shells with a hole in the center, strung on a string). Wouter arrived with his wife at Fort Orange, the early name of Albany, in 1638, and in 1642 fathered Johannes, the first born-American Staats, a noble-headed youth who grew up to serve in the militia as an Indian fighter, gaining knowledge of the wilderness and its inhabitants to such a degree that upon leaving the military he entered the fur trade (beaver pelts) and earned the wealth that began the family fortune.

Johannes was everywhere praised for his honesty but suffered the taint of a curious wife, Wilhelma, who worked as a produce trader during Johannes's long absences in quest of furs, and incorrigibly sold her customers spotted oats and blue wheat. Johannes retired Wilhelma when his wealth permitted, and through his charities erased her stain from the family reputation. He also became a zealot of religious liberty, championed the right of Lutherans, Huguenots, and Jews to worship in Albany, and, upon the appearance of Newton's comet, arranged the day of prayer and fasting that was credited with persuading the Diety to banish the dread missile from Albany's skies.

Dolph Staats, eldest of Johannes's six children, was born in 1664, the year English military might sublimated Dutch power without seriously altering the daily life of Albany Dutchmen. Commerce proceeded apace, pigs roamed the streets, and the old burghers in their cocked hats and worsted caps still filled the air of the town with pipe smoke and, as one English visitor noted, with phlegmatic gravity as well. Dolph Staats came to enjoy the energetic English and traded profitably with them, expanding his father's moderate fortune through mercantility, selling the productions of Europe – Bibles and snuffboxes, fiddle strings and China teapots, love ribbons and dictionaries, satinets and shalloons – to his townfolk. His concern with garmenting impelled him to ask the governor of the province to take pity on the ill-clad English soldiers garrisoned in the town, their tatters so advanced that ladies were advised to avert their eyes when passing lest their gaze intersect with the soldiers' private physical portions. It was also Dolph who left the family signature on two stained-glass windows of the old Dutch church: one the family coat of arms in four colors, and, uniquely, the glazened image of a supine infant whose physiognomy combined the blond ringlets and eyebrows of a Dutchified Jesus, with the crossed eyes of Dolph's only son, Jacobus.

Jacobus, as he grew into ascetic adolescence, loathed his father's mercantile life; loathed also the town's wandering pigs, which he saw as an image of fattable Dutch desire. And so he apprenticed himself to his grandfather Johannes, with whom he sat for long hours, listening while the old man curled pipe smoke around his balding pate and recollected his days with canoe, blade, and rifle, abroad in the land of the red maple, the redwing, and the redskin.

Jacobus married Catrina Wessels, the wall-eyed niece of the Patroon, that absentee landlord who by the fourth decade of our own nineteenth century had held for two hundred years, along with successive heirs, an estate of seven hundred thousand acres, an entity so all-encompassing that arguments prevailed as to whether the Patroon's demesne was within the bounds of Fort Orange, or whether Fort Orange trespassed upon the Patroon, and on which some one hundred thousand tenant farmers and lesser vassals paid rent and servitude *in perpetuum;* and while this colonizing was doubtless the great expansionist stroke that created our present world, it was also the cruelest injustice American white men of the New World had ever known, and would precipitate warfare that itself would continue for decades.

The marriage of the wall-eyed Catrina to Jacobus, who remained cross-eyed into adulthood, was a matter of considerable discussion in Albany, and it was speculated they would give birth to children who could look both left and right at the same time they were looking straight ahead. Social conversation with Catrina and Jacobus together was also said to be a nerve-racking experience since one never knew to which of the four eyes one should properly send one's gaze. But the union was blissful, and the Patroon, mindful of the boon to the family in Catrina's marriage to even a mal-orbed primitive, bestowed a wedding gift of land on the couple, whereupon Jacobus immediately moved out from the town, taking with him the hybrid image of himself and Jesus in stained glass, installing it in the cabin he built in his new and personally owned wilderness three miles to the north in the midst of a primeval forest, and leaving his father to fill the hole in the church wall and to make moral amends for his son's profane deed. On his land Jacobus felled timber, burned it in an ashery, extracted lye from the ashes, boiled the lye into black salts, and then sold the salts to the town's only soapmaker for melting into potash.

He built then (this being the mid-1730s) a sawmill alongside the erratic creek that took his name, the Staatskill, a stream with wellsprings in the western plateau beyond the town, and which, at normal flow, coursed placidly eastward toward the river. But the creek was given to flooding after heavy rain, which Jacobus discovered as the water rose over its banks and diluted into uselessness his large holding of black salts. Jacobus thereafter focused his salvation on his sawmill, which he built on the edge of the stream's lone cataract, Staats Falls, where the waters collapsed with great aesthetic gush and spume into an effervescing pool and then ran for an arrogant mile down the slope of Staats Hill to meet the river at a point by the Patroon's Manor House, near where a handful of Irish immigrants in the employ of the Manor were throwing up one humble dwelling after another in what would eventually be called The Colonie.

Catrina bore Jacobus two sons: the elder called Volckert, a pleasant, boring child of surprisingly normal eye structure; the younger an infant boy whose birth brought about Catrina's sudden demise, but who was himself baptized in time to join his sinless mother in the Dutch Reformed parlors of heaven. With the help of Volckert, Jacobus spent the next decade building the earliest frame building of the mansion in which we fugitives of the wild river would find refuge a century later; and he lived there with Volckert in celibate isolation, an irascible, pointy-headed, and spindly terror to the Irish children who spooked his footsteps on his daily walks through the slowly vanishing wilderness on the mansion's periphery.

Then, in his dotage, the old dog Jacobus kicked up his fleas, traded a pint of gin for an Indian squaw named Moonlight of the Evening, who had been a house servant of the Patroon in her adolescence, installed her as mistress of the Staats ur-mansion without the benefit or liability of wedlock, and with that single act translated his own eccentricity into public depravity and his mansion into a house of miscegenational vice. The affront was not only to white purity but also to the red nations of the New World, for Moonlight's eldest brother had been halved by an ax wielded by a white woman he had sought to rape while drunk on white man's rum. The killing of his favorite son undid Taw Ga Saga, the father of Moonlight and a sachem of one of the five Indian Nations; and yet Taw Ga Saga tempered his hatred of whites with an eloquent plea to the Governor of New York, pointing out that when Indians brought beaver skins and other peltry to Albany for sale, the white men first gave the Indians a cup of rum. They did the same when the Indians sat down to sign a bill of sale for a piece of land. And in the end, said Taw Ga Saga, the peltry and the land always went for more rum: 'For it is true, O our father, that our people crave rum after they get one taste of it, and so long as Christians sell it, our people will drink it. We ask our father to order tap on rum barrel to be shut.'

But it was never shut and Taw Ga Saga, ousted from power because of his son's act, took to drink himself, lost all pelts and all land, and finally died in abject disgrace after selling Moonlight of the Evening to Jacobus for the infamous pint of gin.

Jacobus's son Volckert was thirty when Moonlight of the Evening became his unlawful stepmother and he left home the same day, becoming peerlessly Godful in mortification for the family shame and earning the sobriquet Venerable Volckert. The year after she moved in, Moonlight of the Evening bore Jacobus a son, called Amos after the rustic Hebrew prophet. Amos became the first chronicler of the Staats family, keeping voluminous journal

25

notes of his father's and his mother's memories, from the time he entered adolescence. But Amos lived only to the age of sixteen, dying a young hero, the first soldier of the Continental Army to bring the glorious news to Albany that Burgoyne had surrendered and was no longer a threat to the city. Amos's valiant thirty-mile ride was accomplished with a wound that proved fatal, but he was made an immediate legend. The switch with which he had whipped his horse was salvaged by a woman after he dropped it when toppling from his saddle, and she planted it in her front yard on Pearl Street, where it grew into an enormous tree that for several generations was known as Amos's Oak. Jacobus buried the boy under the floorboards of the cabin he himself had built when he settled the land, and placed a marble sarcophagus in the middle of the main room, which had been long empty but was still of sound construction, and into which the sun beamed at morning through the crossed eyes of the Jacobus-Jesus window.

Thrown into despair at the loss of his son, Jacobus brooded for three years, suffered an apoplectic fit in 1780 while chasing a family of brazen Irish squatters off his land, and died of splenetic outrage. Volckert immediately began proceedings to oust Moonlight of the Evening from the Staats mansion, which Jacobus had left to her alone in his will. But the will was flawed and easily tumbled, and Moonlight of the Evening spent her last year of life in the sepulchral Staats cabin, using her son's sarcophagus as a dining table. Volckert had buried Jacobus with as much restraint as was seemly in the Dutch church, and while maneuvering to take over the land and house from Moonlight of the Evening, he also saw to it that the name of Jacobus became anathema in any society that coveted the presence and probity of Venerable Volckert. Within a month Jacobus's name was only on the tongues of cads and vulgarians, and within a year in the most proper social groupings, Jacobus had faded into a shadow figure of doubtful legend, one who, like the silver-tailed shoat and seven-titted cow, may or may never have existed.

Volckert's wife, Joanna, a woman of mindless piety, bore twin daughters, Trynitie and Femmitie, and they, raised in cloying righteousness, wed men of means from the outlands as soon as it was in their power to do so, and moved to New York and Boston, well out of probity's clutch. Volckert's wife also bore him a son, Petrus, who, as we have said, saw fit to wed and woo the bounteous and bawdy Hillegond in yet another reversal of the moral order in the Staats family, which, in matters of sensual predilection, exhibited all the stability of a Bach cadenza.

Petrus, inspired by the mercantile success of his great-grandfather Dolph, whose early investment in an overland stagecoach line had been passed on to Petrus as a legacy, proved to have economic genius in his makeup. He octupled the Staats fortune, becoming Albany's richest man as the new century began. He also proved the most benevolent of all Staatses, and was loved by his contemporaries, who honored him by naming both a short street and a public water pump after him. He branched into hardware, joining the Yankee Lyman Fitzgibbon in an ironworks and foundry, and was also an investor in several canals (including the Erie), which his peers found quixotic, since canals offered stagecoach traffic its principal competition. But Petrus found such thinking benighted, was in time hailed as a pioneer of transport, and was buried beneath a tombstone bearing a carving of a canalboat.

Petrus died in 1835 at age seventy-two, a nobleman of the spirit and the purse, having built a marble mausoleum around the grave of his uncle Amos, the half-breed (who was only two years his elder), and having also transformed the Staats house into a Federal mansion of such vast dimension that travelers came to Albany expressly to see it. His wife, Hillegond, bore him a stillborn daughter and a son, Dirck, who was destined to play a most significant role in my life, and who, at the time of our arrival at the mansion, was in disgrace with his mother, who had turned Dirck's two full-length portraits, painted when he was twelve and nineteen, to the wall. In the years after the death of Petrus, Hillegond had refused all offers of marriage, certain that her knowledge of men, despite her uncountable intimate encounters with them, was seriously bescrewed. Further, she grew certain from a recurring nightmare that should she ever consider a man as a second spouse, he would strangle her in her bed with a ligature. And so, when she imposed her bosom on Maud and me and welcomed us into her life, she was also keeping one wary but wavering eye clearly fixed on the most virile man to have crossed her doorstep in years, my master, John the Brawn.

How virile he, how wavering she, is the matter next at hand, for when I felt myself fully cooked by the fire in Hillegond's kitchen I stood up and found myself (still wrapped in the blanket) face-to-face with Maud, who was dressed most curiously in clothes that had belonged to Hillegond when she was Maud's size. The dress was drabness itself, but Maud was glad of the gift, and I was exuberant, both from the warmth the fire had kindled in my blood vessels and from being reunited with this magical child.

'What do we do now?' she asked me.

'I couldn't say. Perhaps we should find the mistress.'

'She's ever so frightful-looking, but I am fond of her,' said Maud.

Matty, the Negro woman, breezed by and waved us in the direction of the front end of the house, then went about her business in the kitchen. Maud and I stepped gingerly toward the main salon but were caught by the sight of Hillegond's full-body profile standing just inside the door of the *Dood Kamer*, which gave off the foyer. Hillegond was rigid, both her hands gripping the insides of her thighs. We looked past her and saw my master attending to the corpse of Magdalena, which lay supine on the room's catafalquish bed, to which one ascended by climbing two steps. John the Brawn, in shirtsleeves and trousers, was, with notable delicacy, raising the chemise of the dead woman from her knees to her thighs, having already raised and carefully folded her skirt above her waist.

'What is he doing?' Maud asked me in a whisper.

'I can't be sure,' I said, though that was a canard. I knew very well what he was doing, as did Hillegond, who stood wide-eyed as John exposed Magdalena's nether regions and then undid the cincture at his own waist.

'You mustn't look at this,' I said to Maud, and I interposed myself between her and the brazen necrophile. But she shoved me aside rudely and barked in a whisper, 'Get out of my way, you ninny, I've never seen anyone do this before,' which I came to know as Maud's battle cry in her witnessing of this life. And so we squatted in the doorway, unnoticed by the principals in the vivid scene unfolding before us.

John the Brawn climbed aboard Magdalena Colón and began doing to her gelid blossom what I had heard him boast of doing to many dozens of other more warm-blooded specimens. The sight of his gyrations aroused Hillegond to such a degree that she began certain gyrations of her own, uttering soft, guttural noises I associate solely with rut, and which grew louder as her passion intensified. Magdalena looked vapidly toward us as John gave her the fullness of his weight, her one eye still open and staring, her hair fanned out in handsome peacock show on the pillow.

Hillegond's moans came forth with such uncontrolled resonance that when John turned and discovered her pelvic frenzy he pushed himself away from the inert Magdalena and bobbed brazenly toward our hostess, who swooned into a bundle; whereupon my master did to her skirts precisely what he had done to Magdalena's and, with what seemed to me magnified elevation (proving the truth of the adage: fresh comfort, fresh courage), crawled aboard the supine Hillegond and renewed his roostering. This taking of her infernal temperature restored Hillegond to consciousness and she threw her arms around John and yielded herself with a long crescendoing moan that concluded when our lady of the catafalque opened both her eyes and said aloud from the frigid beyond she had been inhabiting, 'Why did you stop doing me?' raising her arms and stupefying us all, not least my master, who backed outward from Hillegond and, with undiminished extension, walked to the unfinished Magdalena, inspected her center (whose visibility she heightened at his approach), and then clambered once again aboard this abused flower, now resurrected from wilt by the sunny friction of joy. The spent Hillegond rose to one elbow and studied the sight as she might the resurrection of Lazarus, her sensual zealousness giving way to a vision of the miraculous. She covered herself and bore witness while my master, having quickly moved beyond amazement, resumed the thumping of his newly sanguinolent slut with vile laughter and swollen vigor, creating a triadic climax, not only in his own member and its hostel, but also in the bite wound of La Última's face, which, as she bent herself upward to John in consummation, began to ooze the blood of her life, demonstrating that she was again at corpuscular flood in every vein and vessel of her being.

When the orgiasts ceased to move they looked pensively into the glut in their own psychic interiors, Maud and myself perfectly invisible to their eyes. But I sensed they would see us soon enough and know by our expressions what we had seen, and I could not be sure what they might do to us for such knowledge. I pulled Maud away and led her to the front parlor, where we sat upon a green velvet sofa very like the color of Maud's eyes in subdued light. I did not know what to say to her about what I felt, but she, never at a loss for comment, announced:

'He is a low beast, and they are both fools for a man. Would you want to do that to me?'

'I think so,' I said, though I had not considered it in such an individualized context.

'I'm not at that stage yet,' said Maud.

'I guess I am,' I said.

'It seems to be very affecting, what happens to one.'

'That's what I've heard.'

'I should have thought you'd have already tested it.'

'I've not had the opportunity,' I said.

'When I'm ready to do it,' Maud said, 'I shall seek you out.'

'I look forward to that,' I said.

We were both utterly calm – a great lie, of course, for the agitation we felt was not only beyond words but would take decades to be sifted of significance. An image recurred for years in Maud's mind of a voluptuous woman giving birth to an infant skeleton; and I, for years, dreamed of a woman who owned bilateral pudenda. We sat on that vernal sofa staring at a primitively painted portrait of a child wearing a white dress with a lace collar, holding a hoop in one hand while her other hand rested on the neck of a gander two-thirds her size.

'I never want to be old,' said Maud. 'I want to be young forever and ever, and then, when I'm of a certain age, I want to be very suddenly dead.'

'You can't be young forever and ever,' I said.

'Yes I can.'

'No you can't.'

'Yes I can.'

'Not anymore,' I said; for ignorant as I was, I knew.

I had never seen anyone return from the dead before Magdalena Colón was resuscitated by love, the same commodity used by the Christ to effect a similar end. I draw no blasphemous parallels between John the Brawn, the amatory instrument, and Jesus; or between Jesus and Magdalena, especially in light of what she reported to us about her deathy interlude. But the power of love is more various and peculiar than we know.

Once out of the orgiastic moment, Magdalena became the cynosure of our curiosity, for what usually follows the enactment of human improbability is the quest for proof it has really occurred. And, indeed, we all craved the gossip of her soul. And so after Magdalena had dressed herself in dry clothing, after John's tucking of cincture, after the smoothing of all skirts and with the dissembling smiles that follow satiety, the adults gathered in the east parlor, where Maud and I were sitting, I amid a personal rapture that intensified with every moment spent in her presence, awash in desire for I knew not what; not, certainly, the simple raising of her skirts in emulation of John the Brawn. Such vulgarity (though I have since learned not to demean it) was insufficient response to my yearnings, which were destined to intensify even further during this singular evening.

Hillegond took maternal control of Magdalena's bite wound, bathing it, bandaging it, sitting the patient close to the fireplace, whose fire Capricorn faithfully stoked. Then we huddled in front of the flames as Magdalena relived for us her time in the underworld.

'When I first died,' Magdalena began, speaking with a dramatic fervor befitting her thespian nature, 'I saw a child looking up at me from the bottom of the river as I was slowly sinking from above. She was a pretty little thing, and she looked like a doll I used to own. I remembered the dress, a blue gingham.'

'Did she speak to you?' Hillegond asked. 'They like to speak, dead children do.'

'She gave me a welcome, is how I'd put it,' said Magdalena.

'I knew it,' said Hillegond.

'"I welcome you," she said, "to the birthplace of dreams, where even dolls live forever."'

'Isn't that just like a child?' said Hillegond.

'Do you mean,' asked Maud, 'that you remember those words, just as the little girl spoke them, and you were both under water?'

'Not only under water,' said Hillegond, 'they were both dead too, weren't you, dear?'

'Well, I think so,' said Magdalena. 'I mean, you never get to hear that sort of thing when you're up and about.'

'Never,' said Hillegond. 'It's a special event, being dead and then coming back. I never thought I'd see it with my own eyes.'

'But here I am,' said Magdalena.

'Here you are,' said Hillegond. 'Aren't you the wonder?'

'Was there anything at the bottom of the river except the child?' asked Maud. 'I should think there'd have been dead fish and lots of muck.'

'Dead fish rise to the top of the water,' I said, expert at last on something.

'I don't remember any muck,' said Magdalena. 'The most I remember is how bright it was. "It ought to be dark at the bottom of the river," I kept saying to myself, but it was like the light of a thousand lamps. It was ever so cozy.'

'Were you in heaven or hell?' Maud asked.

'I really couldn't say, Maudie, but I think it must've been heaven.'

'You in heaven?' said John the Brawn, and he let out a great guffaw. 'That'll be the day, me love. I'll show you how to get to heaven,' and he guffawed again.

'You are too crude for words,' Maud told my master, stamping her foot as she addressed him. 'You are the piggiest man that walks the earth and I hope you rot so awfully that your feet fall off.'

'Now, now, dearie,' said Hillegond. 'He's only making a joke to lighten the subject. Your auntie was dead, you know.'

'I rather doubt it,' said Maud. 'I believe the symptoms of her life vanished, but not life itself.'

'She's a savvy little brat, ain't she?' said John. 'She'll grow up to drive men batty, is what she'll do.'

'I was *very* dead,' said Magdalena. 'Don't tell *me* I wasn't dead. You think I wouldn't know it if I was dead?'

'Of course you wouldn't,' said Maud. 'Nobody knows anything when they're dead.'

'Oh, that's very wrong, child,' said Hillegond. 'All sorts of people come back from the dead to tell what it was like. I've heard of folks who saw dead women with their feet on backwards, and dead dogs climbing trees, and dead men covered with feathers. You mustn't be too smart about the dead, child, or they'll catch you out when you don't expect it. Be friends with the dead is what Hillegond says, and it's served her well.'

'Anyway, I'm glad I'm not dead anymore,' said Magdalena, who saw Hillegond usurping her stage.

'What'll you do now, dear,' asked Hillegond, 'now that you're not dead?'

'Oh, I have plans,' said Magdalena. 'I've got bookings to dance all the way to Buffalo. They'll want me more than ever, now that I've died and come back.'

'You'll want bodyguardin' for certain,' said my master, 'or the crowds'll tear you apart. A strong man's what you'll need.'

'I imagine I will,' said Magdalena, nodding, and when I saw the way Maud looked in that very moment, I knew she felt trapped and that she would soon remind me of my promise to steal her. But before anything of that order could happen, a fierce knock came at the door, and as Hillegond opened the portal to the arctic night, a tall, cadaverish man, his hat and greatcoat covered with snow, stepped across the threshold to utter the single word 'Lunacy.'

'Lunacy?' echoed Hillegond.

'Prisoners,' said the stranger, and he doffed his hat, revealing a thick head of hair, white as the snow that spattered about the foyer when he whacked his hat against his leg. 'Wrap yourself up, Hilly. Your mansion has been defiled by madness and I need help in coping with it.'

The man who brought us this grim news was Will Canaday, one of Albany's most powerful citizens, the founder and editor of the *Albany Chronicle*, a sheet of considerable power and political brash. His newspaper had brought us to this house, for it was in the columns of the *Chronicle* that Magdalena had placed her notice about crossing the river. And now here appeared the owner of those columns, bringing us news not only of the prisoners he had been tracking but also of the ongoing madness of nature and its consequences to all forms of life.

The cold had descended upon the city so suddenly after the flooding of the riverbanks that men were forced to bring their livestock to high ground. Canaday mentioned one man who brought his horse into his front room, and wisely so, for horses tethered untended in water found their legs frozen in the instantaneous ice that rose 'round their bones. Before the night was out, one man in Greenbush would grow furious at his inability to extricate his horse from deep ice and, in watching the horse dying standing up, the man himself would die of a congested brain. Carriages would become ice-locked, birds would freeze to the limbs of trees, and not only ice but fire would ravage the city wildly and indiscriminately. The bonnet of Bridie Conroy, an Irish washerwoman, would catch fire from sparks on the burning quay and Bridie would run crazed into the night, tumbling headlong into a shed full of hay, and igniting what history would call The Great Fire – six hundred buildings, many of them shops, all burned to cinders: five thousand people without lodging from the blaze that would yield its fury only to the heavy fall of snow that was just now beginning.

None of us, not even Will Canaday, knew of this new curse sent down upon Albany by the maddened gods on this day of hellfire and ice, for Bridie Conroy was not yet aflame when Will cast his glance upon our comfort near the fireplace. He spoke to us with such solemn intent that we were all moved outside of ourselves.

'I would not normally recommend that any man, woman, or child look upon what I am about to show to Hillegond,' he said. 'But by all that is holy in this world, I feel that everyone alive should see this sight, so that its vision may endure for as long as we are able to hand it on.'

As if summoned by Mesmer himself, we all slowly arose and wrapped ourselves in heavy garments to fend off the night, and we trekked single file through the new snow into a coppice in what I, from my vantage point at the rear of the column, saw to be the same procession of pilgrims I had witnessed in the once-dead eyeball of Magdalena Colón, even to the presence of Will Canaday's black dog at my heels.

Carrying a torch, Will led the way to where Amos Staats, adolescent hero of the Revolution, lay buried in his marble mausoleum, and where his Indian mother, Moonlight of the Evening, had spent her final days eating meals off his sarcophagus.

Hillegond entered behind Will and John, and she gave a shriek that bespoke the power of this madness Will had invited us to witness. One by one we entered, Maud again clutching me in her passionate way.

What we first saw when we edged around the sarcophagus was a dance of light and shadow from the torch upon an image I could not discern with certainty. In truth, its abnormal position was such that no man would have understood the sight at first glance. What was clear was the head of the hanging man. The light revealed his crooked neck, and the rope around it suspended from a decorative protrusion of marble. But the top half of the corpse was awry, in a way no hanging man's logic would recognize, angled unnaturally, as if he were lying asleep on the very air.

In time our eyes perceived that the dead man's arm was pulled earthward by something unseen, and what lay at the end of that arm proved to be another being in total shadow. Only when Will Canaday moved the torch closer to the tableau did we see the dead arm manacled to the living arm of a Negro, a man in such debilitated condition that he looked more dead than the corpse above him. Yet his eyes were open and staring.

'He's alive,' said Maud.

'It's Joshua,' whispered Hillegond, leaning close to the man.

'It is,' said Will. 'That's why I tracked them.'

'But who is the other?'

'A Swede who spoke no English and whose name I don't know,' said Will, handing me the torch and moving a wooden box to use as a step stool. 'He was driven wild when he lost his wife in a throng at New York. Swindlers put him on a boat to Albany to find her, then abandoned him and took his life savings. Once in Albany, realizing he was lost and in penniless despair, he dove headlong into a well to kill himself, and when a good samaritan pulled him out before he drowned, he brained the samaritan with a club. Constables shut him in prison and he grew ever more demented, screaming constantly of his losses.'

'God save us from madness,' said Magdalena, and she blessed herself with the sign of the cross.

'Only a madman could understand what has happened today in this mad city,' said John the Brawn, his first admission in my hearing that he was not equal to all that passed in front of his face. Will clambered atop the tomb of Amos to cut down the Swede and I noted then that the covering slab of marble atop the tomb was already dislodged from its straight angle. As Will stood on tiptoe to cut the rope his foot moved the slab farther and it fell to the floor, marble onto marble, splitting into four irregular pieces as neatly as might a well-cut diamond. For an instant Will dangled in air, his arm around the dead man's waist. Then, with full awareness of his position, he deftly sliced the rope and, quite agilely for his fifty years, leaped to the floor clutching the corpse, avoiding the violation of Amos's exposed coffin by either his own or the dead Swede's heavy feet.

Certainly our priority now was the rescue of Joshua from his torture: removal of the manacle that was still tearing his flesh. With the dead man's weight it had cut into the bones of Joshua's wrist and hand, and he had lost such blood as would bestow death on most men.

Will and my master tried ways of carrying him so as not to injure him further, but whichever way they lifted, the Negro's pain was compounded. And so I spoke up.

'If each of you support one man, I can walk between them and hold up their arms. That way there won't be any pressure on the wounds of the man called Joshua.'

'That's good thinking, lad,' said Will.

'He's a ready one,' said my master.

'We can't leave the tomb open like that,' Hillegond said. 'I'd be afraid some animal would come in.'

'We'll put boards over it,' said Will.

'I'd be afraid of rodents. No, he's got to come into the house.'

'You want the coffin in the house?' said Will.

'In the *Dood Kamer*,' said Hillegond firmly, and she turned to leave.

'Come, Maudie,' said Magdalena. 'Back to the house.'

'I prefer to go with Daniel,' said Maud, the first time she had pronounced my Christian name. 'I can come to no harm in the company of three men, and I shall carry the torch to show them the way.'

'She has a mind of her own,' said Hillegond, who then took the arm of Magdalena; and with heads bowed against the billowing snow, the two compatriots in lust strode out into the night toward the mansion.

Will led us to a secondary entrance of this enormous house, where we were met by Capricorn, who expected us. We followed him through a long corridor, down two dozen steps to a basement, and then, by the light of Maud's torch and Capricorn's lamp, we walked the length of the enormous cellar to a cavelike room whose existence became obvious only after Joshua moved two foundation timbers, which were, in fact, a door.

We lowered Joshua to a padded pallet that lay ready on the

floor, and the manacles cut again into his wrist, shooting agony even through me. Capricorn squatted beside Joshua to study his condition, then rose and spoke to us.

'I thank you gentlemen, and you, too, Master Daniel,' he said. 'I'll take care of him now.'

He turned back to Joshua, and as he did so, his lamp cast a beam into the deeper region of the cave and I caught sight of three forms, one a female, all Negro, all crouching in the darkness. I gave off a startled grunt and Will saw my surprise.

'Whatever you see, boy,' he said to me, 'you see nothing,' and he shook a finger in my face. 'Nothing.'

I nodded at this and he added, 'I'll join you in a few minutes at the mausoleum to bring in the coffin,' and Maud, John, and I retreated from the cave while Will conferred with Joshua. As we went my master remarked, 'They got themselves a regular nigger factory in there.'

'You mustn't use that word,' said Maud.

'What word might that be?' said John.

'You know what word I mean,' said Maud, 'and if you use it again in my presence, I shall find a hatpin and stick you with it.'

John shut his mouth at that, the first of his many silencings by Maud, and we retraced our steps to the mausoleum. Will eventually enlightened me on Joshua, an intrepid fugitive from Virginia who had escaped from slavery, later returned to Virginia by stealth to free his woman, and on subsequent trips led six other slaves through the night forests to freedom in the North. He had been recently captured near Albany by slave hunters, the quest for him sweetened by a three-hundred-dollar reward, and he was jailed under the federal law that honored the property rights of Southern slaveholders.

News of a fugitive slave's capture reached Will Canaday at the newspaper and he discovered it was Joshua in custody. A conspiracy among antislavers to snatch Joshua away from the law was plotted, but the day's madness intervened yet again: the driver of the carriage transporting the prisoners to a southbound train was struck by a flying prism of ice, and before Will Canaday and his conspirators could intervene, Joshua and the Swede to whom he was manacled took the reins themselves, fled from both captors and liberators, lashing the horses into such furious flight that at one turning both men were thrown off the carriage, whereupon they fled by foot to the sanctuary offered by the mausoleum of Amos Staats, where Will found them. Once inside the tomb, which over the years had become as much a storage shed as a burial site, the Swede decided that death was his destiny. He choked the weakened Joshua out of his lights with a single hand, and then, with a length of rope, hanged himself with great skill and effectiveness, full certain, I conclude, that no horrors of the beyond could match those of this world.

We waited in the mausoleum and Will returned presently. Then we three, two men and a boy, with Maud lighting our way, lifted Amos from what proved not to be his final resting place, carried him up from the earth and into the *Dood Kamer*, which was thereby hosting its second resurrection of the evening, and placed his coffin on the same raised platform from which Magdalena had arisen. The coffin was remarkably clean and dry in spite of its years of burial, and the odor of its occupant's decay had been banished by time.

The entire household, servants included, gathered in front of the coffin when we set it down, witnesses all to sanctity disturbed, a hero encased, though I knew nothing of Amos's history in the Revolution at that moment. The coffin had been hand-hewn by Amos's father, Jacobus, who had also sealed its edges and surfaces with a substance waxen to the touch and which seal I now could see had been broken, an infinitesimally fine crack running the length of coffin where the lid closed.

'I would like to see what he looks like,' Maud said.

'Dead these seventy-odd years, he wouldn't be a pretty sight, child,' said Hillegond, more amused than affrighted by Maud's suggestion. But Maud did not wait for approval. She walked to the coffin and lifted the lid on a stunning sight: Amos in his soldier's cap and uniform, arms crossed on his chest, a warrior's medal over his heart, lying as if asleep. His skin was a gray transparency, the color of exhausted night, the perfection of his death exuding a radiance that awakened swooning sounds in the onlookers.

'He hasn't decayed,' said Will. 'An amazing achievement. It must be the way the coffin was sealed.'

'I always thought corpses rotted from the guts out,' said my master.

I moved alongside Maud, and as naturally as breath itself we intertwined our hands and stared at Amos from the end of his coffin.

'He's so beautiful,' Maud said. We stared together at his beauty until she turned her gaze to my own face. 'And you are beautiful as well,' she said, and she kissed me with her mouth upon my mouth. She kept her mouth there and my arms went 'round her. We kissed under the spell of death's beauty, then stopped kissing to gaze again at Amos.

'Oh my God, look what's happening to him,' said Magdalena. His face had begun to swell: cheeks, forehead, neck, eyelids all rising as might a loaf of leavening bread, a shocking sight from which we could not take our eyes. And then he exploded – his perfection, I suggest, rent by the air of our pernicious age – exploded upward and outward, his hands and face disappearing beneath a great grayish puff of dust tinged with pale blue, a puff that ascended fully six feet above the coffin and spread over us all in a melancholy haze. The dust demarcated the end of something, the final burst of heroism, perhaps, whose like was no longer accessible to our commonplace lives. The sadness of lost glory was implicit, most especially to Maud, who cried as if a demon held her in its jaws. She clutched me, threw her arms about my neck and kissed me again with passion and energy, ground her pelvic center against my own and kissed all of my face with a ferocious gluttony.

She kissed me, she kissed me, and I kissed in return, quite well, too, I thought; for in one sweet instant she had taught me the true purpose of the lips in matters of profound affection. The dust was falling onto our heads and shoulders, the air slowly clearing; and though we did not interrupt our kissing, I could see from my eye's corner that the face of Amos was gone, as were his hands. His chest had collapsed, as had his legs, so that the uniform seemed to have lost its inhabitant entirely, replaced by a skeletal stranger. Having seen this and understood none of it, I returned my eyes to Maud and kissed on until we were pulled apart by angry hands and a wild woman's scream; and I turned to face Magdalena, who slapped me viciously across the cheeks: front of the hand, back of the hand.

'Loutish child,' she yelled.

I forgave Magdalena her anger but I ripped myself away from her and again thrust my face against Maud's, kissing with all my soul until they rent us yet anew. In the frenzy that followed I remember uppermost a remark by Hillegond. 'They are fortunate children,' she said. 'They know love.'

But fortunate was not the word for what was to become of us.

They separated us that night, Maud and me, and we slept in isolation with our newborn love. I made no protest. I had no rights where she was concerned, though I cared nothing at all for rights when it came to her presence in my days. She, contrarily, complained vigorously about her aunt's behavior toward me, argued that I, more than anyone else alive, had the right to her company, for without me she would have been on the river bottom with Magdalena's doll. In outrage over the situation she refused to eat.

I came to this information belatedly, for no one told me what was afoot. Hillegond spoke sweetly but inconsequentially to me, Magdalena was remote and growing more ill, and John the Brawn sold his boat and told me he was done with the river. I asked if that meant I was out of a job and he said, 'We'll see.' He patted my head and said, 'Don't worry, lad. You'll get your crust of bread.'

Magdalena grew so monstrously ill from her wound that she ceased coming to table and remained abed. Feverish, and in hellish pain, she was the belated victim of her attacker's vile mouth. Her room's door was ajar when I once passed it and I peered in to see the wound, having only heard of its festerment second-hand. The bite had swelled into a yellow-and-purplish horror and was oozing a green slime that filled the room with a repellent odor. Hillegond took to burning incense of two kinds in the room: one to keep down the odor, another to ward off the blood devils that threatened Magdalena. But the combination produced a new mélange of smells that was miasmic in its effect on the patient, and so out went the incense, worse grew the stink. The wound was a menacing sight and made me wonder how any of us ever survive our own interior poisons. With ghastly speed the beauteous Magdalena had been transmogrified into a rancid hag, sister death beginning yet again to take residence in her eyes. My brief glances at her satisfied my inquisitiveness, for none but the perverted could have long fastened an eye on that befoulment.

It fell to the Negro servant, Matty, to bathe and dress the wound according to the doctor's instructions. But when the treatment failed of healing, Matty began a treatment of her own: a poultice of herbs, flowers, dried goat dung, minced crickets, and other improbable ingredients, all boiled, strained, reduced to a powder, mixed with the whites of two duck eggs, and then applied to the infection beneath a bandage made from a fresh bedsheet. Within two days healing began. Within a fortnight Magdalena was growing new tissue, which would in time leave only the slightest evidence of what had once prevailed beneath her skin. I saw the miraculous improvement when I eavesdropped on her lecture to Maud about the evils of Maud's fast (which I persuaded Maud to rescind, for my sake as well as her own; for of what value would my love be if it had no object upon which to resplend itself?). I saw the radiant Maud standing attentively by the sickbed and my heart sped.

'How dare you put your life in such jeopardy?' said the angry Magdalena. 'How dare you, when I am so hounded by fate. Clara, my own sweet serving girl, uselessly drowned, my face almost the ruination of us all, for where would any of us be without it? And you, spiteful child, you take it upon yourself to starve your body, your only salvation. Do you think men care for a woman's mind, especially the mind of a wicked twelve-year-old like you? Do you think you can live by your wits alone, with no help from the talents you inherited with your flesh? Do you think that silly canal boy can save you from ruination, when he cannot even save himself? He's a penniless orphan, seeking to steal you away from me with his urchin ways.' (This remark cut me deeply.)

'You fail to see in him the high quality I see,' said Maud (and I recovered immediately from La Última's cut).

'Child,' said the courtesan, 'you have a strong mind, but you are little schooled in the ways of men. And now it is *you* who must take Clara's place as my social companion. It is *you* whom I must dress as I dress myself. It is early for you, but this is an inheritance we must learn to accept.'

'You want me to love men for money?' asked Maud.

'I shall teach you to talk to men, to disarm them of their harsh moods, to entice them into sweetness, to pleasure them. I shall turn you into a songbird, a dancing swan. I shall teach you how to survive this life, child Maudie.'

'Dear Auntie,' said Maud in a tone of affectionate iron, 'I am your niece of blood and I love you more than I ever loved my mother. But I won't be a carnal woman for you, or for us, or for me. I love only Daniel Quinn and I want to give him half or more of my life.'

Was ever a more precisely self-apportioning line uttered by woman? But Magdalena was not as impressed by it as I. 'Oh pish, child,' she said. 'Pish, pish, pish.'

I saw that I was not a consideration in Magdalena's plans. John the Brawn continued his dalliance with Hillegond, their periodic thumpings a comic ritual to the entire household, and he paid me small heed. I gravitated to our neighbor Will Canaday, who visited us often, first to rid us of the dead Swede, then to aid in the reburial of Amos's dusty skeleton, and more mysteriously to spirit away Joshua from his hiding place in the netherworld of the mansion, an event I witnessed without Will's knowledge during my exploration of the great house (an entity of such enormousness that one needed one's wits always at full brim to avoid being lost in the maze of corridors, tunnels, staircases, chutes, dropaways, cul-de-sacs and other oddities – unopenable doors without handles or locks – that abounded in the multiple wings, towers, and catacombs of the place).

'Where did you take Joshua?' I asked Will the day after I saw them leaving. 'Did you take him to the doctor?'

'Master Quinn,' Will said to me, and I knew from this formality, as well as from his tone, that seriousness was about to descend upon me, 'you will put Joshua out of mind and forget you saw him here if you want to preserve his life.'

I nodded instant agreement to this and Will smiled at me. He inquired of my family, which was the beginning of my friendship with this splendid soul, an irregular man of this world, cut to no cloth save his own, neither in his garments, which rarely matched or fit him, nor in his morality, which was vigorous, impious, peculiar, and steadfast.

I told Will I had no family, that I'd gone to work as a canal boy for four months and run away from a master who not only beat me but refused to pay me for my work, that I'd met John the Brawn and liked him by contrast, since he never hit me, that I'd worked with him three months on the canal till his boat sank, and lately as a river rat, but was now a waterless orphan with a most uncertain future.

Will began instantly with his generous counsel, telling me of my need to keep working, fanning my already burning dread of orphanages, which were proliferating not only in the wake of the cholera but as havens for children, safe retreats from parents ready to murder them rather than feed another mouth. Will also decided I should know more about the world than I did (he was appalled that I thought the Mexican War had taken place over the border in Canada) and he counseled me on books to read – storytellers and poets, historians and playwrights of ancient days. I had learned to read from the nuns in school, and liked it well enough. These books from Will were much beyond my ken, but I plunged into them with a duty that in time became the most subtle of my pleasures in this world. Will also saw to it that his newspaper turned up at the Staats mansion every day so I might educate myself. The newspaper's arrival was anomalous in the home of Hillegond, who cared little for any world outside her own mystical province, even though her son, Dirck, was an editorial employee of Will's. I loved and devoured the paper, reading of murders and thievery, rapscallions and heroes. I read the commercial notices for pianofortes, ever-pointed pencils, and remedies for evil results arising from early abuse and unhappy contamination. The endless political bickering over issues that I could not follow bored me, but I grew fascinated with the wars between Spaniards and Arabs, between Britons and Kaffirs, between the Ch'ing dynasty and the Taiping rebels. I cheered for fugitive slaves in the Carolinas and for the rebellious farmers of Ireland who, under the leadership of one William Smith O'Brien, were defying the English (my father's father had lost his land to the English). But my partisanship aroused no serious animosity toward the forces that opposed my favored side, I being smug and comfortable, far from such violence. But I did begin to see that violence was the norm of this bellicose world.

Will took me on my first visit in sunlight to the city of Albany several weeks after The Great Fire. The weeks of the new year had been deep with cold, snow, and ice that was at last giving way to a spring thaw, permitting a view of the cold ashes of disaster: the center of Albany's ancient commerce and density, its quays, its Great Pier, so many canalboats and sloops, all reduced to char and cinders save for an odd chimney fragment untoppled, or a lone house standing because of its owner's grit in bringing hundreds of buckets of water to wet down his walls and to douse the blankets on his roof, upon which flying embers would futilely spend their heat.

The good weather was also catalyzing the area's charred garbage, sending aromatic blossoms abroad to the citizenry, and this brought out packs of dogs and cats, and herds of roaming pigs, those enduring scavengers who joined the city workers in the ruins. The searchers sought three citizens still unaccounted for, and about whom I had read in Will's newspaper. Then, as Will and I picked our steps through the soft rubble, there before me rooted a pig, snuffling in the sludge. The animal brought forth with its jaws first the arm of an infant and then the attached torso, dragging it up from the dire muck and about to make off with it when I intervened, whacked the waddling ghoul with a charred board, distracting it, but insufficiently, for it would not open its jaws. I struck again and again at its back, but its jaws remained clenched,

47

and then in desperation I kicked at its throat, whereupon it yielded up its booty and squealed off into deeper ashes, soon slowing to a lope and snuffling once again in the ruins.

Will and I stared down at the infant corpse, a black doll, rigid with ice, more rigid with death: hairless, faceless, sexless, yet a residual presence demanding attention. Will summoned a constable patrolling the erstwhile street and the dead child was taken by authority to a place of more secure rest.

'The child's father will thank you for what you did,' Will said to me. 'I know the man. His name is Bailey.'

'How could anyone know whose child that was?'

'Only one child is missing. Would you object if I included a report of what you did in the newspaper?'

'It's what anyone would have done.'

'Perhaps. But you did it, and there are people who loathe the pigs, and fear them, and would never do such a thing. Pigs can be nasty.'

We walked to Will's newspaper office on lower Broadway, a street that sometimes flooded when the river overflowed its banks, but the newspaper was safe on the second floor. Three young printers were actually bouncing as they worked at the typecase and stones, and among the tables that bore long metal galleys of copper-faced type. They all wore long white smocks and black derby hats, the smocks as protection against ink stains, the hats against the crumbling ceiling's falling plaster, which, as all know, rots the follicles in the scalp and, as some say, sends carbonic acid to the brain.

Will led me into his own work area, where his desk stood under a gas jet, next to a window, and beneath a vivid assemblage of chaos. Atop, beside, and on shelves adjacent to his desk lay a strew of magazines, clippings and letters, stacks of encyclopedias, dictionaries, new books, old books, boxed files, files not-so-boxed, with dust on some but not much of this clutter, and in the center of it all, an unopened copy of the morning *Chronicle:* the perfect centerpiece for the anarchy out of which it had come.

At an adjacent slanted desk, a model of neatness, sat a man

writing in a ledger. Will introduced me and I made the acquaintance
of Dirck Staats, the son of Hillegond. Will said to him, 'Dirck, this
young man is one of the guests in your house.'

I extended my hand and said, 'Daniel Quinn is my name, sir,
and I am enjoying your house.'

'I wish I could say the same,' said Dirck, 'but that she-devil of
a mother of mine won't allow it.'

'I recognize you from your portrait,' I said to him.

'I was told she had my portraits turned to the wall.'

'Oh, she has,' I said, 'but I turned one about to see the looks
of a man who could rile a woman to such a point.'

Dirck smiled at Will. 'You speak directly,' he said to me. 'Are
you a devotee of the word?'

'I can't be sure,' I said, 'since I don't know what "devotee"
means.'

'It means you like something quite well and you pay close
attention to it. Something such as words. I myself am such a
devotee of words that I'm writing a book full of them.'

'Words are useful,' I said. 'My dog might not have died if he'd
been able to tell us what ailed him.'

Dirck laughed at that and said, 'Yes, yes, yes,' and I was equally
amused, for I'd never owned a dog.

Dirck Staats: if Will Canaday was a slender citizen, then Dirck
was Will halved. He had a wild crop of dark hair around the back
and sides of his head, his legs were long, his trousers not long
enough, his waist no larger 'round than my own, and as a result
of this design he looked as top-heavy as a hatstand. His face and
high forehead were half as long as his chest, he wore unusually
small spectacles across the top of his broad forehead when he was
not reading, and, if such a thing were possible, his clothes fit him
worse than did Will's. But I liked Dirck Staats during our meeting,
and I liked even more the ambition with which he confronted the
arcane elements of the life around him.

'What is your book about?' I asked.

'It reveals a mystery,' he said, 'but the people in it would like
to keep it a mystery.'

'Give the boy something to read while I write a piece about him,' said Will. 'He retrieved a child's corpse from the pigs awhile ago. A hero in the city's ashes.'

'I am always glad to meet a hero,' said Dirck, bowing profusely before me, offering me his chair at the desk. 'By all means read what I am writing and give me your candid opinion. I confess I am at a loss for an intelligent response.'

He went off then and I sat down in front of his two large red ledger books and looked at his writing. It is now, in memory, very like the mirror writing of da Vinci, the runes of the old Norsemen, the cuneiform writing of the Assyrians. It had about it a world of its own design, an impenetrable architecture that was a fascination by itself. What eventually I came to know was that this was his own language, invented for the purpose of composing this secret book about the secrecy that had come to obsess him. I studied his figures and letters-of-a-kind but could understand nothing. He came back at length and smiled at me.

'What have you discovered?'

'That I cannot read even one word.'

'Excellent.'

I stood up and offered him his chair, but he reached for his coat, which hung on a hook beside his desk. 'We must to lunch,' he said, and I knew not whether this included me and Will, whether he was speaking of another group entirely, or of himself as the collective.

'Is it all right that I can't read a word?' I asked.

'Of course it is.'

'I do understand the print in Will's newspaper.'

'Of course you do.'

'Why do you draw pictures when you write?'

'So no one will understand what I say.'

'If you don't mind my saying so, that is an odd reason to write things.'

'I am as odd as ripe birdseed,' said Dirck.

That was the last word Dirck spoke personally to me, for people were coming up the stairs and as Dirck made ready to leave he was confronted by a man I knew later to be the sheriff. Two other men were with him, one a deputy, the other a citizen of Utica named Babcock. The latter seemed to be the cause of this doing in that he claimed Dirck owed him four dollars, the value of a shirt and cravat Dirck had borrowed from him two years previous and not returned. Will Canaday heard the commotion and joined it, and I hung back and listened.

Questions flew: Could this good man Dirck really be a petty thief? Why was such a paltry event now the occasion for his arrest? Why was this happening now and not two years ago? Could Babcock be serious? Could the sheriff? Dirck offered to pay the four dollars, but the sheriff said that was no longer possible, that he must go to Utica to stand trial for petit larceny. Will offered double payment for the shirt and cravat, but the sheriff was negatively adamant and ordered Dirck taken down the stairs. We all followed to the street, where a carriage waited with two more men. One of the men wore a memorably drooping mustache and was sharpening a long knife on a small whetstone in the palm of his hand. Will pointed to the man and called out, 'Aaron Plum,' and he turned swiftly to the sheriff and told him Plum was one of the toughs who had stoned the newspaper's windows two days earlier and then fled when Will fired a pistol over the heads of the toughs. The sheriff said this was nonsense, that the man had showed him credentials and was a deputy sheriff from Utica. But I knew Will was right, for I had met Aaron Plum on John the Brawn's skiff when we carried four crates of harnesses for him from Troy to Albany. John told me the harnesses were stolen, and so we made the run at night to avoid spectators. I learned Aaron Plum's name because he had his brother with him as a helper, Eli Plum, a schoolmate of mine. We called Eli Peaches after they caught him filling a sack with peaches from the Corcorans' tree.

All this was coming back to me when Aaron Plum and the second man jumped from the carriage, grabbed roughly at both of Dirck's arms, and pushed him toward the carriage, whose door the sheriff opened.

'Murder!' screamed Dirck. 'They will murder me!' Upon which

remark he was thrown headlong into the carriage, the men climbing in behind him. Dirck screamed out to us before the carriage flew away behind the same matched pair I had seen in La Última's dead eyeball. 'They want my book!' he yelled. 'Save my book!'

And then poor Dirck was gone.

Will turned and ran back up the stairs to his office, I at his heels. After we entered the office a man rose from where he had been crouching behind Dirck's desk and ran down the stairs. Will yelled and ran after him and I did likewise. The man was clutching Dirck's ledgers, and as he ran headlong across the street to another waiting carriage, he fell. One ledger flew out of his grip and landed at my feet, and I immediately snatched it up. As the man arose and turned to me I had a full look at him. He had red hair, a poor crop of muttonchops, and the top of his left ear had been sliced or bitten off. He stared at me and I took that stare as a threat. But Will was closing fast on him, and so the one-eared burglar leaped onto the step of the waiting carriage, clutching Dirck's second ledger, and held on to the window as the carriage raced away. I looked at the ledger in my hands and saw it was the one in which I had studied Dirck's hieroglyphics.

'You did well, Daniel Quinn,' Will said to me, and I handed him the ledger. 'This is a terrible event and I must set it right. You'll go home now to the mansion, and I'll see you when I can.' He signaled one of his printers in white smock and black derby who was standing (and bouncing) in the small crowd that had gathered. Will told the man to see that I got to Hillegond's house, and then he shook my hand.

'You are a friend of more things than you know, young man,' Will said to me, and then he went to his office.

The printer found a cab for hire and took me to the Staats house. He said little as we rode, but I noticed he was bouncing even as he sat, and that I was not. I told him I had seen him bouncing at the newspaper and again in the crowd and that he was bouncing still. I asked him why.

'It is because of my hat,' said the printer.

'I see,' I said, and I said no more.

At the mansion I told my story to John the Brawn, but it made so little impression on him that he told me not to bother Hillegond with it, for she had no use for her son. I said I could hardly do such a thing after seeing Dirck kidnapped at knife point. John agreed I should tell her since there was a knife involved, which is a measure of the man's logic. We went to the music room, where Hillegond was sitting with Maud, listening to Magdalena playing the pianoforte and singing a love ballad:

> 'Hangman, hangman, hold the rope!
> Hold it for a while.
> I think I see my father coming,
> Coming on the mile.
> Father, did you bring me gold,
> Or come to set me free?
> Or did you come to see me hang
> Upon that willow tree?'

> 'Daughter, I did not bring you gold,
> Nor come to set you free,
> But I have come to see you hang
> Upon that willow tree.'

I grew to love the song because of its message. All the daughter's relatives come to see her hang but it is her sweetheart alone who sets her free. Maud and I exchanged glances and then John the Brawn announced I had a story to tell. And I told it.

'Then Dirck is truly in trouble, the poor boy,' said Hillegond when I had finished my tale. She arose and went to the east parlor and turned outward the two portraits of Dirck at ages twelve and nineteen. At twelve Dirck was fat as a dumpling; at nineteen he was emaciation incarnate – the pair of portraits telling the story of his improbable progress as an ascetic. 'He will feel better knowing they're set right,' said Hillegond.

'How will he know such a thing?' Maud asked. 'Hasn't Daniel told us he was abducted?'

'He will get my message no matter where he is,' said Hillegond.

'With trouble in the family,' said Magdalena, 'we must be on our way.'

'You needn't leave,' said Hillegond. 'I do enjoy your company.'

'We've overstayed already,' said Magdalena. 'This is such a madcap time for you. And I must get back to my work in the theater.'

'What will happen to Daniel?' asked Maud.

'Why, he'll come with us,' said John the Brawn. 'A group like this needs a slavey.'

'I'll be lost for conversation,' said Hillegond, who saw her new world of thumping, music, mysticism, and children about to vanish. 'I will wither,' she added.

'Nonsense,' said Magdalena. 'You'll blossom. And you'll find a purpose in life, working to help your son. Life must continue. We've loved being here, in spite of all the death.'

I was bewildered. Nothing seemed to conclude. I was in the midst of a whirlwind panorama of violence and mystery, of tragedy and divine frenzy that mocked every effort at coherence. I now felt a physical sadness overtaking me, my body and brain losing their security and being thrust into hostile weather. I knew that apart from my family's being swept away by the cholera, what had happened to me in recent weeks was the most significant phase of my life thus far, the core of that significance being, and preeminently so, Maud. I longed only to watch her, talk with her, touch her hand, kiss her mouth. I had unholy longings to explore certain regions beneath her clothing, but I withheld such unschooled enterprise, for it seemed certain to generate trouble beyond my control. I had only one chance to talk alone with Maud in the next few days, an encounter in an upstairs hallway, outside the room filled with mirrors.

'You must not forget your promise to steal me,' she said in an urgent whisper. 'The chance will come very soon. I must take my life out of the hands of these people.'

'But how will I ever do it?' I said to her. 'I can't even find a way to get near you. Where would we go? And with what money? It's true what your aunt said. I'm penniless.'

'You will have to figure it out,' said Maud.

Then she was gone and we were busy with our goodbyes. In the kitchen I embraced Capricorn and Matty, with whom I had spent a great deal of time. In the foyer Magdalena and Hillegond wept grand tears on each other, and as we left the great house John the Brawn surreptitiously (though I witnessed it) thrust his hand high under Hillegond's skirt to give her a farewell stroke. Into the carriage we lofted Magdalena's trunk, John's suitcase (which he'd retrieved from our old landlady), and the small traveling bags Hillegond had given Maud and me for our belongings.

I leaned out the carriage window for a final look at the mansion, which aroused pity and terror in my breast, but without Aristotle's cathartic effect. I pitied myself both for my inability to ever dream of living in such a place again, and also for my loss of its comforts as I reentered the world outside its doors. And its receding presence aroused in me the terror of John the Brawn, the terror of the unknown, the terror of once again being a penniless orphan.

Hillegond's driver took us to the pier at the Albany Basin, the mouth of the Erie Canal, which was opened because of the weeks of warm weather. Hillegond had suggested we save time by taking the train to the Schenectady highlands and boarding the packet boat there, as did everyone else. But Magdalena was against it, fearing for her safety behind a locomotive. Our final destination was Buffalo, but our first stopping point was to be Utica, where, said Magdalena, the opera house manager would welcome her, for on her last visit she had sold out the house for two weeks. Soon after we boarded the packet the boatmen hitched up the mules and we began our journey westward, scrunched in the salon with a half-dozen lumberjacks and drummers. I won no bed and John told me I could sleep on deck with the spare mule. I will refrain from reporting on the trivial details of the hours that followed, for they were hateful. I loathed being back on the canal, being looked upon as another higgler's boy, one of those shiftless and worthless rungates who deserve whatever their drunken masters mete out to them in whippings, kicks, and cuffings, and whose destiny is either the penitentiary, the Almshouse, or an early grave.

The mules moved us along as I schemed in silence on ways to steal Maud away from John the Brawn and La Última. I conceived of first stealing a horse and carriage, sweeping her into my grasp, fleeing down a gravel carriageway, leaping to the reins, and driving off into the cherished night of freedom, into the unchartable challenges of love. We would ride with the west wind and the flight of wild geese, imposing on each other the most exquisite splendors of which our adolescent imaginations were capable.

As I entered my world of romantic intention I fell into a sleep that, for reasons I judge escapist, proved narcotic. Unable to resolve the theft of Maud, I thrust it even out of my dreams and awoke from that comatose condition facing the rising sun, curled up on dry ground. I was at the edge of the towpath, and what I saw in my first glance was a meadow to one side, canal to the other, no canalboat anywhere, no people and no houses, only a lone cow beside a small shack in a far field. My small clothing bag was beside me and, atop that, wrapped in a greasy newspaper, a ragged chunk of stale bread, the crust John the Brawn had promised me. Slowly I realized I was desolate. But far worse was the intolerable dawning that while I'd been trying and failing to bring about the theft of Maud, scurrilous John the Brawn had stolen her from me.

I wept desolated tears and felt the spiny urchins invading my soul. I shouldered my bag and walked eastward along the towpath, not knowing what town I was near, knowing only my position beneath the sky. Boats, mules, horses, and men passed, but I had commerce with none of them. I screamed, or thought I did, but wasn't certain. I began a new scream that I would surely hear, but the sound was inconsequential to the rising sun. I stifled it and picked up a green stick. I walked until I found the correct rock and then I beat the rock until the stick was limp sinews. This also was inconsequential and I began to believe then that no act, no thought of mine, could shape a response equal to the feeling the theft of Maud had generated in me.

I began to dwell on what it meant to find your love and then to have it taken from you, framing the question with a fifteen-year-old brain and a body in transition toward nefarious impulses. Even so, I could instantly see what a hollow game this was. If *my* condition was desolation, what, then, was Maud's? I was at least able-bodied, male, unsubjugated, and capable of self-sustenance, whereas she was this fragile and precocious visionary in a state of peril. Who would save her from the ritual bawdry that awaited her? What guardian quality in John the Brawn, that overmastering Priapus, would protect her from lifelong invasion by the lust of strangers? The child was, to my mind, about to become a spangled womb, a witch of beauty wasted on the bloody and pecunious bed of ravaged hymen.

I yelled to a passing boatman, who told me I was twelve miles from Schenectady, and as I walked on I thought of telling Maud now all that had befallen me before I met her, those events that had brought me to the moment when I saved her from the bottom of the river. I thought the telling might even reach Maud in Utica, just as Hillegond had faith that her feelings would reach the kidnapped Dirck.

Coupling Dirck and Maud I realized I had witnessed the theft of two lives, and I brooded that Dirck, Maud, I, and all the others were parts of a great machine, generating immeasurable power in the universe. I drew little comfort from this thought for I seemed too minuscule a part to be of any significance. Men like John the Brawn with his strength, Will Canaday with his brain and his newspaper, and the captors of Dirck with their will to evil were the great turbines, were they not? Children like myself waited their turn at power.

But then I thought, no. Age alone does not determine whether one wields power, or even whether one remains a child. My own childhood had been terminated for me on a warm morning in April 1850, under the rising sun on the banks of the Erie Canal. There and then, Daniel Quinn, late a boy in possession of neither safety nor joy, a boy being shaped by fire, flood, ice, and the less comprehensible barbarities of men and women, was entering into a creaturehood of a more advanced order: young animal confounded – solitary, furious, eccentric, growing bold.

This is the message I sent through the sky to Maud about my new condition:

Maud, I begin on an event that took place a month before the raging of the plague. A stranger in old clothes walked crookedly up Van Woert Street and collapsed on Rhatigan's front stoop. Old Lydie Rhatigan came out in her apron, her broom in hand to shoo him away. But one look at him changed her mind.

'You're sick, is it?' said Lydie.

'My left leg is dead,' the man said to her. 'I couldn't walk another step. Feel the leg if you like.'

'I'll do no such thing,' said Lydie.

'Death is moving in me,' said the man, and he shifted his position so that his back rested against the stoop's iron railing and his dead left leg dangled off the bottom step. The right leg he stretched along the width of the stoop.

'It's going into the right leg now,' he said. 'Two more minutes and the right'll be as dead as the left.'

'What ails you?' asked Lydie.

'The death is what it is.'

'What kind of death?'

'The only kind.'

'Get on with ye. Is it a plate of food you're after?'

'Not anymore.'

'Well, you can't clutter the stoop like this.'

'It's in both arms now,' said the man, and his left arm went limp. With his right hand he took off his hat, exposing a bald head, and put the hat on a step above him.

'At least get the last bit of sunshine on the pate,' he said, and his right arm went as limp as his left.

Lydie dropped her broom. 'God bless us and save us,' she said.

'A prayer is a blessing,' said the man, 'but it doesn't bother death. Now it's in the stomach. And now the neck.' He closed his eyes. 'There it is in the chest,' and he opened his eyes like two full moons. 'Now I'm dead,' he whispered, and dead he was, with his eyes as open as the sky.

Everyone thought of this as an isolated incident. Not until the others died was the man who had tracked the course of his own death seen as both carrier and emissary of the plague. It was a fiery hot summer, the worst time for it, the time when death grows fat. I was working for food with Emmett Daugherty, my father's great friend, helping him rebuild his shed and privy. Emmett lived two miles north of Van Woert Street, and because of the distance I stayed with him, and so I wasn't home the week death first walked up our street.

The McNierney family across from us had four die in two days that week, and the four others who lived on fled to no one still knows where. Two desperate stragglers from Vermont found the McNierney house empty and open (Pud McNierney didn't even close the front door when he ran out), and they went in and helped themselves to food, drink, and beds. Both were dead in those beds three days later.

Maud, I won't tell you all the horrid matter that comes out of the body when the cholera invades people; you probably know for yourself. But the sight of such things recurring so often put the fear into everybody in the city. A good many remembered the plague of '32 that killed four hundred in Albany, and so people locked their doors, wouldn't go out, wouldn't let anyone in. Prayer vigils were called and some brave souls came out to hear our preachers tell them their sins were causing people to die. One stranger stood up and called the preacher a madman for saying that and yelled out how it was pigs running loose in the city, not sin, that caused the cholera. But he didn't get far with that. They hit him with a plank and he stopped yelling.

My mother got sick while I was at Emmett's house, and when I came home she was in bed, smothered in blankets, shivering. She'd had the sickness for two days and the doctor gave her Veratrum to take on a piece of sugar. It didn't help at all, even with greater dosage, so Pa gave her Spirits of Camphor and she said she felt better. That same day Pa came home from work at the lumberyard (they wouldn't let him stay home) and found my sister Lizzie face down on the paving stones near the house. She was alive but very ill. Pa carried her to bed and gave her the Spirits of Camphor right off, along with the Veratrum. That was the day I came home from Emmett's house. I sat vigil with my mother and Lizzie both, and I never got sick, though I still don't know why I didn't.

We heard that looting was going on down the block, which was news, because after the first flurry of deaths nobody went near any of the death houses; for who could be sure which things were uncontaminated and safe to steal? But for some the lure of larceny is greater than the fear of death, and soon every empty house was a target for thieves in masks and gloves. When my mother heard this she told me to find our birdcage and bury it. I asked her why.

'Because I brought it from Ireland,' she said, 'and because a birdcage isn't all that it is, but you needn't mind about that. Just remember what I say. Study it well and mind you that there's value in it you can use someday. God knows the value. Now do it, boy, do what I say, and tell no one where you bury it.'

The cage was empty. When my father lost his old job laying railroad ties he blamed our yellow bird, said it brought bad luck, and he let the creature loose in the trees, even though we'd had it for years. My mother cried and put the cage in a crawl space under the roof, up with the suitcases and blankets she and Pa carried for the months they spent on the boat coming over. When Pa saw me with the cage he asked what I was doing. I told him and he said, 'Remember where you bury it and cover it with leaves or they'll see the fresh-dug dirt and go in after it.' And then he said, 'Take care of it, lad, and it'll take care of you.'

When I came back from burying the cage Pa was sitting vigil with Ma and he said to me, 'Go see Lizzie.' I went down to our room and saw she was gone from us. Pa had put a rosary in her hand but it hadn't helped her. I looked at her awhile and went up to Pa's room and sat with him while Ma shivered and wailed. I heated the hot-water jars for her and rubbed her with Spirits of Camphor but that didn't do any good either.

After she died Pa never shed a tear, but his face went loose. He couldn't control its blinking and twitching, or keep the whiteness off it, or banish its shapeless grief. He went to get the priest because Ma was close with the church. She used to go to mass three or four mornings a week, whenever the weather was good. She loved the religion and was good friends with the pastor. But Pa found out the pastor was sick himself from visiting so many people with the plague, so he only brought back Jigger Kiley and his wagon, which was the hearse on our street that month. Pa said there wouldn't be any mass or funeral for Ma just now. Maybe later. Then he took himself to bed and let himself be sick all the way. I sat vigil with him, doing the same useless things I did for Ma, until he, too, shivered and died without a word. I went and got Emmett

Daugherty, and he came back with his own wagon and helped me pack the things he said were valuable and the things I wanted to keep. We locked up the house and got in Jigger's wagon with Pa, and we dropped Pa off at the new body depository near the arsenal, because that was the law. The old Dead House out at the Almshouse couldn't handle so many corpses. The rats were eating them before workers got them into their graves.

I went to stay with Emmett at his house beside the canal and live out the summer and winter there. I cried a good deal over my sister and my lost parents and I stopped going to church. I couldn't abide it anymore, all the talk about Christ. I liked Christ fine, but who didn't? I felt like that stranger who didn't believe the preacher's talk about sin. I didn't know what to make of things, but I knew I had to do something for myself, that I had no more time to be a child. And so in the spring of '48, when Emmett heard that a canaler named Masterson needed a helper, I asked for the job and got it, because I couldn't live off the Daughertys forever. Emmett's niece was about to arrive from Ireland, and Emmett himself was still ailing with the lung trouble he'd picked up on a land-buying expedition with Lyman Fitzgibbon, the merchant-scientist.

I thanked Emmett for all his help, for saving me from God knows what, for being as close as blood. He said I was welcome anytime and he'd keep my things till I wanted them, and then I went off to work on the canal with Masterson for four of the worst months of my life. He beat me like a mutt and refused to pay me wages. I ran off when I saw how to get away clean, and I found work on John the Brawn's boat for three months till it sank. Then John bought the skiff and we worked the river out of Albany as ferrymen and haulers, water rats who'd go anywhere with anything between Albany, Troy, West Troy, and Greenbush.

One day on our river I saw you step into Carrick's boat and saw the boat hit by an ice floe. We put out to rescue you, I saved you from drowning, and that's how we met. My life was used to subtractions, not additions of beauty the likes of yours.

Maud, I send love.

*   *   *

When I reached Schenectady I asked a stagecoach driver for a ride, since I had no money to ride the train. The driver, for helping him load baggage, let me ride on the roof of the coach. I knotted myself in among the baggage tie-down ropes and we bounced away into the wind toward Albany. We came in on the Turnpike, which was rotten with mud, the wagon traffic moving so slowly outside the city that I leaped down and walked. I thought first of my old house, of which I had had no fear when the family took sick. But now the possibility of contamination waiting in it sent me into shivers and I decided to go instead to Emmett Daugherty's.

I cut across the city's western plateau and headed northeast in the direction the cattle drovers took when they moved the herds toward the river and swam them across to the Boston and New York trains. Emmett's house was a cabin, primitive and temporary. He planned to build a proper house once he married, but it was still a cabin in this year, and when I neared it I saw his niece, Josephine Daugherty, feeding chickens in the front yard.

She eyed me oddly until I told her my name, and then she said she was Josie and that she'd heard of me. She was a small redheaded girl of twenty-five with more freckles on her nose and chin than any woman ought to be burdened with. She was a greenhorn, in from Clonmel only a few months, and keeping house for Emmett, who had overcome his lung illness and was again working for old man Fitzgibbon at his Albany ironworks. Josie invited me in for tea, fed me cold chicken and potatoes, and I was glad for it. Her presence clearly meant there was no bed for me in the house, and so I would need money. What arose in memory was the birdcage, so valued by my parents. I remembered our broken spade I'd left with Emmett, and that would be tool enough to dig up the cage.

'Will you sit with us till Emmett comes home from work?' Josie asked me, and I said no, that I had to move along and pick up something I had left behind.

'I've got an old spade with a broken handle stored out in your shed with our other stuff,' I said to her. 'I have to do a little digging.'

'Are you digging a garden?' she asked.

'No.'

'Then you're shoveling ashes or some such.'

'No.'

'You won't say what it is.'

'No.'

'Then you'll hear no more foolish questions from me,' she said, and abruptly left the room. I was sorry, but it wasn't any of her business. I went out the back door. I found the spade, took it back to the house and showed it to Josie, and she was all right again. She had a round face and a low forehead, both of which I have associated with nosy people ever since. There was nothing pretty about her and I made a wager with myself she would never marry. She was not smart, like Maud, and Maud was beautiful and the opposite of nosy.

'I'll be going now,' I said to Josie. 'I'll come back someday and wait for Emmett to come home.'

'You're very young to be alone on the road,' Josie said.

'There's younger than me on the road,' I said.

'And the same in Ireland. It's a desperate time to be a child.'

'I don't feel like a child anymore.'

'Well, now, aren't we the grown-up?'

'We might be that,' I said.

Josie made me two sandwiches and it was four in the afternoon when I left her, a day in mid-April, clear and sunny but growing chilly, with sundown an hour away. I would wait until dark to dig up the cage, but what I thought to do was approach our old house, imprint its image on memory, and say farewell to it forever.

I walked toward the city, down the West Troy Road, and when I neared Van Woert Street I gave myself a choice: to approach our house from the rear, over our hill and down through the trees, or walk directly up the street and perhaps meet old neighbors. Explain solitariness if you can: that I, more alone than I had ever been in life, did not want to encounter old neighbors, not even boys my age who'd been close friends. I was such an outcast from all that was home that I craved the intensification of exile. I believe

I avoided friends from fear of what proximity to their comforts might arouse in me: anger, perhaps, or envy, or even the desire to steal from them. I saw their rooves and chimneys, their back doors and windows as I neared the street, saw Gallagher's spavined horse tethered in the back lot of Carney's grogshop, where my father used to drink. I saw the food store run by Joe Sullivan, who had only one arm. I veered from it all and came at the street from behind the house of the widow Mulvaney, whose husband raised goats before he ran off with a fancy woman and died of intense pleasure.

As I came onto the street proper I saw our house. The railing was off the stoop on one side, the windows all broken in front. Grass grew tall along the walls and in the cracks between the paving slates of the sidewalk. I had heard our landlord died of the cholera and that no one had cared for the house since we left it. The inert quality of the place, the absence of life, gave off a stark aura of isolation, and I now wonder whether I myself was giving off the same aura as I neared the place.

I was no sooner on the path from the Mulvaneys' to our house than I saw Peaches Plum. He was with one of his brothers and they looked as alike as two peach pits: both blond and skinny, both shoeless. They were prowling about our house, I suppose scavenging, a late moment for that, though truly entrepreneurial scavengers believe in the bottomlessness of others' dregs. They saw me approaching and Peaches called me by name.

'Yeeouuu been diggin',' he said to me.

'No,' I said.

'Then why you totin' that shovel?'

''Cause it's mine.'

'Ain't nothin' in *your* house,' Peaches said.

'We took most stuff out when the family died,' I said. 'What we left wasn't *worth* nothin'.'

'You a smarm,' Peaches said. 'Smart little poop.'

'You think what you want, Peaches,' I said, and I walked around him toward the house.

'You gonna dig somepin' with that spade?' he said.

'No, I'm just totin' it,' I said.

'What good's a broken spade? Lemme look at it.'

'Leave it alone, Peaches,' I said, and I picked up a rock the size of a potato. 'And you leave *me* alone, too. I ain't in none of your way, so don't you go bein' in mine.'

Peaches respected rocks. He and his brother (we called him Outa) stared me down and picked up rocks of their own. I kept my eye at a level with Peaches's and picked up a second potato, which made Peaches respect me twice as much. Peaches nodded at me and smiled. Then he wagged his head at Outa, and they went their way and left me alone with two fistfuls of rock. I stood where I was and knew they would look back, both of them, and they did, for the snake is the primal contortionist.

At last they were gone and I dropped the rocks and went to where I had buried the cage: the grove of trees behind the house, a stand of elms and cedar that had grown tall and interwoven their family virtues into a small but quite lovely haven of shade and intermittent sun that allowed for an almost tropical arousal of plant life. A fist-sized rising of water came from the ground halfway up the abrupt hill that sheltered us from northerly winds, and then it trickled down into the grove. This was a spring I had discovered at an early age and claimed as my own, and its water had the dark, sweet taste of the silent stones at the center of the earth.

I went to the spring and drank of that cold clarity to cleanse my mouth of the dust from the road, then sat in the fading light of the grove to await the safety of darkness. When the moon gave me light to work by, I dug up the cage that had been so indefinably valuable to my parents.

I looked at it in the moonlight but saw nothing beyond its basic shape. I could not tell whether it had rusted from being underground or was merely discolored from the soil. I yearned for light but yearned more to be indoors to evade the chill that was sinking into my bones. I looked steadily at the black shadow that was our derelict house and grew brave enough to argue with my fear. Had I not already survived in that house during the plague's heat? Would I not now survive its cold ashes?

I picked up my spade, pack, and birdcage, and at the back door

I reentered the circus maximus, where my family had battled and died under my spectator's eye. I sealed all doors against the night, found the kitchen windows to be intact, and I closed off that room as my retreat. I lighted a candle from my pack and set the birdcage on the floor beside it. I made ready to eat some of the food Josie had given me but then in the window I perceived my image, illuminated by the reflected candlelight. What I saw was a body and a face I barely knew. I was too big for my clothes and I was urchin dirty, but urchin no more. My face had been wrenched out of the puffy adolescence of reasonable expectation. That condition, said my mouth and eyes, is a luxury that is part of your past.

I sat beside the birdcage and studied it. Its slender bars had rusted, as had the round, heavy plate that was its bottom. I let the candlelight search out its secret, but I could find no secret. As I handled it, two of its bars snapped from the rusting.

What was I to do with such a worthless object? What was its meaning? I stared at it while I ate a sandwich. I wondered whether my mother and father had made a talisman of the cage, imposing upon it the values of the people of Clonmel, Cashel, and the towns in Mayo and Tyrone where the family had flourished. My father's life was troubled from the time he was two, his father running off then to America. When Pa came here himself he never tried to find his father, nor did I, nor will I. Maybe Pa came with a birdcage instead of memories, but if he did, that was years behind us, all value long gone certainly from this rusty relic on the floor in front of me. My parents were gone themselves, along with their unknowns, all now remaining of what they deemed valuable embodied in me, this urchin particle floating in time, waiting for the next blow to fall.

My candle died with a guttering hiss; I lay my head on my pack of rags, and I fell asleep thinking of the cool and soothing quality of water. I awoke to a noise and opened my eyes in daylight to see a form moving away from the kitchen window. I sat up and immediately gathered my belongings to move out, and as I did, the kitchen door opened and Peaches and his brother walked through it, carrying clubs.

'I seen where you dug,' said Peaches, looking around the room.

William Kennedy

'You dug up that cage,' and he picked it up and looked at it. It looked even more worthless now than it had by candlelight.

'It belonged to my mother. I wanted to see it again.'

'I think I'll jes take it with me.'

'Take it,' I said. 'It ain't worth a penny. I was just gonna leave it where it sits.'

Peaches opened the cage door and one hinge broke. He grunted and dropped it and the bottom came loose.

'I remember when my father buried it,' I said. 'I thought he might've put a bag of money in it.'

'Bag of money? I'd like to have some o' that.'

'Wasn't no money in it. You find any money in this house I'll cut it up halvies with you.'

Outa Plum tipped the contents of my sack onto the kitchen floor: clothes, candles, matches, a sandwich, and a glove that belonged to Maud.

'You got no money at all,' Peaches said.

'None.' I pulled my pockets out to prove it.

'Then I'll just take this birdcage,' Peaches said, picking it up.

'Take it. Only thing you can't take's my spade. Worth a lot of money, that spade. My daddy used it when he dug the grave of Andy Jackson. People'll pay me a lot of money for it when they know it buried a President of the United States.'

Peaches dropped the cage and picked up the spade.

'I just better take this ol' spade,' he said.

'Hey, you can't take that,' I said and I moved toward him. He threatened me with the spade and Outa raised his club at me.

'I'm gonna tell somebody,' I said. 'I'm gonna tell your folks.'

Peaches and Outa smiled. 'You tell 'em,' said Peaches. 'You jes tell 'em.'

They backed out the door and ran with the heirloom. I smiled myself and put my things back in my sack. I looked at the cage. I could not abandon it, despite its being worthless. As I picked it up, the ruptured base separated further and I saw the cage had a false bottom. I pulled the covering off and found beneath it a circular metal disk bearing an odd trompe l'oeil design. Now it was a screaming mouth with vicious eyes, now a comic puppy with bulbous nose and tiny mouth. Depending on where the light hit the eyes they were glassy, or sad, or hypnotic. I had no time to dwell on the disk for I feared Peaches would change his mind about the spade. But I believed the disk was valuable in some way yet to be understood. It was like nothing I'd ever seen. It might be a platter. It might be gold, or silver, for it had not rusted. But even if it wasn't precious metal it had value as a thing to look at. I stuffed it into my sack and left the house, brimming with a brand-new faith in the unknown that I had found at the bottom of a birdcage.

That mystery reveals itself quickly only to those without the imagination to perpetuate it is a fact that came clear to me when I decided my newfound disk might have been a serving platter for potatoes.

'Potatoes?' exclaimed Will Canaday. 'Why, it's too small for potatoes. And what's more, it's flat as a coin. They'd roll off.'

I saw Will had a point and the mystery of the disk continued. That mystery, along with my desolation and my desire to abdicate forever the river and the canal, had an hour earlier led me into a reverie as I left Van Woert Street. You know nothing, the reverie began. You are a penniless, ignorant orphan who thought the Mexican War was fought in Canada, and you let John the Brawn steal your most valuable possession. You are inferior to everybody in something, even to Peaches Plum, who knows stealth and violence better than you. Quinn, when will you become wise, or even smart?

This question brought back Will's words to me when we were leaving Hillegond's mansion: 'If you find yourself interested in an education, or in the life of the mind, come and see me.' And so in my reverie on ignorance I thought of the *Albany Chronicle* as a source of enlightenment about both the disk and my future.

Will was at work in his office, coatless with shirtsleeves rolled, writing one of the editorials about the abduction of Dirck Staats that would bring him national attention. He finished writing on a page of foolscap, tossed it into a box marked 'copy,' and then he saw me, his face registering genuine surprise.

'Back so soon?' he said.

I told him straightaway of being put off the canalboat.

'Who would do such a thing?'

'It must have been John the Brawn.'

'The man's a villain.'

'I think I will have trouble forgiving him.'

'And I as well,' said Will. 'But more important than that is what do we do with you? If you want to peddle the *Chronicle* you're welcome to live with our other orphan newsboys on the third floor,' and his finger pointed to the ceiling.

'That would be good,' I said, and already I felt rescued. 'But I think I am interested in a life of the mind. Would I get that as a newsboy?'

'A life of the mind?' said Will, much amused. 'In that case we'd better make a reporter of you.'

'On what would I report?'

'On the nature of things,' said Will. 'Does that seem a fit subject?'

'On the nature of what things?'

'All things.'

'It sounds a bit more than I can handle.'

'Nonsense. Before you know it you'll be as expert on everything under the sun as all the other reporters in this world.'

'When shall I begin?'

'Now is as good a time as any. Do you have something in mind to report on?'

'I could report on my platter,' I said, and I fished in my sack for it and told Will my story. I've recounted his response about the potatoes, but I was thinking of my parents' stories about bad times in Ireland, and of the presence on their table of very small potatoes, when there were any potatoes at all, while Will, I suspect, had the superabundance of the American potato in mind. Will stroked the platter with his fingertips. 'It seems to be bronze,' he said. 'Very old, and very handsome at that. Did your parents get it in Ireland?'

'I suppose so,' I said. 'Except for Albany that's the only place they ever lived.'

'It's possible this is the work of the Vikings, or even the Romans. In any case I suspect it's worth considerable money.'

'Is bronze worth money?'

'When it's shaped this way it is.'

'Who would buy an old platter?'

'A museum curator, or someone who values relics from another age.'

'My parents wouldn't want me to sell it. They said it would take care of me.'

'Yes,' said Will, smiling one of his patient smiles of forbearance in the face of idiocy. 'But I suggest that money may be a way in which one is taken care of.'

'Then why didn't my parents sell it themselves? They never had any money.'

'A good question,' said Will, a bit vexed, 'and one you must answer for yourself. Rest easy, Daniel. We'll not sell your relic against your will. But you must protect it. You can't carry it around in that sack.'

'I could bury it again.'

'There are tidier ways to protect things,' said Will. 'For the moment you may put it in our safe, if you find that agreeable.'

'Very agreeable,' I said. 'But I think I would not want to live upstairs. I've lived with orphans on the canal, and they stole from me and fought over everything. I'd rather live with Mrs Staats, if it's all the same to you.'

'It's all the same to me,' said Will, amused again, 'but I can't say how it will sit with Mrs Staats.'

'I'd work for my keep,' I said.

'Work for me and work for your keep both?' said Will.

'I don't need much sleep,' I said.

Will forbore, then said he'd take me to see Hillegond. He put my platter in his safe, told me to stop calling it a platter, then gave me a file of *Chronicles* to read while he finished his work. He pointed out what he and others had written about Dirck. 'If you are going to live with Mrs Staats,' he said, 'you had better understand what is happening to her son.'

Dirck's abduction appeared under Local Events at first mention in Will's newspaper, written straightforwardly, not unlike the way I have already recounted it. But Will also took the liberty of charging the sheriff with provocative behavior, said he intended to follow the case with intensive fidelity to the facts and would pursue 'the deeper darkness that lies beyond this black deed.' He also said Dirck never reached Utica, that his arrest was a fraud, and that Aaron Plum was a felon thrice-accused (always for grievous assault with a weapon), after which Plum became a wanted man. The sheriff was relieved of his duties but charged with no crimes, and vanished from his home. In all, the case of Dirck Staats overnight became synonymous with violence, collusion, and mystery.

Will did not, at first, write of Dirck's secret ledgers, though they loomed large; and I began to understand the power of the word to transform this simple abduction of a man into an event that alters the trajectory of history's arrow. I asked Will about Dirck's book and when he would publish it.

'I would publish it tomorrow,' he said, 'but no one can read it without the key to Dirck's code, and we haven't yet found that.'

The search for the code had been ongoing at the newspaper, also among Dirck's friends, in the places he frequented, in the rooms he kept, and at the mansion. Nothing had turned up.

I ended my reading when Will appeared in coat and hat, saying it was time to visit Hillegond, and on the street he hailed a passing carriage. I anticipated the mansion with excitement and affection, as if I were going home, the complacent impoverishment of my former self now thoroughly transformed by the vision of luxury.

As we rode up the gravel driveway I thought that the house's splendor was probably unmatched in this world, and though I have since seen greater monuments, such as Versailles and the Alhambra, I have not changed my mind about the Staats house's singular beauty, or its wondrously eclectic sprawl.

Capricorn answered our knock, told us Hillegond was with a visitor in the east parlor, then announced us to her. Out she came, devoid of the bright colors that were her style, and wrapped instead in a slate-colored dress and black lace shawl, her uniform of mourning for lost kin. Her face was a mask of gravity, but she brightened when she saw me, and she hugged me.

'Master Daniel,' she said, and smothered me in her abundantly dark bosom. 'Why are you here, and where are the others?'

'Gone,' I said. 'John the Brawn put me off the canalboat while I slept, and I walked back to Albany.'

'A dreadful deed,' said Hillegond, but I knew she was of two minds about John and his deeds.

'The boy wants to stay here with you,' Will said.

'Well, he surely can,' said Hillegond, and my future exploded with rainbows. Only hours out of my family's tumbledown house of death, now I was to become a dweller in this grand villa of life.

'You're both just in time to see me magnetized,' Hillegond said with a verve that reversed her bleak mood. 'It's a very daring thing to do.'

She led us into the parlor and I saw that Dirck's two portraits, face out, were draped with bright red ribbon – red the color of protection in Hillegond's spiritual spectrum. A man in his thirties, wearing a hemisphere of whiskers along his total jawline, the rest of his face clean-shaven, rose to greet us.

'And this is Maximilian Schiffer,' said Hillegond. 'He's a wonderful animal magnetist. He's helping me to find Dirck.'

Maximilian shook hands stiffly with both of us, then inquired grimly of Hillegond, 'Are these visitors to be present during experiment? Witnesses can be distraction.'

'They won't be a distraction,' said Hillegond. 'My son worked for this man, and this boy was one of the last to see him before his abduction.'

Max nodded at that, which ended the sociable aspect of our visit. He then picked up a single piece of paper from the table in front of Hillegond and handed it to her.

'Put this alongside head. You will read it with ear when I tell you.'

'With her ear?' said Will.

'Correct,' said Max testily.

'Maximilian is a world-renowned phrenomagnetist,' said Hillegond. 'He's examined the bumps on my skull and he says the one behind my ear gives me the gift of vision. He's certain I'll be able to see Dirck by reading his scrawlings through my ear bump.'

'Do you really think your bumps are so special?' asked Will with a small smile.

'I have always thought so,' said Hillegond.

'Please, no talking,' said Max, and he guided Hillegond's hand with the paper, on which I was able to see some marks. Max positioned it behind Hillegond's left ear, then moved both his hands over her head, arms, and lap, humming like the lowest note on an organ. In time I recognized the word 'sleep,' by which moment Hillegond was deep in her magnetic trance.

'Now tell about son Dirck,' said Max.

'He's a nuisance and a most foolish child,' said Hillegond, her eyes closed. 'He won't go to church, and he talks back to his mother. He won't play with other children, for all he wants to do is draw pictures and read books, which isn't healthy in a young boy. I tell him he'll turn into an idiot from being alone so much, and I only allow him to wear clothing that doesn't fit him so he'll look even more foolish than he is. "When you behave properly you shall have proper clothing," I tell him, but he doesn't change. I would have my husband whip him if I had a husband. I had such hopes for the boy. I thought he would grow up to make us proud of the Staats name again. I thought he would make new money for us and preserve our mansion, but he can't button his own shoes.'

'Please tell of Dirck, and where is,' said Max.

Hillegond pressed the paper closer to her ear, opened her eyes in a gaze at nothing in particular, and then in a voice several tones higher than her previous pronouncements, spoke with the articulation of a masterful actress.

'My son is a splendid man. He is tied to a chair and watched by a man with a mustache and an old woman in a plaid dress. My son is unhappy to an immoderate degree. People are cruel to him but he is strong and healthy. My son worries about his work and his books, and they are not feeding him. My son will not let these inferior people destroy his will to persevere on behalf of rectitude. My son is a grand citizen of the republic and serves his country with the same nobility that marked the careers of his ancestors. My son is in a black state of mind. My son is vomiting. My son—'

'Where is son?' asked Max.

'I don't know the place.'

'Talk about place.'

'The place is . . . on a road. I can't see the place. The place is in the country? I don't know. By a hill? I can't see the place. I can't, I can't—' and Hillegond swooned in her chair, the paper fluttering to the floor at my feet. I picked it up and saw it to be two very short lines of runic writing comparable to the script in Dirck's ledger. I handed the paper to Will as Max spoke urgently into Hillegond's ear and brought her out of her swoon. She awoke from the trance complaining of a severe headache, and Max immediately lowered her head between her knees, passed his hands over the back of her neck, raised her up, and poof, her headache was gone.

'That was quite fascinating what you said,' Will told her.

'What did I say?'

'You were talking about Dirck. You said he might be on a country road. Which road?'

'I have no idea,' said Hillegond. 'I don't even remember saying it.'

'She will remember if I tell her remember,' said Max.

'Then you should tell her.'

'In time.'

'Where'd you get this paper?' Will asked her.

'Dirck's room,' she said. 'I found it in an old envelope. It's those crazy drawings he's been doing all his life.'

'Do you know what they mean?' asked Will.

'Of course not. They don't mean anything.'

Will nodded and stuffed the paper into his pocket.

'You mentioned a man with a mustache,' Will said. 'Do you remember him?'

'Nothing,' said Hillegond.

'Make her remember,' Will said to Max.

'Is too soon,' said Max with a defiant lip.

'Can't be soon enough if there's anything genuine in all this hocus-pocus,' said Will. 'You make her remember right now or I might forget I'm a gentleman.'

Max paused long enough to suggest his imperviousness to threat, then turned to Hillegond. 'You will remember everything you tell about son,' he said.

'I remember the man had a long, drooping mustache and a bald head and very shifty eyes,' said Hillegond immediately.

'Was it Aaron Plum?' said Will.

'Yes, I think it was. How could you know that, Will?'

'I have special bumps of my own,' said Will.

Hillegond continued recalling all she'd told us and Will quizzed her further on the Plum family. She knew them, but not well. I told Will then for the first time about how John the Brawn and I had carried what were probably stolen harnesses for Aaron Plum and his brother Peaches, and I also added the story of Peaches's theft of my broken spade.

'I think we should pay another visit to the Plums,' Will said. He had gone to the Plum farm immediately after the kidnapping but found only a handyman, and no family.

'You must be careful,' Hillegond said. 'They're dangerous people.'

'It will only be a social call,' said Will. 'We'll inquire about Daniel's spade.'

'It's worthless,' I said.

'Maybe so, but that worthlessness is yours, not theirs.'

We excused ourselves from Hillegond and she said she would have Matty get my old room ready for when I returned. I thought of Maud and how we had lived under this same roof for months, and I grew sad and vowed we would live together again one day. But of course that was an empty wish and Maud was God knows where.

Will and I walked to Will's house through the open fields, the sky cloudy bright. In his barn he hitched one of his three horses to a wagon and gave me my first lesson in Plum history, about which he had written much.

The first Plum in the New World was Ezra, who came to Albany from England in 1759 at age eighteen and hired on as the city's official whipper. In 1786 he was promoted to city hangman, expediting into the beyond numerous robbers, counterfeiters, and forgers until 1796, when whipping posts and execution, except for murder, were abolished. In 1801, when Ezra was sixty, an unknown assailant cut off his head with an ax – the assailant widely believed to be his grandson, Jeremiah.

Jeremiah was the son of Ezra's only child, Bliss, who first proved that murder ran in the family. At age twenty, married only three weeks, Bliss informally executed two of his young cousins, newly arrived from England, clubbing one, hanging the other, thus removing them as competition for an inheritance Bliss coveted. Bliss feigned innocence but in time confessed and was hanged before he turned twenty-one.

Bliss's son, Jeremiah, was conceived during Bliss's three-week marriage to a woman named Blessed Benson. Jeremiah, born the year his father swung, inherited all Plum property and became family patriarch in our time-present, 1850.

Jeremiah married Priscilla Swett of Vermont, who, at a later moment, was convicted of almost eviscerating a woman neighbor with a carving knife in an argument over the neighbor's fur hat, which Priscilla, called Priss, had stolen. Priss was sentenced to twenty years in jail but that was reversed in higher court through the influence of her son, Mason Plum, a lawyer who earned fame for keeping his family out of jail.

Other Plums: Aaron, a blond hunter thrice charged with near murders; Hanna, a beauty; and Eli (Peaches), whom Priscilla claimed as her own in order to cap a scandal, for Peaches was actually the offspring of his own sister, Hanna, when Hanna was fifteen. And the sire was Hanna's father, Jeremiah. There was also Fletcher Plum, a cousin, whose talent for stealing horses and altering their color and markings with charcoal and dye was so well developed that even the owners of the horses were deceived. There were other Plums, but enough.

Will put a pistol in his belt, and another under a blanket on the seat between us as we drove toward the Plum farm. Will assured me there would be no violence, that the pistols were only to fend off highwaymen, but I didn't quite believe that.

'All I want you to do when we get to the Plums',' Will said to me, 'is to identify that spade if we come across it. Otherwise let me do the talking.'

The Plum estate – house, barns, and outbuildings – sat on a knoll about two miles from Will's house, back in the woods on a road that was all but uninhabited except by the Plum family and their poor cousins, who lived in shacks and worked the land for the Plums. Cows grazed in a low meadow, goats on a hillside, and in the corral you could count two dozen horses.

Will pulled up in front of the house and handed me the reins. He mounted the steps but before he could knock, Priss Plum came to the door in what some people might have taken for a plaid housedress. Her hair was a flaming, unnatural red, and she was a bit of a looker, even at sixty.

'Who are you? Whataya want?' she asked Will.

'Canaday is my name,' said Will. 'I'd like to speak with Jeremiah.'

'He ain't here.'

'Is Peaches here?'

'What's anybody wanna see *him* for?'

'It's about a piece of personal property,' said Will.

'You claimin' he stole somethin'?'

'Not at all. Is Aaron here?'

'He don't live here no more.'

'When did he move out?' Will asked.

'That ain't none of your business.'

'You wouldn't know the whereabouts by any chance of a man named Dirck Staats? Last time I saw him he was with Aaron.'

'Never heard of no Dirck Staats.'

In the doorway of the barn I could see a man with a heavily

waxed black handlebar mustache, and with slick, ridiculously black hair, watching us. This was Jeremiah Plum, his hair dyed the way the Plums dyed spots on horseflesh. I also saw my spade leaning against the barn door. Then from around behind Jeremiah came Peaches, and I called out, 'Hey, Peaches, I want my spade back. That's my spade.' I wanted all my worthlessness in my possession, now that Will had told me that's how it should be.

Will turned and walked off the porch. I saw Jeremiah reach to his right and come up with a shotgun, which he almost pointed until he saw the pistol in Will's hand.

'Howdy, Jeremiah,' Will said as he walked toward the barn.

'Didn't know you carried a pistol, Will.'

'Only when I go into the forest,' Will said. 'Like to protect myself from the wild animals.'

'What brings you all the way out here?' said Jeremiah. Peaches wrapped his arms around Jeremiah's midsection and peered out at Will.

'Just lookin' for my good friend Dirck Staats.'

Jeremiah said nothing.

'Also came by to pick up that spade your boy Peaches borrowed from my young friend here. You know this boy, don't you, Peaches?' Will said, pointing to me. Peaches didn't answer.

'You're right talky today, Will,' said Jeremiah. 'Carryin' a pistol, yappin' like a magpie, lookin' for shovels.'

'A spade, Jeremiah, a spade is what I'm looking for.'

Will half turned to glance at the spade, then turned back to Jeremiah. Without looking at the spade Will fired a shot from belt level that put a hole in the center of its blade.

'That your spade, Daniel?' Will asked, his back to me.

'That's it,' I said.

'That spade ain't worth a whole lot,' Will said. 'It's got a hole in it. But I guess we'll take it along just for old times' sake. You know there's folks in this world'll do anything to get back an old spade they feel sentimental about. Sentiment's a powerful thing, Jeremiah, and you ought to take stock of what I'm sayin' because, well, you take this barn here. I know you love barns and I know how many you've burned. I raise this issue because I want you to know how anxious I am for news of Dirck Staats, and how if I don't hear about him by tomorrow, I'll be comin' back out here with more than a boy and a horse. And Jeremiah, if I find somebody's hurt Dirck, then I'll start doing things to people the way I did when I was ridin' with Big Thunder in the Rent War, and I know you remember those days, and how I was one barn-burnin', tar-and-featherin' son of a bitch, and not a bad shot either, Jeremiah,' and Will let go another shot from the hip that went into that spade no more than a cat's whisker distant from the previous bullet hole, the sweetest shooting I ever saw. Then Will said to me without turning, 'Daniel, come and get your spade.'

I didn't want to move. Against all logic I felt protected in the wagon. But I climbed down and walked across the yard toward the spade, which was no longer worthless now that it had those two bullet holes of Will's in it. I saved that spade for years to remind myself that courage is a worthy commodity, but that courage alone wouldn't have gotten me back what was mine. I looked in at Peaches when I picked up the spade.

'Hey, Peaches,' I said. 'I ain't gonna let nobody take this spade no more, so don't come askin'.'

Peaches stuck his tongue out at me and then ducked back behind Jeremiah. I went back to the wagon and Will backed toward it also.

'We'll be moseyin' now, Jeremiah,' said Will. 'Can't socialize like this or I'll never get my newspaper out,' and he climbed up onto the wagon, still holding his pistol. He turned to Priss in the doorway and said, 'I'll say so long to you, too, Mrs Plum, so long for now anyway.' He took the reins from me with his free hand and whacked the horse, and then we moved slowly, much too slowly for my internal fluids, down the wagon path to the road.

Dirck's book was published in an extraordinary edition of Will Canaday's *Chronicle* two weeks after our visit to the Plums'. Will did not publish a paper for three days running, offering no public explanation for the uncommon lapse, then came forth with a twenty-page issue carrying all he possessed of Dirck's manuscript. I am pleased to report that it was my adroitness in snatching up the paper that fell from behind Hillegond's ear during her talk with the phrenomagnetist that led to the breaking of Dirck's code.

The paper had on it two carefully inked lines of Dirck's runic designs. Will's unavailing scrutiny of them led him to think of the lines as a code and he took the paper to a scholar at Columbia College in Manhattan. The scholar saw instantly that the designs came from more than one language: ancient Teutonic runes and Hebrew and Arabic characters forming most of the consonants, and signs of the zodiac serving as vowels. Dirck wrote words in normal sequence but also spelled them backward. Knowing this, a translation became possible; and the opening sentences had this to say:

Maleficence flowers, malevolence reigns in the ranks of The Society, a secret organization that dominates many thousands of American lives. Evidence has accrued that leaders of The Society are often the same men who hold leadership positions in this community, this state, this nation, in commerce, finance, politics, industry, and invention, and that as a way of preserving power over what they consider lesser beings, they are, in seriate accumulation, as guilty of fratricide as was Cain, as guilty of ritual murder as are the disciples of Kali, as devout in their myriad hatreds as any demon from the caverns of hell.

> Whom do they hate?
> Thee and me.
> Which brothers do they kill?
> Thine and mine.

Dirck carried on throughout with such shameless rhetorical flourishes, also interposing an appalling study of clandestine conspiracy to defraud, destroy, debase, and eliminate not only men but families and entire organizations that obstructed the aims of The Society, and to ostracize foreigners from public office, power, and lofty social position. Sudden death on a dark pier, legal theft of an iron foundry's ownership, burning of barns, poisoning of livestock, terrorizing of immigrant and religious gatherings – all such events had been reported in the newspapers, and Dirck cited dates and places. Taken discretely, the events reflected a randomly base quality to much of human behavior. But linked by Dirck's genius for correlation, they coalesced as the scheme of a ruthless and invisible oligarchy.

Dirck's writing went well beyond summary of the plotted web. It also named beneficiaries and heretofore untouchable agents of the vile deeds. Even when his proof was firm but unsubstantiable, he described his targets with a partial fidelity that ensured identification; for instance: 'The corrupt magistrate D— van E— of the nearby village of C—.'

The recklessness of this attack (Will was sued numerous times for libel) was a calculation that placed Will's and Dirck's moral positions above anything purporting to be a fair-minded rendering of reality. Damn fair-mindedness! We are in possession of dastardly truth!

The community response was swift. Committees assembled to

confront The Society's suddenly visible leaders with a cascade of shame and alarm that such secrecy had been so powerfully loosed upon the land. A spate of resignations from the order also followed in protest against the criminal revelation. Many of the accused denied The Society even existed, but sudden departures from the city by certain bankers, politicians, artisans became known, and a few notorious members of the lower classes also vanished, men known to have been available for hired thuggery. Dirck's book was widely reprinted, or paraphrased by cautious editors, elsewhere in the nation, and Dirck, in absentia, became a hero, as did Will for publishing him.

Two known deaths ensued from what Dirck wrote. A magistrate renowned as a temperance advocate shot himself through the right eye after Dirck revealed him as the actual owner of a brothel and four grogshops; and an actors' dresser, one Abner Green, was found hanging from a crossbeam backstage at The Museum. The City Physician rendered a report of suicide on Green, but Will believed it to be murder, for he knew Green had been one of Dirck's informants. Green's death convinced Will that Dirck also had been killed, for Abner Green had given Dirck certain data on the oath that members took to gain entry to The Order of the Cross, the elite group responsible for discipline within The Society. Dirck wrote:

> Deprived of clothing, food, light, and the right to speak, naked in the darkness for as much as twenty-four hours, the candidates for this Order are at last given food to eat, then are told it has been befouled by human waste. The food has not been befouled, only tainted with certain odors. Yet believing it excrementalized, the candidates dutifully devour it. If they retch they must devour a new portion.

Of the oath, Dirck quoted this cautionary segment:

> I will defend The Society with my life, not only its known aims, but those yet to be defined. I will punish its enemies

without fear of reprisal by any man, any law. If ever I betray this oath, I agree that my stomach should be opened by a blade, and my organs and entrails exposed to the tooth and fang of ravenous rats.

Since Abner Green had not died in this manner, Will was not sure it had been a ritual murder. He distrusted all official information from the city, and so called me into his office.

'How would you like to become an actor?' he asked me.

'I would not like it at all,' I said. 'I've never set foot in a theater. Just thinking about being onstage gives me chilblains.'

'Nonsense,' said Will. 'All actors are terrified. But they overcome that and find something of themselves worth presenting to public view.'

'Not me,' said I.

'Frankly,' said Will in his forbearing tone, 'I'm not interested in your lack of dramatic ambition. I only want you to go to The Museum to audition for the new show, and to keep alert for talk of Abner Green and Dirck. They won't suspect anything of a boy your age. Tell them you can act. Tell them you can sing.'

'You want me to do this all by myself?'

'I do.'

'But I'm afraid,' I said.

'You are not afraid,' said Will.

'Oh yes I am.'

'Oh no you are not.'

'Then why do I think I am?'

'Because you are a boy who still believes in fear, and it's time you grew out of that.'

And so, browbeaten by my elder, I took myself to The Museum, which had begun its existence more than twenty years earlier as a showplace of curiosities – a rhinoceros purportedly shot by Benjamin Franklin, a living Chinese torso without arms or legs, a wax effigy of the last man legally hanged in Albany, the unique one-hundred-and-forty-pound Amazonian rat (stuffed). The Museum, in the '40s, had turned to melodrama, but also had

seen Edwin Forrest incarnate Hamlet, Lear, and Othello on its
boards. Several live-horse dramas gained popularity on its huge
stage, but all were eclipsed by the success of Magdalena Colón's
sensational dancing. Since Magdalena, the audiences had been a
thin gruel, and theater manager Waldorf (Dorf) Miller now hoped
to woo people back with a production bridging two genres: the
minstrel show and the Irish frolic. Its title: *Tambo and Paddy Go
to Town.*

A dozen workers were in assorted forms of frenzy – sweeping,
painting, doing carpentry work – as I entered. One man was sawing
a huge, decrepit rhinoceros into thirds to get it out the door (its
skin had been stuffed years earlier inside the theater), and onstage
a cadaverous white man was shuffling to the music of two banjos
and singing:

> Dere's music in de wells,
> Dere's music in de air
> Dere's music in a nigger's knee
> When de banjo's dere.

When the singer finished, Dorf Miller, a somewhat round man
in a silver leather vest, with sprouts of hair behind his ears but
nowhere else on his head, told him he was hired and asked did
he have a costume for the show. The man said he did not, and so
Dorf nodded and pulled aside a curtain onstage, revealing people
fitting costumes on performers. I went to the manager and gave
my name and said I would like a role in his new show.

'A role, you say, Master Quinn?'

'Yes, sir, a role.'

'Are you an actor, Master Quinn?'

'I hope to be,' I said, a great lie that slid so easily off my tongue
that I realized I must be very close to damnation. 'And I sing. My
mother said I had quite a good voice,' another lie that amused Dorf
Miller, and he announced to all present, 'Hear, hear. This boy says
his mother likes his singing,' and all laughed. 'What brought you
to *our* door?' he asked me.

'My mother was a close friend of Mrs Hillegond Staats and my father knew Abner Green. Both of them spoke often of The Museum, and Mr Green told my father to send me here if I needed work. Are you Mr Green?'

'No,' said the manager, 'my name is Miller. Who is your father and how did he know Abner Green?'

'Davey Quinn was his name, and he's dead and buried, God rest his soul. He and Mr Green were members of the same organization.'

'Organization,' said Dorf, growing somber, and I noted two carpenters within earshot looked at me and then at each other. They nodded their heads knowingly and then kept nodding long after any meaning had been conveyed.

'The Society, I think they called it,' I said.

'Your father was in The Society? I didn't think they allowed the Irish in.'

'I'm sure I don't know what they allowed,' I said. 'All I know is what was said.'

One carpenter whispered to the other, both of them nodding furiously. Then one of them went out of the theater.

'Abner Green,' said Dorf reflectively.

'My father said he was a good man.'

'Yes, he was all of that. It's a shame what they—' and he caught himself. 'It's a shame he died.'

'Oh, is he dead?'

'He is. But I'll attend to you myself in his absence, young sir, and if you've a mind to, let us hear this voice that your mother loves so well.'

'Oh indeed, sir. But my mother is dead and buried too, God rest her soul. And sir, if my voice fails to please you, is there another sort of job here for me?'

'Let us have first things first. What song will you sing?'

'"Kathleen Mavourneen." It was my father's favorite.'

'A lovely song, but very difficult,' said Dorf, and he sat on a chair while I faced the banjo players and others. I then sang, a capella, and very badly indeed, the only song whose words I knew to the end, pounded into my memorious brain by my relentlessly lyrical father. I could see from Dorf's face that my talent lay in a direction other than music. He was about to tell me as much when a young man in a plug hat and galluses, and only slightly older than myself, joined me in my progress toward a high note I knew I would never hit. His voice overpowered mine with such mellifluity that all in the theater were thrown into a fit of awe. It was the purest voice I could imagine, and what's more he also knew the words.

> Oh hast thou forgotten
> How soon we must sever,
> Oh hast thou forgotten
> This day we must part.
> It may be for years,
> And it may be forever,
> Oh why art thou silent,
> Thou voice of my heart . . .

I desisted from singing when he began, but continued humming along somewhat unobtrusively, reluctant to abandon my own song entirely. When the song ended, all in the theater (myself included) burst into applause, so obviously grand and crystalline was the fellow's talent. He had not been in the theater when I arrived, but must have come in behind me to unite with my song like a usurper. But his usurpation was justified: he talented, I without a shred. He extended his hand to me.

'I apologize for interfering with your song,' he said. 'But I saw you were in difficulties. Perhaps if you did a different song . . .'

'I don't know a different song,' I said, shaking his hand.

'That is a pity, then. I've ruined it for you.'

'You've ruined nothing,' said Dorf, coming between us. 'I believe it's a wonderful act. This lad here with a very small voice, terrified of performing and quite sympathetic for all that, and then you, rising from the audience like the deus ex machina himself and booming out your splendid tenor's gift. And then, yes . . . yes, yes, you climb onto the stage, singing all the while, and the two of you finish together in grand elevation. The lad is rescued, the tenor triumphant. Oh, I'm fond of it, very fond. How do you call yourself, young sir?'

'Joseph K. Moran,' said the usurper.

We all exchanged names and Dorf told us to come for rehearsal tomorrow at ten. He then busied himself with the next aspirants, a pair of twins who had been dancing in the wings to the jangle of their own tambourines when I came in. I discovered that Joseph Moran had just arrived from Utica after visiting his ailing mother. I quizzed him on La Última and he said she'd sold out the theater there for two weeks, as she had here. I inquired after Maud and he vaguely recalled hearing of a young girl who appeared on stage with La Última, but doing precisely what, he could not say. I liked Joseph Moran in spite of his usurping ways. He was only a year older than I, though he looked to be near the age of twenty, and carried himself with a sophisticated swagger I mistrusted without knowing why.

A man entered as we talked and said to Dorf, 'I'm looking for a young fellow called Daniel Quinn.' Dorf pointed me out and the man came over to me.

'I've a message,' he said in a whisper. 'Mr Staats awaits your visit.'

'Mr Staats?' I said. 'Mr Dirck Staats?'

'I wouldn't know that,' said the man. 'Staats is all they told me.'

'Who is they?'

'Mr Staats. He was with others.'

'Where is he?'

'Out the road north. I'm to take you. You're not likely to find it alone.'

'Is he all right?'

'All right? What constitutes all right in this life?'

'Is he well?'

'He's among the living, if that's what you're asking.'

'Then I think I must go.' I said this more to convince myself than anyone else, but I don't think I succeeded, for Joseph Moran spoke up.

'Is there trouble? You look worried.'

'Not at all,' I said. 'Nothing to be afraid of.'

'Then we'll meet here in the morning.'

'Ten o'clock,' I said, and went out with the man.

He was the driver of an open carriage drawn by two horses, and I rode alone beside him, staring out at the dismally gray afternoon, seeing the houses move farther and farther apart as we left the city. The trees were in early leaf and the grass was as green as April can make it. We'd had a week of heavy rain and the overcast sky threatened us today as well. We turned off the main highway and onto a narrow dirt road, rutted with mud but navigable with the help of the two animals. Certain wooded landscapes in the distance seemed familiar to me, and then I realized we were nearing the Plum spread. I asked the driver, 'Are we going to the Plums'?'

He did not answer. I asked a second time, and a second time won no response. At the road leading into the Plum place the driver stopped. I chose not to move. He was a stringy man of anxious mien, a jittery presence inside his scruffy clothing.

'Up there you go,' he said impatiently, pointing over his shoulder with his right thumb. 'In the barn, they said.'

'What's in the barn?'

'Your friend Staats.'

'Then why don't we drive to the barn?'

'I go no farther than this,' he said, brushing his lapels with the backs of his fingers. I saw no alternative but to climb down. I stood beside the carriage and looked to the barn, then again to him.

'You'll wait here for me,' I said.

'I go no farther than this,' he said, and he again brushed his lapels.

I walked toward the barn, looking for signs of Plum people, but saw no one; nor did I see any Plum animals. The horses were gone from the corral, and no cows grazed on the hillside. The barn door stood open, as it had when Will and I last visited. I looked back at the carriage and saw the driver still on his perch, holding the reins, looking straight ahead. I entered the barn cautiously, hearing no sound. I surveyed the interior from one step inside the door, discovering an open area for carriages and wagons, a hayloft, and two dozen animal stalls. I saw no sign of Dirck, and so stepped forward, making silent inquiry to the Deity whether in the next instant I would be exploded by a shotgun blast or impaled on the prongs of a rusty pitchfork.

I found Dirck in the farthermost stall, face down in soiled hay, wearing the same ill-fitting clothes he'd been wearing when abducted. On close look it was not animal droppings but his own blood that had soiled the hay. I rolled him over to see his face and found it a total wound, a horrifying smear of blood, gash, and swelling. His eyes told me he was still alive, but not for long, I judged. I did not know how to help him, but my instinct was to clean his face, find his bleeding and stop it, just as I had aided John the Brawn in conserving what remained of his blood after a street fight.

Dirck gave me recognition with his eyes, then closed them. I thought he'd died but he hadn't; and on he breathed. I lifted him, found he had no power to stand alone and that I was of insufficient strength to carry him. I ran to the door to call the carriage driver and found the low buzzard had driven off. I felt sure now that no one remained on the Plum place except myself and the bleeding Dirck. I spied a pump near the house, a bucket beside it. I filled the bucket, which leaked, and so ran with it to Dirck. I soaked my shirttail to wash the blood from his face, saw his lower lip was split open at the left corner, and his mouth full of partly clotted blood. I blotted and cleaned what I could, fearful of disturbing any clot, and Dirck made no move except to breathe. It appeared he'd been smashed in the face, so swollen was he. After the cleansing I could see his blood flow was mostly stanched, perhaps by time, or by the downward pressure of his wound onto the straw; and that gave rise to small hope in me. He was, nevertheless, all but dead, and would surely die with thoroughness if I did not find help. What I needed was a horse and wagon, and the Plum barn offered neither. I ran to the house, went 'round it to see what was behind, but found nothing. I peered in a window and saw the house had been emptied of furniture, and I began to understand not only how deeply the

Plums had been involved in, but also how radically their lives had been changed by, the events set into motion by Dirck.

Beyond the outhouse I saw a shed that probably once held pigs, or possibly chickens, or both, and I went toward it with renewed trepidation, but also thinking I should run for help, find someone with a wagon. But run where? Find whom? The Plum house was near nothing and no one. Will Canaday's house was miles away. Emmett Daugherty was perhaps a bit closer, but of that I was uncertain. Would either of them be home? How long would it take to run those miles? And what if . . . ?

The chicken-pig house door was open and I entered through it into a black dream, finding a man lying spread-eagled on the floor, a railroad spike driven into each of his hands, each of his feet. He was long dead and much of him was absent, but his red hair, his muttonchops, and his ear partially sliced or bitten away identified him to me as the man who had stolen Dirck's ledgers from Will's office. He had been stripped to below the waist, slit up the middle, and now a globular rat was eating his liver. When I came in, the rat scurried off, then paused near an exit hole to observe me, waiting for me to decide whether he should, or should not, be allowed to resume his gluttony.

I am impressed by the practicality of the human mind, even in times of terror. I do not join with those who see terror superseding all other emotions, for what I did at this moment was to cast my glance dutifully about the henhouse and discover a four-sided barrow with wheel and handles: a vehicle. Sent. I glanced anew at the sliced man to reassure myself it was he, to convince myself that he had indeed been crucified and split and was now rat-ridden, proving it to my incredulous eye so I would not later think I had merely imagined it. Then I lunged toward the barrow with sufficiently broad gesture to scare the rat into his exit hole, and I wheeled my vehicle out the door and toward the livid lump that Dirck Staats had become.

Dirck had not moved, but his eyes were open when I arrived. 'Can you move at all? Can you stand?'

He tried valiantly to sit up, but his pain had stupefied him, and he fell back. I heaped straw into the barrow as a cushion for him, then lifted him so he was sitting in the barrow's center. His legs dangled and touched the ground, making it impossible to wheel him. I found a filthy tethering rope in one stall, wrapped it 'round Dirck's ankles, and then pulled it taut and fastened it to the barrow's handles, thus lifting his legs and pointing them straight ahead. I wrapped the rest of the rope around his arms and torso and secured that also to the handles, making him my somewhat upright prisoner. His head was bouncing up, down, and sideward, but that seemed to me irrelevant to his safe passage.

I wheeled him out of the barn and off Plum land, then went a mile at least before I saw another dwelling, high on a hillside. I left Dirck on the road, climbed the hill and knocked at the door. A bearded old man leaning on half a crutch answered.

'What is it, boy?'

'An injured man,' I said, 'very badly hurt and bleeding. I have him tied up in that barrow down there. Could I borrow a horse or wagon, or could you take me to get help?'

'What kind of thing is that, tying up a sick man in a barrow?'

'It's all there was, and I couldn't carry him, or even lift him. Is there a doctor near here?'

'No doctor'd put a sick man in a barrow.'

'You don't understand. I'm trying to help him. He'll die if he doesn't get help.'

'Whatever ails him, that barrow'll make him worse. Who is he?'

'His name is Dirck Staats.'

'Never heard of him.'

'That doesn't matter,' I said with maximum exasperation. 'Can you help him?'

'Where'd you get him?'

'About a mile up the road. In a barn.'

'The Plums'?'

'It used to be their place but they're all gone now.'

'Plums are gone? Where'd they go?'

'I don't know. Can you *please, please*, help us?'

'I wouldn't help a Plum if he was dyin' on my doorstep.'

'He's *not a Plum*!' I yelled. 'His name is Dirck Staats! The Plums are the ones who *hurt* him!'

'Why'd they hurt him?'

'I don't know! *I don't know!*'

'I wouldn't help a Plum if he was dyin' in my barn. If a Plum got kicked by a horse right in front of me I'd let him lay. If a Plum was being pecked to death by woodpeckers I'd buy a ticket and watch.'

Then he closed the door on me.

I wheeled Dirck toward the main road, another half mile at least, some of it uphill and much of it through mud. I often had to go off the road into a field to get past the mud, and climbing crisscross on a hill, I almost lost Dirck overboard twice, his head bobbing like a dead chicken's.

When I got to the highway I waved down two carriages, but they both kept on. A man carrying a sack of flour on his shoulder stopped to look at Dirck, then went on his way without a word. I sensed Dirck was giving forth an efflux of dread to all who came near him, and felt also that the Christian virtues of charity and compassion were little heeded by my neighbors.

At the next house I roused only a barking dog. At the next I found a feeble woman, useless to my cause except for her remark that I was near the West Troy Road, and so I knew I could find my way to Emmett Daugherty's. Fixing on Emmett as my destination seemed superior to the futile beseeching of strangers, and so I pushed our barrow with renewed vigor, trying not to dwell on Dirck's painful descent into hell. I grew impermeable to all glances, certain that any imagined court of mercy along the way would turn into a waste of Dirck's diminishing time.

I was not even sure Dirck could still hear me. But if he *was* alive I knew he'd welcome distraction from his pain and discomfort, and so I talked to him aloud of my meeting with Joseph Moran and of our duet on 'Kathleen Mavourneen.' I involved Dirck in my future plans at the newspaper and said I hoped he would tutor me in the writing arts. I told him I was grateful beyond measure for this chance to help him, especially after being allowed to live in his own house with his mother, to whom I was growing very close, and as well to Will Canaday, who, through his newspaper and his tutelage, was opening my eyes to the world in ways not accessible to the being I used to be. I gave thanks to Dirck himself for his revelation to me of the significance of the word, which, I could now see, releases boundless emotion and mystery, even into the lives of such folk as the Plums. I did not mention the fate of the sliced man. I focused on Dirck as someone who could change the world with his writing: a maestro of language, a champion of the heroic sentence. Of course I said these things in my limited way, and Dirck had no choice but to accept them in that form.

I ended my monologue wondering silently whether I should tell Dirck about my love for Maud, and my loss of her, but then we were at Main Street, entering into the most easeful steps of my life: that short walk down the sloping grade to Emmett's house. I saw Emmett sitting on his front step as I turned the corner. He was smoking his pipe, and when I saw smoke rise from it, I knew salvation.

'We're here, Dirck,' I said, and I almost broke into laughter, for he raised his head and blinked vitally at me.

Quickly now I sharpen my point. We put Dirck to bed in fresh nightclothes, washed him, made him warm. When Josie saw Dirck's condition she blessed herself, said a silent prayer, and went to a cupboard for a ball of string. With a length of it she took Dirck's measure from scalp to toe, cut the string, then went to the yard, dug a hole, and buried it.

'They'll not now take his soul,' she told us.

Emmett sent Josie for the doctor and gave Dirck a warm spoonful of the chicken soup Josie had made. Dirck ejected it violently, at the same time loosening a ball of coagulated blood and straw that had settled in the front of his mouth. Emmett moved the oil lamp close to Dirck's face to study his wound, and when he turned to me, his eyes were afloat in tears.

'The cruel, cruel bastards,' he said. 'They took his one and only tongue.'

The *Albany Chronicle*, as we had known it, failed of business one month after Dirck's return to the human race. Four attempts to set the premises ablaze were foiled, but nighttime vandals finally overpowered our sentinels and destroyed Will's press with aggravated sledgings. Within one week Will was printing at the shop that published *The Paddle*, a penny-awful sheet of scandal and mayhem from around the globe (the terrible fate of eunuchs in a Persian harem, the Mouth Murders by the mad dentist of Baltimore); but by then The Society's many members had withdrawn their paid notices. Even advertisers loyal to Will, finding themselves threatened, withdrew also. Will pressed on with his waning capital, being but a week from closing when Hillegond bought out *The Paddle* and installed Will as editor. Will merged the publications, fusing the inherited mayhem with his own politics, and naming the new publication the *Chronicle-Paddle*, a grotesque and short-lived fusion. Will kept it long enough to ensure an orderly transition of readers, but then diminished the word *Paddle* to minuscularity and, after a year, banished it altogether.

Dirck recovered his health but found his tongueless words no more than idiot grunts; and so he went silent. Because he believed I had saved his life (actually, he might have survived alone, even in the filthy hay – unlike Maud, who required my intercession to remain among the quick), Dirck made me his intermediary. He would scrawl swift messages with his everpointed pencil, then thrust the scrawls at me to read aloud. He wrote of his ordeals in fragments that belied their own truth: 'Held me in wonderful chicken coop ... The gentle Jeremiah Plum took orders from kindly bass-voiced stranger who visited me wearing black veil on his face ... Unfortunate man with partial ear guarded me with kindness ... I nevertheless felt selfish need to loosen ropes to escape and return to work at *Chronicle* ... Hid in barn, too weak to run ... Surely against his wishes, Aaron Plum smashed my face with plank and severed my tongue while holding it with pincers ... Man with veil cautioned Aaron not to kill me while severing tongue ... My father, wondrous man, saved my life.'

This euphoric response to Plum captivity and torture was peculiar indeed. Will viewed Dirck's behavior as akin to that of the Christian martyrs who found in all horrors the glorification of that which was greater than themselves: vileness is beauty, punishment is reward, death is life. I saw this equation then, and I see it still, as crackbrained. Dirck's remark about his father was the most peculiar of all, for Petrus Staats had died in 1835, fifteen years before these events took place.

Petrus entered my life indirectly upon the arrival at the mansion of Lyman Fitzgibbon, the merchant-scientist. He was the godfather of Dirck, the former business partner of Petrus, and an inventor of infinite and ingenious improvements on metal-working machines. He was also the father of Gordon Hamilton Fitzgibbon, who would become one of the most confounding figures in my life, an ambivalent man of prodigious energy and erudition, also a writer of sorts, who on this night was away at law school in Yale College.

I was in the foyer when Lyman rapped with the knocker. I opened the door to see this tall and muscular man with a full white beard, full head of white hair, and beside him his handsome wife, Emily, in a long gown of black satin.

'Who are we here?' the man inquired of me.

'We are Daniel Quinn, sir, and we live here through the kindness of Mrs Staats. May I announce you to her?'

'A quick tongue on you, boy. I like that. Tell Hillegond Lyman has come back.'

He had returned from Washington, where in recent years he

had been serving in an English diplomatic post. London-born, Oxford-educated, Lyman Fitzgibbon had come to America at the age of twenty-six, met and married the wealthy Emily Taylor (her wealth came from shipping), and swiftly joined his wife's wealth with Petrus in the nailworks that would become an ironworks and then the largest stove-making foundry in the city. Lyman became an investor in banks, insurance, railroads, and assorted commerce as far west as Buffalo and, not least, a land speculator of grand proportion, the speculation generally in service of a commercial enterprise higher than itself. He would, by the mature decades of his life, be Albany's richest man, his vaunted power, when coupled to nothing more than resolute silence, capable of turning men of perfectly sound ego into cringing and snivelous whelps.

I led the Fitzgibbons to the east parlor to await Hillegond's appearance. Lyman stopped before Dirck's portrait on the east wall and spoke toward it.

'How is the boy?'

'He's recovering, but cannot speak,' I said.

'You were his rescuer,' he said, turning to me.

'I helped him in his trouble,' I said.

'You're quick, and you're modest. You will go far in this world, young man.'

'I thank you, sir.'

'Don't thank me. Thank whoever it was taught you to be quick and modest. You'll shed that modesty in time.'

I nodded, perceiving in myself not modesty but inadequacy, and wondering with what one replaced modesty, once shed. I found Dirck and told him of Lyman's arrival, and went with him to the east parlor. Lyman embraced Dirck, saying, 'You shouldn't have written that book, son. You know it was wrong.'

Dirck stared at Lyman, neither contradicting nor agreeing. The knocker sounded again, and Capricorn this time admitted Will Canaday and his ladylove, the handsome widow woman Felicity Baker, a teacher of needlework and deportment at the Albany Female Academy. Our spate of visitors on this evening had been summoned to a musical soiree through which Hillegond hoped to buoy the warped and muted spirit of Dirck. Long a benefactress of The Museum, Hillegond had asked Dorf Miller to choose among his current talent and provide us with an hour's entertainment. Dorf arrived with pianoforte, violin, tambourine, and banjo virtuosi; also with Joseph K. Moran and a young woman I'd not seen before. Dorf introduced her as Heidi Grahn, a songstress late of Sweden, and at the first sight of her, Dirck's dark mood faded. He separated himself from his godfather and entered into a fury of note writing: 'Be sure she stays after performance,' said the first note he thrust at me. 'Tell her I am taken with her voice' (she had not yet uttered a note) . . . 'Is she married, betrothed? . . . Ask whether she enjoys poetry . . .'

I had no chance to do this, for by then our guests had filed into the music room, a polygonal extension from an eastern wall of the mansion, a semicircular room with mullioned windows and an intricately carved oak ceiling that gave one the sense of being in the apse of a cathedral. The guests besat themselves on plush mahogany benches beneath a pair of murals painted by Ruggiero and depicting the contemporary Staatses: Petrus and Hillegond, whose peripatetic excursions in Europe (in company with the Fitzgibbons) had been the source of many of the works of art, and not-art, that abounded in the mansion. In his portrait Petrus played a great gilded harp (which remained in the far corner of the salon, as Petrus did not), and the image of Hillegond ebulliently fingered the pianoforte, from which she was, in life, incapable of extracting even minimal musical coherence.

Joseph K. Moran saw me and waved from the front of the room. Our plans to do the tenor-to-the-rescue act for Dorf had collapsed when I became linked to Dirck in his infirm time, and well enough so, for Joseph needed no collaborators. His two songs on the opening night of *Tambo and Paddy* had engendered two encores, so Dorf gave him four songs the second night, engendering four encores; and even that left the audience unsated. The talk abroad in the city was that Joseph Moran would be a performer of great magnitude ere long.

'We meet again,' Joseph said, coming over to me. 'I have

William Kennedy

something for you,' and he handed me a letter, the first article of mail I had received in my fifteen years of life. 'It came from Rochester,' he said. 'I mentioned to a traveling actor your interest in La Última, and when he met her he spoke of you.'

I took the letter in hand and at the sight of the handwriting the life within me gathered great potency. I knew the letter was from Maud, for in my possession since before she left were four words she had written on a piece of stationery in a near-perfect hand: 'The sadness of bumblebees' – this meaning I knew not what. When I saw her throw it away, I salvaged and kept it.

'I'm very grateful to you,' I said.

'We must keep track of our friends,' Joseph said.

He spoke of my rescue of Dirck, said he adjudged me a hero and was proud to know me. He carried on in that vein, asking me questions as Dirck thrust more messages into my fist ('Ask her age . . . where she lives . . . what her religion . . . her favorite flower . . .'), and so, with my head full of questions and my hand full of scraps of paper, I had to relegate Maud's communiqué to my trouser pocket.

'What a grand house this is,' said Joseph Moran. 'I would like to live in it one day.'

'Yes,' I said, feeling possessive, 'I live in it now.'

Dorf set his tambourinist and banjoist to playing and followed their medley with an introduction of Heidi Grahn singing an air from *The Marriage of Figaro* that Jenny Lind had often sung, and in truth I know not how the Swedish Nightingale could have sung it more melodiously. Dirck's pencil fell silent at last, he in rapture at the sound of the young woman's voice, and I, at last, was able to open Maud's letter and read her salutation, 'Dearest Daniel,' at which my heart began a percussive thumping. My eye followed down the page, running ahead of itself too quickly to allow me to make sense of anything. But then I read these words: 'am awaiting the fulfillment of your promise to steal me,' and I could read no further, so rich was my excitement. Then the ecstasy was violated by a loud knocking that intruded as well on Heidi's melody.

We turned to the foyer to see Capricorn admitting, to my great

100

surprise, a most serious-visaged Emmett Daugherty, and with him a weeping girl of perhaps eight years, a boy somewhat younger than myself who was tilting his head back and blotting his nose with a filthy and bloody rag, and a woman, the children's mother, in a state as wretched as womanhood can inhabit. The music trailed off as we stared at these representatives of a gravely negative unknown.

Emmett led the woman and children to a sofa in the foyer, then asked to speak with Lyman, who heard Emmett's request and rose from his seat in the music room. I followed but kept my distance, seeing Matty run to the kitchen and return with a wet towel to clean the boy's bloody face, take the old rag from him, and lay him full-length on a bench with his head back.

'It's a tragic thing,' Emmett said. 'Alfie Palmer, one of the moulders let go in the layoff, he did this to them.'

'Why do you bring them here?' Lyman asked.

'It's a foundry matter, Lyman,' said Emmett. 'And it's your foundry.'

'Does Harris know about this?' Lyman asked, Harris being the Yankee engineer who ran the foundry in Lyman's absence.

'I've no use for that man, Lyman. It's his layoffs began this trouble. Your good self is what's needed. None other. Alfie was always a hard-luck man, and with the layoff he had no doctor money when his son got sick, and he could only watch the boy die. It maddened him, as it would any man, and he took to the drink, though I don't know where he got money for that. And there's been fights – dozens – between the new hired men and the old let go, and Alfie in more than his share of those. But he went beyond a punch-up tonight. He followed Toddy Ryan home when Toddy left the foundry, giving him heat, don't you know. But Toddy's only the half-pint, with no health to him at all, and he knew if he fought Alfie he'd be killed sure as sure is, and so he ran to his shack and barred the door, but Alfie broke it in and split Toddy's skull with an ax handle. Then he went after young Joey here, and it looks like he broke the lad's nose. Toddy's wife throws the boilin' tea in Alfie's face, gets the children out, and brings them to the foundry to find me. But her Toddy's dead on the floor and there's no peace for it now, Lyman, no peace. Alfie's on the run and the men are in camps, the old and the new. They'll fight in bunches, and they're forming already. There'll be blood in the streets by morning.'

Emmett, his craggy face overgrown with two days' stubble of beard, was a scolding presence. He was foreman at Lyman's North End foundry, and had risen in eleven years, despite his lung ailment, from apprentice to moulder to chief grievance spokesman, a voice of righteous reason from below. His rise in status began when he hired on as coachman for Lyman on an expedition to buy land in the Adirondack region for a new railroad line. Animosity toward the venture was strong, the natives convinced the railroad would before long destroy their pristine world (and so it would), and the animus peaked when half a dozen mountain men set upon Lyman and his lawyer with plans to tar and feather both.

While Lyman contemplated probable death by absurdity, Emmett garroted one of the attackers and bargained the man's breath for the two captives, an act of bravery that ensured not only his own security ever after through Lyman's gratitude, but also the education of any Daugherty heir not yet born, or even conceived, on this night of tribulation in the foyer of Hillegond's mansion.

Maud, I speak to you now of the Irish, knowing you are in my pocket, to tell you of the Ryans and their misery and how it distracts me, for it is part of me: Joey Ryan – with broken nose, dead father, sickly mother – is surely myself in another guise, just as Molly Ryan, that tiny waif, could be you. They are the famine Irish, Maud, and they are villains in this city. It wasn't this way for the Irish when I was little, but now they are viewed not only as carriers of the cholera plague but as a plague themselves, such is their number: several thousand setting up life here in only a few years, living in hovels, in shanties, ten families to a small house, some unable to speak anything but the Irish tongue, their wretchedness so fierce and relentless that not only does the city shun them but the constabulary and the posses meet them at the docks and on the turnpikes to herd them together in encampments on the city's great western plain. Keep them moving is the edict of the city's leaders, and with obscene pleasure the Albany wharf rats and river scum (some Irish among these, preying on their own) carry out this edict by stoning the canalboats that try to unload newcomers here. It is no wonder the greenhorns grow feral in response, finding in this new land a hatred as great as that which drove them out of Ireland, that suppurating, dying sow of a nation.

Looking at the Ryans one could believe them carriers of any perniciousness: defeated, low in spirit, clad in rags, their skin flaked, pale, and dirty, their hair matted, their eyes raw with the disease of all victims. Who would invite their like? Who would give them bread or bed? None in this city today, and yet not quite none, for Hillegond is doing for them what she did for us: telling Capricorn to find them street and bed clothes; telling Matty to cook for, cleanse, and accept them on their night of trouble here in this haven for ravaged souls.

People are breaking into groups in the mansion, Maud. In the east parlor Emmett, Will, and Lyman are in dark communion. In the music room Dirck is boldly handing notes to Heidi Grahn. In the foyer Joseph Moran is extolling to Hillegond the virtues of her home. 'It's more splendid than any house in Utica,' he coos, and she receives his word as if he mattered. I want with desperation of heart to read the rest of your letter and yet I cannot. I am beginning to sense what it will say and I choose postponement until I have intuited your full message, believing if I am right in my intuition we will be closer than ever and this communion across the miles will be with us for the rest of our lives.

And so I have sought out the person with whom I have most in common: Joey Ryan of the bleeding nose – but bleeding no more – seated now at the kitchen table eating Matty's chicken soup and corn bread. I told him I was sorry for his trouble and that my father was dead also, and at least he had his mother with him, but that my mother was dead and so was my sister.

'You're an orphan, then,' he said.

'I am.'

103

'What do they do to orphans? Do they kill them?'

'I've never heard of that,' I said, 'and they haven't killed me yet. But sometimes they put them in orphan homes, and sometimes they let them run loose.'

'I'd fancy to run loose,' he said.

'I would too,' I said.

'Run loose till I grow up enough to solve the man who killed me father.'

'How will you solve him?'

'I'll break his skull.'

'You aren't big enough for that.'

'I'll get bigger and find him and break his skull like he broke me father's.'

'They'll hang you.'

'Do they hang orphans?'

'They hang you for breaking a man's skull.'

'Will they hang the man that killed me father?'

'If they catch him they might.'

'I'll hang him meself, and then I'll cut off his head.'

Maud, the boy is a little fellow, no bigger than yourself. But vengeance burns in his eyes, and if he doesn't break one man's skull before long, he'll break another's. Anger took seed in him farther back than the clubbing of his father, as I learned when I asked where he came from in Ireland.

'From a ditch near Cashel,' he said. 'The landlord tumbled our house and put us off our land, and me father piled all we owned in a cart and we pushed it till we couldn't climb the hill. Then we lived in the ditch and used the wagon as a roof. We could see the Galty Mountains from the ditch. They tumbled our house to make room for the landlord's cows. "They're in grave need of pasture," the landlord told me pa. Then we left the ditch, threw things away to lighten our load, and the three of us hauled the cart up the mountain, a terrible high mountain of four hundred feet it was, and me sister settin' the block at the wheel. We done it at last and got over the mountain, but goin' down the back side was near as troublesome as goin' up the front, and we almost lost the cart two or three assorted times. We begged food, and when we couldn't get any we stole it, or we ate grass. Then we went to me uncle's place on the road to Tipperary, and he took us in and paid for Pa to go to America. Pa himself is all of us that went over. The night before he left we had a wake for his leavin', with me ma keenin' for hours over his goin'. "Ye won't come back for us," she kept saying. It was near to bury him, is what it was. But he sent remittances and got us all over here, me and me sister and me mother. And didn't we all come to this town of Albany, because we couldn't fit in New York in the wee room Pa lived in. We was here just a few weeks and no money left when he got the foundry job, and then, a little after that, they broke his skull, the man did, the bastard man.'

I talked more with him, Maud, but it was so painful I soon left him and thought of going to bed, for I could find no one else to talk to. People were all over the house talking of the coming fight and how awful it would be, and I knew I would watch it when it came. More death is what I thought, and that put me in mind of the *Dood Kamer*, where you and I watched John and Magdalena and Hillegond love each other, after a fashion, and that was where I sat and read your letter.

Dearest Daniel [you began],

I write to you because a person named Joseph K. Moran has said he met you and that you asked for my well-being, for which I send gratitude. I worry, too, about *your* well-being, for you know I consider you my true love for all time and ever after, and am awaiting the fulfillment of your promise to steal me away from my loving but inconstant aunt and her companion, the ridiculous John McGee. That man had the boldness to tell me you stole money from us, then jumped off the canalboat and ran away. I told him he was a poor liar and a worse scoundrel, and when I received the full impact of your absence I went into a swoon and as in the past I refused to eat, coming so near to death I terrified everyone. I think you would have been quite proud of me. A most peculiar thing happened in my starving condition. I could see what people around me were thinking, not an uplifting thing to be able to do. I also was able to communicate with spirits of the dead, or at least I think they are dead. They certainly seem to be spirits, for no one can see them, not even I. Yet they make violent sounds, of which everyone save myself is terribly frightened. I rather like their rhythms.

Please note that we will soon be in Saratoga Springs, where my aunt is to perform her dancing. I have assisted in some of her performances and may again, but will not now say how, as I wish to surprise you. We arrive in Saratoga May 30th, and I expect to see you soon thereafter, at which time we shall make plans for you to steal me. You have my love forever and a day, and another forever and another day.

Maud

P.S. I saw Joseph K. Moran perform in Utica and thought him an affecting person. Please thank him for putting me in touch with you. I await you, Daniel Quinn.

Maud, nothing in my life has been equivalent to the thrill of reading this letter. I confess I had hoped for a hint of your affection, but am overwhelmed by what you have said. I must add that your meetings with spirits and your plans involving me give me great unrest that I cannot solve of the instant. You consider me more powerful than I am. However, I will do what I am capable of doing.

Maud, I send you love.

Capricorn brought the news that the warring factions from the foundry were assuming positions. Lyman said he feared that if word of the presence of the Ryans in the mansion reached Alfie, he and his cronies might seek satisfaction of the bloodlust that was upon them. Before sunrise the call went out for all in the mansion to be ready, and so Hillegond took Petrus's pistol from its case, loaded it, and sat with it in the lap of her night robe; and Capricorn laid four rifles and two more pistols on the dining table. I could not believe we were anticipating that men from the foundry would invade this grand home to kill children.

As for Joey, he kept himself busy through the night creating a slungshot, a bludgeon fashioned from a rock wrapped in oilcloth and wound tight with string. I saw him in an upstairs hallway flexing his creation cleverly: slapping it with thuds against his left palm. When I saw his mother, Margaret Ryan, and his sister, Molly, at morning, they looked no less affrighted than they had the previous evening, but immeasurably more comely with clean skin and hair and fresh clothing.

Dorf Miller and his company, as well as Emmett and Will, had left the mansion during the night. Lyman stayed in the room long reserved for him on the fourth floor – his aerie, he called it – which gave him his preferred morning view of the Staats woodland and creek, and of the pond Petrus built when Hillegond first became enamored of the wild ducks that inhabited the swamp.

By the first rays of the morning sun the tea was steeping in the kitchen, Matty was taking bread from the oven, and our cluster of souls was gathering near the warmth of the fire. The good feeling among us all seemed inappropriate with a death struggle in the offing, but I attest that thirteen years hence the same feelings would prevail in me when, as a correspondent in the war, I'd speak with soldiers and other journalists around a fire. We would drink coffee of the rankest order and convince each other it was fitting nectar for those about to conquer, or die, or both, or neither.

I must convey now that the fated stroke that aligned Alfie Palmer against the Ryans was an event of historical moment in Albany, for it defined boundaries, escalated hatreds, and set laboring men of near-equal dimension and common goal against each other. In years to come, periodic battles would be waged anew as a consequence of what was about to happen this day. These battles, which invariably took place on Sundays, when men were off work and free to maim one another, raged for hours without interference from the constabulary. The battles (the first was called the Ryans against the Palmers) were in time called the Hills against the Creeks, the Hills being the neighborhood to which Alfie Palmer, and others like him, had risen: high ground that represented a social ascendancy from where the Creeks lived – the low-lying slums, the mean and fetid nest of hovels on the shores of the Foxenkill, that foul creek where the shacks of the Irish erupted overnight like anarchic mushrooms and where the killing of Toddy Ryan took place.

Will Canaday returned after breakfast, and he, Lyman, and Dirck made ready to leave the mansion. I followed behind, and Joey Ryan behind me.

'No, no,' Will said to us. 'You stay here. Down there is no place for children. Take care of the boy here,' and he pointed to Joey.

'It would be good for my education to see such a thing,' I said.

'I want you alive to get an education,' said Will as he and the others climbed into the carriage. Hillegond stood in the doorway as the carriage pulled away, and then called Joey and me inside.

'Come in where it's safe,' she called.

'No,' said Joey, and he broke into a run, following in the wake of the carriage.

'I'll get him,' I said, and then I, too, was running, with Hillegond's screams fading behind me.

I couldn't catch Joey. He was fleet as a wild animal, and more fit than I for such a run, which was two miles or more across open fields, down the gully, and over the footbridge that spanned the Patroon creek, then up the hill on the far side, where I lost sight of him amid distant houses. It was my assumption he would head for Canal Street, where he lived, and it was toward that notorious thoroughfare that I headed.

Bells welcomed me to the populated city, and I saw women and children walking – toward church, I presumed. People were also moving into a vacant field that began the long slope eastward toward the canal and the river. At the crest of the field I saw forty or more men below me, standing, talking, many with clubs in hand. I sensed what they were about and that they would not be likely to give allegiance to Toddy Ryan.

I kept walking south and approached Canal Street, with its creek coursing beside it. This was the neighborhood called Gander Bay, named after the sassy fowl the Irish kept in the Foxenkill. It was a place of dread and danger, of woe and truculence. Its dirt pathways, which became deep and pervasive mud when it rained, were narrow, crooked, and violable by the sudden erection of hovels that would force a detour. Many of these hovels looked as if they'd been thrown together in a day, an upthrust of uneven boards with no windows, buttressed by sod or raw earth. Looming up among them was the occasional giant of an ordinary house, half a century old, built when this was open space and the crowd had not yet arrived.

I'd been in the area before, but not often. It gave no welcome to strangers. In one of the big houses near the creek lived two old brothers, Dinny Reilly, who collected grease from neighbors to make soap (for a certain amount of grease he'd give you a bar of soap), and Johnny Reilly, called Johnny the Cats, who went to jail at cholera time for throwing dead cats into the Foxenkill. Johnny won his name by living with four dozen cats, and the neighborhood rhyme about the men was known to many:

> Pitty-pat, sugar and fat,
> Old Dinny Reilly
> And Johnny the Cats.

Children were running free, and women were doing their washing in the creek, clothes already drying on tree limbs in Gander Bay's early sunlight. A man sat astride a backless chair in the doorway of one shanty, arms folded, pipe in teeth, back stiff and straight: prepared for events. Around him lay half a dozen cats and I took him to be Johnny of the rhyme.

'Good morning, sir,' I said.

'It's a good morning if ye think it is,' he said.

'Do you know where the Ryans live?'

'There's Ryans the world over.'

'A boy. Joey Ryan. His father was Toddy.'

'Aaah, those Ryans. Ye'd best stay away from *that* house.'

'I know Joey. I want to help him.'

'Then folly your nose that way and ye won't miss it.'

My nose led me along a dirt lane, soft from the previous day's moderate rains, to a turning where I saw a crowd of people, and above them the head and shoulders of a young man in sweater and cap, standing in a wagon, haranguing the crowd in vibrant oratory: 'This what is comes of bein' an Irish workin'man,' and he turned his gaze downward, then up again to the crowd. 'A good man . . . alive with the family last night . . . then murdered in front of his children . . . Toddy Ryan gone today . . . who'll go tomorrow?'

The silent crowd was with the man, nodding its reverence.

Children on the edge moved away when his pause broke their attention. A gray-haired woman in a threadbare shawl pushed forward, her hair tight in a bun, her jaw jutting out with anger.

'I knew Toddy Ryan,' she said. 'He was a good man and he deserves better than you're givin' him. Look at him there, shameful.' (We all looked toward the wagon, but I could see nothing because of intervening bodies.) 'Bring the man indoors and wake him properly. It's sacrilegious, this is.'

'Ah, close your mutt, woman,' said the man in the wagon. 'They'll be after you next, and then after your children.'

'Where's this fight you're talkin' about?' a man in the crowd asked.

'We start at the foot of Lumber Street,' came the answer. 'There'll be clubs there for all. We'll move in a body and meet the divvil himself if he's a mind to fight us.'

Satisfied with the answer, the questioner nodded and moved away. Others followed him, leaving an opening that let me see the wagon. Toddy Ryan lay on three boards nailed together, tied down with a rope around his waist so he wouldn't slide off, the boards slanted to allow us full view of his final image: hands folded on his chest, toes of his shoes too long and turned up, ill-fitting clothes full of stains and holes – a runt of a man who, in addition to being horridly dead, had died in terrible health. His cranial cleft and the caked blood of his wound were the unforgettable focus of the cautionary tableau he offered us: here lies a dead Irishman.

The speaker resumed his harangue and some in the crowd fell away. But newcomers kept arriving in a steady stream, and I learned that Toddy, since daybreak, had been on tour of all Irish neighborhoods in the city's north and west ends, a traveling theater piece: drama in the flesh. I asked a woman beside me where the dead man had lived.

'Over there, isn't it?' she said, pointing to a board shanty. I went to it and saw the door and wooden latch Alfie Palmer had kicked in. I called Joey's name but got no answer, then saw the interior was dark and barren, lit only by the light from the open door, and on the floor a broken clay pot and rusty tin cup. Whatever else of life's things the Ryans once owned had been removed by scavengers. Sunlight shone across the large bloodstain on the dirt floor where Toddy Ryan bled his profuse last.

I considered what I should do in this place, then stepped fully inside, closed the door, and shut out the day. The room became blackness of a deep order. I breathed the smell of earth and tried to imagine the life of the Ryans in this tiny room, then tried to imagine them living in a ditch with their wagon as a roof. Poor as we Quinns had been (and we had gone weeks without money, our food all charity from relatives), never were we dirt poor, nor ever before had I understood the meaning of that phrase: to live day and night inhaling the odor of raw earth. I felt like a burrowing animal, and thought how the Ryans must have cursed all things and people that had brought them to this condition, and how they must have envied all who lived above it.

I stepped back into the sunlight and saw that Toddy, the wagon, the recruiter, and his crowd were all gone. I followed the lane and fell in line soon enough behind the wagon, the recruiter now seated and holding the reins but still hailing all gawkers with his spiel: 'Hullo and listen to us now . . . look here on the corpse of Toddy Ryan . . . killed for being Irish . . . clubs for all at the foot of Lumber Street . . . we'll show them who we are . . . we'll send them to blazes . . .'

We passed Patroon Street, several dozen of us now in the growing parade with Toddy's wagon, and we moved north on Broadway in the warming sunlight of the morning. I could see the crowd of men looming ahead of us, twice as large as the group I'd seen on the hill. These were young men, mostly hatless and in shirtsleeves, vibrant in their gestures, anticipating the greater vibrancy of battle. A dozen or two smaller boys were fighting mock duels with the promised clubs that were being handed out from a wagon. I knew a few of the men: Walter White and Petey Carey from Van Woert Street; Midge McTigue, who had worked at the lumberyard with my father. I guessed that my father would have been with these men had he been alive. I could not find Joey Ryan but I saw Emmett, still unshaven, probably sleepless, and looking gravely upset as he grabbed two men by their shirts. I heard his words: 'It's madness to fight uphill . . . madness to fight at all this way.'

'Too late for that jabber, Emmett,' one man said, knocking Emmett's hand from his shirt.

Emmett pushed through to the head of the crowd to yell to them all, 'Don't do this, men . . . we'll have a dozen corpses among us before the day is out . . .'

One hoarse voice called out, 'By the Christ, let's get on with it,' and at that the men, numbering sixty at least, strode forward up Lumber Street, some of them pocketing stones as they went. And then came the rap of the clubs on the cobblestones in steady tattoo: rap, step, rap, step, rap, step, rap – this in march cadence, which the men's feet found compatible; and they moved to it. Emmett saw me, came to me, grabbed my arm.

'You're not in this, boy. I say you're not.'

'I was looking for Joey Ryan. He's out to get Alfie Palmer.'

'That puny little thing after Alfie?'

'He wants to cut his head off.'

Emmett shook his head. 'Madness everywhere,' he said. Then he looked at the men moving up the hill. 'I've got to get with them.'

'Are you going to fight, Emmett?'

'Not if I can help it. But maybe I can do some good.'

'I'll go with you.'

'No.'

'I want to see it.'

'Then see it, but stay on the sides.'

I had no animosity toward Alfie Palmer, whom I didn't know; nor did I feel it my responsibility to champion the cause of Toddy Ryan beyond keeping track of Joey. I walked with Emmett and we caught up with the men as they turned a corner. Spectators joined us: old men, young men, women and children – all on the run from other streets as word of the battle spread; and we moved like a Roman parade, marching the gladiators to the arena. The men kept themselves a tight body as they marched, but when they sighted the enemy waiting two blocks up Colonie Street hill, some behind barricades, their cries went up: 'Kill the bastards . . . go now . . . get 'em,' and they broke ranks and with wordless screams ran forward.

The Ryans, doing themselves no favor running uphill, ran into a hail of stones and paving blocks. They returned them in kind, but the Palmers, galloping downhill with the help of gravity and raised clubs, flung their bodies at the uphillers and felled sixteen into varying states of unconsciousness, losing only half a dozen of their own number in that opening charge. The smack of fists on flesh, the whap of club on skull collided with the curses and whoops of the warriors. Iron bars came into use, though the dominant fashion was the club, either of these tools cumbersome in close combat and some quickly discarded so as to allow fighting with fists and teeth, the battlers rolling and tussling into the proper position to gouge an eye, chew an ear. The battle opened itself and tumbled down new streets and into the pasture that sloped toward Van Woert Street, the growing mob of spectators ringing the fighters, moving with the most vicious, cheering them on to ever grander gouging and bashing.

There exists in the spectacle of a mass of men in fistic battle a love of punishment and pain, a need to be smashed in the mouth by life or else risk losing sight of what is necessary to survival. In the war I would see much worse, but I'd seen nothing before to equal the violence of this day: the ripped shirts, the bloody faces, the noses and ears bitten half off, the torn and bloody fists with their naked bones, men spitting out teeth, men unable to stand, one man shot but the pistol never found, a dozen men stabbed, two dozen with fractured heads, and some to die of these things and be buried in secret, one of the Palmers stabbed in both arms and never the same after. I saw Emmett remove from the fray the man who did that stabbing, a Ryan, but one not to Emmett's liking, and so he punched him, but once, on the side of the head, and the man fell like ten pounds of liver. Emmett took the man's dirk from his hand and rolled him down the hill.

Women ministered to fallen battlers, blotting their wounds,

pulling them to safer turf. I spied a man whose face was the color of a ripe tomato, a scorch in full bloom, and I wondered, is this Alfie Palmer? The raw look of him just might have come from a bath in boiling tea. (How had the Ryans boiled their tea in that closed shack? I saw no chimney, nor any opening for one. Did they live amid smoke?) Such was Palmer's face (and it *was* his) that it could not have heretofore eluded me, and I concluded he was a latecomer to the battle. But that face was known, and when it appeared, it magnetically convened the Ryan lust for vengeance, Alfie quickly ringed by more men than could possibly reach him with club or fist. He knocked down two Ryans with his club before he went under: under by choice, I must now think, for what reasons other than guilt, or suicidal madness, could have compelled him to enter this battlefield of hate as a willful target?

He went down and felt the rain of kicks by Ryan brogans until a group of Palmers moved in for the rescue. But rescue the principal Palmer of the day they could not; for while other Ryans beat the Palmers back, a man all in Albany would come to recognize from this instant forward as Horse Houlihan, a lumber handler of immense size and girth, picked up the inert Alfie and, with great strength and unerring method, broke both his arms and both his legs, cracking each arm over bent knee, stepping on each leg and then snapping it upward, the reverse of its natural flex. The pain of the first break revived Alfie into a scream, but he then lapsed back into his coma and accepted the other fractures without a whimper.

The battle moved in splintered struggles away from the useless Alfie, the last of his reduction being the gob of spit Horse Houlihan loosed on him. And there he lay, a man of spoiled body and soul, a testament to what? To an incomplete understanding of the forces that had been unleashed through his loss of job and death of son; of even less comprehension now of what he himself had released with his random vengeance on the tragic Toddy.

Madness was insufficient designation for what had come of it, for what arose among the battlers was not pathology but something more conscious of itself: the final horrific begetting now blossoming in Joey Ryan, who came out of the crowd after the spectators had shifted with the flow. He found himself standing alone, moving slowly forward and then kneeling to perform with stunning malice the final coda of Alfie's saga: pummeling the near-dead face of his father's murderer with his slungshot as he shouted 'Bastard man, bastard man' over and over, until I pulled him away and was, myself, struck by inadvertence with the weapon, no less painfully for Joey's lack of intent. My intervention came too late, for the slungshot had created bloody craters on Alfie's face and permanently blinded his right eye, a total blinding having been Joey's intention from the moment he espied the inert form.

I cuffed Joey and flung his weapon away from him, pulled him by the arm off the battlefield in the general direction of the mansion, and we left all Ryans and Palmers behind us. The Ryans, after several retreats, regroupings, and two hours of blood, finally routed the Palmers. Alfie Palmer survived to become the half-blind cripple of Arbor Hill, spent four years in jail after confessing the murder of Toddy Ryan, and lived out his remaining days as drunken beggar and infamous martyr to the unfathomable rhythms of rage.

Newspapers reported on the battle, calling it a feud between Papists and Americans, between the Irish and the Know-Nothings (who numbered in their political ranks the enraged nativists and assorted hybrid-haters bent on shaping a balance in this republic of equals by expelling the unequals). Will Canaday, in a departure from reasonableness, noted that a number of probable deaths, and an unmeasurable maiming of heads, had been effected in the battle, and he concluded: 'It is not enough. Let them keep at it until there are no more of their heads to be broken.' Will's view was widely shared, for it had been brought home to us all that the mob at fury's peak has no politics, no ethnic allegiance, no religion, but is a rabid beast with bloody claws, and must be neutralized.

On the Monday after the battle I went with Dirck to hear Lyman Fitzgibbon as he mounted a loading platform on the wharf of his foundry and delivered his gospel to the work force at the hour of high noon. He announced he would sustain the cost of repairing Alfie Palmer's bones but would otherwise leave the fool to his fate;

that he would, with great heart, give moral and financial support to the widow and children of Toddy Ryan; that his foremen would hereafter monitor all comparable battles and would note, for purposes of effecting terminal discharge from foundry employ, the name of any worker involved; that he would write his will to encourage his heirs and assigns to do likewise; that he believed in his soul that we are here on this earth to court peaceful ways in the name of the good Christ, and may those who choose otherwise boil forever in the fluid caldrons of hell.

The silent men, surely not persuaded into pacificity by any such pietisms, began the antcrawl back to their furnaces, boilers, puddles, and moulds to ponder the vagaries of existence. Then, in this peculiar ironbound world under one benevolent God, the making of stoves was resumed, for now and forever, amen.

Lyman held forth later that evening in the drawing room of the Staats mansion, eulogizing Dirck, about whom, he said, he felt a certain guilt, but also recollecting with heartfelt agony the probable stirrings of Petrus in his grave over Dirck's book and the furor it generated in this city; for he knew Petrus feared that precisely such, as did, would occur: that Dirck would fall victim to the low pursuit of the word and with mischievous results.

Hillegond corrected Lyman, saying Dirck's pursuits were in no wise low or mischievous, but of a high moral order such as others rarely reach. It is true, she said, that he is peculiar and ill-clad (and she eyed my own attire with disdain); but Dirck was also kindly, courageous, and brilliant, and she was proud of him.

'Yes, of course,' said Lyman. 'We are all proud of the boy. Proud, proud, proud. But his father would have loathed the publication of that ruinous book. Didn't your son know that his father was a founder of The Society?'

Dirck promptly stood and wrote his answer at the inkstand under the portrait of Petrus in his senescence, wrote with unerring speed of quill, after which I, with rounded vowels, read his words to all: 'Of course I knew. Masked man who ordered my tongue cut, and also ordered against my murder, was giving

117

obeisance to power of Father's residual status in The Society.'

'Yes, yes, yes,' said Lyman, addressing his remarks to me. 'But I'm suggesting you apologize on behalf of your father for what you wrote. If you do, I myself will resign publicly from The Society on grounds that this once splendid brotherhood's high moral aim has fallen into low estate, corrupted by latterday scoundrels.'

Dirck exploded into a furious quilling of counterthrust, then stood beside me and said through the medium of my voice that he considered Lyman 'great man, great friend of family and of father, but I will never retract one word, for book cost me eternal voice, and what recanting will return that? Neither apology nor resignation will change Society, an evil needing violent overthrow.' Then Dirck sat down in a swim of silent passion.

Lyman stood and shook his fist at me, saying he could not resign 'without history's awareness that The Society was *not always* vile, and that *all* present members are not villainous men.'

Dirck scratched out his reply and I read: 'Well enough. Then *you* put Society in historical niche. Please reveal secret dogmas of yore that have led to crucifying of men and slitting of their gizzards to create pasture for rats. For I do not understand such moral evolution.'

Lyman said that nothing he could say would reveal such progression, and that no matter *what* he said, 'it would not clear the name of Petrus for having founded the local chapter of The Society. The words of Dirck Staats are required for that.'

Dirck, dismissing this remark with a wave of his hand, wrote his conclusion: 'Am not dead father's keeper. Nor yours either.'

The sociality of the evening deteriorated with that remark and before long we took to our beds. All that had passed weighed on my brain, but shining epiphanically through it all was the face of Maud. With her visit to Saratoga approaching within weeks, I knew a decision loomed: one that would also involve my bronze disk, which had been recurring in my dreams. On this burdened and sleepless night the disk's face spoke to me in a pair of cryptic phrases: 'Under the arches of love,' it said, and then 'Under the banner of blood,' neither phrase holding intimate meaning for me. Only an intuition persisted that one day I might find the grand significance of this oracular object, as well as how it related to Joey Ryan and his slungshot, to the bumblebees in Maud's script, to the bleeding wrist of Joshua the fugitive slave, and to the exploding soldier's melancholy dust. The message emerging from my febrile imagination during these tumultuous days was a single word: 'linkage'; and from the moment I was able to read that word I became a man compelled to fuse disparate elements of this life, however improbable the joining, this done in a quest to impose meaning on things whose very existence I could not always verify: a vision, for instance, of a young girl holding a human skull with a sweetly warbling red bird trapped inside, the bird visible through the skull's eye sockets.

In an earlier day I would have dismissed such a tableau as nightmare. But now I was propelled into an unknown whose dimensions grew ever wider and whose equal in spanning them I knew I was not. But even as I knew this I knew also I might never be their equal, and that remaining as I was, out of deference or timidity, would keep me ever distant from Maud. My life would then, I knew, fall into desuetude, like the lives of so many men of my father's generation, men who moved through their days sustained only by fragments of failed dreams, and who grew either indolent in despair or bellicose in resentment at such a condition.

And so, on a morning not long after the peaking of these pressures, I rode in silence with Will Canaday and Dirck to the *Chronicle-Paddle*, and when I saw the pair of them together in editorial conference beside the woodstove, I summoned the courage to present them with my decision, saying, 'If you please, sirs, I think I must resign from this job and leave Albany.' They regarded me with silent surprise.

'Leave for where?' Will asked.

'For Saratoga, to the north.'

'I know where Saratoga is. Have we treated you so poorly here?'

'No, sir. I feel very happy here. Nobody is more grateful

than I for what I've been given, but I have to meet someone.'

'A relative?'

'No,' I said, almost adding, 'not yet.'

Will sat down in the chair beside Dirck and stared at me with
what I took to be incomprehension compounded. I believe he felt
me bereft of common sense. 'When does this departure take place?'
he asked.

'About two weeks,' I said.

'You'll stay in Saratoga? Live there?'

'I'm not sure.'

'How long will you be gone?'

'I really can't say.'

'Do you plan to look for another job?'

'I was hoping,' I said, 'that you would help me figure that
out.'

'Ah,' said Will. 'So I'm to be an accessory to your flight.'

'I would rather work here for the *Chronicle* than anywhere else
in the world. But I have to help this person.'

Dirck scribbled a note and handed it to me. It read: 'Maud?' I
nodded and handed the note to Will.

'Then your journey is really a romantic quest,' said Will.

'She asked me to meet her. She seems desperate,' I said.

'Of course you're fully equipped to solve all the random cares
of desperate young women.'

'Probably not any of them,' I said, 'but I promised to try.'

Will and Dirck then listened with mock solemnity while I spoke
about Maud's life with La Última and John the Brawn. But the more
I talked the more I saw how ignorant I was of everything about
Maud except her desire to be stolen by me. I did not say this. I
said in summary that I couldn't be sure when I'd return to Albany.
At that moment I saw in Dirck's face his realization that he was
losing his voice yet again. I had become adept as his surrogate,
but surely others could replace me; and I couldn't say the same
for Maud's role in my affection, or mine in hers.

Will raised the question of my disk and I said I'd leave it in his safe, but he said no. What if they burgled the safe? What if the place caught fire? What if he died? No. We needed proof of my ownership, and then safekeeping for the disk in a bank vault, in my name. As usual, Will was thorough.

During subsequent days my departure was much discussed, especially by Hillegond, who couldn't believe I was going off on my own. She stared me up and down and said, 'If you are going to be an adventurer, you must stop looking like a crossing sweeper,' and she summoned a tailor to the mansion to measure me for wool and linen trousers, dress coats (the wool coat had a velvet collar), two silk damask waistcoats to match and contrast with the dress coats, and a long gray frock coat for cold weather. She personally took me to the city for dress shoes and shoeboots, six new shirts, six cravats, two pairs of braces, and an abundance of stockings and undergarments. All this was topped off with a tall black hat that I thought somewhat silly, but that Hillegond insisted was the true mark of a young gentleman.

'I only wish Dirck had been like you,' she said to me.

When we had done with clothing she took me to the stationer's and fitted me out with a writer's travel kit that included a writing box, a portable lamp, candles and holder, two everpointed pencils, a dozen pen points with pen, ink, and inkwell, and a roll of writing paper.

'Now you are a writer,' said Hillegond.

'I think I will have to write something first,' I said.

I came back to my room in the mansion, marveling at all my acquisitions. But one may be an acquisitor for only so long, and then the emptiness of it comes to the fore. And so I went down to the kitchen to see Matty and Capricorn, who had become my friends. I always wanted to hear their stories of Negro life in old Albany, and their tales of fugitive slaves, which sometimes were happy stories of escape, sometimes tragic with death and separation. I wanted to know what had happened to Joshua, and so I asked them how he was getting on after his ordeal and where he was. This won me a profound silence and brought our talk of slavery to an abrupt end.

Two mornings before my leave-taking I was breakfasting in the dining room with Dirck when he placed a message alongside my plate as we finished our tea. I read:

Daniel,

Our society seems ever to be confessing its flaws to you, just as you seem to have been born to witness tragedy and to elevate people from trouble. I owe you my life. My banker is setting up an account in your name and will be here today to talk with you. You will now have an income for the next fifteen years of your life. By then you should be wealthy in your own right.

Luck,
Dirck

When I realized what he had written and raised my head in grateful wonderment, Dirck was gone. As good fortune embraced me, baleful new shadows fell upon the Ryan family. The young Molly erupted with sores and boils over her entire body, a disease of no ostensible origin that was finally ascribed to the terrors that had taken seed in her upon her witnessing Toddy's murder. Joey Ryan was set upon twice as he ventured little distances from the mansion, and one boy sought to pluck out his eyes. Hearing this, Margaret Ryan ran to Hillegond and fell prostrate on the parlor rug, cursing the enemies of Ireland, cursing America, cursing God and His mother, cursing the murderer of her husband and all his heirs and ancestors, cursing the curse that was on her and her children. She stopped cursing when Hillegond patted her head and cooed at her; then she sat up and swore she would leave Albany for a new place, swore it on the suffering body of Molly Ryan, on the threatened eyes of Joey Ryan, on the hate that lived in her own body and which was the blood, fire, and venom of her will to survive this hell of black devils.

Lyman Fitzgibbon rescued the Ryans from family dementia by finding Margaret a charwoman's job in a Syracuse orphan asylum, where her children could find haven away from Albany; and so one day they were gone from the mansion, yet frozen forever in my memory as paradigms of helpless, guiltless suffering. I sensed in the days after they left that a life such as theirs would probably not be my lot; that any troubles befalling me in later days would emanate more from my own willfulness or sapheadedness; that I was not destined to be a passive pawn of exterior forces. One exposes great hubris with such confession, but there was truth in my intuition.

On the day I was to leave, Hillegond supervised the farewell breakfast, for which she baked bread from an old Dutch recipe. Laden with cheese, raisins, sugar, and walnuts, the bread, for Hillegond, was symbolic of plenty, her parting wish for me. Dirck kept his farewell as brief as he could, but his handshake was as strong as a bear's trap as we separated.

Will, who had already given me a letter recommending me as a gracious, trustworthy young soul of plentiful talent and potential, an effusion of praise I was sure no one would believe, came to pick up Dirck and report to us that Lyman had sent him a letter, to be printed in the *Chronicle*, publicly repudiating The Society and resigning from it.

Will gave me his personal copy of Montaigne's essays, telling me it contained enough wisdom for several young men like myself, and he urged me to read it constantly and in small doses. He also gave me some agates of advice. Sitting at the end of the dining-room table, where Hillegond and I were eating alone, holding his hat in one hand and his walking stick in the other, he delivered his message to me in words whose precise shape I cannot reconstruct, for I felt terrible leaving Will's newspaper, which had become the home of my soul; and the thought of departure clouded my memory severely. Though I searched for those precise words all the rest of that day, my findings fell far short of Will's impromptu eloquence. What he said, as best I could reconstitute it, was this:

'Remember, Daniel. The only thing worth fighting for is what is real to the self. Move toward the verification of freedom, and avoid gratuitous absolutes.'

123

I confess I did not know what he meant by the two final words, but which are exact, for I recorded them indelibly on my memory because of their strangeness. Will also added that I should be wary of marriage 'before the age of comprehension,' which he placed at twenty-five. 'No man younger than that has any idea what women are all about,' he said. 'And while after twenty-five they have even less, they are somehow readier for the game.'

His speech brought tears to Hillegond's eyes, for it made my departure increasingly real to her: yet another adventure of the heart taking its leave. She gave me quite contrasting counsel as to matters of love.

'I know you and Maud saw what happened on the night Magdalena came back from the dead,' she said. 'I did not see you there, but John did, and he enjoyed the audience. I won't apologize for what you saw, but I do say that life is never what you think. We seem to discover love in the most awkward places, and not always with the appropriate people. But Daniel, young dear of our hearts, love is better than wheat. Love is worth what it costs to find it, and I do know you've found it. I also know you know everything that I say before I say it. You are such a smart boy – smarter than Dirck was at your age, and he was smart as a Dutchman's thirst. I shall miss you, Daniel Quinn, and I *demand* that you come back as soon as you can and make your home here. Bring Maud if you like, and if not her, then another. But you have made yourself valuable to the Staats family, and you shall never want again as long as we live. God bless your good sense and Godspeed on your new journey.'

I had my train ticket in hand and was packed and ready for departure well before the appointed hour. Emmett Daugherty came to pick me up, and said we'd have to watch the Irish circus before I left, a comment that confused me. But he explained that today was the departure day as well for the new immigrants: homeless Irish who had come to Albany to find life, and finding none, were being ushered elsewhere – driven, really, from the city by authorities unable to cope with the mounting cases of Ship Fever the newcomers had brought with them. It was widely held that fever could not prosper in open spaces, and so the immigrants were being sent to the western plains, where they could build cabins, and forage in the outdoors for their lives, becoming as one with the wilderness, safely distant from the fetid city, where fever seeds wax strong.

I embraced Matty and Capricorn in turn, vowing I would see them both again, then was smothered in my final enfolding by Hillegond and her abundant bosom, which made me weep with love for the woman to whose open arms I swore anew that I would filially return.

I climbed onto the seat of Emmett's open wagon as he threw my baggage aboard, and I turned my final gaze upon the mansion, its shrubbery, its turrets, its gables and conical towers, its sprawling porches and beautiful lawns of intense verdancy, its acres of bosky slopes, and that vast metabosky terrain I had always judged to be the Staatses' primeval forest, and along which their road coursed toward the city. All this I surveyed with saddened eye, for I knew that this time I was truly leaving, perhaps never to return, despite my avowals, and sensing in my most anxious reaches that this was all slipping away forever, even before I had begun to command power over its lushness. This was no longer mine, and I was to be alone on the road, a waif in gentleman's clothing, aimless and homeless, pointing myself in the vague direction of an even more vaguely defined duty to a stranger I barely knew but loved with unquestioning fervor.

I wept openly upon my separation both from the grandeur of this vision and from Hillegond's chest full of heat. And then, as I accepted the unknowable emptiness of my future, Emmett clucked his horse into motion.

And so goodbye.

We saw signs of Emmett's circus as we neared the railroad station: mobs of people being herded out of the city by constables and sheriff's men on horseback. I sat beside Emmett in his wagon and we watched them pass.

'Pay heed to these people and remember what you see,' he said to me, and I remember him as vividly as the rest, his great wavy mane of black hair crowning him with handsome abundance, his eyes as strong as nuggets of iron. And so in memory I heed him as much as I heeded that troubled throng. Here came a man with two children on his shoulders and three more in tow, a woman nursing slung babies at both naked breasts as she walked along. The day was chill, but some men walked bare-chested, galluses holding their trousers, their feet in rotting boots. A man with a bull terrier under his arm had grown neck whiskers like a dog collar, his face otherwise clean of hair. A boy in a small cart drawn by a jackass played on the pennywhistle a Gaelic air I remember my father whistling, and naughty women with chemises visible and skirts flying threw visions of hip and thigh at men and women both (one of them eyed me), taunting in the Irish tongue all who watched the parade from windows and doorways. One man wore no shoes, his feet wrapped in cloth. Another carried a short club, the Irishman's gun, ready for impromptu battle. Men wore hobnail boots, hats of straw and felt, caps of leather and fur, tall hats, plug hats, sailor hats, vests. Women wore bonnets and shawls or nothing on their heads, sweaters, tattered coats, threadbare cloaks, long skirts. They carried brooms, and straw boxes, bags and valises tied with rope. Their stockings were rolled, their hair in buns or loose to the middle of their back like my mother's, some of the loose-haired ones loose as well with affection to the men who pawed and patted them as they walked, those patters clad in tailcoats and knee britches with holes in the knees, men carrying pails and whiskey bottles and a small pig in a basket. One man pissed like a horse in the street, and an entire clustered family of six gripped one another's hands in fearful dignity.

Emmett told me stories of some of these people. He had been moving among them for a week to hear their tales, discover news from Ireland, help where and how he could. His concern for them was missionary: he had been one of them himself when he came here. His fervor to work for their betterment would grow in him with the passing years and affect my life profoundly. He told me of one man who stole a sack of horsehides, was arrested trying to sell them back to their owner and went to jail for it, leaving his family destitute. He told of a man long off the whiskey who came home drunk and singing and urged his sullen wife to sing with him, but she would not, and so he beat her with a crock and went to jail for it, leaving her destitute.

'They're lost, most of them,' Emmett said to me. 'And who wouldn't be? They've left all they knew, and all they've got is what they can wear and carry. But if lost it is, then some say this is the land to be lost in, for it all comes right again here. Would you agree to that, lad?'

I nodded my head yes, but I thought of Dirck and his absent tongue, and of lost Joshua and his fugitive life, and of the dead Swede who could no longer agree life would come right again; and it remained to be seen whether the lives of the Ryans would ever again be other than a tissue of days with open sores.

'Look at them,' Emmett said to me. 'Study the face and the eyes and the gait of the walking misery that's come to visit.'

They passed on then, the last of them, and Emmett followed their steps with his horse and wagon. Ahead we could see them climbing into the railroad carriages that would take them west, the carriage windows down, some wet wash and portable bedding already getting the air, the children barefoot and on holiday, racing on the cobbles and gravel, a snarling dog clubbed by a militiaman's rifle, a piglet dropped and running loose beneath a carriage. I scrambled under the car to catch it, but the pig could run faster than I could crawl, and it ran into the tall grass by the tracks, lost forever to the old man who dropped it.

Thirty-four cars they occupied, not the longest train I ever saw but the one whose memory is vivid still. We watched until they were all on board. A man of middle years, his shirt in tatters, a half-eaten chicken leg in his hand, stood alone on the steps of the train and began a song in the Gaelic, that strange tongue rendered brilliant by the man's plaintive voice. Silence came onto the crowd and we listened to the minstrel, I with a growing wonder in my heart at all the joy and misery that simultaneously commanded so many unknown lives. The train whistle interrupted the sound of the song but not the singer, and as the cars moved out, his voice reached us in fragments, audible between the whistle blasts, a fervent melody struggling to be heard. And then it was gone.

While we waited for my train Emmett and I talked of Ireland, and of family, and of my future, and of how I was always welcome at his home, which I well knew, and then my train was there, bound for Saratoga.

I boarded knowing, with every willful step, that I had once and for all obliterated the image of myself as helpless, hapless orphan, tossed off a canalboat like so much offal. Nor was I a greenhorn victim, not anymore. I still do not know why I knew this so firmly, but it was true. It remained to be seen whether fate would again ravage my life, but at the moment luck was with me, and I felt an extraordinary rapture, full of the music of sunrise. As I waved farewell to Emmett, I and my train moved northward with that same boiling energy that we had, at the dawn of the light, stolen from the gods.

The Dumb Cake

Saratoga

Spring 1850

When Magdalena Colón stepped onto the stage at Utica, her first public appearance after leaving Albany, her overarching impulse was to tell the audience of her death and resurrection. But with John's words strong in her brain, she stifled the urge. What John had said to her was, 'You talk of that and they'll think you're daft as a bloody owl.'

By Syracuse Magdalena could stifle herself no longer. In a voice reverberating with all the humility of a heavenly choir's frailest angel, she stepped delicately to center stage and offered her thanks to God for resurrecting her from the dead. She told her story of the child at the bottom of the river who had welcomed her to the birthplace of dreams. She expatiated on her pleasant time under water in the land of luminous dolls and, with a great surge of her mystical wisdom, told her listeners they should not fear crossing over into death, because it was so attractive over there. 'Also,' she said, 'there is always the chance of turning around and coming right back.' She concluded by saying, 'I can't imagine a more pleasant experience than dying.'

She then went into her performance: a song first, then her famed Spider Dance, in which she shook off an attack of imaginary arachnids that were climbing her skirts and bodice, and in so doing revealed more flesh than was generally provided to American audiences outside of brothels. Alas, her report on the beyond had taken its effect. The audience tittered at her dancing, and her vaunted sinfulness was paled over with an aureole of humbug sanctity.

131

William Kennedy

A Syracuse newspaper reported on Magdalena's disquisition:

DANCER CLAIMS RESURRECTION

The Spanish dancer Magdalena Colón, who calls herself La Última, performed for an overabundance of spectators last night but failed to arouse either the condemnatory or the lascivious reactions her dancing has produced in other cities. After evoking the Deity by describing Him as a small female child clutching a doll, the dancer spoke of her own experience drowning in the river and of being resurrected from death at a much later hour by the ministrations of love. It might be said of her performance that while it, too, perished, resurrection was not a consequence.

Magdalena, undaunted, repeated her tale to a Rochester audience. By then the word of her bizarre story, and not her sensuality, sold out the house. Hearing the laughter and hooting that met her remarks about resurrection, Magdalena swirled in frenzied pirouettes across the stage and fled into the wings. Witnessing this, hearing the hoots, Maud walked onstage and faced the hostile audience, whose derision subsided at her advent.

'Only fools and martyrs laugh at death,' she said to them. 'Which are you?'

She then asked the orchestra leader to play the music for the Spider Dance, and in learned emulation of her aunt she whirled about in recklessly flying skirts, her wild abandon silencing all hooters, and at length provoking them into cheers and long applause as the curtain fell. She took no curtain call. Backstage the wounded Magdalena embraced her, saying, 'What a wonderful child you are.'

'I'm not a child any longer, Auntie. No child could dance as I just have.'

'Whatever you are, Maudie mine, I love you.'

'You needn't go on about that. Go out there now and sing your songs or the theater manager will deny us our money.'

Thus began the stage career of Maud Fallon.

La Última, in subsequent days, experienced a falling off, an attack of despair that prevented her from venturing on to Buffalo. She stopped eating and faded languidly into a vale of melancholy.

'I have lost the voluptuary in me,' she kept saying. 'My life is a bore, and in boredom I shall surely die.'

She did not say this to John McGee, especially when he was providing her with the only kindness he fully understood: the thrust of his pelvic appendage. She received his thrust with artificial passion, but such politeness also bored her, and so she eventually accepted John's largess in immobilized silence.

'You had more life when you were dead,' John told her.

She arose one day from her passionless bed to perform the usual ablution, and the coolness of the water between her legs seemed to renew her spirit. The idea of the healing power of water, so capable of assuaging even the agony of death, preempted all her thought.

'I must have a lake,' she said to John.

'A lake, is it?'

'I must lie in a lake and recover my passion,' she said.

'By the Jesus, I'm all for that,' said John.

And so Saratoga Springs, famed for its lake and its healing spas, famed also as a place where voluptuaries were as commonplace as clover, became the destination of Magdalena, of John the Brawn, and of that chrysalid creature of the future, Maud Fallon.

Upon arriving in Saratoga, Daniel Quinn bought a newspaper and read of the cancellation of Magdalena Colón's performance that night at the Union Theater. The brief story referred to unexplained noises in the theater during an earlier performance. Quinn went to the theater and found it closed. He went to the print shop where the newspaper was printed and confronted its publisher, Calvin Potts, a small man with a white pigtail, who was wearing an apron stained with a generation's worth of ink. Potts was working at a type cabinet, a stick of type in his hand, when Quinn introduced himself and handed him the letter Will Canaday had written on his behalf.

'A man of substance, Will Canaday,' Potts said. 'You must be worth a scrap of something if he thinks well of you. Did you ever set type for him?'

'Setting type isn't what I want to do,' said Quinn, and he groped for the word that would define his goal. Editor? Not likely. Writer?

133

Too ambitious. 'I think just now I ought to learn how to be a paragraphist,' he said.

'You'd best learn to set those paragraphs in type if you want to earn a living, boy. Words are flimsy things. Type is solid and real.'

'I can see that,' said Quinn. 'But paragraphs are also real in their way. I've seen how they can change things.'

'Ah, so you're out to change things.'

'No, sir. I just want to write paragraphs and see what happens. I thought I might write one or two for you about Magdalena Colón, the dancer. I know her quite well and I saw this story about her in your newspaper.'

'Did you read that about those noises? Folks think spirits made them.'

'Yes. Magdalena is quite good with the spirits.'

'You talk to spirits too, do you?'

'No, sir. I talk only to living people.'

'A blessing if you want to be a reporter.'

'I don't know where to find Magdalena, though.'

'She's out at Griswold's place, but I don't know as they'll let you in out there.'

'I'm expected,' said Quinn.

'You certainly do come equipped,' said Potts, and he told Quinn how to find Griswold's. 'I'll look at your paragraphs, if you write any,' he added, 'but hold down that spirit nonsense. People want real stuff, not all that folderol about spooks.'

Quinn nodded as he went out, not quite agreeing.

Calvin Potts gave Quinn directions to the home of Obadiah Griswold, the carriage and sleigh manufacturer at whose home on the shore of Saratoga Lake Magdalena Colón and her entourage were guests. Obadiah had become smitten with Magdalena after seeing her dance in New York, and offered her the run of his mansion, his stables, his vast acreage, and his lake whenever she cared to visit. In her melancholy period at Rochester she remembered Obadiah and wrote him, accepting his invitation.

Obadiah welcomed his guests with one proviso: that Magdalena alone occupy the room next to his own. He kept her constantly in his sight during the first days of her visit, catering to her every whim. Magdalena accepted him as an oddity, a foppish middle-aged widower who frequently wore an ankle-length robe to hide his bowlegs, a descendant of English Puritans who had long ago rejected all Puritanical inheritances. Anticipating Magdalena's early capitulation to his desire, Obadiah took her on a tour of his secret third-floor room that housed his erotic sculpture, paintings, etchings, and pornographic books dating to the dawn of printing. Magdalena relapsed into melancholy at the sight of so many erect phalluses and lubricious vaginas, and she retreated to her room, insisting that only Maud and John the Brawn attend her bedside.

Obadiah took up a vigil outside Magdalena's door and left it only to eat, sleep, and perform bodily functions, a gesture of concern that so bored Magdalena that she sent John theaterward to book her a performance as soon as possible as a means of escape. John returned, accomplished, but warned her the theater manager would brook none of her humbuggery.

'Just keep mum on what you found at the bottom of the river,' John told her, 'or he'll throw us all out in the alley.'

And so Magdalena performed as she had prior to her death: a blithe entrance to the orchestral melody, several pirouettes of restrained torsion, then a medley of French and Spanish songs. She followed with her interpretation of a Viennese waltz, *andante*, and concluded with the Spanish tarantela, her spectacular Spider Dance, *allegro* – oh yes, quite. Hisses, hoots, wild applause, and huzzahs, the miscellaneous wages of Terpsichore, followed her performance.

On the next night Magdalena had barely begun her Spider Dance when a thunderclap shook the theater, vibrating orchestra seats, rocking the boxes, loosening plaster dust from the ceiling, and spilling oil from the burning wall sconces into running pools of fire onstage. Maud, standing in the wings, swiftly smothered them all with a piece of canvas.

Magdalena was convinced an earthquake was in process, but

135

then calm returned, audience panic and screaming subsided, and except for a few who fled at the threat of fire, people returned to their seats. Magdalena signaled the orchestra to resume, and she began her dance anew. At her initial steps another noise erupted, smaller of force, but formidable even so; and then another, and another. Magdalena stood frozen, and the orchestra trailed off. The booming from above, fixed in no single area, seemed to be a storm floating free inside the theater. The concussions came yet again, four this time, and rhythmic; then three more, and rhythmic. Such noises were man-made, were they not? Earth had never quaked in regularized tempo, had it?

Magdalena knew only confusion in that moment, and then she saw Maud walking onto the stage and staring up at the theater's stormy ceiling. Maud clapped her hands four times, then three. The noise instantly echoed: four sounds and then three, all subdued in keeping with the softness of Maud's clapping. Maud clapped twice more, then once, and the source of the noise responded in precise kind.

'What are you doing?' Magdalena asked.

'I'm having a conversation with the noise,' said Maud.

People in the audience began to clap their hands, but the noise would not echo them. When audience clapping subsided, Maud looked toward the nearest ceiling and wall from which the noise seemed to come, and said, 'Are you a human being making these noises? If you are, then rap once.'

No rap followed.

'Then are you a spirit? If so, rap twice.'

Instantly two raps were heard, along with gasps from the audience and the swift exodus of the timid and the incurious. But most of the audience stayed, fully as transfixed by Maud's performance as was Magdalena, who atavistically blessed herself.

'Good Lord, Maudie, what's going on?'

'How many letters in my first name?' Maud asked the wall.

Four raps followed, and Magdalena immediately told the audience, 'That's true. Her name is Maud.'

'How old am I?' asked Maud, and thirteen raps followed.

'Correct again,' said Magdalena.

'Now, how old is La Última?'

'No, no,' said Magdalena, but there followed then a rapid series of raps like the long roll of a drum (forty-one in all) and the audience exploded with laughter. At this Magdalena shook the front of her skirt, exposing her saucy response to mockery, and won applause from the crowd. But from the wings came another response: the hisses and wild fulminations of the theater manager, demanding a resumption of music and dance. Nonplussed by the condition of life around her, Magdalena gestured her agreement. Maud shrugged, nodded to the audience, and walked off the stage. The orchestra resumed the music of the Spider Dance, but before Magdalena could begin, a thunderclap descended with more power than at first, swaying the chandelier in a dangerous arc and scattering the audience beneath it. The thunder clapped a second time, then a third, and more of the timid folk took their exit. Only when Maud walked back onstage and clapped three times at the noise did it clap thrice in return. *Lento*. Politely *lento*.

Thus began the spiritualistic career of Maud Fallon.

Throngs came to the theater on subsequent nights to hear the indoor thunder, but after three nights of only pregnant silence the crowds dwindled and the accusation of humbug again attached itself to Magdalena. She cancelled all performances and reluctantly retreated to Obadiah's lakefront sanctuary.

Four days after the first onset, the noise returned, this time at morning in Obadiah's plant-ridden conservatory-breakfast room. Maud paused in the midst of her shirred eggs and told the noise to mind its manners and not interrupt her and her aunt's breakfast.

The noise desisted but returned at midafternoon, sliding an empty chair across the porch and thumping lightly on its wooden back. Maud spoke to it in French and Spanish, and the noise responded in a way Maud found unintelligible. The following day the noise returned while Maud was in the kitchen talking to the cook and the scullery maid. She told it to go away and stop bothering people, and it exploded with a thunderbolt that broke four teacups.

Word of all this spread through Saratoga and crowds converged on the Griswold property, cluttering the road and carriageway, many asking to see Maud in action. Obadiah posted servants outside to deflect the crowds. He also invited the mayor, the constable, two bankers, four judges, the head of the women's auxiliary of the county orphan asylum, and asked them to help define the nature of this visitation.

It was at this point that Quinn arrived at the mansion. Having left his traveling bag at Mrs Trim's rooming house on Phila Street, he hired a cab to take him to Obadiah's home, his first expenditure of money from the Dirck annuity. He arrived quite the young gentleman, thinking of himself for the first time as a journalist of independent mind and means, in debt to no man, woman, or relative, and full ready to carry out the task at hand, the nature of which eluded him utterly.

To the servant who answered his knock he said he was a friend of Magdalena and Maud. The servant summoned John McGee to establish Quinn's validity, which John did with a middling smile and a lifted brow.

'Damned if it isn't Danny me boy.'

'I'm no boy of yours, and that's the truth of forever,' said Quinn.

'Does he know Madame Colón?' the servant asked.

'He does. She knew him in Albany. We all knew him when he had no hat.'

At this Quinn doffed his hat and the servant made way for him to step inside. The servant took him to Obadiah in the library, where Quinn introduced himself as an emissary from the newspaper of Calvin Potts. Obadiah instantly recruited him as a witness to the proceedings upcoming with Maud the wondrous, who could converse with the insubstantial air.

'Do you believe she can do that?' inquired Obadiah.

'I believe she can do anything she sets her mind to,' said Quinn. 'I believe she has the magic.'

'The magic?'

'Yes, sir. The magic.'

*　　*　　*

Here is what Maud was thinking as she entered Obadiah Griswold's drawing room to face eleven witnesses, including one woman who would make a body search of her prior to her planned conversation with the voluble dead.

First came the vision of Daniel Quinn, whom she saw as soon as she entered the room, he sitting there with a broad grin on his young face, wearing well-tailored clothes, new boots, and waving his new hat at her, the ninny, as if she hadn't seen him the instant she walked into the room. She nodded her awareness of his presence but refrained from smiling, for when one converses with the dead, one must observe proper decorum.

Second, she had the moving image of a tall, emaciated man riding a horse across an open field. Here is what she was seeing: When the man becomes aware of the two carriages coming rapidly along the road he is nearing, he leaps down from his mount and, at a run, climbs a slight incline. He halts in the center of the road so that the deadly onrush of horses and vehicles will run him over.

Third was her thought on the cause of this image, which was a mystery, for it was neither memory nor dream, but a fully developed panorama, even to the brightness of the sun and the brilliant green of the hills behind the oncoming carriages. It arrived in her brain in all fullness at the moment she saw Quinn enter the drawing room of the mansion. Quinn was none of the men in the image.

Maud nodded at Quinn and turned her mind to her inquisitors, who all looked to her to be believers in the plausibility of conversing with a spirit. Maud felt lost in such a world of belief. Her classics teacher in Madrid had spoken of enantiodromia, the ancient Greek concept of running in contrary ways: believing in the unbelievable, for instance. Maud could not so believe. She believed in noise but not in spirits. Dead is dead, she believed. Noise came from the living. Minds were as noisy as the howling of a terrifying windstorm. Minds made noise: the collision of minds – hers, Magdalena's, Quinn's across the room, the ninny. I love him and his mind.

With her vision of Quinn came the continuing visual story of the emaciated man, who was climbing now to the road as the horses bore down on his life. The noise came then, rappings synchronized with the thudding of the horses' hooves, growing louder, louder, louder.

'Enough!' yelled Maud, jolting her witnesses in their silent seats.

And so began the séance.

Talking with spirits can be tedious, and so Maud quickly devised a code: one rap is yes, two is no, spell out the rest with numerical equivalents of the alphabet. The noise quickly understood this, and while Maud was establishing her rules, witnesses left their seats and sought out hidden rappers or rapping devices. They moved furniture in their search, kept vigil in rooms adjacent to, above, and below the drawing room, and they found nothing at all.

'Can you see this spirit?' Obadiah asked Maud.

'Not a shred of anything,' said Maud. 'But it is sending me pictures.' And she told them of the emaciated man.

'There he is in the road,' she said, 'and the horses are coming at a fierce gallop. The man is facing the horses and won't budge. Now the driver of the oncoming carriage is veering the horses to avoid running the man down and the carriage wheel strikes a rock on the rough ground. The right carriage door, it's flying open, and oh, a woman, a woman is thrown to the ground. Now we're on the road again, and a second carriage and pair are coming at a furious pace, directly behind the first. The second driver reins in his steeds and comes to a stop just where the emaciated man is standing with his eyes closed. The man is standing there between the frothing mouths of the second team of horses. There, now, there comes the driver jumping down from the second carriage. He grabs the emaciated man by his shirt collar and drags him from between the horses. He punches him once in the center of his face, and the man falls backward and rolls down the incline. Now I can see the first carriage, halted in the distance. The punched man is rolling toward where the woman was thrown from the carriage and he bangs his head on a stone. Oh. Oh, oh, oh, the poor woman is impaled through the chest on a protrusion of rock. Oh dear, oh dear. She is dead.'

Here is what Maud and the spirit said to each other:
  'Are you the dead woman?'
  No.
  'Are you one of the men in the vision?'
  Yes.
  'Are you the emaciated man?'
  Silence.
  'Was the dead woman your wife?'
  Silence.
  'Do you want to talk about this or don't you?'
  Yes.
  'Then tell me something. Are you the driver who punches the man in the road?'
  No.
  'Then you must be the emaciated man.'
  Silence.
  'Goodbye, then, whoever you are.'
  Yes.
  'You are the emaciated man?'
  Yes.
  'You're not proud of that.'
  No.
  'You were trying to kill yourself.'
  No.
  'Then what was it?'
  L-o-v-e.
  'Love. Pish-pish-pish, as my aunt would say. Love indeed.'
  L-o-v-e.
  'You were chasing the woman because you loved her?'
  Yes.
  'And you tried to kill yourself because of her?'
  L-o-v-e.

'Because of love.'

Yes.

'Instead of killing yourself, you killed her.'

Silence.

'Didn't you?'

L-o-v-e.

'Yes, I understand the motive. But you can't escape the facts. You killed the woman you loved.'

THUNDER.

Long rapping on walls, floors.

THUNDER.

'It upsets you to hear the truth. I can see that. Did you kill yourself after this?'

Silence.

'So. You didn't. You couldn't. Am I right?'

THUNDER.

'Do you tell this story to many people?'

No.

'Why me?'

L-o-v-e.

'Ah. So you love me the way you loved the dead woman.'

Yes.

'Then I'd better watch out.'

No.

'Suicidal people don't care who dies with them. My mother was that way. She left me alone when I was an infant and when she tried twice to kill herself, I almost died both times.'

THUNDER.

'Maybe you stood in front of the carriage because you wanted it to go off the road and kill someone.'

THUNDER.

'I don't believe you. I think you're lying.'

THUNDER.

THUNDER.

THUNDER.

And down came the chandelier, only inches from Maud's head.

'I knew it,' said Maud, and she left the room.

Here is what Quinn eventually decided he was thinking as he watched Maud conversing with the spirit of the emaciated man:

Her frown belongs to the devil.

Her frown is paradise lost.

Her left eye sees through brick and mortar.

Her mouth is cruel with love.

Her mouth is soft with invitation.

Her lips exude the moistness of temptation.

Her glance will break crystal.

Her nose is imperious.

Her eyebrows are mistrusting.

Her hair is devilishly angelic.

Her eyes are golden beauty.

Her eyes are as hard as Satan's heel.

Her teeth are the fangs of a devil bat.

Her cheeks are the pillows of a kiss.

Her cheeks are the soft curves of abandon.

Her hair is full of snakes.

Her hair is a bed of warmth.

Her hair is a tiara of desire.

Her throat is the avenue to passion.

Her face is a white tulip.

Her face is a perfect cloud.

Her face is virginal.

Her smile is an oriflamme of lust.

Her smile is paradise regained.

Quinn, studying Maud's face as she conversed with the spirit of the emaciated man, wondered whether all her talk, all her responses were an effort to create a reality superior to the one she was living.

If so, Quinn feared Maud was a candidate for madness.

You cannot talk to spirits.

Dead is dead.

Maud's face is a dream that cannot be imagined.

*   *   *

Maud insisted on dining alone with Quinn in the gazebo of the upper gardens so they could speak without fear of being overheard. Together they left behind the witnesses to the séance, who were babbling with great verve. Maud refused to talk about the spirit with anyone, including Quinn. Instead, she talked to him of the decline of Magdalena into solitude, depression, and prayer of a peculiar order: asking God for the return of her lost lust, that electrovital force that made people pay to see her dance. She prayed that when it returned she would no longer lust for men seriatim, for she was weary of sex and longed to give her body a vacation from friction.

'How do you know these deeply personal things about her?' Quinn asked Maud.

'She confides in me,' said Maud. 'She wants me to understand men.'

'And do you understand them?'

'I don't understand what she has against friction.'

'Neither do I,' said Quinn, who did not understand why anyone would be interested in it to begin with. All it did was cause things to wear out, or break, or burst into flame. Even so, he perceived that Maud was learning things from Magdalena that he was not learning from anybody. Women handed their wisdom on to each other, but boys were supposed to discover the secrets of life from watching dogs fuck. Quinn listened to Maud with as much patience as he could tolerate, and then refused to hear another word about Magdalena.

'No more of that,' he said. 'I want to kiss you.'

'It's not the right time,' said Maud.

'Then until it is the right time, we'll talk about how I'm going to kidnap you.'

'I can't be kidnapped now,' said Maud. 'There are too many interesting things going on.'

'You mean like talking to spirits?'

'There are no spirits,' said Maud.

'Then who were you talking to?'

'I don't know. I might have been talking to myself.'

'You mean you made it all up?'

'That's a possibility.'

'How do you do thunder? How do you make a chandelier fall?'

'I don't know. Maybe I didn't do that.'

'Then how can you say it wasn't a spirit if you aren't sure you did it?'

'There are no spirits.'

'That well may be,' said Quinn, admiring how deftly he was getting back to the point, 'but even so, I want to kiss you. I didn't move to Saratoga to be rejected.'

'You're absolutely right,' said Maud.

She stood up and took his hand, and they walked across the lawn in the early darkness. They saw Magdalena sitting under an arched pair of trellises at the entrance to the lower gardens, with John the Brawn and Obadiah Griswold both seated facing her. They could hear John say, 'All he wants is a bit of a look. He's been a proper gentleman, and very accommodating, if I might say so.'

'No,' said Magdalena. 'I can't be immodest.'

'You can be the bloody whore of Babylon when you put your mind to it,' said John. 'Give him a look. Go on. Get it out.'

Maud and Quinn watched as Magdalena stood up and, by the light of the early moon, and swathed in the shadow of a great weeping beech tree, undid her buttons. Then, holding her dress open with both hands, she allowed the men to violate her with their gaze. As she undulated her body ever so slightly, John the Brawn leaned back in his chair to take in the view of his eminent domain. Obadiah, seeking a more proximate vista, leaned closer to the subject at hand. Magdalena swayed on. Obadiah's right hand moved toward her *vestibulum gaudiae*. Magdalena backed away, closed her dress around her, and sat down.

'That's enough of that,' said Quinn, and he grabbed Maud by the arm and moved away from the tableau, down the long, sloping lawn toward the lake.

'She's such a fool,' said Maud.

'She seems to have a body that men desire.'

'Men desire any woman's body if it's naked.'

'Would you ever be naked like that?' Quinn asked.

'I can't predict what I'd do. I'm not ready for that. But I am ready to kiss you.'

She stopped at the edge of the dark water and turned her face to Quinn's. Obeying an inherited impulse, he put his arms around her waist, thrust his face toward hers, and placed his lips upon her lips. They kissed, just as they had in front of the dusty soldier's coffin, with lips tight. Then, with the lips loosened somewhat, with tension rising, with everything new and the pressure of each kiss increased, with Quinn's teeth and gums turning to sweet pain, they broke apart, came together again, tight, loose, looser; and then Maud's lips parted and she eased the pressure totally, without breaking the kiss, and Quinn found his own lips growing fuller and softer and wetter. Then Maud's mouth was open, and so he opened his own, and here came revelation. He tasted her tongue. This so undid him that he stopped to look out over Maud's shoulder, out at the lights playing on the dark water, and to whisper into her ear, 'This is a terrific kiss. This is the best kiss I ever had.'

'Keep quiet and open your mouth,' said Maud, and she pressed her lips again to his.

At this point Quinn fell in love with the secluded night.

Obadiah decided the only way to lay hands on the flesh of Magdalena was to dance with her. He could hold her hand, perhaps stroke her neck, or, given the proper gown, even stroke her shoulder. He could press himself against her bosom, feel the full whirling weight of her body as they moved about the dance floor. And so he arranged for them all to attend the weekly ball given by the Union Hotel.

A month had passed since the séance, and Maud's fame as a spiritualist had spread, fueled at first by a report on her behavior written by Quinn for Calvin Potts's newspaper and reprinted by Will Canaday. Horace Greeley's *New York Tribune* sent a reporter to talk to Maud and to the witnesses to her séance, and in time published a lengthy story on the 'miracle at the spa.' A scout came to hire Maud for P. T. Barnum's museum of freaks, but upon discovering Maud's lack of belief in the very spirit with whom she had talked, the scout decided such skepticism was commercially useless.

Magdalena received offers to perform in many places, and she sensed a rebirth of both her passion and her talent for seduction. Wriggling into the shoulderless pink dress Obadiah had bought her for the ball, she counseled Maud on the display of a bodice. 'Precisely three inches of cleavage is proper,' she said. 'Two inches is denial, and four is basely vulgar.'

Magdalena insisted that Maud and John the Brawn attend the ball, and Maud chose Quinn as her escort. The five alighted from Obadiah's splendid barouche and moved with sartorial elegance into the hotel's vast lobby, where fashion ruled tyrannically and ostentation at its most fulsome was the crowd's principal pleasure. John looked overdressed in cravat and tailcoat, Obadiah was original in black silk trousers and opera cloak, Maud virginal in white frock, and Quinn felt brand-new, wearing, for the first time, the gray dress suit Hillegond had bought him.

A group of men and women turned their full attention to our group upon a remark by one of the women. 'There are those fraudulent spiritualists,' she said in stentorian whisper. 'We saw them at the theater and nothing happened at all. They're all charlatans.'

'How,' asked another woman, 'are such low people tolerated here?'

'Ignore them,' said Obadiah to Maud and Magdalena. But John had already turned to address the insult.

'If I was you,' said John, 'I'd keep that kind of talk to meself, ya old pissbats.'

A man whose brawn matched John's, who wore a full beard and a dress suit, stepped in front of the women. 'Hold your tongue, you pup,' he said to John.

'Hold me fist,' said John, and with the right jab Quinn had seen him deliver so often, the punch Quinn called The Flying

147

Sledgehammer, John caught the whiskered man on, as they say, the button. The man fell like a wet sock, his legs betrayed by his devastated brain. On his back, the man found it difficult to believe such a thing had happened.

'No man knocks down Michael Hennessey,' he said.

'This man does,' said John the Brawn, 'and if Michael Hennessey stands himself up from the carpet I'll knock him down again.'

'He knocked Hennessey down,' said another man's high-pitched voice from the crowd that suddenly surrounded the group.

'You knocked Hennessey down,' said the owner of the voice, a nattily dressed runt who grabbed John by the hand and shook it. 'You put Hennessey on his back.'

'I see that I did,' said John.

'Do you know he's the champion?'

'No.'

'Well, he is.'

'Champion of what?'

'Of the world entirely.'

'Is that a fact?' said John.

'It's a positive fact,' said the runt.

Hennessey was up then, and smiling.

'You've a grand right hand there, bucko,' he said.

'I don't deny it,' said John.

'There's damn few right hands like that,' said Hennessey.

'There's none at all that I know of,' said John.

'There's one or two,' said Hennessey, extending his own right hand for a handshake. The two men shook hands and smiled at each other. Then Hennessey swung a left and caught John on, as they say, the button, and he went down like a wet sock.

'You see what I mean,' said Hennessey. 'They're here and there, and sometimes they're on the other fist.'

John smiled and picked himself up.

'If you get rid of those old bats you're with,' said John, 'I'll buy you the best drink in this house.'

'You're a drinkin' man, are you?' said Hennessey.

'It runs in me family,' said John.

'What a coincidence,' said Hennessey. 'It runs in me own as well.' He clapped a hand on John's shoulder and the two men went off to the bar, leaving the ladies and the younger folk to fend for themselves in this argumentative world.

At the ball Quinn and Maud danced all dances that required no special skills, since Quinn had none. They danced what they knew until boredom ravaged their legs, and then they sat. At this point, and with ritual avuncularity, Obadiah asked Maud to pursue a schottische with him, and she accepted. As she danced with Obadiah, Maud realized she had never been alone with him in the months they had lived at his house. She looked at him and saw a skull being abandoned by its hair, revealing bony lumps that had the fascination of a mild deformity. Obadiah was a creature unlike most. Maud thought he would be much at home in an aquarium. He danced much worse than Quinn, and he told her she was a remarkable child, that few in this world had her gifts.

'Such people as you make the world spin on its axis,' he told her.

'You're very nice to say that,' said Maud, 'but I am not a child. I'm thirteen years and two months old.'

'Well, of course you are. But in a way—'

'Not in any way,' said Maud.

'Of course not.'

They danced in silence. Maud saw Magdalena dancing with Quinn and talking to him with her eyes closed, and jealousy rose up in her.

'There is a difference between a child and a woman,' said Maud. 'I can't say I'm a woman yet.'

'When do you become a woman?' Obadiah asked.

'When I make love to a man.'

'Have you chosen the man?'

'I may have.'

'I presume young Mr Quinn is the lucky one.'

'He may be.'

'If he is not . . .'

'If he is not I will find someone equally exciting.'

'Yes,' said Obadiah with a sigh. 'Exciting. I'm not sure I was ever exciting.'

'What an unusual thing to say,' said Maud.

'What?'

'That you were never exciting. People don't say that about themselves.'

'They do if they are me.'

Obadiah was a uniquely homely and boring rich man, but his abnegation thrilled Maud, gave her gooseflesh. She said to herself: I love Obadiah. I love what shall not be. I am never what I was. I am always new, always two. I am, and I am, and so I am.

After Maud accepted Obadiah's invitation to dance, Quinn, obligated in the breach, asked Magdalena to dance. He found his feet not nearly so bored, and Magdalena floated in his arms. He told her as much and she told him he was a sweet boy. She apologized for John the Brawn's throwing him off the canalboat like a sack of oats. Quinn's newly assured self had already decided to relegate that event to useless memory, especially after watching John knock down the world champion, and so Quinn smiled and said of his canalside odyssey, 'It was nothing. I just walked home and it was fine.'

The dimension of this lie convinced Quinn he had a future as a confidence man. He'd always felt bound for hell, convinced of it by his early confessors, and also by his great maiden aunt from Ireland who told him he was 'a devil dog if I ever saw one,' when what he was doing – cutting his dead cousin's hair with his father's knife – was not devilishness but tidiness, for the boy's hair was full of nits and cockleburs. And what way was that to bury anybody?

'You are becoming a reporter for the newspaper, I understand,' Magdalena said.

'I'm trying,' said Quinn.

'I, too, write,' said Magdalena.

'I thought you were just a dancer.'

'Dancers have souls with myriad planes,' she said. 'Every step of the dance is like a line from a poem.'

'I didn't think of that,' said Quinn.

'I write poetry that dances.'

Quinn nodded and danced on, fearing she would recite to him.

'Would you like to hear some of my poetry?' she asked.

'Oh, that would be fine indeed.'

Magdalena cleared her throat and prepared to recite and dance all at once.

'The moon followed me home,' she began, her grip on Quinn tightening.

'But a cloud covered it

'And I made my escape.'

Quinn nodded and smiled. Magdalena needed no more.

'If a butterfly

'Turned into a caterpillar,

'Where would be the loss?'

Quinn narrowed his smile, spinning with Magdalena as he did so, wondering how to respond.

'Those are quite short poems,' he finally said.

'I never write long poems,' said Magdalena. 'My longest was about my trip to the bottom of the river.' She closed her eyes, straightened her neck.

'Four gleaming clamshells.

'Danced for my pleasure.

'The mud fairies made me a shawl

'Of luminous eelgrass.

'I died of death

'Until the sword of the sailor

'Pierced my heart,

'And I ascended again

'Into the land of sorrow.'

'Someday I must write about your poetry so people will know you are more than a dancer,' Quinn said, shamed by his deception, pleased by his politesse. He wanted to be as honest with Magdalena as she was being with him. Perhaps he *would* write about her. She was a striking woman. He could even write of her body, of which he had had privileged sightings, in the *Dood Kamer* and under the garden arch.

'That would be very kind of you,' Magdalena said to him. 'When are you going to kidnap Maud?'

'What's that?'

'I know she's asked you. Hasn't she?'

'She told you?'

'She didn't have to. She's been asking men to kidnap her ever since she was eight years old.'

'No.'

'Everybody knows that about Maud.'

'I didn't know it.'

'She doesn't tell her kidnappers.'

'She's been kidnapped before?'

'Never.'

'I don't understand this.'

'She doesn't want to be kidnapped. She only wants to talk about being kidnapped. That way she doesn't have to make any decisions about the future. When things get difficult she invites someone to kidnap her.'

'That seems madcap.'

'Yes, doesn't it?'

'Has Maud always been madcap?'

'As long as I've known her.'

'How long have you known her?'

'Since she was born.'

Maud Lucinda Fallon was born in 1837 of a twin and a tenant farmer, and distinguished herself at the age of two by reciting the Ave Maria in its entirety, in Latin. Her mother, Charlotte Mary Coan, and her father, Thomas (Thomsy) Fallon, both denied having instructed her, and both claimed utter ignorance of Latin.

Maud began a diary at age four and filled notebooks with poetic language her parents could understand only marginally. The source of her gift was made suspect by the parish priest in Athlone and her writing was not encouraged. When she was five her notebooks were sent to a schoolmaster for evaluation and Maud never saw them again.

Maud's life lost what little formal structure it had when her father joined a tenant farmers' rebellion and was arrested and shipped to an English prison. He escaped en route and found his way to Canada, from where he sent money back to Charlotte, a young woman of spirit, whose gift was for music and dance. Charlotte, in short order, took herself and her child to Dublin, resolving to wrench them both up from the depths into which Thomsy Fallon's arrest had plunged them.

Charlotte joined a traveling theater company, became its principal dancer, the lover of two of its actors, and by the time the troupe reached England, she was its sensual public flower. From London she was whisked to Paris by a plutocrat in the July monarchy of Louis Philippe, changed her name to Lila Márquez to distinguish herself from the French, and was kept in circumstances proper to her burgeoning ambition.

Maud grew to be an encumbrance on her mother's *vie amoureuse*, and so Charlotte-Lila sent the child to Spain to live with Maud's aunt (and Charlotte's twin), Magdalena Colón, that surname a gift from her most recent late husband. Like the intrepid general who refuses to die in battle but is thwarted in the charge by having his horses repeatedly shot from under him, Magdalena had bid farewell to three husbands at graveside and was on the brink of acquiring a fourth when Maud arrived in Spain and changed her life, generating in it the wise child's mystery, and giving Magdalena new vistas beyond sensuality and security.

While Charlotte-Lila abandoned the Parisian plutocracy to pursue the devil amid the royal resplendency of Bavaria, Magdalena imposed tutors, dancing masters, and dolls on the five-year-old Maud, who became trilingual in a trice, and at six could also emulate her aunt Magdalena in the flamenco and the tarantella (which Magdalena had learned from a Zincali Gypsy queen).

In 1848, as revolution swept through Europe, Magdalena saw her fortunes fading in Spain and, upon the advice of a cosmopolitan lover, turned her attention to the United States of the New World, a nation only moderately cultured and given to irrational frenzies toward beautiful dancing females.

And so it came to pass in the summer of 1849 that Magdalena, known as La Última after the death of her third husband, arrived at New York with serving maid and Maud, now twelve, and began a theatrical tour that included a capsizing and sudden death in the icy river at Albany, a spiritual communion in Saratoga, a reluctant companionship with John McGee (a well-hung lout), an empty dalliance with Obadiah Griswold (a generous fool), and a dance in the arms of Daniel Quinn (a boy of compelling charm).

Maud, witness to this, adolescent savant-seer, child of the emotional wilderness, discovered one night in Obadiah's mansion at Saratoga the presence of bloodstains on her bedsheet and fell instantly into raptures at their significance, judging them to be the geography of a long-awaited unknown. She sought counsel from Magdalena in coping with the flow.

'Well, Maudie, it's about time,' said Magdalena. 'Your body is several years late in catching up with your mind, but here you are, at last. Maybe now you'll understand what your auntie is all about.'

Poor Quinn. Consider him. He saves a life, discovers love, finds it reciprocated, is obsessed and rightfully so, alters his life to yield to his obsession, finds worlds beyond worlds that he cannot understand, finds the object of his obsession to be madcap, takes her home, kisses her, all but swoons with confounded desire, goes to his rooming house, fails to sleep, rises, lights his writing lamp, plucks from his writing case his pointless pen, finds a point, imposes it upon the pen, unrolls his paper, uncaps his inkwell, poises his pen above the well with the intention of wetting the point and writing, refrains from dipping because his condition allows no clarity of thought, puts down the pen, paces up and down in his bedchamber, takes up his collection of Montaigne's essays, opens it, and finds two passages underlined: 'What causes do we not invent for the misfortunes that befall us? What will we not blame, rightly or wrongly, that we may have something to fight with?' and also this: 'And we see that the soul in its passions is wont to cheat itself by setting up a false and fanciful object, even against its own belief, rather than not have something to act upon,' and piqued by this, turns back to the beginning of the essay, which is called 'How the Soul Relieves Its Feelings on the Wrong Objects, When the Real Are Wanting,' reads it through, then resumes his pacing, considering the current state of love, of men and women, of his life past and future, wondering what will become of himself, a novice in all things, now that he is lost to love and probably about to set out in several wrong directions, linked as he is to a radical child, a deluded poetaster, and John McGee, a scurvy bastard, but who did knock down Hennessey with Quinn as a witness, and at that memory Quinn picks up his pen, dips it in his ink, and writes one sentence: 'They call him John the Brawn and he doesn't know enough to pull his head in when he shuts the window, but he knocked down the best fighter in the world,' and having written that, puts down his pen, smiles, walks up and down the bedchamber, and understands that he has just changed his life.

Quinn's mood elevated once he discovered his control over the word. He envisioned a thrilling future for himself, sitting alone in hotel rooms, ruminating on epic events, then imposing his conclusions on paper for the world to read in the morning newspaper. He felt a surge of power and also vague intimations of wealth. He made plans to hire a carriage and take Maud to the High Rock, the Iodine, and the Empire Springs, whose multiple chlorides, bromides, sulphates, phosphates, and bicarbonates of magnesia, iron, soda, strontia, and lime had been vitalizing and restoring the health of multitudes since the age of the Indian, most notably the health of the 'high livers,' whose love of good food, abundant drink, and nocturnal revels was a proven ravagement. Quinn did not consider himself a high liver, but he intuited that he might become one; and Maud, too, though of a different order. Quinn's intuitions about Maud had all the fixity of a cloud in high winds.

William Kennedy

Quinn's plan was this: hire the open carriage, promenade through the city to the springs, stop at an appropriate place for tea, and, while the carriage waited, stroll with Maud through the first available park, lead her into a wooded grove, throw your arms about her, kiss her passionately with lip and tongue, declare your eternal love for her face, her form, her brain, her soul.

Upon Quinn's invitation to an outing at the springs, Maud brooded on the uncertainties that had been keeping her wakeful during recent nights. Most disturbing was the dream that had arrived after her talk with the emaciated man. Walking by a lake she saw a living, pulsating, disembodied eye sitting on a large rock. The eye was her own and when she reached for it to put it back in its socket it slithered through her fingers into the sand. She cupped it in the palms of her hands and as she lowered it into the water to rinse it, the eye swiftly melted into corrupt slime.

Maud read this as an omen of confusion, especially in regard to Quinn. It was true that only he and she would do each other justice in this life. But what but a proper botch would they make of an adolescent marriage? It was a peasant dream, laughable. Furthermore, Maud was mutating: communicating with herself through the techniques of Mesmer, willing herself into states that were alien to her waking self. Become a loveless Japanese wife, she would tell herself. Become a sibyl in the Delphic mode. Become a child of slaves at the auction block. Become an actress who works with Shakespeare himself. She would allow herself to pass hours of waking and sleeping in these foreign moods, and come away from them only reluctantly, and with written messages she could not reconcile. 'The sadness of bumblebees and the longitude of pity exist only for lovers,' she wrote to herself. This poetic turn she found to be at odds with her pragmatic self, and pleasingly so. But her ability to communicate with the emaciated man was a disturbing extension of the condition, for it existed outside what she deemed the realm of the possible. She therefore disbelieved it, albeit hollowly: full of mocking echoes.

I must decide what to do about Quinn, Maud told herself, and so she fasted for the rest of the day, then set about making a dumb cake, as Magdalena's Zincali Gypsy had taught her. She waited until Obadiah's household was asleep and then in the kitchen she created her cake from eggs, salt, flour, and water in which she had lightly bathed her privities. She sat in silence with her back to the stove until it was time to take out the cake. She then revealed her breasts to the cake, covered herself, drew her initials with a knife on the top of the cake, and set it on the hearthstone in front of Obadiah's drawing-room fireplace. She opened the front door of the house and left it ajar, sliced out a small piece of the cake for herself, and walked backward with it up the stairs to her room.

She put the piece of cake on her bedside stand, took off her dress, and unbuttoned her underclothing. She then ate the cake while standing, awaiting the spectral double of the man she would marry to enter the drawing room, carve his own initials on the cake downstairs, and perhaps then come up the stairs to pursue her with phantom hands. The loosening of her shift would allow her to free herself from such a grasp. He might get her underclothing, but not her. She would fall upon the bed at such an attempt, thus banishing him from the house.

The charm drugged her into sleep, and upon waking, and after inspecting the cake on the hearth at morning, she dressed herself and awaited the arrival of Quinn and his carriage.

Quinn walked through the village streets with Maud, envying the behavior of other strolling couples, all of whom seemed to be either in complacent love or in varied stages of flirtation. None seemed to exude the intensity of what he himself felt, and yet he could not touch Maud, not even her hand with his fingertips. Nor could he take hold of her arm to guide her; and so they walked as strangers along the grass-trimmed sidewalks, out of the area of stores, shops, hotels, and onto a street of stately homes and private gardens. At a wooded area past the last of the homes, Quinn stopped to regard the residue of a careless picnic: bits of bread, a strew of paper, a chicken bone, the core of an apple, a cork, a cigar butt, a woman's handkerchief with a hole burned in it. An irrational sadness overtook Quinn.

'Look at that mess,' he said, shaking his head.

'The remnants of beauty,' said Maud, nodding.

Quinn and Maud were entering a new condition. Despairing of more intimate conversation, Quinn told her of a story he was writing about John the Brawn and that Calvin Potts was interested in printing in his newspaper.

'You will be very good at what you do,' Maud said. 'I myself am riding horses again for the first time since we lived in Spain. Obadiah has wonderful horses.'

'I've never been on the back of a horse,' Quinn said.

'It's a majestic experience,' said Maud.

Quinn nodded, uncertain of the meaning of 'majestic,' and how riding a horse could be conducive of that.

'We ought to walk through the woods,' Quinn said, and in a gesture that defied the static present tense of his life he grabbed Maud's hand and stepped over the picnic leavings and onto a path that led he knew not where.

'You want me to walk in the woods?' said Maud.

'Are you so delicate?'

'I'm not at all delicate.'

'Then we'll go into the woods,' said Quinn. 'I don't like what's been going on with you today.'

'Nothing has been going on with me.'

'Nothing indeed, and more nothing. What I expect from you is something. I expect you to love me as I love you. I expect you to want to kiss me and hold me as I want to kiss and hold you.' Quinn thought he might have stolen this line from a poem.

'Yes,' said Maud. 'I understand that. But what happened is that I spent the night baking a dumb cake to find out how to behave with you.'

'Why would you bake a dumb cake? Why wouldn't you bake a smart cake if you wanted to know something?'

'All cakes are dumb.'

'I think I always knew that.'

'The true dumb cake helps you discover who will be your husband.'

'Ah, I see,' said Quinn. 'More spirits.'

'If you like.'

'What do you do with a dumb cake after it's baked?'

'You put your initials on it, you eat some of it, and you wait for your future husband's double to come and also put his initials on it.'

'And that's it?'

'No,' said Maud, and she paused. 'You also show your breasts to it.'

'You show your breasts to a cake?' said Quinn.

'That's part of the ritual.'

'It would make more sense if you showed your breasts to me, if I'm going to be your husband.'

'My breasts are too small to show to anyone. Especially you.'

'Am I so much less than a cake?'

'It's not less or more, you ninny. It's what must be. I didn't invent this ritual.'

'I'm glad to hear that,' said Quinn, and he grabbed her hand and pulled her along. Suddenly he stopped and threw his arms around her and kissed her with lip and tongue, but could say nothing. He finished his kissing and pulled her toward the street.

'Your face is very rough,' Maud said to him, stumbling along behind him. 'You should shave.'

'I don't shave,' Quinn said. 'People who are lower than cakes don't have to shave.'

'You're not lower than a cake, Daniel,' said Maud. 'You don't understand my situation, and you don't understand me.'

'It's true I don't.'

'If you shave I'll tell you everything.'

'Then we'll go to the barber right now.'

'No, we'll go back to Obadiah's. I'll get you John's razor.'

'I don't know how to use a razor. I'd cut off my nose.'

'Of course you wouldn't. If a primitive like John McGee can use a razor, so can you.'

159

'John also knows how to use his fists and knock out the champion of the world, and I don't know how to do that.'

'Then it's time you learned,' Maud said, stepping up into their hired carriage.

Quinn stood before the mirror of the shaving stand in an upstairs bathroom and looked at himself. His shirt was hidden under the towel Maud had tucked into his collar. She had fetched all of John's shaving gear: soft-bristle brush, mug of soap, bone-handled straight razor, also a jar of alum to cauterize cuts – medical wisdom she had come by while watching John shave. Maud opened the razor and put it in Quinn's hand.

'You know how it's done, don't you?' she asked.

'Of course I know how it's done. I saw my father shave a thousand times.'

'Well, don't cut yourself in any vital spots. Go careful till you get the knack of it.'

'I don't need to be told.'

'Then I shall tell you no more for now. Ta ta.'

And she left.

Quinn touched the razor to his right cheek, a fly's weight on the skin, and moved it gently downward. Some of the dry, soapless stubble gave way before the razor's formidably sharp edge, but with the pain of snagged hair. The truth was that Quinn had never seen his father shave. The man wore a beard. Quinn now looked at John's brush and soap as hostile objects, for if you cover your face with soap how will you see what you're supposed to cut? He continued his dry shave. It hurt. Still, he had not gouged himself. He pressed on. It hurt.

Eck.

A cut.

Reluctantly he wet his face and soaped one side of it and around the mouth, making small dabs with the brush, using the circular motion he remembered from watching a barber work. He moved his lower jaw to the left and puckered his lips as he lathered his right cheek, moved jaw to the right and made opposite pucker when lathering left. With his first finger he wiped his lips clean of soap, picked up the razor and began anew the elimination of his downy whiskers. Blood was coloring the soap on his cheek, but he tried not to watch. He shaved on.

Eck.

Another cut. More blood.

He pressed on, carefully, learning to let the razor glide over his skin, shearing the whiskers with newfound ease as the blood flow intensified. He finished, rinsed his face in the now pink water, then set about applying alum to the cuts as Maud had instructed him. His blood stopped leaking but he felt new pain from the alum's stypticity. He dried his face and stared at himself in the mirror. He concluded he would have to shave regularly from now on, a relentless obligation. He would, in spite of all, develop an awesome talent for shaving himself. He could feel that. He would be very good at what he did: Maud had predicted that.

Life does seem to conspire against the lofting of the spirit, does it not? Quinn came down clean-shaven from the bathroom and looked for Maud. He asked the footman if he'd seen her and the man said he had not.

Quinn went to the veranda and sat in the largest wicker rocker in North America. In the waning sunlight of the afternoon he mused on beauty, wealth, women, and the brilliance of the person who had invented shaving soap. He studied the architecture of Obadiah's veranda with its twisted columns and the perfection of its paint, which seemed ever new. He relished the rolling symmetry of the lawn and gardens, the trellises and arches, the beds of roses and lush stands of mature trees. He felt a profound serenity overtaking him and he began to doze. He was awakened by the footman, who asked if he cared for tea. Obadiah had seen him napping and thought the tea might brace him. Quinn smiled and said yes, tea would be pleasant.

He rocked, no longer worrying where Maud might be. He knew she would be along, probably in a new dress, or in a peculiar costume, or with a new hairdo. Whatever her look, her mood would be the reverse of what it had been when they parted. She would be effusive, flirtatious. She would open her mouth and pretend to kiss him. She would tell him stories of old Spain, or of majestic horseback riding, or of her mother and the King, or she would reveal arcane secrets of love that Magdalena had passed on to her.

Quinn equated Maud with his Celtic potato platter: both of them agents of change and illusion, both of uncertain origin and significance – the platter waiting underground for another generation to unearth it, quantifying its own value and mystery in the shallow grave; and Maud propounding mysteries of the cosmos with every Maudbreath. Buried, they eluded. Resurrected, they grew lustrous.

The footman brought tea and cucumber sandwiches. Quinn apologized for not liking cucumbers and asked was there an alternative. The footman said he would speak with the cook, and returned with caviar canapés, diced celery, and raw peppers. Quinn tasted and loathed each in turn, an awareness dawning in him that something was amiss. It was unlikely that so many foods chosen by a chef should all displease him. Negative matter was being imposed on him. He wondered if Maud's spirits were stalking him. He saw dusk settling on Obadiah's landscape and imagined himself starving to death while the footman brought him an unending stream of food samplers: lamb's eyes and bull's testicles, goat fritters and fried pigskin. These would be perfectly cooked, elegantly offered. Quinn would reject each, and passersby would soon notice his weight loss.

Obadiah sat down in the rocker next to him.

'Enjoying yourself?' Obadiah asked.

'I enjoyed the tea, but I wonder what's keeping Maud.'

'No one has seen her since last night. She's not in her room.'

'I was with her today. We took a carriage ride and came back here so I could shave with John McGee's razor. I sat here to wait for her. She's a girl of a different sort.'

'A different sort exactly,' said Obadiah. 'No one has seen her since last night.'

'I was with her today. We took a carriage ride.'

'If you say so.'

'What do you mean, if I say so?'

'Well, you're a young lad.'

'I *was* with her.'

'If you say so.'

'I do,' said Quinn.

'A horse is missing. From the stable.'

'A horse?'

'One of my horses. A horse.'

'Where did it go?'

'Well, that's certainly a question. Where *did* it go?'

'Do you think Maud took the horse?'

'It's been suggested.'

'Maud wouldn't steal a horse.'

'Perhaps she's only out riding. But she's been gone since last night and so has the horse, and no one has seen either one of them.'

'I have. I was with her today. We took a carriage ride.'

'So you've said. That's quite extraordinary. But no one has seen her since last night.'

'I have. We took a carriage ride.'

'I think you should stop saying that.'

'It's the truth.'

'It's your truth. It's certainly not my truth. I wasn't out for a ride with anybody today.'

'I didn't say you were.'

'But you keep contradicting me. The fact is that no one wants you around here. You come in and use the razor and sit on the veranda and reject my food and now you tell me I'm a liar.'

'I didn't say that. Where is Maud, anyway?'

'We would all prefer it if you went somewhere else and asked your questions.'

'I want to see Maud.'

'You'll have a long wait. She's run away with my roan stallion.'

'She knew I was waiting for her.'

'She took her bag.'

'She took her bag?'

'No one has seen her since last night.'

'I have. Where is Magdalena? Where is John?'

'They don't want to see you. You better go along now, like a good fellow. My carriage will take you to the village.'

'How do I know Maud is gone?'

'No one has seen her since last night.'

'I have, we took a carriage ride.'

Obadiah stood up. Quinn resisted standing, but here was the man ejecting him from his home. Quinn stood.

Two days later he returned and asked for Maud. The footman said she had not been seen in three days. Quinn asked to see Magdalena and John but was told they were not at home. The footman told Quinn he was no longer welcome at the Griswold estate.

Quinn returned to Mrs Trim's rooming house on Phila Street and stood looking out of the window of his room at people walking and talking with one another on the sidewalk. He grew irrationally jealous of these amiable strangers and decided to lie upon his bed until the jealousy passed. He lay there, staring at the ceiling, until he felt the energy of his hostility wane. He perceived that he was not angry with Maud. He dwelled on that and felt humiliated, abandoned, and lost yet again. This condition sickened him, an emetic to his soul.

He went back to the window and looked down at the people on the street. They had become normal. He liked them now, liked the way they preened in their finery: fashion on the hoof, style on parade.

He framed Maud's face in his memory.

This girl, he said to himself, is beyond your control. She has excluded you from her future. Well, so be it. Forget her. This part of my life is over and I will suck up to no one. I am done with all the tattered nonsense of first love. The word itself caught in my throat: love. In the years ahead I would be unable to abide all the fatuous love palaver that would assault my ears. Humming 'Kathleen Mavourneen,' I packed my bag. But I caught myself humming and knew what it meant. I stopped humming, thinking: Done. Yes. Done.

Book Two

The malevolent and terrifying thing shall of itself strike such terror into men that almost like madmen, while thinking to escape from it, they will rush in swift course upon its boundless forces.

— LEONARDO DA VINCI

A Bazaar of Enticement

Albany

Summer 1864

We will now talk of events that take place in fact and memory after Daniel Quinn, that orphan of life, now twenty-nine years of age, arrives by train at Albany from the mudholes of hell. Quinn, for more than two years, has been traveling with the Union Army, interviewing generals, captains, and soldiers of the line, writing about their exploits at Spotsylvania, Cold Harbor, Monocacy, and elsewhere, describing their casualties, camp life, army food, the weather, incompetent surgeons, Southern women.

The day in Albany is intermittently sunny and overcast, and the clerk of the weather says no rain is expected, that Albany's long drought will continue, and that passing rain clouds are merely illusory elements in a dry world. Quinn has already bought a horse and saddle, the mode of travel that has become part of his being, and is riding, at an ambling gait suited to the slowness of his mind, toward the Staats mansion of revered history. The waters of the Staatskill course toward him as he ascends the hill, arousing in him thoughts of time spent near other water . . .

He was then riding with the Forty-fourth out of Albany, camped on one bank of the Rappahannock, with rebel troops camped on the other. For two days men of both camps swam in the river under an unspoken truce. Jim Lynch from Saratoga broke the silence when he swam to the rebel shore and yelled to the nearest reb, 'You got a newspaper we can read?' The reb waved one at him and Lynch waded to shore, naked, took the paper and thanked the reb, swam

171

back with one hand high, and gave the paper to Quinn. It was from Richmond, only days old.

In a day's time the swimmers were killing each other. In three days' time Quinn, walking the battlefield seeking survivors among the dead thousands, heard a wounded reb ask for water. Quinn gave him his canteen and let the reb drink his fill. Then he wet the reb's leg wounds with the remaining water. Quinn considered this a fair exchange for the Richmond newspaper. The reb could not move, but he would not die of his leg wounds. The water will cool, it will loosen, it will cleanse. It will be interesting, important to the reb. But do not touch him.

The reb thanked Quinn by telling him of his optimism before battle. Such optimism was an inversion. It was based upon the vision of his wife beckoning him into the barn with their secret love gesture. The reb knew this was a temptation sent to him by the devil. He knew the barn was death and that his wife would never invite him into death's hayloft.

The reb was of North Carolina stock, strong of face and form, and Quinn knew he had farmed all his life. He revered Longstreet and grieved over the outcome of the battle. He had not known defeat in two years of war. Quinn covered the reb's legs with a blanket taken from a dead reb's bedroll, then found a rebel canteen and filled it for the reb in the river. He filled his own canteen and rinsed the taste and touch of the reb from its neck. He walked across the darkening field, where the broken artillery was strewn, but found no other survivors. Six horses stood hitched to a limber, all with limp necks, all erect in harness: twenty-four legs in an upright position, dead.

Quinn patted the neck of his new horse of the Albany instant, thankful for its life, trustful of its strength. It may be that I am coming out of death, he thought, though he sensed this was untrue, or at least a confusion. Probably he was still in death's center and losing ground. But even the possibility of leaving death behind cheered him, and always there was the banal reality: he had survived and others had not. Such a thought made him as optimistic as the wounded reb before battle. Rubbing elbows with optimism calmed Quinn and he rode on toward the mansion.

At first glimpse he knew the mansion had grown. More rooves and towers rose up from it, more porches spanned its new girth. A Chinese roof topped one new wing and on another rococo carvings spun and curled upward and around new doors and archways, new pillars and dormers. Hillegond and Dirck are manic builders. Lost in a house suited for multitudes, they create yet more space for their solitary comings and goings.

Quinn circled the mansion to see what had become of the structures and gardens of his memory. Amos's tomb and the pump and boat houses were as he remembered. A small, elegant structure was new (this was the shooting villa), but the gazebos and trellises looked as they always had, and today were brilliant with flowers, though the lawns that surrounded them were brown from the drought. All buildings were newly painted in the uniform colors of yore – a rich brown with beige trim – and all the brickwork was that same pale, rusty red.

In replenishing his vision of it all, Quinn sought not what was new but what was not: the elusive thing that endured unchanged in spite of growth. He tethered his horse in the front carriageway and knocked at the portal of first entrance, the carved wooden door looming before him with the same majesty it owned on the night he arrived a fugitive from the wild river. He stood on the same spot where he had stood then, feeling the strength of ritual rise in him. Repetition of past gestures suddenly seemed to hold the secret of his restoration to . . . to what? He could not say. He would not repeat a single day of the known past, would he? Would he willingly relive the days in which Maud was revealed to him, full knowing that the brink of that ecstasy gave onto a chasm of loss and waste? He had kissed Maud and known love, and then descended from beauty into the valley of putrefaction, where lay a generation of blasted sons: seven thousand dead in a single battle, dead in a great wedge of slaughter, their brains and bowels blown out of them, and they then left to rot on a field consecrated by national treachery and endemic madness. And the killing moved on to greener pastures.

William Kennedy

The front door opened and Quinn recognized Capricorn, hair gone to white, skin gone to leather, eyes waning. The old man did not recognize the long, lean Quinn in his soldier's shirt (he was not a soldier), his riding breeches and boots, and the wide-brimmed slouch hat beneath which he had lived so long. But when Quinn took off the hat to reveal dense waves of hair the color of earth, then the old man's eyes remembered history.

'You're Mist' Quinn.'

'Cappy, you've kept your wits intact, unlike most of us.'

Quinn entered a house refurnished: gone the cherrywood sofa on which the widow Ryan and her terrified children had sat, replaced by a resplendently huge oval settee; gone the musicroom portraits of Petrus and Hillegond, the walls covered now with huge tapestries; gone, too, the foyer's Dutch colonial chandelier, and pendulous now in its place one of crystal, twice the size of the old one and exuding thrice the former elegance. This place does not shrink in memory. It waxes in breadth, and its opulence thickens.

'Is Dirck home?' Quinn asked.

'No more. He marry that singer and he move to Sweden. That's where he live now.'

'Sweden. I remember his wife always wanted to go back there.'

'Said he didn't wanna be here no more. Sold the house to Mr Fitzgibbon and went away.'

'Sold the house? What about Hillegond?'

'Mist' Quinn, Miss Hilly's gone.'

'Gone where?'

'Gone. Killed. They strangle her. Wire her neck. They say she musta died right off.'

Quinn took off his hat, ran his hand through his hair, falling into the void, groping for a word.

'When?'

'Last Feb'ary sometime. Six months now. Worst thing ever happen in this house.' Capricorn sighed mightily and his voice broke. 'They do my Matty too. Killin' women like that.'

174

'Who did? Why? What is all this?'

'Don't really know. Some thinks they knows. But nobody knows why they do my Matty too.'

Capricorn was near tears, and Quinn motioned the old man toward the east parlor.

'Can we sit and talk about this?'

'Capricorn don't sit in there. New butler, he don' allow that.'

'A new butler. Everything's changed. What about the porch?'

'Don' think so.'

'We won't go to the kitchen. All right if we walk?'

'Walkin' is fine.'

And so they walked on the road under a relentless sun, with Capricorn immediately talking of the great wealth of the new owner, Gordon Fitzgibbon, son of Lyman, and passing on then to Hillegond. Sadness smothered Quinn with each vision of her that came into his memory, and he knew he would have to turn the conversation away from her. He would find out the details of her murder from Will Canaday, read all the stories Will must have written about it. Quinn could drown in such evil but he would not. He would survive Hillegond's death as he had others in the war: move past them; control the power of grief and anger to destroy the vessel. But he could feel the impetus for control weakening with each new death that touched him, his survival drive waning like Cappy's eyesight. Soon there may be no drive.

And Capricorn talked on.

'This woman, she open her house to colored folks. She feed them, help them go to freedom. She save Joshua from jail, then give him money so's he can bring other coloreds up from Carolina. Joshua's woman stop here too. Miss Hilly a sainted lady. She in heaven for sure. She be a queen up there.'

'I was here the night Joshua came in as a prisoner, manacled to the Swede,' Quinn said.

'I recollect.'

'After that I asked you about him, but you wouldn't tell me anything.'

'I recollect that too.'

175

'I saw Joshua in New York.'

'We ain't seen him here. How that boy doin'?'

'Long time ago, but he was all right then.' Quinn the liar.

'Aw, that's fine.'

'He was working in John McGee's saloon. You remember John? The fighter? John the Brawn they called him.'

'Nobody forget *that* man once they meet him.'

'Joshua had a new name first time I caught up with him. Called himself Mick the Rat.'

'Go on. Mick the Rat?'

'That's it. He was handling rats for John.'

'Handlin' rats?'

'A special show to bring people into the saloon. They see the rat show free, then maybe they drink and gamble some. Joshua had a bag full of rats. He'd catch a fresh bunch every night at the slaughterhouse. Throw a light on them and while they stared at it he'd grab 'em with long pincers and drop 'em in the bag.'

Capricorn shook his head. 'Joshua do that? Joshua?'

Quinn nodded. 'Then he'd bring the rats into John's place and put one into this pit in the back of the saloon. People all around the pit watching, and then somebody'd put a bull terrier in with the rat. Terrier'd kill it quick. Then Joshua'd put two rats in and the terrier'd kill them too, sometimes just one bite apiece. Then they'd put a Mexican hairless in and Joshua'd dump in four rats and the Mex'd get them all. Then five rats, then six. The rats had no chance. It was a matter of time.'

'Can't say as I like that game.'

'No. But Joshua needed money. He was hiding two fugitive slaves and trying to move them north.'

'He always doin' that.'

'Asked me to help him. He didn't really know me, but he trusted me. Said that was his talent, knowing if he could trust you.'

Joshua told Quinn the bounty on one of the runaways was three hundred dollars, which made his work of hiding the pair doubly difficult. The second slave had no price on his head, being possessed of only one eye, the other destroyed by the lash of a whip from his master's hand, marking him as an evil-eyed source of ill luck to all. Joshua had led the slaves from Philadelphia to a farmer's cabin south of Kingston that was only marginally secure; and when he learned the slave hunters were closing in he put the problem to Quinn: We need a white man. Quinn said he was a white man.

Joshua had allies, but the known local abolitionists were of no value in this situation. Quinn, a stranger, could bring the necessary word to the inns and the grogshops where the deadliest gossip thrived and where the slave hunters had been biding their time to hear it. The slavers were also a pair, not from the South (by their accent) but Yorkers, clearly. They came equipped: ropes, manacles, rifles, pistols, money to loosen tongues. They called each other by name – Fletch and Blue – and made no secret of their ambition: 'Catch niggers.'

And so when Quinn sat in the Eagle Tavern and ordered his whiskey toddies and grew garrulous, dropping the news that he'd seen niggers moving around near a cabin up the pike, then repeated his performance at the Bump Tavern at the next crossroads, well, it came as no surprise when Fletch and Blue turned up at his elbow, inquiring about particulars.

'You hunt niggers, is that it?' Quinn asked them.

'We take property back to its rightful owners,' said Fletch.

'A wonderful thing,' said Quinn. 'Man owns somethin', he shouldn't oughta have to give it up, just on accounta the thing he owns don't want to be owned no more. Man could lose all his cows that way.'

'Cows,' said Fletch, and he thought about that.

'You think you could show us where you seen them niggers?'

'Can't really tell it,' said Quinn. 'Don't know the names of none of these roads, don't know where nothin' is, rightly.'

'You figure you could show us?' asked Fletch.

'I s'pose.' And Quinn mused on the possibility. 'What's the profit for a fella like me shows you what you're lookin' for?'

'You want profit, is that it?'

'Most folks do.'

'We'll give you profit.'

'That case, we probably got us a deal.'

'Then let's go.'

'How much profit you figure we're talkin' about?'

'We give you two dollars. You can buy a new horse with two dollars.'

'Not no kind of horse I'd wanna ride.' And Quinn fell silent.

'We'll give you three,' said Blue.

'We'll give you five, never mind three,' said Fletch.

'All you gonna give me is five? I was thinkin' twenty ain't a bad price for a couple of niggers.'

'Twenty; all right, twenty. Let's go.'

'I'd like to get the feel of the twenty 'fore we go,' said Quinn.

'Give him twenty,' said Fletch. And Blue opened the flap of his shirt pocket and took out a fold of bills.

'You ready now?' Blue said when Quinn took the money.

'I'm ready,' said Quinn. 'You ready?'

'We're ready,' said Fletch. 'But if'n we don't get no niggers I'll be lookin' to get back that twenty.'

'Fair's fair,' said Quinn, and he led the way out of the tavern, mounted his horse, and headed north on the turnpike.

Wrapped in blankets, the fugitive slaves squatted on the earth in a pit under the floorboards of the cabin, their retreat in times of threat. Planks covered their heads. Long slivers of light from the oil lamp in the second room of the cabin found their way down between the boards and into the soft clay cubicle of the slaves' secret dwelling place.

Joshua added wood to the fading fire, the first time the stove had been used in the eight days the slaves had been here, for smoke is a traitor. In the second room of the cabin sat two white men with blackened faces, each with pistol and shotgun. When they heard the horses approach, the men took up prearranged positions and Joshua stood by the cabin door, carrying no weapon, and waited for the visitors to knock.

Quinn rode to the rear of Fletch and Blue when they neared

the cabin and in his mind heard the music the two banjos made
when the cadaverous dancer at The Museum sang his ditty:

> Dere's music in de wells,
> Dere's music in de air,
> Dere's music in a nigger's knee
> When de banjo's dere.

And then Fletch was telling Joshua that they were working for
the federal marshal to track runaway slaves. Joshua spoke in a
voice foreign to Quinn, whining and mewling.

'I's a free man,' he said. 'Don't know nothin' 'bout no 'scaped
slaves. Lived here all my days. You don't believe that, go ask
anybody here'bouts.'

'Ain't you we're lookin' for,' said Fletch. 'We're after two
niggers got only three eyes between 'em.'

'Don't know nothin' 'bout three eyes,' Joshua said. 'You wanna
come in and look, you can. I ain't fightin' no federal marshal. But
ain't nobody here but Mick the Rat, and that's me, and that's
what is.'

'We'll have a look,' said Fletch. He dismounted and tied his
horse to a bush, and then with Blue behind him and Quinn
bringing up the rear, the three entered the cabin. What Quinn
saw was a long shadow of a man in the second room, and Fletch
and Blue both drew their pistols and moved toward it. Joshua
backed into the room ahead of them and turned toward the
shadow, which was made not by a man but a coat and hat
on a stick, at which Fletch and Blue pointed their guns. As
they did, the shotguns of the blackfaced men rose out of the
shadows to the level of their faces, and both slavers dropped
their pistols.

'You lookin' for us niggers?' said one of the blackfaces. 'You
wanna take us to Virginia?'

Fletch shook his head.

'Thought you did,' said blackface.

Joshua drew a knife from the scabbard on his belt and with

179

deft strokes cut the belts and waistbands on the trousers of Fletch and Blue.

'Sit,' said Joshua, and Fletch and Blue sat.

'Take off your boots,' said Joshua, and they did.

'Stand up and drop your pants,' said Joshua, and they did.

Joshua left the room, lifted the planks, and helped the slaves up from their pit as the blackfaces led Fletch and Blue to the pit's edge. The slaves huddled by the stove and watched as Joshua and one of the blackfaces tied the arms and ankles of the slave hunters. Fletch wore long underwear to his ankles. Blue's went to his knees. Neither man wore stockings. When the slavers were bound, Joshua and one of the blackfaces rolled them into the pit.

'We gonna be leavin' now,' Joshua said to them. 'But thinkin' about how you gonna be all alone down there, we got you some company.'

Then from a corner of the cabin, he dragged out a canvas bag the size of a small child. He undid its drawstring, then upended it, dropping two dozen live rats into the pit. The men yelled, the rats squealed. Fletch and Blue kicked at the rats and backed themselves into a corner together.

As Quinn raised the lamp to see what was happening, a courageous rat began climbing Fletch's bare foot.

Fletch kicked it, and the rat flew against the wall and rolled over.

Then it righted itself, undaunted.

Quinn, at this point, let the twenty dollars he had taken from Fletch and Blue flutter back down to its rightful owners.

Capricorn was laughing so hard that tears were on their way.

'Oh, that Joshua, he wicked. That man, he know how to do it. How all that come out?'

'Joshua took the horses and they all rode north,' Quinn said. 'I guess they made it. I never saw any of them again, except Joshua. Never did know those fellows in blackface.'

Quinn and Capricorn turned toward the house, walking past the pond Petrus built for the wild ducks, six of which were in residence. Quinn looked toward the house and saw Hillegond in the window fourteen years before, and he thought: Queen mother of compassion, I loved you.

But he would not weep.

He would not be diminished.

Joshua, a saint, could diminish Quinn, but not death, not even the death of queenly love. The war, wondered Quinn, astonished anew at his toughness – has it turned my soul into a lump of lead? He pictured the city of corpses where he had lived, and a fear gripped him. He was growing strong because of that city, preening with survival. One by one the corpses struggled upright, began a ragged march in his direction. He remembered his Celtic disk and he imposed its memory on this vision, raised it before his eyes like a monstrance, like a shield. Protected from corpses, he breathed deeply and walked toward the mansion.

As he approached his tethered horse he saw a coach and four coming up the carriageway from the new turnpike that now passed the Staats property, and Capricorn said, 'That's him now. Mr Fitzgibbon.'

And so it was: Gordon Fitzgibbon, son of Lyman, a man Quinn knew by name but had not met. Beside him in the carriage Quinn saw a woman.

Then he saw it was a woman of love.

Saw Maud.

He could not have suspected or even intuited her presence here, and yet neither was this coincidence. We could call it Quinn's will to alter existence, to negate life's caprice and become causality itself. This was not the first time he had willed history to do his bidding, but it was the first time history had obeyed him. He'd come here seeking not Maud's presence but the ethereal fragrance of her memory, all he could hope to find. Given that, he felt he would be able to trace her. Now here she arrives, and so begins a new confluence for these two strangers of love.

The coach halted at the mansion, and the coachman leaped to the ground, opened the door. Out first stepped Maud Fallon, dressed in black and white silks, her abundant auburn hair upswept into a crown encircled with a white ribbon, her skin exquisitely white; and upon seeing Quinn she said, 'Daniel, I feared you were dead,' and gave him her hand, which he took and held.

'I seem to have survived,' he said, 'but it may be an illusion.'

Maud turned then to Capricorn and said, 'Cappy, will you bring in my boxes?' Then, nodding once at Quinn, she entered the mansion. Gordon Fitzgibbon approached Quinn with extended hand.

'You're Quinn,' he said.

'That's a fact,' said Quinn.

'I've heard about you and read your writing. You're quite a famous fellow.'

'I think you exaggerate.'

'Not at all. Everybody knows Quinn.'

'I would have thought almost nobody knows him.'

'I'm a true admirer. You've projected me into battles and set me alongside those wounded soldiers. I could feel the weight of their haversacks. You have a talent for creating the vivid scene. Won't you come into the house?'

'I was just leaving. I came to see Hillegond.'

'Poor Hillegond. But at least they caught the villain.' Gordon nodded sadly and, without waiting for Quinn's response to his invitation, strode purposefully into the mansion.

Quinn debated whether to follow, stunned by Maud's brusqueness, then decided he had not exhausted his fate's capacity for surprise (and that's why they call it your fate). Also he wanted to hear more about the villain, and so he left his horse and followed Gordon into what he now was forced to think of as the Fitzgibbon mansion. In the drawing room Gordon offered him whiskey, Quinn's first under these multiple rooves. The two men then settled into facing armchairs, a table between them, and on it a bowl of grapes and apples. Gordon positioned himself so that he was framed from behind by his own enormous portrait: a figure of abundant black hair, strong of jaw and dark of eye, wearing a cloak flared over one shoulder, holding a sheared beaver hat in his right hand, and standing in boots and breeches on the steps of his newly acquired mansion: arrived – for the ages.

'A very good likeness, that,' said Quinn, perceiving the jaw in the portrait to be stronger than the jaw beneath it. Of Gordon's past he remembered only Yale law school, but he would come to know the man as the successor to his father in running the family foundries, a serious churchgoer who abandoned his father's Presbyterian life for the Episcopal high church, who translated Vergil's *Aeneid* from the Latin and then dramatized the story of Aeneas and Dido for the stage; a man of many interests. One too many: Maud.

'It's only been up a week,' said Gordon of his portrait, 'but I am pleased with it. The artist worked on it five months. He began it even before I took title to this place.'

'You were very sure of yourself.'

'Once I heard Dirck was selling it, I had to have it. I bought it for Maud, really. She's mad about being here.'

'It was quite a surprise to see Maud.'

'She's spoken of you, but then again, who hasn't? She's here only a few days and then we're going to Saratoga for the racing. She has a relative up there.'

'She looks well.'

'Indeed she does. She's dazzling. We'll be married soon.'

'Now, that's a surprise, Maud married,' Quinn said, reaching for the grapes.

'She's trepidatious about it.'

'Maud is always trepidatious about relationships,' said Quinn, popping grapes into his mouth.

'We're solving it,' said Gordon.

'You're a sturdy fellow,' said Quinn.

Quinn popped his final grape, then stood up and drank his whiskey in a gulp. 'I must be going,' he said, 'but first tell me about Hillegond.'

'The killer went upstairs and found her sleeping, looped the garrote around her neck and dragged her from the bed with it. It was clear she died in a moment and did not suffer.'

'Some suffer in a moment what takes others twenty years to feel.'

183

'I'm sure you're right,' said Gordon, and his voice was receding for Quinn, only sporadic words registering: '. . . strangled Matty . . . the stairs . . . she fought . . .' For Quinn there was only Maud's coldness, and he silently recited the old Irish poem of warning:

> Wherefore should I go to death,
>> for red lips, for gleaming teeth? . . .
> Thy pleasant mien, thy high mind,
>> Thy slim hand, O foam-white maid,
> O blue eye, O bosom white,
>> I shall not die for thy sake.

Repeat it now. Repeat.

For this is your fate.

'. . . the fellow was shameless . . . dressed like a priest . . . Hillegond's young lover, can you imagine? . . . But he shows up in no records as a priest . . . Did you know him?'

'Who?' asked Quinn.

'The priest fellow. Finnerty, if that's his name. It's what he went by in the theater. A bad apple, to say the least.'

'What about him?'

'Aren't you listening, Mr Quinn? He's in jail. They've charged him as her killer. He had her jade ring. He said she gave it to him.'

'Hillegond?'

'Damn it, Quinn, are you all there? I took you to be acute. Are you ill, or what ails you?'

'I'm distracted, forgive me,' and he turned to leave, turned back. 'Thank you for the whiskey.'

'I hoped to hear of your war experiences.'

'Another time.'

'Perhaps tonight if you're not busy. Join us at the Army Relief Bazaar.'

'Perhaps,' said Quinn, straining.

'It's for the sick and wounded, you know. I'm chairman of

the thing. I've been so involved with the war that my father considers me a practical amalgamationist. I actually recruited an entire company of army volunteers out of our two foundries. A good many were Irish.'

'That's very patriotic,' said Quinn.

'You *must* come to our bazaar,' said Gordon. 'We'll lionize you if you'll let us.'

'I doubt I could handle that.'

'We'll be going at seven. We could pick you up. Where are you staying?'

'I'm not sure.'

'You mean you don't have a place? Why, stay here, then.'

'That's generous, but I think—' and Quinn, in this instant, could not think at all.

From the doorway Capricorn intruded on the hesitational moment. 'Mr Quinn, Miss Maud say she got a letter she want you to read. She be upstairs in the sittin' room.'

Quinn turned to Gordon, who was smiling.

'It's pleasant in Maud's sitting room,' Gordon said.

Quinn returned Gordon's smile, feeling the sudden urge to stuff several grapes up the man's nose. Then he followed Capricorn out of the room and up the stairs.

As he walked, Quinn perceived that with a brusque offering of her hand, with a summons to come hither for a letter, with a decorous public invitation to chat in proper confines, Maud again proved herself a creature of quixotic ways, social fits. Quinn made the first turning on the mahogany staircase, that broad, expansive work of art that rose out of the foyer into the mystery of the mansion's upper labyrinths, and he measured the distance from his last meeting with Maud: six years – the year 1858, when, as journeyman paragraphist and sometime essayist on sporting events, theater, crime, and judiciality for Will Canaday's *Albany Chronicle*, he was present as Maud made her debut in *Mazeppa*.

This was a hippodramatic spectacle, an innovation within a hoary melodramatic theatrical corruption of a Lord Byron narrative poem that had been inspired by a passage in Voltaire's history of

Charles XII of Sweden; and it proved that Maud Fallon not only possessed a singular body but was willing to demonstrate said fact to the world at high risk to that very same singularity.

Lo, the poor Mazeppa. A Tatar foundling who comes to young manhood in the court of the King of Poland, he shares love with the King's daughter, who is abruptly promised to the Count Palatine. Professing his love for the princess, Mazeppa assaults and wounds the Count in a duel and for his effrontery is strapped supine to the back of a wild horse. The horse is then lashed into madness, loosed upon the Ukrainian plains, and runs itself to death. Grievous torture is the lot of Mazeppa during this wild ride, but he survives, is discovered near death by his father (what a coincidence is here), who is the King of Tatary. And Mazeppa soon returns to Poland with the Tatar army to wreak vengeance on Poland and marry his beloved.

In early years of the play the Mazeppa ride had been accomplished onstage with a dummy athwart the live animal, the dummy role in time giving way to intrepid actors. But not until Maud's day had the intrepidity been offered to a female, this the idea of Joseph K. Moran, Albany's Green Street Theater manager and erstwhile tenor turned theatrical entrepreneur, who invited Maud (a horsewoman all her life, as well as a danseuse with acrobatic skills and risqué propensities – her famed Spider Dance, for example) to impersonate the male hero, ride supine and bareback upon Rare Beauty, a genuine horse, and to rise, thereon, up from the footlights and along four escalating platforms to a most high level of the stage, and to do this as well at a fair gallop while clad in a flesh-colored, skin-tight garment of no known name, which would create the illusion of being no garment at all. And so it followed that Maud, barebacked, perhaps also barebuttocked and barebusted, and looking very little like a male hero, climbed those Albany platforms to scandalously glamorous international heights.

Witnessing all this on opening night in 1858, Quinn confirmed his suspicion that he and the truest love of his life (whom he had not seen since she disappeared from Obadiah's home in Saratoga eight years previous) were at this moment incompatible; for who could marry a woman of such antics? That raucous lasciviosity of the audience would madden Quinn in a matter of weeks. And so he called upon Maud in her dressing room, waiting for the wildness of her success to subside into a second day, to tell her as much.

'My God, Daniel, you're my savior,' she said when she saw him, hugging him vigorously, talking as if only days and not years had elapsed since their last meeting. 'You've come just in time to rescue me from this dementia. Can you imagine what this will do to my life?'

Quinn, nonplussed as usual, sat next to Maud, bathing in her presence and her gaze, and could say only, 'You are quite spectacular. I love you incredibly. I'll always love you.'

'I know that,' said Maud. 'Never mind that now. How am I going to get out of this? They want me for as long as I'll stay. They want a contract. They think they'll draw capacity houses for weeks, or months. They say I'll be rich in a trice.'

'Money is nothing,' said Quinn.

'Don't be a nincompoop, Daniel,' said Maud. 'Money is everything to me. How am I to live without money? I've schemed for years to accumulate wealth but it eludes me. I'm incompetent.'

'I'll take care of you,' said Quinn.

'How much do you make?'

'Twenty dollars a week.'

'I'll make four times that tonight,' said Maud.

'Then marry your horse,' said Quinn, and he left her.

Quinn made the second turning on the grand staircase, contemplating the nature of love and money, inquiring to an unknown authority whether there was such a thing as pure love, or was it as much an illusion as Maud's sham nudity? If there was such, he wondered further, was it what he now felt? And if what he now felt was *not* love, could the real element ever be begotten by his like?

He repeated to himself:

> I shall not die for thy sake,
> O maid with the swan-like grace . . .

And then, trepidatious, he entered the sitting room of Maud the Brusque, and encountered her in a pale pink dressing gown, her auburn hair now flowing to her shoulders, her pink chemisette visible beneath her gown, and beneath that, three visible inches of cloven line between her breasts. Never before had Quinn seen this much of Maud's flesh. Never before had he known it to be so abundant; and the sight of it stopped his movement.

'You have a letter for me?' he asked.

'I do,' said Maud, 'but that's not why I invited you here. I thought you might like to see my breasts.'

'Ah,' said Quinn, 'have I at last become the equal of a cake?'

Maud loosened the belt of her dressing gown and moved closer to Quinn.

When she saw Quinn standing tall by the door of the mansion, Maud assumed he was a spirit, so certain had she been of his death; for she had seen in her mind how he crumpled when hit by the cannonball, and how he lay still. And from then forward she received no further visions of his distant life. She thought often of him, and wept always at the memory of his face, his infectious smile of the so-white teeth. And yet there he stood, not a spirit at all, so she knew she must act quickly.

From the first landing on the staircase she watched him as he talked with Gordon, ready to call his name if he started to leave. When she saw him enter the house she knew she had gained time, and so came to her rooms, found the letter she had written him in 1858, and prepared herself to greet him in the manner she had so long imagined. With the help of her serving maid, Cecile, she stripped off her clothing, then donned the chemisette and the robe, placed the letter on the long table, lighted the candles in the two candelabra to frame the letter (and in due course, herself), drew the drapes so the room would not be visible from the upper porch, and sent Cecile away.

She sat on the green velvet sofa, thinking of how angry with her Quinn would be after his talk with Gordon. But that anger would pass and she would impose on him a *geis*. He would then, in due course, be hers, never again to talk of money. They would live together, or separately, it would not matter, for they would be equals in love, something they never had been since love began.

When he came into the room she saw his expression was a stone of feigned wrath, which only made him more handsome, more appealing. Maud always saw through Quinn's masks. He threw the cake up at her when she spoke of her breasts, but she pacified him by offering herself to his eyes. He will not resist me, was her intention. But one must not dismiss Quinn's dispositions too easily, for he is a willful man and at times must be cajoled into the behavior he most desires. With him love must be sat upon, like an egg. It will hatch with warmth, with envelopment. On its own it could rot.

She let her robe fall open, revealing the chemisette, the same order of undergarment Magdalena had worn the night of her death in the river of ice. It clung to Maud from shoulder to middle thigh. Maud imagined herself floating to the bottom of the icy river, snared by John's hook, lifted aboard a skiff, then dragged, bitten, and bounced through the night toward this mansion, which Maud ever since had known as a place where the miracle of love rises gloriously out of death, relinquishes its scars, and moves on to the next order of fulfillment.

She opened the tie of her robe, cradled her breasts with both hands, removed them from constraint, and introduced Quinn to her matured bosom.

He stared.

He almost smiled.

He looked at her eyes.

He looked again at what was revealed.

He kissed her on the mouth.

He held her shoulders.

He stepped back from the kiss.

He touched her left nipple with his right fingertips, lightly. It was the color of cinnamon sugar.

He put his lips on her left nipple, tasted it.

He lifted her left breast in his right hand, moving it slowly from east to west, then west to east.

He attended her right breast with his left hand.

He put his lips on her right breast.

He lightly bit the nipple of her right breast.

He kissed her on the mouth, holding both her breasts in both his hands.

He stepped back from the kiss, levitating both breasts, moving them from west to east, north to south, and so on.

He kissed the cloven line between her breasts.

He licked the line and tasted her salt.

He held both her breasts with both his hands and pressed their softness against both sides of his face.

He raised his face to hers and kissed her on the mouth.

'Do you like me?' she inquired.

'That's the most ridiculous thing I've ever heard you say, and I've heard several.'

'Have you known a lot of women?'

'A fair number. It's been a bazaar of enticement, you might say.'

'I've had six men.'

'A round number.'

'And several hundred suitors.'

'The fellow downstairs is one of the privileged half dozen, I presume.'

'He is not.'

'Has he ever put his mouth on your body?'

'Never. But even so, he is quite jealous. We must hurry. I want you to see all of me.'

'You're very determined.'

'Only fools are otherwise.'

She picked the letter off the table and stuffed it into Quinn's trouser pocket, then moved the candelabra farther apart and sat on the table.

'Do you remember how John came to Magdalena when she was dead, how he raised her clothing?'

190

'I remember it vividly.'

'I want you to do the same with me now. My breasts are blushing. Can you see?'

'I can.'

'I feel a sharp rush of blood to them when I get excited.'

'I could feel their pulse when I touched you.'

'They make the rest of me function. They're the brains of my sex.'

'I'll remember that.'

'Now, I want you to look at me, but you must be precise in what you think. I'm accessible to the man who knows exactly how he loves me. No voyeur will ever reach me.'

She lowered herself into a supine position on the table, freeing up her robe and chemisette. Quinn, seeking precision but astonished by Maud's behavior, could only watch with awe her reenactment of Magdalena's posture, the array of her apparel before resurrection.

'For God's sake, hurry up,' Maud said, and Quinn folded her robe and chemisette upward to reveal the inversely triangulated center of his dreams, more striking than he had imagined, more symmetrical, the auburn crest of it an arc, an emerging sunrise of irresistible invitation. Maud closed her eyes and let her arms fall into the same position as Magdalena's of yore. Quinn put the palm of his hand on her sunrise and she opened her eyes.

'No,' she said. 'We're not ready.'

'Who says we're not?'

'My blood.'

'Why are you with him?' Quinn said.

'I have to be with someone once in a while. He's bright.'

'And he's rich.'

'That doesn't matter.'

'It used to.'

'Why are you talking about money when I'm in this position?'

'You should leave him.'

'Why don't you take me away from him?'

'I wondered when you'd get around to kidnapping.'

'Look at me, Daniel,' she said, and she spread herself.

Quinn looked. 'You are a most willful woman,' he said.

'Everyone has a right to a willful life,' said Maud. 'I dare you to take me away.'

'And so I shall,' said Quinn. 'But first I must know. Have you ever done this in front of a cake?'

She sat up and covered herself, moved the candelabra to where they had been before her ritual, snuffed the candles, opened the drapes to the upper porch, and sat on the velvet sofa precisely where she had been prior to Quinn's arrival. Gordon then knocked on the door of the sitting room.

'Maud, may I come in?'

'Of course,' she said, and Gordon entered, smiling.

'I have to change for this evening,' he said, 'and I wondered whether we should prepare a room for Mr Quinn. I invited him to join us at the bazaar tonight.'

'What a good idea,' said Maud.

'I guess it would be valuable to see it,' said Quinn.

'It's quite a spectacle for Albany,' said Gordon.

'Albany has spectacles and spectacles,' said Quinn.

'Then I'll have them go ahead with the room.'

'If it's not too much trouble,' said Quinn, 'I wonder could I have the one I used to sleep in. Next floor up, opposite the stairs.'

'We have much grander rooms than that,' said Gordon.

'There's grandeur also in repeating history.'

'Then you shall have it. I'll have Cappy bring up your things and stable your horse.' Gordon looked at Maud. 'You seem to be in your nightclothes.'

'I'm about to bathe,' said Maud.

'We'll meet at a later hour, then,' said Quinn, moving toward the door.

'An excellent idea,' said Gordon, standing pat.

My dearest Daniel [Quinn read, lying in the bed he last lay in six years earlier, the careful handwriting before him composed six years earlier also], I am appalled by your unfeeling ways. You are a man of mercurial moods, and if you do not change,

I shan't promise that our love will survive, which would be lamentable. I have never ceased of loving you, but when you came into my dressing room and I hugged you as a savior, I felt something I had not felt since our kiss by the shore of Saratoga Lake (and I have known certain compelling intimacies with men in the intervening years). I conclude from this feeling that I have an enduring element in my makeup, one that, unlike most mortal characteristics of our species, resists change. Poets have talked of this but I have never credited them with propounding anything except romantic twaddle, and yet I must now confess they knew something I heretofore did not.

But you left me in such haste that I did not even gain the moment to tell you what led to our separation in Saratoga. I saw all that happened to you on the veranda that afternoon. I did not ride off on the roan stallion, as some thought, but created the ruse of my departure by convincing a stableboy to take the horse to a neighboring farm. I then hid in the hayloft with my bag and observed all events, for I was in need of time to think what I should do. Intuitively I knew you would never accept my solution to the situation in which I found myself that afternoon after our return. I was, of a suddenness, sorely pressed to provide for Magdalena in light of John McGee's decision to leave us and pursue a career as a prizefighter.

Magdalena, headstrong of course, decided to depart Obadiah's farm immediately and resume our life on the road. She thought of accepting an offer from a New York producer who wanted her to travel and dance and then meet with visitors curious to observe her beauty up close. She was to charge one dollar for each personal handshake. But I was fearful of her health, and knew it would worsen with travel. She was in a most sorry and withdrawn condition and I felt it my duty to bring her to a less grueling fate. This I achieved by shifting Obadiah's obsession from Magdalena to myself. I discovered he was a man of peculiar predilections, obsessed by the backs of women's knees, and so I agreed to make such parts as I owned available for his periodic scrutiny in exchange for his solace and support for the dwindling Magdalena, and a curb on his attentions to her.

In short order Magdalena grew easeful and serene, and in time I hired a woman companion, a French immigrant girl named Cecile, and began my life as the sojourning spiritualist, which afforded me small income and much danger from malevolent Catholic Irishmen. During one visit at Troy a group of them sought my destruction, thinking me an apostle of Satan. I eluded them and struck out from those shores soon enough to become the successor of Mother and Auntie, which is to say, I became the daring danseuse, which I remained until you saw me in my triumph as Mazeppa. This, I fear, will be the bane of my days, as well as my financial salvation. A new life opens before me now, with bookings everywhere. I do loathe these particulars, but I am comforted by the memory of our last embrace, and I send you my fondest caresses.

Until we meet again, I remain, your truest love, Maud Fallon.

In the carriage Maud asked Quinn's permission to practice aloud what she would be reading later in the evening: excerpts from Scott and Keats; and from her handbag she took a slim volume, *Marmion* and *The Lay of the Last Minstrel*. The reading, she explained, was her contribution to the Army Relief Bazaar. Tonight she would take no fee for her work, which, of late, she had been doing in salons and temples where the arts flourished.

'Elocution in the salon has replaced horses in the hippodrome for Maud,' Gordon said.

'Elocution in the salon. Exotic in the extreme,' said Quinn.

'I needed something less convulsive than an upside-down horse-back adventure every night of my life,' said Maud. 'I crave tranquillity.'

'We seem to crave that as we wind down,' said Quinn.

'Winding down has nothing to do with it,' said Maud in miffed tones. 'I'm winding neither down nor up. The problem was boredom and physical torture. I'm sure my body has suffered more than Mazeppa's.'

'She was a tapestry of black and blue,' said Gordon.

'A tapestry,' said Quinn.

'I had to wear long sleeves and high collars,' said Maud.

'What a shame,' said Quinn.

'It was punishment without sin,' said Gordon.

'I hope you were well paid,' said Quinn.

'I loathe money,' said Maud.

'My romance with money is enough for both of us,' said Gordon. 'That's why I took her over.'

'I hardly think I've been taken over,' said Maud.

'You shall be,' Gordon said with a smile.

Maud then decided not to practice her reading and said nothing for the rest of the ride.

When he entered the bazaar Quinn experienced a rush of black wisdom and felt himself moving toward the crags of a new nightmare. This was irrational and he knew it. Tension rose in his throat and chest. He followed Gordon's lead, walking beside Maud, threading himself through handsomely dressed crowds, breathing in the bright and busy oddness of this peculiar building: a sudden upthrust built in two weeks and designed in the shape of a double Grecian cross.

They walked beneath the elevated orchestra stand, from where a waltz by Strauss energized the evening. Arches festooned with flowers and evergreens led Quinn's eye to booths celebrating England, Ireland, Russia, Schenectady, Troy, Saratoga. Hundreds of flaming gas jets imposed brilliance on the bodies below, which exuded in their finery a light and power that for Quinn paralleled the luminous battlefield dead. Irrational. Quinn knew it.

'It's a veritable palace of Aladdin,' said Gordon. 'And all these fair ladies, why, they seem like the nymphs and graces of mythology.'

'By and large, dumpy and frowzy,' said Maud, who explained that one of the graces was really doing public penance by working

195

here since her husband was in jail for selling horseshoes to the rebel army.

Gordon ignored Maud's remark and led the way to the Curiosity Shop, explaining that they would see Myles Standish's pistol, carried by Myles on the *Mayflower* and purchased by Lyman Fitzgibbon after his genealogist discovered a link between Myles and the Fitzgibbons.

'It's merely on loan from Father,' said Gordon. 'Not for sale, by a long shot. A curiosity of history, as they say.'

Quinn looked at the pistol, wondered how many savage breasts its power had pierced, then moved along to the writing bureau owned by George Washington, upon which George had signed Major André's death warrant. He saw Madison's cane, Lafayette's pistol, Grant's autograph, and the Bastille model (made from the Bastille's own stone) that Lafayette had presented to George Washington. Such lovely revolutions. Such a grand Civil War. We must not forget how they are done. He noted a pair of leather shoes that had been made for Union troops by prisoners at the Albany penitentiary. Five hundred and six prisoners were busy making the shoes. Half of their number were Negroes.

Then Quinn saw and quickly found focus on handwritten words in a locked cabinet, under glass, difficult to read: '. . . gradual abolishment of slavery within their respective limits . . . the effort to colonize persons of African descent . . . upon this continent . . . all persons held as slaves within any state, or designated part of a state . . . shall be then, thenceforward, and forever free . . .'

Quinn read the related sign explaining that one might, for one dollar, purchase a ticket and perhaps win, and thereby own forever, this document donated by the President to the Albany Bazaar, and described as the

ORIGINAL DRAFT
of the
PRESIDENT'S FIRST
EMANCIPATION PROCLAMATION
dated September 22, 1862

Whereupon Quinn fumbled in his pocket for a dollar and purchased a ticket from one of the nymphs.

Maud took Quinn's arm and said, 'I must show you something at the Saratoga booth,' and Gordon, noting this, followed in their wake. Crossing the transept Quinn sensed an easing of his tension at the touch of Maud the cynosure. Then he saw Will Canaday standing by the Irish booth and he felt a surge of joy at the convergence of the two people he valued most in this life, and he moved Maud toward the Irish booth. When Will saw them he grasped Maud's hand and kissed her cheek; then he embraced Quinn, neither of them speaking.

'You didn't say you were coming home,' Will finally said.

'I wasn't sure until I actually got on the train,' said Quinn.

Six years had passed since Quinn last saw Will, who was more stooped than Quinn had ever seen him, and walking with a limp. He had always carried a handsome walking stick but now a stout cane supported his steps.

'What happened to your leg?' Quinn asked.

'Aaah, they knocked me around one night and shattered a bone.'

'Who did?'

'A few of the boyos. I didn't know them.'

'The Society?'

'It could have been. I've all sorts of new enemies as well, and they didn't identify themselves.'

Will's reputation for being the scourge of the city had not abated since Quinn left Albany in 1858 to test out New York and expose his soul to other than clement weather. He left with an invitation from Will to write anything he pleased, and so he had, until he hired on at Greeley's *Tribune*. Even then, Will reprinted all that he recognized as coming from Quinn's pen.

'And yourself,' said Will. 'Are you well?'

'I wouldn't say that,' said Quinn.

'I'll introduce you here tonight. You'll say something about the war, I understand.'

William Kennedy

'I don't think so,' said Quinn. 'I have nothing to say.'

'Then no one else on earth does, either. It can be brief. Everybody here knows your name.'

'I'm not up to it, Will.'

'You'll do it. People need the war's reality.'

'They do? You can't mean it.'

'I mean it.'

'I'm the wrong choice. I wouldn't know reality if it knocked me down. And it did.'

'Just a few minutes will do,' said Will. 'And how are you, Maudie? You look thunderously beautiful.'

'I wanted to show Daniel the Saratoga booth, and our old friend.'

'Oh yes,' said Will, 'our friend.' He looked at his pocket watch. 'We'll be ready for your reading in about five minutes. Are you doing the Keats?'

'Yes, and I may also do Scott,' said Maud.

'Scott is always a pleasure.'

'Perhaps "Lochinvar."'

'Splendid,' said Will, and he winked at Maud.

Will left them then, and Quinn saw what had been shielded from view by Will's presence: a photograph of General McClellan framed in marble, and beside that a huge morocco-bound Bible donated to the booth by Mr R. Dwyer, superintendent of the County Idiot Asylum. Quinn moved closer to a large framed photo of a military unit and saw it was the Irish brigade, led by Batt Connors from Wexford. Quinn had ridden with them for two days and told a bit of their story: wild men all, daredevil heroes their superiors thrust into lost or impossible causes. Using a steady supply of replacements off the boat, the brigade recapitulated the fate of ancient Celtic warriors: they went forth to battle but they always fell.

At the Saratoga booth Quinn found the usual antiques and art objects, as well as photographs and sketches of the great hotels, the ballrooms, the long porches, the ladies in promenade, the parks, the springs, the pines. What was new to him was a sketch of jockeys on racehorses, and an excited throng rising in the grandstand of the new racecourse that was opening this week.

'This is what I wanted to show you,' Maud said to Quinn. 'Do you see who owns it?'

Quinn then saw a photo of a man standing beside a chestnut filly called Blue Grass Warrior. The man was well dressed, with a full black beard.

'That's my horse,' said Maud.

'Really? Well, you always loved horses.'

'It was a gift from a suitor. Not one of the six, to anticipate your question. He's from Kentucky. I met him at Saratoga just before the war, and he gave me a horse and a slave girl as gifts.'

'I hope you kept the slave girl too.'

'Of course. And I sent her to Canada in case he changed his mind about her.'

Quinn read the printed matter explaining the photo.

'Why that's John,' he said. 'John McGee.'

'It took you a while to notice.'

'It's his beard. I never saw him with a beard.'

He studied the most recent incarnation of John the Brawn, handsome figure of substance and money, as wealthy as he is hairy. The last Quinn had seen of him was in 1863, when, as always, John was leaping into a new future, linking his fistic notoriety to the politicians who ran New York City, using his name as a draw for gambling parlors: John the Brawn becoming John the Grand and John the Mighty, his power and his fortune as expansive as his chest.

'He owns the track?' Quinn asked.

'He's one of the principals. A handful of millionaires.'

'Our John has truly risen.'

'He's wonderful to Magdalena,' said Maud.

'Isn't she living with Obadiah?'

'She married Obadiah five years ago. But you know Magdalena. She was never content with one man.'

'That seems to be a family trait.'

'It's stupid that you're jealous,' said Maud.

As Quinn smiled his skepticism, it became evident to him that his possessiveness stemmed not only from desire and love but also from seeing Maud as the instrument by which he would rid himself of death and war, put life once again on horseback. He had felt such rumblings of possibility for himself on Obadiah's veranda, anticipating Maud's arrival after his first shave. He'd reveled merely in waiting for her there amid the architecture of dynamic serenity, that vast, sculpted lawn sloping to the lake, leading him to the edge of all that was new, centering him in a web of escalating significance. And in such privileged moments his life became a great canvas of the imagination, large enough to suggest the true magnitude of the unknown. What he saw on the canvas was a boundless freedom to do and to think and to feel all things offered to the living. In Maud's presence, or even in waiting for her to arrive, the canvas became unbearably valuable and utterly mysterious, and he knew if he lost Maud he would explode into simplicity.

'Ah, there you are, cousin,' came a female voice, and here toward Gordon, with hand outstretched, came a handsome woman in her thirties, artfully coiffed, regal in maroon silk dress, its hoop skirt bouncing as she came.

Gordon took her hand, kissed her cheek. 'Phoebe,' he said.

'We expected you for tea,' Phoebe told Gordon. 'But here you are, all bound up with an entourage.'

'Two friends,' said Gordon. 'Miss Maud Fallon and the war journalist Daniel Quinn.'

'A pleasure indeed, Mr Quinn,' said Phoebe. 'You've educated us all on the terrible battles you've seen. And how quaint to meet you with clothes on, Miss Fallon. You're usually naked on horseback, aren't you?'

'I was born naked,' said Maud.

'How charming,' said Phoebe. 'We'll look for you at tea tomorrow, Gordon. Please come alone.'

'Excuse me, madam,' Quinn said to her, 'but you have the manners of a sow,' and he took Maud's arm and walked her away.

*   *   *

Will Canaday found them browsing at the Shaker booth and led Maud to the elevated platform in front of the booth of Military Trophies. This, the focal point for the bazaar's public moments, was crowned by Washington's portrait, crowded with cannon, bristling with crossed rifles and muskets, and grimly but passionately brilliant with the regimental flags and the colors of the nation from before the Revolution to the present Civil War. Many of these proud silks had been reduced to gallant rags, the most notable being the flag of Albany's Forty-fourth Regiment, shredded with eighty bullet holes, and for whose constant elevation in battle twelve standard-bearers had died and eighteen more had been wounded.

'A peculiar place for a poetry reading,' said Quinn.

'A perfect place for it,' said Maud.

'Why are you doing these readings?'

Maud cocked her head and considered a reply before ascending the stairs ahead of Will. 'I suppose,' she said, 'that one's brain also craves distinction.'

Will addressed the crowd then, explaining Maud's international renown as an actress and how in recent years she had been a popularizer of the great poets as well as a woman asserting an intellectual stance on behalf of all womanhood. 'And,' he added, 'if any of you have had the pleasure of talking with our Maud, you know the keenness and originality of that mind of hers,' which, he concluded, was tonight a gift to the bazaar, and that after her reading a basket would be passed for donations.

Maud smiled and stared out at the crowd, found men's faces beaming at her, many women scowling. At what did they scowl? At the dancing spiritualist? The sensual horsewoman? The actress who reads poetry? The woman of fame who represents the power of the intuitive life? Well, whatever it is, Maud, they are scowling at you: you who merely by breathing in, breathing out, grow ever more singular.

Maud looked down at Quinn and saw neither the boy nor the young man (however briefly met) that she once knew. She saw a pacific smile and knew she was the cause of it, but saw, too, the

201

trouble that lay behind it, had noted that trouble the instant she
saw him in front of the mansion. It was the war, of course, and
so she would begin with Keats, telling Quinn that he was perhaps
half in love with easeful death.

'Thou was not born for death,' she read, and eyed Quinn
secretly, finding his smile gone, his face at full attention. Her
geis was functioning. He was in the spell of her suggestion about
the kidnapping. When they talked later she would invite him to
Saratoga as her and Gordon's guest. And once there . . . and once
there . . . ?

She opened her second book and told the audience she had not
publicly read this poem before this moment, and then began:

> O, young Lochinvar is come out of the west
> Through all the wide Border his steed was the best;
> And save his good broadsword, he weapons had none,
> He rode all unarmed and he rode all alone.
> So faithful in love, and so dauntless in war,
> There never was knight like the young Lochinvar . . .
> But ere he alighted at Netherby gate,
> The bride had consented, the gallant came late:
> For a laggard in love, and a dastard in war,
> Was to wed the fair Ellen of brave Lochinvar.

Maud read with great verve and sensitivity the next four stanzas,
banishing male beamings and female scowls and replacing both
with rapt attentiveness to the narrative, wherein Lochinvar avows
to the bride's father that he has come only to drink one cup of
wine with the bride denied him and, when it is drunk, to have but
a single dance with fair Ellen. And they do dance, as parents and
bridegroom fume, and as bridemaidens watch approvingly. Then
does Lochinvar assert himself:

> One touch to her hand, and one word in her ear,
> When they reached the hall-door, and the charger stood near;
> So light to the croupe the fair lady he swung,

So light to the saddle before her he sprung!
'She is won! we are gone, over bank, bush, and scaur;
They'll have fleet steeds that follow,' quoth young Lochinvar.
There was mounting 'mong Graemes of the Netherby clan;
Forsters, Fenwicks, and Musgraves, they rode and they ran;
There was racing and chasing, on Cannobie Lee,
But the lost bride of Netherby ne'er did they see.
So daring in love, and so dauntless in war.
Have ye e'er heard of gallant like young Lochinvar?

Maud descended the stairs to stout applause, perceiving with pleasure that Quinn's was the stoutest of all.

'Will Canaday has suggested I talk of the war's reality,' Quinn said to the audience. 'These cannon here look like reality to me . . . and these flags all full of holes. And those things over there in the Curiosity Shop made by rebel prisoners at Point Lookout: rubber buttons turned into rings, and carved with the word "Dixie." You could walk right over there now and buy a rebel button and that might qualify as reality. Albany boys in rebel prisons down in Carolina and Alabama are making things too, carving pictures of Abe Lincoln and the flag out of kindling so the rebs can buy them and pitch them in the fire.

'Reality in this war is not always what you think it is. Take the fight at Round Top, when the Forty-fourth from Albany was part of the brigade trying to take that hill. Just a hill like a lot of others in this world, but ten thousand of our men went after it, and only twelve hundred came out alive. A pile of dead people, that's the reality I'm talking about. The bigger the pile, the bigger the reality. We did get that hill before the rebs, and that's reality too. A lot of hand-to-hand fighting. When it looked like our boys might get their tails whipped, our batteries opened up and dropped a whole lot of cannon shot on top of everybody – the point, of course, being to stop the rebs. Fact that our boys were mixin' it up with the rebs wasn't all that important, and so they got themselves killed by their own cannons. Reality.

'Then there was the major that the general wanted to see but nobody could find him. This major, he was from Buffalo. He was one nice fella, and I knew just how good a soldier he was. The best. We didn't want him to get into trouble, so we all went out looking for him. I found him under a bridge, having what some folks like to call carnal relations – with a brown chicken. That may not seem like it, but that's reality.'

Several women exchanged glances at this remark, rose instantly from their seats, and left the gathering. Men snickered at one another and some squirmed. Quinn fell into a natural pacing up and down the platform as he talked, unintimidated by the task for which he claimed to be so ill suited.

'This reb from Texas,' he went on, 'when our boys got him in their sights at Round Top he called out to them, "Don't shoot me," and threw down his rifle. Soon as he did, one of his fellow Texans shot him in the back. Reality coming up from behind.

'And the attack at Cold Harbor, where seven thousand of our boys died in eight minutes trying to break through Lee's line. Couldn't do it. Our dead boys were spread shoulder-to-shoulder over about five acres. You could hardly find any grass wasn't covered by a dead soldier. That was unnatural reality down at Cold Harbor.

'I remember a letter I helped a young boy from the Forty-fourth write. He wrote what an awful mistake other boys back home had made by not joining up with the glory of the Forty-fourth. He died of inflammation of the brain, somewhere in Virginia. There was also a measles epidemic that killed a bunch of our lads before they ever had a chance to get themselves killed by reb muskets. Sort of a reductive reality, you might call that.

'Then there was this close friend of mine from Albany who was a captain, and we used to talk about things that were real and things that weren't, though we never put it quite that way, and one day I heard he got shot three times in less than a minute. Shot sitting down and so he stood up, and before he could fall over he got shot again, and then on the way down they got him again, and he didn't die. Still kickin' after twenty-three battles, and that's one of the nicer realities I ever heard of in this war.

'I got my own reality the day I was hit by a spent reb cannonball. Just touched by it, really, and it wasn't moving very fast. But it knocked me down, broke my leg and made me bleed, and I thought maybe I'd die alone there on the battlefield. I couldn't even give a good explanation of why I was hit. The battle was long over and I wasn't a soldier. I was just out there looking for survivors and some reb cannoneer maybe figured, why not wipe out that Yankee bastard? He let one go I never paid any attention to, and it got me. I might be out there yet, but then along came this grayback doctor and I see him working on hurt rebs. I called out, "Hey, doc, can you stop my bleeding and set my leg?" And he said, "I cain't set no laigs. I got soldiers of my own dyin' here." And he went on helping rebs. So I called out and said, "Hey, doc, I got money I can pay you if you stop my bleeding and set my leg." And the doc looks me over and says, "How much you got, son?" and I say, "I got twenty-five dollars in gold I been savin' for my retirement," and he says, "Okay, I can help you retire." And he comes over and looks me up and down and says, "Where's the gold?" And I fished in my money belt and showed it to him, and he smiled nice as peach pie at me and went ahead and stitched me up and put a splint on me, and then he wrapped that leg so fine I got right up and started to walk. I gave him the gold and says to him, "Thanks a lot, doc," just like he was a human being. And he says, "Don't mention it, son, but don't put too much pressure on that leg," just like I was a goddamned reb.'

The squirmers in the audience, spellbound since the mention of bestiality, were at last roused to indignation by the profanity, and a dozen or more men and women rose from their seats, a few shouting out to take Quinn off the platform. But as they left, Quinn moved to the platform's edge, pointed after them and shouted, 'Do you know the reality of Eli Plum of Albany?'

He stopped some in their exit and riveted the hardy remainder. Then he genuflected in front of them all and blessed himself with the sign of the cross.

William Kennedy

'We called him Peaches Plum,' said Quinn, 'and he was never worth much in any context you might want to discuss. He was one of your neighbors, and he and I went to school together here fifteen, twenty years ago. We were in Virginia, and we heard the drum corps beating a muffled Dead March in the woods near us and we all knew what was coming. Before long, orders came down to form with the whole First Division, and the Forty-fourth moved out onto elevated ground, facing an open field. The men formed a line, division front, facing five fresh graves.

'That, my friends, was a fearful sight. Also very rousing somehow, with all those brass buttons and rifles shining in the sun, and kids watching from trees, and older men alone on horses, or on top of rooves, and everybody's eye on Peaches and four other boys as they came walking: two, two, and one. Peaches was the one, walking behind the drum corps, and followed by the provost guard, fifty of them with bayonets fixed. Five clergymen walked along, too, reading scriptures, and thirty pallbearers carried five new coffins. The procession went up and back the length of the whole line of battle and then the pallbearers stopped at the fresh graves. The five prisoners stopped, too, and stood there with their hands tied, a guard alongside each one of them. Then those five young men sat down on their coffins.

'I never got to talk privately with Peaches, but I dug up his story, once I saw it was him. Never wrote it, though, and I'm only telling it now because Will Canaday says you folks are hounds for reality.

'Peaches was a bounty jumper who joined the army eighteen times. You only got a fifty-dollar bounty for joining up when Peaches started his jumping career. Used to be there was enough henpecked husbands, and third sons, and boys who got girls in trouble, who were glad to go to war and improve their outlook. But the war kept on going and volunteers fell away to a trickle, and so the price of bounties went up, all the way to a thousand dollars, which is what they're paying right now. Peaches, he made lots of money enlisting but he never got to keep it. When he'd light out he'd always bring the cash back home to his pa, like he was supposed to. Then one day after the draft came in, Peaches's pa told him, "Go join up the army again, Peaches, only this time don't come back because you're going in place of your brother." This brother was a lawyer, a son the father couldn't do without, the way he could do without Peaches.

'All those times Peaches joined up he never got close to a battle. He'd just disappear during the night off a train, or on a march toward some regiment, then head back home to Pa. But this time Peaches finally went to war. He saw a lot of corpses and didn't want to become one of those, so he drew on his talents and his instincts, and he took out for points north. And he ran right into another unit and got court-martialed for desertion along with the four other boys who ran with him. They were all found guilty and the President approved they be shot as a warning to cowards and mercenary men in the army. I guess we all know how many good soldiers have the impulse to run, but somehow don't, either out of fear, or good sense, or because they want to kill rebs. One youngster told me, "I'm stickin' because we got justice on our side." Lot of rebs think the same way, but that doesn't matter. Death's all that matters, and I know you all want the reality of that, just like the folks back home in the real olden days who wanted to know how their war was going. And their soldiers would collect the heads and genitals of the enemy and bring 'em back home for inspection to prove the army was doing its job. Peaches never got into any of that kind of fun. He was just one of those poor souls who fumble their way through life, never quite knowing the rules, never playing by them even if they think they know them, always fated to be a pawn of other folks.

'Poor Peaches. Grizzled men around me were crying as the provost guard took up its position, ten guardsmen for each of the five prisoners, rifles ready, standing about fifteen yards away, while the captain of the guard read the five orders of execution out loud. The clergy came by and talked to each of the prisoners for a few minutes, and then the officers started putting those white blindfolds on the chosen five.

'I could see Peaches really clear, see him crying and quaking, and before I knew what I was doing I'd called out, "So long, Peaches, and good luck," which wasn't very appropriate, I admit, but that's what I said. Peaches looked toward my voice and nodded his head. "Okay," he yelled. Then his blindfold was on, the black cap was placed over his face, and it was ready, aim, fire. Four of the prisoners fell backward onto their coffins. Peaches took the bullets and didn't let them knock him over. He crumpled in place and I never felt more an outsider in this life. All that pomp and panoply in service of five more corpses. It's a question, I'll tell you. But that's all that's left in me – a kind of fatal quizzicality, you might call it. I hope my sharing it with you has been of some value.'

And Quinn left the platform.

Quinn, that formidable folklorist, walked along amid throngs of other souls like himself and he took sight of a picture photograph that revealed how a man will sometimes stand alongside of a horse. Quinn then said to himself, 'I have a horse, but not so fine a horse.' This was a truth that served no purpose for Quinn, and yet he felt a goad. He went to his friend the editor, who wrote wisely about the great warps and goiters people must bear in this life, and his friend said to him, 'I think it is time you took up with your platter.'

Quinn then went with his friend to a place where they met a man with chinwhiskers who opened a great door and took out from it The Great Platter of the Unknown that Quinn had long ago found at the bottom of a birdcage.

'This is a great thing,' Quinn said when he felt the heft of it. 'I wish I knew what it was.'

'Well, you'll never know that,' said his friend, 'for you're not smart enough.'

'I'm smarter than many,' said Quinn.

'We'll not dispute that. Just carry it with you and it won't bother anyone at all that you don't know what it is.'

And so Quinn went to the slaughterhouse and bought a pig's bladder and blew it up like a ballon and then soaked it in whiskey until it was strong and put the platter inside it and slung it over his back with a thong.

'You're on your way,' said his friend.

'I am,' said Quinn.

'Do you know where you're going?' said his friend.

'I do not.'

'Will you know when you get there?'

'I might,' said Quinn, 'or I might not.'

'Then I'll go with you,' said his friend. 'I'm going in that direction myself.'

And so the two rode their horses, one each, and found themselves at the house where the woman known as The Great Mother had lived until she was done in severely. As they entered they heard the voice of an archangel in the music room. They stopped where they stood and Quinn said, 'It is a man's duty to sing.'

'And when one man sings,' said his friend, 'it is another man's duty to listen.'

So listen they did until the song came to a full stop. Quinn knew then that the archangel was a fellow named Moran.

Quinn and Will Canaday walked into the music room and saw that Maud was sitting at the pianoforte, looking into the smiling eye of the Moran fellow, and Quinn saw more in her eye than a beam of light. He resolved to tell her of this.

'I'm so glad you came,' Maud said. 'We've been waiting for you both.'

'We didn't know we were coming until we got here,' said Will.

'That's true,' said Maud. 'But don't let it bother you.'

'You're dressed in mourning,' Quinn said to her, and she was: hair upswept and bound with a black ribbon, wearing a severe black bombazine dress with long skirt and half sleeves, the severity relieved by a descending bodice line designed for provocation.

'We're having a wake,' said Maud.

'Who died?' Quinn asked.

'Hillegond.'

'Again?'

'Six months to the day. We're remembering her, aren't we, Joseph?'

'We are,' said Moran, 'and I remember this fellow as well. He can't sing a note.'

'You've a good memory,' said Quinn, and the two shook hands even though Quinn was of a mind to knock him down. He had not seen Moran in six years, which was also the last time he'd seen Maud. The man's face was prematurely ravaged, probably by drink, which was what had done him in as a performer. In his cups he mocked his audiences and drove them away, making himself a pariah with theater managers. And so he gave up the drink and became a manager himself, of the Green Street Theater, establishing a reputation for recognizing talent by casting Maud as Mazeppa.

'Joseph was just singing to Hillegond's memory,' said Maud, and she gestured toward the Ruggiero mural of Hillegond seated at the same pianoforte at which Maud now sat, Hilly in the obvious midst of supernal music. Quinn looked at the opposite wall, to find the matching mural of Petrus Staats totally covered with a tapestry of a brilliantly white unicorn on a field of golden flowers.

'I'm glad to see Hilly out in the open again,' said Quinn. 'But why is Petrus still out of sight?'

'Gordon covered them both so they wouldn't haunt him,' said Maud, 'but I had him uncover Hillegond. I couldn't stand her being completely gone.'

'You did well,' said Quinn. 'And where is the master of the house today?'

'At the foundry,' said Maud.

'I thought you were down south dodging musket balls,' Moran said to Quinn.

Quinn regarded Moran's large, flashing, and breakable teeth, then put his sack on the table in front of his chair.

'I gave that up,' said Quinn.

'You're right to come back here,' said Moran. 'I love this place.'

'We all love this place and we love one another, don't we, Joseph?' said Maud.

'Love lasts forever,' said Moran, staring at the portrait. 'I loved Hilly.'

'Who didn't love Hilly?' said Quinn.

'The fiend who murdered her,' said Maud.

'Ah now, that's a truth,' said Moran. 'Bad enough to kill one woman. An act of passion, perhaps. But to turn on Matty.'

'Murderers have their logic,' said Maud.

'Who is the killer?' asked Quinn.

'Ah,' said Will Canaday. 'There's a question.'

'Finnerty,' said Moran. 'Ambrose Finnerty.'

'Joseph brought him to Albany,' said Maud.

'I saw him in Boston,' said Moran. 'I never heard a more stirring orator.'

'He's in the penitentiary,' said Will. 'He claims innocence and says he's an ex-priest, but nobody can find the truth of that yet. He traveled with a woman and babe, his wife and child, oh yes. But she's a known cyprian who says she's a nun and that Finnerty, her confessor, plugged her up with child in the convent. She loved him all the same, and he her, and they knew the world was good and the church wasn't. So they went into theater with their peculiar love of God, and their hatred of all true priests and Catholics. And may the rightful Jesus and all his saints stand strong between us and the likes of such faith.'

'The Catholics have a lot to answer for,' said Moran.

'As do the heathens and Hottentots,' said Will.

'Finnerty could sing, too,' said Moran.

'Bawdy songs about religion,' said Maud.

'He kissed and fondled his wife onstage,' said Will. 'In their nun's and priest's costumes.'

'It was very effective,' said Moran. 'We filled the house twice a night for three weeks at thirty-five cents a ticket. Think of it.'

'Hillegond was in bed,' said Maud, 'reading Gordon's play about Dido. Joseph was going to produce that at his theater, too, with some help from Hillegond, weren't you, Joseph?'

'I had hopes,' said Moran.

'She was wearing her rose-colored nightdress,' said Maud, 'and her worsted stockings, too, because there was a chill in the air. And her silver earrings. She would never be caught without her earrings, even in sleep. It was near midnight when she looked up from her book and heard the step outside her door.'

'How do you know she looked up from her book?' Quinn asked.

'I have my ways.'

Quinn nodded and opened his satchel. He took out his bronze disk with the angry face. Was it a fat man with a round tongue? Was it a walrus? Was it a bespectacled woman screaming? Quinn put the disk on the table in front of him.

'What is that?' Moran asked him.

'It's a thing of a kind. A round sort of thing,' said Quinn.

'I can see that.'

'Quinn puts tubers on it,' said Will.

'Hillegond,' said Maud, 'had come to the part of the play where Dido pleads with Aeneas to stay in Carthage with her, but he says he cannot. I'm so sick of self-sacrificing women, immolated by love.'

'How do you know where she was in the play?' Moran asked.

'There are things one knows,' said Maud.

She stood up from the pianoforte bench, walked across the room with regal poise, and sat in a cushioned chair that gave her a vision of both Hillegond's portrait and her own listeners. Quinn rotated his disk so that its face had proper perspective on Maud. He did not know why he did this but he did it. Why should I have to know why I do what I do? he said to himself.

'Finnerty was intriguing to Hillegond,' said Will from his own plush bench. 'She invited him to dinner one night to hear his full story and he admits they had a dalliance.'

'More than a dalliance, I'd say,' said Moran.

'They found her jade ring in Finnerty's rooms,' said Will. 'That's what did him in.'

'He said she gave it to him,' said Moran. 'But there's no proof. His wife said he was with her that night, but that's a wife talking.'

'Hillegond took fright at the footstep,' said Maud, 'for it was heavier than it should have been. But when the door opened and

213

she saw him she gave him a smile. "Ah love," she said to him. "Look at you, sneakin' around like a nighthawk."'

'You even know the words she used,' said Moran.

'It's quite remarkable what I know,' said Maud.

'You used to do that sort of thing all the time,' said Moran.

'She made her living at it,' said Quinn.

'She moved sideways on the bed to let him sit beside her,' said Maud. 'He kissed her gently on the forehead, then on the lips – not a real kiss, which she expected – and then he took off her spectacles and kissed her on the eyes. When he had closed both her eyes with his kisses he put the garrote around her neck and tightened it. She flailed but she wasn't strong. She was big, but age had drained her and she soon stopped her struggle. He continued twisting the garrote and pulled her off the bed with it. Her feet knocked over the ewer pitcher with the tulips on it.'

'A pair of owls are roosting in Hillegond's room,' said Will.

'I would like to see that,' said Quinn.

'They'd be asleep now,' said Moran. 'Owls sleep in the daytime.'

'Even so,' said Quinn.

'I see no reason not to see them, even if they're asleep,' said Maud, who stood up from her bench and led the way out of the music room. Quinn put his disk into his sack.

'Are you coming, Joseph?' Maud asked at the foot of the stairs.

'What is the point of looking at owls?'

'Indeed there is none,' said Will.

'But they must be a sight to see,' said Quinn.

'They're quite beautiful,' said Maud.

'I have no objection,' said Moran.

And so up the great staircase they went to Hillegond's room, whose six windows offered a view of the river and the sunrise, and where the pair of owls were asleep on the valance above the glass doors to Hillegond's balcony. The room was a vista of peace and order. Murder was nowhere to be seen, though the aroma of villainy hung in a vapor alongside the lushly canopied bed, and all four visitors to the room walked 'round it.

They stood by the glass doors and stared up at the sleeping owls, which were two feet tall, one a bit taller, being female. The birds were both solidly pale gray, great soft puffs of matching and matchless beauty, both feathered to their talons and sleeping side by side, facing into the room with closed eyes.

'They'll die in here,' Quinn said.

'They go out to eat,' said Maud. 'The servants open the doors for them at dusk and again at dawn. They know no one lives in this room anymore, and we all welcome their presence.'

'An owl can turn its head completely around and look backward,' said Moran. 'I once made a study of birds.'

'The room isn't quite like it was,' said Maud. 'The Delft vase and the double-globed lamp with the lilacs were both broken when Matty came in and fought for Hillegond's life.'

'I thought they found Matty on the stairs,' said Quinn.

'The struggle carried out of the room. Matty fought fiercely. She was a strong woman and she loved Hilly.'

'She heard the fighting going on?' asked Quinn.

'She only heard the pitcher fall and break,' said Maud.

'You know it all, don't you?' said Moran.

'Yes,' said Maud. 'I also know it wasn't Finnerty.'

'You can hold these owls when they're asleep, and they won't wake up,' said Moran. He carried Hillegond's baroque silver dresser bench to the glass doors and stood on it. He reached up and grasped the sleeping female owl with both hands and stepped down from the bench. The owl slept on.

'That's quite a trick, Joseph,' said Will.

'Not a trick at all if you know anything about owls,' said Moran.

Maud opened the double doors to the balcony and the breeze of summer afternoon came rushing into the room. Quinn studied the behavior of the owl held by Moran and observed that owl sleep is comparable to coma, a step away from death. He studied the behavior of Moran and marveled at the man's concentration

215

on the bird: eyes as hard as iron spikes. Quinn felt his old resentment at Moran's ability to differentiate himself from the normal run of men.

'Joseph and I became lovers during my time here as Mazeppa,' said Maud. 'Everybody knew, didn't they, Will?'

'Joseph tends to boast about his conquests,' said Will.

'He was very attentive in those months,' said Maud, 'but I don't think I made him happy. As soon as I left the city he began to court Hillegond.'

'Assiduously,' said Will. 'It was peculiar.'

'Which of your six was he?' Quinn asked.

'Number three,' said Maud, 'and the only one in theater.'

'Joseph wanted to marry Hillegond,' said Will, 'and she considered it for a time. But finally she wouldn't have him.'

'We remained great friends,' said Moran. 'May we change the subject?'

'He loved this mansion,' said Maud, 'and all that went with it. And all that went with Hillegond.'

'Then he saw he couldn't have it,' said Will.

'Hillegond came to think it was ridiculous, the idea of them marrying,' said Maud.

'It was not ridiculous,' said Moran. 'Profound aspirations must not be mocked.'

'How lofty of you, Joseph,' Maud said.

'I admit error.'

'The news will thrill Hillegond in her grave.'

'It's a great pity,' said Moran, 'all this plangency so close to the heart.'

'Closer to the throat,' said Maud.

Quinn pondered these remarks and concluded that for some men a fatal error is the logical conclusion of life, and may not really be an error at all but the inevitable finale to an evolutionary evil. He watched as Moran the covetous sat on the bench, holding the owl aloft above his lap. Suddenly the bird was awake and staring, and Moran instantly released her upward. Perversely, she settled downward and sank her talons through his trousers and into the tops of his thighs. He screamed pitifully as he fell backward, and at the sound of flowing blood the male owl's eyes snapped open. Soundlessly he flew down from the valance and, in an act of providential justice, drove his talons into Moran's face and neck.

Tambo and Paddy
Go to Town

Saratoga

August 1864

Horseless now, I, Daniel Quinn, that relentless shedder of history, stepped aboard the horsecar, the first of three conveyances that would take me to Saratoga Springs and Maud and the others who had gone before me, and I sat beside a Negro man in whose face I read the anguish of uncertainty, an affliction I understand but not in Negro terms. The man was bound for a distant place, his bundles and baggage revealing this fact, and I began to think of Joshua. I then tried to put Joshua out of my mind and opened the satchel containing my disk. I studied the disk rather than people who would take me where I did not want to go again. I discovered the disk looked Arabic with all that cursiveness in its design. Were the Celts really Arabs? Perhaps they were Jews: the lost tribe of Tipperary. The lost tribe of Ethiopia, some say. Go away, Joshua. I will remember you when I am stronger. I concentrated on my disk and it changed: convexity into concavity – a fat tongue into a hollow mouth; and in this willful ambiguity by the Celtic artist I read the wisdom of multiple meanings. Avoid gratuitous absolutes, warned Will Canaday. Yes, agrees Quinn, for they can lead to violence.

How had Maud known about the violence to Hillegond? Well, she knew. Psychometry is the most probable. How did she make the chandelier fall? Psychomagnetic pulsation, most likely. Quinn has neither of these gifts. Quinn is a psychic idiot. Quinn experiences everything and concludes nothing. *Tabula rasa ad infinitum*. Still, when the owl tore out Moran's throat there was a purgation of sorts. Quinn perceived that he himself had wanted the mansion as much as Moran did, but so hopelessly that he did not even know that he wanted it. What good is your brain, Quinn, if you can't even read your own notes? Yet, once free of secret covetousness, Quinn moved outward: another leaving off of false roles, false needs. In beginnings there is all for Quinn, a creature of onset. Will Quinn ever become a creature of finalities?

For this newest onset I was, as usual, unprepared except financially. I'd used less than a thousand dollars of what Dirck had given me over the past fifteen years and had allowed the rest to mount up in Lyman Fitzgibbon's bank; and so for a reporter I was a modestly wealthy man, without need of work for hire.

Freed from the history and the penury of war, at least for the moment, Quinn was about to embark on a life of thought, or so he thought. And there he went, west on the train to Schenectady and north on another to Saratoga, crowding his brain with unanswerable questions and banishing unwanted memories that would not stay banished, especially since he was about to enter the gilded and velvet parlors of John McGee, the gambler who could fight, and would, and did, and whose life is not separable from Joshua's anymore.

John never gambled when I first knew him, preferring to store up his savings for drink. But we find new targets for our vices as we move, and when he knocked down Hennessey, the champion of the world entirely, John's life entered an upward spiral that took him into bare-knuckle battles in Watervliet, Troy, the Boston Corner, White Plains, Toronto, and home again to Albany. I wrote John's ongoing story for the *Albany Chronicle* until the Toronto bout, Will Canaday then deciding not to finance expeditions quite so distant. I grew audacious enough to tell Will he was erring in news judgment, for John McGee and his fists had excited the people of Albany and environs like no sportsman in modern memory.

'Sportsman? Nonsense,' said Will. 'The man is loutish. No good can come of celebrating such brutes.'

It is true that John's brawling was legendary by this time, his right hand a dangerous weapon. He knocked over one after the other in his early battles and in between times decided to open a saloon in Albany to stabilize his income. He set it up in the Lumber District, an Irish entrenchment along the canal, and called the place Blue Heaven. Over the bar he hung a sign that read: 'All the fighting done in this place I do ... [signed] ... John McGee.'

A brute of a kind John was. Nevertheless, he was a presence to be understood, as even Will Canaday perceived when John fought at Toronto. In that fight, ballyhooed as Englishman against Irishman, John knocked down, and out, in the twenty-eighth round, a British navvy who was Canada's pride. John escaped an angry crowd, bent on stomping his arrogance into the turf, only with the help of the fists, power, and guile of the man who had been his sparring mate, and whose talent for escaping hostile pursuants was also legendary. I speak of Joshua.

And so it thereafter came to pass that John the Brawn was, at the age of thirty years, polarized as the heroic Irish champion of the United States, and matched against Arthur (Yankee) Barker, the pride of native Americans. The fight took place on a summer afternoon in 1854 at the Bull's Head Tavern on the Troy road out of Albany, a hostel for wayward predilections of all manner and scope, where, as they say, cocks, dogs, rats, badgers, women, and niggers were baited in blood, and where Butter McCall, panjandrum of life at the Bull's Head, held the purse of ten thousand dollars, five from each combatant, and employed a line of battlers of his own to keep excitable partisans in the crowd from joining the fight, and whose wife, Sugar, kept the scrapbook in which one might, even today, read an account of the historic fight taken from the *Albany Telescope*, a sporting newspaper, and written by none other than Butter himself, an impresario first, perhaps, but also a bare-knuckle bard, a fistic philosopher, a poet of the poke.

Wasn't it a grand day [Butter wrote], when we all twenty thousand of us gathered in the Bull's Head pasture to witness the greatest fight boxiana has ever known? It was a regular apocalypse of steam and stew, blood and brew that twinned

223

John (the Brawn) McGee, also known as John of the Skiff and John of the Water (from his days on the river), and Arthur (Yankee) Barker, also known as the Pet of Poughkeepsie and The True American — twinned and twined the pair in mortalizing conflict over who was to be bare-knuckle champion of this godly land.

John came to the pasture like Zeus on a wheel, tossed his hat with the Kelly-green plume into the ring, and then bounded in after it like a deer diving into the lakes of Killarney. His second bounced in after him, Mick the Rat, a stout Ethiopian who, they say, all but broke the nozzle of the God of Water in a sparring meet. The Mick tied the Water's colors to the post as the Yank trundled in, no hat on this one, just the flag itself, Old Glory over his shoulders.

Peeling commenced and the seconds took their stations while the flag was wrapped around the Patriot's stake. Referees and umpires were appointed, the titans shook hands, and yo-ho-ho, off they went. The odds were even at first salvo, but the grand bank of Erin was offering three-to-two on the Water.

ROUND ONE

Both stood up well but the Pet in decidedly the handsomest position. Hi-ho with the left, he cocks the Skiffman amidships and crosses fast with a right to his knowledge box, but oh, now, didn't he get one back full in the domino case and down.

ROUND TWO

The Pet didn't like it a bit. He charged with his right brigade and hooked his man over the listener, which the Brawn threw off like a cat's sneeze and countered with a tremendous smasher to the Patriot's frontispiece, reducing him to his honkies. Said Mick the Rat from the corner, 'Dat flag am comin' unfurled.'

ROUND THREE

The Patriot came to his work this time with anger at the Mick's funny saying, rushed like a hornet on ice at the Waterman, firing pell-mell, lefts, rights, and whizzers at the Water's nasal organ. Water comes back bing-bing, and we see the claret running free from the Brawn's nostrilations. First blood has been declared for the Pet, which raised the clamor of three-to-one on Patriotism and plenty of takers, including Brawny Boy himself, who ordered the Rat to take a cud of the old green from his jacket and offplay the action. The Water let his bottleman second him while the Rat did his duty at the bank.

ROUND FOUR

The boys came up to scratch, the Pet again for business with vigor from Yankee heaven, pinning the Water boy on the ropes and hitting him at will. What happened to yer brawn, Johnny boy? Oh, it was fearful, and the claret thick as pea soup. Was he gone from us? Hardly. The skiffer outs with an ungodly roger up from the decks of Satan's scow; evil was that punch and it hit the True One in his breadbasket, loosing the crumbs it did, for a great noise came out of the Patriot's bung and he went flat as Dutch strudel.

ROUND FIVE

The Brawn lost blood, all right, but he's a game one. Up for mischief again, he leveled a terrible cob on the Pet's left ogle, leaving Pet's daylights anything but mates, and the blood of the Patriot gushed out like the spout on a he-goat. The Skiffer grabbed the Pet's head of cabbage around the throttle and used every exertion to destroy the Patriot's vocal talent, which we thought a pity, for the Patriot loves to sing duets with his sweetpea, that lovely tune, 'I won't be a nun, I shan't be a nun, I'm too fond of Arthur to be a nun.' The seconds separated the battlers and it was called a round.

ROUND SIX

Oh, the punishment. The Yankee Pet came up to scratch, erect on his pins, and lit out at the Skiffer's cabbage bag, but an uppercut sent him sliding like a chicken in a blizzard. The Brawn follows with the lefties and righties to the ogles, the smeller, and the domino case, but the Pet won't go down. Tough he was and tough he stayed, but dear God the blood. No quarter now from the God of Water, who goes after the Pet's chinchopper and schnotzblauer, which is a bleeding picture, and one of Erin's poets in the crowd observes, 'Don't our John do lovely sculpture?'

ROUND SEVEN

The Patriot came to the scratch in a wobble of gore, both eyes swollen and all but closed, his cheek slit as if by a cutlass, the blood of life dripping down his chest and he spitting up from his good innards. Was ever a man bloodier in battle? I think not. Yet the Pet of Patriotism, a flag himself now – red, white, and blue, and seeing the stars and stripes – moved at the Skiffman, who had contusions of his own, but none the worse for them. And the Skiff let go with a snobber to the conk that put the Pet to patriotic sleep. Old Gory went down like a duck and laid there like a side of blue mutton. A sad day for the Natives, and Green rises to the top like the cream of Purgatory.

We would judge the victory a popular one in this pasture, city, state, nation, and hemisphere, opinions to the contrary notwithstanding. John McGee proved himself a man of grain and grit, and the True Yankee now knows the measure of his own head. For those who wanted more fight, well, more there was – and plenty, too, which the Yankees found to their liking, loving punishment as they do.

A good time was had by all, nobody got killed that we know of, and the nigger carried off John the King on his shoulders.

*　　*　　*

John McGee, the black man's burden, retired after this fight, claiming the American championship, and rightly so. He left his Blue Heaven only for occasional trips to Boston, New York, and other centers of manly vice to box with Joshua and a few select sparring mates in exhibitions for the sporting crowd. He was heroized everywhere and he approved of such. But in New York (he once told Joshua) he felt kin to all that he saw: the antlike mob of Irish, the Irish political radicals, the city politicians, the gamblers, the brawlers, the drinkers, and oh, those lovely women.

John always said he retired from fighting for the sake of his nose. 'No sensible woman,' he said, 'wants a man whose nose is twice as wide as itself, or that travels down his face in two or three assorted directions.'

The power that our hero manifested in galvanizing the attention and loyalty of other men, the magic of his name and fists, generated wisdom of the moment in Manhattan's Democratic politicians. And so they hired John to round up a few lads and fend off the gangs hired by politicians of the Native American stripe, the most vicious and fearsome of these headed by Bill (The Butcher) Platt, whose method was directness itself: invade the polling places in Democratic strongholds and destroy the ballot boxes. But the presence of the newly fearsome John McGee was a countervailing influence, which by dint of bludgeons, brickbats, and bloody knuckles proved the superiority of several Democratic candidates for public office in the great city.

For his accomplishments John was rewarded with the right to open an illegal gambling house, and assured he need never fear the law as long as there were honest Democratic judges in the world. He began his career with humbleness: three faro tables that catered to gamblers with no money. Perceiving limitations in this arrangement, John persuaded men of foresight to back his expansion, and in a few years owned sixteen gambling hells, including the most luxurious in the city, a Twenty-fourth Street brownstone furnished in high elegance (a taste

John had acquired in the mansions of Hillegond and Obadiah), replete with sumptuous dining and endless drink, and featuring a dozen faro tables, two roulette wheels, and private poker salons where John on occasion, or by challenge, played for the house.

I never heard John utter a word on behalf of slaves or against slavery, but as he rose in the world, so did Joshua, working for John as Mick the Rat, as sparring mate, as doorman in the gambling house, and eventually as the most adept of faro dealers, nimble-fingered fleecer of rich men in John's lush parlors. Joshua did this work when he could, but more than half of his time was spent conducting on the Underground Railroad. By the time the war began he had shunted more than four hundred fugitive slaves toward the North Star. He also owned his own policy house a block away from John's faro palace on Barclay Street and had four freed slaves working for him, running numbers.

I spent a fair amount of time with Joshua when I moved to New York. After I broke with Maud on that unpleasant night in her dressing room, I suddenly felt stifled by Albany. The year was 1858 and I had sharpened my writing skills to the point that I felt I could function as an independent. Will Canaday promised to print anything I wrote, I made contact with other editors, and so began a life in New York City. My aim was to work at the *Tribune* for Horace Greeley, a man whose principles seemed as worthy as Will's, and in time I summoned the courage to present myself and my clippings at his office.

'Your dudgeon is admirable,' he told me, and so I went to work on the greatest newspaper in the metropolis. I wrote first of what I knew well: an interview and reminiscence with John McGee about his great boxing days. I also used John's connection to gain access to the dominantly Irish gangs of the Five Points section (the Dead Rabbits, the Plug Uglies) and write of their ongoing feud with nativist gangs (the American Guards, the Bowery Boys). This warfare was a constant in the city, as many as eight hundred to a thousand young men in deadly battle in the streets at a given time, and the police helpless to curb it.

I also wrote of Joshua and his former slaves, revealing none of their identities. I printed slave stories as they came out of Joshua's mouth:

'Slave named Bandy tried to run away and master slit his feet.

'Slave named Mandy lost a plow hook plowin' and master tied her to a tree and whipped her till blood ran down her toes.

'Slave named Julius was flogged bad for callin' his master "mister."

'Slave named Pompey worked for a man had a wife wanted a nigger whipped every time she see one.

'Slave named George had a master got hisself into a rage in town, came home drunk and shot George in the foot.

'Slave named Abram got old and useless but master wouldn't send for no doctor. "Let him die," said master, and old Abram died with creepers in his legs.

'Slave named Hanson had a master so mean that two hundred lashes was only a promise.

'Slave named Darius, all he lived on for a year was Indian-meal bread and pot liquor off boiled pork.

'Slave named Adam ran away and they caught him and tied him to the ground and whipped him to death.

'Slave named Caroline runnin' stuff up a hill fell down, got up, kept runnin', and master whipped her, sayin', "How come you can't get up that hill faster?"

'Slave named Tucker got punished for goin' to a church meetin' at night. Next mornin' master called Tucker in and whipped him on the head with the butt of the cowhide, got his gun and hit Tucker on the head with the breech, got the fire tongs and hit Tucker on the head with it, got the parlor shovel and beat Tucker on the head with it; then when Tucker went to leave, master got his knife and sliced Tucker across the stomach and hit him on the head with the knife. But Tucker got away holdin' his guts in, ran and walked sixteen miles and found a doctor, and almost died for five days but didn't.'

So wrote Quinn.

Quinn, looking starched and fresh in a new shirt and dark-blue dress suit, the only one he owned, wearing also his slouch hat over his day-old haircut, sat in one of the hundred or more rocking chairs on the busy two-hundred-and-fifty-foot porch of the United States Hotel, holding in his lap the Saratoga morning newspaper for today, August 3, 1864, reading a story reprinted from the *Tribune* about the recent battle at Atlanta, the most disastrous of the war for the rebels: immense slaughter by Sherman's army. Quinn also read a letter found on a Confederate soldier captured by Grant. The letter was from the man's brother, a rebel officer, and he wrote: 'The capture of Vicksburg and our army last year has proven to be fatal to our cause. We have played a big game and lost. As soon as I am exchanged for a Yankee prisoner I shall leave the Confederacy and the cause for Europe.' And under the headline 'Democratic Patriotism' Quinn read: 'The Democratic leaders opposed the use of Negro troops as an admission that white men of the North could not vanquish white men of the South. This prevented the raising of many thousand Negro troops. But when the government calls up white men through conscription, the same Democrats strive to defeat it, even inaugurating mobs against it. They won't let the Negro go, they won't go themselves, and they claim to be patriotic!'

Feeling the fear and anger rise in him again, Quinn put the paper aside to watch the arrival of three people, affluent parents with two grown daughters, a pair of petted beauties, or so it looked.

231

Their carriage stopped at the hotel stairs and four young Negro men descended to them instantly, one assisting the women, two attending the abundant luggage, the fourth, with whisk broom, sweeping travel dust from the shoulders of all.

Quinn, as usual superimposing Joshua's valiant face on other Negroes, could not complete this picture. He could not imagine Joshua allowing himself even an instant of overt servility, though he'd often worked as a servant. How had the man avoided it? There is a painting of him done by an artist-gambler who frequented John's gaming house, which, thought the artist, captured Joshua from life: standing against a wall in his white doorman's jacket, listening to music being played for John's dinner guests in the next room. There is a smile on Joshua's face, a benign and folksy response to the music, excavating the simplicity of the Negro soul that is so lulled by, so in harmony with, the sweet melodies of the oboe and the violin.

But if anything, Joshua's smile in that painting is a mask of dissimulation, a private recognition that all that exists in this music is the opposite of himself, and that he understands the racial enemy better for having this privileged audience to his pleasures. I have never presumed to truly understand Joshua, but certain things are so self-evident that even the abjectly ignorant are entitled to an opinion, and I therefore aver that Joshua did not aspire to this veranda on which I was sitting, did not aspire to the glut of wardrobe trunks that were being hauled down from the roof of the carriage, did not aspire to join the parade of strutters and predators marching up and down the posh hallways, salons, and drawing rooms of this cavernous hotel, or along the preening streets of the old village, not only did not aspire to own or be owned by such ostentation but despised it for its distance from the reality to which Joshua did aspire: that landless, penurious freedom that was the newborn, elementary glory that followed after slavery.

I saw Joshua in New York not long after John McGee discovered that Limerick, his purebred Irish setter, for which he had paid eight thousand dollars in a public gesture of contempt for the poverty of his early days, had disappeared. The dog was widely known in the city, trumpeted in the gossipist newspapers as the luckiest dog in town, not because it was owned by an affluent world-champion fighter but because a rub of its head had propelled more than a few gamblers into great winnings as they fought the tiger at John's faro tables. John, of course, had invented this story.

When John discovered Limerick's absence from the house, the bedrock of Manhattan trembled with crisis. John sent emissaries into the streets to find him, dispatched Joshua to the police lockup for animals, this being the priority, for stray, unmuzzled dogs were poisoned daily at sunrise and carted to the dump by noon, and owners, if traceable, were fined five dollars for letting a cur run loose in the rabid months of summer. And we were in July. I caught up with Joshua on the street and learned of the impending tragedy as we walked.

'Damn dog don't know when he's well off,' Joshua said.

'He run away before?'

'He try. Seem like he need the street, that dog. He ain't no house dog.'

'Maybe they already poisoned him.'

'May be,' said Joshua. 'Then look out. John gonna desecrate any cop kill his dog.'

We found the dog poisoners taking their leisure, somewhat removed from the doomed bayings that erupted beyond a wooden partition in a warehouse built of failing brick, crude slatwork, and chicken wire. We confronted the sergeant in charge, presented our case, and were led by a rankless lackey to the wire pen where two dozen dogs, most of them mangy mongrels, but among them a fox terrier, a bull, a husky, and a collie, were all leaping and barking their frenzy at us. Limerick was among them, suddenly beside himself with joy at recognizing Joshua.

'How much it cost to take that red dog outa here?' Joshua asked the lackey.

'One dollar, but you can't take him out without a muzzle.'

'You got a muzzle I can buy?'

'Yep.'

'How much it cost?'

'One dollar.'

Joshua counted the dogs in the pen.

'You got twenty-six muzzles?'

'Yeah. Got a hundred.'

'Then we gonna muzzle up these dogs and take 'em all.'

'Take 'em all?'

'That all right with you?'

'Whatayou gonna do with twenty-six dogs?'

'Gonna make me a dog house.'

Joshua pulled a roll of bills from his pocket to prove his seriousness. Then we muzzled the dogs and turned them loose. With luck they'd find a way to get rid of the muzzles before they starved to death. But poison at sunrise was no longer their fate.

Gordon and Maud arrived at the hotel porch precisely at eleven, the hour of rendezvous, Maud ebullient in a pink frock with matching silk shawl, wide skirt with sweeping train, and her burnished red hair in large, loose curls. Gordon, striding purposefully beside her, looked so brilliantly fresh in his starched cravat, tan linen shirt, claw-tailed coat, and new brown boots that Quinn felt he should return to his own room and find dandier clothes. Having none, he loathed the thought and vowed to become unkempt by midafternoon.

'Ah, you have the newspaper,' said Gordon. 'I just heard it has an item that must be read.'

Quinn handed him the newspaper, and Gordon sat in a rocker and busied himself with print.

'You look like a bouquet of roses,' Quinn told Maud.

'How poetic of you, Daniel.'

'What do you have in store for me today?'

'Something beyond your imagination.'

'Nothing is beyond my imagination,' said Quinn.

'Opening day at a brand-new racetrack, you can't know what to expect.'

'I thought you might have something more exotic in mind.'

'Your old friends John McGee and Magdalena will be on hand. They're quite exotic in their way, wouldn't you say?'

'You're pulling my leg.'

'Perhaps later,' said Maud. 'Do you find Saratoga changed?'

'More crowded, more money, more hotels, more women.'

'You've kept busy watching the women, then.'

'It seems like the thing to do when you sit on this veranda. Clearly they come here to be looked at.'

'Do you like my new dress? It's the same color as the one I was wearing when we met.'

'Very nostalgic of you, my dear.'

'Nostalgia is not my purpose,' said Maud.

'This is vile,' said Gordon, rustling the newspaper angrily. 'It's a letter. They're referring to your aunt.'

'What could they say about her that hasn't already been said a hundred times?' Maud asked.

'It's clearly a threat because of her party tonight,' said Gordon. He thrust the paper at Quinn and Maud, and together they read the letter:

Mr Editor – I would advise a certain aging ex-theatrical performer to keep a sharp eye out today for revelations of what she and her kind mean to this community. We who try to elevate the life of Saratoga are appalled at the degradation she is imposing on our society with her ridiculous social ambitions. We suggest she depart across our borders as soon as possible and rid us of the repugnant memories of her scandalous life. Courtesans are of the lowest order of mammal, and performing courtesans who kick up their legs for the edification of the rabble are a pox on our community.

PURITY KNICKERBOCKER
(Who speaks for a multitude)

Quinn, deciding the letter and Gordon's response to it were fatuous and depressing, let his eye roam over the rest of the page, found an advertisement for hashish candy, exhilarant confectionized: produces the most perfect mental cheerfulness. Also (remembering Magdalena's five abortions) a medical salute to the Ladies of America: 'Lyon's Periodical Drops! The Great Female Remedy! But Caution!!! Dr Lyon guarantees his drops to cure suppression of the menses, but if pregnancy be the cause, these drops would surely produce miscarriage and he does not then hold himself responsible. BE WISE IN TIME.'

'That kind of letter is commonplace, just ordinary jealousy,' Quinn said. 'You can't let it bother you. It carries no more weight than these frivolous advertisements.'

'Easy to say,' said Gordon, 'but they warn of something coming. They'll try to spoil her birthday party, I'll wager.'

'I'm sure Magdalena can take care of herself,' said Maud. 'She's as invulnerable as the *Monitor* on things like this.'

'But her heart is weak. You know that,' said Gordon.

'What's wrong with her heart?' Quinn asked.

'She's had trouble for six months or so. She's collapsed twice now, but she's doctoring,' said Maud.

'I worry she'll be harmed by this business, whatever it is,' said Gordon.

'Is she joining us here?' Quinn asked.

'She and Obadiah will meet us at the track,' said Gordon.

'Has she kept her looks?' Quinn asked.

'And her figure,' said Maud.

'Splendid. She's one of our national physical treasures.'

'I agree,' said Gordon.

'You do?' said Quinn. 'I wouldn't have expected that of you.'

'I don't know why not. I'm fond of the whole family.'

'As am I,' said Quinn, and he leaned over and kissed Maud on the mouth.

'That's a bit familiar, I'd say,' said Gordon.

'With reason,' said Quinn. 'I'm deeply and forever beyond familiar, and beyond that, I'm irrevocably in love with Maud, and I intend to kidnap her.'

Gordon broke into laughter and his tall hat fell off.

'How wonderful,' he said. 'You speak as well as you write. Wasn't that wonderful, Maud?'

'It was wonderful,' said Maud.

'Of course you know I mean it,' said Quinn.

'Of course you do,' said Maud.

'Did Maud ever ask you to kidnap her?' Quinn asked.

'Not that I can remember,' said Gordon.

'Good. She asked me, but I was never quite equal to it, and she was a vacillating kidnappee. But now I've decided to carry her off into the night, out of bondage to money, power, and fame, and do arousing things to her soul. Would you like that, Maud?'

'I don't think you should answer that question,' said Gordon.

'I have no intention of answering it,' said Maud.

'I think it's rather insulting,' said Gordon.

'Love is never an insult,' said Maud. 'Let it pass.'

'I'm not sure I like your attitude,' said Gordon.

'Oh, you like it, you like it,' said Maud.

'I'm not sure I do.'

'Are we going to the track or not?' said Quinn.

'We're going,' said Maud.

'Having professed love for you, am I still welcome or should I engage my own carriage?'

'Oh, Daniel, don't be twice a boor,' said Maud.

Our triumvirate at this point descends the porch stairs and, settling into Gordon's handsome landau drawn by a pair of matched grays, recedes now, necessarily, into the moving mosaic that Saratoga has become at this hour. The landau moves into a line half a mile long, extending from the front of the hotel on Broadway out past the elms on Union Avenue and onto the grounds of the new Saratoga track. The carriages are a study in aspiration, achievement, failed dreams, industrial art, social excess, tastemaking, advance and retrograde design, cherished fantasy, inept pretension, and more. They are the American motley and they carry the motley-minded denizens of a nation at war and at play. Quinn, aware the Union Army uses up five hundred horses each day of the war, is uncomfortably gleeful to

237

be a part of this many-horsed motley. In his woeful solitude he embraces the crowd, famished for significance that has not been sanctified by blood. Before the day and the night are over, Quinn will observe, speak with, or become friend of, among others en route to the track:

Price McGrady, John's gambling partner in New York City, a faro dealer of such renown that John pays him forty-five hundred dollars per month plus fifteen percent of the house winnings at all faro tables, and who is now in a fringe-topped surrey alongside his lady for today, ready for his horse, Tipperary Birdcatcher, to win the principal race of the day, or, failing that, ready for it to lose, either outcome an exercise in ecstasy;

The Wilmot Bayards of Fifth Avenue, he a horseman and yachtsman, investor in the racetrack with John McGee, and owner of Barrister, a horse that will run in the feature race, Bayard today among the most effulgent presences in the parade, riding in a barouche made in France, drawn by eight horses, and monitored by a pair of outriders who are wearing the silks of the Bayard Stable, gold and green, the colors of money;

Lord Cecil Glastonbury of Ottawa, the iron magnate (and sympathizer with the Confederacy), in a wind-colored four-passenger brougham, he the owner of Royal Traveler, the horse favored in today's feature race;

Jim Fisk, the stock speculator and financial brigand, in a six-passenger closed coach, the largest vehicle in the line apart from certain omnibuses owned by the hotels, in which the brigand carries five cuddlesome women, all six drawn by six horses that follow behind the German marching band Fisk has hired to travel with him for the week;

Colonel Wally Standish of the 104th Regulars, who rides alone in his two-wheeled cabriolet, proving that the wound he earned in the Second Manassas campaign may have left him with a malfunctional left arm, but that his right is still powerful enough to control his spirited sorrel mare;

Magdalena Colón and Obadiah Griswold, he the carriage maker and principal partner of John McGee in establishing the racetrack, and for whom the feature race of the day, the Griswold Stakes, has been named – this notable pair riding in Magdalena's demi-landau with its leather top folded down, she holding the reins of what is known to be the most expensive two-passenger vehicle in Saratoga: Obadiah's masterpiece, gilded rococo in decor, doors of polished ebony, with Magdalena's initials inlaid in white Italian marble on each door; she and Obadiah both eminently visible to all whom they now pass, he entirely in white including white cane and white straw boater, she in a summer dress of gray foulard silk with blue velvet buttons, the dress created in the *postillon* body design with tripartite tail, the new fashion favored by young women with slender figures; and rising from the right side of her straw bonnet the feathered plume of changeable color – gray today – that plume her vaunted symbol of resurrection ever since her time at the bottom of the wild river and which has made her the most instantly recognizable woman in Saratoga, in or out of season.

Along with these, in assorted buggies, phaetons, chaises, coupes, and chariots, come bankers, soldiers, politicians, Kansas farmers and Boston lawyers, litterateurs from Philadelphia and actors from Albany, reprobates with dyed locks and widows so tightly laced that breathing does not come easy, young women with tapering arms and pouting lips, full of anxiety over the adequacy of their *botteries* and *chausseries*, gouty sinners and flirtatious deacons, portly women with matching daughters who are starting their day, as usual, full of high hope that they will today meet the significant stranger with whom the hymeneal sacrifice may at last be offered up – these and five thousand more of their uncategorizable kind all move forward at inch-pace progress into the brightest of bright noondays beneath the sunswept heavenly promise of life at Saratoga.

A quarter of a mile from the track the carriage line intersected with a moving crowd of Negroes singing a song to the music of their own marching musicians, the singing spirited and full, the music rousing, the crowd en route to a celebration (to be marked by song, speeches, and prayer, I would discover in tomorrow's newspaper) of the emancipation of slaves in the rebellious states of the American union, as well as a commemoration of the thirtieth anniversary of the abolition of slavery in the British West Indies. The marchers were singing this:

No more peck of corn for me, no more, no more;
No more peck of corn for me, many t'ousand go.
No more driver's lash for me, no more, no more,
No more driver's lash for me, many t'ousand go.

I observed that the faces of all the marching Negro men brought back, as always, the face of Joshua and his myriad masks of power.

I saw John McGee as soon as we came within sight of the track's entrance, where all carriages were discharging their passengers. Here, looking more prosperous and fit than I'd ever seen him, handsomely garbed in starched white linen, black broadcloth, and patent-leather boots, and with a full and perfectly trimmed beard as black as coal tar, stood the redoubtable God of Water and Horses, guarding the portal like the three-headed dog of Hades. He truly did seem to own three heads, so busy was he greeting and weeding the crowd. Up to a half-dozen people sought to pass through the gate and into the track proper at any given time and John knew many by name. He kept up a steady monologue:

'Ah, there you are, Mrs Woolsey, lovely day for the races . . . Mr Travers, your uncle is upstairs . . . Hold it there, Dimpy, we'll have no blacklegs among us today [and with a rough pluck of Dimpy's sleeve, John sent the man back whence he came] . . . And none of yours either, darling [gently turning back a painted doll] . . . Ah, we'll all enjoy ourselves this afternoon, won't we, Henry? . . . And welcome, Mrs Fitz, how's your mother? . . . You've an escort, do ye, Margie, well, so be it, but if I find you with your hands in anybody's pocket, I'll whip your hide and put you in rags . . . Your cousin's horse had a splendid workout this morning, Mrs Riley, and I'd play him in the pool if I was you . . . Throw that hoodlum off the premises . . .' Etc.

John left the weeding of undesirables in the hands of two burly associates and came to greet us, shook my hand vigorously, gripped Gordon by both shoulders, then kissed Maud's hand with tender affection.

'Ah, Maudie girl, there's devilish news.'

'Magdalena?'

'There's no news of her except she's a year older. It's the Warrior. They poisoned him.'

'Noooooo,' groaned Maud, and she collapsed into herself so quickly that I grabbed her arm, fearing a fall.

'They cored an apple, filled it with opium, and fed it to him. But he had the good taste to spit it out, and we don't think he was hurt.'

'Who did it?'

'Ah, now,' said John, 'I wouldn't accuse anyone. But I have my notions.'

'I want to see him,' said Maud.

'I thought you would.'

And so John took Maud's hand and led us to his carriage and then across the street to the workout track, where we found Blue Grass Warrior coming off a final lap. The jockey, a Negro lad of about sixteen years, rode him toward us, and when John grabbed the reins the jock dismounted. Maud stroked the horse, which was lathered with sweat.

'Are you all right, baby?' Maud asked the horse, and he dipped his head.

'He's doin' fine,' said the jockey.

'I'd horsewhip anybody who'd harm such a beautiful animal,' said Maud.

'It's dastardly,' said Gordon.

Maud felt easeful after a time, and so we walked toward the stables with the Warrior and watched other horses being readied for performance. The jockeys were about, and the Negro grooms and handlers, and we had close looks at two of the Warrior's competitors: Tipperary Birdcatcher, newly purchased by Price McGrady after a particularly fruitful month at the faro tables, the Catcher being a gray colt bred in Pennsylvania by the Dwyer

241

brothers, the noted gamblers and horsebreeders; and Comfort, a bay filly owned by Brad and Phoebe Strong of Slingerlands, an Albany suburb, she a former Fitzgibbon (cousin to Gordon) and an enduring shrew.

Both animals looked splendid to my uncritical eye, for I had knowledge of horseflesh only at its most general and practical level, and was wanting in the specifics of Thoroughbreds, this an evaluation that could have applied to my entire life: he knew things in general; his specifics lacked direction.

We bade farewell to the Warrior and, for luck, I stroked the centered white rhomboid above his eyes. John led us then on a brief tour of his racetrack, orienting us to the betting enclosure, where we might make bid on the auction pools, past the several reception rooms and saloons where beverages, viands, and oysters might be had, along the colonnade with its thickening growth of crowds, and up the stairs to the covered galleries, where Obadiah and Magdalena awaited us in their front-row seat at the finish line.

My first response upon seeing Magdalena after a hiatus of fourteen years was that she was an evolutionary figure. Age had wrinkled her, of course, and comfort had broadened her, her posterior in particular. Her bosom remained handsome, a somewhat amplified garden of promise and romp, but there was an organic pursing to her mouth line, and her hands were birdlike in their animation. Yes. A bird was what she had become. Had she always been a bird? Possibly. Once a ravenously sensuous Bird of Paradise; now, with that upward cascade of throat, an aging swan with fluttering eye.

'Oh, good,' she said when we neared her. 'Daniel is here. He's smart about these things. On which horse should we wager, Daniel? Maud's silly animal or the Canadian?'

'My horse is not silly,' said Maud.

'I know that,' said Magdalena.

'You look splendid,' I said to her. 'But I'm sorry to say I can't counsel you on this.'

'Of course you can't,' said Magdalena. 'You just got here. You haven't even looked at the program.'

'He certainly ought to look at the program,' Obadiah said.

'That's none of your business,' said Magdalena. 'Let the boy alone. You've grown up to be beautiful, Daniel.'

'You're very kind,' I said.

'One doesn't say beautiful to a grown man,' said Obadiah.

'Will you shut your mouth and let me talk? Sit down here by me, Daniel,' and I did.

'If you don't bet on Maud's horse,' said John, 'you'll be wasting your money.'

'I heard you tell a woman to bet on another horse, down by the gate,' I said.

'Well, you can't have everybody betting on the same horse,' said John, and he excused himself to attend to the pool betting, pledging to return and inviting us to join him if we felt inclined to gamble, which I did, believing only in Maud's horse, believing Maud could not lose at anything in the world. John moved off into the crowd, which by the day's peak moment would number five thousand. Bodies filled every seat, seemingly every square inch of space under the covered and roofless galleries. In the open area within the tall fence the crowd was equally dense, the movement to own space on the rail already having begun, the men's tall hats a liability for those to their rear. Women in clusters of finery, their vertical hats also a bountiful obstruction, and women with opera glasses observing the judge, the grooms, the horses, and other women, elevated the day into a vision of royalty and its court of ladies and their courtiers enthusing at races run solely for their relentless amusement. What exquisite privilege! What exaltation, that these animals exist to give us pleasure!

'Where do you keep your horse?' I asked Maud.

'She keeps it at my stables,' said Obadiah.

'He didn't ask you,' said Magdalena. 'You must learn to keep your mouth shut.'

'I keep him at Obadiah's stables,' Maud said.

'You see?' said Obadiah.

'It's very peculiar,' I said.

'Keeping a horse in a stable?' asked Obadiah.

'Will you shut up?' said Magdalena.

'Peculiar that we are all here, and how and why it happened,' I said. 'It's Magdalena's doing. If you hadn't died at the bottom of the river, and if you hadn't accepted Obadiah's invitation to come to Saratoga, we'd all be somewhere else. Of course it's possible, even if you'd *never* crossed the river, that we'd all be here anyway. But that's a fated way of looking at things.'

'Daniel is so smart,' said Magdalena. 'If I were younger I'd steal his heart away.'

'Well, you're not younger,' Obadiah said.

'Shut up, I know I'm not young. I'm sick and I'm dying and nobody cares.'

'Who said you were dying?' I asked.

'It's my heart. It's always fluttering and giving me sharp pains. But we all have to die sometime.'

'Don't be morbid, Auntie,' said Maud.

'Especially don't be morbid on your birthday,' said Gordon. 'How old are you?'

'Older than Methuselah.'

'You look wonderful,' said Gordon.

'That's what I tell her,' said Obadiah.

'Shut up. I look like a chicken with its neck wrung.'

'Why are you having a party and calling attention to your age if you feel that way?' I asked.

'When one is ill,' said Magdalena, 'one feels it incumbent upon oneself to say proper farewells to one's friends.'

'But what if you don't die after this farewell?' I asked.

'She can do another party next year,' said Maud. 'It's all very silly. You're in excellent health.'

'She's strong as an ox,' said Obadiah.

'You shut up about how strong I am. I'm weak as a kitten.'

'Did that letter in the paper this morning disturb you?' Gordon asked.

'I don't bother with such tripe,' said Magdalena.

'Good for you,' said Gordon.

'What did it say?'

'It was just tripe, as you say,' said Gordon.

'I thought so. Did they mention me by name?'

'No names were used. Even the signature was a pseudonym. Purity Knickerbocker.'

'They're all cowards,' said Magdalena.

'Precisely,' said Gordon.

'They said I should watch out for something.'

'They implied that,' said Gordon.

'Extremely silly. What do you suppose they meant?'

'I wouldn't worry about it,' said Maud.

'It's totally ridiculous,' said Obadiah.

'It's ridiculous when you open your mouth,' said Magdalena.

At this point I decided to maintain my sanity by separating myself from Magdalena's quixotry. I stood up and suggested to Gordon, who was beginning to take on the appearance of a loathsome animal of indeterminate species, that we should go to bid on the race.

'I want to go, too,' said Maud.

'No,' I said. 'You stay and keep your aunt company.'

'I want to bid. I want to buy a pool on the Warrior.'

'I'll buy one for you,' said I.

'*I'll* buy one for you, never mind him,' said Gordon.

'I'll buy it myself,' said Maud.

'Then go by yourself,' I said and I sat back down.

'You're a mule, Daniel,' Maud said.

'If I were a mule I'd be in battle at Atlanta,' I said.

Maud chose to stay, at end, and Gordon and I walked off like school chums.

'Is it true you're going to run for Congress?' I asked him. I had no need to be sociable with him, but Will Canaday had told me he truly was a man of decent principle, a Unionist, staunchly (though belatedly) for Lincoln – unlike his father, Lyman, who thought Lincoln a tyrant and usurper – and good with the workers at the Fitzgibbon foundries. I thought him a bit too full of himself, but he did have the good taste to pursue Maud.

'I probably will,' he said. 'The party offered it to me.'

'The Republicans?'

'Of course.'

'You may find yourself running against John. The Democrats are talking of him as a candidate, too.'

'I've heard that. I'm afraid I can't worry about the Irish.'

The idea of a man entering into a new career at midlife was strange to me, and appealing. I had thought only of continuity since I began educating myself, and so the idea of a mind change – industry into politics, in Gordon's case – seemed like a mutation of the species; and I date to this moment my change of mind on the word.

All that I had written for Will and for the *Tribune* seemed true enough, but a shallow sort of truth, insufficiently reflective of what lay below. Joshua's life, or John's, or my own could only be hinted at by the use of the word as I had been practicing it. The magnificent, which is to say the tragic or comic crosscurrents and complexities of such lives, lay somewhere beyond the limits of my calling. My thinking process itself was inhibited by form, by the arguments and rules of tradition. How was I ever to convey to another soul, even in speech, what I felt for and about Maud, what grand churnings she set off in my inner regions? How could I know those workings, even for myself alone, without a proper language to convey them? I was in need of freedom from inhibition, from dead language, from the repetitions of convention.

If I had not left my disk at the hotel, I would have taken it out of its sack and studied its mystery. And with that thought I knew that what was wrong with my life and work was that I was so busy accumulating and organizing facts and experience that I had failed to perceive that only in the contemplation of mystery was revelation possible; only in confronting the incomprehensible and arcane could there be any synthesis. My wretched inadequacy in achieving integrity of either mind or spirit after having witnessed so much death, deviltry, and treachery was attributable to this. I had become a creature of rote and method at a time when only intuitions culled from an anarchic faith in unlikely gods could offer me an answer. How could I ever come to know anything if I didn't know what I didn't know?

'Well,' I said to Gordon as we neared the betting enclosure, 'I hope you're getting used to my plan to kidnap Maud.'

'You haven't gone soft in the brain, have you, Quinn? Kidnapping is a serious affair.'

'They have to catch you, and I can't conceive of that.'

'You're unorthodox, all right. I can say that after hearing you talk at the bazaar. But you know I intend to marry the girl.'

'Does she intend that as well?'

'We've talked of it often.'

'I don't think Maud is very taken with marriage,' I said. 'I think she much prefers to live in sin.'

'You'd best watch your language, fellow.'

'You're totally correct. I was just telling myself the same thing.'

We were by then at the center of the exquisite vice of gambling on Thoroughbreds, the auctioneer standing on an elevated platform with a pair of spotters watching the crowd of about three hundred for their bids. Bidding on the pools had been frenzied since early morning at John McGee's local gambling house on Matilda Street in the Spa, but now it was reaching an apex of zeal at the track. As post time neared, a chalkboard gave the bids on each horse in the first pool. And now each horse was being auctioned separately, yet again, the folks with the fat bankrolls raising the bid on their favorites to levels beyond the reach of everyday gamblers. John held all bets, giving the winning bidder a ticket on the horse of his choice, with which he might claim all the money bet on his particular pool if his horse won. John took three percent of all bets, and so stood to win perpetually and lose never a whit – odds that pleased him quitesome.

There would be two races today, the first and most important being the Griswold Stakes, named for Obadiah: best two out of three heats, each heat one mile, carry ninety pounds, $50 entrance, purse $1,000 added, for all ages. These were the entries:

Lord Cecil Glastonbury's ROYAL TRAVELER, four-year-old, highest pool price thus far $1,200

Maud Fallon's BLUE GRASS WARRIOR, five-year-old, pool price $950

Wilmot Bayard's BARRISTER, four-year-old, pool price $600

Bradford and Phoebe Strong's COMFORT, five-year-old, pool price $255

Price McGrady's TIPPERARY BIRDCATCHER, three-year-old, pool price $180

Abner Swett's ZIGZAG MASTER, four-year-old, pool price $60

By the time Quinn and Gordon focused on the betting the Warrior was up to $1,100. Quinn bid $1,150 and was topped by a Negro woman with a fistful of money who bid $1,175. Quinn went to $1,200, the Negro woman to $1,225, Quinn to $1,250 and quiet. And so Quinn took the ticket, knowing it was madness to spend so much money. But spending it on behalf of Maud reduced the madness substantially. Also, the total for his pool was $3,805. So if he won, as he intuited, he would triple his money.

'I'm glad you didn't fight me,' he told Gordon.

'I wasn't tempted.'

'There'll be other chances,' said Quinn.

They observed the presence of five-hundred- and thousand-dollar bills in hands of newcomers bidding feverishly on the next pool. The two men observed the selling of this last pool before the first heat and noted Maud's Warrior moving into favored position, the pool now bringing $1,050 on the Warrior, and only $990 on Royal Traveler, the other horses standing more or less the same; and then the pair walked back toward their party, observing the jockeys sitting in wire baskets to be weighed, the horses in the paddock circle waiting to enter the track, and on to the gallery to see the first horse already on the track with jockey up and stewards leading the parade past all connoisseurs and ignoramuses in residency on the subject of horseflesh. The buzz of the crowd was growing in volume, the judges alert in their elevated viewing stands on either side of the finish line, the track a mix of sandy loam and clay, sere and pale now from the long drought. It was blazing noon on this inaugural racing morning of August third, and the five thousand all looked out from their privileged galleries, out from the less-privileged standing area below, and still more looked on from perches in trees or atop tall wagons parked on the periphery of the mile-long track, sandy scrub pines visible in all directions beyond the sea of grass planted in the center of the track's oval.

Looking down from his perch between Maud and Magdalena, Quinn saw the Negro woman he had outbid standing with a group of Negro men and women in their own preserve along the rail's final edge, the woman with an unobstructed view of the race. She and her male companion had been the lone Negroes in the betting enclosure, and Quinn now sought to define her from a distance. Her ample self was singular, to begin with; her aggressive presence here a fact that set her apart from the four million slaves and the half-million free Negroes in this divided Union. How does she come to be here when war rages around the heads of her enslaved kith and kin? Why are any of us here, for that matter? Quinn would take bets that the prevailing evaluation would be that she was a madam. She well may be. Quinn knew such madams in New York, drank in their establishments, knew their girls. But Quinn knew also that the woman could be a gambler on the order of Joshua, an entrepreneur who saw her chances and understood them. She could be the inheritor of a fortune left by a guilty white man, or a queen of industry in the great Negro netherworld so little understood by white entrepreneurs. Or was she a mathematical wizard who had discovered the investment market? Well, Quinn had a good time trying to place her in the cosmos, and knew he'd be wrong no matter what he decided, just as no man alive looking at Joshua could imagine his achievement in money and survival skills. Was the woman a sculptress from the Caribbees? A sorceress from Sierra Leone?

Joshua's father, known as Cinque, had been stolen by slavers from Sierra Leone, but offshore from Puerto Rico he led a revolt of slaves on board the ship, killed the captain and mate as other crewmen fled in small boats, then with one sailor's help sailed eight weeks toward America and freedom, landing in starving condition at Virginia, where the sailor had vengefully steered them, and there Cinque and other surviving slaves were charged with murder. But instead of trial, and because of his physical value, Cinque was sold to a planter with a reputation for curbing arrogance. In time Cinque found a woman, sired Joshua, and after an escape attempt was hanged by his feet and whipped until he bled to death through his face, leaving a legacy of rebellion and unavengeable suffering for the three-year-old Joshua to discover.

When his own time came for rebellion, Joshua, who had educated himself in stealth, had no need of murder. He fled from master in the night and made his way north to New York, where he gravitated to the first cluster of Negroes he found, that being at the Five Points, the pestilential neighborhood dominated by the Irish, but where Negroes and Italians, in smaller numbers, also lived and worked in the underworld that that neighborhood was, where every stranger was a mark, and where no human life was safe from the ravagements of the street and river gangs: the Daybreak Boys, the Short Tails, the Patsy Conroys.

Joshua learned rat baiting at the Five Points, learned how to draw blood from bare-knuckle wounds with his mouth, this taught to him by an expert named Suckface, a member of the Slaughterhouse gang, who for ten cents would bite the head off a live mouse, and for a quarter off a live rat. Joshua learned to deal cards in a Five Points dive owned by a three-hundred-and-fifty-pound Negro woman called The Purple Turtle. She, like Joshua, lived on a street called Double Alley, and when Joshua told all this to John McGee in a later year, an enduring bond was forged between them; for John knew the Five Points intimately, had cousins there from Connacht (considered by some the lowliest place in Ireland, although not by the people from Connacht), had been in The Turtle's place often, and for years sang the song of Double Alley and its poetic alias, Paradise Alley.

Now Double Alley's our Paradise Alley,
For that's where we learned how to die.
We suckled on trouble and fightin' and gin,
And we loved every girl who was ready to sin.

Old Double Alley's our Paradise Alley
For nobody ever got old.
We fought for a nickel and died for a dime,
We knew there was nothin' but having' a time.
Oh, I'd sure love to see the old place in its prime,
Double old Paradise Alley.

The Five Points harmony, though quitesuch it never was between the Negroes and the Irish, waned perceptibly when the war fever came on. The fight to free the niggers was all idiot stuff to the Five Points paddies, whose principal interest was freeing themselves from the woes that ailed them. And so it happened that many Negroes wisely moved out of Paradise to less hostile quarters. Joshua, by then, was long gone from Double Alley, and by the time the war erupted he'd been conducting on the Railroad for more than a decade.

At a brisk tap of the drum the Griswold Stakes got off with as even a start as ever was. Blue Grass Warrior and Tipperary Birdcatcher led a tight pack by a pair of noses, Barrister and Royal Traveler neck and neck behind the leaders, Zigzag Master two lengths off, and Comfort trailing. So it went until the half mile, when Zigzag made his move and challenged the leading duo, his nose at the Warrior's saddle girths, Barrister falling back after a spent burst of speed, and Comfort trailing. At the three-quarter turn it was a three-horse race, the Birdcatcher ahead by a length, Zigzag's jockey freely using the whip to stay close, and the Warrior no more than a neck off in third, the rest far back and Comfort trailing. At the top of the stretch the Catcher lost wind, and Zigzag took the lead by a head, but the Warrior on the outside, attentive to the Negro jockey's whip and whisper, moved alongside Zigzag, and then with a surge of power moved in front by a full length, then two, and in the stretch was going away to win the heat. The results:

Blue Grass Warrior	1
Zigzag Master	2
Tipperary Birdcatcher	3
Royal Traveler	4
Barrister	5
Comfort	6

The betting was scrambled for the second heat, Comfort and Barrister withdrawn by their owners. Grooms started their rubdowns of the horses as soon as they left the track, and a keen-eyed steward, by chance and nothing more, noted that a long white marking on Zigzag's nose had taken a shape different from what it had been at the start of the race; whereupon the overheated animal was examined and found to have been dyed. Under interrogation, owner Abner Swett professed ignorance. But it was quickly learned he was the brother-in-law of Jeremiah Plum, the patriarch of the notorious Plum family, which was famed throughout northeast Christendom for dyeing stolen horses to prevent them from being identified and reclaimed. Before the day was out we would all learn that Zigzag's record had been fabricated as well, that his true name was Wild Pilgrim, and that he was a four-year-old with so many victories that he would have been at least a co-favorite (at much lower and less profitable odds) with the Traveler or the Warrior had his true history been known. The Pilgrim had beaten the Traveler twice, and so only Maud's Warrior was feared as his competitor on this sunbright noonday, which was why John's investigation into the doping of the Warrior focused on Abner Swett of Watervliet, a man of irregular values.

As the horses were about to enter the track for the second heat, a carriage drawn by a single horse, and another horse and rider behind it, came onto the track from a gate at the top of the stretch, and at moderately high speed they approached the finish line, there slowing enough for the crowd to view them in full detail. In the carriage, an old demi-landau gilded like Obadiah's masterwork, and with the letters M.C. painted on the door, rode a Negro wearing women's clothing, including an unmistakable copy of Magdalena's hat with a scarlet plume rising from it, the plume and the Negro waving to the crowd as they passed. Behind him, clad only in long white underwear and a woman's red wig, and riding backward and belly-up in the pose well known to multitudes from newspaper advertisements and theater posters – Maud as Mazeppa – rode another Negro, who also waved at the crowd and showed them his backside, to which was pinned a large green shamrock. Then, with a trick rider's expertise, he righted himself, and the two Negroes galloped down the track and out the gate by the far turn before anyone had the wit to stop them.

In the upper gallery, while the crowd exploded with laughter, Magdalena fell unconscious in Quinn's arms.

Soon after the mockery of Maud and Magdalena, the second heat of the Griswold Stakes was run. Three horses were entered: Blue Grass Warrior, Tipperary Birdcatcher, and Royal Traveler. They finished in that order, the Warrior winning by a length, the Traveler a far third. After crossing the finish line, Maud's horse stepped into a hole in what seemed like a perfectly smooth section of the track, twisted its left foreleg, and broke it. The jockey pulled him up and the Warrior stood with his leg bent and dangling. Track handlers went to him and wrestled him down onto his side atop a tarpaulin; then they strapped him into the tarp and dragged him away. After discussing the matter with Maud, John McGee went to the barn where they had taken the Warrior and personally fired two bullets into the animal's brain.

Quinn again perceived inevitable death in the dangling leg of Blue Grass Warrior, just as he had seen it in 1863 during the second day of a week of violence now known as the New York Draft Riots. Rioting was entering into a crescendo on that day as Quinn and John McGee turned a corner onto Ninth Avenue, heading for the house where Joshua was waiting out the riots with another man, a newly arrived fugitive slave.

Quinn himself had arrived only a week earlier, back from the battle of Vicksburg to write his personal tale of that ordeal, and having done that, he rested, sipping lager and communing with other ink-stained wretches at Charlie Pfaff's Cave at Printing House Square about the nuances of war correspondency, literature, and Charlie's German pancakes. Quinn's time spent with the lower orders at the Five Points worked against his need for rest, and a doughty *Tribune* editor tracked him down and assigned him to roam the Five and assess the rampant resentment to the draft, the first list of conscripts having just been released by the federal government.

In the Five Points and other like slums of the metropolis there was all but solid opposition to the war and to the race of people whose plight had brought it about. Also in the Five Points, Quinn found that the Copperhead politicians, great friends all of John McGee, were viewed as heroic figures. Denizens of the Five, 'outscourings of humanity, the dregs of Europe' commonly called, abided in harmonious squalor with the city's criminal element, and numbered, in all, perhaps eighty thousand in a city of eight hundred thousand, a statistic with wicked potential.

Given the normal antisocial elements of such a group, its antipathy to the war and to the government waging it, given its natural thirst for vengeance, the balance of social madness, in retrospect, can be viewed as easily tippable with the imposition of a hateful law. Such was the conscription law, drafting men for the first time (volunteers and bounty seekers had heretofore sustained the army's needs), but exempting from service anyone able to pay the government three hundred dollars. We need not elaborate on the crystalline injustice of this to the poor man in general, and in particular to the poor Irishman (a quarter of the entire city was Irish), mired in generational denial and humiliation as he was, and for whom free Negroes meant a swarm of competitors for the already insufficient jobs at the bottom of the world.

And so in the heat of a midsummer weekend in July 1863, while Lee was licking his wounds from Gettysburg, the first polymorphic mob, estimated at ten thousand, drank itself into a frenzy in the greengroceries, the dance halls, and the dives of its choice, then took to the streets with baleful intent: Burn the draft office, burn the *Tribune*, that abolitionist rag, and pillage and destroy all that is not of us.

John and I found that mob as we turned the corner onto Ninth Avenue. The screaming that greeted us was horrendous, a battle already engaged between fifty policemen and the uncountable rioters who, in this moment, were led by a gigantic bare-chested, one-armed man, and at his side a young man I'd seen haranguing a crowd at the Five Points two days earlier. I remembered him at that time screaming anti-Negro invective at a crowd, urging rebellion, riot, revolution, no draft, and concluding with huzzahs for Jefferson Davis.

This younger man now fought like a pit bull, felling policemen with his club and with the force of his rage; and beside him the giant flailed outward with his enormous bludgeon, an extension of his Herculean right arm, cracking heads and backs with a vehemence,

255

his own head and body remarkably invulnerable to clubbings by police truncheons.

The mob moved relentlessly forward, the police valiant but unequal, routed and forced to flee for their lives as we watched. I do not know how they found Joshua's house. Perhaps they saw a Negro face in a window, or perhaps a neighbor was aware that Joshua had been there in recent days. But they singled out the house, beat open its doors, and swarmed inside.

'If he's still in there, he's dead,' said John.

The howling of the mob grew fiercer, more shrill, a wordless yawp of animal frenzy, the mob hearts all linked now in a single feral pulsebeat as they sensed a quarry and a kill. And then, from a second-story window in the house, a man screamed in triumph words I could not understand, but the mob could, and it responded with a roar. The man gave a signal and the mob obeyed. It moved backward into the street and was rewarded with a Negro (not Joshua) being pitched headfirst out the window, whereupon the mob closed in over him and I saw no more of what was done.

Joshua they brought out the door, his head bloodied but he still able to walk, and at the sight of him John broke into a run and pushed his way toward the center yelling, 'Don't kill him!' only to be met by the one-armed giant and his cudgel and dealt such a blow as would have killed two normal men. John fell unconscious, bloodied, dead I thought, and death might have been his lot had not the mob's focus been on the preferred quarry: Joshua. The swarm turned its attention from the dissenter, and I pulled John off the street and toward the basement of the nearest house, found it doorless, black, and empty. I propped John in a corner, and, as best I could, tried stanching the flow of his blood. He was breathing, but I dared not move him toward help now, for the sight of that bloody head was too likely to whet the mob's appetite for another kill. And so I was fated to guard the wounded John and watch from my darkness as the mob took its pleasure with Joshua. Here is what they did to him:

They beat him with their cudgels
And they stabbed him with their knives
    and he did not die
They dropped stones onto his chest
They dropped stones onto his head
    and he did not die
They poked holes in him with sticks
They roped his legs and dragged him
    and he did not die
They gave him to the harpies
And they opened up his flesh
    and he did not die
Then the harpies oiled his wounds
And they lit him with a match
    and he did not die
Then they hanged him from a lamppost
Lit a fire underneath him
    and he died

The mob moved on, and so I was able to get help from a family on the block to carry John to a bed; and a woman bandaged his head. Two samaritans cut down Joshua but a fragment of the mob came back and found him on the ground and hanged him a second time. When quiet came upon the street I shinnied up the lamppost and cut him down again. His left hand had been severed. I could not find it. I dragged him into my cellar and left him, then explored the neighborhood until I found a peddler with a pushcart. I rented him for two dollars, but when I told him my purpose he reneged. I threatened him and he went with me. When we got to the cellar, Joshua was gone.

When Magdalena Colón decided she was about to die for the second time, she announced from her bed that the only way she could die properly was lying by the water under a tree. Her intuition about death came at home at midafternoon, two hours after she collapsed in the gallery in my arms. She summoned Obadiah, Maud, her doctor, and her servants to her bedroom and insisted that someone find John McGee and bring him to her to reorganize the evening. Instead of a birthday party to celebrate her being alive for fifty-five years, what she now wanted was a wake to acknowledge her passing over into lovely death, but held while she was still alive and able to enjoy both sides of existence at the same time.

'You can't have a wake if you're not dead,' said Obadiah by her bedside.

'I won't even let you come to the wake if you don't mind your mouth,' said Magdalena.

The doctor had diagnosed her condition as palpitation, arrhythmia, and syncope, and ordered her to sip brandy, lie with her head below the level of her ankles, with her clothing loosened at neck and waist, with smelling salts on hand for revival in the event of further fainting, a coffee enema if necessary, and with the utmost ventilation to her room.

Maud entered into a weeping rage at Magdalena's plight, but Magdalena delighted in the attention, ordered her maid to find her a loose-fitting blouse, strip her of all undergarments, daub her face with powder, etch with pale crimson the lines of her lips and the hollows of her cheeks, brush her hair forty strokes, impose upon her throat the pendant emerald Obadiah gave her for her fiftieth birthday, heighten her eyebrows and eyelashes with charcoal, push her feet into her silver slippers, and find a pair of strong men to carry her out onto the lawn beneath a tree, where she might freely breathe her anticipated last. She then sent for me to ask my advice in publicizing her wake, since she wanted all her friends and enemies to come. I suggested a handbill.

'Fine,' said Magdalena, 'and I also want you to write something about me and how I changed the world.'

'How did you change the world?' I asked.

'I have no idea. That's why I want you to write it.'

'I'll do what I can,' I said.

'Splendid. And you can read it tonight at the wake instead of some poopy old prayer.'

I was alone at this point in the day, John off in places unknown, and Oba, as people called him, having donned his at-home costume of dressing gown and thigh-length kid boots, puttering around the servants' quarters. Maud closeted herself in her private reverie, emerging only to check on Magdalena's condition, which was improving. When she collapsed in my arms her face was ashen, but by now she had become sanguine and relaxed and was moving toward death with all her summonable beauty.

I took myself to the library, where Oba's butler brought me Magdalena's half-dozen scrapbooks, thick with newspaper cuttings in Spanish and English. I browsed through them and saw an outline of her life, the topography of a notorious career, the mockery of her first death, and on forward into the social notices of her life with Obadiah. What she wanted me to write, I supposed, was an obituary that would heap glory upon her achievements as performer, as mystic, as hostess; but the very thought of that bored me. If I was to do justice to the woman, I needed to move beyond the barricade of empty facts into some grander sphere – charting, for instance, what I myself found significant: her ability to survive as a solitary woman in a hostile world; her love affair with death; and, most important of all (to me), her nurturing of the incredible Maud, and then imposing that hallowed creature on my life.

The decision I had made so long ago, to live my life according to the word, reached its apogee in the war and then descended into the bathetic dumps of faceless slaughter. Yet in writing about what was worst in this world an unconscionable pang of pleasure dogged my every line. Mine was clearly a life fulfilled by language, and I was coming to see that through that, and only that, could I perhaps in some unknown way gild the eccentric life of Magdalena, or the tragedy of Joshua, or my own thrumming symphony of mysteries. By devising a set of images that did not rot on me overnight, I might confront what was worth confronting, with no expectation of solving the mysteries, but content merely to stare at them until they became as beautiful and valuable as Magdalena had always been, and as Maud now was.

It was in this elated frame of mind that I picked up a pen and set down a handful of words that I hoped would begin the recovery not only of what had been lost but also of what I did not know had been lost, yet surely must have been. I was persuading myself that if I used the words well, the harmony that lurked beneath all contraries and cacophonies must be revealed. This was an act of faith, not reason.

And so, rather than writing Magdalena's obituary, I began to write her story, taking the facts not from her cuttings but from my imagination, where, like a jungle flower, she had long since taken root.

I, Daniel Quinn, neither the first nor the last of a line of such Quinns (of this I was hopeful), would, with the courage false or real that comes with an acute onset of hubris, create a world before which I could kneel with awe and reverence as I waited to be carried off into flights of tragic laughter.

I did not write Magdalena's obituary but I did compose the notice of her death and carried it to town to have it printed as a handbill for distribution throughout the city. It read:

NOTICE OF PROXIMATE DEATH

The social leader and former international theater star Magdalena Colón Griswold, with all sincerity and affection, invites the visiting and resident citizenry of Saratoga to a viewing of her last remains, so to speak, this evening at her home, Griswold Gardens, on the eastern shore of Saratoga Lake. Her passing will take place on the Griswold lawn, and so, to facilitate the viewing, it is suggested that visitors carry with them either candle or lamp. Dinner and libations will be served, and dancing on the lawn will begin sharply at eight o'clock.

Magdalena had not anticipated anything more than a solemn parade of mourners filing past her, uttering condolences, shaking her mortal paw. But when John McGee arrived he put an end to such thinking.

'We're having a party,' he said. 'You can't spoil everybody's evening just because you've decided to die.' And so the final sentence was added to the handbill's invitation.

The guests began to arrive by seven. Those invited to the birthday were received in the mansion; those invited to the wake were directed to the lawn. John, when present at the mansion, clearly became the man of the house, Obadiah no more than a potty little wisp in the cosmos. John took up the welcoming position at the front gate, just as he had at the track, but now he turned away no one, including known thieves.

'Just stay outside the house,' he told the thieves he recognized, 'or I'll eat your gizzard for lunch.'

Champagne, Bordeaux wines, squab, and lobster were served to the birthday guests; beer, oyster stew, and crackers to the mourners on the lawn. John had ordered a stage built at the edge of the reflecting pool and at seven sharp Adolph Bernstein's orchestra from the United States Hotel began the music of the evening with a Chopin medley. John also asked Jim Fisk to bring his German band to the party, Fisk said he would, and did, and so music was continuous for Magdalena's presumably farewell performance. Milo, the Master of Magic from Albany, performed hat and animal tricks at an intermission, and when the music resumed Milo waltzed with a dancing bear, who was actually Cornelius Gómez, an idiot-savant Mexican dwarf, who told fortunes for a quarter afterward on the veranda.

Magdalena watched it all from her vantage point at the cusp of the lawn's principal slope, Maud beside her dotingly, responding to all her whims, which grew fewer as the line of strangers who came to wish her a pleasant passing grew longer.

'What a lovely idea inviting people to your wake ... Are you dead yet, Magdalena? ... When do you die? ... Will we see it happen? ... Have a good time in heaven, Magdalena ... We'll miss you ... Will there be a party for the funeral, too?'

'You're all such dears to come,' said Magdalena. 'I hope we don't run out of food. Maud, will we run out of food?'

'No, Auntie.'

'That's nice, dear. Keep them moving.'

No one mentioned the mockery of the afternoon to Magdalena, this warning passed on to all in line by order of John McGee, who said that if anyone talked of the thing to Magdalena he would break both their legs. Of the mockery, John discovered through informers that the two Negroes were both transient stable hands who had no knowledge of what they were doing and earned three dollars apiece for what they thought was entertainment for the crowd.

Gordon Fitzgibbon grew so pensive and melancholy over the mockery that Maud could not bear his presence and sent him away to elevate her own spirits. She told Gordon to cure himself of gloom and come back to the party in jubilation or else she would have nothing to do with him for the entire evening. Gordon went off and drank gin at the United States bar and returned at sunset with a rakish angle to his tall hat and a crooked smile on his face, the first time Quinn ever noted anything likable in the man.

Gordon arrived on the arm of his cousin Phoebe Strong, whose horse had also suffered humiliation during the afternoon, finishing a ridiculous number of lengths behind the winner. What Gordon did not know, nor did Quinn, was that Phoebe had been the architect and executrix of the mockery, and of the letter penned by Purity Knickerbocker – these facts unearthed by John McGee and his Hawkshaw network of social spies. John told only Maud of his discovery, and so Phoebe arrived at the wake with the serenity of a criminal who has committed the perfect crime.

Humanity arrived in great droves to mourn for Magdalena and grieve in its free beer. The lawn was asprawl with a vast multitude, the night a wash of flickering brilliance from a thousand lamps, lighting up the lawn more brightly than a full moon. John took it upon himself to summon a Presbyterian cleric, who was part of Magdalena's social set, to utter a prayer on behalf of the imminent decedent's soul, but the uniqueness of the occasion thwarted the man and instead he uttered a homily on the therapeutic quality of night breezes. Magdalena lost patience and shooed him away.

'Daniel,' she said, 'you say a prayer for me.'

'No,' I said, 'I can't do that sort of thing anymore. But I shall write about you as one of the great philanthropists in the entire history of sensuality.'

'He's so brilliant,' said Magdalena. And then she pulled me to her and kissed me on the lips.

'I envy Maud,' she whispered.

'You are the queen of the night,' I told her, and she feigned a swoon.

The mourners' line undulated across the entire lawn, and at the level area atop the slope the dancing began.

'I should like to dance,' said Magdalena. 'It may help me die. I should like to dance with John McGee.'

'And so you shall,' I said, and we organized the bearers, who carried Magdalena and her chaise longue across the lawn to the dancing area. I summoned John and told him he was wanted. He had never stopped being Magdalena's lover, even after her marriage to Obadiah – their assignations, whenever John was in range, being an open secret, and always conducted on Wednesday afternoons, Magdalena's preferred day of the week ever since a young lover told her Wednesday had been named for the god of poetic frenzy.

And so we danced: Magdalena and John, Gordon and Phoebe, Maud and I, and several hundred others, all waltzing to the music of 'Beautiful Dreamer,' so very popular at this moment. Seeing her dance I did not believe Magdalena would die. She looked irrepressibly radiant. How could such a vivid creature cease to be?

'I think we should change partners,' Maud said, and she broke from me and went to Gordon. 'I would like to dance with Phoebe,' she said.

'With Phoebe?' said Gordon, stunned.

'With Phoebe,' said Maud, and she grasped a reluctant Phoebe in a waltzing position and moved her forcefully away from Gordon, all of us suddenly turned into spectators. But dancing was not Maud's intention, as she proved by spinning Phoebe around and ripping her dress down the back. Phoebe tried to turn and strike Maud but Maud was far stronger and quite ready for the countering. She then flung Phoebe onto the floor, face down, and sat on her back. Gordon and another man started to intervene but John stopped them.

'Let them be,' said John. 'History needs elbow room tonight.'

Maud continued ripping Phoebe's dress, and then her petticoat and fluffy netherings, Phoebe squirming and screaming to the death, of course, howling for help. I thought Maud must have lost her reason, and yet her method exuded such control that a purpose was obvious.

'For heaven's sake, what are you doing, Maudie?' Magdalena asked, hovering over the struggling women.

'This is Phoebe Strong, Auntie, Gordon's first cousin.'

'I know it's Phoebe,' said Magdalena. 'Of course I know Phoebe. What are you doing to her?'

'I'm ripping her clothing.'

'Yes, but whatever for?'

'She's the hateful bitch who planned the mockery of you and me this afternoon.'

'Phoebe did that? Did you do that, Phoebe?'

'I did and I'm glad I did,' said Phoebe between screams.

By this time Maud had ripped the full length of every garment Phoebe was wearing and as the circle around us grew dense with interrupted dancers Maud fully uncovered the screeching Phoebe's buttocks for all to see.

'I thought of asking her to apologize,' said Maud, 'but this seemed a superior solution. Do you agree, Auntie?'

'Oh, quite,' said Magdalena. 'Quite indeed. But you know that is a most unpleasant sight. All full of pimples and dimples. Oh, do cover them.'

At the roar of laughter Maud stood up, and the humbled Phoebe, screaming and crying, clutched her rags about her and ran off toward the mansion. The orchestra took up the music again and the beautiful dreamers of Saratoga resumed their dancing under the stars.

As the evening moved on, four whores who had been the recipients of Magdalena's charities (she supported cyprians, waifs, and actresses) turned up, crying helplessly as they bent to say farewell to their benefactress. Their spirits improved when they saw how well she looked, and after several beers they were all in chorus singing 'Father's a Drunkard and Mother Is Dead,' which took the evening into a new phase.

The crowd was thinning and the light dimming. Many couples moved through various stages of romance by the shore of the lake, or in the shadowed woods, or in the sanctuary of Obadiah's shrub gardens. Gordon could not stop apologizing for his cousin's behavior, he assuming the guilt himself. But Maud wanted to hear no more of it and she left him to dance with me.

'I think it's getting time now to kidnap you,' I said.

'A perfect ending to a perfect day,' said Maud.

'I would like to sit under that arch,' I said, pointing to the trellis where we had watched Magdalena reveal herself to Obadiah at John's urging. We sat on the benches where they'd sat, the roses on the trellises around us all colored a vivid blue by the dark light of the night sky and the dancing flames of a thousand lamps and candles. And then, for the first time since our rendezvous at Hillegond's house, I kissed Maud. I had felt estranged from her after our meeting on the hotel piazza at morning, but I reclaimed our intimacy with the kiss, my brimming passion organizing my mind in a most salutary way. What flooded back to me was not just every memory, every loving response I'd had to her, but the opening also of an entire emotional landscape that I truly knew must exist somewhere but had never been able to find: the discovery of a new place in which to live. It vanished as quickly as it appeared, a trompe l'oeil of the imagination, but I knew as long as I had Maud with me I could reconstitute it. I took her by the hand just as Gordon arrived.

'You're monopolizing Maud,' he said to me.

'I was about to take her somewhere and make love to her,' I said.

'You had better quit that sort of talk, fellow.'

'It's more than talk, Gordon.'

'*I'm* going to marry this woman,' he said.

'I've loved her for fifteen years,' I said. 'Do you think now that I've found her I'll just walk away from her?'

'Maud,' he said, 'I want you out of this situation.'

'She has a will of her own, Gordon. Why do you suppose she's with me?'

'You're an arrogant bastard,' he said.

'And you're an insufferable prig,' I said.

I stood up and he rose to come at me, but I merely pushed and he went backward onto the bench. He stayed sitting.

'I'll have satisfaction for this,' he said.

'You will,' I said.

'Oh, no,' said Maud. 'Never.'

I took her hand and pulled her away and across the lawn, seeing Magdalena in the cradle of John's arms, he walking down toward the shore. We stopped and watched and saw her bearers following with her chaise longue, which they placed at the water's edge along with two large candelabra. John put Magdalena on the chaise in a position that allowed her to look out over the great expanse of water, then sat down on the grass beside her.

A storm was developing on the lake, and in an hour the wind

would rise and extinguish most of the candles and the party would end. Tomorrow would be a day of fast and humiliation, called for by the President to rekindle the nation's attention to ending the war. Quinn would contemplate a duel with Gordon and remember Joshua's duel with life and his conclusion about it: 'If you lose it's fate,' Joshua said. 'If you win it's a trick.' Quinn would dwell on this and perceive that he himself had changed, that he was forever isolated into the minority, a paddynigger and an obsessive fool whose disgust was greater than its object, who was trying to justify in this world what was justifiable only in another cosmic sphere. There were no explanations that satisfied Quinn, only a growing awareness of dark omissions in his life and a resolute will to struggle with the power the past seemed to have over him: power to imprison him in dead agonies and divine riddles. He would wake dreaming of his disk and its faces, a savage dream of a new order: faces as old as the dead Celts, forces in the shape of a severed hand and a severed tongue that would bring Quinn great power over life.

'You will go to war,' the Mexican dwarf had told him on the veranda. 'You will live a long life, raise sons, and have a happy death.' Quinn believed none of it, believed it all.

Maud did not want to go to her room, or to the hotel, but led the way to an upper floor of the mansion on the side that gave a full view of the lawn and the lake. She tried one door and they were greeted with a privileged vision: Obadiah on his knees, holding aloft the skirt of Adelaide, a parlormaid, and licking the back of her right knee. They moved on and found a room and locked themselves in, and then kissed at such a pitch of passion that Quinn thought his chest would explode, so acutely aware was he that at last he had stolen Maud.

'Slow,' he said, and he loosened the dark ribbon that held Maud's dress at the bodice. She removed the ribbon from the dress and tied it around her neck as a choker, and he took her dress from her, then the rest of her garments, and she did the same for him. The ribbon was long and uneven and fell the length of her torso to obscure part of her private hair. Quinn's eyes studied her with

William Kennedy

a wondrous lust and a love that was as limitless as the universe. Maud rolled backward onto the simple iron bed, her legs rising, the ribbon falling naturally between her open thighs, leaving her gift mostly secret. Quinn moved between her legs and gently lifted the ribbon to one side. And then Maud and Quinn were at last ready for love.

THE FLAMING
CORSAGE

Here's a how-de-do!
If I marry you,
When your time has come to perish,
Then the maiden whom you cherish
Must be slaughtered, too!
Here's a how-de-do!

With a passion that's intense
I worship and adore,
But the laws of common sense
We oughin't to ignore.
If what he says is true,
'Tis death to marry you!
Here's a pretty state of things!
Here's a pretty how-de-do!

— GILBERT AND SULLIVAN, *The Mikado*

The Love Nest

October 17, 1908

When the husband made his surprise entrance into the Manhattan hotel suite, his wife was leaning against a table, clad in a floor-length, forest-green velvet cloak, and wearing a small eye mask of the same color, her black hair loose to below her shoulders.

The second woman, her light-brown hair upswept into a fuss of soft curls that bespoke an energetic nature, and wearing a floor-length, peach-colored evening gown embroidered with glass pearls, was in conversation with the man who had rented this suite months earlier, and who at this moment was wearing a frock coat, evening trousers, wing collar, gray ascot and pearl stickpin, the two dressed as if for a social evening. They were standing near the window that gave a view at dusk of the falling leaves and barren branches of the elms and maples of lower Fifth Avenue.

The husband's entrance to the suite was made with a key. How he came into possession of the key has not been discovered. The husband spoke first to his wife, saying, according to one witness, 'You Babylonian whore, everything is undone'; or, according to the other witness, 'Babylon, *regina peccatorum*, you are gone.' Turning then to both the man in the wing collar and the second woman, the husband spoke of 'traitors' and 'vixen,' his exact phrase unclear to both witnesses. The husband then opened his coat, drew a .45-caliber Colt revolver from his waistband, parted his wife's cloak with its barrel, placed the barrel against her left breast, and shot her precisely through the heart. The position in which she fell onto the carpet revealed that she wore nothing beneath the cloak.

The husband turned to the man by the window and fired two shots at him, hitting him with one, the force of which propelled him backward into the windowpane, which shattered. The second woman screamed, ran into the bedroom, and locked its door. The wounded man watched the husband staring at his pistol and heard him mumble, 'Confido et conquiesco,' which translates from the Latin as: I trust and am at peace. After saying this, the husband put the revolver barrel under his chin, pulled the trigger, and fell dead beside his exposed wife.

Edward in the City of Tents

September 1885

It was the year the State Fair came to Albany, and as Edward Daugherty walked through the vast city of tents and impromptu structures that had sprung up in a matter of weeks at the Fairgrounds on the Troy Road, he felt a surge of strength, a certainty that he was changing substantially, at the breaking dawn of a creative future.

He could see the tents on the midway where seven newspapers had their offices and seven sets of reporters wrote yards of daily copy about Shorthorns and Clydesdales, Cotswold sheep, and Poland China swine. In the *Albany Evening Journal*'s tent he found Maginn writing at a table.

'What news do you have of the swine?' Edward asked.

'What a coincidence that you ask,' Maginn said, and he thrust what he was writing at Edward, who read:

> Country maidens in their best bib and tucker shot coy glances at robust lads of brawny arm and sun-browned face as a brilliantly sunny day brought thousands to the midway of the Fair yesterday. Flirtations were numerous and many lords of creation succumbed before batteries of sparkling eyes.

'Splendid,' said Edward, 'but what about the swine?'

'They are the swine,' said Maginn.

Edward was twenty-six, dark-haired and tall, considered by women young and old to be the handsomest of men. Thomas

William Kennedy

Maginn, lanky and lean at twenty-eight, was considered a ragtail beanpole with an acid tongue. The two worked for rival Albany newspapers, Maginn on *The Journal*, Edward on *The Argus*, had known each other a year, but now, as working rivals on the Fair's midway – better than a circus, as all knew – they had tested each other's attitudes toward this instant city and were impressed with its two miles of stables, its racetrack, its complete farm, its vast Hall of Machinery with the latest thermostatic chicken incubators, potato diggers, sulky plows, and type-writers, the oyster pavilion, the temporary lockup/courtroom where troublemakers won swift justice, and the curiosities – the solid-silver razor, the huge pyramid of sacked salt, the embalmed dog in a casket.

'A confected metropolis,' Maginn had called the Fair, and Edward agreed that its rapid construction, and its appeal to both the elite and the crowd, reflected a creativity that could harmonize the wonders of existence with a flick of the mind. To such creation both young men aspired, seeing themselves as citizens of a world beyond newspapers. Edward had graduated with honors from Albany Academy and Columbia College. Maginn had been expelled from Columbia for drunkenness in his sophomore year, an autodidact ever since.

'Luckiest day of my life when they kicked me out,' he said. 'Unburdened forever of pedants and pederasts.'

One night after the Fair closed, Maginn cajoled Edward into joining him at the Freethinkers convention at the Leland Opera House in Albany for a lecture on 'The Aristocracy of Free Thought,' and they heard a man named Palmer aver that 'a true gentleman would always embrace the highest forms of culture and contribute most to the good of his fellowmen. And the true gentleman will maintain that woman's consent is as requisite as man's.'

'I don't know as that's necessary,' Maginn whispered.

'The best must rule,' Palmer declaimed. 'No man can prevail among the true elect if he remains imprisoned in the bastille of a dwarfing environment.'

Just such an environment, Maginn said, he and Edward inhabited

276

as Albany newsmen, but only temporarily. Edward was about to publish a novel, *The Mosquito Lovers* (about Irish convict laborers as expendable martyrs in the building of the Erie Canal, men who elected to risk a dig through malarial swampland rather than rot their souls in jail). Maginn regularly published reviews of fiction and belles lettres in the *Atlantic Monthly*, had just finished revaluing Melville's *The Confidence-Man* as an underrated work on human treachery, and was writing a novel.

This imminence of large-minded success convinced the young men they were vastly smarter than the run of Fairgoers, including their fellow reporters, and would soon inhabit a lofty perch in America's high culture. Maginn had shown Edward his Melville essay. Edward's response was 'Well written but perfunctory. It would improve if you didn't view your own opinions as unmatched in human thought.' Edward let Maginn read his novel in manuscript. Maginn found it 'seriously wanting as fiction, but you write such effective dialogue you should be a playwright.'

This critical honesty formed a bond of truth-telling between them, and their friendship deepened when they found they could talk to each other about anything at all.

As they strolled the trim rolling field that came down from the western rise of the valley, they eyed passing females and tried to recall all women they had ever desired. Maginn observed that a voluptuous woman was the greatest gift the universe offered to an imaginative man, a statement that seemed true to Edward; but the word 'voluptuous,' 'How do you define it, Maginn?'

'A woman who delights in her body and what a man does to it,' said Maginn. 'A woman who loves the encounter.'

'You mean a *loose* woman, then?'

'Not quite, but all women are loose at some time or other,' Maginn said.

'I disagree,' Edward said. 'The most voluptuous woman I've ever met I know in my soul isn't promiscuous, and is undoubtedly a virgin.'

'They become loose after they cease to be virgins.'

'You are very down on women.'

'Every chance I get,' said Maginn.

'I may marry a woman who doesn't conform to your view of promiscuous females.' Then, without wishing to, but in defense of his putative bride-to-be, he blurted out her name: 'Katrina Taylor.'

'Katrina Taylor! She said yes to you?'

'Not yet. I'm waiting for her answer.'

'You are one extraordinarily lucky son of a bitch if you snare her, my friend. She's a woman in a million. I met her last February skating on the canal, but I doubt she knows my name.'

'She may not have me,' Edward said.

'Ye gods! Katrina Taylor! Thinking about a woman like that must drive you mad. What do you do when the urge comes on you?'

'Which urge? I have many.'

'The only urge worth yielding to. It's on me now just talking about women, and I thought I'd yield over at the Pasture.'

'The Pasture?'

'You are benighted, Daugherty. You've been here a week and haven't heard of the *other* tent city? We must complete your education.'

As dusk enveloped the Fairgrounds and the Fair's seven gates closed for the night, the young men walked to the Bull's Head tavern, beyond the fenced pasture where six bulls rested beside a barn. They walked across the tavern's open meadow, where prizefights were staged, to four small tents standing in a clearing of the bordering woods. This was the Fair-spawned Night Village, where the Ladies of the Pasture sold bucolic love. The brothels downtown in Albany and across the river in Troy were servicing multitudes of visiting Fairgoers in quest of passion's two-bit nocturne; but the higher-paid Ladies of the Pasture opened for business at high noon and worked well past moonrise, catering to postmeridian libido, and to lust which lacked the time or inclination to quit the Fair's environs.

The night was brisk and Edward and Maginn both wore fedoras and three-button suits. A man sitting in front of one open tent lit by a kerosene lamp was accepting money from a tall, brawny farm boy. The boy paid, then bent himself into the tent and closed the flap behind him.

'You boys in the market?'

'We're shopping,' said Maginn.

'Anything in particular?'

'They should be pretty.'

'Hell, they're all pretty once you're in that tent. Just go say hello and see what you like. Last three tents. The first one's busy.'

'We'll take a look,' Maginn said.

As he and Edward walked to the farthest tent, Edward stopped and asked aloud, 'Why am I doing this?'

'What is it you're doing?'

'I don't know.'

'Then you're making a discovery,' Maginn said. 'Like Lewis and Clark charting the Northwest Territory, we're about to enter the heady hemisphere of love.'

'I'm already in love.'

'Love may look virginal, but also whorish. You have to differentiate the forms.'

'This will serve me well?'

'You will earn medals for your service.'

'Who awards the medals?'

'The whores of the world, by which I mean most of the human race.'

'You have a dark view of life, Maginn.'

'Dark, like French pussy,' Maginn said.

At the last tent Maginn raised the flap and they walked in on two young whores who looked about twenty, bundled in coats, sitting on chairs.

'Good evening, ladies, we came to say hello.'

'Is that all you came for?' asked the one with blond bangs and a crossed eye.

'We'd like to see what you're offering.'

The girls stood and took off their coats, showing matching bodies clad in chemisettes and black stockings.

'My name is Nellie,' said the girl with normal eyes, lowering her shoulder strap. She was dark-haired and chesty. 'We came to see the Fair,' she said.

'And have you seen it?'

'Not yet. We found this job, and when we get through at night the Fair is closed.'

'Well, we're glad *you're* not closed,' Maginn said. 'You look lovely from the anterior perspective, but may we now have your posterior revelation?'

'What's that?' the cross-eyed girl asked.

'He means our fannies,' Nellie said. The two turned their backs and bent from the waist.

'Very intriguing,' Maginn said. 'We'll be back.'

'Thank you kindly, girls,' Edward said.

'Don't mention it,' Nellie said, and she raised the front of her chemisette for Edward. Maginn pulled Edward by the arm outside and toward the next tent.

'She was nice,' Edward said.

'Not bad for starters,' Maginn said, 'but we shouldn't accept the first offer.'

'What if you like the offer?'

'You're fond of busty women.'

'I liked her style.'

'She lacks all style. What you like is subliterate quim.'

'Whatever you call it, it's worth some attention.'

'Take a squint here first,' Maginn said, and he opened the tent flap. A woman in her thirties, her long brown hair streaked with gray, smiled at her visitors. She was sitting on her cot, wrapped in a blanket, only her black stockings visible.

'You boys looking to get warm?'

'Maybe even hot,' Maginn said.

'That can happen,' the whore said, and she stood and spread her arms to open the blanket. 'Here's the stove.'

She had penetrating eyes that gave her face a smartness Edward liked. She wasn't as chesty as Nellie, but ample, and her symmetry raised the issue of sexual aesthetics in Edward's brain.

'I wish we had a camera,' he said.

'Camera ain't what you point at this,' the whore said.

'What should we point at it?' Maginn asked.

'You really asking me that question?'

'He's making a joke,' Edward said.

'I ain't here for jokes.'

'I apologize for him. How much do you charge?'

'Six bits, same as the others, unless I do more. You know what I mean?'

'I guess I do,' Edward said.

'I guess you don't, if you gotta guess about it.'

'What's your name?' Edward asked.

'Rose,' the whore said. 'And I got the pink petals to prove it.'

'I think I'll stay,' Edward said.

'There's another tent to check out,' Maginn said.

'You check it and give me a report. I'm with Rose.'

'That's my cute boy,' Rose said.

'All right, since you insist,' Maginn said. 'I'll meet you in the tavern in fifteen minutes.'

'Fifteen minutes?' said Edward. 'What if it's two hours?'

'You take two hours,' Rose said, 'you get your money back.' She unbuttoned Edward's suit coat.

'Don't wait for me past Tuesday,' Edward told Maginn.

Edward wondered at his own choice, decided he was behaving instinctually, without accessible logic, but knew his behavior was full of awe and pity and reverence and some bizarre desire yet to be understood. As Rose moved through her early performance Edward adjudged her a woman of imaginative display: skilled in revelation, exalted by self-communion, who yielded herself without haste. 'A gift of flint, nest of tinder' is how he would describe such a woman in one of his short stories. She moved Edward slowly into fervency.

'Tell Rose you like her and you're gonna take her.'

'I like Rose so much I'm taking her for a ride.'

'That's my cute boy.'

'This train is moving.'

'All aboard. Going home to your best girl.'
'Rose is my best girl.'
'Rose is the only girl you ever wanted.'
'Rose is there from the first day.'
'You couldn't go no place without Rose.'
'We're going to heaven, me and Rose.'
'This boy is so nice that Rose is in love.'
'I'm in love with Rose.'
'The cute boy's in love with an old whore.'
'Rose isn't old.'
'The cute boy's in love with an ugly old whore.'
'I'm in love with a beautiful whore named Rose.'
'The cute boy makes Rose happy.'
'Is Rose happy making love?'
'Rose is happy making money.'
'Which comes first, the money or the love?'
'They all come before Rose.'
'Gotta go, Rose.'
'Not yet, cute boy.'
'Rose is so nice it's nice, but I'm going away.'
'It's not two hours.'
'Two hours couldn't be better than now.'
'My cute boy.'
'Goodbye, Rose.'
'There goes the cute boy.'
'There goes Rose.'
'Cute boy is gone.'
'And Rose?'
'Rose is where she is.'

At the crowded bar in the Bull's Head tavern, Maginn greeted Edward with a triumphant smile.

'Two for the price of one,' he said. 'I went back to the first tent and opted for the bung-eyed bitch, but she was so lackadaisical I departed her corpus and threatened not to pay for such inertia. Her tenting twin – Nellie, wasn't it? – came to the rescue. Very vigorous, Nellie. Bicameral bawds. Unexpected dividend. How was Rose?'

'Splendid.'

'In what way?'

'In all ways.'

'You went all ways?'

'She was splendid. Let it go at that.'

'The details are important, Daugherty. As a reporter you should know that.'

'This place is too noisy,' Edward said. The bar was two deep with drinkers, fogged with cigar and pipe smoke, and in a corner a fight seemed about to happen. 'Let's go someplace quiet. I'm hungry.'

'Venereal delight stokes the appetite.'

They took the West Shore train from the Fairgrounds to downtown Albany, and at Edward's insistence walked up from the station to the Kenmore for dinner.

'I can't afford their prices,' Maginn said. 'I'm not yet part of the plutocracy, like some of my friends.'

'It's good that I am,' Edward said. 'I'll buy dinner.'

'Done,' said Maginn. 'A plutocratic gesture if there ever was one.'

In addition to wages from *The Argus*, Edward had an annuity from birth given to him by Lyman Fitzgibbon that would keep him from starving until he reached age thirty, four years hence, and this allowed him to keep rooms on Columbia Street, close to the newspaper and just up from the Kenmore, where, unlike Maginn, he dined often.

He went to the men's washroom and soaped off the residue of Rose's body from his hands and his privates. Then he went back upstairs and with Maginn sat in the tan leather chairs of the hotel's lobby lounge while they waited for a table. Maginn bought a cigar at the newsstand, bit off the end and spat it into the brass cuspidor, then lit the cigar with a match he struck on the sole of Edward's shoe.

Edward saw Katrina entering with her parents through the

hotel's side door on Columbia Street, avoiding the lobby and the vulgar stares of the loungers. The three went directly to the dining room – reserved table, of course.

'Isn't that the magnificent woman you proposed to?' Maginn asked.

'That is she. With Mama and Papa.'

'Her beauty is exhilarating.'

'I agree.'

'I wonder how she compares with Rose.'

'Wonder to yourself,' Edward said.

'Protective already,' said Maginn. 'I can see the transformation. "Once the favorite of whores of all ages, Edward Daugherty has evolved into the perfect husband."'

Edward perceived that Maginn, the gangling whoremonger, was miffed that women in both tents had given their preferred eye to Edward; and he would, in a later year, remember this day as the beginning of his relationship to Maginn's envy and self-esteem, the beginning of competitive lives, even to evaluating the predilections of whores ('They picked you because you picked them, no trick to that'). It would be Maginn's oft-repeated credo that 'the only thing that can improve on a lovely whore is another lovely whore.' Edward's unspoken credo toward Katrina-as-bride-to-be was: 'If she becomes my wife, then my wife is my life.'

The Kenmore's maître d', a light-skinned Negro, came toward them. 'Your table is ready, Mr Daugherty,' he said.

'Very good, Walter.'

He led them to a table next to Katrina and her parents. But Edward asked for one at the far end of the crowded dining room, Albany's largest, where Parlatti's orchestra was playing a medley from Gilbert and Sullivan's *The Mikado*, all the rage.

'I'd like to meet your bride formally,' Maginn said. 'Will you introduce me?'

'Another time. And she's not yet my bride.'

They walked past the Taylors without a glance. After they'd been seated beside a thicket of potted palms, Edward walked back and greeted Katrina, Geraldine, and Jacob Taylor. He stared at

Katrina, her golden hair swept into an almost luminous soft corona, and was about to bend and kiss her hand; but then he thought of his mouth on Rose's body, and only bent and nodded and smiled his love toward her.

'Your friend Giles Fitzroy won two gold medals today at the Fair, for his saddle horses,' Edward said to her.

'The Fitzroys do breed champions,' Jacob Taylor said.

'I've been reading what you write about the Fair,' Katrina said. 'You make it so exciting. I want to see it.'

The sound of her voice, the cadence of her speech, seemed musical to Edward, a fragment of a Mozart aria. Everything about her had the aura of perfection. He knew his perception must be awry, and he thought he should try to find flaws in the woman. But to what end? Is it so wrong to embrace perfection? Am I a dunce to believe in it?

'Come tomorrow,' he said. 'I'll give you an insider's tour. You come with her, Geraldine; you, too, Jake.'

'I think not,' Geraldine Taylor said. 'I'm told it's overrun with a vulgar crowd.'

'There are some of those,' Edward said, and he understood that Geraldine could accept no generosity, not even a meaningless invitation, if it came from beneath her station.

'People like the Fitzroys and the Parkers and the Cornings are exhibitors,' Edward said, 'and they're frequently around. I'll stop by in the morning, Katrina, and see what you decide.' He nodded farewell and went back to Maginn, who was buttering a biscuit as a waiter poured his wine.

'I sit here and look at these good burghers with their gold watch chains dangling over their pus bellies,' Maginn said, 'and I all but drown in my loathing.'

'That's juvenile,' said Edward. 'They're only people who've found a way to make some money.'

'Come on now, Edward. They're another breed. With them and us it's like thoroughbreds and swine. Those mosquito-loving Irish canal diggers in your novel are sewer rats to them. But I loathe them just as much as they loathe me. Is there *one of them* in this dining room who'd invite you home if they knew you drink in a saloon that has an encampment of whores in the backyard? Or me – if they found out my old man salvages hides and bones of dead horses and sells their flesh to pig farmers?'

'I would,' said Edward.

'You're a rare specimen,' said Maginn, 'and I drink to whatever makes you say that.' He sipped his wine, put down the glass. 'But then you still tote the baggage of the sentimental mick, offering alms to forlorn souls. You're really not that long out of the bog yourself, are you?'

'Long enough that I'm at home in this room, no matter what company I keep.'

'Touché. Yet you wouldn't introduce me to Katrina. Too obvious a bogtrotter, is that my problem?'

'It's a family situation. Let's move on to something else, shall we?'

Edward imagined Maginn unloosing his gutter candor in the presence of Katrina and her parents, and he winced. Just what Geraldine expects from the Irish. Maginn, you're great company, and you own a fine mind, but you are a problem.

'You keep complaining about your editor at *The Journal*,' Edward said. 'How do yo get along with him?'

'Like a tree gets along with a dog.'

'If you're interested, I'll put in a word at *The Argus*. I know my editor would like to have your lively style in our pages. He's said as much.'

'My present editor loathes my lively style.'

'There's a lot of loathing in your life, Maginn.'

'You connect me at *The Argus*, my loathing will dissipate like warm sunshine lifting fog off a bog.'

'I'll do what I can.'

'You're a princely fellow, Daugherty, a princely fellow, for a mick. I'll buy the wine.'

Edward Rediscovers Katrina

November 1884

Edward had entered Katrina's world at the adolescent moment when he registered at Albany Academy to begin the education Lyman Fitzgibbon, Geraldine Taylor's father, had ordained for him. Edward's father, Emmett Daugherty, came to this country from County Galway in 1836 at age fourteen, and at eighteen hired on as coachman for Lyman's Adirondack expedition, an extended trip to acquire land for the railroad, lumbering, and mining interests that were central to Lyman's bountiful life. The expedition encountered hostility in a remote Warren County hamlet that was so new it lacked a name. Lyman and his lawyer were taken captive by townsmen, who foresaw accurately that these interlopers were about to change life as they knew it; and they prepared tar and feathers for them. Young Emmett Daugherty, as truculent as the next man when called upon, picked up a fallen tree branch and felled the townsmen's ringleader, then garroted him with a horsewhip and, by legend, told the man's cronies, 'Turn those men loose or I twist the tongue out of his head,' the tongue already halfway out.

That was July 1840, and Lyman vowed Emmett would never want for anything again, and that his children would have the best education available.

Edward was born to Emmett and Hanorah Sweeney on Main Street in the North End in 1859, went to the North End public school for five years, then three years to the Christian Brothers boys' school on Colonie Street in Arbor Hill, Emmett insisting that Edward first discover the workingman's God before going off to study among pagans and Protestants.

Lyman Fitzgibbon was London-born (1805), Oxford-educated, a translator of Tacitus' *Germania*, wealthy early in life, a British diplomat at midlife, and, as British consul in France, rescuer of Louis-Philippe in the revolution of 1848. For his inventions relating to metalworking machinery he was called 'the merchant-scientist' and, along with his stove-making foundry and investments, he became not only Albany's richest man, but its most variously eminent. He was also Edward's godfather.

Through the benediction of this eminence, Edward, when he enrolled in the Academy, entered the elite circle of Albany's social life, became close friends with boys whose fathers ran the city, was invited to dances with debutantes, sleigh rides and tobogganing expeditions out to the Albany County Club, and dinners at the Fort Orange Club as Lyman's guest. On such occasions he came to know the young Katrina Taylor, Lyman's granddaughter, but she was six years his junior, a child. They grew up as friendly 'common-law cousins,' as he called their relationship. They were separated by Edward's years at Columbia College, when he lived in New York City, and later by his western trip to research the lives of the Irish workers who had built the Erie, men whose achievement his father had invoked often, and about whom Edward was writing his first novel. And so it was not until the night the Democrats marched in the vast torchlight parade celebrating Cleveland's defeat of Blaine in the presidential election that Edward encountered the maturing Katrina.

The city was explosive with lights, bonfires, fireworks, and parties to hail the new chief of state from Albany, and a line of thousands of marchers, their oil-lit torches creating a dancing serpent of lights, moved past more thousands of cheering spectators in a triumphal procession up State Street's steep incline. Edward watched from the stoop of Lyman's home, an august four-and-a-half-story brownstone facing on State Street and, like other homes on this night, festooned with Chinese lanterns. More lanterns bloomed like bizarre forms of fruit on Lyman's trees, and buildings across the street displayed the American and Irish flags, and huge images of Grover Cleveland.

In the crowd on the sidewalk a woman caught Edward's eye when she opened a yellow parasol and held it aloft over her yellow bonnet as the parade approached. The band played and the marchers yelled in left-right cadence: 'Blaine, Blaine, James G. Blaine, the continental liar from the state of Maine,' and Edward recognized the woman with the yellow bonnet as Katrina. He went down the stoop and stood behind her and patted her shoulder. When she turned to him he saw a Katrina (she was 'Katch' to him as a child) he'd never known.

'My God, how lovely you look, Katch,' he said. 'What have you done to yourself? You're positively beautiful.'

'I suppose I've grown up. But so have you. You look very much a man of the world, Edward.'

'And so I like to think that I am. But even as a man of the world I don't understand why you open your parasol when it is neither sunny nor raining.'

'It well might rain oil on my new bonnet from those dreadful torches. And I would not like that at all.'

The marchers broke into a new chant: 'Ma, Ma, where's my Pa?' a Blaine campaign slogan about Cleveland's bastard son. But the electorate shrugged off this scandal, and the marchers now voiced the new, answering gibe: 'Gone to the White House, ha, ha, ha!'

'That is so funny, and so just,' Katrina said.

'Didn't his fathering a child out of wedlock scandalize you?'

'He never denied the boy, and he took care of him. He's a courageous man, Mr Cleveland.'

'You have a modern outlook on the matter, for a woman.'

'I am a modern woman.'

'So you say. And so you may be.'

Katrina spotted Giles Fitzroy riding with a dozen men from the Jacksonians. She called his name and waved to him.

'It's Giles,' she said. 'He's riding Phantom Guest. What a beautiful horse. This is all so wonderful. We really, really won. It's staggering, isn't it?'

'Cleveland owes his election to me, did you know that?'

'No, you must tell me. Did you vote a thousand times?'

'Not quite. Are you going to Lyman's party?'

'Of course.'

'Then I'll tell you there.'

They watched the paraders: all the Democratic clubs, many carrying brooms for a clean sweep, and the Irish-American Association (with which Emmett Daugherty marched), and the German Democratic Business Men, the Dry Goods Cleveland Club stepping to the rhythms of the Tenth Infantry Band, and the Flynn Fife and Drum Corps, and so many more, moving up to Capitol Park, where the President-elect waved down from his executive chamber.

When all paraders had passed, Edward and Katrina went into Lyman's house, where bustling servants were setting out punch bowls and placing vases of flowers on tables and mantels.

'We're early,' Edward said, and he greeted the servants and steered Katrina by the arm into the conservatory. She sat on a bench with her parasol in her lap, and Edward looked long at her and studied the phenomenal change in her face, the way she combed her hair, the way she held herself with such poise, such an air of certainty about who and what she was.

'You are dazzling tonight, Katch,' he said. 'How old are you now?'

'I'm about to be nineteen, thank you.'

'Is anybody paying court to your radiant self?'

'I have my admirers.'

'Permit me to join their number. Where have I been?'

'You should control yourself and tell me how you elected the President.'

He leaned on the back of her bench and put his eyes in line with hers. Looking at her face silenced him.

'Well?' she said.

'Yes, the election. I'd much rather look at you. I went to a dinner party at the Fort Orange Club to meet the Governor, and Lyman introduced me as "the talented son of a fine Irishman whose vote you need." Mr Cleveland agreed the Irish vote was important and asked who my father might be.

'"Emmett Daugherty, foreman at Lyman's foundry," I told him, "but I doubt he'll vote for you, Governor. He's very angry with all politicians, and so is the whole North End. Father Loonan, the pastor of Sacred Heart church, talks of it every Sunday from the pulpit, and a North End saloonkeeper with a keen political eye says his customers are talking Blaine. North Enders are Democrats, but this year it's up for grabs."

'"Why are they so angry with me?" the Governor asked me.

'"You, the Mayor, the aldermen, everybody who forces them to live in mud," I said. "Anybody who hasn't delivered any pavement to North Albany's streets or sidewalks. It's an old, old promise nobody's ever kept. They see Elk Street, where your wealthy friends live, being paved with granite blocks, while they're still riding on rotting planks in a sea of mud. After a rain they have to put bog shoes on their horses to get home. And they blame you."

'"Do you know Father Loonan?" says the Governor.

'"I do," says I.

'"Bring him and this saloonkeeper – what's his name?"

'"Jack McCall. Black Jack, they call him."

'"Bring Black Jack and the good father up to see me. We'll have a chat."

'"I'll do that tomorrow," says I.

'"Do you know anybody else who doesn't like me?" the Governor says.

'"Aren't the North End Irish enough?" says I.

'I had no trouble convincing Jack and Father Loonan to visit the Governor. He saw us straightaway and had Mayor Banks in the office with him. They listened to the complaints about mud and the Governor asked the Mayor could he get the contractor paving Elk Street to start on Broadway in North Albany? The Mayor said the city had let no contract to pave Broadway.

'"Well, *let* one," said the Governor. "We'll get you reimbursed.

But get the crews out there tomorrow." And the Mayor said he'd get on it.

'The Governor thanked me for my enterprise; then he and Black Jack got off on fishing and it was as if they'd known each other forever. "We'll have to go to the mountains one day and get some trout," the Governor said, and on the way out Father Loonan told me I ought to run for governor when Cleveland leaves. I said I couldn't, that I was a writer.

'The next day, workers put granite blocks on Broadway, starting in front of Sacred Heart church. We had a rally five nights later and five hundred heard Jack's speech. They marched and chanted against Blaine, the highway robber from the state of Maine. It was the biggest political turnout in neighborhood history. And Blaine's support went the way of North Albany mud.

'Cleveland carried the state by one thousand one hundred and forty-nine votes,' Edward said. 'Only five hundred and seventy-five votes would have reversed those results, and the Democratic plurality in North Albany was six hundred and seventy-seven.'

'Why, you're a miracle worker,' Katrina said.

'I'm glad you understand that about me,' Edward said.

People were arriving from the parade, and Lyman's valet was helping him down the stairs to the parlor to greet them.

'He looks so frail lately,' Katrina said.

'Only his body. His mind is very astute.'

'He's terribly fond of you,' Katrina said.

'He's like a second father,' Edward said. 'And he's crazy about you. But right this minute I'm crazier about you than he is.'

'You are turning this girl's head, sir.'

'I mean to do nothing else, as soon as I'm able. I have obligations for a month or two.'

'I'm abandoned before I'm courted.'

'You will not be abandoned. I intend to pursue you with a fervid Irish passion, unlike anything you've ever imagined. But I must finish what I've begun.'

'And what is it you've begun?'

292

'A novel I've been writing for more than a year, the key to my new life. One key. You are the other.'

'You've become an impetuous man, Edward.'

'I am a man instantly in love. Do you mind if I love you?'

'I have never been so flattered, or so quickly.'

'I have just begun to flatter you. I have just begun to worship you.'

Edward Begins a Serious Dialogue with Katrina, While Dancing

September 1885

In the months that followed his rediscovery of Katrina, Edward took a leave from *The Argus* and devoted his days to the final research and writing of his Erie Canal novel. He finished by late summer 1885, and began, with great earnestness, a campaign to have himself invited to all social events he knew Katrina would attend. Katrina's mother noted this.

'That man is a pest,' Geraldine said.

'He's a perfect gentleman, and very intelligent,' Katrina said. 'I'm always happy to see him.'

'I don't care how intelligent he is, he's not the right sort for you,' her mother said.

September's major social event was the ball for the coming-out of Felicity Grenville, held in Bleecker Hall on Maiden Lane. Edward found Katrina besieged by suitors and only at the cotillion did he discover she had saved a place for him on her dance card. As soon as they were arm in arm in the dance he said to her, 'I've decided. Yes, I've made the decision.'

'Oh? And what did you decide?'

'To ask you to marry me.'

'I believe I knew that.'

'Wasn't that presumptuous of you?'

'I'm a student of love, Edward, and you seem to be a proper subject for my scrutiny.'

'You considered my proposal even before you heard it.'

'I wouldn't have dared.'

'But in your scrutiny you had passing thoughts. Is your answer yes?'

'No.'

'Is it no?'

'I don't think so.'

'Not a very satisfactory response.'

'You have no right to an instant answer to that question.'

'But you expected the question.'

'Yes, but I must confirm the reality.'

'How do you do that?'

'By testing myself. For instance, how do I know if I should marry you when I haven't even kissed you?'

'I could rectify that immediately. Here and now.'

'It would cause a scandal. "Woe be to him who gives scandal to my brethren."'

'Upstairs, then? Downstairs? Outside?'

'If it happens, I don't want even the birds to see.'

'I'll find a secret place where we can be alone.'

'I'll find it when the time is right,' Katrina said.

Edward and the Bean Soup

September 25, 1885

Edward walked the three miles up Broadway from *The Argus* to Black Jack's saloon, marking the trail through the North End with whatever psychic spoor it is that would-be bridegrooms create when they make plans to abandon home territory. He came to where the pavement used to abruptly end: at the carriageway into the pasture of the Patroon's Manor House (where his mother had worked as a cook for the last Patroon's widow). The Manor House was the northern boundary of civilization as Albany's roadbuilders judged it, and after it you entered the wild Irish neighborhood where Edward was raised, and for which plank roads and mud had sufficed.

Now new granite pavement continued past the Manor entrance, past the gasworks. And where the moulders and lumber handlers of the North End had built their houses, slate sidewalks covered the old dirt paths. It pleased Edward to have been partially responsible for this, though the public heroes of upgraded life were Father Loonan and especially Jack McCall, who, in return for staging the rally that reversed the voting slide toward Blaine, had been named Democratic Leader of the Ninth Ward.

Jack had been born into saloon life. His father, Butter McCall, ran the Bull's Head tavern on the Troy Road until his liver stiffened, whereupon he sold the place, outraging Jack, who considered the Bull's Head his future; so Jack then opened his own saloon on Broadway, now headquarters for anyone seeking favor with the Democratic party.

296

'Short one,' Edward said to Jack, who was talking to Maginn. Jack, behind the bar in white apron and collarless white shirt, was a formidable presence, thick head of hair, Roman nose, cleanshaven, and muscular from hefting beer barrels, first at the Bull's Head, then for the Quinn and Nolan brewery. The time now in Black Jack's saloon was the lull before the invasion at six when the lumber mills' whistles would blow the twelve-hour workday into oblivion, and those handlers with money to quaff would move single-mindedly into liquid pleasure. The remains of the bean soup simmered in the pot on the woodstove behind the bar, half emptied by the lunch crowd; the ham was getting down to the bone; the bread growing stale; but soup, ham, and bread would all be eaten by six-thirty, and the hell with food after that hour, was Jack's dictum.

Edward, when marriage became a possibility, had thought of Jack for his best man, and his visit here today was to tell Jack of his proposal to Katrina, and the resistance he was meeting from her parents. Finding Maginn here was a surprise. Maginn, now reporting for *The Argus*, was at the end of the bar behind his new mustache, his suit hanging loosely on his lanky frame. He was talking to Jack, pumping him about the invitation he'd received from his newfound friend, the President of the United States, to go fishing. The election poster for Cleveland and Hendricks dominated the wall of the back bar.

'He telling his White House fish story?' Edward asked.

'He's telling about the letter,' Maginn said.

'He wants the mountains,' Jack said. 'Trout he wants. "Pick any place in the Adirondacks," he tells me.'

'And what did you pick?'

'North Creek. They got trout up there big as dogs. They jump out of the water to shake hands.'

'That'll be some circus, fishing with the President,' Edward said.

'No it won't,' said Jack. 'We won't tell anybody where we're gonna light. He don't want a circus, he wants to fish.'

'I know how important the President is,' Maginn said, 'but did you hear this young lad here may soon be stretched on the holy rack of matrimony.'

'No,' said Jack. 'Is that true?'

'It could be true,' Edward said. 'But there are things to be done.'

'Buy the bed and spread the sheets, he means,' said Maginn. 'He's marrying up. Beautiful, smart, and rich. Altogether too much for him.'

'Too much for me, but just enough for Maginn, if he could only get his hands on her.'

'Who is she? Not Ruthie.'

'No, not Ruthie,' Edward said.

'Does Ruthie know?'

'No. It's Jake Taylor's daughter Katrina. I proposed. She hasn't said yes yet.'

'Jake Taylor? That royal son of a bitch. What's Emmett say to that?'

'He doesn't know about it either, but he won't relish it.'

'He wouldn't, after Davy.'

'Davy?' said Maginn.

'My father's brother,' Edward said. 'Jake's goons beat him so bad when he tried to organize the lumber handlers, all he can do now is shovel sawdust.'

Edward and Jack had courted the same girls (Ruthie was the last), fished, hunted birds, and played baseball together, lived in houses back-to-back, went to school together, and grew apart only when Edward left the Christian Brothers school and moved into Lyman's home downtown to be closer to Albany Academy.

'Jake's family's Protestant,' Jack said.

'Very true,' said Edward. Jack's look judged him a traitor.

'Where's the wedding gonna be at?'

'I haven't even talked to her parents yet.'

'You worry about them?'

'She does.'

'There's no problem,' Maginn said. 'Why should a mudhole mick from the North End have any problem marrying into one of Albany's first families?'

'Who's a mudhole mick?'

298

The voice came from a table where two men had been eaves-dropping on the presidential talk. The bigger of the two came over to Maginn. He wore a sweater and a cap, had the slouch of a man whose back had lifted too much weight, and his drooping right eye gave him a permanent squint. Edward knew him as Matty Lookup, a lumber handler and ice cutter on hard times, suspected of breaking into Benedict's lumber office in the District and stealing four rubber coats and pieces of harness; and so no one would hire him now. He had come by his name when he chased somebody into Tommy Mullon's icehouse on Erie Street and lost him, but three boys in the icehouse loft called out, 'Look up, Matty, look up,' and when he did they dumped a bag of horseshit on him.

'Who's a mudhole mick?' Matty Lookup said a second time.

'I don't remember,' Maginn said.

'He's making a joke,' Edward said. Always explaining Maginn's jokes.

'You calling me a mudhole mick?'

'I don't even know you,' Maginn said. 'Why would I call you anything?'

'You don't like the Irish?'

'I am Irish.'

'You look like a goddamn Dutchman.'

'I don't have enough money to be Dutch.'

'You talk like you don't like the Irish.'

'Why don't you go find a mudhole that'll accept you, and lay down and take a bath,' Maginn said.

Matty Lookup grabbed Maginn's throat with both hands, lifted him off his stool, then off the floor, and swung him around like the ball of a hammer. While Maginn the splinter flailed helplessly with his fists (like pummeling a sack of grain), Jack came around the bar to pull the two apart but was staggered by Matty Lookup's backhanded wallop. Matty was pinning Maginn to a tabletop, positioning himself to bite off Maginn's right ear, when Edward vaulted the bar, lifted the cauldron of bean soup off Jack's stove with both hands, and moved with it toward the unequal struggle. He yelled in his most urgent vibrato, 'Look up, Matty! Look up!'

and, as Matty's teeth parted to release Maginn's ear and his glance turned predictably toward those mocking words, Edward hurled the boiling soup into his face; and Matty knew agony. He rolled off the table onto the sawdust of Black Jack's floor, screeching the song of the scalded beast. Edward stood over him, the pot raised above his head with both hands, ready to break the brute's skull if his belligerence revived. Matty wailed in pain and Edward lowered the pot. Jack, a short club in his right hand now, nudged Matty with his foot.

'Get out you crazy son of a bitch, get out,' Jack told him. 'Come in again, you'll get worse.'

Matty Lookup, whimpering out of his ruined flesh, stood up and shuffled his crumpled form out the door.

'How's your ear?' Edward asked Maginn, who, with a handkerchief, was blotting the blood that oozed from his lightly chewed ear. 'Did he eat much of it?'

'Don't worry about it,' Maginn said. 'I've got his nose in my pocket.'

'You hurt any place?' Jack asked him. 'I thought you were all done.'

'I would've been, except for our nimble novelist here. Quick thinking, old man. I myself might've reached for a bottle to club him with, but I'd've never gone for the soup. A genteel weapon. Your prospective in-laws would doubtless approve the choice.'

Don't say anything, Maginn.

Jack tapped Edward's arm with his club.

'Good, Eddie,' he said. 'You did good.' Then he went behind the bar to get the mop.

The whistle blew in the Lumber District. Six o'clock. The men would be pouring in, any minute. Edward now hated this saloon, hated Matty Lookup, Matty Beansoup, Matty Noface, hated his own savage response to the oaf. What was served by your attack and your sacrifice, Matty? What rubric of resistance did I serve with the soup? He held the empty pot in his hand. He looked at it: foot and a half deep, blue enamel, chipped rim, charred bottom, implement of retribution. He looked up and saw Maginn staring at him and smiling, blotting soup from his coat. Jack came with the pail and mop and went to work on the beans.

Edward could not now ask Jack to be his best man. A great fellow, Jack. A generous man if ever there was one, and now he's got Ruthie all to himself. But he doesn't approve of Katrina. Everybody's generosity ends somewhere.

Maginn was still smiling.

'Shut up, Maginn,' Edward said.

Edward Delivers a Manifesto

September 27, 1885

Edward mounted the stoop of Katrina's home on Elk Street, a quiet shaded thoroughfare on Capitol Hill that because of its monied residents was known as Quality Row. This was his first visit to this house since his proposal to Katrina. He'd seen her often, exchanged letters with her daily, but was *persona non grata* until her insistence wore down her parents. She had written Edward this morning that her determination had triumphed, that they would talk to him about the future; and so now, at afternoon, when he rang the pullbell of the Taylors' Gothic Revival town house, Fletcher, the family butler these ten years, opened the door to him. As Edward entered the foyer, Fletcher took his hat, put it on the hall hat rack.

'Miss Katrina will meet you in the library, Mr Daugherty.'

'Thank you, Fletcher. How goes the horseshoe season?'

Fletcher, a precise and florid man of some wit, and with a day laborer's constitution, was horseshoe champion of Elk Street servants. A summer-long competition ran in the court alongside the Taylor stables, and Edward, being of neither master nor servant class, occasionally joined the games.

'Somewhat predictably, sir,' Fletcher said.

'You mean you're ahead.'

'Yes, sir, I do mean that.'

'I almost beat you last time,' Edward said.

'You did, indeed. But, alas, you did not.'

'My turn will come, Fletcher.'

'It's always good to believe that, Mr Daugherty.'

Fletcher led him to the empty library and lighted the gas in the six globes of the chandelier. The library was part sitting room with tea table and cane-bottomed straight-backed chairs, walnut bookcases with glass doors and perhaps two hundred books, blue velvet drapes on the windows, and Jacob Taylor's orderly walnut desk, with two leather armchairs facing it. Edward sat in one of these chairs, staring at the books. He waited, listened to the silence of the vast house, stood and searched for two particular books he'd read when he came here with Lyman years ago. He scanned the English and Dutch history books, such a burden when he first opened them, and now they weighed on him again: all that confirmation of ancestry. But where are the books of *my* lineage, *my* ancient history? My history has not yet been written.

He found books on Albany's Dutch origins, volumes in the Dutch language, studies of the first Dutch and Episcopal churches of seventeenth-century Albany, lives of the Van Rensselaers, Albany's founding family and its dynasty of patroons, lives of the Staatses, Jacob's family, and shelves of Shakespeare, Dickens, Thackeray (which Katrina read avidly before she was allowed to have them), Washington's memoirs, *The Federalist Papers*, and books on the English in Ireland, yes: what Edward was seeking.

He took two volumes from the shelf and sat and skimmed them: 'The Irish are abominable, false, cunning and perfidious people . . . The worst means of governing them is to give them their own way. In concession they see only fear, and those that fear them they hate and despise. Coercion succeeds better . . . they respect a master hand, though it be a hard and cruel one . . . Cromwell alone understood this . . .'

The same Cromwell, Lord Lieutenant of Ireland, writing of his 1649 attack on Drogheda: '. . . the enemy were about 3,000 strong in the town . . . I believe we put to the sword the whole number . . . I forbade them to spare any that were in arms in the Town . . . about 200 of them possessed St Peter's Church-steeple . . . I ordered the steeple . . . to be fired, when one of them was heard to say in the midst of the flames: "God damn me, God confound me; I burn, I burn." . . . I wish that all honest hearts may give the glory of this to God alone . . .'

And then to Wexford to slaughter 2,000 more: 'I thought it not right or good to restrain off the soldiers from their right of pillage, or from doing execution on the enemy.'

And Sir William Petty's estimates: that the war reduced Ireland's population from one million, four hundred and sixty-six thousand in 1641 to six hundred and sixteen thousand in 1652, much more than half exterminated; and three-fourths of Irish land and five-sixths of Irish houses taken over by British settlers; and, twenty years after Cromwell, three-fourths of the Irish population existing on milk and potatoes, living in cabins without chimney, door, stairs, or window.

Wrote Gookin: 'They were strong, they are weak; they were numerous, they are consumed by sword, pestilence and famine; they were hearty, they are out of courage; they were rich, they are poor and beggarly; they had soldiers, they are left naked; they had cities, they have but cottages.'

'So,' Petty concluded on Cromwell's achievement, 'they will never rebel again.'

Cromwell: Lyman's presumed ancestor. Geraldine's. Katrina's. And here you are, Edward, seeking the hand of a woman bred of Cromwellian dust, you, whose father, by memory passed on, traces your lineage back to Connacht then and now.

Katrina entered the library and came to him, reached out her hand and stared into his eyes.

'I'm pleased you're here at last,' she said. 'Mother and Father will meet you alone, and I'll come back when your conversation is over. I love how strong your face looks today.'

'I hope it's strong enough,' Edward said. 'Will you be able to hear what is said?'

'Oh yes, I shall,' she said.

He watched her vanish beyond the doorway, stood with book in hand conjuring his own seventeenth-century forebears: more than two centuries gone since the ancestral Daughertys' lands were taken in Donegal, the clan reduced to lowly cottiers tilling the land of others; some of them turning into the plundering rapparees who preferred the pike to the hoe; but, in time, all of them thrust into the barrens of western Connacht like flung dogs.

Whether my people were marked because they had slaughtered English landholders in the bloody rebellion of 1641, or were unslaughtered remnants-in-arms after Cromwell's 1649 conquest, it matters not, for they go into exile by Cromwellian fiat – the transplanting, he called it – to the far western part of Ireland's most desolate province, without houses, adequate clothing, cattle, or farm implements, prohibited from living within five miles of the River Shannon or the sea. Women and children perished in ditches, dead of starvation or eaten by wolves. In their desolation the Irish fed upon dead bodies dug from graves, the survivors condemned to till the earth of Connacht's hellish landscape and discover its essence: ubiquitous rock.

How goes the family lineage?

It hardens.

And how grows the rock's foetus?

With neither tongue, nor brain, nor soul: doomed creature mutilated in the womb, conceived with one foot, webbed arm, vertical eyes, a row of teeth in its belly, suitable for frightening devils, born on a rock so wide the people of Connacht made it the altar of Jesus, worshiped it in Gaelic prayer, lived off its might, starving as they prayed, their priests axed or hanged, their young men and maidens sent to slavery in the Tobacco Islands where they toiled at a level below the Negro bondsmen; the leftover faithful withering by the tens of thousands, living amid a world of rock fences, those man-high sculptures that ride the contours of hills and valleys still, lace-made to foil the wind, an endless, timeless memorializing of rock in order to live free of it: fences visible for miles, miles, and miles beyond that, each rock a gravestone, each fence testament to the ingenuity of survival: leaving, where the rocks were liftable out of the earth, scrubby patches of soil for planting.

The lineage leads from Connacht's fences forward to famine, when even potatoes die, then into modern exile on Connacht Block in Albany, raucous overcrowded neighborhood at Madison Avenue and Quay Street, where greenhorns cluster till they find footing, send money away for others to quit the rock, then move uptown, to the North End like the Daugherty brothers, Owen and Davy first, then Emmett, or they rise like you, Edward Daugherty, to heights where you can court the modern get of an ancient devil.

I am demonizing my love, Edward thought, to make her the equal of what her parents think I am.

He returned the Irish books to their shelves, and he waited. Fletcher brought sherry and three glasses. Edward stared at it: Waterford crystal, brought here by Lyman.

'The Master thought you might like a bit of sherry,' said Fletcher, setting one glass apart.

'They *are* going to see me,' Edward said.

'They will be along presently,' said Fletcher, nodding.

'I've already read all the books.'

'You are accomplished at many things, Mr Daugherty.' And Fletcher left the room.

Edward knew what Jacob and Geraldine would say to him, had long absorbed their hostility in the foreshortened glance, the abrupt tone, the bristling at his closeness to Lyman: for that closeness differed in kind from Lyman's behavior toward his children. It was Lyman's duty as an unmurdered man to see that Edward escaped what fate had ordained at birth for his kind. Edward *was* transformed, and Lyman lived to know his godson had grown and flourished, would even publish a novel, though Lyman would not live to hold it in his hand. But what Edward's transformation would win him remains to be seen. Now here he sits, waiting to be judged, and he feels his brain on fire with ancient yearnings for justice and comprehension.

But I will not kiss their foot.

Well enough. Do you know what they'll say to you?

They'll say the disparity between families and religions will cause friction among friends and relatives, be a curse on the marriage. They will never mention the Irish or that they see us as a race of beasts.

They will imply, with exquisite finesse, that you are of lowly financial status, that Katrina stands to inherit great wealth, and that this wealth has given her her life as she knows it. You, a writer, could you, in a lifetime, ever earn enough to preserve her birthright? Not likely.

They will praise you as a cultured man and wish you well in your literary pursuits, but they will continue to believe Katrina's attentions should be from a suitor of an established profession. You, Edward, being no such thing, stand as a living impediment to a harmonious marriage, in Katrina's mind if not in your own.

He poured himself a sherry, bolted it. It tasted like the Irish Sea.

He leaned back in the leather chair, considered his position, moved a straight chair to a point where it would face the two leather chairs. He sat in the straight chair and leaned forward – no, too close – moved the chair back a foot, poured another sherry, bolted it.

They came in together, Geraldine still growing wide with age, wearing a long black dress that covered her from throat to toe and could have passed for a mourning vestment (anticipating the death-like eventuation of losing Katrina to this man?). Jacob came in with his high white collar and his unruly graying hair, and Edward stood to greet them, blocking Jacob's access to his desk chair.

'You have something to tell us?' Jacob asked.

'I do,' Edward said.

The Taylors made no move to sit down.

'Jake, Geraldine, please sit,' Edward said. 'I have a few things to say, no sense standing.'

Geraldine sat in one of the leather armchairs, and Jacob, not taking his eye off Edward, sat warily beside her. Edward reseated himself on the hardback, facing his captive audience.

'I'm here,' he said, 'to say directly to you that I've asked Katrina repeatedly to marry me, and she has not said no, but neither has she said yes. I know she's indecisive because you have questions and uncertainties about such a marriage, and about me, which is natural.'

Jacob moved as if to speak, but Edward pressed on.

'I don't want to trouble either of you to speak of this now. I want only to reveal to you who I am, for even though you think you know me, you truly do not.

'I begin with this room, where the worlds of your family and mine exist side by side on your bookshelves: Dickens and Thackeray, giants in the world I aspire to, alongside chronicles of your exalted ancestral civilization. I'll live my life writing, books now, perhaps plays in the future, a noble profession, playwriting, as you know from Shakespeare on your shelves.

'I'm sure you've heard what the gossips say about Katrina and me, that I'm aiming above my station. I don't answer such gossip and Katrina admires me for it. After all, who's to say what my station is? Am I fresh from the low life of the Dublin slums? Am I a rude peasant late off the stony fields of Connacht? These things may have been part of my ancestry, just as you two derive from a culture of avaricious land barons who kept farmers in unspeakable peonage for two centuries, from generations of soulless men who grew rich off the slave trade. Is that low life, or—'

'What's that about the slave trade?' Jacob asked. 'If you're implying—'

'Don't reduce yourself, Jake, don't give it a second thought. I don't,' and Edward quickened his speech, eliminated pauses, breathed on the run.

'I know these are old and generic accusations, and I also know how high you've risen above those early scoundrels who populate your ethnic history. Only a fool would hold it against you. What a glorious heritage you have in the Staats family, paragons of religious liberty, vigorous giants of commerce, and yet there *was* old Jacobus Staats who scandalized his townsmen by marrying a squaw, did he not? Yes, he did, and so what? Who cares who marries whom if the bride and groom are blissful?'

Jacob squirmed, his mouth forming a rebuttal, but in his eyes the question: What exactly is this man saying? Edward poured three glasses of sherry as he spoke and, without losing a beat, put two of them in the hands of Jacob and Geraldine, downed his own, and stood and paced before them, a dynamo of pent energy made visible and audible.

'Henry James, the old man – you both know him, he went to Albany Academy before me – argues that Adam's fall from Eden was necessary for Adam to achieve a higher plane of existence. And I mean to tell you that Katrina and I are now together at the gates of our own Eden, and we couldn't be more sure of our happiness. If a fall is fated I believe we'll rise to that higher plane, just as Adam did. We'll thrive, we'll transcend whatever society tries to do to us. We'll move onto the grand stage and I'll prosper formidably and achieve heights no lawyer or doctor who might court Katrina could ever know; for I have talent and I have energy and both will last me a lifetime.

'I have a name descended from Irish kings who preexist Oliver Cromwell by six centuries, and I fervently believe in the aristocracy of my lost ancestral world. I'm vividly aware also that your ancestors, Geraldine, going back as they do to Cromwell's England, your ancestors, in the name of God, tried to eliminate the entire population of Ireland, and almost succeeded. Then I sit here and all that self-glorifying butchery leaps out at me from the pages of books in this room – clear proof the past is behind us, that we're in a new world with a new light on our own days, and you, Jake, and you, Geraldine, have the strength and courage to keep – *in your own library* – the record of those unspeakable crimes. Hurrah, I say to this. Hurrah for you both, hurrah for facing the worst history has to offer, and moving forward to honorable success in every realm worth inhabiting – civic, business, ecclesiastical, social, but, most of all, success in conceiving and raising the peerless Katrina, icon of beauty and wisdom. And so my congratulations to you both, and don't say anything yet. Just think on my words. Think on me as the husband of your sublime daughter. Consider the uncritical love she and I have for each other, and what a rare thing this is in anyone's life.'

Then, as these final words of what Edward would come to call his Manifesto of Love and History hung in the air, he backed quickly away from Jacob and Geraldine (who still stared at him, gripping their sherry), found the library door and opened it, and then he was gone.

Katrina Visits the *Angel of the Sepulchre*

October 10, 1885

Headaches were coming gradually to Katrina, then they became intermittent, and, after two weeks, incessant; and so she took to her bed with valerian drops, the only avenue to sleep. When the sedatives worked she slept day into night, read poetry (especially Baudelaire and Verlaine, who, she had learned in school, were abominable writers to be avoided), read them to tire herself with the pleasure of words, and told her family she was not ill, only full of bodily weariness.

Katrina took her meals from a tray and kept reading, marveling at Baudelaire's misogyny: *I have always been astonished that women are allowed to enter churches. What can they have to do with God?*

God, on the arm of the Episcopal Bishop (very high church), came regularly to dinner at Katrina's home. God ate well, stayed late, and the discourse, while boring, was not without merit: for it reinforced the family conviction that evil resided elsewhere, and that divine providence hovered just above the dining room chandelier.

One night she awoke dreaming of panthers running loose in the forest. Her vantage point from an upper story of her house gave her a full view of the threat, and then one of the panthers was inside the stable. Katrina went downstairs to the kitchen, and as she reached for the butcher knife to defend herself, a blue panther, jaws wide in a snarl, sprang out of the bread box. She sat up in a silent scream, her headache gone. She put on her night robe, walked down to the kitchen, and opened the bread box. She found the butcher knife, cut a corner of bread, and ate it sitting at the window, staring out at that patch of her garden that was illuminated by streetlamps. She could see the Venus fountain, after Botticelli, that her father had bought in Italy, and, around its base, the yellow and orange leaves that were falling from the trees.

Of course the dream was Edward.

She got up from the window and boiled a kettle of water, then went to the china room and took down the Berlin cup and saucer that had belonged to the King of Holland, and the tea service owned by Oliver Cromwell. She made the tea, put the pot and china on a tray, carried it to the front drawing room. She had no precedent for her behavior, but she believed the rightness of every thought, every impulse that came to her.

She lit four candles in the candelabra her mother said was once owned by the Bonaparte family, and sat down for contemplative midnight tea amid family treasures: the Ismari vase mounted in ormolu, the Washington portrait by Rembrandt Peale; the Wentworth mirror, its border embroidered by Lady Wentworth; the portrait, as handsome widow, of Femmitie Staats, ancestor of her father, and direct descendant of Johannes Staats, who had been born in 1642 into Albany's original settlement.

Femmitie's and the Wentworths' presences were reinforcements of family links to the origins of the city and the nation: American life predicated upon Dutchness without end, Albion evermore. I do believe this house is paradise, Katrina thought. I believe it is a palace of brilliant crystal, softest velvet, golden light, pervasive elegance; and memory overflows with beauty and the holiness of history. I see a proud elevation of spirit and mind in the splendid people of my life. I will lose my birthright to these things if I marry Edward.

She slept and at painless morning took breakfast in the dining room with the family, an occasion of relief for all, the cause noted by Katrina's sister, Adelaide: 'She's gotten over her love-sickness.'

'That Daugherty is ruining the peace of this family,' Jacob Taylor said.

Katrina said nothing and after breakfast gave Cora, the chamber-maid, her daily fifteen minutes of tutoring in elocution in Katrina's sitting room.

'Is it true as Miss Adelaide says that you're desperate sick in love with Mr Daugherty?' Cora asked.

'I'm not such a fool,' Katrina said. 'I know the difference between my body and my soul. Love is the soul's business. I'm sick because my body seems to want this marvelous man. I would never call it love.'

'Oh, Miss Katrina, I think you got it backwards.'

'You're an expert on love?'

'I'm commonsensical on it. I loved a boy well and do yet, and it's body and soul, Miss, body and soul.'

'You do speak your mind, Cora.'

'I wouldn't know what else to do with it, Miss.'

Katrina's clearest memory of Cora McNally was of the white stone china cup with the broken handle, a memorable stub of unmanageable clay. It was the day Geraldine Taylor hired Cora for scullery work (from which she swiftly graduated), and cook was giving Cora her first lunch, setting her chair and dishes at a solitary place at the drainboard of the sink: a sandwich of turkey scraps and skin dabbed with cranberry sauce, and tea in that unforgettable stone china cup. Cora came in from the scullery, saw this offering, and said not to cook but to Katrina's mother:

'Mrs Taylor, on the poorest day of me life in Cashel I never ate a meal on the drain of a sink, and if ever a cup in our house broke its handle, we threw it out.'

Geraldine nodded and said quietly to cook:

'Sit Cora at the servants' table and give her a proper cup.'

And from then forward the Taylor family and its servants knew who Cora was, as you shall know me, Katrina announced silently to all future obstructionists.

Katrina's dilemma: whether to decide in silence to accept the offer of marriage, suffer all losses privately in advance, and move beyond loss, or allow family and peers to mount the inevitable attacks on such outrageous wedlock. Katrina knew her decision would not be influenced by the views of others. The problem lay in protocol, distortion of which would leave scars.

As the days passed, it began to decide itself. Mother must be allowed to invite the Bishop to lecture Katrina on marrying someone outside the religion. Father must be permitted to agree to finance a tour of the Continent to take Katrina's mind off the papist lout.

Katrina looked at the portrait of Femmitie clutching the red rose of love, her shawl over her left shoulder emphasizing the fullness of her right breast; and in Femmitie's mouth Katrina read the flirtatious curl of a smile, supporting the legend that Femmitie fled her parents' unbearably pious Albany home to marry a seductive Boston confidence man (a Dublin rascal masquerading as an Ulsterman) who made her insanely rich, then was, himself, hanged for murdering a wealthy Presbyterian cleric. These events had been irrelevant to Femmitie's sensuous smile, which survived religion, money, and the gibbet. Wrote B: *Woman cannot distinguish between her soul and her body. She simplifies things, like an animal. A cynic would say it is because she has only a body.* You are not talking about me, Katrina told him.

Katrina decided her resurrection from indecision and reclusion would take place two days hence, and she wrote letters organizing the event, the first to Giles Fitzroy, asking that he take her for an afternoon ride to brighten her pallid complexion, expose her weakened spirit to the restorative of fresh air and sunshine; and the second to Edward, asking that he meet her at one-thirty in Albany Rural Cemetery near the *Angel of the Sepulchre*, the one landmark of whose location everyone was certain.

In her parents' estimation, Edward, despite his long-standing family link through Lyman, was now a figure to be kept as remote from Katrina as possible; but Giles, Katrina's childhood friend, was eternally welcome in this house, his father being the Taylor family physician, his mother Geraldine Taylor's colleague in maintaining standards for Albany's social elite.

314

'Where shall I take you?' Giles asked when Katrina had settled into his cabriolet (top down), his horse leading them at a sprightly pace up Broadway. Katrina covered her lap and legs with Giles's blanket. It was the time of sublime autumn in Albany, the day bright and warm with sunshine, explosive with the reds and oranges and yellows of the dying leaves.

'We should go to the most beautiful place we know,' she said. 'The cemetery.'

'Oh you are cheerful,' Giles said.

'But I'm serious. I want to see where the Staatses and Taylors are buried, and decide should I be buried there.'

'What puts you in such a morbid mood?'

'Contemplating death isn't morbid, Giles. It's liberating.'

'But why now? You're so young and healthy. Why not think of life instead?'

'But I do. And death is so important to it.'

'You're as odd as you are beautiful, Katrina.'

They drove past St Peter's Hospital, where Giles was a medical intern, following his father's career, and past her grandfather's foundry. Without Lyman, Katrina and Edward might never have met, and most certainly would not now be contemplating marriage.

'What do you think of me these days, Giles?'

'I think you're heavenly, a goddess among us. I love being with you.'

'Will you be my slave?'

'Gladly.'

'Oh that *is* good.'

They rode over the small bridge where the Patroon's Creek crossed Broadway, through the tollgate by the sandpits onto the Troy Turnpike; then they turned west up the Loudonville plank road toward the cemetery.

'Do you like Edward Daugherty, Giles?'

'He seems a fine fellow, but he's a few years older than I, so we're not close.'

'I'm going to meet him.'

315

'When?'

'This afternoon.'

'Aren't you with *me* this afternoon?'

'You're taking me to him.'

'Katrina, I don't understand anything about you.'

'That's all right, Giles. I understand everything about you and I'm very fond of you.'

'"Fond" is a terrible word.'

'A true one.'

'Where are you meeting him?'

'At the cemetery. By the *Angel of the Sepulchre.*'

'This is ridiculous. I feel like a fool.'

'But aren't you my slave?'

Giles fell silent and they turned and drove along the crest of the hill that was Rensselaer Avenue, past the Fitzgibbon country mansion, where her mother's eccentric brother Ariel dwelled in baronial excess, and where Katrina had never been at ease. When she saw that Giles's silence had become a sullen pout, she reached over and took his hand in hers. By the time they passed through the south gate of Albany Rural Cemetery and were approaching the Angel, his pout had melted into an abashed smile.

'Come back for me at four o'clock,' Katrina said as she stepped down from the cabriolet near the statue of the Angel. She folded Giles's blanket over her arm. 'I'll take this in case I have to sit somewhere and wait.'

'Why are you meeting him?' Giles asked.

'I'm not sure. If I find out I may tell you.'

'You know he just writes for the newspaper. He's only a writer.'

'I read him with great appreciation for his intelligence. Have you read the novel he just published?'

'I don't bother myself with novels. But I've heard it said he keeps fast company.'

'There is none faster than I,' Katrina said.

'At that the slave exits,' Giles said, urging his horse forward.

A quarter hour early for Edward, Katrina walked to the Angel,

316

who was sitting on the rock he had rolled away from the sepulchre of Jesus, atop the gravestone of the Banks family from Albany. Since his arrival in 1868, this heavenly, white-marble emissary had become the best-known resident of the cemetery, eclipsing magnates and governors, even heroes of the Revolution, and daily drew crowds of the curious and the reverential, although today only two women were standing off, staring at him. The Angel had also enhanced the fame of his creator, Erastus Dow Palmer, neighbor of Katrina's for as long as she had been able to look out the window and see him striding along Elk Street with his walking stick and his great white beard. Instrument of the resurrection, the Palmer Angel, in flowing white nightshirt, hair of Jesus length, folded wings as tall as his seated self, stared out into Katrina's afternoon and thrilled her, bringing her again to the edge of tears with the beauty of his irreality, the perfection of his fingers and toes, the strength and certainty in his mouth and eyes. He was speaking to the known and unknown Marys who had come to weep over the dead Jesus: 'Why seek ye the living among the dead?' he asked them.

Sentinel of salvation, rock of redemption, he knew what he was about. No perfection in bedridden indecision, Katrina. The Kingdom of Heaven belongs to the clear of heart; you know that. (Yes, yes, of course. But what, besides clarity, inhabits the heart of an angel?)

'Beauty regards beauty,' came Edward's voice, and Katrina turned to see him in his phaeton two-seater, looking so spirited, so ebullient, even sitting still: as fine a figure, she suddenly decided, as she would find this side of the angels. She walked toward him and he took off his hat to greet her and leaped down to take her hand, help her up into the seat beside his own.

'I didn't expect this day,' he told her: 'Your invitation thrilled me. But how did you get here?'

'I have my slaves,' she said.

His dark-brown eyes focused only on her and she thought he owned the handsomest head of brown hair imaginable, and she thought: I'll bet he took off his hat to woo me with his hair.

317

'Do we have a destination?' he asked.

'Where the road leads,' she said, and Edward told his horse to take them along it.

Katrina could navigate all of the cemetery's vast natural beauty, knew each vale, brook, and ravine, knew the cypress grove, the pond by the elm woods. And she knew many of its residents, could identify the replica of Scipio's tomb where Jared Rathbone, Lyman's old friend and business enemy, was buried, and the thirty-six-foot Doric column commemorating Albany's heroic Revolutionary general, Philip Schuyler, and the granite sarcophagus of General James Rice, once of Elk Street, who, dying at Spotsylvania, said, 'Let me die with my face to the foe,' and Thurlow Weed, founder of the *Albany Evening Journal*, whose Republican politics her father detested, and the very, very rich William James, whose grandson Henry wrote novels of great convolution that intimidated Katrina, and the banker Billings Learned, Katrina's favorite capitalist, who wrote on his wife's headstone: 'Wife, I thank my God upon every remembrance of you.'

These notable graves gave comfort to Katrina in her pursuit of love, perhaps marriage. This gilded world of the familiar dead, a world into which she had been born and raised, filled her soul with cultivated joy, for her mother had sensitized her to the splendor of an eminent death, which, as all know, perpetuates an eminent life.

But now the beat of her heart also importuned Katrina, and as they came to a grove of blue spruces, with no monuments or people in sight, she said to Edward, 'Stop here. It's all as I remember. No corner of the world more beautiful.'

While Edward tethered his horse, Katrina climbed down from the carriage and, with blanket in hand, walked to a shaded place beneath the holy trees, whose wood was one of the principal sources of her father's abundant wealth. The tall spruces had shed needles and cones in a soft carpet upon the earth, and atop this carpet Katrina spread Giles's blanket. She unpinned her hat and set it on the blanket, then sat and looked up at Edward, who was watching her private drama play itself out.

'Come and sit,' she said.

'You seem to know exactly what you're doing,' Edward said. 'This is indeed a secret place.'

'I've been thinking about it endlessly, ever since your talk with my parents.'

'The hymeneal event,' he said. 'Does this mean you finally have an answer to my question?' He took off his coat and sat beside her.

'Put your face near mine,' she said. 'I want to know how I'll react.'

Edward moved close and, when their noses almost touched, he smiled.

'Stop smiling,' she said.

They studied each other's eyes, mouth, hair. She parted her lips and moved her mouth onto his. She held the kiss, stopped it, withdrew to a distance of inches.

'I like it,' she said.

He took the game away from her and kissed her, as he well knew how to, and she folded herself into a condition for which anterior planning could not have prepared her.

'Oh that is *very* good,' she said, and she resumed the kiss. When it came to a stillness she stared for a long time at Edward, decisions being made by her eyes and by a pervasive bodily tension that was thrilling.

'It's clear,' she said, 'that we now have to do the rest. I've worn as few garments as possible.'

'The rest?' Edward said.

'I've read all about this,' Katrina said. 'It's nineteen days since my time. I now have nine days when I cannot conceive. It's an ideal moment for the estrus to strike, and strike it has.'

'This is a very bold act, Katrina.'

'You don't accept me?'

'I accept with great heart but wild misgiving. We're marked forever if something happens.'

'I sense the ecstasy I've heard about. I want to be certain it exists.'

'I love you for this, Katrina, more than I loved you yesterday, and I didn't think that possible. You're a wonder.'

'You're all the world to me now, Edward. But I must confirm that you are truly real. Do you understand?'

'I don't think I understand why we're establishing my reality in the cemetery.'

'We'll die before we get to it if you don't shut up,' and she arched her buttocks off the blanket, raised her skirts to her waist, and unbuttoned the top of her dress as Edward fell on his knees in front of her.

'Why seek ye the living among the dead?' the Angel asked Katrina, and her answer came that, in her, there had taken root the truths of her poet: that death is the divine elixir that gives us the heart to follow the endless night, that it is the mystical attic, the poor man's purse, the mocker of kings, the accursed's balm, the certain loss that vitalizes possession. She feared it not at all, and chose to behave as if each moment were the ultimate one; and this consistency, to the end of her days, would astonish all who knew her.

Edward, who had won her eye with his brash flirtation, and now was gaining her virginal body, believed *he* was the privileged one to be given such a sumptuous gift as the mythic ideal that was Katrina. And he told himself: You, Edward Daugherty, you, now prostrate on this exquisite altar, you own a fortunate heart.

After a time that he would remember not by its length but by the intensity of his joy, he felt and heard her approaching her peak, felt it also in himself, and he moved out from her sweet place to spill his seed on the carpet of brown pine needles; for God can be tempted only so far.

'Are you always so cautious with life?' Katrina asked.

'I don't want to lose you, now that I have you,' he said.

'Because you did that, did you love me less?'

'Because you court danger,' he replied, 'do you love me more?'

'You don't understand,' Katrina said.

'Perhaps it's you who don't understand.'

'We'll marry in the spring, I understand that,' she said.

'People are already trying to stop us.'

'We'll overcome them.'

'Love will prevail over everything.'

'We'll live like no other people ever lived.'

'Only death will undo us,' he said.

'Amen,' she said.

Confirmed anew that a voluptuous woman is the universe's greatest gift to a man, Edward turned back to Katrina, bent low and kissed her mouth. Stroking himself then, because this must not end, and seeing and feeling Katrina's blood on his hand, he made his inward thrust, thinking: Do whatever you will, Lord. This is worth it.

Edward Brings Katrina Home to
Main Street

October 20, 1885

Main Street was the second-last street in the North End, one of
five block-long streets that sloped down from Broadway to the
railroad tracks and the Lumber District. After these streets only a
few isolated houses dotted Broadway before the Bull's Head tavern
and Island Park racetrack, and then came the open road that ran
north toward Troy. Houses stood only on the north side of Main,
the south side as wooded with oak and maple and elm as it had
been the day Dutchmen first left their boat to set foot on this
land of the Mohawks. The five small streets were a community to
Edward, a cul-de-sac of rustic, harmonious life, lived adjacent to the
chug and clatter of Albany's three lifelines: the rail, the canal, and
the river. As he turned the corner in his carriage, Edward saw his
mother and the Whites standing in front of the Daugherty house,
then saw his father's head halfway out the bedroom window.

'They're talking to neighbors,' he said to Katrina, beside him.

'Is that bad? Do you want to come back later?'

'No, neighbors are good. They'll cut the ice. It's Cappy and
Mamie White.'

'Such a large woman.'

'She's larger than that. Cappy drives the Lumber District
horsecar and when she gets on the front of it the back end
goes up.'

'Does she have to be so big?'

'They've had doctors, but she keeps growing. It's been like

watching the slow inflation of a balloon for as long as I've known her.'

A brown chicken ran into the street as Edward pulled up, and his mother, an apron over her long housedress, ran after it, snatched it up and held it under her arm. Edward reined the horse, and as he jumped down to tether it, Katrina said to him, 'That's your mother.'

'It certainly is.'

'I remember her.'

He helped Katrina down from the carriage, then walked her over to introduce her first to his mother, then to the Whites, as his fiancée. His father was gone from the window.

'Katrina says she remembers you,' Edward told his mother.

'From the Manor House,' Katrina said. 'My mother took me to visit the Van Rensselaer girls when I was eight or nine, and when we played in the kitchen, you were there. I remember how young you were, and yet your hair was pure white.'

'I do remember your mother came often,' Hanorah Daugherty said. She smiled at Katrina. 'But I wasn't so young, I don't think.'

'Oh, but you were,' Katrina said.

'We'll move along, Hanny,' Cappy White said. Cappy was a burly six-footer with a thatch of bristle on his upper lip, and already graying at thirty-eight. 'Congrats to you, Eddie.'

'Thanks, Cappy. I deserve them.'

'You have a beautiful, beautiful bride,' Mamie White said. She stared at Katrina, then gave Edward the saddest of smiles.

'She's not my bride quite yet, Mamie. But we're getting there.'

The Whites said their goodbyes and walked off slowly, Mamie's shoulders rocking from side to side.

'Go on in, go in,' Hanorah said, shooing them toward the front door. 'I'll put this one back in the yard,' and she walked to the rear of the house with the chicken in her arms.

Edward opened the door for Katrina and led her into the parlor with its huge chrome stove, the beaded valances on the windows, the doilies on the arms of the horsehair chairs. A small braided rug in front of the rocking chair was the only covering on the wide pine-board floor.

Edward moved the wicker rocker into the sunlight for Katrina, and took three tintypes off the otherwise bare white mantelpiece: individual studio shots of his father in a suit and derby, his mother in a full-length flowered skirt, white blouse, and black bonnet tied under her chin with a ribbon; and one photo of them sitting together, with little boy Edward on Emmett's lap.

'This is what we no longer look like,' he said, handing Katrina the pictures. 'I'll be right back.'

He went to find his father, bring him out of hiding. Emmett had said he would go to no wedding, nor would he hear any argument aimed at changing his mind. Edward had revealed this fact to Katrina and vowed he'd confront his own parents as he'd confronted hers.

Katrina said her mother thought him 'a rude social climber' and was furious at his suggestion that her family had committed violence against the Irish; and her father, baffled by Edward's 'babbling about atrocity and slavery,' wondered, 'What world is that overeducated maniac living in?'

'But what did they say about the marriage?' Edward asked.

'They disapprove but they honor my choice, and they certainly won't stay away from the wedding, as your father threatens to do. My father wouldn't abide anyone but him giving me away, and Mother will insist on buying my dress and shoes and choosing the flowers and decorating the church. She lives for such things.'

Decorating the church. Which church?

Emmett was a different problem.

'I'm thinking of marrying Katrina Taylor' was all Edward had said, and Emmett exploded: 'Any kin of Jacob Taylor has to be poison . . . that polished fool . . . that felonious rodent . . . a family of pretenders . . . merchants without souls . . . They aspire to nothing but money . . . It's traitorous marrying one of them after what he did to Davy . . . smashed his mind because he pushed for a better wage . . . I dream of seeing them in rags and clogs. No good can come of it, boy, it's a wrong idea.'

'It's not an idea, Papa. She and I, we're a matched pair. We've a great love and she's as bright as any woman alive. She's a woman you only dream of knowing.'

'Marry your dream, then,' Emmett had said. 'I'll not witness it.'

Edward now climbed the stairs and glanced at the framed tapestry of the Daugherty crest (a leaping stag) hanging on the stairway wall. The Pittsburgh chapter of the moulders' union Emmett helped establish gave it as a going-away gift when Emmett left Pittsburgh to come back to Albany. The family name was stitched under the crest in the Irish: *docararch*. Emmett was fond of explaining that it translated as either 'unfortunate' or 'disobliging,' take your pick.

Edward found his father shoeless, in a fresh shirt and his everyday pants, sitting in his bedside rocker, cleaning his fingernails with a six-inch knife. His hair was the color of granite now, and as wild as the mind beneath it.

'So you brought her home,' Emmett said.

'She's in the parlor.'

'You know what I think about this.'

'Nobody could know what to think about Katrina without talking to her. You don't even know what's going on in *my* head.'

'I won't argue,' Emmett said. He closed the knife, pocketed it, and bent over to pull on a shoe.

'You won't hear me out? You, the one who's always fighting for the right to be heard?'

Emmett leaned back in the rocker and stared at his son. 'What is it, then?'

'It's me, it's what I've become,' Edward said, and he felt the same energy rising that he'd known in delivering the Manifesto. He could not taunt his father as he'd taunted the Taylors, for the man wouldn't sit for it. So, then, he would neither pace nor gesticulate. He would keep his energy leashed. He sat on the bed and faced Emmett.

'You raised me and Lyman educated me,' Edward said, 'and now I'm some kind of new being with no known habitat – not North

Albany, not Elk Street. Katrina knows this without my saying it. She's as smart as the edge of your knife. She knows exactly who I am and she loves me and wants to marry me. And God knows I want to marry her. I've never felt anything even close to what I feel with her. It's thrilling, Papa, unbelievably thrilling. I'm not marrying her father, and I'm not condoning what he did to Davy. But is this a blood feud that carries on for generations? Do the wars of the father have to be the wars of the son? I wrote *The Mosquito Lovers*, didn't I? You planted that in my head and I'm glad you did, but I've got other things to write. I'm no soldier in the class war. If I'm geared to do anything it's to celebrate the mind and the imagination. Rise in the world with your brain, not your back and your fists – if you can. And I believe I can. And I believe others can as well as me. Where are the minds of *our* people? Why aren't we running the foundries and lumber mills instead of being moulders and handlers all our lives? I'm not against radicalism, but I want to get beyond it. I want to leap over the past and live in a world where people aren't always at each other's throats. I know some of our roots are in the hovels of Connacht and we shouldn't forget that. But there was Donegal before Connacht, and before Donegal who can say? Were we ever anything besides tribal warriors? We were bards, weren't we, some of us? And we were architects of the book. And we had the music, as you always said. If they reduced us to breaking rock to stay alive, those other qualities were still in us, and I see them now in myself. They're not new to me but I look in the mirror and I think, "You're a new being," and I wonder what to do about that. Do I lose my past by shaping a future? Do I disinherit myself? No matter what you think, I haven't abandoned the struggle. If you'd heard what I told Jake and Geraldine when I asked to marry Katrina, you wouldn't have turned a deaf ear. I probably made lifetime enemies of them. I don't want to fight with you now, Papa, or ever, just as I don't want to give up this woman, who is everything I value. My love for her seems like a primal force, as basic and as strong as what I feel for you and Mama.'

Edward stopped talking. He stood and took two hesitant steps toward the door.

'Now that you know this,' he said, 'can you still tell me to abandon Katrina to satisfy your vengeance against Jake Taylor? If you can, then I think you're wrong, and I don't believe I ever said that to you before, or even thought it. Now I'm going downstairs and talk to Katrina and Mama. I hope you come down and join us.'

Katrina had left the parlor. Edward found her in the kitchen, sitting at the table, watching Hanorah at the stove stirring something in a frying pan. The kettle was sending up wisps of early steam and the table was set for five, one extra, of course.

'I saw those children grow up and move off,' Hanorah was saying. 'Twenty-six years I was with them, from when I went in there to wash pots. Then they found out I could cook and I cooked for the Patroon till he died, and for Mrs Bayard until she died, too. Then they closed the place up. I still cook for some of the family when they stay the month at Saratoga, but mostly I only cook for himself, and for this one, whenever he comes to see us,' nodding at Edward as he entered the kitchen.

He walked to Hanorah and looked over her shoulder at the frying pan.

'Bubble and squeak?' he said.

'You don't like it?' Hanorah said.

'I don't like it, I love it with a passion I reserve only for beautiful women like yourself.'

'Listen to the mouth, will you?' Hanorah said.

'Bubble and squeak,' Edward said to Katrina, 'is this cook's way of joining potatoes and cabbage in God's secret recipe. I presume we're having lunch.'

'Miss Taylor said you didn't eat.'

'Miss Taylor is Katrina.'

'I just met her, if you don't mind.'

'You set five places. Is Hughie Gahagan joining us?'

'He might.'

'Hughie Gahagan is dead,' Edward said to Katrina, 'but my mother doesn't give up on him. My father brought him home

327

one night for supper and put him to work in the lockhouse. He stayed five years and we buried him out of the parlor. He had nobody else.'

'Emmett brought men home for a meal all his life, especially if they were down on their luck,' Hanorah said. 'He still does it, so I always set an extra place.'

Emmett's step on the stairs silenced the conversation.

'There's a boat in the lock,' Emmett said as he came into the kitchen. He looked at no one and walked to the kitchen window that gave a view of the canal at the foot of North Street. He stood looking out, his back to those in the room.

'It's a passenger packet,' he said.

No one reacted. After a while he said, 'Cappy White, he's a hard-luck man.'

'He has more than his share of trouble,' Hanorah said.

'He lost a thousand dollars' worth of horses in a fire last year. And then Mamie like that.'

'Well, she's getting about,' Hanorah said. 'She walks the block and she does the garden. She sat in the chair this summer in the garden. She leans sideways and pulls the weeds she can reach. Those she can't she tells Cappy to pull. Sometimes he pulls up the flowers.'

'Cappy and I raced horses on the canal in the winter,' Emmett said, still staring out the window, 'and sometimes up at Island Park on a Sunday, when we had the money. We had fast horses them days.'

'We have a very fast horse,' Katrina said.

Emmett turned slowly around and stared at her.

'This is my father, Emmett Daugherty, Katrina,' Edward said. 'He sometimes forgets to say hello to people. And this is Katrina Taylor, Papa. I mentioned her to you.'

Katrina nodded at Emmett. 'Chevalier is his name,' she said. 'He's a trotter.'

Emmett continued to stare at her.

'We're having bubble and squeak,' Hanorah said.

'Is it your horse?' Emmett asked.

'No, my father's,' she said.

'Unh,' Emmett said and he sat at the table across from Katrina and stared out the back door. The brown chicken pushed through the broken screen of the door and stepped into the kitchen.

'That hen is in again,' Emmett said.

'Let her be,' Hanorah said.

The hen came over to Hanorah and moved in a circle near her, pecking at the hem of her dress.

'It's all right, Biddy,' Hanorah said to the hen.

'My mother's pet,' Edward said. 'A hen that behaves like a cat.'

'She's a bloody nuisance,' Emmett said.

'She just comes to see me,' Hanorah said. 'I bought her as a chick last year at the fair. I saw her born in one of them machines and I paid ten cents for her.'

The hen beat her puny wings and lofted herself onto a chair and sat on its cushion.

'Now she'll lay an egg on the chair,' Emmett said. 'For the love of Jesus will you look at that.'

'She lays the egg for me,' Hanorah said. 'She doesn't know anything about Jesus.'

The hen sat, adjusted her rump, stared at her audience and spoke to it – '*took-a-takaawk*' – shook her rump, laid her egg on the cushion, batted her wings anew, and lofted herself back to the floor.

'She came upstairs and laid one in the bed one morning and Emmett rolled over on it,' Hanorah said.

'Isn't it good luck, a hen in the house?' Katrina asked.

'There are those who'd argue with that,' Hanorah said.

She picked up the hen and carried it out to the yard, then came back and rinsed her hands under the pump by the sink and wiped them dry with her apron. She picked the new egg off the chair and put it in the icebox with the other eggs and took out the butter and put it on the table. She poured boiling water into the teapot, spooned the potatoes and cabbage into a dish, and took warm bread out of the oven and sliced it. She put it all on the table and said, 'We're ready.'

She and Edward then sat on either side of Katrina, the spirit of Hughie Gahagan separating Edward from his father. Hanorah caught Emmett's eye and he bowed his head and said silent grace. Then Hanorah passed the bread and the bubble and squeak, and they all helped themselves.

'There's talk now of a wedding,' Hanorah said.

'There is,' said Edward.

'When did you meet?'

'When we were children, or at least Katrina was a child. Then all of a sudden she grew up and I saw her at Cleveland's victory parade, and she looked like this,' and he opened his hand to Katrina's face. 'I was conquered, or maybe I was victorious, finding what I didn't even know I'd been looking for all my life.'

'Did you feel that way, too?' Hanorah asked Katrina.

'I thought him quite perfect,' Katrina said. 'I've tried to discover ways to improve him, but I've found none at all.'

'You may find some. You're still young,' Hanorah said.

'I'm almost twenty. Juliet, had she lived, would've been married six years at my age. Perhaps I'm older than I seem.'

'Where would the wedding be?' Hanorah asked.

Katrina looked at Edward. He waited for her to answer, but she did not.

'We've made no plans,' Edward said. 'We wanted to talk to you before we did anything.'

'My parents want it to be at the Cathedral Chapel of All Saints,' Katrina said.

'That's where the Episcopalians go,' Hanorah said.

'Yes. Bishop Sloane is a friend of the family.'

'What do you say to that?' Emmett asked Edward.

'I hadn't heard this,' said Edward.

'You marry in that church, you're excommunicated,' Emmett said, and he turned to Katrina. 'Do you know what you're doing to the man, taking him out of his religion?'

'I had no idea,' she said.

'We'll find a way to solve it,' Edward said.

'Which is your church?' Katrina asked Edward.

'Sacred Heart, here in North Albany.'

'Then we'll marry there. Will that solve it?'

'Are you sure about this?'

'You can't marry in the church if you're not Catholic,' Emmett said.

'Then I'll become Catholic. How long does it take?'

'You have to take instructions,' Edward said. 'A few months, maybe?'

'That's fine. I was thinking of a spring wedding anyway, weren't you?'

'Just like that, you become a Catholic?' Emmett said, snapping his fingers.

'I don't believe it matters which language we use when we talk to God. It's possible I'm really a pagan. If so, I shall now be a pagan Catholic.'

'What will your parents say?' Hanorah asked.

'They'll be furious.'

'You certainly make quick decisions,' Emmett said.

'I do what I think I should do, so I can become what I feel I must be.'

The Daughertys fell into silence. Edward stared at Katrina, understanding that with a few words she had transformed herself, become as rare to his parents as he already knew her to be, yet he could not have predicted any word she said. Emmett and Hanorah stared at her, rancor gone from Emmett's face, Hanorah a study in bewilderment. What Katrina had done was akin to her action at the cemetery, and Edward now knew she would have this effect on everyone, that the directness of her idiosyncratic behavior was a singular gift. He coveted it, felt the young man's ambition to conquer life with a stroke, as Katrina just had. But he knew he would live a long time before he understood even where to direct such a stroke. Yet, credit where credit is due, Edward: you intuited the rightness of bringing her here unannounced, and for that much you should congratulate yourself. Blind navigation, a maestro's talent, won the battle for today.

The bells for the noon hour rang in the church belfry.

William Kennedy

'Those are the bells of Sacred Heart,' Edward said.

'It sounds like a requiem,' Katrina said.

'No, just the time of day, the noon hour, time for the Angelus.'

Katrina framed a question in her eyes.

'A prayer to the Immaculate Conception and the mystery of the Incarnation,' Edward said. '"Behold the handmaid of the Lord. Be it done unto me according to thy word. And the Word was made flesh. And dwelt among us."'

'It sounds like bells I heard at a neighbor's funeral,' Katrina said. 'I remember his widow getting out of a carriage in front of St Peter's church just as the bells began, and, as she stopped to listen, she swooned and fell on the sidewalk. I thought the slow pealing of the bells was very sorrowful, and yet it was the most beautiful sound I'd ever heard. Will they ring that way for our wedding?'

'I'll see that they do,' Edward said.

And he remembered Aristotle: as the eyes of a night bird relate to the bright glare of day, so the soul's understanding relates to those things that are the clearest and most knowable of all. Oh, Katrina, most knowable, you speak the dead language of the soul with dazzling fluency.

The Bull on the Porch

October 16, 1908

Fintan (Clubber) Dooley, a butcher living on Van Woert Street in Albany, came forward to reveal his role in the decapitation of a bull the day before the Love Nest killings. This was, he said, a practical joke popularly known as the 'Bull-on-the-Porch Joke.' The bull's owner, Bucky O'Brien, told an interrogator he was asleep upstairs over his Bull's Head tavern on the Troy Road (where drovers had penned and watered Boston-bound herds of cattle in years past) and did not hear the rifle shots that killed his bull. He was awakened by raucous singing, accompanied by the banging of a dishpan as percussion, but O'Brien judged this a normal happening in the vicinity of his tavern, and he went back to sleep. Dooley said he had banged the dishpan while singing the song 'I Want My Mommy' to cover the sound of the rifle shots.

The bull, named Clancy, a long-familiar denizen of the pasture behind the tavern, had only one eye and was known as a peaceful animal. Dooley said Culbert (Cully) Watson, a sometime hotel clerk, known pander, and erstwhile member of the Sheridan Avenue Gang, shot the bull, whereupon Dooley climbed the pasture fence and, with cleaver, handsaw, and knife, and the expertise gained in the slaughterhouses of West Albany, cut off the bull's head and lifted it by the horns over the fence to Watson, who put it in the back of Dooley's wagon. Dooley and Watson then rode down the Troy Road to Albany and left the head on the stoop of the Willett Street home of Dr Giles Fitzroy. Dooley said he had known Dr Fitzroy for many years, that the doctor was a noted practical joker, and that, in a bygone year, Dooley had helped the doctor stage the elaborate 'Fireman's Wife Joke.' Dooley was persuaded by Watson that putting the bull's head on the doctor's porch was a hilarious way of joking the joker. Dooley was unaware that the presence of the head might have other than comic implications.

The whereabouts of Culbert Watson are unknown at this time.

Dinner at the Delavan is Interrupted

December 30, 1894

'Evening, Mr Daugherty,' the hall porter of the Delavan House said to Edward.

'Evening, Frank. Cold as hell out there tonight.'

'Back again, Mr Daugherty,' said Willie Walsh, the liveried bellhop.

'Only place to be on a night like this, Willie,' Edward said, guiding the golden-haired Katrina to the door of the elevator, her hair swept upward into a brilliant soft bun atop her head, the lynx collar of her coat high around her exposed ears. Toby the dwarf, also in livery, gave the Daughertys a half-bow, and bade them enter his elevator.

'Going up, Mr Daugherty?'

'Indeed we are, Toby,' Edward said.

Toby closed the door of the small wooden cubicle that accommodated himself and four people, no more, and the car moved upward. Edward and Katrina stepped out at the second floor, walked toward the dining room, and were greeted by a plump and pretty housemaid, in black dress and starched white apron, sitting on a chair just inside the cloakroom doorway.

'Why it's Cora,' Katrina said.

'Miss Katrina,' said the housemaid, standing to greet them. 'Mr Daugherty.' She curtsied and smiled. 'Don't you both look elegant. Let me take those coats from ye.'

'Welcome to them,' said Edward.

'Oh it's terrible frigid out, isn't it, sir?'

'Even polar bears are inside tonight,' Edward said.

'Is your sister well?' Katrina asked Cora.

'Oh she is, Miss, she's just fine. Your sister and parents and all, they're inside already.'

'They all miss you, Cora. And so do I. I have no one to tell my secrets to anymore.'

'Them were good times, Miss Katrina. I'll never, never forget them. I miss you all so much, but isn't that just the way it is?'

Katrina kissed Cora on the cheek. Edward pressed a dollar bill into Cora's hand and then took Katrina's arm and walked with her into the dining room. People were eating at all but two of the dozen tables, and in one corner a harpist and violinist were playing 'After the Ball,' a song Edward loathed and Katrina loved. Edward saw Tom Maginn across the room, dining with two couples, and recognized one of the men as a powerful New York City Assemblyman. Edward caught Maginn's eye, waved. Katrina nodded to Maginn and smiled.

'Maginn,' said Edward. 'Busy at work.'

Edward's dinner guests were already seated at a round table in the far corner. The party numbered six: Edward and Katrina, Jacob and Geraldine, Katrina's sister, Adelaide, and her new husband, Archie Van Slyke, bright young man out of Harvard Law School, now an assistant vice president of the State National Bank, and whose great-grandfather, in collaboration with Jacob Taylor's grandfather, had assembled a pair of family fortunes by confiscating Tory estates after the Revolution.

Dinner would begin with oysters, be followed with choices of foie gras, shad with sorrel, partridge and cabbage, tenderloin of beef, lobster gratiné (a Katrina favorite), an array of wines, fruit, and cheeses, charlotte russe and Roman punch, Napoleon brandy and Spanish coffee. The menu was chosen by Edward to please the palate of Jacob Taylor, who believed the Delavan served the best food in Albany.

'Can you read your father's mood at this stage of the evening?' Edward whispered to Katrina as they neared their table.

'He doesn't see how this dinner can do anything to stop him from loathing the sight of you,' Katrina said.

'I hope to reverse his expectations,' Edward said, and with smiles and formality he greeted Jacob and the others, kissing the hands of his female in-laws.

He had ordered small bunches of violets to be at the place settings of the women, and when they arrived Katrina picked hers up and pinned them as a corsage to the breast of her gown. 'Flowers, like love,' she whispered to Edward, 'should lie easy on one's bosom.'

Her mother pushed the violets to the center of the table, disowning them. Adelaide sniffed hers, threw Edward a kiss.

'How thoughtful you are,' she said.

Of the Taylors, only Adelaide had no censure for Edward; for she had coveted him when he was courting her sister. 'If you don't marry him,' Adelaide told Katrina when she was abed with indecision, 'you're a fool.'

Edward had reserved this table in the Delavan's second-floor dining room, which was decorated with sketches and photographs of the luminaries whose visits gave credence to the Delavan's boast that it was one of the nation's greatest hotels. Here was Abraham Lincoln, who supped here before and after he became president, and Jenny Lind, when the hotel was a temperance bulwark, and P. T. Barnum, Oscar Wilde, Boss Tweed and a generation of his plundering ilk, who had made the Delavan a political mecca. Here were actors Edwin Booth and James O'Neill, Albany's Irish tenor Fritz Emmett, the dancers Magdalena Colón (La Última) and Maud Fallon, the actresses Mrs Drew and Charlotte Cushman, plus one actress who inhabited the American demimonde, photographed in a gown revealing all of her right breast except the nipple, and whom Edward once glimpsed in the Delavan bar, coquettishly urging a swinish, kneeling pol to swill champagne from her slipper.

On this penultimate night of 1894 the hotel was in its political but not yet swinish mode, abuzz with the noise, money, and power of the politicians who had come to Albany for the legislative session that would begin on New Year's Day. The ritual was familiar to

Edward, who had dined here often during the years he covered politics for *The Argus*. The festive air, he decided, would be a useful distraction from the heavy mood of this dinner party. The opposing political forces were already feasting and roistering in the two grand suites at opposite ends of the second floor when oysters on the half shell were served to Edward's table.

The maître d' and two liveried Negro footmen approached carrying a box almost the size of themselves.

'Would you give that to the elegant lady over there?' Edward said, and the bellboys set the box on its end beside Geraldine.

'What might this be?' she asked.

'You could open it and find out,' Edward said.

'Is this some sort of joke?'

'I assure you it isn't.'

'Shall I help you unwrap it, Madame?' the maître d' asked.

'If I must, then please do,' Geraldine said.

The maître d' cut the twine that bound the box, then gently ripped away its festive holiday wrapping.

'Open it, Mother,' Katrina said.

'Are you in on this?' Geraldine asked. But Katrina only smiled.

'I'll open it,' said Adelaide, and she revealed an ankle-length black sealskin coat with high collar and abundant cuffs.

'Gorgeous, it's gorgeous,' said Adelaide. 'Full-length.'

'It's a coat,' said Geraldine.

'I'd be abashed if it wasn't,' said Edward.

'But what is it for?'

'For you, my dear, for you,' Edward said, 'a belated Christmas from your daughter and me. You know how things were at Christmas.'

Adelaide lifted the coat out of the box.

'I'll try it on for you, Mother,' she said, and she slipped into it, with Edward's help, and twirled about so all could see the coat's glory from every angle. 'It feels divine,' Adelaide said.

Edward noted that the room's other diners regarded the display with smirks and smiles, disdaining the ostentation, admiring the exquisite garment.

'I suppose you want one now,' Archie said to Adelaide.

'I wouldn't say no if you brought one home.'

'I can't accept this,' Geraldine said.

'Of course you can,' Katrina said.

'It's too much.'

'Not for you,' said Edward.

Adelaide took the coat off and held it for her mother.

'Must I?' Geraldine asked.

Then, without standing up, and offering a small smile, she thrust her left arm, then her right, into the sleeves of the coat. Edward could see Jacob relax, not quite into a grin, but that enduring owlish frown of his was fading.

'Very becoming, Gerry,' said Jacob.

'It feels so silky,' Geraldine said, rubbing the fur with her palms. She took the coat off and folded it into its box. 'It's a lovely gift,' she said to Katrina.

'It was all Edward's idea,' Katrina said.

'Yes. Well, then. Thank you, Edward.'

'My pleasure totally,' Edward said, snapping his fingers to the maître d', who came forward with a much smaller package and handed it to Jacob.

'Another gift?' Jacob said, squinting at Edward. 'Wise men say that gifts make slaves like a whip makes a cur.'

'Or a horse,' said Edward as Jacob undid the gift wrapping, revealing a pen-and-ink sketch of a racehorse pulling a sulky and driver.

'Very pleasant,' said Jacob. 'I didn't know this was a night for gifts.'

'The picture isn't the gift,' Edward said. 'The horse is. It's Gallant Warrior. I know how you value a good trotter, and I know how you felt when you lost Chevalier.'

'You bought me a horse?'

'He's in Baltimore,' said Edward. 'And he's yours. We can have him brought up now, or wait for the spring meeting at Island Park, whatever you prefer. He's a handsome animal, and a winner if there ever was one.'

'Gallant Warrior is a very classy animal, Jake,' Archie said. 'He did very well on the circuit this year. He ran second in the Kentucky Futurity.'

'Where did you get the money?' Jacob asked Edward.

'You'd be surprised how much novels and plays earn when people like them.'

'Which play?'

'Several. Does it matter?'

Jacob smirked, then looked again at the sketch. 'You bought me a horse,' he said.

From the inside pocket of his coat Edward took a fold of papers and set them in front of Jacob.

'The bloodline, and the ownership papers in your name.'

'This is astounding,' said Jacob. 'Gallant Warrior. He must have cost you a fortune.'

'What good is money if you don't spend it on something of value?' said Edward, and he raised his wineglass. 'And now, may I wish a joyful holiday to all here, with the sincere hope that harmony settles on our lives in the new year.'

The others answered his toast, amid small smiles and waning tension. Katrina surreptitiously patted her husband's hand.

'I must add,' said Edward, 'that the last play I wrote will earn neither me nor my producers any more money. When its run ends next month in Philadelphia, I'm withdrawing it from performance forever. You probably know which play I'm talking about.' He stared at Jacob Taylor.

'You're a clever fellow, Daugherty,' Jacob said. 'A very clever fellow.'

'So they tell me,' Edward said.

The play was Edward's latest work, *The Baron of Ten Broeck Street*, a satiric social comedy about a wealthy lumber baron (very like Jacob Taylor) that had earned Edward considerable money and a notable increment of theatrical fame. It owed its existence to Edward's quest to balance his bias; for his previous play, *The Stolen Cushion*, had satirized Albany's lofty Irish bourgeoisie as they were reduced socially by an influx of crude Irish immigrants.

Those Irish vied with the Negroes for the nadir of American social status, and, some thought, won. In the play Edward mocked social rising based solely on money. His private quest, he told himself, was to raise the Irish to the intellectual level of nativist Americans, prove the educability of greenhorn multitudes, as he had proven his own, and show those same multitudes how to transcend the peasant caste into which they'd been born.

Instead, the *Cushion* brought down on his crown not only the wrath of the acquisitive Irish, which he had expected, but also the hostility of his father.

'Who isn't looking for a better life?' said Emmett, who had never forgiven Dickens ('that arrogant beggar') for his scurrilous portrait of Irish peasants near Albany in 1842, a year when Emmett himself was struggling upward from the shame of being least; and he now found it necessary, half a century later, to scold his son for the similar dishonor the *Cushion* represented.

Edward had written the *Baron* in part because of Katrina's estrangement from her father, not only for her marriage, but for converting to the Roman Catholic faith. Despite the family hostility, Katrina clove to Edward with fierce loyalty, and married him in Sacred Heart church. Her father endured the formalities of the wedding and gave Katrina away, but as the meaning of her decision pressed in on him he grew more hostile and distant. Because of this, writing a satire on Jacob Taylor's image had seemed to Edward not only apt, but safe. But when the play appeared to resounding huzzahs, first in Albany, then New York and Boston, Katrina quixotically reembraced not only her father, but also the lush comforts of the house on Elk Street, where he had raised her with nannies and servants; and she now yearned for this house in ways Edward judged to be nearly irrational.

Withdrawing the *Baron* from performance was a small loss, a stroke that Edward hoped would render all Taylors respectful of his apparently selfless ways. But in fact he was done with satire and social tracts that aim to reform scoundrels and pave the way to proletarian heaven. Changing the world is elevating work, but

341

better if he could dramatize the mind of Katrina, that complex creature who so dominated his life.

He looked at her sitting beside him, in awe, as always, of her gifts: that serene beauty which masked such lambent passion, those prismatic charms that had taken root in his soul and made him her slave: as a whip makes a cur.

'Are you enjoying your dinner, Katrina?' he asked her.

'You were quite brilliant, my love,' she said softly. 'You did it all with such panache.'

I did it all for the venal streak at the bottom of your elegant heart, he said silently; for his capitulation to Jacob Taylor was, above all, his recognition that unless he acted swiftly, his marriage would bleed to death from Katrina's imagined wounds. He had built their house on a Colonie Street plot next to the Christian Brothers school he had attended. Jack McCall touted him to availability of the land and also built his own home on the same street.

Colonie was an Irish street in the erstwhile aristocratic neighborhood of Arbor Hill, where many of Albany's lumber barons lived. Edward built the house for Katrina as a scaled-down replica of the Taylors' Gothic Revival town house, and, to assuage her loss of the resplendencies she had left behind, he was now refurnishing the interior of the Colonie Street replica in that halcyon Elk Street image – crystal, engravings, chairs, fabrics, lamps – all in the Taylor mode, so that she might simulate her past whenever her fits of neurasthenic nostalgia descended.

While the remodeling proceeded, Edward, Katrina, and their seven-year-old son, Martin, were staying on Main Street with Emmett, who was alone there since Hanorah's death in the spring of '94.

Since the *Baron*'s first production, in spite of Edward's elaborate efforts to comfort her, Katrina had lapsed into prolonged silences, offered him vacant stares and listless, infrequent sex. Edward at first perceived these as her quirkish reaction to his play, but came to believe in a deeper cause: her vengeance against him for luring her away from her maidenly joys with his eloquent tongue, his hot love.

Now his resentment was growing: a muffled fury accumulating toward his wife of eight years. He was stifling it at this instant, admiring the assertive swatch of color the corsage of violets made on her breast, when the waiter served the lobster gratiné. For no reason except his strange intuition to monitor portent, Edward then took his watch from his waistcoat pocket and noted the hour, eight forty-one o'clock, and that Toby, the elevator operator, was waddling, at the highest speed his stubbiness allowed, across the dining room to the maître d'. Edward saw Toby whisper a message, and then return on the run to the hallway, from which Edward now saw smoke entering the dining room.

'Ladies and gentlemen,' the maître d' announced in a loud but thoroughly courteous voice, 'I suggest that everyone leave with all swiftness. The hotel is on fire.'

Edward grabbed Katrina and Adelaide by the arm and moved rapidly away from their table toward the rushing and already whimpering throng that formed an instant clot in the dining room's double doorway. Edward saw the maître d' and Maginn already in the hallway beyond the clot, turned to see Jacob and Geraldine just behind him, and then he rammed himself into the edge of the clot, his force breaking the impasse and sending people stumbling into the hallway toward the stairwells.

In the hall Edward heard Archie behind him saying, with a voice full of panic, 'The stairway's jammed and the hallway's full of smoke. We should go to the roof.'

'The roof?' Edward said. 'How will you get down? Look, this hallway has two staircases.'

'The elevator,' Geraldine said with a high-pitched gasping that wanted to be a screech, 'where is the elevator?'

'Hunker down, get under the smoke if you can, and follow me,' said Edward, and the family did as he said and followed him in a crouch along the hall. Edward heard Toby calling, 'Here, here, the elevator, I can take one more!' and Edward grabbed Geraldine's shoulder and thrust her at Toby, who pulled her inside the crowded car, slammed the door, and descended to the street level in a rush.

'Mother's coat,' said Adelaide, and she ran back to the dining room before Archie could grab her, and vanished in the hallway's thickening smoke.

'Don't die for a coat,' Edward yelled to her.

'The roof,' said Archie in a voice broken with panic, 'we've got to get to the roof! The firemen will get us down.'

'You don't even know how to get to the roof,' Edward said, but Archie was already on the run into the dining room, pursuing Adelaide.

Two people came toward Edward on their hands and knees, coughing, crying in their fear and asphyxia, a woman in a blue gown and a man Edward recognized as the New York Assemblyman who had been at Maginn's table. He was dragging a trunk as he crawled, and when he reached the staircase he pushed the trunk down the steps ahead of him.

'Come on, Edna,' he called to the woman in blue. But Edna had stopped moving, and Edward saw Jacob wheezing badly, immobilized by the smoke.

'His heart,' said Katrina, and Edward lifted Jacob and dragged him toward the narrow southern stairway. Through the thinning smoke Edward saw that the New York politician had gotten ahead of his trunk and was pulling it down the stairs behind him, oblivious of the loss of Edna.

Edward began to cough, and Katrina, who could not stop coughing, fell on the stairs. 'We're in hell,' she said.

'Only on the outskirts,' Edward said. 'Don't panic on me. Hold my coattail so I know you're here.' He saw the winding stairway below, pocked with flame.

'We'll go,' he said, but Katrina's cough revealed her weakening strength, and Edward took off his jacket and wrapped her head with it. 'Breathe through the cloth,' he said, 'and wait one second,' and he crawled back toward the collapsed woman.

'Let's go, Edna,' he said, and he dragged her by one arm to the stairway. Behind him the hallway's carpet in front of the elevator was a running pathway of flame. No one else would get through that.

344

'Grab her other arm,' Edward told Katrina, and together they moved down the stairs, Edward holding his father-in-law under his left arm like a sack of grain, Jacob's head forward, and he and Katrina pulling Edna, faceup, by her arms. The smoke lessened dramatically, for reasons Edward could not understand, as they descended to the first-floor landing. They moved down the final flight to the ground floor, the fire erratically licking only two walls, and when they reached the billiard room they found four sawhorses blocking the nearest street doorway, which had been painted earlier in the day. Edna's husband was throwing his weight against the door with no success. Edward left the women and Jacob near the door, picked up the man's trunk and used it as a battering ram, smashing the door outward and letting in a rush of cold air. He tossed the trunk out onto the sidewalk and its latch snapped open, revealing a score of wrapped packages of cash lying atop folded shirts.

He turned back to the women, saw that both were safe from flame, Edna regaining her wits. He went toward them and lifted the now-unconscious Jacob over his shoulder just as Katrina bent down to help Edna rise. Edward then heard a great whooshing sound and in the same instant saw the elevator shaft fill with a sudden rocketlike uprush of flame and gas, a blazing cylinder made visible as the elevator door exploded outward, showering sparks and embers on all in the room, setting fires on the green felt of the pool tables, and hurling into the air blazing splinters and sticks, one of which pierced the breast of Katrina and instantly set her gown aflame. She screamed, bewildered by the wound as she looked at it, and Edward could see the flame blackening petals of her violets. With his left hand he pulled the burning stick from her breast and hugged her to his chest to quench the flaming corsage.

As Edna and her Assemblyman ran to the street, frantically brushing sparks from their hair, Edward moved through the doorway, clutching Katrina ever more tightly with his left arm, the inert Jacob doubled over his right shoulder, a family fusion of three bodies inching toward the outer darkness of the frigid world.

Katrina Visits the Ruins

January 1895

On the second day after the fire, despite the pain in her violated breast, Katrina dressed in her winter bloomers and long woolen stockings, two of her warmest sweaters, woolen muffler, heaviest skirt and cape, skating cap that covered her ears, and she rode the trolley downtown. On this cold and sunny morning she left the car and walked to the corner of Steuben Street and Broadway and joined the crowd of a thousand who were watching firemen with hoses wet down the smoldering bricks of the Delavan's ruins so that the search for the missing bodies could begin. She watched people pick up a brick or a piece of pipe as souvenirs, watched three workers trying to pull down a standing wall so it wouldn't topple on the firemen. One worker threw a rope, with a hook at the end, over the wall and, with his mates, then tried to pull the wall down. They tried half a dozen times, but the wall stood. A man in the crowd told the worker with the hook, 'Tie a noose around the end of that rope and hang yourself, you dumb mick.'

A fireman passed by and Katrina asked him, 'Aren't you going to dig for the bodies?' The missing, estimated at a dozen, were all hotel workers. Cora. Her sister Eileen.

'Not today, ma'am. Still got some fire under there, and in some places maybe eight inches of ice on top of that.'

Workers would need a month to move ten thousand cubic feet of stone and brick to recover all the dead.

Katrina stared up at where the third floor had been, only the brick facade standing now. On the night of the fire the firemen's hoses wouldn't reach that high, their streams turning into broken plumes just above the second floor and coating the hotel's lower exterior with the glitter of instant ice, a scandal: low water pressure in the city, pressure turned off at night in the antiquated pumping station, and for twenty minutes after the fire started, nobody there to turn it back on.

In two third-floor windows, when they were still windows, when there was still a third floor, Adelaide and Archie Van Slyke appeared in Katrina's memory, Adelaide wearing her mother's sealskin coat. She climbed out and sat on the window ledge to escape the smoke pursuing her. She said nothing, but Archie was cajoling her to be calm while he uncoiled a rope fire escape, a single braid, and fed it out the window and down toward Broadway, where his in-laws, and a crowd that would grow to twenty thousand, watched. Firemen inched the great weight of their ladder along the icy wall to a point beneath the imperiled Van Slykes, and two firemen began the upward climb. It was suddenly clear that the ladder would not reach the third floor (four stories up), clear also that Archie's escape rope (designed for a room two floors down) did not even reach the top of the ladder.

Jacob Taylor said then, 'They're as good as dead.' He was lying propped in the doorway of Iligan the Bootmaker's shoe repair shop across from the hotel, awaiting a carriage to take him to St Peter's Hospital.

'They'll get them,' Edward said to him, and Katrina ripped her petticoat to make a bandage for Edward's blistered left hand.

As the flames rose up wildly behind her, Adelaide chose to make her silent leap. She clutched the sealskin coat around her and, to the shrieks of the crowd, pushed herself feet-first toward the firemen on the ladder, swiping both men with her leg (neither man lost his grip on the ladder), bounced onto the trammeled snow cushion of Broadway's sidewalk, and landed at the feet of the half-dozen firemen holding the ladder.

'She's dead,' Katrina said, and she wailed like a wounded hound and buried her head in Edward's embrace.

Then Edward saw Adelaide stand up and talk to the firemen. 'She's *not* dead,' he said. 'Look at her, she's up.'

Katrina looked and saw Adelaide, then kissed Edward.

'God help her live,' Jacob Taylor said.

The firemen on the ladder reached upward toward Archie, who now dangled from the end of the rope just above the second-floor window. A chorus of voices in the crowd yelled to him, 'Hold on . . . they've nearly got you . . . don't let go.' The topmost fireman's hands reached Archie's shoes, then touched them (to a cheer, Katrina remembered), then gripped them both, and at that moment Archie let go of the rope and let himself fall palms-forward to meet the hotel wall. The second fireman grabbed his pantleg and then his knees, and together the two firemen eased him down atop their backs and shoulders onto the ladder. The crowd sent up its roar.

When Katrina learned there would be no digging for bodies today, she took the trolley back to North Albany.

Edward explained to Katrina how it was possible that a flaming stick could fly through the air and pierce her breast.

A porter emptying ashes from the furnace, he told her, had spilled embers on a pile of rags in the basement, without knowing what he'd done. Allowed to kindle unseen, the smoldering rags became the cellar fire that sent foul smoke, and eventually sparks, up the stairwells and heating vents, igniting the south wall of the staircase, and creeping along that wall to the elevator shaft.

The shaft's four wooden walls glistened with spattered oil, Edward said. The wooden elevator cab was built to glide on its cables three inches away from all walls, making the shaft a perfect chimney with perfect draft. The fire licked that oily interior but once, and then blew skyward with instantaneously-cubed ignition that shaped the shaft as a fiery skyrocket, as perfect in its elemental power as the stack of a blast furnace. It swiftly turned the elevator cab into a blazing coffin, and then shot fire through the roof, exploding disaster onto the attic superstructure. The ravenous blaze trapped a dozen employees in their windowless bedrooms under the attic eaves, the only exit door to the roof nailed shut by management to keep housemaids and kitchen boys from loafing, from watching parades pass by on Broadway, to keep them from sleeping on the roof on those summer nights when temperatures in the attic hit a hundred and five. The door burned to ashes, and there was no proof of the nailing. But surely, Edward said, those trapped people must have tried to reach the roof to save themselves, for the hotel had no fire escapes, no fire axes, no hand grenades, no standpipes; and the fire extinguishers hadn't been examined for eighteen months, and many did not work.

Not a dozen but fourteen people lost. Cora and Eileen.

The stack of a blast furnace.

You can see how it could blow a stick through the air to stab you, Edward said.

Geraldine Taylor, recounting her escape for her family, said she had moved through the main lobby, coatless in the early exodus, and out onto Steuben Street, where firemen pointed her toward the Dutch Kitchen, an all-night lunchroom that had become one of several havens for the dispossessed and the injured. She stood in the zero-degree night, searching the thousands of faces, watching the hotel entrance for a glimpse of her family, until she could no longer bear the cold, then went to the lunchroom, which was already out of all food except bread and coffee. Two doors away, in the sheltered doorway of the bootmaker's shop, Jacob Taylor would soon lie in the care of his daughter and Edward.

Geraldine would not see Alelaide's leap, or Archie's rescue, would not see Jacob lifted into the same carriage with Adelaide and Katrina, to be taken together to the hospital. She heard from Maginn, that vulgar reporter, that all were alive but injured, and had gone to St Peter's Hospital.

'And Edward is still looking for you, Mrs Taylor, searching the crowds,' Maginn said. 'They don't know whether you're alive or dead.'

Geraldine did not wait to be found by Edward. She walked the eleven blocks to the hospital without a coat and caught such a cold that Dr Fitzroy thought it might turn into pneumonia; and so kept her home in bed for a week.

Adelaide was hospitalized, and in three days, willful woman, walked out of the hospital without help. Three days after that, she developed such pain that Dr Fitzroy readmitted her, fearing for her life.

Katrina was a presence in the ruins, whatever the weather; two hours a day, or more, watching the work crew grow from six to sixty, coming to know the foreman, the fire chief, the coroner, the policemen, watching ice hacked and shoveled off the debris as the January thaw arrived, hydraulic mining having failed to loosen the debris: for the stream from the hose was too weak. Relatives of the missing sought out Katrina, confided in her; and she locked in memory the names of the fourteen: Florence Hill, housekeeper; Anna Reilly and Mary Sullivan, linen-room workers; Ellen Kiley, laundress; Thomas Cannon, sweeper; Toby Pender, elevator man; Ferdinand Buletti, cook; Nugenta Staurena, vegetable cook; Bridget Fitzsimmons, kitchen girl; Simon Myers, coffee boy; Molly Curry, Sally Egan, and Cora and Eileen McNally, chambermaids.

Tom Maginn of *The Argus*, Edward's bohemian friend, crossed the street toward Katrina. She'd met Maginn before she became involved with Edward, met him skating on the canal when she was nineteen, a flirtatious afternoon. He was tall, had a bit of a shuffling walk, a mustache now that grew long and drooped, a strong jawline, some might say. At their first meeting he said he knew who she was, 'the yellow-haired princess of Elk Street,' and he confessed he could never court her, for he had no money, no prospect of any.

'You are the most sublime woman I've ever met,' he had told her, 'but I'm below your class. I'm a slug in the cellar of your palace.'

She had not spoken to him again until he came to the wedding rehearsal as Edward's best man. Edward had asked his father to be best man, but Emmett said he would not stand on any altar in front of God with Jacob Taylor.

Now, hands in his pockets, Maginn tipped his hat, smiled.

'The city is talking about you,' he said. 'My editor wants me to write about why you come to the ruins every day.'

'I want to bury the dead.'

'Which dead?'

'The McNally girls. Cora was our housemaid until her sister came from Ireland, and they got a job together.'

'You're here because of a housemaid?'

'Cora was very special. We told each other things.'

'Did she tell you she was married?'

'Cora?'

'I talked with her husband. He was a pastry chef at the Delavan, but was let go. They married secretly a month ago to bind themselves together, no matter what happened.'

'Oh, the poor man, he must be devastated.'

'I told him I'd let him know when they find her. What about yourself? I heard you were seriously burned.'

'It's nothing compared to what others suffered. And you? We saw you at dinner. Were you hurt?'

'Not a scratch, not a singe.'

'You were fortunate.'

'Yes, and your husband, he's one of the heroes of the fire. He always seems to rise to the occasion.'

'He saved my father's life. And my mother's. And that poor woman from New York.'

'You helped save that woman, too. You needn't be modest.'

'I did what Edward told me to do,' Katrina said.

'Anything I can do for you? The slug, as always, is at your service. You only have to ask.'

'I can think of nothing to ask. Please don't write anything about me.'

'It wouldn't embarrass you, I assure you.'

'Any story would embarrass me. Please don't. This is what I ask you.'

'All right, Mrs Daugherty,' Maginn said, and with a smile added, 'Now you owe me one.'

At dusk this day the workers found the first body. Until then the chief discovery had been the safe owned by Ozzie Parker, who ran the cigar stand in the lobby. The safe had protected Parker's ledgers, gold and silver coins, and seven boxes of cigars, still unlit. The found body was a legless torso, head and one arm attached, sitting erect. It was Mrs Hill, the housekeeper, identified by her protruding teeth; and under her arm an album of tintypes, all defaced by the heat, no one recognizable.

As the light of day faded, a dozen lanterns surrounded the dig with ceremonial light, and families of the dead moved closer to the ruins, Katrina in the vanguard. One worker with a spade brought up a blue worsted vest. When he held it up to the light of two lanterns, a man came out of the crowd and said, 'That's Simon Myers's vest.'

'How might you know that?' the foreman asked him.

'I gave it to him,' the man said. 'He's my son.'

'I'm sorry for that, Mr Myers, but we won't be digging him up tonight.'

'Why not, in heaven's name?'

'Just too dark. These men been here eleven hours, and I hate to say this, but the smell up from there is tough to work in. We'll let the grave here air out and get back at it in the mornin'.'

Most workers were smoking pipes to mask the odor of the malignant vapor that rose from the ruins. To Katrina the odor had been an onset of reality, a proof that death was more than an assumption. Workers put the lanterns in a circle around the open grave and the coroner ordered police to guard the dig. Twice during the night they chased away a bulldog.

On the next morning at half after midnight, the seventh day after the fire, Adelaide died in the hospital. Katrina and Geraldine were with her. Jacob, on the floor above, was unaware she'd been readmitted, for Dr Fitzroy cautioned against shocking him. He would sedate Jacob when it came time to tell him his daughter died of a ruptured spleen, suffered in her leap from the window. Edward brought the carriage to take Katrina and her mother home.

Katrina put her mother to bed and told Edward she would stay the night at Elk Street.

She lay on the canopy bed in Adelaide's old room, a room of memory now: her old hobbyhorse, and the dozen and a half dolls of all nations, a new one every Christmas, and the Phrygian cap of liberty that was a gift from the French Ambassador when he came to the Taylor home for a dinner in his honor (the cap was supposed to be Katrina's but was handed to Adelaide by mistake), and the Cleveland for President poster, and the toy sailboat, differing only in color from Katrina's, that the sisters had sailed together on Washington Park Lake.

Katrina, incapable of sleep, imagined how she might have diverted the course of life from the dreadful conclusion it had come to this night: by not letting Adelaide run away from them at the fire, by not siding with her parents against Edward, by not yielding to Edward's plan to win back their goodwill with his dinner and gifts. By not marrying him.

She told her mother's servants to monitor Geraldine, make her breakfast, keep her in bed through the morning. Then she dressed, ate freshly baked bread with butter and coffee, and walked down Elk Street, past the city high school, and down Columbia Street to the Kenmore Hotel, where she bought an *Argus* at the hotel's cigar stand. The paper reported there would be a Catholic mass for the dead at St Mary's Catholic church. Eleven of the dead were Catholic, three Protestant. Protestant ministers and mourners would be welcomed. When all bodies were presumed recovered they would be buried in a mass grave at St Agnes Catholic Cemetery unless relatives claimed the remains. But who could say whose remains were whose?

Toby Pender might have been buried in an unmarked grave had not Edward bought not only a grave but a sculpted sword-bearing granite angel to mark the resting place of the fire's principal hero, the man who saved Geraldine, among many, and who deserved more than anonymity in death. When he first discovered the smoke, Toby rode his cab to every floor to alert all in earshot, picked up passengers, returned for stragglers, returned again, and yet again on a fourth trip, and was rescuing a lone woman guest when the blast of fire incinerated them both. Toby's and the woman's presences were verified four weeks later, in the final stages of the dig, days after the mass burial, when the woman's melted diamond ring and Toby's tiny crooked spine were found at the bottom of the shaft, along with fleshless, disheveled bones that crumbled at the touch.

Katrina left the Kenmore and walked down to Broadway and stood at her post by the ruins. She was there ten minutes before the digging resumed at eight o'clock. By ten-thirty parts of eight bodies had been resurrected: part of a thighbone and a pelvic bone, both looking like coal; a wristbone with crisp flesh; the cloth of two dresses, one brown, one black with a weave of dark blue on the skirt's hem, both fragments of cloth found adhering to the same flesh.

'It looks to us that these two died in each other's arms,' said the coroner to a group of reporters, Maginn among them. 'We guess they were under the bed, and fell through to the kitchen, where the fire was hottest. The kitchen and bakeshop were both full of grease and just fed the fire.'

'Those dresses may have belonged to the McNally sisters,' Maginn said to the coroner. 'Her husband here recognizes the design in the black one.'

Katrina approached Maginn and Cora's husband. She stared at the husband, who was holding the piece of dress and weeping. She touched the man's arm.

'I knew Cora very well,' she said. 'Please let me help you bury her and her sister.'

The husband looked at this stranger, then at Maginn.

'This is Mrs Daugherty,' Maginn told him.

'We can't help whom it is we love,' Katrina said to the man. 'We must learn to avoid love. Love is a mask of death, you know.'

'What's that?' asked the husband.

'Death is venerable. You can always count on death.' Katrina began to weep, dabbed her eyes with a handkerchief, saw Edward pushing through the crowd toward her.

'Forgive me,' she said to Cora's husband. 'I weep all the time lately. I weep for everybody. It's a pity what people come to be.'

'What's going on?' Edward asked.

'I think you should take her home,' Maginn said.

'Yes,' said Katrina. 'There's other death at home, isn't there, Edward?'

'Yes, there is, my dear,' Edward said. 'I know how you love death, how you need it,' and Katrina smiled at him and wept anew. Maginn and Cora's husband could only stare at the two of them.

In a subsequent diary entry Katrina fixed on the fire as the point of transformation of Edward's and her lives into a unity that transcended marriage, love, and a son:

We were united through the fire in freakish fusion, like Siamese twins with a common heart that damned us both to an intimacy that not only *knew* the other's every breath, but knew the difference between that everybreath and the signal breath that precedes decision, or unbearable memory, or sudden death. We now live out an everlastingly mutual curse: 'May the breath of your enemy be your own.'

Two months after the fire, in the unbanishable melancholia that followed the death of his daughter, Jacob Taylor died of a massive heart attack. Katrina was not the one to articulate the accusation, but she came to believe what her mother had said first: Edward killed Adelaide and Jacob.

Katrina at Emmett's Sickbed

July 17, 1903

The day was warm and brilliant with light when Katrina entered the Daugherty house on Main Street with a bouquet of asters and zinnias just cut from her garden on Colonie Street: reds, oranges, pinks, and yellows to brighten the sickroom where Emmett Daugherty, eighty-one, lay dying of decay and disuse.

Katrina had come to see this as a house of death, for just before she and Edward stayed here, in the months the Colonie Street house was being renovated, Hanorah died of a heart seizure. And they were still here when Adelaide, Jacob, Cora, and all the others died from the fire. Now death was claiming yet another soul, and the imminence was giving meaning to Katrina's life in the way her vigil at Cora's exhumation had vitalized her days. The sun was shining brightly on this latest visitation.

The front door was open (Emmett had not locked it since he built the house) and Katrina strode into the hallway and past the front parlor, which had gone all but unused since Hanorah died. The parlor always seemed to Katrina to be Hanorah's museum: the rocking chair where she sat to sew, and to monitor the passersby on Main Street; the huge woodstove she always tended that was now ornamental with the advent of the coal furnace; the dusty valances, the chair doilies – when were they last washed?

She walked down the hallway into the kitchen, found two empty milk bottles in the pantry, and filled them with water and flowers. A woman in a housedress and a clean white apron that covered the dress from waist to ankle came in through the kitchen door. Who is she? A face Katrina knew. Annie Farrell, from next door, that's right. I haven't seen her since '95. So pretty. So plain. And not Farrell anymore.

'Mrs Daugherty, I'm not interrupting, am I?' Annie said.

'Oh, hello, hello, not at all,' said Katrina. I can't call her Annie. Mrs Phelan? No. 'I brought some flowers.'

'So beautiful,' Annie said. 'And I baked some beans and bread, just out of the stove. I know nobody cooks in this house.'

'That's sweet of you,' said Katrina. She thinks I should come every day and cook?

'With all the sickness and trouble, I mean,' Annie said. 'How is he?'

'I just this minute got here. But I know he had a very bad night. Go up and say hello.'

'I wouldn't intrude,' Annie said.

'He'd love it. He speaks so fondly of the Farrells next door.'

'There's always been a closeness. He and my father helped each other build their houses.'

'But you're not a Farrell anymore,' said Katrina.

'Right you are, Mrs Daugherty. I'm a Phelan these four years. Francis, you know. He worships your husband.'

'Yes.' And I worshiped him. *Worshiped* Francis. Before you did, Mrs Phelan.

'He always mentions your kindness when you were neighbors and he worked for you,' Annie said.

'Does he? That's nice.' Kindness he thinks it was?

Katrina picked up the two bottles with the flowers.

'We'll go see Emmett,' she said, and Annie followed her up the stairs to the sickroom, where Edward, in his late-afternoon ritual, was sitting with Frank McArdle, the Daugherty family doctor, an ample-bellied man with a white brush of a mustache, here on his daily visit. Edward and the doctor were delivering up stories and gossip to keep Emmett alive with words alone. As the women entered they saw Emmett, raising phlegm from his ruined lungs, propped on pillows under a large colored likeness of Pope Leo XIII, the man Emmett loved better than Jesus.

357

Katrina remembered an angry Emmett invoking Leo when the trolley strike of 1901 was looming. He would rant over supper about the injustice of the traction company for bringing in scab labor and not only refusing its workers a pittance of a wage increase, but cutting their wages and extending their workday. She could see him pounding the table, bouncing potatoes out of the dish, declaiming to all: 'Don't take my word. The Pope of Rome himself said it. Workers are not chattels, and it's shameful to treat them like that. Shameful, that's the Pope's word for those traction company frauds. "To defraud anyone of wages that are his due is a crime that cries out to the avenging anger of heaven." There's Pope Leo for you, a real man he is, and by the Jesus, no man ever spoke truer. Amen to Leo, I say. Amen to Leo.'

Now Emmett lay beneath the image of the Workingman's Pope, his eyes half closed, giving fading attention to Dr McArdle, who was talking of a woman who married a man for his money and the man then went bankrupt and stayed that way twelve years.

'It's a rare day,' said the doctor,' that people marry for love anymore, the way you and I did, Emmett, and the way Edward did. Am I right, Edward?'

'I hear you, Frank,' Edward said. 'But love isn't enough, and anybody who thinks it is, is demented.'

Katrina, hearing this as she entered, said, 'You are so right, my love,' and she put one bottle of flowers on Emmett's dresser, the other on his bedside table.

Edward took her aside, held her hand.

'There are impediments to love,' she said softly.

'How well I know that,' he said.

'I'm glad you accept it.'

'I don't accept it.'

'But you must,' she said.

Edward pushed love away, whispered to her that Emmett was very weak, and that they had decided to go for the priest. Emmett heard him.

'Yes, get Father Loonan,' Emmett said with more strength than

Katrina expected. 'And have a pitcher of ale to pour when he gets here.'

Annie Farrell walked to Emmett's bedside, touched his hand with her fingertips, shook her head.

'Giving drink to the priest, now is that a good thing, Emmett?'

Emmett almost smiled and answered her in such a scratchy whisper that Annie had to lean over to hear him.

'He says ale is God's greatest handiwork,' Annie said.

'Then we should get some right away,' said Edward.

'I'll get Father Loonan,' Katrina said, 'and then I'll stop for the ale.'

'You?' said Annie. 'You surely wouldn't be seen in a saloon.'

'It's time I would be,' Katrina said, and she bent over Emmett and kissed his forehead. 'Don't you dare go anywhere till I get back,' she said.

'I'll get the ale,' Edward told her, 'you get the priest.'

'I'll get both,' said Katrina. 'You stay here with your father, where you ought to be.'

In the kitchen Katrina rinsed out Emmett's two-quart pewter growler with the snap-on cover and put it in a wicker handbasket. Edward was right about love. The impulse to love is a disease. Is disease a proper reason for marrying? No sane person would do anything for such love. What had loving Francis meant? When he went away she was left with dead memories, cold as a corpse. Try drawing love out of a corpse. It's never who or what you love that drives you, Katrina, but who or what loves you. A cat. If a cat loves me, I am alive.

She left the house and walked the two and a half blocks to Sacred Heart church on Walter Street, the church Emmett helped build with his monthly payments and the strength of his back. She rang the parish house bell to rouse Father Loonan, who had performed the marriage ceremony for Edward and Katrina seventeen years ago. He opened the door, fresh from his prayers, or was it a nap? Well, he seemed to be elsewhere.

'Emmett Daugherty is dying, Father. He needs you. He needs the sacrament.'

359

'Ah, the poor devil, he's all done, is he?'

'He's no devil, Father. He's a virtuous man.'

'Oh he is, he is. I've got someone coming in ten minutes, my dear, and then I'll be along.'

'Emmett can't wait ten minutes, Father.'

'He can't. It's that way, is it?'

'Your visitor can wait, but Emmett is losing the light.'

'Then I'll be right along, dear, right along.'

'Excellent, Father,' Katrina said, and turned to leave.

'Have you candlesticks in the house?' the priest asked.

'I believe we do.'

'And a crucifix. You must have a crucifix.'

'We have one.'

'Holy water. Do you have that?'

'We do.'

'And the chrism?'

'The what, Father?'

'The chrism, child. The holy oil.'

'I never saw any.'

'Then I'll bring it. And a piece of palm from Palm Sunday. You must have that.'

'There's some stuck behind Jesus on the crucifix.'

'All right. And a lemon, do you have a lemon?'

'I'll buy one if we don't.'

'And water, and a spoon, I'll need that.'

'Are you going to make lemonade, Father?'

'Don't get flibbertigibbet on me,' the priest said. 'And a piece of cotton. And some bread. And salt.'

'We'll have it all,' Katrina said.

'Then we'll get Emmett ready for his journey,' Father Loonan said.

Katrina left him in the doorway and walked toward Jack McCall's saloon on Broadway. Lemon and cotton and salt and oil. What a peculiar religion she had joined, its mysteries endless. She walked with a dynamic erectness, straight back, narrow waist, wide-brimmed straw hat flat on her yellow hair, her walk, almost a military pace, surging with the energy of youth, though she was now thirty-seven. She moved toward McCall's with an all-but-visible purpose, a change of mood for Katrina, who did daily battle with absence of purpose, boredom, pervasive ambivalence toward every waking act. Why should I get up? Why go to bed? Why try to reimagine Francis? Why write the diary? Why not? It's as meaningful as anything else you might do, and as meaningless. You have a lazy soul, Katrina. You will die with such slowness, such slight daily reduction, that no one will notice that you've left the room until the clusters of dust accumulate around your empty chair.

But today could be different: today on Main Street, at the parish house, heading for the saloon, immersed in the life of the people you inherited when you wed Edward, today you know that change is so real it can almost be touched. You will be free, Katrina, when you know what drives you. When Emmett, that wonderful man, at last ceases to linger, you will be liberated from the street that marriage has imposed upon you. Won't you be free? I do love my husband and his family. I do, I do. And I do think them alien to all that I am or will be.

There were no saloons like McCall's in Katrina's private domain. She entered it through the front door, walked to the bar and put the basket on top of it. As she lifted out the growler, the bartender and six men at the bar stared at her. This was a small, two-room saloon with black window curtains that were closed only on Sunday mornings, when it was illegal to serve spirits to any but the neediest cases. Such cases entered as quickly as possible through the side door, for you wouldn't be seen going into a saloon's front door on a Sunday. Also, women always entered through that same side door, the ladies' entrance, and sat at one of three tables in the back room, where ladies were supposed to sit. And not for long.

'We don't have women at the bar, Ma'am,' the bartender said. His name was Jimmy McGrath and he had managed the saloon for Jack McCall ever since Jack became a county undersheriff. Jimmy was known as the most honest bartender in Albany, for no drunk ever lost the money he didn't know he'd left on Jimmy's bar. Jimmy would put it in the register, with a note specifying the credit, and he'd tell the drunk about it on his next visit. Katrina did not know such things about Jimmy, but she liked his kindly face, and the clever way he parted the remains of his silky white hair.

'I don't plan to stay,' she said to Jimmy. 'I only want this filled with ale,' and she pushed the growler toward him. He didn't touch it.

'Ladies generally come in the other door and sit in the ladies' section,' he said. 'And ladies never come in without an escort. For politeness and protection.'

'I shall be very polite, I assure you. And I need no protection.'

'Ladies sit back there, Ma'am, no matter what.'

'Is there a bar back there where I can get my ale?'

'No, Ma'am. This is the only bar.'

'Then I'll stay here, and when I get it I'll leave.'

'But we don't serve ladies here, Ma'am. House rule.'

'And a silly one, I must say. My father-in-law is dying, and the ale is for him, and for Father Loonan when he comes to perform the last rites, ten minutes from now.'

The men nodded at the solemnity of use to which this ale was about to be put.

'You probably know the man who's dying,' Katrina said. 'Emmett Daugherty is his name.'

'Ah, Emmett. So that's who it is,' Jimmy said. 'I knew he was ailing.'

'Emmett is dying?' said one of the men. He was tall and brawny and wore a brown derby with a hole in it. He took off his hat, looked at it reverentially, then put it back on. 'I've known him all my life. A grand man.'

'He's very close to death,' Katrina said. 'Now may I have this container filled?' She put a dollar on the bar.

Jimmy McGrath uncovered the growler, put it under the ale spigot, and pushed the dollar back to Katrina.

'Tell Emmett this round is on Jimmy,' he said.

He capped the full growler, put it in Katrina's basket, lifted it and came around the bar to hand it to her.

Outside, a dog yelped in pain. Katrina looked out to see a man kicking a collie dog tied to the tailgate of a wagon loaded with red bricks.

'That man is kicking a dog,' Katrina said, and all the men came to the window to look at the spectacle. The man kicked the dog again. A heavyset woman, sitting on the wagon and holding the reins of the two horses, watched the kicking.

'Somebody should stop him,' Katrina said. 'Help that poor animal that can't help itself.'

'Yes, Ma'am,' said the tall man with the derby. He went out the saloon's screen door and spoke to the dog-kicker.

'You oughtn'ta kick that dog,' said the tall man.

'It's my dog. I'll kick him all I want,' said the dog-kicker, and he kicked the dog again. He was short and muscular from lifting bricks, and he wore a sleeveless undershirt.

The tall man effortlessly shoved him to one side, then reached down and untied the rope that held the dog. The dog ran away. Katrina came out of the saloon with her basket.

'You did very well,' she said to the tall man. 'I thank you, and I'm sure the dog does too.'

'You better go bring my dog back,' the dog-kicker said.

'No, I ain't gonna do that,' the tall man said. 'You'd only kick him some more.'

The dog-kicker swung his fist, but the blow only reached the left side of the tall man's neck. The tall man threw two short, powerful punches, one with each hand, and knocked the dog-kicker backward into the street. When he went down, the back of his head hit the granite-block pavement. He started to sit up but fell back and stayed down. Everybody stared at him. The woman climbed off the wagon. She was as burly as the man on the ground (Katrina thought of them as a matched pair), and wore a man's shirt with sleeves rolled, her muscular arms bare well above the elbow. She lifted the fallen man up onto the sidewalk and raised him with a hand under his back. His head wobbled.

'You killed him,' the woman yelled at the tall man.

'I didn't kill him,' the tall man said. 'He hit me and I hit him.'

'He shouldn't have kicked the dog,' Katrina said.

'Who asked you?' the woman said. 'Maybe he shoulda kicked you. Maybe I oughta kick your tail across Broadway.'

'I'm harder to kick than a tied-up dog,' Katrina said.

'You think so?' the woman said, and she flexed her right bicep, the size of a grapefruit, and walked toward Katrina. She tightened the muscle and held it and the veins stood out like branches of a tree. She stared at Katrina and tensed the muscle, splitting a vein and spurting blood onto Katrina's yellow dress; then she raised the bloody bicep in front of Katrina's face.

'I don't have to kick you,' the woman said. 'I'll squeeze you like a bunch of grapes.'

The tall man stepped between the women. 'Nobody gonna squeeze this lady.'

'I'm gettin' the cops after you, Mister,' the woman said.

'That's good,' said the tall man. 'I'll be waitin' for 'em here in the saloon. You go along, now, Miss,' he told Katrina. 'This ain't your business to worry about.'

'If you need a witness, my name is Katrina Daugherty. Second-last house on Main Street.'

'Okay, Miss Daugherty, and we thank you,' the tall man said. He tipped his hat. 'You tell Emmett, but only if he's really dyin', that Hoggie Ryan wishes him a happy death.'

'Does he know you, Mr Ryan?'

'He seen me fight bare-knuckle many a night.'

'I shall certainly tell him. Hoggie Ryan. Thank you.'

Katrina shook hands with Hoggie and then walked toward Ronan's grocery to buy a lemon. She saw the collie sitting in the shade of a porch. As she passed, the dog wagged its tail.

Katrina put a chiffon scarf around her shoulders to hide the blood on her blouse; then she and Annie carried the ale and three glasses to Emmett's room. Katrina gave a glass to Edward, one to Dr McArdle, and put one on a table for Father Loonan, drawing an instant rebuke from Emmett.

'Do you think I wouldn't have a glass meself?' he asked. 'And one for each of you.' The speech cost him strength, and he coughed, and slumped, then closed his eyes to rest for the next challenge.

'I'll go,' Annie said, and while she went for more glasses, Katrina spread a white table scarf on Emmett's bedside table, then set out the paraphernalia Father Loonan requested: the holy water, a table-spoon, glass of water, wad of cotton, salt cellar, heel of bread, lemon sliced in two, two candleholders with blessed candles, the crucifix, and the palm fronds she undid from behind the torso of Jesus. The table was so crowded that she and Edward brought down a long table from the attic to give proper space to the final necessities.

When Annie came in with the glasses Emmett opened his eyes. 'Is no one goin' to pour the ale?' he asked.

'At your service,' said Dr McArdle, and he poured for those in the room, giving the first to Emmett, who took the glass and looked at it, then set it beside a blessed candle.

'I think you did this just to have a drink your doctor couldn't object to,' Katrina said. 'You don't look like you're dying.'

'Half me life I didn't look like I was livin'. It evens out,' Emmett said. And he closed his eyes again.

When Annie came back with Father Loonan, Doc McArdle poured an ale and handed it to him.

'What's this?' the priest asked.

'I know you like your ale,' Emmett said.

'I never denied it,' the priest said. 'But I never had any with the last rites.'

'It goes good with everything,' Emmett said.

'Emmett Martin Daugherty,' Edward said, 'we're all present and accounted for. What's your pleasure? Where would you like your body anointed first, on the inside or the outside?'

'First I want to know what he does with that lemon,' Emmett said.

'It cleans the oil off my fingers,' the priest said.

'That's clever,' Emmett said. He reached for the ale and raised the glass to the light. 'By God that looks good. We'll just have a taste.' He took a sip and others in the room did likewise. 'All right,' Emmett said, 'get it over with.'

'I was told you were dying,' the priest said. 'But I'm not sure you're dying.'

'That's what I told him, Father,' Katrina said.

'I'm dyin' nevertheless,' Emmett said. 'I can't stand on me pins anymore, and with every breath there's a pain, and when I close me eyes I see somethin' comin'.'

'What does it look like?' the priest asked.

'Like the inside of a fireman's boot.'

'That's not what heaven looks like.'

'Then I'm goin' someplace else.'

'Since you're able to talk, we'll want to have a confession,' the priest said, and turning to the others he said, 'If you'd all please leave the room . . .'

'There's no need,' Emmett said. 'I've nothin' to confess.'

'You're a saint, then, is that it?' the priest said.

'Not hardly, but I've nothin' to confess.'

'Confess the sins you forgot and I'll forgive those.'

'I forgot none I ever committed. The memory of them kept me smiling for forty-five years.'

'I'll forgive those. Anything else?'

'I let my wife work too hard.'

'You've got company on that one.'

'And I thought too little of meself,' Emmett said. 'I paid too much attention to the work, and the trees in the yard, and Reilly the dog, God rest his soul.'

'Dogs don't have souls,' the priest said.

'This one did,' said Emmett. 'He went to mass every Sunday with me. And he never ate meat on Friday.'

'And did he do his Easter duty?'

'He did. On the parish house lawn.'

'Is that all the sins?'

'I could make some up,' Emmett said.

'No need for that,' and he made the sign of the cross, saying, '*Te absolvo in nomine Patris et Filii et Spiritus Sancti*. For your penance say one Hail Mary and have some more ale.'

Emmett blessed himself, closed his eyes for a ten-second prayer, then reached for his glass and took one long swallow, all he could tolerate. Father Loonan did likewise, then opened his prayer book and said, 'Now we'll get on with it,' and, holding the holy oil, read in the Latin: '*Per istam sanctam Unctionem, et suam piissimam misericordiam, indulgeat tibi Dominus quidquid deliquisti . . .*'

Emmett said to him, 'Will ye say it in English so I know what's goin' on.'

And the priest spoke the formal prayers of Extreme Unction, anointing, with holy oil on cotton, Emmett's eyes, ears, nose, lips, hands, and feet, the sensory entrances of sin, saying to him, 'Through this holy Unction, and of His tender mercy, may the Lord pardon thee whatsoever sins thou hast committed by thine eyes . . . thine ears,' and repeating it on through to the chrismal swabbing of the foot from heel to toe, whereupon Emmett spoke up and said, 'There's no need to bother with the toes. I never sinned with any of them.'

Katrina giggled, then broke into sobs she tried to stifle. This gallant man really was dying and by loving him she felt like a traitor to her own dead, for he loathed her father and spiritually worked against him all his life, and against the world that had shaped her family and her life. She looked at Edward and her sobbing intensified: my husband who put my sister and father in their graves, guiltless, honorable man now losing his own father. And all her love for Edward seemed remarkable and perverse. This Main Street, this North End, where the Daugherty seed took root, was, in all its guises, a foreign place, and yet its river and its foundries and its traction barns and its Lumber District and its dying canal were the sources of life that sustained *her* family in all its lineages – the Staatses, Bradfords, Taylors, Fitzgibbons, Van Slykes. Here were the wellsprings of power and wealth that had gilded the heart, soul, and lifetime of Katrina Taylor Daugherty, weeping child of the new century, wounded by the flames of hellish flowers, who can now find no substitute in life for her loss, her diminishment, her abasement known so intimately: loving and losing Francis Phelan, that angry, lovely boy who defeated the abstraction of power with a flung stone. Katrina, faithless, sobbing wretch, you are adrift in this Irish Catholic fog that envelops your elegantly patrician self. (That woman with the bloody bicep must be Catholic. She would be all wrong as an Episcopalian.) What does your poet say to you now, Katrina? He says that the world goes round by misunderstanding, the only way people can agree: for if they understood each other they would never agree on anything, such as marriage to the enemy: that man across the room whom you say you love, who woke you into a terrifying nightmare, who had you screaming for release before you even made the bond with him, who led you, docile woman, out of fire into salvation; that man who is the son of this virtuous man dying in front of you. What part of this dying father has passed into that living son, do you know? When the soul's light goes out forever, what is the loss to those who have stood for so long in that light? Your sobs are evidence of an uncertain mind, Katrina. You should not cry at the death of a beloved man to whom you once gave only hostility. Your allegiance is as fickle as the rain. Your giggle at his sinless toes is a proper response.

The priest ended the sacrament and made the sign of the cross over Emmett. Katrina breathed in, straightened her back, and raised her glass in emulation of Edward's celebratory gesture.

'All praise to Emmett Daugherty,' she said. 'All praise to a great man, I say. The truly great men are the poet, the priest, and the soldier, and Emmett Daugherty is a soldier of the righteous wars.'

Then, between sobs, she willfully drank all of her ale.

'Cully Watson Hanged'

Albany Argus, *May 24, 1910*

Culbert (Cully) Watson, known in Albany for years as a hotel sneak and petty hoodlum, was hanged from a telegraph pole in the French Quarter of New Orleans last night after being taken off a train at gunpoint by four men in kerchief masks. Watson was en route to New Orleans for trial on an attempted-murder charge, and was in custody of two New Orleans detectives when the four masked men disarmed and tied up the detectives, and fled the train with Watson.

His corpse was found hanging on Bourbon Street, near the hotel where ten days ago, police say, he raped, robbed, and left for dead a twenty-seven-year-old woman. She had been smothered, but revived to find the room filled with gas from an open jet. She said she'd seen her attacker working at the hotel desk as night clerk. Police said the attacker had gained entry to and left the woman's room through the transom, and that Watson was slim and agile enough to accomplish this. He has a known history of such unlawful entry and assault on women.

Police caught Watson with the woman's diamond brooch and $2,000 in cash as he stepped off a train at Memphis. To bargain with police, Watson told of his connection to the infamous Love Nest killings of 1908, when a prominent Albany physician, Giles Fitzroy, murdered his wife, shot and wounded the Albany playwright Edward Daugherty, then killed himself. The shootings took place at the Millerton

House in Manhattan, where Watson was then working. He disappeared after the killings.

Police said Dr Fitzroy and Daugherty testified against Watson at a hearing into a river-barge brawl in 1906, and Watson may have held a grudge against them. Police have a lengthy statement from Watson about the Love Nest case but have disclosed no details about Watson's role in it; but they did say that others may be involved.

A Picnic on the Barge

June 17, 1906

Edward, in his white suit and white Panama with the flowerpot crown, walked at sunbright morning with a stream of other men, women, and children down Columbia Street past the new Union Station. Where the goddamned Delavan stood. Handsome new building and they used plenty of the Delavan's scorched bricks. Some things can be salvaged from any wreckage. Katrina?

He headed toward the old red bridge that spanned the Albany Basin, then out toward the pier, where two covered, double-deck barges, and the tug that would pull them, rested at anchor in the placid water of the Hudson. He saw Maginn coming toward the bridge from another direction, and he waited for him.

'You're alone,' Maginn said.

'So are you,' said Edward.

'I'm always alone, except when I'm with a beautiful and accessible woman, which I fully expect to be before this day is over.'

'My own beautiful woman decided not to come.'

'That's truly a pity,' Maginn said. 'How is she? I haven't seen her in months.'

'She's all right. You know she doesn't favor the drinking.'

Despite Edward's arguments to Katrina that today they could celebrate something *together* for a change – the river's summer glory, the gift of a lustrous day – she said she couldn't abide all that family sweetness, all those dowdy biddies, all the rowdiness. So she stayed home. Avoiding the class struggle.

'Then we're a couple of bachelors for the day,' Maginn said. 'Like the old days. Tent city at the State Fair, when you were still a lowly reporter? Remember?'

'Things have changed since then,' Edward said.

'Not I. I find myself a lowly reporter still. And I still dandle the doxies, don't you, old man, once in a while, just for the hell of it? Tell the truth.'

'Part of my past,' Edward said.

'You've tamed the tendril. How resolute.'

At the gangway, a policeman was backing a man down the ramp, poking his chest with a billy club. Five others backed down behind him. Edward recognized the cop, Willie Glass.

'It's not a free ride,' Glass said. 'Buy a ticket.'

'Go scratch your ass, Glass,' said the ejected man, who was short, wiry, and thirtyish, with long black hair parted in the middle, a full mustache, and sufficiently irregular good looks that Edward judged him a pimp. He mumbled to the men with him and they went away.

'Sheridan Avenue boys,' Maginn said. 'The one sassing the cop is Cully Watson. He doesn't like to pay for things.'

'He has the look of a man who uses women,' Edward said.

'Very perceptive,' Maginn said. 'He's also very wild.'

Edward and Maginn boarded the barge for the impending voyage, a neighborhood outing of North and South End church groups, social clubs, and singing societies. They'd all been accumulating food in their club rooms and vestries for days for this, the Eintracht excursion, which took its name from the city's premier choral group, the Eintracht Singing Society, a mix of working and professional men, Protestants and Catholics, Germans, Dutch, English, and Irish, who once a year embarked together on this exercise in social leveling.

The excursion was financed by boarding tickets, and the sale of prepaid tickets for beer and soft drinks. People had been boarding since eight o'clock, fifty cents a head; and the two barges (used to haul ice, hay, or produce on weekdays) were already a floating small town. At ten-thirty, with more than two thousand aboard, the sailors hauled up the gangway. *Old Hellbound,* the tug, towed the first barge under and past the narrow draws of the Maiden Lane and South Ferry Street bridges, then went back for the second barge; and when the two were side by side, sailors lashed them together, then opened the rails of their top decks so the two boats became one, doubling the conviviality. Then the tug moved them downriver at low speed, toward the Baerena Island picnic grounds.

Edward and Maginn searched for a table on a lower deck, where women were already passing out knockwurst, pork sandwiches, plates of beans and cabbage, and men were clustered at the bar, where two bartenders steadily drew mugs of beer from tapped kegs. Johnny Daugherty, the famous fiddler, Edward's distant cousin through unchartable family links in Spiddal, broke into 'The Wind That Shakes the Barley' for anyone ready to jig this early in the day, and there were a few. Card games proceeded, and Edward saw Midge Kresser unfolding his portable three-card-monte table, about to begin his day's work parting suckers from their nickels and dimes. Ministers and priests were eating with their flocks. Policemen Willie Glass and Joe Anthony strolled the deck, keeping the peace.

'I see Giles,' Edward said, and they found him in line for drinks, wearing his commodore's cap and lemon-yellow vest.

'Felicity come with you?' Edward asked, expecting Giles's wife would have absented herself today for the same reasons as Katrina.

'She did,' Giles said, and he pointed toward a table where Felicity was sitting with a woman in her late forties. Felicity was quintessentially summery in a white linen frock and white straw boater with pink ribbon. The other woman was older, slender, bosomy, and narrow-waisted, her pale-green dress subtly décolleté.

'That woman with your wife,' Maginn said, 'she's suitable for a saddle, wouldn't you say, Fitz?'

'I knew you'd notice her, Maginn,' Giles said. 'Felicity's Aunt Sally, a handsome woman. To tell the truth, I wouldn't be surprised if she went for you. She has a weakness for your type.'

'What's my type?'

'Worthless lout with a wit,' Giles said. 'Her husband has no sense of humor.'

'She has a husband but fancies witty men.'

'I hear he's not much of a husband. He's a fire chief down in Westchester. You see before you the fireman's wife.'

'The fireman's wife. And why is she here?'

'Visiting Felicity. The fire chief rents a summer place near Glenmont, and Sally stays there all summer. The chief comes up weekends.'

'Weekends,' said Maginn. 'Is that a midweek knock at the door I hear?'

'I wouldn't go so fast,' Giles said. 'She's a proper lady all the same.'

'Of course. Aren't they all?'

Giles's procuring for his wife's aunt at first mention of her existence baffled Edward. It was out of character for the man, but it certainly energized Maginn.

'What do you want to do, Maginn? As if I didn't know.'

'I'll go chat with Giles,' Maginn said.

'You do that,' Edward said. 'I'll see you later.'

And Edward then roamed the barge alone, seeing who was aboard. He saw Jack McCall sitting with Ruthie, and Father Loonan with a glass of ale in front of him, and men Edward knew from the Eintracht, to which he, Giles, and Maginn all belonged. Lyman had initiated Edward into the singing group at age sixteen ('The Daughertys always had the music' was Emmett's line), but as he grew older, traveling as a writer, Edward lost connection with the group, except for this excursion. He had no desire now to join anybody's company. The fraternal impulse to spend the day with his fellow Eintrachters and North Enders, to celebrate family serenity and midsummer's sweet pleasures, had faded totally. If he could get off the barge now, he would.

He heard half a dozen singers in an impromptu rendering of 'Believe Me, If All Those Endearing Young Charms,' Tom Moore's ballad about the constancy of love:

Thou wouldst still be adored,
As this moment thou art,
Let thy loveliness fade as it will . . .

He walked to the rail and felt the day warming, saw the sky as a
wash of peaceable blue. He stared out at a field full of grazing cows,
at the great trees along the river's edge, at the riverfront mansions,
and fields of early-sprouting corn growing above the floodplain,
and he felt invincibly depressed, trapped in his shriveling skin: a
man in motion to save himself from stasis. Tom Moore's song
mocked what he felt about his increasingly silent marriage. The
only constancy was Katrina's steady withdrawal into her world
of poetry and fantasy, the endless interiorizing of her life in
diaries, which she did not hide, but which Edward would not
intrude upon. Her behavior had been eccentric always, but after
the Delavan she backpedaled into silence, her life a chamber
of secrets and venerations of all that is sad and solitary: in
communion is contamination; in isolation the suffering soul's
beauty is enhanced.

'Where have you gone?' he had asked her this morning after
she decided not to join him on the excursion.

'Where I have to be,' she said.

'You should be here with me.'

'I am here.'

'You're not.'

'Let me be.'

'I apologize for trying to make you look at us as we are, and
what we have become. I know it's terrible to force someone to
accept reality.'

She smiled and grew more beautiful.

Francis Phelan tapped him on the shoulder.

'You ain't thinkin' of jumpin' overboard, are you, Ed?'

Edward shook hands with Francis.

'Just thinking about things that can spoil a great day,' Edward
said. 'How come you're not playing ball?'

'We got us a day off and Annie wanted to spend it on the river.'

Francis, maybe the best baseball player in the city, played short-stop for Albany in the New York State League. Edward had written a play, *The Car Barns*, about the Albany trolley strike of 1901, and modeled his hero on Francis, a young man who, with uncanny accuracy, threw a stone the size of a baseball and killed a scab motorman, an action that started the riot in which the militia killed two men, unacceptable violence in defense of scabs that hastened a strike settlement and made Francis a hero of the strikers.

'Your family all okay?' Francis asked. 'Katrina and Martin?'

'They're fine,' said Edward, looking at Francis now as Katrina seemed to see him: her bauble when he'd lived next door to the Daughertys on Colonie Street, before he married Annie Farrell: handsome young handyman in whose presence Katrina went fluttery. Very thrilling, no doubt. You know, said La Voluptueuse, I'm only interested in youth.

'Martin's started to write stories, father's footsteps,' Edward said.

'He can do it. Smart kid like Martin puts his mind to it, he could stand on his ear, do anything he wants.'

'Sometimes it's not that easy.'

'Maybe not,' Francis said. 'Can I buy you a beer? I got too many tickets in my pocket.'

'No thanks, Fran.'

'That play you wrote,' Francis said. 'People always tell me it's me and your father.'

'It's some of you and him, all right, but not really.'

In the play the hero is counseled by a labor organizer, as Emmett had counseled the young Francis, told him about the Pittsburgh steel mills, and the Sons of Vulcan Emmett had helped organize to give voice to the workers. 'Identify the enemy,' the organizer keeps saying in the play, and the hero identifies one with a stone.

'I ain't no godalmighty hero for what I did and never thought I was,' Francis said. 'I had a good time watchin' your play, but I sure don't talk like that hero.'

'You have your own eloquence, Francis, and people know it. You're a fellow to reckon with.'

'I learned a lot from Emmett. Most clearheaded man I ever come across. Anything I asked him he had an answer. You don't find people like that. They're a gift. One day you get lucky and meet one, and after a while you find out you're halfway smart, smarter'n you ever thought you'd be.'

'Emmett was serious about every day of his life.'

'That's the truth. I'm serious too. If the Daughertys ever need anything, I'm there.'

Edward nodded and thought: I'll pass the word to Katrina.

When he went back to Giles's table, the women were gone, Maginn and Giles were sitting with Jimmy Cadden, another Eintrachter, a prankster who battened on the comic discomfiture of his friends, especially Maginn.

'Where's Aunt Sally and Felicity?' Edward asked.

'Maginn chased them away,' Cadden said.

'Not true,' said Maginn. 'I paid them such compliments they couldn't sit still. Sally is crazy about me.'

'She thinks Maginn is demented,' Cadden said.

'We'll see what she thinks,' Maginn said.

'Let's say Sally was amused,' said Giles.

'I saw you talking to the hero of your play,' Maginn said to Edward.

'If you mean Francis Phelan, get it right,' Edward said. 'He inspired part of the hero's character, but only part.'

'The radical part,' Maginn said.

'Some of that, yes,' Edward said.

'How's that play doing?' Giles asked.

'Played to sold-out houses in Albany for a month and a half last year,' Edward said. 'Did well in Boston and Philadelphia, and it's still running in New York.'

'I'm writing about it for the *Century*,' Maginn said, 'an article on using fiction and theater for political ends, writers telling us how the world ought to be. I seriously warn you against running with those pimps of transformation, Edward. You're a talented man, and *The Car Barns* is a talented play, but radical work like that strikes me as a justification for labor violence. I'm fond of politics, but let's not call it art.'

'Some art is political, whether you like it or not.'

'And some plays are so political they cease to be art.'

'I write what I believe. My soul is open for inspection.'

'Read my inspection report on your soul in the *Century*.'

'What about *your* novel? When do we get a look at it?'

'Let's say my novel is in abeyance,' Maginn said.

'You've quit it,' said Edward.

'Maybe,' said Maginn.

Excellent move, Edward thought. You never wrote a fictional paragraph I believed. More intelligent than talented, that's your condition, Maginn.

'We all do some things better than others,' Edward said.

'I envy you your naïveté, Edward,' Maginn said. 'You still think that everything you do matters. I think it's all a chase after the great cipher.'

'Time to chase the beer,' Cadden said.

'I'll go,' Maginn said, and he collected the drinkers' prepaid beer tickets. When he moved toward the bar, Giles quickly unfurled his plan for the Fireman's Wife Joke. He'd heard about it in New York, where it had had great success, but now said he needed Cadden and Edward to make it work.

'Leave me out,' Edward said. 'I'm too old for this.'

'Of course you are. That's what makes you credible.'

Edward was only five years older than Giles, but five seemed like twenty to Edward. Giles, dedicated physician, good and amiable friend, was the perennial adolescent, a fireman himself since the Delavan, reveling in the excitement of a flaming building, riding with firefighters as their doctor, treating injured firemen and burn victims.

'What do you expect me to do?' Edward asked him.

'Be the voice of authority.'

'Who else are you bringing in on it?'

'Somebody whose voice Maginn won't recognize. Clubber Dooley, maybe. Maginn doesn't know Clubber very well.'

'Can you trust Clubber not to give it away?' Cadden asked. 'Isn't his brain a little wrinkled?'

'Clubber'll do me a favor,' Giles said. 'I eased the pain in his bad foot last year.'

'Maginn is smart,' Edward said. 'He'll figure it out.'

'Maybe not,' Cadden said. 'When he's hot for a woman his brain moves below his belt.'

Very accurate on Maginn, Edward thought. The man, unfortunately, was a freak. He could be the greatest of friends, great talker, witty and oddly wise. Edward had had misgivings asking him to be best man at the wedding, but Maginn behaved impeccably, a notable contributor to the elevated spirits of that marvelous day. And he was embarrassingly grateful for being asked: an imprimatur on the friendship. But you are also a pain in the ass, Maginn. Your mouth is out of control and so is your critical faculty. You need comeuppance. Edward decided to help with the joke.

Maginn returned with the news that a roll of the prepaid tickets used for buying beer had been stolen, and bartenders were accepting only cash. Maginn, short of cash, suggested they all buy their own drinks. So he, Cadden, and Edward moved toward the bar at the stern of the barge.

Cully Watson and the five other toughs from the gangway incident, all in their twenties, all in shirtsleeves and caps, hovered near the bar. Only Watson was bareheaded. He had an empty glass in one hand and tickets in the other.

'You're saying my money's no good,' Watson said.

'Tickets are no good,' the bartender said. 'Our tickets were stolen. You want a beer, you pay cash.'

'I paid cash for these tickets when I got on this shitbucket.'

'Maybe you did, but now it's cash only.'

'He says our tickets are no good,' Watson said to his friends.

'Maybe he's the one that's no good,' said one.

'He says he only takes cash,' Watson said.

Edward saw the toughs were already in a fight stance, coiled with energy. Watson's talk was a gambit. Cadden stepped up to the bar.

'I got cash money and I'd like three lagers,' Cadden said. He turned to Watson. 'You guys don't mind, do you?'

The barman filled three mugs. Watson stared at Cadden.

'This is trouble,' Maginn said. 'Let it go, Cadden. We'll go to the bar on the upper deck.'

'I got 'em already,' Cadden said, reaching for the beers.

'You wait your turn,' Watson said, and he put his tickets on the bar. 'I'll take them beers.'

'Not with tickets you won't,' the bartender said, and he pushed the beers closer to Cadden. Watson reached for the mugs but Cadden blocked him.

'You ain't very polite,' Watson said. He shoved Cadden with one hand and knocked him off-balance, then swept the mugs off the bar.

'Bad news, Cadden, I told you,' Maginn said. 'Don't push it.'

'Cheap hooligan,' Cadden said.

As Cadden faced down Watson, one tough picked up a fallen beer mug and stood staring at him. Suddenly the tough swung the mug and hit Cadden on the side of the head. He staggered and fell across the bar. Willie Glass and Joe Anthony arrived, swinging nightsticks. Glass rapped the tough who had floored Cadden and he buckled. Maginn and Edward pulled Cadden away from the bar and sat him on a bench. Edward felt his head. No blood. Cadden shook his head, trying to focus.

'Break this up,' Willie Glass was saying, shoving the toughs away from the bar. He and Joe Anthony had their backs to each other as they swung their clubs.

'I'll get that son of a bitch,' Cadden said.

'Cadden,' Maginn whispered, 'that's Cully Watson. He's a killer.'

'Where's Giles? Get Giles to come and look at Cadden's head,' Edward said to Maginn.

Two toughs leaped on Glass, took away his stick, and brought him down. Two other toughs were showing knives, and one said, 'The cop says break it up, so we'll break it up,' and he kicked Glass in the mouth, then bashed his face with a beer mug. Anthony clubbed the kicker, but another tough hit Anthony with a mug and blood spurted from his left eye.

Two fell on Glass, punching his face, which was drenched in blood. One tough took his revolver and two others pulled off his uniform jacket, then his pants and shoes. Jack McCall moved out of the crowd and next to Edward, a club in his hand.

'Let's move in,' Jack said.

'Gimme his gun,' Cully Watson said, and a tough threw Glass's gun to Cully, who fired it into the deck, halting Jack and Edward's forward motion. Another tough took Anthony's pistol and pulled his uniform off. With their knives the toughs sliced the uniforms into rags. Cully, pistol in hand, shoved aside the two elderly bartenders, and with his other hand held a mug under the open tap. One tough pointed Anthony's pistol at the crowd of picnickers, keeping reinforcements at bay. Men from the excursion sent women and children to the upper deck.

Cully drew more beers and slid them across the bar to the toughs, who guzzled it. Cully left the taps open, the deck awash in beer, then tucked the pistol in his belt, picked up an empty keg, and tossed it over the bar to a tough, who caught it.

'Give Glass some beer,' Cully said, and the tough dropped the beer keg on Willie Glass's back. Glass was unconscious, clad only in underwear, his and Anthony's uniforms in shreds. Anthony was conscious, but bleeding profusely.

'Take a uniform away from a cop,' Cully said, 'you can't tell he's a cop no more.'

Edward saw Francis moving up behind the tough who held the pistol, and he decided to act.

'You goddamn pack of jackals,' Edward yelled, and he threw a beer mug at the tough with the gun and hit his chin. The man fired once and hit a stranger next to Edward. Francis came up behind the tough and pinioned him with a life preserver, then kneed him in the crotch and kicked the gun toward Edward. Cully fired a second shot into the deck before Edward could pick up the pistol. Another tough rushed to pick it up, but Cadden, with the energy of rage, stood and grabbed the attacker's arm, smashed his nose with his fist. Cadden snapped the man's arm like an ear of corn, dragged him to the railing.

'Let's move,' Cully yelled, and he fired again into the deck. The toughs backed away from the bar as Cadden flung the man with the broken arm into the river.

Edward picked up the fallen gun as Black Jack and men from the crowd with knives and clubs moved toward Cully and crew. Cully led his toughs up a ladder, firing over the heads of the crowd as they went. Nobody followed them.

Giles was suddenly there as Edward and Maginn lifted the wounded stranger and the two savaged policemen onto tables where Giles could treat their wounds. Edward saw Maginn going up the ladder the toughs had climbed.

Word reached the captain and he pulled his tug close to a man in a rowboat to tell him of the riot on board and to send a message to the Albany police. The captain turned the tug and the barges in a semicircle and moved at high speed back toward Albany. Edward saw the rowboat man pulling the tough with the broken arm out of the water.

Edward thought: When you look at Cully Watson you know what you're looking at, but when you look at Maginn you don't know what he's become since yesterday. You could not know he would follow Cully and his gang, which scattered among the crowds on the four decks of the two barges. You might have predicted that by the time the Albany police rowed out to the barges at the Columbia Street pier, Cully and his toughs would be elsewhere. But you could not have predicted that Maginn would row Cully to the Rensselaer shore across from Albany, then row back to the barge.

When Maginn climbed back aboard from the lifeboat, he said he'd found Cully at the stern of the second barge, taking up slack on the rope of the lifeboat that trailed the barge in the water. Cully told Maginn to drop into the boat and row him and the boys ashore or he'd shoot him.

'What could I do?' Maginn asked.

'Why couldn't he row himself?' Edward asked.

'He wanted to see who was following him.'

'Why didn't he have one of his pals row?'

'He thinks they're stupid.'

'But you're intelligent enough to row a boat.'

'Cully doesn't like me, and you don't argue with a man with a pistol.'

'Why doesn't he like you?'

'Something I wrote about him in the paper.'

'Will you write about this?'

'Of course.'

'Naming names?'

'Do you think I'm suicidal?'

A police sergeant, finding no culprits on either barge, arrested Maginn for aiding a felon, and for taking a lifeboat from a river vessel, a federal offense. As police led Maginn away, Felicity's aunt waved a handkerchief at him, and Maginn, in hand chains, vigorously waved back with both hands.

Edward and Giles posted bail for Maginn, but after his interrogation, the charges against him were dropped. Cully left Albany a fugitive, the only one of the gang known by name. At a hearing Edward and Giles testified to the beating of the police, and to one tough's shooting a man in the crowd. Police arrested three men, but ten witnesses in their behalf testified they were sunning themselves on an upper deck during the fight. No other witness came forward to testify against the wild boys, and all charges were dismissed: a victory for numerical perjury, and triumph of the worst and the least.

Maginn never wrote about the brawl for *The Argus*. His editor said nobody believed his rowboat-kidnapping story.

Courting the Fireman's Wife

July 1, 1906

Two weeks after the excursion Giles called Edward to say Cadden's head was mended, and they were ready to play. They all met at Keeler's men's bar and Giles revealed that Sally would welcome a visit from Maginn tonight, after nine o'clock, when the house was empty. She wanted to hear of Maginn's encounter with the hoodlums, and had heard he was a writer, as was she. She was writing a love story on the order of *Wuthering Heights*.

'Where are these rooms she's taken?' Maginn asked.

'About three miles down the river road,' Giles said.

'Then I need a ride,' said Maginn. 'The trolley doesn't go that far.'

'Are you serious about this, Fitz?' Cadden asked. 'That lovely woman really wants this clown to visit her in her rooms? At night?'

'She did seem excited.'

'This is unbelievable,' Cadden said.

'It's normal,' Maginn said.

Maginn, at forty-nine, could not be called good-looking. His hairline had moved backward, his drooping gray mustache was ineptly darkened with mustache wax. He did not fit the lothario image, but his sensuality gave him an exotic appeal to many women. Why shouldn't the fireman's wife be one of his herd?

'I can take you down,' Giles said, 'but you'll have to find your own way back.'

'Maybe I'll stay the week.'

'Just be careful. Her husband's got a temper.'

'Isn't he in Westchester?'

'That's what she said.'

'Then why shouldn't we believe her?' Maginn asked. 'What do you think, Edward?'

'I don't know what to think about you, Maginn. And I certainly don't know what to think about this woman. You're making a career out of intrigue.'

Edward said he had a meeting but would drop by at Giles's house later to learn the outcome. Giles and Cadden drove Maginn to the house of assignation, which was dark.

'Doesn't look like anybody's home,' Maginn said.

'You want us to wait?' Giles asked as Maginn stepped down onto the carriage drive.

'I'll go with him, make sure he gets in,' Cadden said.

Maginn mounted the steps, knocked, won no response. He turned to Cadden, who stood in the moonlight at the bottom of the stoop, and shrugged, knocked louder. A light went on and Maginn smiled at Cadden.

'Who is it?' a voice from inside whispered.

'Is that you, Sally? It's Thomas Maginn, your admirer from the barge.'

The door flew open and from interior shadows a male voice boomed, 'So you're the one who's seeing my wife! Well, you've seen her for the last time, you home-wrecking son of a bitch!'

A man loomed from the shadows, pistol in hand, and fired two thunderclaps at Maginn, who was already on the run down the carriageway with Cadden.

'Hurry up, for God's sake,' Cadden said.

'So there's two of you!' yelled the man with the gun, and he fired another shot. Cadden fell on his face and Maginn kept running, turned to see the man coming toward him, and clambered wildly into the carriage.

'He'll kill us all,' Giles said, whipping the horse. And the carriage careened down the drive. Maginn looked back and saw the man pointing his gun at the inert Cadden.

'Christ,' Maginn said, 'that bastard shot Cadden for no reason. He's killed him. He's a lunatic!'

'Some men are like that about their wives,' Giles said, urging the horse to a wild gallop.

'We should go back for Cadden,' Maginn said.

'You want to get us shot too?'

'But he's hurt. We've got to call the cops.'

'And tell them what?'

Maginn did not answer. They drove to Giles's town house and found Edward waiting, sipping whiskey in the drawing room. Maginn manically recounted the terror, the fall of plucky Cadden, incoherent flight, his desire to straighten things out. Edward listened with head-shaking sympathy.

'If Cadden is dead he's dead,' Edward said. He paused for reflection. 'If he's not dead he'll probably admit to that irate man what was happening. But if he mentions Giles's carriage, they'll come here looking for you.'

Edward stood and paced.

'What you need is an alibi,' he said to Maginn. 'We'll go upstairs and get you into bed and if anybody comes we'll swear you've been here for hours.'

'You'd do that?' Maginn asked Edward.

'What happened wasn't your fault, was it?'

'You think it'll work?'

'An alibi worked for those fellows who beat up the cops on the barge,' Edward said. 'And what choice do you have?'

'I'd get into that bed if I were you,' Giles said. 'We'll figure out what to do about Cadden. I'll get in touch with Sally. Here, have a drink.'

He poured a whiskey for Maginn, who swallowed it in a gulp.

Giles led the way to an empty bedroom and lighted a lamp. Maginn sat on a chair and took off his clothes.

'Underwear too,' Giles said. 'If you're naked it's a better alibi. Am I right, Edward?'

'It's logical.'

Giles handed the lamp to Edward, diminishing bedside light,

then pulled down the covers so Maginn could crawl beneath them.

Cadden walked into the room.

'Aren't you in bed a little early, Maginn?' he asked.

Maginn by then had rolled fully under the covers and was lying in ten pounds of soggy gingersnaps that had been mixed with four quarts of warm chicken fat and spread between the sheets.

The puerile reduction of Maginn was a supreme success, but gave no satisfaction. It generated a predictable withdrawal in Maginn, but also in Edward, whose guilt was such that he stopped work on his new play, yet another confounding of intentions. Whatever seemed the right thing invariably proved otherwise. Could it be, Edward, that you were meant to be confounded unto the grave, that your destiny is linked to the everlastingly wrong choice? Was Katrina the wrong choice? Weren't you ambivalent about your *Stolen Cushion*, about *The Baron*? Hasn't Maginn made you doubt even *The Car Barns*? Is the play-in-progress a mistake? You're a mindless achiever, moving toward you know not what. 'Edward Daugherty, a formless lump of matter, was born into this world yesterday for no known reason.' Your sadness is a pose, Edward, your Weltschmerz sliced like liverwurst. You are different from everyone you know. You can't afford to consider Maginn's idea that all effort is a quest for the great cipher. You need a pair of spiritual spectacles to see things as they are. Understand this, Edward: you are still living your preamble.

Dinner at the Daughertys'

July 4, 1907

The heat worsened. All screened windows of the parlors and dining room were open, all curtains and drapes tied back to the extreme; but the house was without a breeze. Dinner would be wretchedly uncomfortable and Edward was almost ready to take off his coat and tell Giles to do the same.

The women were another matter. Neither Felicity nor Katrina could easily shed a layer of clothing, nor were they likely to, whatever the degree; but then they were used to suffering for their plumage. Why do they do that to themselves? Edward decided he would wait for the missing guests before suggesting a dinner in shirtsleeves. Sweating through the city's hot spell, instead of spending the holiday week in the Adirondacks, was his choice: a chance to meet socially with Melissa Spencer, the young actress Maginn was bringing to dinner.

With great verve in projecting the volatility of young love, with a face that demanded one's attention, and a foxish smile that kept it, Melissa had taken Edward over when he saw her onstage; for she seemed the incarnation of the female lead of his new play. Suffer the heat for such gain.

And so he had begun this Independence Day holiday by taking Katrina to Washington Park for the morning band concert and reading of the Declaration of Independence, then lunch at Keeler's and out to the Woodlawn Park track to see Giles's trotter, My Own Love, foal of Gallant Warrior, the horse Edward had tried in vain to give to Katrina's father. He had given it, instead, after neither Katrina nor her mother would accept it, to Giles, who had won frequently with it for years, then put it to stud, and now was reaping second-generational benefits; today the foal won its heats and also tied a track record, 2:01 for the mile.

Edward poured sherry for the Fitzroys, a pony of very old port for Katrina, and a Scotch whisky and water for himself. They were all in the Daugherty drawing room, sitting near the windows to harvest the breeze, should it arrive, rubber plants and ferns in lush leaf among them. The room's personality reflected Katrina's devotion to the revered dead. Geraldine, Jacob, and Adelaide, in hanging portraits, and Katrina's poet, Baudelaire, in a pen-sketched self-portrait, all stared down at the occupants of the room. On a table between French porcelain vases and jade dragons the marble bust of the naked Persephone (a Katrina look-alike Edward had given her for their first anniversary) now seemed apt, chiefly as an adornment for the tomb of the Katrina-that-was: full woman then, now suitable only for admiration. Jacob Taylor's pendulum clock hung silently on the wall, permanently stopped at 8:53 to memorialize the approximate instant when the burning stick pierced Katrina's breast. And atilt on its hook opposite the mantel, a large gilt-framed mirror ensured that with even a cursory glance, one could monitor one's own or the collective image of this overheated quartet: all eyes, including her own, always on Katrina and her chamber of venerated memory, her sumptuous crypt of exhausted life.

'Maginn is late, as usual,' Edward said.

'When we're gathered around his deathbed,' said Giles, 'he'll be someplace else.'

'Do you have him to dinner often?' Felicity asked Katrina.

'Now and then. Why do you ask?'

'I find him so coarse, rather low-class in his tastes. And he paws you if he finds the opportunity.'

'He's tried to get next to Felicity for years,' Giles said, 'hasn't he, love?'

'He has. It's quite obscene what he once said to me.'

'Whatever did he say?' Katrina asked.

'I wouldn't repeat it.'

'Paraphrase it,' Edward said. 'Give us a thrill.'

'It had to do with anatomy,' Felicity said. 'Mine.'

'And a splendid anatomy it is,' said Giles.

'Maginn does like women,' Edward said. 'He's also tried his hand at Katrina.'

'Not at all,' Katrina said. 'It's all talk.'

'He went after you in our garden.'

'No, no, no. He was flirting.'

'What I saw was beyond flirting.'

'We are never sure of what we see.'

Edward let it go. She would forever deny the slightest dalliance. On Francis Phelan, she was vehement. Even Giles's pitiful effort at a beach picnic ('May I touch your naked shoulder?') she dismissed as an excess of friendship ('Just a lovable, silly man'). Like flies after sugar. The veneration of sugar.

'Maginn is afflicted, like a man with a stutter or a limp. He can't help it,' Edward said.

'When God was handing out social graces,' Giles said, 'Maginn was elsewhere, trying to seduce an angel.'

'Aren't angels sexless?' Felicity asked.

'That would merely present Maginn with a challenge,' Edward said.

'But he's just a reporter, such a common person,' Felicity said.

'I used to be a reporter,' Edward said. 'Is that your view of my social position?'

'You're very different.'

'You really mustn't speak about people as "common,"' Giles said. 'You shouldn't type people that way.'

'Not even if it's true?'

'It's snobbish. Not everybody has the good fortune to be born into money and social status.'

'Are you quite sure that's good fortune?' Katrina said.

'Who is this woman he's bringing?' Felicity asked from her severe pout.

'Melissa Spencer, an actress,' said Katrina.

'Oh dear,' said Felicity. 'Isn't "actress" just another name for, you know . . .'

'Felicity,' Giles said, 'you have no idea who this young woman is. She's only eighteen and she's going to be in Edward's new play.'

'Oh I am sorry,' said Felicity.

'Don't waste your sorrow on Melissa,' Edward said. 'She's a very talented young lady. I saw her in a Sardou play in New York, and I knew if she toned down the melodramatics, she could act my heroine. She's at Proctor's this week in a comic opera, and so I sent her a script, and yesterday my producer came up from New York and we auditioned her. She was perfect – articulate, with an open heart, and a beauty that's hard to define. She commands one's attention.'

'She certainly commands yours,' Felicity said.

'Why shouldn't beauty be appreciated?' Katrina asked.

'It should, I suppose.'

'It should be cast in bronze, carved in marble like Persephone there,' said Giles, pointing to the marble bust. 'Beauty is how we stay alive. It's why I married you, my love,' and he patted Felicity's wrist.

'That's a ridiculous reason to marry, Giles,' said Katrina. 'I don't believe that's what drew you to Felicity.'

'I swear it's true,' said Giles.

'I doubt it. People want an unknown they can embrace. Something mysterious.'

'Do you really think we're so anxious for the exotic?' Giles asked.

'But of course,' Katrina said. 'What else is love but the desire for prostitution?'

'Oh my,' said Felicity. 'You don't mean that.'

'She means prostitution as a metaphor,' Giles said.

'Not at all,' said Katrina.

'I've been dying to ask what you've chosen for dinner,' Felicity said. 'I always love your menus.'

391

'We start with prostitute soup,' Katrina said.

'You do say the most outlandish things, Katrina,' Felicity said. 'You like to shock us.'

'Do I? Is that true, Edward?'

'Offending people has always been one of the pleasures of the upper class,' Edward said.

'I left the upper class when I married you,' Katrina said.

'Perhaps you did,' said Edward. 'I remember Cornelia Wickham's saying I made you *declassée*. In spite of that, you certainly brought your elite social codes to the altar.'

'Cornelia was jealous that Katrina was the true princess of Albany's social life,' Giles said. 'I remember her coming-out cotillion, the most elaborate the city had seen in decades. Cornelia looked radiant, and her dress, made by a London couturier who had gone on to design for the Queen, was the talk of the city. Yet every eye was on Katrina. All the men had to dance with her, including myself. The women, polite as they were, were wretchedly jealous, and it got into the social columns. Cornelia still hasn't forgiven her.'

'Cornelia was a vain and brainless ninny,' Katrina said. 'I went to her cotillion determined to annoy her, and I flirted outrageously with everyone.'

'You became the belle of someone else's ball,' Giles said, 'a mythic figure in society. And Cornelia married bountifully and grew fat as a toad.'

'Is there something wrong in being fat?' Felicity asked.

'Nothing at all,' Giles said. 'After I lose interest in you, my dear, you may get as fat as you like.'

'I will never be fat, Giles,' Felicity said. 'And it may be I who lose interest.'

Footsteps on the porch announced that Maginn and Melissa had arrived.

At dinner, Maginn-by-candlelight looked less like Melissa's escort than somebody's ne'er-do-well uncle, with his waning, scraggly hair and mustache, expensive but wrinkled blue-silk tie, and his trademark coat with velvet collar: a coat for all seasons. His shirt collar was freshly starched, but only when Edward was sure he was wearing the complete shirt, and not just a dickey, did he give the word for the men to doff jackets. Edward and Giles, in their tailored shirts, ties in place, seemed aloof from the heat. Coatless, Maginn looked steamed.

Edward suggested the women could follow suit in whatever way feasible, and Melissa removed her diaphanous tunic, revealing shoulders bare except for where her light-brown hair fell onto them, and the string straps holding up her loose-fitting beige gown. It was clear she wore no corset, nor could Edward see any evidence of that new device, the brassiere. Her gown became the object of silent speculation: would it offer the table, before dinner's end, an unobstructed chest-scape?

'The play by Edward is so exciting,' Melissa said. 'I'm so flattered to be asked to even *read* for the role of Thisbe. There's such pathos in her. It's too good to be true, but it is true, isn't it, Edward?'

'We can't be sure about anything,' Edward said, 'but you will have the part if we're not all stricken by disaster.'

'There's always the odd chance,' Maginn said, 'that the play will be a disaster.'

'Oh no,' said Melissa. 'It's a wonderful play.'

'That has nothing to do with it,' Maginn said.

'Here now,' said Giles, 'let's not have any sour grapes.'

'Maginn is right,' Edward said. 'Even great plays, and I make no argument for my own, are often badly received. *The Seagull* was mocked in its St Petersburg premiere, and this year a horde of benighted Irishmen rioted at the Abbey Theatre over Synge's language in *Playboy of the Western World*.'

'I won't hear of any disasters,' Melissa said. 'Have you read Edward's play, Mrs Daugherty?'

'Of course. It was enthralling.'

'I agree. It's gotten even better as I commit it to memory.'

'You've memorized it already?' asked Katrina.

'Rather a lot of it,' Melissa said. 'Actors must read a play countless times, although I know some who memorize only their own lines and cues.'

'Some do even less,' Katrina said. 'They bumble through and think it enough just to stand there and shimmer in the footlights. Have you known actresses who only shimmer?'

'I've only been in theater a year,' Melissa said, and she turned to Felicity. 'Does theater thrill you as it does me?'

'I rarely go,' Felicity said. 'In New York I went once and found it extremely improper. Women in tights, that sort of thing.'

'Felicity is easily shocked,' Giles said.

'I saw Edward's last play,' Felicity said, 'but I didn't entirely understand it.'

'What didn't you understand?' Melissa asked.

'The words,' Maginn said.

'The play has a political theme,' said Giles, 'and my wife doesn't understand politics, do you, my love?'

'I'm not a simp, Giles.'

'Let Felicity speak for herself, Giles,' Katrina said. 'Don't be such a mother hen.'

'Those pearls you're wearing are gorgeous,' Melissa said to Felicity. 'I've never seen anything like them.'

'Giles gave them to me for our anniversary.'

'And your hair,' said Melissa. 'I wish I had such beautiful hair.'

'How nice of you to say that,' said Felicity. 'Your own hair is very lovely. I'm sure you shimmer beautifully onstage, and I'll bet you don't forget your lines.'

Edward saw Felicity as not unattractive, a hint of the hoyden in her manner, and with a flouncy appeal, undergirded by that heralded anatomy. Her hair, a mass of thick black waves, loosely plaited and gathered in soft coils to just below her shoulders, was truly beautiful, but neither bronze nor marble could rescue her long nose and small eyes. Edward also decided Melissa was extremely shrewd, with the good sense to back off an argument about acting with Katrina, and with instant insight as to where Felicity was most susceptible to flattery.

Loretta came to take the soup bowls and Katrina introduced her to the table as 'Loretta McNally, just here from Ireland. Cora's youngest sister. Lovely Cora who died in the Delavan. Loretta isn't a servant. She's like family.'

Katrina: reconstituting Cora through her sibling, replaying the psychic games she invented for that bygone girl: taking Cora to tea at the homes of social friends, teaching her how to sit a horse, and the names of flowers and jewels, correcting her posture, her speech, coiffing her hair, giving her clothes, lifting Cora up from Irish peasantry into Katrina's own shining world.

'You're arousing expectations that can't be fulfilled,' Edward had argued.

'Nonsense. When she knows how to move she'll rise.'

'All she'll have is a mask of pretense.'

'Then she'll be like everybody else.'

And which mask are you wearing tonight, Katrina? Princess of the social elite? Benefactor of proles? Beloved of cats? Iconic prostitute before her mirror?

Loretta was serving individual silver bowls of cold crabmeat on beds of cracked ice, with the pale-green sauce Edward recognized as his mother's, created for the Patroon's table. Katrina, knowing the sauce pleased Edward's palate, learned the recipe from Hanorah, then saw to it her own cook, Mrs Squires, made it to Edward's satisfaction.

'Let's go back to your play, Edward,' Maginn said. 'Why did you write it? I find its structure extremely strange.'

'You've read it?'

'I borrowed Melissa's copy last night.'

Edward looked at Melissa, whose eyes were on the crabmeat. 'That wasn't for circulation,' he said.

'I cajoled her,' Maginn said. 'I told her we were very old friends. I told her I was best man at your wedding and you wouldn't mind. I know you've been working on it for years. Was it a major problem, getting the form?'

'It took the necessary time,' Edward said. 'You can't rush it. When the matter is ready the form will come.'

'I prefer to think that when the form is ready the matter will come,' Maginn said.

'I was echoing Aristotle. Your remark is pure Oscar Wilde.'

'There is no pure Oscar Wilde,' said Maginn.

'You don't like my play?'

'It's so ethereal,' said Maginn. 'Where's your trademark realism? Or those cherished political themes?'

'I left all that out.'

'But without that the play flies off into myth, and artsy romanticism.'

'You faulted *The Car Barns* for being *too* political. "Radical art," you called it. Now, with no radicalism, I'm artsy. I can't find a happy medium with you, Maginn.'

'What is this play about?' Giles asked.

'It's a somber love story,' Melissa said. 'Beautiful and very romantic.'

'But what is it about?'

'It starts from the myth of Pyramus and Thisbe, Ovid's version,' Edward said. 'Two lovers, kept apart by their families, find a way to meet. Thisbe arrives by the light of the moon, sees a lioness who has just finished a kill and has come to drink at a fountain near the tomb where she is to meet Pyramus. Thisbe drops her veil and flees, the lioness finds the veil, mauls it with bloody paws and jowls, and leaves. Pyramus arrives, finds the bloody veil, and assumes Thisbe has been killed. Disconsolate, he kills himself with his sword. Thisbe emerges from hiding, finds her lover dying, and also kills herself. That's the myth. I alter it considerably. No lioness, no sword.'

'But it's so fated,' said Maginn, 'all wrapped up in God's intellect. God is mindless, Edward, don't you know that? The random moment is what's important, not the hounds of fate. It's time we left Oedipus behind. We should be our own gods, not their pawns. I believe in whim, not wisdom.'

'Your random moment,' Edward said, 'means to live like a blown leaf. I do believe in impulses, but I believe they come from something central to what we are, that they're signals for action – a craving for sacrifice in exchange for love, an instinct for evil we can't escape. We're mostly ignorant of what's really going on in our souls, but we should give the signals a chance.'

'Instinct for evil,' Maginn said. 'You sound like a Catholic missionary saving heathens from original sin.'

'And you,' said Katrina, 'sound like a misanthrope. What ever pleases you, Thomas?'

'You please me, Katrina, the way you please the world. I'm overcome with pleasure when I see beauty and wit come together. And I value our visiting Miss Melissa, a young woman with a future. I do have my moments, and they arrive quite randomly.'

'I remember one of your random moments,' said Giles. 'Your date with the fireman's wife.'

'You never forget that, do you, Fitz?'

'That was so funny,' said Felicity.

'Depending on your perspective,' said Maginn.

'Who is the fireman's wife?' Melissa asked.

'An invention of these grown-up boys,' said Katrina, pointing to Edward and Giles.

'Consummate actors, both,' Maginn said. 'They set out to humiliate me and they did it extremely well.'

'Humiliation wasn't the intention,' Giles said. 'It was a joke. If we weren't close friends we wouldn't have bothered.'

'They took advantage of Thomas's infatuation with Felicity's aunt,' Katrina said, 'and convinced him she felt the same way.'

'I told my aunt all about it,' Felicity said. 'She was amused and flattered, but she'd never cheat on her husband.'

'An exceedingly rare woman,' said Maginn. 'Almost extinct in our time.'

'Oh, you are a wretched man,' Katrina said.

'Hateful,' said Felicity. 'Devilish.'

'You know what Chaucer said, my dears. "One shouldn't be too inquisitive in life either about God's secrets or one's wife." Do you hear what I'm saying about God, Edward?'

'I do hear,' Edward said.

'*Mundus vult decipi*,' said Giles.

'What's that again?' Edward asked.

'The world wants to be deceived,' Giles said. 'Don't you think so?'

'What happened with the fireman's wife?' Melissa asked.

'When Thomas went to meet her,' Giles said, 'a jealous husband shot at him and he fled for his life. The husband was played by a friend of ours, Clubber Dooley. He screamed at Maginn as a home-wrecker and fired blank cartridges. Grand melodrama, a high point of Clubber's life.'

'Dooley is pitiful,' Maginn said.

'I wouldn't say so,' said Giles.

'He drinks in Johnny Groelz's saloon, morose, all but toothless, swilling beer till he's senseless. Once a week a boy comes in and Dooley hands him money and the boy takes it home to Mother, a slattern who once indulged Dooley – what way, precisely, I'd rather develop bubonic plague than try to imagine. But ever since then she's been on dreadful Dooley's dole, and he dreams of another go at her someday, if he can only find a way to get off the barstool. Pitiful, needy sap.'

'That's perverse,' said Giles. 'That boy is related to Clubber. His mother raised Clubber.'

'Intimacy within the family is not a new thing in the universe,' Maginn said.

'Always sex,' said Katrina. 'Thomas the satyr, eternally pursuing the nymphs.'

'The Greeks made bucolic gods of the satyrs,' Maginn said, 'and I find it a jovial way of life, bouncing through the bosky with divine goatishness, spying one's pleasure, taking it, then moving on to the next pasture. Is there a better way to spend one's day?'

'You are moving into depravity,' Katrina said.

Edward saw she was smiling.

Loretta appeared at Katrina's elbow to say dessert was ready, and Katrina announced it would be served on the back piazza, with fireworks to follow.

Edward had put his son in charge of the fireworks, and now here he came: Martin Daugherty, twenty, home from his day's wandering. He stepped onto the piazza carrying his dish of Mrs Squires's ice cream, looking, Edward thought, like himself at that age: tall, with abundant brown hair all in place, still not quite grown into his teeth, wearing a fresh white shirt with cuffs turned. Edward saw Martin's eyes go directly to Melissa.

'This is our son, Martin,' Edward said. Martin stopped at Melissa's chair and took her hand in greeting. 'Melissa Spencer.' And they smiled. Both of an age.

'You look like your father,' Melissa said. 'A handsome family indeed.'

A beginning? Two beginnings?

'Melissa will play the lead in my new play, all things being equal,' Edward said.

'That's exciting,' Martin said. 'A pleasure, Miss Spencer.'

'All things are never equal, Edward,' Maginn said. 'You should avoid inaccurate clichés.'

'Are you in school?' Melissa asked Martin.

'Going into my third year at Fordham.'

'He may be a writer like his father,' Katrina said. 'He writes well.'

'No, not like my father. I'm not serious about it.'

'It takes time to be serious,' Katrina said. 'He's a fine student.'

'I might write for the newspapers,' Martin said.

'That's such an exciting world,' Melissa said.

'It's about as exciting,' said Maginn, 'as being attacked by fleas.'

'Are you really so bored by your work, Maginn?' Edward asked.

'I would infinitely prefer setting off fireworks as a way of life,' Maginn said.

'I just came from the fireworks at Beaver Park,' Martin said. 'A huge crowd. A horse ran wild when somebody threw a cannon cracker at him. He was pulling an Italian peddler's vegetable wagon and he ran into a moving trolley. He was on his side and bleeding badly, two legs obviously broken.'

'Oh that's awful,' said Melissa, and she hid her face in her hands.

'The peddler kept asking the policeman to shoot the horse, but the cop said he couldn't kill an animal like that.'

'You have to, if they're in that condition,' Giles said. 'You have to shoot them.'

'A man came out of a house with a rifle and said he'd shoot the horse. The Italian got down on his knees and begged him to do it, and the man shot the horse in the head.'

'Horrible,' said Melissa, and she wept for the horse.

'I also saw Jack Apple do his annual jump into the river,' Martin said, breaking a silence. 'He jumped off the top of the Maiden Lane bridge.'

'He only jumped *off* it?' Giles said. 'Anybody can do that. The trick is to jump *over* it.'

'Oh Giles,' Felicity said.

'Giles is warming up his jokes,' Maginn said. 'Edward, have you considered casting Giles as Pyramus in your play? You'd have them tumbling out of their seats. Or rolling in the aisles, as you might put it.'

'The fireworks are in those bags at the foot of the steps,' Edward said.

Martin inspected the skyrockets, Roman candles, flowerpots, cherry bombs, strings of Chinese crackers; and Edward watched the women as they watched each other, a study in optics: Katrina aware of Giles's and Felicity's fascination with Melissa's unblushing attitude toward her body; Melissa aware of Edward's eyes on her, her own eyes on Katrina, evaluating. Edward monitored the shifting glance, the recurrent stare that extended an instant too long to be insignificant. He observed Maginn giving equal attention to all three women: failed with Felicity, failed with Katrina – didn't he? Will he fail with Melissa, or does she collect men as he collects women? Her smiling eye lingered on Edward an instant too long not to be significant. Edward saw that Maginn saw.

The fireworks sizzled, glowed, exploded with great bangs and a thousand small, oriental poppings, and the Roman candles thup-thupped toward where the lawn sloped down toward the brickyard on Van Woert Street, all this under Martin's expert hand. Edward had taken him to see fireworks the first year of his life and ever after taught him caution in their handling.

'I suppose all over Albany right now,' Edward said, 'boys are having their fingers blown off and their eyes blown out.'

'Giles, how come you're not with the firemen tonight?' Maginn asked. 'Don't you usually help them out on the Fourth?'

'I took the night off to have dinner with you, you lout,' Giles said. 'I'm tired of stupid people blowing themselves to pieces. But if you decide to blow yourself up, Maginn, I have the tetanus antitoxin in my bag to treat you.'

'If I decide to blow myself up,' said Maginn, 'there won't be anything left to treat. I will very thoroughly atomize myself into the circumambient air.'

'What a grisly thing to say,' Katrina said.

'Grisly? I thought it was quite poetic. You're very severe with me tonight, Katrina.'

Grisly the whole thing. And unacceptable. Edward rose from his rocker and walked down onto the lawn to get away. Something magnetic in him attracts her lashing tongue. Of course she knows he lives for these lashings. What is the recourse?

'Time for the skyrockets,' Martin said.

'Oooh, can I light one?' Melissa asked, and she left the piazza and came to the bottom of the garden, where Edward and Martin stood beside a dozen skyrockets stuck into the ground on their launching sticks. Martin handed her the lighted punk and showed her where to touch it to a skyrocket's fuse. She bent over the skyrocket, very probably giving Martin an unobstructed view of the chest-scape; and, as they all watched the rocket ignite, soar into the moonlit sky, and explode, Melissa touched another rocket, then another, sending them all to heaven. From the piazza came applause for the spectacle.

As Edward and Melissa walked back toward the house she touched his arm. He turned to see her leaning toward him, offering him her beautiful moonlit breasts.

'I just wanted to say I'm incredibly grateful for your belief in me,' she said. 'You're a very special man.'

'I recognize talent when I see it,' Edward said. He offered her his hand and they went up the steps together.

Maginn rose from his chair and came over to Edward.

'Are you taking her away from me?' he whispered. 'Is that what you're doing?'

Before Edward could answer, Felicity said, 'Look, a shooting star!' and he turned to see in the northern sky the dying arc of the meteor, or was it a comet, or a falling angel?

'Oh dear,' Melissa said, blessing herself. 'That's bad luck. That means one of us here will be dead next year.'

'More fatalism, Edward,' Maginn said. 'This superstitious child is perfect for your play.'

'I don't believe such things,' Katrina said.

'On the other hand, the Trojans didn't believe Cassandra's prophecies,' Maginn said, 'and look what happened to them.'

'We're all too healthy to die,' Felicity said.

'I agree,' Edward said. 'I refuse to play dead just because the sky is falling.'

'I second that motion,' said Giles.

At the stroke of midnight Martin lit the last fireworks of the evening: half a dozen red lights that burned brightly together for a long minute at the bottom of the garden, then weakened until their lambency was spent, and the light on the Daugherty lawn came only from the vigilant moon.

The Rape of Felicity: Two Versions

She was there when I came into the apartment, wearing that exotic cloak and mask, moving nervously around the parlor, and exploding with her story. She said she was napping on the sofa in her room, fully dressed, when she saw a man crawling over the transom, half into the room through the fanlight's opening; and what awakened her was the sound of his shirt buttons scraping on the wood.

'I would have screamed,' she said, 'but he waved a knife at me in silent warning. I ran to the buzzer to ring for help, but he was at me before I got to it, and he searched my purse and valise. He took all the cash I'd drawn from the bank in Albany, more than three hundred dollars, and he touched the long strand of pearls I was wearing, the ones Giles gave me. He seemed to know jewelry. "Now," he said to me, "get out of your clothes."'

She wept as she said this, lifting her eye mask to dab at her tears. I asked her why she was wearing the mask but she just waved both hands impatiently.

'He led me to the bedroom and pushed me onto the bed and raped me, hurt me so much I thought I must be bleeding. When he was done he made me draw water for a bath and told me to sit in the water and soap myself. He knelt by the tub and lathered me with one hand, his knife always at me.

403

He helped me out of the tub and handed me a towel to dry off, then opened the wardrobe and took out this mask and cloak. I never saw them before and can't imagine how he knew they were there. Maybe he'd put them there.

'He told me, "Lady, you got one great shape," and made me put on the mask, cloak, and shoes and walk across the room, holding the cloak open while he looked at me. Then he pushed me down on the sofa and raped me again. And he left. I knew you [me] had an apartment here, and this morning I saw Melissa in the lobby and I assumed she was visiting you. So when he was gone I grabbed my clothes and came straight here, afraid he'd come back for another go at me, or even kill me, that's how these men are. Oh the foul dog.'

Melissa told me she was shocked to see a masked woman at the door, and wasn't sure it was Felicity until she spoke. Felicity's arrival was a quarter hour before my own, and all that time, Melissa said, she was hysterical, talking of being raped and robbed of her money and pearls by a man she'd seen working in the hotel. When I arrived Felicity told me the rapist looked like one of the gang who beat up the policemen on the barge. When she described him I knew it was Cully Watson. Melissa knew Cully only as Hopkins, a sometime hotel elevator operator.

Melissa, Felicity, and I were together half an hour, sifting what had happened, when Giles arrived. Never has a man been more deceived about what he thought he was seeing. Such costly, ghastly error. The questions remain: What led to his insane behavior? How did he know Felicity would be in my room at that moment, when neither we nor Felicity could have predicted it?

CULLY WATSON: FROM HIS STATEMENT TO POLICE

I was in Ohio first I heard of those killings. It was the Doc's wife and the actress, and Daugherty. Something going on there. Same day as the killings a guy says the Albany cops are looking for me, want me for trial, so what I needed was a bundle to get gone. The Doc's wife liked me, so when I took her stuff up to her room I patted her on the ass. She opened her bag to duke me and I saw a fold of bills thick as a steak. I told her, 'I don't want money, just a little lovin'.' I already had her three times before when she was at the hotel, so I muzzled her up. Not now, somebody's comin' to see me, she said. I said I'll be quick, and I opened her up some and she let me do this and that but pushed me away.

'We'll do it all later,' she said, but I'm hot so I kept going and we did it on the davenport.

She liked it but she was pissed at me mussing her hair, she's got company coming. Then the door opened and in came the actress. She didn't know what to make of us, both half naked, and she backed out, but the Doc's wife said, 'He's raping me, don't go.'

I said, 'No, I'm just fucking her. We're friends.' And I pulled out of her.

'I wanna take a bath,' the Doc's wife said, and she turned on the tap in the tub, bare-ass, except for that long string of pearls. I told her I liked the way she looked in 'em so she took 'em off to spite me and threw 'em on the bed. They said I took 'em but that ain't so. Fencing jewels on the run, you gotta be stupid. The other woman kept looking at me and she wasn't afraid.

'Are you busy?' I said.

'Forget it,' she said.

'Maybe you wanna take a bath too.'

'No thanks,' she said, but I pulled her clothes off. She fought me pretty good, but I got it into her too, short time, just to say I did it, a hell of a sweet-looking bitch. I put 'em both in the tub, soaping each other up. I coulda diddled the two of 'em all day, but with the cops after me I slipped out, took the cash from the purse, and left the women playing foot-in-the-crotch. I don't know who was doing what to who in that crowd. Maybe everybody was doing everybody. For me, I was long gone before the killings. When I heard about them I didn't blame the Doc. His wife was no good. But she was a pretty good fuck.

Edward Visits a Movie Set

June 10, 1910

Miss Innocence of America. If a headbirth by Aphrodite and The Prince were possible she could have been the progeny: born with passion's mouth and sacred swath, and wisdom from below. There are lessons to be learned by brushing a wing against such as she, and the lessons continue. In Melissa's nest of tinder I remembered Rose from tent city: vivacious, talented, driven, exuberant, bright, cunning strumpet. She answered when I wrote that I wanted to talk about Felicity.

Can you remember the dress I wore when we met? It no longer fits me, I'm so thin. The Kinegraph people think I'm ill or dying. They even say it to my face. I still wake up calling your name over and over. You've never left me. Some weeks I hardly eat anything. I'm wasting away, they tell me, and you know an actress can't afford to lose her profile.

Sickness plagues her imagination. She falls mortally ill when life goes awry, when fortune balks, when love loses its luminescence; for if you are ill, God cannot refuse you sustenance. It was because I genuinely believed her inability to either sleep without night sweats, or draw breath without pain, that I was with her when death came at us out of Giles's pistol. She and I were finished, but I had been unable to reject that face: not beautiful, but so robustly young, and illusory. Believe that face and lose your way. Study the transformation as she applies the powders, rouges, and charcoal stripings. Discover in that colored mouth, in those magnified eyes, the lure of the virgin-into-vixen: kill my innocence and I'll reward you with my fur.

> I've made thirty-five films this year and until two months ago nobody knew my name. And I thought I'd be anonymous forever: Of course I'd love to see you. Always. I was supposed to make two films last week and I missed both because of my weakness, but now that we're leaving the city I'm wonderfully well, for we're going to a marvelous lake with wild woodland. Do you know where I'm talking about? I can't believe it. I'm so excited. I told them everything I knew about the place, and my director couldn't wait. We'll be at our hotel four weeks, so come, love, please come, and everything will be just as it was.

Her success as my Thisbe had been supreme, she famous overnight, her photo in all the magazines. The play ran five months and when it closed Flo Ziegfeld was ready to put her in his *Miss Innocence* to replace Anna Held, but along came Giles's Wild West performance and Ziegfeld said nobody tainted by scandal would ever be in a show of his. For a time no one in theater would hire her, but the scandal faded into gossip and instead of being branded as the vixen she emerged as destiny's waif, the innocent darling corrupted by the 'eater of broken meats,' as the *Police Gazette* labeled me.

She sought work in the pictures, brought her photographs to Kinegraph, and was hired at fifteen dollars a week. Her salary rose to six hundred a week and is still climbing. She's become Kinegraph's chief asset: The Kinegraph Girl, nameless, chameleonic face of sorrow and rapture and fury and terror and wickedness and determination and invitation.

During one of her illnesses rumors spread that she'd been killed by a burglar, or run down by a drunken motorist. The public wondered: Where has our girl gone? Kinegraph publicists advertised in the newspapers to disprove the lies about her death, and announced she was coming to New York for a new picture. Squadrons of police had to hold back fans waiting for her train at Grand Central – a greater crowd than greeted the President the previous week. Kinegraph promptly abandoned its policy of anonymity for actors and agreed the public should know the Kinegraph Girl by name: Melissa Spencer ... Melissssssssssa Sssssssssspenccccccccer, how sweet the sibilance!

My sickness flared up when the police came to talk about Cully Watson. All lies. How can such a man be believed? If they put it in the papers again my career is ruined. Why would he slander me? I never said a word to him, and I swear this on my breasts, which you know how much we both value. Please meet me at Cooperstown and we will erase the horror and relive our loving days there and I'll be well again just from the sight of you.

Her film-in-progress was *The Deerslayer*, Cooper's five-hundred-page Natty Bumppo novel condensed to a twenty-minute movie. Her role was Hetty, the simpleminded daughter of scalp hunter Thomas Hutter. When I found my way to the village and then to the set, there she was, Melissa-into-Hetty, lying on her bed beneath a quilt, her face powdered into a death pallor; for Hetty had been shot by a stray bullet as the British troops rescued Deerslayer and Hetty's sister, Judith, from torture at the hands of the Huron Indians. Hetty was dying, and her secret love, Hurry Harry, another scalp hunter, was by her deathbed, along with Judith, heroic Deerslayer in his fringed buckskins, and his bare-chested Indian friend Chingachgook, noble Delaware chief. The actors mouthed Cooper's cumbersome dialogue as if it meant something to the film.

'How come they to shoot a poor girl like me and let so many men go unharmed?' Hetty wondered.

''Twas an accident, poor Hetty,' said Judith.

'I'm glad of that – I thought it strange: I am feebleminded, and the red men have never harmed me before ... there's something the matter with my eyes – you look dim and distant – and so does Hurry, now I look at him ... my mind was feeble – what people call half-witted . . . How dark it's becoming! . . . I feel, Deerslayer, though I couldn't tell you why . . . that you and I are not going to part forever . . .'

'. . . Yes, we *shall* meet ag'in, though it may be a long time first and in a far-distant land.'

'Sister, where are you? I can't see now anything but darkness . . .'

'Speak, dearest,' said Judith. 'Is there anything you wish to say . . . in this awful moment?'

Cooper has Hetty blush, which to Judith means Hetty is undergoing 'a sort of secret yielding to the instincts of nature,' and, on cue from Judith, Hurry Harry, nature's lusty pawn, takes Hetty in his arms. She utters her love for him, then dies.

Melissa, no stranger at death's door, rose up from Hetty's bed twice, fell back twice to die twice, one of the film's notable scenes. When it ended and the camera ceased its clatter, she rose up again to embrace me, kiss me lightly but with promise. The director eyed our kiss with disapproval, and I sensed he was Melissa's new conquest. He was early thirtyish, boyish, and rumpled.

'Our next film's in California, where we'll never have to worry about the weather,' he said. 'And it gets us away from the patent wars – movie companies suing each other over who owns the camera technology. You know about that, I guess.'

'Of course,' I said, knowing nothing of such wars.

'Melissa has no interest in these things,' said the rumpled boy, 'but she'll thrive in California. Inspiration under the sun. You'll have that every day, Mel.'

'A life of sunshine,' Melissa said. 'What luxury.'

When Rumples ended the day's filming, Melissa changed clothes, leaving Hetty's shroud and heavy eye makeup behind, converting that face that launched a thousand nickels (ten thousand thousand nickels) back into its faux pristinity. We went to the hotel and found our way to the rear piazza with its same rockers, same hammock, same view of the lovely lake that Cooper called Glimmerglass, and its vast, lush forests. Here we had spent ten idyllic days in the summer of 1908, convinced life was a dream of sensual indolence.

Melissa took up her familiar position in the hammock, and we ordered the same drinks (gin and quinine water), set them on the same wicker table, and we studied each other as if the 1908 dream had not dissolved in cordite reek and blood spew. Two years gone and the residual bone pain from the bullet (which had entered my left chest where the burning stick pierced Katrina: God's own symmetry) continued to plague my sleepless nights. Yet it was the forgotten wound, spoken of by neither Katrina nor Melissa; for I'd behaved badly, had not summoned the penitential grace to die from my bullet.

'Tell me about your play,' she said. 'Am I in it?'

'Someone like you is in it, but it isn't you.'

'But I could play the role.'

'You could if I cast you.'

'Of course you'll cast me.'

'Maybe you won't want this role.'

'If you wrote it I want it.'

'That's your only interest, a role. You don't even know what the play is about.'

'What *is* it about?'

'It's about a marriage that fails and the partners stay together but take lovers, not very original. Then the husband is caught with his mistress in a love nest, there's a shooting and two die. The husband is shot but doesn't die. People wish he had. He is condemned as a lecherous cad by priests, newspaper editors, and other custodians of the high moral ground. His son abandons college to escape his father's scandal. Thoughtless of the father not to perish from shame. To spite others, the man lives on. His life grows bleak. He can't understand why this tragedy happened, why people died. It's a mystery. He begins a journal, fills ledgers with ruminations, theories, then decides writing a play will combat the lethal determinism of the universe. He fills his imagined stage with a riot of scenes that synthesize events, discover answers. He discovers little and falls depressed at the pointlessness of wild endeavor. In time he humbleheartedly reunites with his estranged wife as a way of saving his soul. Magnanimous woman, she doesn't loathe him. She has her own sorrows. She has always loved him and he her.

William Kennedy

This is such a commonplace story. It happens to everybody, don't
you think? Finally, as he's framing a conclusion on the cause of
the killings, he turns up facts that dramatically contradict his
conclusion, so he visits his old paramour to confront her with
the news. That's as far as I've gotten.'

'When he goes back to his wife, do they make love?'

'I haven't decided if love is what they make.'

'But they do sexual things.'

'I haven't decided if what they do is sexual.'

'You've forgotten what's sexual?'

'Not at all.'

'Do you remember me making myself sexual in this hammock?'

'I do.'

'Shall I do it again?'

She was nuding herself belowskirts. She could do this expedi-
tiously.

'Is anybody watching?'

'I am.'

'I mean others.'

'No.'

'Is anybody coming?'

'No.'

'You see how I still love you?'

'I see the contour of a sunrise.'

'Shall we go to the room?'

'If you like.'

'You're not enticed.'

'I seem to be.'

'Then say it.'

'The room. Yes.'

We went to her rustic chamber: bed, dresser, commode, basin
and pitcher, wallpaper with pink roses on a field of mattress
ticking. We shed our garments and I remembered vividly what
I felt whenever I took this journey; but I felt none of that now,
could not invest my movement with the pelvic arrhythmia she

412

would remember, if she could differentiate mine from others. She perceived the problem and initiated variations on the theme, but while I remained full-blooded, I did so with ice in my heart.

'You're like a hanged man,' she said. 'Erect but dead.'

'I *am* a hanged man. At the end of my rope.'

'You don't look dead. You look wonderful. You look like the man I fell in love with at your dinner party.'

'That man is dead. Did you fall in love with your director? And what would he say if he saw you now?'

She was, just then, a moving picture, stirring the air with my verticality as if it were the tiller of a boat in a rowdy sea. My question becalmed her.

'Ah, you're jealous. How silly.'

She always viewed my objection to her flirtations as the fettering of her soul.

'He knows about us,' she said, 'but he assumes we're a thing of the past.'

'Would this scene convince him otherwise?'

'He's not important to me the way you are, and he's not very good at this.' She jostled the tiller. 'I told him we had a legal matter to discuss.'

'And so we do.'

'Not now.'

She went to the dresser and found a long strand of pearls, put it around her neck and knotted it so the knot lay in the deep fallaway of her breasts. She straddled the tiller and let the pearls caress my chest, my face.

'Those look like Felicity's pearls,' I said, and she reacted as if I'd lashed her with a bullwhip.

'Why would you say such a thing?' She knelt up straight, then put one foot on the floor, so beautiful in her angularity, her pudendal equipoise. 'You think I stole them?'

'Cully Watson says he didn't take them, yet they did vanish. Odd he admits the money but denies the pearls.'

'Maybe the police stole them. What do I care? How could you think I took them?'

'I never saw you wear pearls like these before.'

'I loved Felicity's pearls, so I got my own.'

'Saved your pennies, did you? Giles paid five thousand dollars for Felicity's.'

'Mine were a gift from an extremely wealthy gentleman. You're being rotten.'

'Cully contradicts everything you and Felicity told me.'

'Cully!' she screamed. 'I'm sick of Cully. He's a murderer. You take his word over mine?'

'Have you seen his statement?'

'Yes, and he's a maniac. It's all lies. ALL LIES! *ALL LIES!*'

She was kneeling on a pillow. She stood up, grabbed the pillow, and threw it at me.

'You son of a bitch, you believe him, don't you! You think I had sex with him! You think I was in the bathtub with Felicity! *YOU'RE A MANIAC TOO IF YOU BELIEVE THAT!*'

She threw a box of body powder at me. It missed my head, hit the wall, and showered talcum over the bedclothes. She reached for the toilet water but I wrapped her fury in a bear hug and made her put it down.

'That cape Felicity wore,' I said. 'I found the costumier where you bought it. I saw a similar cloak in his display window. He remembered you.'

Her body went limp in my arms. I eased her backward so she could sit on the bed, and she blanched, summoning a stroke, or the black plague, anything to solve this crisis of contradiction. She buried her face in her hands as she had when she wept for the dead horse on the Fourth of July.

'You don't know anything,' she said.

'I agree with that. Why don't you enlighten me?'

She fell backward on the bed and stretched her arms over her head, eyes closed, her cave of opulent nuances assisting her in negotiating a new reality.

'I gave Felicity the mask and cloak to wear for you.'

'For me?'

'She wanted you. Wanted to be with you.'

'Felicity wanted *me*?'

'For years. She could never tell you.'

'Did it occur to her I might not want her?'

'You'd have wanted her if you saw her in that cloak.'

'I did see her in it. Alive and dead.'

'She had a beautiful body and she wanted to give it to you. I thought you'd like that. I said I'd arrange it. We made a game of how we'd both dress up for you.'

'You never mentioned such a thing.'

'It was new. We talked about it the week before. We wanted to surprise you.'

'But Cully was the surprise.'

'Yes.'

'And he, not I, put you both in the tub.'

'*NEVER!*'

She fumed in silence, stoking herself for an explosion of logic that would defy all argument. I pacified her with gin and in the ensuing half hour she cobbled together her story.

She bought the cloak for Felicity a week before the famous day, she said, kept it in a closet in our apartment (*ours* for the previous two months; but we were finished, for I'd wearied of her feigned illnesses, her absurd jealousies – over an actress who smiled at me at the theater, or a buxom waitress where we breakfasted – and her rage over these imagined dalliances. That rage would end as irrationally as it had begun: she on her knees asking forgiveness, I touching away her tears and reaffirming my loyalty with prolonged vaginal stroking). Melissa, having seen Felicity arrive in the hotel that morning, took cloak and mask to Felicity's room, the proposed site of our ménage. She put the garments on a chair but saw no Felicity; nor was she in the bedroom. Melissa called out, 'Your wardrobe mistress has arrived,' and from the bathroom came male and female voices, then Felicity's voice saying she would see Melissa later.

'I left immediately,' Melissa said to me, 'telling myself she was always something of a tart.'

'You didn't hear any fear in her voice?'

415

'I suppose I should have.'

'Wasn't that the bathtub rape in progress?'

'*If* he raped her. He said he raped me too, but I never set eyes on the man.'

'You never told me any of this.'

'She came to our door in that cloak, crying and carrying her clothes, hiding behind that mask. She cried rape and I let her in. She lied to you about the cloak, but how could she tell you what it was really for? Maybe she still hoped to charm you with it. Tarts are tarts. And yet how could I doubt her? She said he held a knife to her throat, that she even feared for *my* life when I was outside that bathroom door. I couldn't tell you this.'

'Not even after her death, to get at the truth?'

'*This is the truth!*'

Melissa stood up and began to dress herself and I too stepped into my clothing, told her I was going back to Albany.

'You make it quite credible,' I said. 'I don't doubt any part of your story. But I'm absolutely certain you're a virtuoso liar.'

Katrina's Diary and the Bovine Poem

June 11, 1910

Edward entered his home and from the hallway he called Katrina.
The house replied with a stillness that plummeted him into gloom.
He tossed his coat and hat on a chair and went to his library where
Katrina would have left him a message, if she had been in a mood
to communicate. He saw the letter from Melissa to Katrina, which
lay unopened on his desk where Katrina had left it, along with two
volumes of her diary for the years 1894 and 1908, their marking
sashes emerging, presumably, from pages to be heeded. He pushed
Melissa's letter aside and opened the pages of Katrina's mind.

The first diary: April 19, 1894

Mother sold her emerald last month. I've only now learned
this. The house was in jeopardy and the emerald preserved it
for at least four years. Father had far less than he let on, lost
almost half a million in the panic of '93, and gave more than
anyone knew to Madame Baldwin. He came to Mother with
his problem. Had he not given her the jewels? Were they
not emblematic of lush times? But now, after the panic, the
times have us in a precarious position. He did not mention
Madame Baldwin. Mother yielded the emerald and kept his
secrets, shoring up the facade of normalcy by forgoing travel
to London and Paris for the year, limiting her shopping, and
letting two of the lesser servants go. Of her truly valuable
jewels only her black pearls and solitaire earrings remain,
and, of course, her priceless tiara, which I covet.

417

Mother chaired her antisuffrage meeting today in our main parlor. Giles came, unable to resist Mother's magnetism. Edward brought me, listened for ten minutes, amused, then left for the club. The room was filled with a hundred of Mother's friends and peers, all so well educated, so certain of their position, so unified and uniformed in their spring bonnets against the amendment that would eliminate the word 'male' from the State Constitution's definition of suffrage. Mother was valiant, insisting an undesirable class of women would swiftly take advantage of the vote, that it is a man's sphere for which women are unsuited. Could anyone, she inquired in her shrillest tone, imagine a proper woman serving in the militia, or on the police and fire departments? One wonders. But as B says: 'I have no ambition. I am not base enough to hold a conviction.'

Giles, sweet Giles, ever the suitor. He persuaded me the antisuffrage papers the women were reading ('. . . educated women would stay away from the polls . . . present relations between men and women are all that could be desired . . .') were making me crimson with vexation, and he insisted we escape. We went to the dining room and sipped punch and he put down his cup and kissed me. 'I want to embrace your unclothed body,' he said, his words squishing at me through the kiss. 'I dream of your intimacy. I picture your head on my pillow. I don't care a fig that you're married. Edward is my valued friend and has nothing to do with this. I've loved you since we took dancing class together.' He tried to kiss me again but I twisted his ear. He yowled like a cat, yanked his head away and I left him by the punch bowl, sweet fool. Did Father treat Madame Baldwin this way? Probably so.

I have no desire for Giles, but the idea of a lover is taking hold. It has everything to do with resisting my age, for I will be thirty soon. I know how vain and foolish this is, but it is no less real for that. Also I must punish Edward for despoiling me. I sought it, yes, but he did it, as he should have, or I would not have married him. But I cannot forgive him. He does not yet understand the craft of dying. I wonder, shall I be truly beautiful all my life?

The second diary: October 17, 1908
Giles arrived this morning in a frenzy but would not say what was causing it. I made him tea to calm him, and it did. He asked for Edward and when I said he was in New York working on the production of his new play he responded, 'As I thought. Are you separated?' I told him Edward and I had been moving apart with glacial slowness, and distance was having antithetical effects, a growing sense of peace, through solitude and the absence of an intolerable presence; but also a deepening fury at being abandoned, however justified the abandonment. I told him I loved Edward profoundly, that in his eyes was a melting tenderness I could find in no other man. Without a word Giles took a folded sheet of paper from his coat and handed it to me. At the center was a well-drawn cartoon of a minotaur cavorting on a theater stage with two near-naked women with the heads of cows, while another and smaller minotaur with excessively large horns was watching from the theater's front row. Beneath the cartoon were six lines of verse:

> Your little wife's gone to the city again
> To dance on the stage with her partners in sin.
> So she and the scribe and the actress will play
> Their bovinish games in Gomorrah today,
> The ladies disporting like September Morns,
> While you sit at home cultivating your horns.

Of course the verse concerns Edward and Melissa Spencer, common gossip by this time, and I have ignored it. But the involvement of Felicity comes as a shock to Giles and a surprise to me; and I saw his frenzy return as a twitch in his left eye. He found the poem in his mailbox this morning. And during the night someone put a severed bull's head on his porch. I wept for the shame of it, for all our shame. I felt extremely close to Giles at this moment, as if what was happening to us with such sudden force was a form of transcendence, thrusting us naked together into some underworld dungeon for abuse by obscene devils. Giles's face was collapsed and flushed with tears, and I then decided to disrobe for him, rid myself of blouse, skirt, petticoat, knickers, shoes, stockings, all. I stood before him as he once said he wanted me, and his weeping ceased. I sat and let him study me, giving him not my body, but the part of my soul that lives in shadow. I told him not to touch me; nor had he betrayed any such plan. He stared at me and we didn't speak, but I felt glorious, basking in the light of my dear friend's wan smile. He stood up and took my chin in his right hand and kissed me just once, then said, 'You are the vestal goddess of sublime pain.' I had banished his frenzy.

Edward Goes to the Slaughterhouse

June 11, 1910

It was already late afternoon when Edward closed Katrina's diary. He hitched up the horse he called Galway Kate to his demi-landau and rode out to the Cudahy slaughterhouse in West Albany. Cattle were being led out of a storage pen and up an inclined wooden runway onto the killing floor of the huge wooden shed, where Edward told a foreman he had urgent business with Clubber. Clubber, the foreman said, worked as a splitter, and Edward found him, heavy cleaver in hand, halving the backbone of a dead cow. Edward called his name, and Clubber turned and stared at Edward, then finished cutting the beast and handed the cleaver to a man beside him to cope with the next carcass. Clubber spoke to the foreman, then limped toward Edward, who was trying not to retch from the stench of the gutted animals. Clubber rinsed blood off his hands with a hose, and dried them on his trousers, which were full of bloodstains.

'Hey, Ed, what got you out here? I ain't ever seen you out here.'

'You got a few minutes, Clubber?'

'I can take ten minutes.'

They walked out of the shed to Edward's carriage.

'We'll go have a drink.'

'Quick one's all,' said Clubber.

'Get up here.'

They rode to George Karl's saloon and Edward bought the beer. Clubber pinched himself a piece of beef on an onion slice from the lunch counter and sat at a table.

'Putting the bull's head on Giles's porch, what exactly happened? Tell it again, Clubber.'

'I told it twenty hundred times.'

'Once more.'

'Cully Watson says help him with the joke. Kill the bull, cut its head, leave it down at Giles's, hell of a joke, you know it, he'll wake up and say, "Hey, that's a dead bull on my porch. Son bitch," he'll say, "who'd do a thing like that?"'

'What did Cully do on the porch? Anything you remember?'

'Lifted the head with me.'

'What else?'

'Said where to set it.'

'Did he have a piece of paper?'

'Paper?'

'With some lines of verse on it.'

'What verse?'

'Any verse at all. Whatever you remember.'

'Verse.'

'What about the paper?'

Clubber drank some beer and searched for the paper.

'I guess he coulda had a paper.'

'What'd he do with it?'

'I don't know. Put it in the mailbox?'

'That's right. He put it in Giles's mailbox.'

'Yeah. That's it. It was part of the joke. Like a valentine, Cully said. He'll get a valentine in the morning. I forgot that.'

Edward handed Clubber the verse he'd copied from Katrina's diary. 'Here's what that valentine said.'

Clubber's eyes moved across and down the page, up and across, down again, up and across again.

'What's this stuff say?'

'It says in a roundabout way that Giles's wife is down in New York having sex with two people, a man and a woman. The man is meant to be me. The scribe. That's what it means.'

'That ain't true.'

'You're right. It's all wrong.'

'No, that ain't true on the valentine. It was a joke.'

'Wasn't a joke, Clubber.'

'It was a joke, I'm telling you. Cully said it was a joke. We laughed like hell at the joke. Just a goddamn dead-bull joke, Ed. That's all it was, a dead-bull joke.'

'When Giles read it he went to New York and murdered his wife, shot me, then blew his own brains out through the top of his head. Nobody thought that was a joke.'

'That couldn'ta been why he done it, not the joke. It ain't possible, Ed. He gotta had somethin' else on his mind.'

'It was this, Clubber, it was this.'

Clubber suffered Edward's words as a succession of blows, a whipped cur cowering from an affectionate hand. He pulled in his shoulder and cried, making no noise. He tried to remove the evidence of such unmanly behavior by rubbing the water off his face, wiping his fingers on his pants. When he did it again, he spread pink streaks of the damp cow blood on his cheeks and around his eyes.

'Couldn't be. It ain't true.'

'Wasn't a joke, Clubber.'

'I wouldn'ta hurt Giles or 'specially you. You know that, Ed.'

'I know that, Clubber.'

Clubber made a noise in his throat, an involuntary blubbering, and ducked his head below table level so none could see. He coughed, a fake cough, and smeared his face in new places with the pink cow blood.

'Who put Cully up to it?'

Clubber only stared.

'Was it Maginn?'

'Maginn?'

After Edward revealed to Clubber the valentine's fatal message, Clubber hid himself in the darkest corner of the attic of his two-story home on Van Woert Street. His sister Lydie saw his lunch pail and knew he'd come home but could not find him. When Clubber heard her step on the attic stairs he climbed out the window and leaped off the roof to kill himself. He broke an arm and an ankle, and sprained a shoulder, all of which were put in casts or wrapped by Doc Keegan at St Peter's Hospital. Lydie took her brother home from the hospital and when she went to sleep he crawled back up to the attic and threw himself off the same roof, breaking a leg and a hip, and earning his ticket to the asylum at Pough-keepsie.

Katrina in the Drawing Room Mirror

May 7, 1912

She stood before the gilt-framed mirror in the drawing room of her home, primping, reimposing a straying hair, ordering the lines of her solid-gray, V-necked satin dress, its skirt gathered into soft billows at the front to reveal stockinged ankles, the shocking fashion at Auteuil this year. She studied what remained of the forty-seventh year of her beauty. It was persistent, vegetative, clarion. In her own reversed eyes it seemed less fragile now than when she married him and had worried about her too-emphatic cheekbones, the early lines at the corners of her eyes. Such empty concern. What does all that mean to anyone now? To him? To other men?

The men in the mirror, behind her. At her. Always at her, in memory or dream, or with their need, or their plangent sorrow at the leave-taking, or their eyes that improve with reversal. And their alcoholic breath on your neck.

She has known the joy of beauty. But, he wrote, joy is one of her most vulgar adornments, while melancholy may be called her illustrious spouse, a strain of beauty that has nothing to do with sorrow.

She had begun the day knowing her obligations and desires, an unusual rising, life rarely so orderly for Katrina. She remembered seeing her father, and dreaming of a monkey, knew what Mrs Squires should make for breakfast: turkey hash, her mother's favorite, and pumpkin patties, knew the tasks of this consequential morning, knew that revelation would greet her afternoon.

She had bathed, dressed, and, first order, taken down her large black leather shoulder bag and opened it on the bed. From her clothes hamper, where she had put it for safekeeping last night, she took her mother's jewel case and put it in the bottom of the bag. She walked to the third-floor storeroom and unlocked the steamer trunk her father had bought for her trip to London and presentation at court. She rummaged under that famous dress of white chiffon over white silk in which she had made her deep curtsy before Queen Victoria, and she lifted out the seven identical leather-bound diaries of her life. She dropped the key inside the trunk, closed it.

In her room she put six of the dairies in her bag. The remaining one (1896–98) she opened to the page where lay a newspaper clipping of a baseball player photographed in close-up as he throws a ball. Francis of the excellent face.

She raised her glance to the window and looked out at the maple tree in the garden where she'd seen him perched on a branch, sawing another branch above his head. Her valentine in the tree. And she had immediately, then, dressed herself naked, in sun hat and evening slippers, and walked out onto the back piazza to induct the young man into her life. And didn't they love each other so well after that induction? Oh they did.

She built shrines to their love: in her bureau, on her dressing table, on the shelf above the bathtub: a piece of paper on which he'd written both their names: Francis Aloysius Phelan and Katrina Selene Taylor, a snippet of the green canvas he'd wrapped around her when he carried her naked in from the piazza, coins he'd held in his hand, a rag of a shirt he'd left with her, a book with the poems she'd read to him, a handkerchief stained with their love. The shrines were palpable proof of time memorious, when love lived in the next house and came to call.

Until one day it did not. And she destroyed the shrines.

She looked at the clipping, his face scowling at the unseen baserunner he is about to throw out at first, scowling at the hidden Katrina he is about to throw out of his life.

She read the open page of the diary:

The end of summer, 1898:

If you saw me plunge a knife into myself would it baffle you? Would you think it a miracle? Do you understand what I mean when I say I have no ability to slide in and out of love? Would you be tempted to pull the knife out of me and cut off my face? Would you kiss me while I bled through my eyes?

She considered ripping the clipping in half, but did not. She put it between pages of the diary, put the diary into the bag, and went downstairs to breakfast.

'I dreamed of pumpkin last night,' she said to Mrs Squires, who was serving her breakfast. 'Does that mean anything?'

'Did you eat the pumpkin?' Mrs Squires asked.

'No, it was just pulp and I threw it at a monkey.'

'Monkeys could mean sharpers are after you, so watch out, Mrs D. But pumpkin is nice. Pumpkin means happiness. Unless you eat it, and then I'm afraid it means trouble's coming.'

'The monkey was a collapsed doll, sitting on a high perch, and I hated it. I hit it with a handful of pumpkin and it came to life.'

'So the monkey ate the pumpkin. You'd best be careful today, Mrs D.'

'I shall indeed, Mrs Squires.'

She relished her food, the taste of bygone breakfasts, when her mother shopped and arranged the daily menu. As she swallowed a forkful of the creamy turkey hash the telephone rang in the hallway. She heard Loretta answer, heard her footsteps coming toward the dining room.

'Martin is on the wire from New York, Missus Daugherty,' Loretta said, and Katrina went quickly to the telephone.

'Martin?' she said into the mouthpiece. 'This is your mother who loves you. Where are you?'

'A hotel lobby on Fourteenth Street.'

'Are you coming home?'

'I'm thinking about it.'

'You should stop thinking about it and get on the train. Your father's play opens in four days.'

'I know that, Mother.'

'Are you coming to see it?'

'That's what I'm thinking about.'

'Martin, my sweet and only child, please stop thinking and make your decision. You no longer hate your father. You told me so yourself.'

'That's right. I don't hate him.'

'Then come and be with him for his play. It will be a momentous event.'

'For some people.'

'For more than you suppose. Now you must come, Martin. You can't hide from the reality of your life. You must confront it and see what it looks like. Your mother insists. Do you hear what she's saying?'

'I believe I'll be coming.'

'You surely will?'

'I believe I will.'

'How very, very good that is. Oh how very, very good, Martin. I was afraid you'd fail me. Is there anything else you want to tell me?'

'I'm staying at Father's apartment in the Village. I've just taken over the rental, as he suggested.'

'You're such a sensible young man. I'm so proud of you, Martin, so proud. Have we finished with our talk?'

'I told you I would call.'

'And so you have. And I told you I would do all in my power to make the rest of your life as harmonious as possible with your father. I do mean that, Martin. I verily do.'

'I believe you do, Mother. I'll see you tomorrow.'

'You've made me very happy, Martin.'

'I'm glad for that, Mother.'

'Then goodbye, my sweet boy. Goodbye.'

And she placed the receiver on its hook.

She went back to the table, her mind sprinting into the day

ahead of her. She sat down to finish her breakfast, but she could not. She took one forkful of hash for old times' sake, then went to the drawing room, where she had left her bag and her hat.

She stood before the mirror, primping, reimposing a straying hair. Her eye swept the reflected room behind her, the room she had created in her own image, and she saw herself unbuttoning Francis's shirt, saw his hand cautiously moving down her shoulder to touch her naked breast for the first time, to touch her scar. Do you like my scar, Francis?

She shook the image away, took her new hat with the ostrich plumes off the table and put it on, pale-gray, wide-brimmed hat that matched her shocking dress. She centered the hat on her head, pinned it to the crown of her hair, which was still the color of the gilded mirror. Maginn, behind her, raised a hand to touch that hair he so worshiped.

'You didn't deserve to have this happen,' he said.

He touched the shoulder of her dress, moved his face so close that she smelled the liquor on his breath.

'I saw it coming. Why would he do this to you?'

He touched her bare neck. In the mirror she saw the faces of persistent desire, and behind them the will to persistent desire.

'It should be enough for any man to make love to a woman like you. Having you in my arms is worth any amount of mayhem and murder.'

She let him turn her around, and as she did she saw the portraits of her parents staring at her. Why do you allow this slumcrawler to touch you, Katrina? Why do you even allow him in the house? Maginn gripped her arms and kissed her. When she could again see his face he was smiling.

'Shall we sit down?'

They sat on the sofa facing the fireplace and he held her hand in his.

'The anger must be consuming you.'

He put one hand on her thigh.

'I was in New York when it happened. I talked to a chambermaid who went in to clean his rooms one day and they didn't hear her key. They were all in bed, making peculiar love. And Felicity was there. The maid knew her.'

He moved his hand between her thighs, spreading them, and with one finger began slowly pulling up her skirt.

'There are ways to reciprocate,' he said.

She turned away from the mirror and crossed the room to the fireplace. She picked up the black iron poker and walked back to the mirror and smashed it with the poker. Mrs Squires came running from the dining room.

'Are you all right, Mrs D?'

'Perfectly fine, Mrs Squires. I broke the mirror. Will you tell Loretta to sweep up the glass and throw the mirror in the trash. Then move my father's portrait into its place.'

'I'll tell her right away.'

'I have to go to the bank and the theater. I'll be back this afternoon.'

'Very good, Mrs D.'

'The turkey hash was excellent, Mrs Squires.'

'Like your mother made, was it?'

'Exactly like Mother made.'

Katrina looped the strap of her bag over her shoulder and left the house, her ostrich plumes bobbing as she walked.

Katrina Sits for Her Portrait,
with a Flower

In the MacDonald photographic studio on Broadway and Maiden Lane, the studio favored by eminent Albanians, Katrina confirmed with the secretary her appointment for a portrait sitting. She sat down to wait and the secretary stared at her exposed ankles, one stockinged leg visible up to the shinbone.

'Is something wrong?' Katrina asked the secretary. 'You seem to be staring at my dress.'

'Oh, nothing wrong at all, Madam. It's a lovely dress. I've just never seen one like it.'

'Do you like it?'

'I wouldn't have the courage to wear it.'

'That's a very silly thing to say. One may wear whatever one chooses to wear.'

'Yes, Ma'am.'

Pirie MacDonald, the photographer who had established the studio, came out of an inner office in his tailcoat and greeted Katrina who shook his hand without standing up.

'Your secretary finds my dress unusual,' she said.

'Does she?' MacDonald stared at her legs, nodded. 'Shall we go into the studio?'

He entered behind her and motioned her to a seat in front of a pastoral backdrop with a sky full of clouds. She shook her head.

'That will not do,' she said. 'I do not want to be photographed with clouds.'

'Whatever you say, Madam.'

He moved the backdrop to one side, revealing a black backdrop behind it.

'Nor do I want blackness,' Katrina said.

'White, then?' And he moved the black backdrop aside, revealing the white wall.

'Do you have any yellow?'

'Color doesn't show in the photograph, Madam.'

'But color is there, whether it shows or not.'

'It's white or that's it, I'm afraid.'

'Then let it be white.'

She sat in the chair he placed in front of the empty whiteness while he organized the placement of lights, creating the fall of shadow on her face. 'When will the photo be ready?'

'Beginning of the week.'

'You'll deliver, of course.'

'Of course.' He was under his focusing cloth, adjusting the camera lens. 'You'll want a torso portrait, I assume. From the waist up?'

'Not at all. I want the entire body.'

She moved her legs to give greatest visibility to her ankles. MacDonald came out from under his cloth.

'Is this how you want to be seen in the photo?' he asked, indicating her ankles.

'It's for my husband.'

'Very lucky man, your husband.'

'No, he's not a lucky man. His life is a disaster, and much of it is my doing.'

'I'm sure you're too cruel to yourself, Madam.'

'I'm not cruel at all. This is just how it happened to be. One is what one is, one does what one does. Isn't that how you find it?'

'I'm not much on philosophy, Madam.'

'But in taking pictures you must see in people's faces how they are.'

'Sometimes I think I do, but other times I know what I see is only an illusion. From what I see here, I'm sure this photo will cheer up your husband.'

'I hope you are right.'

'Then relax, Madam,' he said as he hid himself beneath the cloth, 'relax.'

'I have no intention of relaxing,' Katrina said. 'You'll have to photograph me as I am.'

'Don't move. And look into the camera.'

'Wait!' she said, for she suddenly remembered Femmitie Staats, defined forever in her painting by her flirtatious smile; and Katrina wondered which feature of hers people would fix upon as definitive. She loathed the idea of its being her avant-garde ankles. Then she saw the dried sunflower in a vase on a corner table in the studio, and she spoke up, told the photographer she wished to redesign herself, and would he leave her for a few moments?

The billowy V-neck of her dress was adjustable by hidden buttons, two of which she undid, allowing the neck to open to the edges of her shoulders. The separation of her breasts then became visible, but she concealed most of that with the sunflower, whose stem she snapped to shorten it, then tucked the stem inside her bodice. In her mirror image she had become different, new yet again. And, for the first time, the top of her white, oval scar from the Delavan was visible to the world, above the edge of her dress.

Could one call this appearance brazen?

She thought not. Some might suggest that a flaw such as a scar should be hidden forever, but she disagreed.

She called to the photographer to return, and he raised an eyebrow at what he saw, then proceeded to take what would be unarguably the most important photograph of his later life. In it Katrina's hair is symmetrically divided in an inverted V that falls with slight convex curves from the center of her forehead to the edges of her eyebrows, not one hair straying. Her sharply patrician nose is half in soft shadow, her mouth a small smile that says 'I understand,' and there are deep oval shadowings that enhance her eyes, render them patient with the melancholy she so covets. She is looking directly at us and into us, her torso slightly rightward, her yellow sunflower an oblique presence, her left shoulder in a gently aggressive forward thrust, for she is yielding, but with a will that only very reluctantly recognizes the inevitable; yet it does recognize it. Her ankles, a statement of rebellion, do not dominate the photograph as MacDonald thought they might; but they color it, as Katrina's radical exploration of love colored her entire life, and the lives of those around her.

With the making of this picture MacDonald would elevate himself, for a time, to the status of master photographer of eastern American beauty. Women of privilege, having once seen this photo, would come to Albany from as far as Boston and Manhattan to be photographed by him. But no other photo he took in these years would approach in vividness the image of Katrina and her sunflower with the pale yellow petals: two kindred blossoms of nature's intelligence, caught at the peak of their elegant desiccation.

Katrina Deposits Some Valuables in the Bank Vault

Katrina walked from Broadway up State Street to the State National Bank, where her grandfather Lyman and her father had been directors in their time; the oldest bank in the city, where Archie Van Slyke was an assistant vice president, still. She saw Archie at his desk in a far corner of the main banking room, in his tight suit and his pince-nez. He stood to greet her as she walked toward him, and from the lethargic way he moved she decided he was still drinking too much.

With the Van Slyke and Taylor fortunes behind him, Archie had entered Albany's banking world with flourish and promise. But he skidded at the death of Adelaide, and moped forward in life, focused on the bottle, never remarrying, keeping himself humbled and blurred. Yet he held his job, kept his modest title, one reason being that Geraldine had always placed unqualified trust in his handling of her once-substantial accounts.

Katrina always thought of Archie when she remembered what Henry James had told Edward and her during their luncheon in New York in 1903. When he thought of Albany, Henry said, he remembered his father's stories about his own contemporaries, all of them men with great promise and romantic charm, all of them, in his father's eyes, eventually ending badly, as badly as possible.

'Oh dear, Archie,' she said as she sat beside his desk, 'this is a sad errand. I closed Mother's house last night.'

'How is she?'

'Depressed. But the good of it is she no longer has to fear foreclosure. She'll do fine in the apartment. And she's still in the old neighborhood.'

'I knew it was happening,' Archie said. 'Such a pity. Such a magnificent house it was.'

'I've taken a few pieces of special memory, but the rest is off to be auctioned. I bring valuables for our box in your vault. Mother had a safe for them at home, but I do not.'

As he prepared the paper for her to sign, Katrina saw the descending panorama of Archie's entire life, culminating in the whiskey-blotch of his face; and she realized precisely how this, too, had happened. She would have to tell him.

'We'll go in now,' Archie said, and together they walked across the bank to the armed guard, and Archie presented him with Katrina's identification card; and they entered. Katrina left her bag on the table in the coupon room, and walked into the great vault of the bank with Archie. Together they opened the combination lock on the Daugherty safe deposit box, and Katrina carried the box back to the table.

'I'll be a few minutes with this,' she said.

'Ring the wall buzzer and I'll come back,' Archie said.

She took the jewel case out of her bag and placed all that was in it on the table: her mother's diamond tiara, the silver cream pitcher from the Cromwell tea service, a pair of gold cuff links inscribed with her father's initials in Old English script, two gold rings she and Adelaide had outgrown in childhood, the single strand of pearls Lyman had given Geraldine on her sixteenth birthday, and a miscellany of gold and silver bracelets that might not be gold and silver, since Geraldine had yielded most jewelry of value to rescue her husband from debt. This was what remained of the Taylor fortune, excepting what would come from the auction and the sale of the house, some of which would clear her mother's debt to tradesmen, doctors, and lawyers, the rest to go into the trust fund that would pay for Geraldine's modest room and board for the rest of her life. The melancholy management of reduced expectations.

Katrina took two silk scarves from her bag, wrapped the tiara, pitcher, and cuff links (a set of rainy-day surprises for Edward) in one, the rest of the items in the other. She saw that, as now packed, the deposit box would not accept all she wanted to put into it. She took out the family documents, their birth certificates, and the endowment agreement under which Lyman gave an annuity to Edward, the deeds to the Colonie Street house and the Daugherty house on Main Street, and two plays by Edward she had copied and put here for safekeeping without his knowing: *Pyramus and Thisbe*, which had since been published and no longer needed to be here, and *Lunar Majesty*, his play about a woman's courtship, marriage, and early estrangement from her husband. Katrina cherished this play for its compassion and insight – into her, of course – she the enduring heroine of all of Edward's works. She opened the manuscript to a page and read:

THE HUSBAND: I'm convinced she's walled in behind the energy of her derangement, sane as anyone alive, mad as the queen of Bedlam – the stigmata, the sickness, the lesions visible in her eyes and the clutch of her hand. Such a marvel of womanhood, as pure and as fated as Eve before the serpent.

'A bit overstated, Edward,' Katrina said aloud.

Then she closed the manuscript, laid it flat in the deposit box, arranged the diaries atop it, then put in the jewels wrapped in their scarves. She folded *Pyramus and Thisbe* into her leather bag, closed the box, and rang the buzzer for Archie. He was waiting outside the door. Together they reentered the vault, secured the box in its place, and left the vault.

'I saw my father last night at the house,' Katrina said as they went out.

Archie stopped, looked at her, took off his pince-nez.

'I was standing in his office,' she said, 'and I realized he was in the cellar. I went down with a candle and found him sitting on a stool by the pipe where the city water comes in. The pipe was dripping water onto his shoulder. He was wearing his small spectacles and an old overcoat, which was quite wet. He was hunched over and looked very pitiful. We stared at each other until I summoned the courage to say, "I would take you upstairs, Father, but there's nothing up there now." He continued to stare at me, and the water dripped onto his unruly hair.'

Archie looked away from Katrina, spoke to the floor.

'You know, Katrina, of course you know, that your father is dead. You were at his burial.'

'Of course I was, of course I know that.'

'I suppose these things can happen.'

'Father blamed Edward for Adelaide's death, but I was the one. Edward was only doing what he knew I wanted.'

'You can't blame yourself for such things, Katrina. You seem a bit skewed today, frankly. You should see a doctor.'

'I'm very clear on it, Archie. I truly am.'

Her voice was as bright as morning.

'If I hadn't been what I was, Edward and I wouldn't have needed to make peace with the family. If we all hadn't gone to that dinner of reconciliation, Adelaide and my father wouldn't have died, and you wouldn't have ruined your career with drink.'

'I have hardly done that, Katrina. You are ill.'

'It's you who are ill, Archie, and I'm sorry I had a hand in it.'

'You'll soon be taking blame for the weather.'

'Perhaps I shall. It's quite uncanny what one sets in motion by being oneself.'

She stood up and extended her hand.

'Thank you so much, Archie. I must go up to the Hall now and see a bit of the dress rehearsal of Edward's play.'

'Yes, I saw a notice in the paper.'

'I believe he's written the tragedy of our lives. And do stop drinking, Archie. You're such a good man without it.'

'You should learn to mind your own business, Katrina.'

'Yes, I suppose I should. But I have so very little business to mind.'

Katrina Watches *The Flaming Corsage*

She sits alone at the rear of the orchestra
In Harmanus Bleecker Hall,
Albany's premier
Theater

She sees only Act Four, Scene One

The text of the scene:

The City Club Tea Room on Elk Street (ladies only), summer, 1910. One round white wicker table, two matching chairs, one potted palm tree in white pot.

MARINA *and* CLARISSA *are seated at table with white lamp with white shade, a pot of tea, two cups and saucers, spoons, two small plates, and, in the center of the table, a plate of small sandwiches made from white bread with crusts removed.*

Both women are elegantly dressed in long, white dresses with colossal hats. MARINA's *hat is a garden of puffy white ostrich plumes.* CLARISSA's *hat is a circular fountain of long, narrow white feathers.*

MARINA: Will you have tea?

CLARISSA: If you please.
              (*Marina pours tea into both cups.*)
              You must wonder about my letter.

MARINA: Not at all.

CLARISSA: I thought it important to write you.

MARINA: Did you? Why was that?

CLARISSA: I thought we should discuss Miles.

MARINA: *Did* you? Why was *that*?

CLARISSA: He was so odd.

MARINA: You're absolutely right. Shooting his wife
              that way. Then shooting himself. Odd.
              (*Marina sips her tea, holds cup in air.*)
              Miles suffered from an excess of fastidi-
              ousness.
              (*She sips tea again, puts cup down.*)
              He was appalled by its absence in others.

CLARISSA: Miles was quite wrong about one thing. He
              thought his wife and your husband were
              paramours.

MARINA: But it was *you* and my husband who were
              paramours.

CLARISSA: We were the best of friends.

MARINA: And now that's all past. Now Miles is
              dead and my husband considers you a well-
              poisoner.

CLARISSA: I understand your anger.

MARINA: My anger faded long ago, replaced by other emotions.

CLARISSA: I won't ask what they are.

MARINA: I'm not sure I could say what they are. They're quite mysterious.

CLARISSA: Your husband thinks me a well-poisoner?

MARINA: He blames himself, but thinks you spawned the disaster.

CLARISSA: How does he think I did that?

MARINA: Through Mangan, who conceived the plot to expose your love nest, the most successful creative act of his life.
              (*She sips her tea.*)

CLARISSA: Mangan never forgave Miles for the fireman's-wife joke.

MARINA: Nonsense.

CLARISSA: He was so humiliated.

MARINA: Mangan is unhumiliatible.

CLARISSA: Mangan is really quite sensitive.

MARINA: Mangan lacks fastidiousness.
              (*Pause.*)

441

He told me you were his constant paramour,
even when you were seeing my husband.
Dreadful to reveal such things.

CLARISSA: Did Mangan say that?
              (*She sips her tea.*)
              He's such a liar.

MARINA: He did not seem to be lying.
              (*She proffers plate of sandwiches.*)
              Sandwich?

CLARISSA: Thank you.
              (*Clarissa takes sandwich, bites it.*)
              Delicious.
              (*Marina takes sandwich from plate and smells
              it.*)

MARINA: Raw fish. How repellent.
              (*She puts sandwich on her own plate, wipes
              her fingers with napkin.*)
              Mangan has always envied my husband.
              They were like brothers once, but he envied
              my husband's social position, envied his
              marrying me, envied his success in the
              theater, envied his self-possession.
              (*Pause.*)
              My husband was the true target in the love-
              nest conspiracy, not poor, simple Miles.
              (*She lifts teapot.*)
              Tea?

CLARISSA: If you please.
              (*Marina pours tea.*)
              Mangan told me he once had Miles's wife.
              In a Pullman compartment on the train from

Albany to New York.

MARINA: I did say Mangan lacked fastidiousness, did
            I not?

CLARISSA: But he does seem to know things.
            (*Pause.*)
            He told me you took a seventeen-year-old
            neighbor boy as the light of your life.
            (*She sips her tea.*)
            He believes there is no such thing as fidelity.
            'The fidelity fallacy,' he calls it.

MARINA: He stole that phrase from a speech in my
            husband's unfinished play. Do you know the
            rest of that speech? 'No one understands the
            disease of infidelity until it's upon you. And
            then you are transfigured. Of course you
            have your reasons for what you do, but
            they are generally misleading.'
            (*She sips her tea.*)
            Quite an accurate speech, wouldn't you
            say?

CLARISSA: I'm sure you know better than I. Mangan
            also told me he had *you*, two days after the
            shooting.

MARINA: He tried often with me, but never succeeded.
            I'm not as diverse as you in these matters.

CLARISSA: You have such lofty airs.

MARINA: And you are from womanhood's lowest
            register. You linked yourself to my hus-
            band when he was a rising star, and now,

443

after you've risen on his back, you want to destroy what remains of his life as a fallen star.

CLARISSA: I loved him truly.

MARINA: You began as a frivolous soubrette, full of intrigue, and in short order you've risen to become a sublime slut. Do your sluttish things, as you must, but don't speak to me of love.
(*Marina picks up teapot.*)
Love is vertical. You are relentlessly horizontal.
(*She proffers teapot.*)
More tea?

Katrina Ruminates on What She Has Seen

He makes me cleverer than I am. He knows things I do not know about Maginn. I don't know how he knew Maginn came to see me, and I doubt very much Maginn had Felicity in a Pullman. She wouldn't. Would she? Edward believes he knows the truth about my life without him. 'I know of your dalliances,' he once said. 'Of course you don't,' I told him. He will come to know some of what was. His writing is acute, and bright people will admire it, but the clergy will try to have the play closed. No one can say such things publicly. Edward knows this. He is flaunting his play. 'You made me the villainous eater of broken meats,' he is saying. 'Here then, see what raw fish such a man offers you.'

He is obviously finished with that woman. I do like the well-poisoner line. I wish I had said it. He is giving a shape to the chaos that overtook us. What he said at dinner – when the matter is ready the form will come. I wonder did he see me sitting in the theater? He did not come down. Perhaps he thought I would go backstage. No. He would assume I would not wish to confront them all. He must not have seen me. Nonsense, if he thought I could not face up to people. I've recovered. I've recovered from everything. It's depressing how total my recovery is; as if the condition had not been serious. No one can know what the wound was like. No one would care to know. Even Edward could see only the blood, the scab, the scar. There will be a photograph of my recovery. It's depressing how easily we reconcile the unthinkable. I must let Edward know why I never told him about Giles, and Maginn's doggerel. How to tell him? I want no argument. Tell him also what no one ever knew about Felicity. But I saw it. Tell Edward these things now. Yes. Answer all questions. What was I supposed to do with my life? Was it correct, what I did? Was it worth doing? Write him a letter. A letter, of course. When the matter is ready the form will come.

She left the theater and walked to the cabstand in front of the Armory, full of the memory of significant life on the Hall's grand stage. There she had seen Caruso and Pavlova and met John McCormack after he'd thrilled her with that old ballad (*'Oh! hast thou forgotten how soon we must sever? Oh! hast thou forgotten this day we must part?'*). She had watched Duse and Maude Adams and Richard Mansfield and countless others play out their charades of life, she had danced with Edward on the false floor that covered the theater seats for Governor Roosevelt's inaugural ball. And this week Edward's people, you among them, Katrina, will come to life on that enormous stage. And everyone's legend will grow.

Katrina's hat was so large that she had to tip her head sideways in order to step into the cab.

She entered her empty house, the servants gone until dinner, and left her bag and her hat in the drawing room. She made tea for herself in the kitchen and carried it on a tray to Edward's office, where she set it atop his desk. She sat in Edward's chair and took one of his lined tablets from the drawer. She sipped the tea as she considered the questions she would write answers to on the tablet.

'What, really, was my destiny?' she wrote.

She put her head down on the desk in acquiescence to the drowsiness the question evoked in her. She slept for she knew not how long, and awoke smelling smoke. She went to the window of the office and parted the curtains to see the Christian Brothers school next door in flames. It was clear to her that the fire would make the leap to this room in a matter of minutes. She went back to Edward's chair and put her head down on his desk. The smoke was familiar in her mouth. She had breathed fire before.

Edward and Katrina Revisit the Cemetery

May 10, 1912

After the house burned, and Katrina died in his arms, Edward moved what was left of his life into a parlor suite at the Kenmore Hotel and began the process of gently evicting the Cohallon family from Emmett and Hanorah's Main Street house: his house now, his only house now. He put Katrina in the hands of Ebel Campion, whose undertaking parlors were only two blocks from where she died, with instructions that there would be no wake, only a funeral mass in Sacred Heart church, and then private burial. He would not abide strangers ogling her corpse.

The buzzards were already at work on the leftover carrion from the Love Nest scandal, writing how the debauchery of the ogre Daugherty had shamed Katrina, hastened her death; and cheering – were they not? – for the innocent Melissa, who had replied to the evil done her by gaining much-deserved movie stardom. There they perched, at the edge of Edward's life, anticipating new morsels from *The Flaming Corsage*, which would open May 11, the fourth day after Katrina's death; for the show must go on *now*, Mr Ogre, or not at all.

Sacred Heart church was filled, even to standing room, and hundreds more jammed the church steps, and Walter Street's sidewalk, twenty minutes before the small cortege arrived. Six bearers carried Katrina's coffin up the steps into the church, photographers recording her ascent, then moving their tripods to focus on Edward, impeccably tailored in black suit with cutaway coat and beaver hat, stepping down from the first carriage, with

Martin next, dressed like his father, and then the heavily veiled Geraldine, triadic study in family distance. Geraldine's brother, Ariel, and Archie Van Slyke came in the second carriage, then other relatives, friends.

As they entered the church in procession, Edward saw, first, the blaze of color on the altar: the dozen baskets of yellow flowers he had sent to brighten the solemnity for Katrina, then saw, with sharper focus, faces from North Albany, Colonie Street, Elk Street: Francis and Annie Phelan, and old Iron Joe with them; and Jack and Ruthie McCall, she refusing to measure his eye; and the Phelans: Peter, Chick, Molly, and Tommy, all in one pew; and Bishop Sloane, flanked by a brace of Minor Canons, bowing ecclesiastically to Geraldine as she passed him; and so many, many more neighbors and forever-nameless witnesses to the lamentable truth: that Katrina Selene Taylor Daugherty is no more.

Father Loonan, without the stamina to say mass, sat in trembling witness on the altar, as Edward had asked of him: Katrina's counselor in the faith when she converted. Three other priests would celebrate Katrina's passing with a solemn high mass, and Father Loonan, at the proper moment, feeble but clear of speech, and wearing his simple cassock and surplice, would stand and read the Gospel, not only from the mass for the dead, but also from the mass for the previous day on the liturgical calendar, as if the two Gospels were one; and Edward found the addition of the latter Gospel more than accidental redundancy: '. . . You are the salt of the earth; but if the salt lose its savor, wherewith shall it be salted? It is good for nothing any more, but to be cast out, and to be trodden on by men. You are the light of the world. A city seated on a mountain cannot be hid. Neither do men light a candle and put it under a bushel, but upon a candle-stick, that it may shine to all that are in the house . . .'

Yea, verily, Father. Edward will make Katrina shine for all in the house. Come and see his play.

Ebel Campion and his bearers carried Katrina's coffin out of the church to the hearse, then drove it not to St Agnes Cemetery, as expected, but back to the funeral home, where it remained for hours, until the last of the snuffling press had abandoned its watch. The undertaker then put the coffin into the closed wagon he used for picking up corpses, a vehicle never pressed into cemetery service before; then, with one bearer who could be trusted to keep his mouth shut, rode to the Kenmore to pick up Edward and Martin, and transported the Daugherty family to Albany Rural Cemetery, to the plot Edward had bought for Katrina, twenty yards from the grove of blue spruces where she had offered up her virginity to him.

Without prayer, the four men lowered her into the newest grave in this gateway to the Protestant beyond, the heaven where Katrina would be most at ease, and watched silently as two gravediggers arrived to bury the coffin and fill the grave with fresh earth. When the workers departed, Edward asked his son, 'Do you want to say anything?'

Martin shook his head. 'You really need a ritual at this point?'

Edward smiled at the new clarity in Martin, done with adolescence at last, his face refined to a mature handsomeness, a young man who speaks with a quiet fluency that belies the anger Edward sees in him.

'You're a man who uses words, as am I,' Edward said.

'I've already spoken my words to her,' Martin said.

'Before or after she died?'

'Before.'

'That smacks of excellence,' Edward said. 'I applaud your initiative.'

'Your applause sounds like parental pride for what you've instilled in me.'

'I think your mother would not want us to argue at her grave.'

'She wanted us reconciled.'

'And so we are,' Edward said. 'We're together. We have each other. We have no one else.'

'I don't feel reconciled,' Martin said. 'I seem unable to forgive what you did to us.'

'Understandably so. But it's a pity you see the world from only one perspective.'

'You mean I should take her madness into consideration? I've watched it since I was a child.'

'She wasn't mad, she was original.'

Edward took a step forward and spoke to the grave.

'I don't know what she believed,' he said, 'but it was a belief like none other. She began with God and moved on to death, and made them part of her being. But she abandoned both to astonish her soul. She sought something no one expects out of this life, and sought it with a firm purpose that she defined and executed without the advice or consent of others. She might have been judged an ascetic in another time, for she was much in love with suffering, her own and others'. She was also seraph and voluptuary, of such uncommon ways she seemed to preexist the fall; and there is no name for such a hybrid in our limited world, or our limited heavens. But she does not need justification. Katrina dwelled among us, and we are thankful for that. We will regret forever that she has willfully left us.'

'Willfully?' said Martin. 'What do you mean?'

'Her time had ended. She knew it.'

'The fire killed her.'

'Of course it did,' said Edward. 'It was her element.'

Edward Completes His Play at the Kenmore Hotel

In the spring months when he was trying to finish *The Flaming Corsage*, Edward was accumulating evidence that he owned only half a brain, half a heart, that his talent had decayed, all fire gone from his imagination. With his early plays he had run blindfolded into the unknown and come away with the prize, or believed he had. But now he knew that despite his relentless work, something was missing. This play did not end, it aborted. Three years of writing and he had produced a ridiculous lie, an evasion, a travesty of the truth. Nothing will save it from savagery by all who see it.

There is blood in your mouth, Edward.

The enemy applauds your fate.

He decided Maginn must have lived all his life in this condition: full of desire and effort, but a creative cripple: inadequate strength to imagine the substance of the work, and an intelligence too arrogant to shape it. The love song of the wrong word.

Then Katrina died, and Edward sat at the desk in the parlor of his hotel suite and began a new ending for the play – already in production with the flawed ending. He wrote the night she died; wrote most of the following two days, except for some time with Martin, and arranging the funeral. After the mass, while waiting for the undertaker, he began yet another version of the final scene, one with promise. After the burial he reread the scene and let it stand.

The two as measured distance. The absence that grows in the fertile earth.

451

He hired the young woman typewriter-copyist in the hotel's office to make three copies, and was at the theater to hand them to the director and actors when they arrived in the evening for the final run-through.

Too late to change this much dialogue, the director said. It absolutely *must* be changed, Edward said. I'll never memorize it in time, the lead actor said. Oh yes, you will, said Edward. And the play opened Saturday night with the final dialogue dictated by Katrina.

Edward watched the performance from the aisle of the parquet. When the houselights went up on the clamor that greeted the end of the play, Edward saw Maginn in a forward box with a woman, and moved toward him immediately. But he was met by the exiting throng and lost Maginn in the crowd.

The play closed after one performance.

'Scandalous Play Closes'

Albany Argus, *May 13, 1912*

The forces of decency in the city dealt a sledgehammer death blow to the new play by Edward Daugherty Saturday night. The opening performance at Harmanus Bleecker Hall was greeted with hisses at the first scene of Act Four, and shouts of 'unclean' and 'filth' were heard as the play progressed to its conclusion. A score of people left the theater, which was packed to capacity for the performance, more than 2,500 seats filled. When the curtain came down, the hisses and boos were loud and relentless, especially from the gallery, and extra police were summoned to move the audience out of the theater.

Yesterday morning Episcopal Bishop Sloane and Catholic Bishop Burke, in concert with Mayor McEwan and many leading citizens of the city, pressed the owners of the Hall and the play's producers to cease further performance. At midafternoon the producer announced the cancellation of the play's two-week run. The Hall's manager said he will offer, in its place, the return of last week's immensely popular production of *Regeneration*, with Bert Lytell, the story of an Irish Bowery thug raised to manhood by the power of a woman's prayer.

Daugherty's play, titled *The Flaming Corsage*, purports to be a tragic love story, but is a thinly veiled excursion into the lower regions of human degradation, beginning with the murder, in a 'love nest,' of an unfaithful wife, who is shot by her husband; and the husband then suicides. It carries on from there through such morally repugnant dialogue as has never been heard on the Albany stage. Some phrases would not be printable in this newspaper under any circumstances, yet they are uttered brazenly by two women characters.

'The shame of Albany' is what Bishop Sloane called the play; Bishop Burke said such a writer should be 'damned to hell for such public sin'; and the Mayor, who had not seen the play, said, 'From all accounts it is a degenerate assault on American womanhood. And we won't stand for that in this city.'

It was agreed yesterday by seasoned theatergoers who saw the play that it is little more than a self-exculpation by the playwright, an apologia for his involvement in the Love Nest Scandal of 1908 in Manhattan, whose events closely parallel those of the play, with names of the characters changed so slightly from their real-life counterparts that all are recognizable. And so the old scandal is rekindled to a bright flame.

Letter to the Editor

Albany Argus, *May 14, 1912*

Dear Sir,

I rush to correct the general misapprehension of the play *The Flaming Corsage*, which closed after a single performance on Saturday. The play is seen as a violation of our Magnificent Municipal Moral Code (would that it were!). But it was not that at all, and judgment of it on that basis should be left to the philistines. The play will have, most certainly, a secure place in the history of American theater, as a curiosity. It has kinship with dreadful Ibsen's one great achievement, *Peer Gynt*, and may be as great a literary benchmark as *Beowulf*, that ossified ostrich egg of fictional narrative, though the Daugherty play resembles neither work.

The Flaming Corsage must be judged a failure, a great botch of a work that should probably have been a novel, just as Chekhov's plays, overstuffed with characters and incident, would have shone as novels. Daugherty, the playwright, was, potentially, a novelist of the first rank, but abandoned the genre for playwriting, a major mistake, the success of his last play notwithstanding. That play, *The Masks of Pyramus*, owed its success to its paralleling of *Romeo and Juliet*, just as the Shakespeare work owed its nucleus to Ovid's *Pyramus and Thisbe*. Plagiarism in the arts continues apace.

But *The Flaming Corsage* does have its merits. It casts aside the weeping and wailing of our mouldy melodrama and the contrived realism of our present potpourri of pygmy playwrights, and instead it offers up scenes rich with raw realism, as well as stinging satire of a high order. The bovinish women of the piece, and their hopeless husbands and lovers, all struggle between lofty intentions and hidden animal instincts, much the way Peer Gynt confronts the evil trolls of his life in the Ibsen play.

No one in American theater has ever written with as much insight into the dark quotidian reality as Edward Daugherty. It is a great pity that he is such a paltry buffoon when it comes to organizing his play, and sorting out the fates of his characters. He creates fine china, then destroys it all with his unruly hindquarters.

Like *Beowulf*, which was fated to be unreadable, this play is fated to be judged unplayable by future generations. But it will also be studied as a grotesque curiosity that broke new theatrical ground. It does not surprise me that it was closed, but it was closed for the wrong reasons.

THEATER LOVER
(Name withheld)

Edward Writes a New Play

July 15, 1912

Edward sat now in a long pause, staring out the second-floor window of his workroom at another grotesquely shadowed evening that had become abominably hot. The pages of his nameless play-in-progress lay on the desk beside the marble bust of Persephone, the only artifact of value to survive the fire. And beside that lay Emmett's loaded .32-caliber revolver.

Emmett had bought the pistol to defend himself during labor trouble at the Fitzgibbon foundry, protection against men he'd fought for all his life; for when he became foreman, he became their enemy. Rise in the world and count your friends on your thumb.

'I could shoot it and hit what I shot at,' Emmett said, 'but I never pulled the trigger in anger, or in fear. It was a useless damn gadget and I knew that the day I bought it.'

Edward looked at the pistol. He looked at his pages. He picked up his first page, read the opening scene. Sweat dropped from his forehead onto the paper.

Scene One
The execution chamber of Sing Sing prison. Six WITNESSES *sit on folding chairs facing the empty electric chair.* EXECU-TIONER *stands near large-handled switch that will activate electric current.*

WARDEN *and* PRIEST *enter with* THOMAS MAGINN, *the prisoner. Two* GUARDS, *escorting* MAGINN, *seat him in*

457

electric chair, strap him into it, apply one electrode to calf of his right leg, another to cover his forehead and shaved temples.

DR GILES FITZROY *enters, walking ahead of stretcher wheeled in by another* GUARD, *and upon which lies the pale corpse of* EDWARD DAUGHERTY. GILES *motions to* GUARD *where to put stretcher.* GUARD *tips stretcher on its end so that* DAUGHERTY *corpse stands upright, facing the electric chair.*

GILES (*to* WARDEN): Is the condemned ready?

WARDEN (*to* PRIEST): Is he ready, Father?

PRIEST: Frankly, I don't think he has a prayer.

WARDEN: Are you ready, Mr Maginn?

(MAGINN *breaks into hysterical laughter, which continues as he speaks.*)

MAGINN: My father collected dead horses for pig food. My mother was a one-armed bitch who took in washing for cowboys. My sister was a whore at age six. My kid brother tortured cats with hatpins. My uncle gouged eyes for a dime. My family was saintly in the extreme.

(*His laughter subsides somewhat.*)

I'm a lucky man, the first in my family to be executed for his intelligence. The world will mark today as the day they uselessly martyred a beloved hero, and it will await my resurrection. There's no doubt I'm the

458

smartest man on the North American continent, given to humility at all hours, ready
to play the fool for any woman with pubic
hair. I also admire them shorn.

(MAGINN's *laughter is gone, his face saddens
gradually. He weeps, then cries openly.*)

The worth of my being is proportionate
to the weight of my written work. The
essence of all power in this life is defiance,
malfeasance, the pox, the smile, the dollar,
and comprehension of the nature of time,
which is running short. In sum, I'm as
unprepared for death as I was for life. But
let's get on with it.

(MAGINN *is now sobbing, breathing with
difficulty.*)

Red pig blood, orange sunset and evening
star, pale-yellow pig shit, lime-green urine,
blue sky and meadow, indigo clouds, violet
pussy, white horses, whiteness whitening the
white white . . .

(*He stops sobbing, laughs hysterically.*)

WARDEN (*to* GILES): The condemned is ready.

GILES: Are you ready, Mr Daugherty.

DAUGHERTY: I am.

GILES: Let it be noted for the record that the eyes
                      of the dead Daugherty have been sewn open

to enable him to witness the execution of his murderer, the fugitive whoremonger, the unrequited narcissist. Now, let us proceed.

(*He waves his hand to* EXECUTIONER, *who pulls switch, sending current into* MAGINN, *who stiff*ens. *Steam rises from his skull and from his leg.* GILES, *checking his pocket watch, waves to* EXECUTIONER, *who turns switch off.* GILES *examines* MAGINN *with stethoscope and holds thermometer against his leg.*)

GILES: Let it be noted that auscultation indicates the condemned still has a pulse, and the temperature of the skin is one hundred eighty degrees. All skin contacts show notable burn marks. How are you feeling, Mr Maginn?

MAGINN: Tip-top.

GILES: Then let us continue.

(*He gestures again to* EXECUTIONER, *who pulls switch, with same reaction from* MAGINN. *Not steam but smoke rises from burned flesh.* GILES *times this jolt with his watch, waves to* EXECUTIONER, *who turns off current.* GILES *examines* MAGINN.)

GILES: The condemned heart still beats. Temperature at contact points now two hundred fourteen degrees, nicely above boiling point. Crepitation noted throughout. Anterior epithelial cells of the cornea have desquamated from the action of heat. Sclera of left eye

bulges at its left corneal junction. Scalp
and skin of neck have a dull, purplish hue,
with blisters on temples, cheeks, and eyelids. Epidermis at flexure of knee joint has
been torn away. How are you feeling, Mr
Maginn?

MAGINN (*weakly*): Violet piss, golden pigs.

GILES: Then let us continue.

(*He waves hand again to* EXECUTIONER,
etc.)

Edward stopped reading. He ordered the pages of the play and
walked downstairs to the kitchen, the heat no longer tolerable.
He pumped water, wet his face, hair, arms. He walked, dripping,
to the front porch, sat in his father's rocking chair, and stared at
the corner of the porch. The flood this spring had tilted it another
fraction of an inch eastward: fittingly askew.

He stared up the empty street and saw his young self walking off
it forever (oh yes) and out of this city into worlds no boy, no man
on this block, except his father, could even have imagined. Now
he was back, solitary Main Streeter: no visitors, curtains drawn,
answering no rings of the bell, no knocks, reading no mail, food
delivered by Drislane's.

The oaks and the elms are in full leaf, the honeysuckle bush
his mother planted in 1859, when the house was new, when Main
Street and Edward were new, is a tree now, yielding berries, and
the robins are eating them. Nobody hates these leaves, these
berries, these robins, the way people hate Edward. Neither will
Edward love any of them for their overrated glory, their vaunted
beatitude. You think such mindless things deserve love? Love is
what you feel during yesterday's lightning storms. And then here
come the dogs.

He saw two boys with sticks running down from Broadway,

chasing a dog that was leaving them behind, that ran into the horseshoe court between Joe Farrell's and Edward's houses, across Francis Phelan's backyard, and was gone.

'You won't catch him now, boys,' Edward said, and the boys stopped and looked at him. 'And there's gardens back there. You wouldn't want to run through them.'

'He bit me,' one boy said.

'Did he draw blood?'

The boy, in short pants, looked at his bare leg. Edward could see a line of blood from calf to ankle.

'Yeah, he got me,' the boy said.

'You should go see Doc McArdle,' Edward said. 'You know where he lives?'

'Doc McArdle is dead,' the boy said.

'Is he?'

'His horse kicked him in the head.'

The boy bent his leg to look at the wound, spat on it, and rubbed up the trickle of blood with two fingers. He snapped the spit and blood off the fingers, pulled a leaf off an oak tree and wiped the wound.

'I'll put a bandage on it,' the second boy said, and he took off the red bandanna he was wearing on his neck and tied it around his friend's wound. The boy who'd been bitten took a few steps, limping.

'It hurts,' he said.

He picked up a stone and hurled it at the garden where the dog had fled. The second boy picked up two stones and threw them at the eastern sky that arced toward the bed of the Erie Canal that was: whelps all: the dog, the boys, Edward.

The moon sent down its light to weave an image in the branches of an oak tree, and Edward saw in it Emmett's face: a grid of sinew and wisdom that would not stay in the grave. There, perfectly etched by leaf and moonlight, were the lines of the Emmett nose and jaw, the wry slash of smile, vanishing, then reappearing in the flickering light's gestalt. Keeper of the flame. But there is no longer a flame. Your father is preparing for your departure, Edward.

Under this July moon, now shaped like a battered face, Edward left the porch, walked past the lot where the cattle pens used to be on Champlain Street, parallel to the tracks and the all-but-dead canal. Beyond the canal half a dozen of forty-two sawmills were still active in the Lumber District, which was dying from want of softwood: so many Adirondack pine forests denuded, so few people working in the District that for sixty years gave jobs to men by the swarm: now a zone of quiet. No more overflowing lunch crowds in Black Jack's, no more cardsharps at the tables, no more brawls, no more dead horses in the canal, all work in the foundries now, or over the hill in the West End, at the Central's railroad shops. Purpose vanishing from North Albany, eclipsed like the dead Irish of Connacht. Potential actualized into a living neighborhood. And then? Yes. What, then, is the potential of the *new* actuality?

He walked up Erie Street past the icehouse, and the site of the old wooden Sacred Heart church, where pigs and chickens came to mass, now a vacant lot. He passed the car barns. When he read the *Car Barns* play to his father in his sickbed (for he would not live to see it performed) Emmett had asked:

'Is that fella in the play supposed to be me?'

'Does he sound like you?'

'He does.'

'Did you say those things he says?'

'Never.'

'So there you are. You and not you, reality and fantasy in one package.'

'You're a glib man. If you don't change your ways you'll come to a bad end.'

Prophetic.

He turned onto Broadway, bats swooping though the glow of streetlamps, and saw Cappy White with a growler under his arm. Edward hadn't seen Cappy since his son, Bitsy, a softspun boy born without ears, who'd earned candy money eating live frogs for a nickel, went up in flames in church while lighting a candle for his mother, Mamie. Mamie weighed maybe five hundred pounds – nobody ever found a way to weigh her – and grew wider with the years. When Doc McArdle came to examine her dropped stomach she refused him access: 'I never showed my front end to anybody but Cappy White. He was the first one, he'll be the last one.'

Mamie stayed in the house, could not leave it even for Bitsy's funeral, did not fit into the stairwell. When she died Cappy knocked out siding and two windows, then backed up a derrick to lift her out of bed and carry her to her own funeral. After that he took himself to bed and stayed there, leaving it only to buy food and beer. Hermit of Main Street, punished by the gods for marrying fat and cherishing a freakish child. What peculiar shapes love takes.

'Hi ya, Cappy,' Edward said.

'Who's that?'

'Eddie Daugherty.'

'Eddie, yeah, you're back. I heard you lost everything.'

'That's right, Cappy.'

'So did I.'

'I know.'

'How you livin'?'

'Best way I can.'

'You still got your son,' Cappy said.

'I guess you could say that.'

'I lost my son.'

'I know you did. I hate that, Cappy.'

'So do I.'

'You get out much, Cap?'

'Nope. No reason to.'

'Maybe it'll get better.'

'No, it won't get no better. You oughta know that.'

'I keep wondering whether it's finished.'

'It's finished.'

'How do you know?'

'They ain't nothin' worth doin'.'

'It seems like that, all right.'

'You came back to North Albany.'

'I did,' said Edward.

'What for?'

'No place else to go.'

'That's a good reason. So long, Eddie.'

Cappy turned toward his house and Edward thought: Now Main Street has two hermits. He walked to Jack McCall's saloon for an ale. Respite. But maybe not. The night he moved back to Main Street he stopped at Jack's for an ale. Smiler McMahon and Petey Parker were at the bar when he came up beside them.

'Something stinks,' Petey said.

'Yeah. We don't need that around here,' Smiler said, and he and Petey crossed the room and sat at a table.

'I'll have an ale,' Edward said to the bartender, a man he didn't know, but who obviously took his cue from Smiler.

'One's all you get,' said the bartender.

Edward let him draw the ale. He picked it up and poured it onto the floor, then let the glass drop and shatter in the puddle.

Now, through the screen door, he saw Jimmy McGrath behind the bar. Four men looked at him when he entered, then went back to their beer. Had he ceased stinking after only a month?

'What'll it be, Eddie?' Jimmy asked.

'I'll try an ale. The last glass I had here I never got to drink.'

'I heard about that,' Jimmy said. 'And so did Jack. He fired that stupid son of a bitch. "Nobody tells Eddie Daugherty he can't drink in my saloon," Jack said.'

Jimmy set an ale in front of Edward, then sat on his stool behind the bar.

'Here's to Jack,' Edward said, taking a mouthful. 'I thought you retired, Jim.'

'I did. Had two toes taken off from the sugar. But I come in nights when Jack needs help. Business is kinda quiet, and I'm next door. Long as I don't stand up too long.'

'The whole neighborhood's quiet.'

'Right. But the Tablet Company's comin' in up the road. They're hiring men, and women too, they say.'

'That'll be good for business.'

Edward took another mouthful of ale.

'Eddie,' said Jimmy, 'I'm sorry about the fire, and your wife. They hit you hard.'

'That they did.'

'I remember her coming in after some ale when Emmett was dying. I didn't serve her first, but she kept at me. She knew what she wanted, that one.'

'You could say that,' Edward said.

'The fire take everything, did it?'

'I saved some journals, inside a trunk in the cellar. They got wet but I can read them. A few books, some silver, odds and ends, a piece of marble. The rest is ashes.'

'How you gonna live now?'

'That's a hell of a question, Jimmy.'

'People know you're holed up down there in the house. They see the ice and the food going in. Freddy Doran, the mailman, says the letters he delivers are gone outa the box the next day.'

'I don't read letters. They're all about yesterday.'

'We got a letter here for you,' Jimmy said.

He went to the back bar and opened a drawer, handed a letter to Edward.

'Came about a month ago. "Hold for pickup," it says.'

When Jimmy drew beer for the men down the bar, Edward looked at the letter. Maginn's hand. He opened it.

Old Chum Edward,

Missed you at your opening night. If you're up for a bit of a chat, look me up at 65 Division Street, any time. Always a pleasure to see you.

M

Edward pocketed the letter, finished his ale.

'Another?' Jimmy asked.

'I'll move along,' Edward said.

'Anything I can do, say the word,' said Jimmy.

'If I ever figure out the word I'll let you know.'

He walked back to Main Street and climbed the stairs to his

workroom. He noted the time, nine-forty-five on the mantel clock, as he picked up the revolver from the desk. He put it in his back pocket and walked down the stairs, feeling the bulk of the pistol, opened the front door and stepped onto the porch. He stared at the long shadows the trees made on Main Street's bricks, at the sky incandescent with moonlight. The brilliant blackness was suffusing his being like an elixir of resolution. He took the pistol from his pocket and stared at it. He saw Emmett's finger on the trigger. There is a reason for everything.

He walked into the house and through the hallway to the kitchen, down the back steps and across the yard to Emmett's toolshed. He found matches and candle and lit them. He saw Emmett's vise covered with dust. He broke open the pistol and let the six bullets fall onto the workbench. He opened the vise jaws and put the pistol barrel between them, tightened the jaws. He took down a small sledgehammer from its hook and swung, then swung it again, and again, until the pistol broke in three pieces. He opened the vise jaws, tossed the pieces and the bullets into the trash bucket.

Giles, Felicity, and I bring you greetings even so, Maginn.

Edward Goes to the Tenderloin at a Late Hour

Division Street, five blocks long, ran west from Quay Street on the river, then crossed Broadway, Liberty, Dallius, and Green Streets, which at this hour formed a neighborhood grid thrumming with the revels and lusts of the night city. This was Albany's Tenderloin, and life was open, the streets full of motion, the Palace Lodging House catering to quick turnover, Scambelluri's and Marino's poolrooms, side by side, both busy, Dorgan's Good Life Saloon, which called itself a concert hall, thriving on music for illegal dancing, for thou shalt not dance in a saloon in Albany. And on the stoops of houses with telltale awnings on their windows (business was so good Jidgie Shea had opened an awning shop on the street), whores of the white race, and one *mulata* on the stoop of the Creole house, were taking the air this stifling night; and together they formed a tableau of discrete enticements. Youths too poor to buy any of their offerings walked Division Street, hoping for a charitable glimpse of raised thigh, unsequestered breast.

'Come and get it,' one whore said to Edward. 'Anything you want you can find right here. You don't find it, you ain't lookin' for it.'

Sixty-five Division Street, a three-story brick dwelling, gave entrance off street level. It adjoined the Good Life, and Edward heard the saloon piano and banjo ringing out a ragtime melody he could put no name to as he rang the bell. A well-shaped woman in her forties, wearing high-necked blouse and long, black skirt, greeted him. Edward flashed that she should have one crossed eye, but she did not.

'You looking for company?' she asked.

'I'm looking for Maginn. Is he here?'

'He's here,' she said, gesturing for Edward to enter.

'My name is Edward Daugherty.'

'I know who you are.'

'How is that possible?'

'He talks about you.'

Maginn *talks* about you, of course. He plots to destroy you. Why didn't you know this the instant Giles blew Felicity into naked infinity? Who profited from that explosion? Yes, the cur Cully was a likely avenger. But when myopia wanes, Maginn, without doubt, emerges as the epiphanic presence at the slaughter. And you, Edward, the true target, you couldn't see that; you and Maginn such great friends, brothers of the ink stain, comrades of the imagination. Gainsaying fool is what you were. Now here you stand, believing you can goad evil into explaining itself, wondering what the whore of justice looks like, wallowing in your pathetic desire to mean.

'He's at the bar,' the woman said, and led the way to a large parlor furnished with two sofas and three armchairs of dark red plush, a scatter of Oriental rugs, maroon drapes on the two windows, and lighted by four electrified gas lamps with pale-blue taffeta shades. Music and tobacco smoke came through a half-open door that led to the dance floor of the saloon (Edward could see two women and two men dancing), and at the small bar at the end of the parlor a very young, carrot-haired woman, wearing a blouse that covered little of her large, shapely breasts, was pouring liquor for a man in shirtsleeves who was smoking the butt of a thin cigar. Maginn.

'Ah, Daugherty, you worthless mutt,' Maginn said, 'you're here at last. You look well for a man whose life has been destroyed.'

'You don't look well at all, Maginn. You look shriveled. You look like a chimney sweep's brush. Are you dying?'

'Aren't we all? But I'll live out the week.'

Maginn had lost hair on his head and had blackened his mustache. His skin was sallow and he was thinner by fifteen pounds from Edward's last vision of him. A broomstraw of a man, probably venereally ravaged. His sickly look delighted Edward.

'Have you met Nell?' Maginn asked.

The woman who'd brought Edward in stood next to Maginn.

'Nell runs this emporium,' Maginn said. 'She's also my wife, my strong right arm, my favorite toss, and a font of money and strumpet wisdom. I love her like a sister. I'd be lost without her. Do you remember her?'

Edward looked at Nell and again recognized something but did not know what.

'You met in that tenebrous tent city we visited during the State Fair. You fancied her and she you, but you went forward to a more elderly crotch, while I regressed to the nubile Nell, a relationship that's endured for, what is it now, sweet suck of my life, twenty-seven years, on and off? Nell remembers *you*, Edward. I reminded her how she upped her skirt for you. Would you up it again, Nell? Give him a new look at the old puss?'

'He looks like a real gentleman, is what I say. Such fine duds he's got. The genuine article.'

'A gentleman, oh yes.' And Maginn, visibly perturbed by the remark, turned to the barmaid. 'And this is Cherry. Say hello to Edward, Cherry.'

'Howdja do, Edward,' Cherry said.

Edward smiled at Cherry.

'And pour him a brandy, the best we have for this *gentleman*. Cherry, Edward, played the twelve-year-old virgin in the last house she worked. But she swiftly aged into this million-dollar set of tits, with only irony for a hymen. Does Cherry interest you, Edward?'

Edward said nothing.

'Let the gentleman sit down with his drink,' Nell said. 'Let him get a word in.'

'Of course. Sit, Edward, sit. Get a word in, if you have any left after that theatrical debacle.'

Edward and Maginn sat in the plush, facing each other.

'Gentleman. You called him a gentleman,' Maginn said to Nell. 'This is Eddie, a mick to the heel of his boot, transformed by adroit social maneuvering into the elite, affluent Edward Daugherty, Esquire, famous playwright, a bit infamous lately, though. He recently had a major opening night with his new play, staged with considerable fanfare at the Hall. But, alas, it was only another facade, a mongoloid mishmash, an ambitious botch that closed with a wail and a snivel after one performance. My condolences, Edward. Did you like my critique of it?'

'At what point did you become an assassin, Maginn?'

'Uh-oh, he's getting personal, Nell. Time for the parade, get a bit of life in this party.'

Nell left the room, and Maginn dropped his cigar into the spittoon by his chair, then coughed and spat into it, the spew of rotted lungs, Edward hoped.

'You haven't touched your drink, Edward, and you seem depressed. I can't blame you, given the burden you carry, some of it my doing, I fear. Truly sorry, old fellow. I berate myself constantly for what I did. You can see how I'm suffering here. But listen, when you see the parade you'll perk up, old Edward Edward Edward. But tell the truth, now. Isn't that name a sham all by itself? Why not call yourself Eduardo, or Edmundo, or Oedipus, for chrissake? You always went for older women, didn't you? Why not just be Eddie, like other micks? Edward exudes pretense. But I'll wager it wears well in your social set.'

'You invented a brilliant scheme, Maginn – bravura insight into the very worst human impulses. And I actually might've died, except for Giles's faulty aim.'

'I appreciate the compliment,' Maginn said, 'but you overestimate my intention. It *was* a clever scheme, and I revel at the genius in it. But I was only answering Giles's little joke – at least you got *that* right in your wretched melodrama. Who knew Giles harbored such violence? I saw him as one of the more gentle bigots of his tribe. Remember his joke about the Irishman whose cousin suffered two heart attacks and died, and the mick asked, "Did he die of the first attack or the second?" Giles enjoyed jokes at the expense of others. A pity he didn't live to enjoy mine.

'My plan was to repay your joke with my own, but then Giles decides to atomize the useless Felicity bitch, and his own vapid self. What an oblique bonanza! Sorry he got a bit of you in the doing, but look at you! You've recovered splendidly. And I knew our lovely Melissa would survive, of course. The world loves soiled innocents, when they're beautiful and repentant of their sin. Melissa, it must be said, repents well, but doesn't know what sin is, wouldn't you agree?'

'I'm surprised she's not here working for you.'

'She's beyond my means and always was,' said Maginn. 'But not beyond yours. Did you know she put Cully up to that rape of Felicity? Perverse little twat. She told Cully she'd be his if he'd rape Felicity with her looking on. She wanted to watch, and then comfort the poor, ravaged victim.'

'More lies, Maginn.'

'Cully told me this himself the day he left New York. I was with him before and after his little orgy. I even put him on the road with that story about the Albany police being after him. It was time to be rid of the lowlife pest. Didn't Melissa tell you any of this? I was with her too, earlier that day. In your room.'

'If your fiction was half as imaginative as your lies, Maginn, you'd have been famous years ago.'

'You don't know the truth when you hear it, Edward. You never did. But forget that and cop a sneak at these wenches.'

Nell entered ahead of three women, drew Cherry into the head of the line, then stood aside and let the four whores parade for Edward. Cherry opened her blouse, raised her offerings with her hands.

'We have two more in the stable,' Maginn said, 'but they're busy at the moment,' and he walked to the second whore and caressed her belly. 'This one carries her snake-head dildo at the ready and wears an Egyptian headdress, suitable for the moving pictures. I call her Putonalissa. A French artist I met in New Orleans sketched her costume for me on a bar towel.'

'New Orleans,' Edward said. 'When you went down to settle up with Cully?'

The remark stopped Maginn's spiel, and he gave Edward a twisted look; then continued.

'This young lady with the mask and open robe we call Complicity,' he said, parting the whore's robe with both hands. 'Sweet young thing, but she carries a whip. You don't know what to expect from Complicity.'

The third whore, a blonde, wore only a gown of transparent white chiffon, and Maginn lifted the chiffon to pat her bush. 'You probably guessed the name of this fair-haired beauty already,' he said. 'The lovely Beatrina, our *pièce de résistance*, by far our prettiest, and most angelic. I'd say her dress was suitable for a trip to Paradise, or even a walk down the old church aisle.'

Edward drank his brandy in two gulps to be rid of it. Maginn, seething with archaic rage against the divine arbiter of talent, trying to commit murder-by-whores to avenge his meager inheritance of the myth, droned on, urging the women to display themselves, even Nell, who did up her skirt, and whose freckled thighs, Edward thought with faded memory, had widened since the State Fair.

'So there you have it, Edward. Which one would cheer you most? Or would you like two? Or all five? It's on the house, you know.'

The whores seated themselves on the sofa to await Edward's decision and Cherry went back to the bar, her blouse askew. Nell poured Edward a new brandy and brought it to him. He sipped it, smiled at Maginn.

'I can't tell you how much it's meant, Maginn, seeing all this,' he said. 'Ever since I met you I've overpraised you, especially that beastly fiction no one ever published. I got you a job you weren't equal to, and even abided your envious tirades. I concluded you were the eternally inadequate man, *Homo invidiosus*, but all things keep striving for that higher form that nature designs for them, and I see tonight that you've climbed up from pigsty to pimpdom, up from creative myth to a career in vice, up from skulking whorehound to grand cuntmaster with a troop of trollops. Do

473

you like that phrase? It's very Maginnish. Vaudeville tonight! The Grand Cuntmaster Maginn and His Troop of Twisted Trollops. One night only! When the matter is ready the form will come, as I've been saying for years, Maginn, and you've evolved into absolute parity with nullity. In any world worth inhabiting, you now mean nothing at all.'

'Very good, Edward, very droll. Are you finished?'

'Not quite. There's Cully's confession that you incited Giles to murder. Poor Cully. He asked you for bail money and you failed him.'

'I didn't have it. And there is no confession.'

'True, his confession disappeared from the New Orleans police files, in the same way you disappeared when police came to *The Argus* to ask you about Cully. But my investigator turned up the detective who took Cully's confession, and he's got his notes and he'll testify. So will Clubber. So will I. And I wouldn't put it past Melissa to put in a good word for you. My man also found a fellow who says Cully's killers were paid to hang him, paid by somebody who looked like you.'

'You're pathetic, Daugherty.'

'I often tell myself that. Even so, I've documented this, and when I got your letter I gave my report to *The Argus*. They'll print it this week, with an editorial urging the case be reopened.'

Maginn picked up the spittoon beside his chair and heaved its cigar butts, slops, and globs of phlegm in Edward's face. Edward snatched the spittoon from Maginn's hand and swung it in a backhanded smash against his head. As Maginn staggered, Edward swung forward and smashed him full in the face, and Maginn's face exploded with blood.

'Nell!' Maginn called up out of his weakness, collapsed sideways over his armchair, spitting out pieces of broken teeth, 'Nell, do him! Do him!'

Edward turned to look for Nell and saw her right arm swinging a piece of lead pipe. It hit high on the left side of his head, and as he went down he saw Cherry moving toward him with a rag and a bottle of what he already knew was chloroform.

474

Edward Wakes in the Moonlight at Three o'Clock in the Morning

He felt the tongue on his face and thought of a deer at the salt lick. He'd been walking down the sloping corridor after Katrina and saw steam shovels moving great slabs of broken marble to block the exit. The way out now was down, down the high, grassy slope past the broken statuary. It led him to the edge of a high precipice over an abyss, and he felt the onset of his vertigo. A finger touched his outer thigh and he turned to see the beautiful young whore. 'Pressure makes it pop out,' she said. 'You're less of a sybarite these days, but nobody cares. The sinners are too chaotic.' He realized the paper he'd had in his hand was missing. He looked where it might have fallen, then saw it in his other hand. He touched his hip. His wallet was gone, as was the whore, and he knew that from here forward, something would vanish with every breath he took.

He opened his eye into pain and moonlight and the breath of the animal licking his hair. Will it bite my face? He closed his eye, felt in the dirt and found a small glass bottle at his fingertips. He dug it out and knew from its shape it once held paregoric. The planet Neptune was discovered by mathematical analysis of the movement of another planet. Such has happened. The tongue is a dog, not a deer, licking my pain. He licked his own lips and realized the dog was licking his blood. He tasted a sweetness that was not blood. The chloroform. He raised his hand and swiped the dog's jaw with the bottle. The animal yelped and Edward opened an eye to see it standing off, waiting. It barked once. Edward growled and the dog ran, a whelp.

He could see tall weeds, but the earth was bare and moist beneath his face, and smelled of ashes. The pain was an ax blade. He did not recognize the weeds or the buildings beyond them. He knew only the moon, and the heat of the dark, early morning, and the burned earth where his cheek touched it. He raised his head into new pain that might kill him. If it did not, he would raise himself. Do not go too fast. Up, and roll. Now sit. He saw light in an upper room of a house, another light at street level. By the light of the moon he saw that the weeds around him had grown over, and through, charred remnants of trash. He closed his eyes to see how to get down the precipice to where Katrina was.

The light at street level came from a window whose painted lettering announced 'Saloon.' Edward saw two men talking with the barkeep. He pushed open the half door, went to the bar.

'A double whiskey.'

'Christ, what happened to you?'

'Somebody hit me with a pipe.'

'You know who did it?'

'A woman I knew a long time ago.'

'They don't forget, do they?' the barman said.

He wet a towel and handed it to Edward.

'Wipe your face, pal.'

Edward took the towel while the barman poured whiskey. The blood on the towel was abundant, streaked white with ashes. He wiped his eyes, his mouth. He drank the whiskey, returned the glass for a refill.

'What street is this?' he asked.

'Dallius.'

'How far are we from Division?'

'Three blocks.'

'They didn't carry me far.'

'Who didn't?'

'You know a place called the Good Life?'

'Dorgan's. They closed early tonight.'

'How do you know?'

'I'm gettin' their regulars.'

Edward drank the second whiskey. The barman gave him another wet towel. He wiped his ear, blotted his head, blood still oozing. How much had he lost?

'You wanna go the hospital? I'll get a cop'll take ya,' the barman said.

'I'll go later. What do I owe you?' He reached into his pocket, wallet gone. 'I can't pay you. They robbed me.'

'You had a big night.'

'I'll come back and pay.'

'If you ever get home. You want another shot?'

'The pain is terrific.'

'Have another.'

Edward drank his third double.

'What's your name?' he asked.

'Grady.'

'You're a man worth knowing, Grady. If I don't die I'll be back. Can I keep this towel?'

'Take a new one.'

He wet a third towel for Edward.

'I'll pay your laundry bill, too,' Edward said.

He walked up Dallius toward where Division crossed. The pain was awful but easing. Why did he want to go back to the whorehouse? Explain the riddle of the goat. He turned on Division and walked until he came to Dorgan's. It was dark. He broke a panel of the glass door with a high kick and entered. By the light of the streetlamp he saw the back bar empty of bottles. He walked across the dance floor toward Maginn's, opened the whorehouse door, and stepped into darkness. He found a window and raised a shade, letting in light from the street. The rugs, lamps, chairs, and drapes were all gone. One sofa and small bar, without bottles, remained. He moved the bar and found nothing on its one shelf. They took the lead pipe and the chloroform. On the floor he found a large envelope.

He went outside and left the front door wide open. Let the rats out. On the street he lightly touched his wound. The blood seemed to be coagulating. He stood under the streetlight and opened the envelope, to find two dozen identical postcard photos of a woman in a flat, flowered hat, black stockings, shoes, and a white blouse she was holding partly open. She wore no skirt and was facing front, taking the viewer's picture with her fluffy black camera. Nellie. He would recognize those thighs anywhere. He pocketed one postcard, tossed the rest.

He walked toward the all-night cabstand on State Street, evaluating his latest creation: Cully's lost confession. Not until he'd finished his monologue to Maginn had he thought of resurrecting it. He'd often imagined an investigator would discover it just that way; and it also made perfect sense for Maginn to hire Cully's hangman.

His mood improved as he thought of Maginn, with fewer teeth, and fettered with whores, forced into midnight exile by the power of fiction.

Edward Concludes a Dialogue with Katrina on his Front Porch

Edward reached for his watch when the intern at St Peter's Hospital finished with his bandage. The watch was gone. What else could he lose tonight? The pain in his head was horrible, the whiskey wearing off, the powders they gave him not yet working. They wanted him to stay overnight in the hospital but he would not. He wanted to walk to Main Street but he lacked the stamina. They rang for a cab and the intern gave him a chair. He sat by the door and waited for the cab.

He looked for Giles in the hospital hallway but did not find him. He's here someplace. He saw a wall clock that said four-twenty. It's early. Late. It was not likely that his play would be resurrected. His playwriting days were over. Everything was over. It won't get no better, Cappy said. Nothin' worth doin', it's finished. The only thing that isn't over is the pain. He regretted not having time enough to do the play properly, and to use the real names. Who would care? The play would never be done again. But if it was done, some scenes would be different.

KATRINA *is seated on sofa in the Daugherty drawing room, looking at photo album.* EDWARD *stands with his arms folded, watching her. They are dressed for the evening. She wears a corsage of violets.*

EDWARD: You could never admit your behavior was
                   unacceptable.

KATRINA: Of course I could. I just said you had
                   to accept it. I understood *your* behavior
                   perfectly. You were correct in moving to
                   New York. I was impossible.

EDWARD: You're very understanding of your own
                   contradictions.

KATRINA: I would've gone mad otherwise.

EDWARD: You can seem as mad as the Queen of Bed-
                   lam. The soul obsessed by primal passions,
                   trying to carry out the divine will. That's
                   Peer Gynt but it's you.

                   (KATRINA *picks up photo album, raises it for*
                   EDWARD *to see.*)

KATRINA: Yes, *Peer Gynt*. Look at this wonderful
                   picture of Adelaide and me up at Schroon
                   Lake. What a wonderful summer that was.
                   It was my fault she died.

EDWARD: More madness. You stay alive through the
                   death of others. Pain and guilt, romantic
                   despair, the tragic dimension. If you'd aban-
                   don this melodrama and let the dead stay
                   dead, we'd be happier.

KATRINA: I should have died in the Delavan.

EDWARD: I should have died when Giles shot me.

480

KATRINA: Giles wasn't your fault. You behaved admir-
            ably during that terrible episode. Admir-
            ably.

EDWARD: I behaved like a fool, the only way I knew
            how. Look at me, Katrina. Leave the dead.
            Let's salvage the time left to us.

            (KATRINA *walks to the drawing room mirror,
            looks at her reflection.*)

KATRINA: How much time do we have, Edward?

            (EDWARD *comes up behind her, looks into
            the mirror over her shoulder.*)

EDWARD: You know more than I about such things.

            (KATRINA *turns and faces* EDWARD, *their
            faces very close.*)

KATRINA: If I fainted now, would you unpin my
            corsage? Would you undo the buttons of
            my bodice to help me breathe?

When the cab was halfway down Main Street, Edward saw he had
left a light on in the parlor. His pain was leveling, but would not
go away. He went to the bedroom for money he kept in a jar,
paid the driver, then went to the icebox. The ice was almost
gone. With the pick he chipped some ice into a glass, then
half-filled the glass with whiskey. Quarter to five. The whiskey
and powders would take away the pain. He stared out the kitchen
window at the canal and remembered Emmett in his days as the
lock tender, standing here watching the boat traffic, waiting for
trouble and grievance from the canalers, his problem as well as
theirs to solve. It may be that the existence of the planet Neptune

does not contradict the design of the solar system. How can it if it is really there?

Edward walked out the back door to Emmett's toolshed and found the bullets and broken pieces of the pistol in the waste bucket. He picked them out and carried them to the kitchen.

'Did you ever consider,' he said to Emmett, 'that I never was the Irishman on horseback? It may be I was free of racial and social destinies, and that what I wanted was altogether different from what had gone before.'

He put the bullets and pistol on the kitchen table, where Hughie Gahagan would have been sitting. The dead pistol meant something simple: sycophancy, scorn, false praise, cruelty, rage, narcissism, pain, prayer. Maginn was innocent of everything relating to success. He contrived complexity as a substitute for disuse. 'If you don't find her in one room, try the other,' he wrote on his note with the passkey.

It may be that after the worst has happened, you see that Neptune was there from the beginning, problematically, and the old orbit of death is superseded. Then you see that faith, or its mathematical equivalent, has to do with your discovery.

When Emmett wanted anything he invoked Connacht.

Booming voice.

Shorn of sustenance, shorn of the past, of love, of the theater of action, what's left to a man? The answer, son, is the necessary sin. You won't name it. It's written in a forgotten code. The light's still on in the parlor.

(*The* FIREMAN, *a handkerchief over his mouth and nose, carries* KATRINA *out of the burning house in his arms and crosses the street to where* EDWARD *is standing. The* FIREMAN *lays her down on the street, unbuttons her bodice, puts smelling salts under her nose. She does not move. The* FIREMAN *puts his mouth on hers, breathes into her. She opens her eyes, looks at the* FIREMAN, *then looks past him at* EDWARD, *who moves closer to her.*)

KATRINA: I can see you.

EDWARD: I thought you were lost.

                (*The* FIREMAN *lifts himself away from* KATRINA *and exits. He waves at her as he goes.* EDWARD *kneels beside* KATRINA, *raises her head and kisses her.*)

KATRINA: I remember a poem, a woman dying in her lover's arms. She has come down from the mountain of gold and as he holds her she turns to ashes.

EDWARD: You won't die, Katrina. It's wrong to die now. You won't die, Katrina. You won't die.

KATRINA: Life is something that should not have been.

EDWARD: I loved life when you loved me.

KATRINA: I loved you?

                (*Pause.*)

                Quite likely. I forget.

                (KATRINA *dies in his arms.*)

Edward picked up his whiskey and walked to the front porch. He sat in the chair beside Emmett and decided mockery was a more exalted mode of behavior than was generally assumed. He sat on the porch drinking whiskey with Emmett until he grew ravenous. He thought of what he would cook.

    He would fry bacon.

He would stay up and outlast Emmett. He had outlasted Martin, and the boy went back to New York. That was part of their problem. The father's energy acknowledged the irrelevance of the future, the worship of the present tense.

He could almost smell the bacon. A pig is turned into bacon, bacon becomes food that gives unity and purpose to the imagination. Brother William died in the fire, kneeling, turned into a bent cinder. Katrina, heroine of neighborhood children, had walked into the classroom and whipped William with the same stick he'd been using to whip a boy. Katrina understood the nature of fire.

Edward, seeing the earliest blue line of things to come, finished his whiskey. Then he went to the icebox for the bacon, which will always be with us.

LEGS

This is for Pete McDonald, a first-rate relative,
and for all the archetypes lurking in
Ruth Tarson's lake house

People like killers. And if one feels sympathy
for the victims it's by way of thanking them
for letting themselves be killed.

— EUGENE IONESCO

Jack's Alive

'I really don't think he's dead,' I said to my three very old friends.

'You what?' said Packy Delaney, dropsical now, and with only four teeth left. Elephantiasis had taken over his legs and now one thigh was the size of two. Ah time.

'He don't mean it,' Flossie said, dragging on and then stubbing out another in her chain of smokes, washing the fumes down with muscatel, and never mind trying to list *her* ailments. ('Roaches in your liver,' Flossie's doc had told her. 'Go on home and die at your own speed.')

Tipper Kelley eyed me and knew I was serious.

'He means it, all right,' said Tipper, still the dap newsman, but in a 1948 double-breasted. 'But of course he's full of what they call the old bully-bull-bullshit because I was there. You *know* I was there, Delaney.'

'Don't I know it,' said the Pack.

'Me and Bones McDowell,' said the Tip. 'Bones sat on his chest.'

'We know the rest,' said Packy.

'It's not respectful to Bones' memory to say he sat on the man's chest of his own accord,' Tipper said. 'Bones was the finest reporter I ever worked with. No. Bones wouldn't of done that to any man, drunk or sober, him or Jack the corpse, God rest his soul. Both their souls, if Jack had a soul.'

'He had a soul all right,' said Flossie. 'I saw that and everything else he had too.'

'We'll hear about that another time,' said Tipper, 'I'm now talking about Bones, who with myself was the first up the stairs before the cops, and Jack's wife there in the hallway, crying the buckets. The door was open, so Bones pushed it the rest of the way open and in he snuck and no light in the room but what was coming in the window. The cops pulled up then and we heard their car door slam and Bones says to me, "Come inside and we'll get a look before they kick us the hell out," and he took a step and tripped, the simple bastard, and sprawled backward over the bed, right on top of poor Jack in his underwear, who of course didn't feel a thing. Bones got blood all over the seat of his pants.'

'Tipper,' said Packy, 'that's a goddamn pack of lies and you know it. You haven't got the truth in you, and neither did Bones McDowell.'

'So in comes big Barney Duffy with his flashlight and shines it on Bones sitting on poor Jack's chest. "Sweet mother of mine," says Barney and he grabbed Bones by the collar and elbow and lifted him off poor Jack like a dirty sock. "Haven'tcha no manners atall?" Barney says to him. "I meant no harm," says Bones. "It's a nasty thing you've done," says Barney, "sittin' on a dead man's chest." "On the grave of me mother I tripped and fell," says Bones. "Don't be swearing on your mother at a filthy time like this," says Barney, "you ought to be ashamed." "Oh I am," says Bones, "on the grave of me mother I am." And then Barney threw us both out, and I said to Bones on the way down the stairs, "I didn't know your mother was in the grave," and he says to me, "Well, she's not, the old fart-in-the-bottle, but she oughta be."'

'You never got a good look at the corpse,' Packy said to Tip, 'and don't tell me you did. But you know damn well that I did. I saw what they did to him when he was over at Keenan the undertaker's for the autopsy. Thirty-nine bullets. They walked in there while he was sleeping and shot him thirty-nine times. I counted the bullet holes. You know what that means? They had seven pistols between the pair of them.'

'Say what you will,' I told them, savoring Packy's senile memory, remembering that autopsy myself, remembering Jack's face intact but the back of his head blown away by not thirty-nine but only three soft-nosed .38-caliber bullets: one through his right jaw, tearing the neck muscle, cutting the spinal cord, and coming out through the neck and falling on the bed; another entering his skull near the right ear and moving upward through his brain, fracturing his skull, and remaining in the fracture; and the third, entering the left temple, taking a straight course across the brain and stopping just above the right ear.

'I still don't think he's dead.'

I had come to see Jack as not merely the dude of all gangsters, the most active brain in the New York underworld, but as one of the truly new American Irishmen of his day; Horatio Alger out of Finn McCool and Jesse James, shaping the dream that you could grow up in America and shoot your way to glory and riches. I've said it again and again to my friends who question the ethics of this somewhat unorthodox memoir: 'If you liked Carnegie and Custer, you'll love Diamond.' He was almost as famous as Lindbergh while his light burned. 'The Most Picturesque Racketeer in the Underworld,' the New York *American* called him; 'Most Publicized of Public Enemies,' said the *Post*; 'Most Shot-At Man in America,' said the *Mirror*.

Does anyone think these superlatives were casually earned? Why he was a pioneer, the founder of the first truly modern gang, the dauphin of the town for years. He filled the tabloids – never easy. He advanced the cause of joyful corruption and vice. He put the drop of the creature on the parched tongues of millions. He filled the pipes that pacify the troubled, loaded the needles that puncture anxiety bubbles. He helped the world kick the gong around, Jack did. And was he thanked for this benevolence? Hardly. The final historical image that endures is that corpse clad in underwear, flat-assed out in bed, broke and alone.

That's what finally caught me, I think: the vision of Jack Diamond alone, rare sight, anomalous event, pungent irony. Consider the slightly deaf sage of Pompeii, his fly open, feet apart, hand at crotch, wetting surreptitiously against the garden wall when the lava hits the house. Why he never even heard the rumbles. Who among the archeologists could know what glories that man created on earth, what truths he represented, what love and wisdom he propagated before the deluge of lava eternalized him as The Pisser? And so it is with Jack Diamond's last image. It wouldn't matter if he'd sold toilet paper or milk bottles for a living, but he was an original man and he needs an original epitaph, even if it does come four and a half decades late. I say to you, my reader, that here was a singular being in a singular land, a fusion of the individual life flux with the clear and violent light of American reality, with the fundamental Columbian brilliance that illuminates this bloody republic. Jack was a confusion to me. I relished his company, he made me laugh. Yet wasn't I fearful in the presence of this man for whom violence and death were well-oiled tools of the trade? Yes, ah yes. The answer is yes. But fear is a cheap emotion, however full of wisdom. And, emotionally speaking, I've always thought of myself as a man of expensive taste.

I chose the Kenmore to talk to Packy, Tipper, and Flossie because if Jack's ghost walked anywhere, it was in that bar, that old shut-down Rain-Bo room with its peeling paint and its glory unimaginable now beneath all that emptiness. In the 1920s and 1930s the Kenmore was the Number One nightclub between New York and the Canadian border. Even during the Depression you needed a reservation on weekends to dance in evening clothes to the most popular bands in the country: Rudy Vallee and Ben Bernie and Red Nichols and Russ Morgan and Hal Kemp and the Dorsey Brothers and all the rest who came before and after them. Naturally, limelighter that he was, Jack lived there. And so why wouldn't I choose the place to talk to three old friends, savor their memories and ring them in on my story?

I called Flossie first, for we'd had a thing of sorts between us, and I'll get to that. She was pretty back in those days, like a canary, all yellow-haired and soft and with the innocence of a birdsong, even though she was one of the loveliest whores north of Yonkers: The Queen of Stars, she called herself then. Packy's Parody Club had burned years before and he was now tending bar at the Kenmore, and so I said can we meet there and can you get hold of Tipper? And she said Tipper had quit the newspaper business finally but would be on tap, and he was. And so there we were at the Kenmore bar, me looking up at the smoky old pair of David Lithgow murals, showing the hunt, you know. Eight pink-coated huntsmen on horseback were riding out from the mansion in the first mural, at least forty-five hounds at their heels, heading into the woods. They were back indoors in the second painting, toasting and laughing by the fire while one of their number held the dead fox up by the tail. Dead fox.

'I was sitting where you're sitting,' Packy said to me, 'and saw a barman work up an order for Jack's table, four rum Cokes. All he poured was one shot of rum, split it over the top of the four and didn't stir them, so the suckers could taste the fruit of his heavy hand. "I saw that," I told him after the waiter picked the order up, "and I want you to know Jack Diamond is a friend of mine." The thieving bastard turned green and I didn't pay for another drink in this joint till Jack died.'

'His name had power,' Tipper said.

'It still does,' I said. 'Didn't he bring us together here?'

And I told them I was writing about him then, and they told me some of their truths, and secret lies, just as Jack had, and his wife Alice and his lovely light o' love, Kiki, had years ago. I liked all their lies best, for I think they are the brightest part of anybody's history.

I began by recalling that my life changed on a summer day in 1930 when I was sitting in the second-floor library of the Knights of Columbus, overlooking Clinton Square and two blocks up from the Kenmore bar. I was killing time until the pinochle crowd turned up, or a pool partner, and I was reading Rabelais, my gift to the library. It was the only book on The Index in the library and the only one I ever looked at.

That empty afternoon, and that book, gave me the insight that my life was a stupendous bore, and that it could use a little Gargantuan dimension. And so I said yes, I would take Jack Diamond up on his telephone invitation of that morning to come down to his place for Sunday dinner, three days hence. It was the Sunday I was to speak at the police communion breakfast, for I was one of Albany's noted communion breakfast intellectuals in those days. I would speak, all right, and then I would walk down to Union Station and take the west shore train to Catskill to listen to whatever that strange and vicious charmer had to say to an Albany barrister.

Jack Sauce

I met Jack in 1925 when he and his brother Eddie were personally running booze down from Canada. Jack stopped at the Kenmore even then, and he and Eddie and some more of their crew were at the table next to me, talking about Al Jolson. From what he said, Jack was clearly a Jolson fan, and so was I, and I listened to him express amazement that anybody could be as good at anything as Jolson was, but that he was also the most conceited son of a bitch in shoe leather. I broke into the conversation and said something windy, like: 'He sings, whistles, dances, gives out the jokes and patter and it's all emotion, all a revelation of who he is. I don't care how much he's rehearsed, it's still rare because it's pure. He's so at home in himself he can't make a false gesture. Everything he does is more of that self that's made a million, ten, twenty million, whatever it is. People find this very special and they'll pay to see it. Even his trouble is important because it gives him diversity, pathos, and those qualities turn up in his voice. Everything he does funnels in and out of him through his talent. Sure he's conceited, but that's only a cover-up for his fear that he'll be exposed as the desolated, impoverished, scrawny, fearful hyena that he probably thinks is his true image, but that he can't admit to anybody without destroying his soul.'

It all stunned Jack, who was a sucker for slick talk, and he bought me drinks for an hour. The next day he called to say he was sending me six quarts of Scotch and could I get him a pistol permit from Albany County? I liked the Scotch so I got him the permit.

I didn't have anything to do with him after that until 1929 when I represented Joe Vignola in the Hotsy Totsy case. And a story, which I pieced together very painfully from Joe, Jack, and half a dozen others, goes with that. It begins the night Benny Shapiro knocked out Kid Murphy in eight rounds at the Garden in '29. Jack, a serious fan of Benny's, won two grand that night taking the short end of seven to five.

'Stop by the club later,' Benny remembered Jack telling him in the dressing room after the fight. 'We'll have a little celebration.'

'I got to meet a guy, Jack,' Benny said.

'Bring her along.'

'I'll try to make it, but I might be late.'

'We'll wait,' said Jack.

Herman Zuckman came hustling toward the bar as Jack walked into the Hotsy Totsy Club with Elaine Walsh, a singer and his special friend of the moment, on his arm. Fat Herman had been sole owner of the Hotsy until Jack Diamond decided to join him as a fifty-fifty partner. The club was on Broadway, near Fifty-fourth, top of the second-floor stairs, music by a six-piece jazz band, and tonight Joe Vignola, the singing waiter, doubling on violin.

All thirty tables in the bar area were full, despite Mayor Walker's nightlife curfew to keep decent people away from racketeers, bad beer, and worse liquor. Wood alcohol. Rubbing alcohol. The finest. Imported by Jack from the cellars of Newark and Brooklyn. Drink me. The bartenders were working hard, but there was too much work for the pair, Walter Rudolph, old rum-runner with a bad liver, and Lukas, a new man. Jack took off his coat, a Palm Beach, and his hat, a white sailor straw, and rolled up his sleeves to help the barmen. Elaine Walsh sat at the end of the bar and listened to the music. 'I'm just a vagabond lover,' Joe Vignola was singing. Joe Vignola, a merger of John Gilbert and Oliver Hardy, fiddled a chorus, then went back to delivering drinks.

Saul Baker, silent doorman, sat by the door with two pistols in his pockets, one on his hip, another inside his coat, and smiled at arriving customers. Just out of Sing Sing, a holdup man in need, pudgy Saul had found a survival point in the spiritual soup kitchen of Jack Diamond. Let no hungry thief pass my door. Don't try to tell Saul Baker Jack Diamond is a heartless man.

Charlie Filetti sat at the end of the bar. Filetti, it would soon be disclosed, had recently banked twenty-five thousand dollars in one day, a fragment of profit from his partnership with Jack Diamond in the shakedown of bucket-shop proprietors, shady dealers in the stock market.

'Who won the fight, Jack?' Filetti asked.

'Benny, KO in eight. He ruined the bum.'

'I lose three hundred.'

'You bet against Benny?' Jack stopped working.

'You got more confidence in him than I got. A lot of people don't like him ducking Corrigan.'

'Ducking? Did you say ducking?'

'I'm saying what's being said. I like Benny good enough.'

'Benny ducks nobody.'

'Okay, Jack, but I'm telling you what talk's around town. They say you can make Benny lose, but you can't make him win.'

'It was on the level tonight. You think I'd back a mug who runs? You should've seen him take Murphy apart. Murphy's a lunk. Hits like half a pound of sausage. Benny ate him up.'

'I like Benny,' Filetti said. 'Don't get me wrong. I just like what Murphy did in his last fight. Murphy looked good that night I saw him.'

'You don't know, Charlie. You shouldn't bet on fights. You just don't know. Ain't that right, Walter? He don't know?'

'I don't follow the fights, Jack,' Walter Rudolph said. 'I got out of the habit in stir. Last fight I saw was in '23. Benny Leonard whippin' a guy I don't even remember.'

'How about you, pal?' Jack asked Lukas, the new barman. 'You follow the fights? You know Benny Shapiro?'

'I see his name in the papers, that's all. To tell you the truth, Mr Diamond, I watch baseball.'

'Nobody knows,' Jack said. He looked at Elaine. 'But Elaine

knows, don't you, baby? Tell them what you said tonight at the fight.'

'I don't want to say, Jack.' She smiled.

'Go ahead.'

'It makes me blush.'

'Never mind that, just tell them what you said.'

'All right. I said Benny fights as good as Jack Diamond makes love.'

Everybody at the bar laughed, after Jack laughed.

'That means he's a cinch to be champ,' Jack said.

The mood of the club was on the rise and midnight seemed only a beginning. But forty minutes behind the bar was enough for Jack. Jack, though he had tended bar in his time, was not required to do manual labor. He was a club owner. But it's a kick to do what you don't have to do, right? Jack put on his coat and sat alongside Elaine. He put his hand under her loose blond hair, held her neck, kissed her once as everyone looked in other directions. Nobody looked when Jack kissed his ladies in public.

'Jack is back,' he said.

'I'm glad to see him,' Elaine said.

Benny Shapiro walked through the door and Jack leaped off his chair and hugged him with one arm, walked him to a bar stool.

'I'm a little late,' Benny said.

'Where's the girl?'

'No girl, Jack. I told you it was a man. I owed some insurance.'

'Insurance? You win a fight, break a man's nose, and then go out and pay your insurance?'

'For my father. I already stalled the guy two weeks. He was waiting. Woulda canceled the old man out in the morning. I figure, pay the bill before I blow the dough.'

'Why don't you tell somebody these things? Who is this prick insurance man?'

'It's okay, Jack, it's all over.'

'Imagine a guy like this?' Jack said to everybody.

'I told you I always liked Benny,' Filetti said.

'Get us a table, Herman,' Jack said. 'Benny's here.'

Herman Zuckman, counting money behind the bar, turned to Jack with an amazed look.

'I'm busy here, Jack.'

'Just get us a table, Herman.'

'The tables are all full, Jack. You can see that. We already turned away three dozen people. Maybe more.'

'Herman, here beside me is the next welterweight champion of the world who's come to see us, and all you're doing is standing there making the wrong kind of noise.'

Herman put the money in a strongbox under the bar, then moved two couples away from a table. He gave them seats at the bar and bought them a bottle of champagne.

'You feeling all right?' Jack asked Benny when they all sat down. 'No damage?'

'No damage, just a little headache.'

'Too much worrying about insurance. Don't worry anymore about shit like that.'

'Maybe he's got a headache because he got hit in the head,' Charlie Filetti said.

'He didn't get hit in the head,' Jack said. 'Murphy couldn't find Benny's head. Murphy couldn't find his own ass with a compass. But Benny found Murphy's head. And his nose.'

'How does it feel to break a man's nose?' Elaine asked.

'That's a funny question,' Benny said. 'But to tell the truth you don't even know you're doing it. It's just another punch. Maybe it feels solid, maybe it don't.'

'You don't feel the crunch, what the hell good is it?' Jack said.

Filetti laughed. 'Jack likes to feel it happen when the noses break, right Jack?'

Jack mock-backhanded Filetti, who told him: 'Don't get *your* nose out of joint, partner' – and he laughed some more. 'I remember the night that big Texas oil bozo gave Jack lip. He's about six eight and Jack breaks a bottle across his face at the table, and then *you* couldn't stop laughing, Jack. The son of a bitch didn't know what hit him. Just sat there moppin' up his blood. Next day I go around to tell him what it costs to give lip to Jack and he says he wants to apologize. Gives me a grand to make Jack feel good. Remember that, Jack?'

Jack grinned.

The Reagans, Billy and Tim, came into the club and everybody knew it. They were brawny boys from the Lower West Side, dockworkers as soon as they knew they were men, that God had put muscles in their backs to alert them to that fact. Behind his back people called Billy The Omadhaun, a name he'd earned at seventeen when in a drunken rage he threw repeated football blocks at the crumbling brick tenement he lived in. Apart from the bleeding scrapes and gouges all over his body, an examination disclosed he had also broken both shoulders. His brother Tim, a man of somewhat larger wit, discovered upon his return from the Army in 1919 that beer-loading was no more strenuous than ship-loading, and far more lucrative. Proprietorship of a small speakeasy followed, as Tim pursued a prevailing dictum that to establish a speakeasy what you needed was one room, one bottle of whiskey, and one customer.

'That's a noisy bunch,' Elaine said when they came in.

'It's the Reagans,' said Filetti. 'Bad news.'

'They're tough monkeys,' Jack said, 'but they're pretty good boys.'

'The big one's got a fist like a watermelon,' Benny said.

'That's Billy,' Jack said. 'He's tough as he is thick.'

Jack waved to the Reagans, and Tim Reagan waved and said, 'Hello, Jack, howsa boy?'

'How's the gin in this joint?' Billy asked Joe Vignola in a voice that carried around the room. Herman Zuckman looked up. Customers eyed the Reagans.

'The best English gin is all we serve,' Vignola told him. 'Right off the boat for fancy drinkers like yourselves.'

'Right out of Jack's dirty bathtub,' Billy said.

'No homemade merchandise here,' Vignola said. 'Our customers get only the real stuff.'

'If he didn't make it then he stole it,' Billy said. He looked over at Jack Diamond. 'Ain't that so, Jack?'

'If you say so, Billy,' Jack said.

'Hey, he can get in trouble with that kind of talk,' Filetti said.

'Forget it,' Jack said. 'Who listens to a drunk donkey Irishman?'

'Three of the good gins,' Billy told Vignola. 'Right away.'

'Comin' up,' said Vignola, and he rolled his eyes, dropped the serving tray he carried under his arm, but caught it just before it hit the floor, then lofted it and caught it again, well over his head, and spun it on the index finger of his left hand: a juggler's routine. Others laughed. The Reagans did not.

'Get the goddamn gin and never mind the clown act,' Billy Reagan said. 'You hear me, you waiter baloney? Get the gin.'

Jack immediately went to the Reagan table and stood over big-fisted Billy. He poked Billy's shoulder with one finger. 'You got no patience. Make noise in your own joint, but have a little patience when you're in somebody else's.'

'I keep telling him he's ignorant,' Tim Reagan said. 'Sit down, Jack, don't mind him. Have a drink. Meet Teddy Carson from Philly. We been tellin' him about you, how you come a long way from Philadelphia.'

'How you makin' out, Jack?' Teddy Carson said, another big fist. He shook Jack's hand, cracking knuckles. 'Some boys I know in Philly talk about you a lot. Duke Gleason, Wiggles Mason. Wiggles said he knew you as a kid.'

'He knocked a tooth out on me. I never got even.'

'That's what he told me.'

'You tell him I said hello.'

'He'll be glad to hear that.'

'Pull up a chair, Jack,' Tim said.

'I got a party over there.'

'Bring 'em over. Make the party bigger.'

Saul Baker left his post by the door when Jack went back to

his own table. 'That's a bunch of shitheads, Jack. You want 'em thrown out?'

'It's all right, Saul.' Pudgy little Saul Baker, chastising three elephants.

'I hate a big mouth.'

'Don't get excited.'

Jack said he wanted to have a drink with the Reagans. 'We'll all go over,' he said to Filetti, Elaine, and Benny.

'What the hell for?' said Filetti.

'It'll keep 'em quiet. They're noisy, but I like them. And there's a guy from Philly knows friends of mine.'

Jack signaled Herman to move the table as Joe Vignola finally brought drinks to the Reagans.

'You call this gin?' Billy said to Vignola, holding up a glass of whiskey. 'Are you tryna be a funny guy? Are you lookin' for a fight?'

'Gin's gone,' Vignola said.

'I think you're lookin' for a fight,' Billy said.

'No, I was looking for the gin,' Vignola said, laughing, moving away.

'This is some dump you got here, Jack,' Billy called out.

Herman and a waiter moved Jack's table next to the Reagans, but Jack did not sit down.

'Let me tell you something, Billy,' Jack said, looking down at him. 'I think your mouth is too big. I said it before. Do I make myself clear?'

'I told you to shut your goddamn trap,' Tim told Billy, and when Billy nodded and drank his whiskey, Jack let everybody sit down and be introduced. Charlie Filetti sat in a quiet pout. Elaine had swallowed enough whiskey so that it made no difference where she sat, as long as it was next to Jack. Jack talked about Philadelphia to Teddy Carson, but then he saw nobody was talking to Benny.

'Listen,' Jack said, 'I want to raise a toast to Benny here, a man who just won a battle, man headed for the welter-weight crown.'

'Benny?' said Billy Reagan. 'Benny who?'

'Benny Shapiro, you lug,' Tim Reagan said. 'Right here. The fighter. Jack just introduced you.'

'Benny Shapiro,' Billy said. He pondered it. 'That's a yid name.' He pondered it further. 'What I think is yids make lousy fighters.'

Everybody looked at Billy, then at Benny.

'The yid runs, is how I see it,' Billy said. 'Now take Benny there and the way he runs out on Corrigan. Wouldn't meet an Irishman.'

'Are you gonna shut up, Billy?' Tim Reagan said.

'What do you call Murphy?' Benny said to Billy. 'Last time I saw him tonight he's got rosin all over his back.'

'I seen you box, yid. You stink.'

'You dumb fucking donkey,' Jack said. 'Shut your stupid mouth.'

'You wanna shut my mouth, Jack? Where I come from, the middle name is fight. That's how you shut the mouth.'

Billy pushed his chair away from the table, straddling it, ready to move. As he did, Jack tossed his drink at Billy and lunged at his face with the empty glass. But Billy only blinked and grabbed Jack's hand in flight, held it like a toy.

Saul Baker snatched a gun from his coat at Jack's curse and looked for a clear shot at Billy. Then Tim Reagan grabbed Saul's arm and wrestled for the gun. Women shrieked and ran at the sight of pistols, and men turned over tables to hide. Herman Zuckman yelled for the band to play louder, and customers scrambled for cover to the insanely loud strains of the 'Jazz Me Blues.' Elaine Walsh backed into a checkroom, Benny Shapiro, Joe Vignola, and four others there ahead of her. The bartenders ducked below bar level as Billy knocked Jack backward over chairs.

'Yes, sir,' Billy said, 'the middle name is fight.'

Tim Reagan twisted the pistol out of Saul Baker's grip as Teddy Carson fired the first shot. It hit Saul just above the right eye as he was reaching for his second pistol, on his hip.

The second shot was Charlie Filetti's. It grazed Billy's skull,

509

knocking him down. Filetti fired again, hitting Carson, who fell and slithered behind a table.

Jack Diamond, rising slowly with his pistol in his hand, looked at the only standing enemy, Tim Reagan, who was holding Saul's pistol. Jack shot Tim in the stomach. As Tim fell, he shot a hole in the ceiling. Standing then, Jack fired into Tim's forehead. The head gave a sudden twist and Jack fired two more bullets into it. He fired his last two shots into Tim's groin, pulling the trigger three times on empty chambers. Then he stood looking down at Tim Reagan.

Billy opened his eyes to see his bleeding brother beside him on the floor. Billy shook Tim's arm and grunted 'Timbo,' but his brother stayed limp. Jack cracked Billy on the head with the butt of his empty pistol and Billy went flat.

'Let's go, Jack, let's move,' Charlie Filetti said.

Jack looked up and saw Elaine's terrified face peering at him from the checkroom. The bartenders' faces were as white as their aprons. All faces looked at Jack as Filetti grabbed his arm and pulled. Jack tossed his pistol onto Billy's chest and it bounced off onto the floor.

Jack, out of Doors

Jack lived the fugitive life after the Hotsy, the most hunted man in America, and eventually he wound up in the Catskills. I don't think I'd have ever seen him again if the 1925 meeting in the Kenmore had been our only encounter. But I know my involvement in the Hotsy case brought me back to his mind, even though we never met face to face during it. And when the heat was off in midsummer of 1930, when the Hotsy was merely history, Jack picked me out of whatever odd pigeonhole he'd put me in, called me up and asked me to Sunday dinner.

'I'm sorry,' he said when he called, 'but I haven't seen you since that night we talked in the Kenmore. That's been quite a while and I can't remember what you look like. I'll send a driver to pick you up, but how will he recognize you?'

'I look like St Thomas Aquinas,' I said, 'and I wear a white Panama hat with a black band. Rather beat up, that hat. You couldn't miss it in a million.'

'Come early,' he said. 'I got something I'd like to show you.'

Joe (Speed) Fogarty picked me up at the Catskill railroad station, and when I saw him I said, 'Eddie Diamond, right?'

'No,' he said. 'Eddie died in January. Fogarty's the name.'

'You look like his twin.'

'So I'm told.'

'You're Mr Diamond's driver – or is he called Legs?'

'Nobody who knows him calls him anything but Jack. And I do what he asks me to do.'

'Very loyal of you.'

'That's the right word. Jack likes loyalty. He talks about it.'

'What does he say?'

'He says, "Pal, I'd like you to be loyal. Or else I'll break your fucking neck."'

'The direct approach.'

We got into Jack's custom, two-tone (green and gray) Cadillac sedan with whitewalls and bulletproof glass, armor panels, and the hidden pistol and rifle racks. The latter were features I didn't know existed until the following year when Jack had the occasion to open the pistol rack one fateful night. Now what I noticed were the black leather seats and the wooden dashboard with more gauges than any car seemed to need.

'How far is it to Jack's house?' I asked.

'We're not going to Jack's house. He's waiting for you over at the Biondo farm.'

'That wouldn't be Jimmy Biondo, would it?'

'You know Jimmy?'

'I met him once.'

'Just once? Lucky you. The bum is a throwback. Belongs in a tree.'

'I'd tend to sympathize with that view. I met him during the Hotsy Totsy business. We swapped views one day about a client of mine, Joe Vignola.'

'Joe. Poor Joe' – and Fogarty gave a sad little chuckle. 'Some guys'd be unlucky even if they were born with rabbits' feet instead of thumbs.'

'Then you knew Joe.'

'I used to go to the Hotsy when I was in New York even before I knew Jack. It was quite a place before the big blowup. Plenty of action, plenty of gash. I met my wife there, Miss Miserable of 1929.'

'So you're married.'

'Was. It broke up in four months. That dame would break up a high mass.'

It was Sunday morning, not quite noon, when Fogarty left the station in Catskill and headed west toward East Durham, where Jimmy Biondo lived. My head was full of Catskill images, old Rip Van Winkle who probably would have been hustling applejack instead of sleeping it off if he'd been alive now, and those old Dutchmen with their magical ninepins that lulled you into oblivion and the headless horseman riding like a spook through Sleepy Hollow and throwing his head at the trembling Ichabod. The Catskills were magical for me because of their stories, as well as their beauty, and I was full of both, despite the little crater of acid in the pit of my stomach. After all, I was actually going to Sunday dinner with one of the most notorious men in America. Me. From Albany.

'You know, two and a half hours ago I was talking to a whole roomful of cops.'

'Cops? I didn't know cops worked in Albany on Sunday.'

'Communion breakfast. I was the speaker and I told them a few stories and then looked out over their scrubbed faces and their shiny buttons and explained that they were our most important weapon in saving the nation from the worst scourge in its history.'

'What scourge?'

'Gangsterism.'

Fogarty didn't laugh. It was one of his rare humor failures.

Fogarty was the only man I ever met through Jack who wasn't afraid to tell me what was really on his mind. There was an innocence about him that survived all the horror, all the fear, all the crooked action, and it survived because Jack allowed it to survive. Until he didn't allow it anymore.

Fogarty told me he was eleven when he understood his own weak spot. It was his nose. When tapped on the nose in a fight, he bled, and the sight and feel of the blood made him vomit. While he vomited, the other guy punched him senseless. Fogarty avoided fistfights, but when they were unavoidable he packed his nose with the cotton he always carried. He usually lost his fights, but after he understood his nose, he never again bled to the vomit point.

He was thirty-five when I got to know him, pretty well recovered from a case of TB he'd picked up during his last year of college. He had a Fordham stringency that had gone sour on religion, but he still read books, liked O'Neill, and could talk a little *Hamlet*, because he'd played Laertes once in school. Jack used him as a driver but also trusted him with money and let him keep the books on beer distribution. But his main role was as Jack's sidekick. He looked like Eddie. And Eddie had died of TB.

Fogarty was working as a bartender for Charlie Northrup when he first met Jack. He talked flatteringly about Jack's history when they sat across from each other at Northrup's roadhouse bar. Jack was new in the mountains and he quizzed Fogarty on the scene. What about the sheriff and the judges? Were they womanizers? Gamblers? Queers? Drunks? Merely greedy? Who ran beer in the mountains besides Northrup and the Clemente brothers?

Fogarty gave Jack the answers, and Jack hired him away from Northrup and gave him the pearl-handled .32 Eddie Diamond once owned. Fogarty carried it without loading it, giving it the equivalent menace of a one-pound rock. 'You boys don't know it, but I've got you all covered with a one-pound rock.'

'I don't want to get into any heavy stuff' is what he explained to Jack when he took the pistol.

And Jack told him: 'I know you better than that, Speed. I don't ask my tailor to fix my teeth.'

This arrangement suited Fogarty down to his socks. He could move among the big fellows, the tough fellows, without danger to himself. If he did not fight, he would not bleed.

Fogarty turned onto a winding narrow dirt road that climbed a few minor hills and then flattened out on a plateau surrounded by trees. Jimmy Biondo's place was an old white farmhouse with green shutters and green shingled roof. It sat at the end of the drive, and behind it stood a large unpainted barn as dilapidated as the house was elegant. Three moving shapes sat on the long front porch, rocking in green wicker rockers, their faces hidden from me by the newspapers they were all reading. The faces opened themselves to us when Fogarty stopped on the grass beside the house, and Jack, the first to stand, threw down the paper and bounded down the stairs to greet me. The woman, Alice, held the paper in her lap and looked at me with a smile. The second man was Jimmy Biondo, who owned the place but no longer used it, and rented it to Jack. He detached himself from Andy Gump to give me a look.

'Welcome to God's country, Marcus,' Jack said. He was in white ducks, brown and white wing tips, and a yellow silk sport shirt. A tan blazer hung on the back of his rocker.

'God's country?' I said. 'Fogarty told me Jimmy Biondo owned this place.'

Jack laughed and Jimmy actually smiled. A smile from Jimmy lit up the world like a three-watt bulb.

'Look at this guy,' Jack said to his wife and Jimmy, 'a lawyer with a sense of humor. Didn't I tell you he was beautiful?'

'I only let my mother call me beautiful,' I said.

What can I say? Jack laughed again. He liked my lines. Maybe it was my delivery or my funny old hat. Fogarty recognized me from the hat as soon as he saw me. It was all discolored at the front from where I touched it, crown and brim; the brim was split on the side and the black band raveling a little. It happened to be my favorite hat. People don't understand that some men need tradition as much as others need innovation. I doffed the hat when Alice came down the steps and characteristically asked me after our handshake, 'Are you hungry? Have you had breakfast?'

'Catholic eggs and Irish bacon. That's extra greasy. About three hours ago at a communion breakfast.'

'We just came from church, too,' Alice said.

Oh? But I didn't say oh. I just repeated the story about my speech on the scourge of gangsterism. Jack listened with straight face, and I thought, Oh Christ, another humor failure.

'I know what you mean,' he said. 'Some of my best friends have been taken by that scourge.' Then he smiled, a very small smile, a smile you might call wry, or knowing, or ironic, or possibly ominous, which is how I looked at it and was why I laughed my courtroom laugh. That laugh, as they used to say in the Albany papers, is booming and infectious, and it had the effect of making Jack's line seem like the joke of the year.

Jack responded by standing up and jiggling, a moving glob of electricity, a live wire snaking its way around the porch. I knew then that this man was alive in a way I was not. I saw the vital principle of his elbow, the cut of his smile, the twist of his pronged fingers. Whatever you looked at was in odd motion. He hit you, slapped you with his palm, punched you with a light fist, clapped you on the shoulder, ridding himself of electricity to avoid exploding. He was conveying it to you, generating himself into yourself whether you wanted to receive him or not. You felt something had descended upon him, tongues of fire maybe or his phlogiston itself, burning its way into your own spirit.

I liked it.

It was an improvement on pinochle.

I mounted the steps and shook hands with Biondo and told him how overjoyed I was to see him again. He gave me a nod and an individualized twitch of each nostril, which I considered high graciousness. I would describe Jimmy as a giant maggot, an abominable toad with twelve-ounce eyelids and an emancipated nose that had nothing to do with the rest of his face. He was a globular figure of uncertain substance. Maybe all hotdog meat, goat's ears and pig's noses inside that salmony, shantung sportshirt. You said killer as soon as you looked at him, but he was not a killer. He was more complex than that.

'How's your buddy Joe Vignola?' he asked me. And he grunted a laugh, which went like this: 'Hug, hug, hug.'

'Joe is recovering nicely,' I said, an exaggeration. Joe was in awful shape. But I should give Jimmy Biondo satisfaction?

'Dumb,' said Jimmy. 'Dumb, dumb, dumb.'

'He never hurt anybody,' I said.

'Dumb,' said Jimmy, shaking his head, drawing out the sound

like a short siren. 'Dumb waiter,' he said, and he laughed like a sneeze.

'I felt so sorry for his family,' Alice said.

'Feel sorry for your own family,' Jack said. 'The son of a bitch was a stool pigeon.'

'I'll feel sorry for anybody I feel like feeling sorry for,' Alice said in modified spitfire manner, a trait I somehow didn't expect from the wife of Jack Diamond. Did I think he'd marry a placid cow? No. I thought he'd dominate any woman he chose to live with. We know from the movies, don't we, that one well-placed grapefruit in the kisser and the women learn who's boss? *Public Enemy*, the Cagney movie with that famed grapefruit scene, was touted as the real story of Jack Diamond when it played Albany. The advertising linked it unmistakably to his current escapades: 'You read about him on yesterday's front pages in this newspaper. Now see the story behind the headlines,' etc. But like everything else that ever had anything to do with Jack in the movies, it never had anything to do with Jack.

Well, we got past Joe Vignola as a topic, and then after a few anxious grunts from Jimmy ('Guh, guh, guh,') , he got up and announced his departure. Fogarty would take him to Hudson, across the river, and he'd take a train to Manhattan. His and Jack's presence on this front porch was not explained to me, but I didn't pry. I didn't know until much later that they were partners of a kind. His departure improved the conversation, and Alice said she and Jack had been to mass over at Sacred Heart in Cairo where she, and once in a while he, went on Sunday, and that Jack had given money for the new church organ and that she brought up Texas Guinan one summer to raise money at a church lawn party and Jack was going to bring Al Jolson up and so on. Revelatory.

An old colored man came to the foot of the front steps and said to Jack, 'The tahger's ready, Mist' Jack.' Tahger? Tiger? Could he be keeping a tiger? Was that what he wanted to show me?

'Okay, Jess,' Jack said. 'And will you bring out two quarts of rye and two quarts of champagne and leave 'em here on the porch?'

Jesse nodded and moved off slowly, a man who looked far older than his years, actually a stoop-backed fifty, a Georgia cotton chopper most of his days and then a stable hand. Jack met him in '29 through a Georgia horse breeder who had brought him to Churchill Downs as a stable boy. Jack heard Jesse had made moonshine back home and hired him on the spot at a hundred a week, a pay raise of about eight hundred percent, to come north with his two teen-aged sons and no wife and be plumber for an applejack still Jack and Biondo owned jointly, and which, since that time, had functioned night and day in a desolated patch of woods a quarter of a mile from the patch of porch on which I was rocking.

So the old man went for the rye and champagne, and I mentally alerted my whistle to coming attractions. Then Alice looked at Jack and Jack looked at me and I looked at both of them, wondering what all the silent looking was for. And then Jack asked me a question: 'Ever fire a machine gun, Marcus?'

We walked to the garage-cooler, which is what it turned out to be, as luxuriously appointed a tumbledown barn as you'd be likely to find anywhere in America, with a beer refrigeration unit; a storage room for wine and champagne, paneled in knotty pine; a large area where three trucks could comfortably park; and a total absence of hay, hornets, barnsmell, cowflop, or chickenshit.

'No,' I had told Jack, in answer to his question, 'I am a machine-gun virgin.'

'Time you shot the wad,' Jack said, and he went dancing down the stairs and around the corner toward the barn, obviously leading both me and Alice, before we were out of our chairs.

'He's a nut on machine guns,' Alice said. 'He's been waiting till you got here to try it out. You don't have to do it, you know, just because he suggests it.'

I nodded my head yes, shook it no, shrugged, and, I suppose, looked generally baffled and stupid. Alice and I walked across the side lawn to the barn where Jack had already pried up a floorboard and was lifting out a Thompson submachine gun, plus half a dozen boxes of bullets.

'Brand-new yesterday from Philadelphia,' he said. 'I been anxious to test it.' He dislodged the magazine, loaded it, replaced it with what, despite my amateurism in the matter, I would call know-how. 'I heard about a guy could change one of these drums in four seconds,' he said. 'That's handy in a tight spot.'

He stood up and pointed it at the far end of the barn where a target was tacked on a windowless wall. The target was a crudely drawn face with the name Dutch Schultz lettered beneath.

'I had a couple of hundred of these printed up a few years ago,' he said, 'when Schultz and me weren't getting along. He looks just like that, the greedy prick. I drew it myself.'

'You get along all right now with him?'

'Sure. We're pals again,' Jack said and he let go with a long blast that nicked the Schultz forehead in two or three places.

'A little off,' Jack observed, 'but he'd have noticed.'

'Let me try,' Alice said. She took the gun from Jack, who parted with it reluctantly, then fired a long burst which roamed the wall without touching the target. With a second burst she hit the paper's edge, but not Schultz.

'I'm better with a rifle.'

'You're better with a frying pan,' Jack said. 'Let Marcus try it.'

'It's really out of my line,' I said.

'Go on,' Jack said. 'You may never get another chance, unless you come to work for me.'

'I've got nothing against Mr Schultz.'

'He wouldn't mind. Lotsa people shoot at him.'

Jack put the gun in my hands, and I held it like a watermelon. Ridiculous. I put my right hand on the pistol grip, grabbed the other handgrip with the left, and raised the stock into my armpit. Absurd. Uncomfortable.

'Up a little,' Jack said. 'Against the shoulder.'

I touched the trigger, raised the gun. Why? It was wobbly, cold. I pointed it at Schultz. Sunday morning. Body of Christ still undigested in some internal region, memory of prayer and holy bacon grease on my tongue. I touched the trigger seriously, pulled the gun tighter to my shoulder. Old feeling. Comfortable with a weapon against the pectoral. Like Army days, days in the woods as a kid. Put it down, fool.

'For chrissake, Marcus, give it a blast,' Jack said.

Really childish not to. Raising the flag of morality. Powerful Irish Catholic magic at work that prohibits shooting effigies on the side of a barn. Bless me Father for I have sinned. I shot at Mr Schultz's picture. And did you hit it, son? No, Father, I missed. For your penance say two rosaries and try again for the son of a bitch.

'Honest, Marcus,' Alice said, 'it won't bite.'

Ladies' Auxiliary heard from. Altar Rosary Society Member attends machine-gun outing after mass, prods lawyer to take part. What a long distance between Marcus and Jack Diamond. Millenniums of psychology, civilization, experience, turpitude. Man also develops Milquetoasts by natural selection. Would I defend him if some shooters walked through the barn door? What difference from defending him in court? And what of Jack's right to justice, freedom, life? Is the form of defense the only differentiating factor? What a morally confounded fellow Marcus is, perplexed by Mr Thompson's invention.

I pressed the trigger. Bullets exploded in my ears, my hands, my shoulders, my blood, my brain. The spew of death was a personal tremor that even jogged my scrotum.

'Close, off the right ear,' Jack said. 'Try again.'

I let go with another burst, feeling confident. No pain. It's easy. I leveled the weapon, squeezed off another.

'Got him. Eyeball high. No more Maggie's Drawers for Marcus. You want a job riding shotgun?'

Jack reached for the gun, but I held onto it, facing the ease with which I had become new. Do something new and you are new. How boring it is not to fire machine guns. I fired again and eliminated the Schultz mouth.

'Jesus, look at that,' Jack said.

I gave him the gun and he looked at me. Me. Sandlot kid hits grand slam off thirty-game winner, first time at bat.

'How the hell did you do that?' Jack asked me.

'It's all a matter of the eyeball,' I said. 'I also shoot a pretty fair game of pool.'

'I'm impressed,' Jack said. He gave me another amazed look and put the weapon to his shoulder. But then he decided the shooting was over. What if he missed the target now? Bum of bums.

'Let's have lunch and toast your sharpshooting,' he said.

'Oh nonsense,' Alice said, 'let's toast something important, like the beautiful day and the beautiful summer and having friends to dinner. Are you our friend, Marcus?'

I smiled at Alice to imply I was her friend, and Jack's, too. And I was then, yes I was. I was intuitively in sympathy with this man and woman who had just introduced me to the rattling, stammering splatter of violent death. Gee, ain't it swell?

We walked back to the porch where Fogarty was reading Krazy Kat.

'I heard the shooting,' Fogarty said, 'who won?'

'Marcus won,' Alice said.

'I wiped out Mr Schultz's mouth, if that's a win.'

'Just what he deserves. The prick killed a kid cousin of mine last week in Jersey.'

And so I had moral support for my little moral collapse – which sent a thrill through me, made me comfortable again on this glorious Sunday in the mountains.

We got into the car and left the Biondo place, Alice and I in the back seat, Jack up front with Fogarty. Alice previewed our Sunday dinner for me: roast beef and baked potatoes, and did I like my beef rare the way Jack liked it, and asparagus from their own garden, which Tamu, their Japanese gardener, had raised, and apple pie by their colored maid, Cordelia.

Alice bulged out of her pink summer cotton in various places, and my feeling was that she was ready instantly to let it all flop out whenever Jack gave the signal. All love, all ampleness, all ripeness, would fall upon the bed, or the ground, or on him, and be his for the romping. Appleness, leaves, blue sky, white sheets, erect, red

523

nipples, full buttocks, superb moistness at the intersection, warm wet lips, hair flying, craziness of joy, pleasure, wonder, mountains climbable with a stride after such sex.

I like her.

Oxie was asleep on the enclosed porch when we arrived, more formally known as Mendel (The Ox) Feinstein, one of the permanent cadre. Oxie was a bull-necked weightlifter with no back teeth, who'd done a four-year stretch for armed robbery of a shoe store. The judge specified he do the full four because, when he held up the lady shoe clerk, he also took the shoes she was wearing. Justice puts its foot down on Oxie.

He got up immediately when the key turned in the front door. We all watched as Alice stopped to coo at two canaries in a silver cage on the porch. When she went on to the kitchen, Fogarty sat down on the sofa with Oxie, who made a surreptitious gesture to Jack.

'Marion called about a half hour ago,' he whispered.

'Here?'

Oxie nodded and Jack made facial note of a transgression by Marion.

'She wants you to see her this afternoon. Important, she said.'

'Goddamn it,' Jack said, and he went into the living room and up the stairs two at a time, leaving me on the porch with the boys. Fogarty solved my curiosity, whispering: 'Marion's his friend. Those two canaries there – he calls one Alice, one Marion.' Oxie thought that was the funniest thing he'd heard all week, and while he and Fogarty enjoyed the secret, I went into the living room, which was furnished to Alice's taste: overstuffed mohair chairs and sofa; walnut coffee table; matching end tables and table lamps, their shades wrapped in cellophane; double-thick Persian rug, probably worth a fortune if Jack hadn't lifted it. My guess was he'd bought it hot; for while he loved the splendid things of life, he had no inclination to pay for them. He did let Alice pick out the furniture, for the hot items he kept bringing home clashed with her plans, such as they were. She'd lined the walls with framed calendar art and holy pictures – a sepia print of the Madonna returning from Calvary and an incendiary, bleeding sacred heart with a cross blooming atop the bloody fire. One wall was hung with a magnificent blue silk tapestry, a souvenir from Jack's days as a silk thief. Three items caught my eye on a small bookshelf otherwise full of Zane Grey and James Oliver Curwood items: a copy of Rabelais, an encyclopedia of Freemasonry, and the Douay Bible sandwiched between them.

When he came down, I asked about the books. The Freemasonry? Yeah, he was a Mason. 'Good for business,' he said. 'Every place you go in this country, the Protestant sons of bitches got the money locked up.' And Rabelais? Jack picked up the book, fondled it.

'A lawyer gave it to me when I had my accident in 1927.' (He meant when he was shot three times by the Lepke mob when they ambushed and killed Little Augie Orgen.) 'Terrific book. You ever read it? Some screwball that Rab-a-lee.'

I said I knew the book but avoided mentioning the coincidence of Rabelais being here and also in the K. of C. library, where I made my decision to come here, and in the additional fact that a lawyer had given the book to Jack. I would let it all settle, let the headiness go out of it. Otherwise, it would sound like some kind of weird, fawning lie.

Alice heard us talking and came into the living room in her apron. 'Those damn Masons,' she said. 'I can't get him away from that nonsense.' To rile her, Jack kept a picture of an all-seeing eye inside a triangle, a weird God-figure in the Masonic symbology, on the wall in the upstairs bathroom. Alice raised this issue, obviously a recurring one.

'It sees you, Alice,' Jack told her, 'even when you pee.'

'My God doesn't watch me when I pee,' Alice said. 'My God is a gentleman.'

'As I get it,' Jack said, 'your God is two gentlemen and a bird.'

He opened the Rabelais to a page and began reading, walking to the kitchen doorway to serenade Alice with the flow. He read of Gargantua's arrival in Paris, his swiping of the Notre Dame

Cathedral bells for his giant horse, and then his perching on the cathedral roof to rest while mobs of tiny Parisians stared up at him. And so he decided to give them wine.

'"He undid his magnificent codpiece"' – Jack read with mock robustness; his voice was not robust but of a moderately high pitch, excitable, capable of tremolos – '"and bringing out his john-thomas, pissed on them so fiercely that he drowned two hundred and sixty thousand, four hundred and eighteen persons, not counting the women and small children."'

'My God, John,' Alice said, 'do you have to read *that?*'

'Piss on 'em,' Jack said. 'I always felt that way.' And holding the book and talking again to me, he said, 'You know what my full name is? John Thomas Diamond.' And he laughed even harder.

Jack threw the book on the sofa and went quickly out to the porch, then to the car, and came back with a bottle of champagne in each hand. He put both bottles on the coffee table, got four glasses from the china closet.

'Alice, Speed, you want champagne?' They both said no and he didn't ask Oxie. Why waste champagne on a fellow who'd rather drink feet juice? He poured our champagne, the real goods.

'Here's to a fruitful legal relationship,' Jack said, rather elegantly, I patronizingly thought. I sipped and he gulped and poured himself another. That disappeared and another followed that, two and a half glasses in one minute.

'Thirsty,' he explained, 'and that's prime stuff.' But he was getting outside his skin. He finished what was in his glass and then stared at me while I drank and told him my experiences with bad champagne. He interrupted me, perfectly, at a pause, with obvious intentions of letting me continue, and said: 'I don't want to interrupt your story, but how about a walk? It's a great day and I want to show you a piece of land.'

He led the way out the back door and along a stream that ran parallel to the highway, and at a narrow point we leaped across the stream and into the woods, all soft with pine needles, quiet and cool, a young forest with the old granddaddy trees felled long ago by loggers, and the new trees – pines, white birches, maples, ash – tall but small of girth, reaching up for sunlight. A cat named Pistol followed at Jack's heel like an obedience-trained dog. He was an outdoor cat and had picked us up as we left the back steps, where he'd been sitting, gnawing gently on a squirrel that wasn't quite dead and that still had the good sense to run away whenever Pistol relaxed his teeth. But that old squirrel never got far from the next pounce.

Jack walked rapidly, stepping over the carcasses of old trees, almost running, moving uphill, slipping but never falling, sure-footed as the cat. He turned around to check me out and at each turn motioned to me with his right hand, backs of fingers upright toward me, bending them toward himself in a come-on gesture. He said nothing, but even today I can remember that gesture and the anxious look on his face. He was not mindful of anything else except me and his destination and whatever obstacle he and the cat might have to dodge or leap over: an old log, jutting rocks, half-exposed boulders, fallen limbs, entire dead trees, the residual corpses of the forest. Then I saw a clearing and Jack stopped at its edge to wait for me. He pointed across a meadow, a golden oval that rolled upward, a lone, dead apple tree in the center like the stem and root of a vast yellow mushroom turned upside down. Beyond the tree an old house stood on the meadow's crest and Jack said that was where we were going.

He walked with me now, calmed, it seemed, by the meadow or perhaps the sight of the house, all that speed from the forest faded now into a relaxed smile, which I noticed just about the time he asked me: 'Why'd you come down here today, Marcus?'

'I was invited. And I was curious. I'm still curious.'

'I thought maybe I could talk you into going to work for me.'

'As a lawyer or riding shotgun?'

'I was thinking maybe you'd set up a branch of your office in Catskill.'

That was funny and I laughed. Without even telling me what he wanted of me, he was moving me into his backyard.

'That doesn't make much sense,' I said. 'My practice is in Albany and so is my future.'

'What's in the future?'

'Politics. Maybe Congress, if the slot opens up. Not very complicated really. It's all done with machinery.'

'Rothstein had two district attorneys on his payroll.'

'Rothstein?'

'Arnold Rothstein. I used to work with him. And he had a platoon of judges. Why did you get me a pistol permit?'

'I don't really have a reason.'

'You knew I was no altar boy.'

'It cost me nothing. I remember we had a good conversation at the Kenmore. Then you sent me the Scotch.'

He clapped me on the shoulder. Electric gesture.

'I think you're a thief in your heart, Marcus.'

'No, stealing's not my line. But I admit to a corrupt nature. Profligacy, sloth, licentiousness, gluttony, pride. Proud of it all. That's closer to my center.'

'I'll give you five hundred a month.'

'To do what?'

'Be available. Be around when I need a lawyer. Fix my traffic tickets. Get my boys out of jail when they get drunk or go wild.'

'How many boys?'

'Five, six. Maybe two dozen sometimes.'

'Is that all? Doesn't seem like a full-time job.'

'You do more, I pay you more.'

'What more might I do?'

'Maybe you could move some money for me. I want to start some accounts in other banks up this way, and I don't want to be connected to them.'

'So you want a lawyer on the payroll.'

'Rothstein had Bill Fallon. Paid him a weekly salary. You know who Fallon was?'

'Every lawyer in the U. S. knows who Fallon was.'

'He defended me and Eddie when we got mixed up in a couple of scrapes. He wound up a drunk. You a drunk?'

'Not yet.'

'Drunks are worthless.'

We were almost at the old house, a paintless structure with all its windows and doors boarded up and behind it a small barn, or maybe it was a stable, with its eyes gouged out and holes in its roof. The panorama from this point was incredible, a one-hundred-and-eighty-degree vision of natural grandeur. I could see why Jack liked the spot.

'I know the old man who owns this,' he said. 'He owns the whole field, but the son of a bitch won't sell. He owns half the mountainside. A stubborn old Dutchman, and he won't sell. I want you to work on him. I don't care what the price is.'

'You want the house? The field? What?'

'I want all you can get, the whole hill and the forest. I want this yellow field. Everything between here and my place. Things are going good now and they can only get better. I want to build up here. A big place. A place to live good. I saw one in Westchester, a great place I liked. Roomy. A millionaire owned it. Used to work for Woodrow Wilson. Had a big fireplace. Look at this rock.'

He picked up a purple stone lying at our feet.

'Plenty of this around,' he said. 'Have the fireplace made out of it. Maybe face part of the house with it. You ever see a house faced with purple rock?'

'Never.'

'Me either. That's why I want it.'

'You're settling in here in the Catskills then, permanently?'

'Right. I'm settling in. Plenty of work around here.' He gave me a conspiratorial smile. 'Lots of apple trees. Lots of thirsty people.' He looked over at the house. 'Van Wie is his name. He's about seventy now. He used to farm a little up here a few years ago.' Jack walked over to the shed and looked inside. Grass was growing inside it, and hornets, birds, and spiders were living in the eaves. Birdshit and cobwebs were everywhere.

'Eddie and me did the old man a favor in here one day,' Jack said, reminding me and himself, and, in his way, reminding me to remind the old man too that when Jack Diamond did you a favor, you didn't turn your back on him. He turned suddenly to me, not at all relaxed now, but with that anxious face I saw as he was moving through the forest.

'Are you with me?'

'I could use the money,' I said. 'I usually lose at pinochle.'

I can recall now the quality of the light at that moment when I went to work for Jack. The sun was dappling his shoulders as he peered into the shadows of the empty stable with its random birdshit, with his faithful cat Pistol (Marion later had a poodle named Machine Gun), rubbing its sides against Jack's pants legs, his head against Jack's shoe, the sun also dappling the black and white of Pistol's tiger tom fur as it sent its electricity into Jack the way Jack sent his own vital current into others. I mentioned to Jack that he looked like a man remembering something a man doesn't want to remember and he said yes, that was a thousand percent, and he told me the two interlocking memories he was resisting.

One was of another summer day in 1927 when old man Van Wie came down the meadow past the apple tree, which was not dead then, and into the forest where Jack and Eddie Diamond were firing pistols at a target nailed to a dead, fallen tree, recreation therapy for Eddie, for whom the house, which would later be described as Jack's fortress, had been purchased: mountain retreat for tubercular brother.

The gunfire brought the old man, who might have guessed the occupation of his neighbors but not their identities; for Jack and Eddie were the Schaefer brothers back then, a pseudonym lifted from Jack's in-laws; and Jack was not yet as famous a face as he would be later in that same year when Lepke bullets would not quite kill him. The farmer did not speak until both Jack and Eddie had given him their full attention. He then said simply, 'There is a mad cat. Will you shoot it before it bites on my cow? It already bit on my wife.' Then the old man waited for a reply, staring past his flat nose and drooping mustache, which, like his hair, he had dyed black, giving him the comic look of a Keystone Kop; which was perhaps why Jack said to him, 'Why don't you call the troopers? Or the sheriff. Have them do it.'

'They'd be all week,' said the old man. 'Might be it's got the rabies.'

'How'll we find him?' Jack asked.

'I chased him with the pitchfork and he ran in the barn. I locked him in.'

'Is the cow in there?'

'No. Cow's out in the field.'

'Then he can't get at the cow. You got him trapped.'

'He might get out. That's a right old barn.'

Jack turned to Eddie, and they smiled at the prospect of making a mad cat hunt together, the way they had once hunted rats and woodchucks in the Philadelphia dumps. But Eddie could not walk all the way to the farmer's house, and so they went back and got Jack's car, and with old man Van Wie they drove to the barn which had not yet had its eyes gouged out or holes made in its roof. And with guns drawn and the farmer behind them with his pitchfork, they entered the barn.

'What's going to stop him from biting hell out of us?' Jack said.

'I expect you'll shoot him 'fore he gets a chance at that,' the old man said.

Jack saw the cat first, yellowish orange and brown and curled up on some hay, and quiet. It looked at them and didn't move, but then it opened its mouth and hissed without sound.

'That don't look like a mad cat to me,' Jack said.

'You didn't see it bite on my wife or leap on the lampshade and then try to run up the curtain. Maybe it's quiet 'cause I whacked it with the fork. Maybe I knocked it lame.'

'It looks like Sugarpuss,' Eddie said.

'I know,' Jack said. 'I'm not going to kill it.'

The mad cat looked at the men, orange and silent and no longer disturbed by their intrusion or fearful of their menace.

'You shoot it if you want,' Jack said.

'I don't want to shoot it,' Eddie said.

'Look out,' old man Van Wie said, pushing past the brothers and sticking his pitchfork through the cat, which squealed and wriggled and tried to leap off the fork. But it was impaled and the farmer held it out to the brothers, an offering.

'Now shoot it,' the old man said.

Jack kept his arm at his side, pistol down, watching the cat squeal and squirm upside down on the fork. Eddie put three bullets in its head, and the old man, saying only 'Obliged' and grabbing a shovel off a nail, carried the carcass out to the yard to bury what remained of madness. And Jack then was triggered into his second cat memory of eighteen years before, when he was twelve, when he said to Eddie that he wanted to furnish the warehouse and Eddie did not understand. The warehouse was enormous, longer than some city blocks, empty for as long as they had been alive. It was made of corrugated metal and wooden beams and had scores of windows that could be broken but not shattered. Jack discovered it, and with Eddie, they imagined its vast empty floor space full of automobiles and machinery and great crated mysteries. At one end an office looked down on the emptiness from second-story level. There was no staircase to it, but Jack found a way. He rigged a climbing rope, stolen from a livery stable, over a wooden crossbeam, the stairway's one remnant. He worked two hours to maneuver a loop upward that would secure the rope, then shinnied up. It was 1909 and his mother had been dead two months. His brother was eight and spent two days learning how to shinny up to the office.

The brothers looked out the office windows at a fragment of Philadelphia's freight yards, at lines of empty boxcars, stacks of crossties, piles of telegraph poles covered with creosote. They watched trains arrive and then leave for places they knew only from the names painted on the cars – Baltimore and Ohio, New York Central, Susquehanna, Lackawanna, Erie, Delaware and Hudson, Boston and Albany – and they imagined themselves in these places, on these rivers. From the windows they saw a hobo open a freight-car door from inside, and they assumed he'd just awakened from a night's sleep. They saw him jump down and saw that a bull saw, too, and was chasing him. The hobo had only one shoe, the other foot wrapped in newspaper and tied with string. The bull outran him and beat him with a club, and when the hobo went down, he stayed down. The bull left him where he fell.

'The bastard,' Jack said. 'He'd do the same to us.'

But the Diamond brothers always outran the bulls, outscrambled them beneath the cars.

Jack brought a chair to the office and a jug of water with a cork in it, candles, matches, a slingshot with a supply of stones, half a dozen pulp novels of the wild West, a cushion, and, when he could steal it from his father's jug, some dago red. He kept the hobo's hat, which was worn through at the crown from being fingered and had spots of blood on the brim. Jack took it off the hobo after he and Eddie went down to help him and found he was dead. The hobo was a young man, which shocked the brothers. Jack hung the hat on a nail in the office and let no one wear it.

The brothers were asleep in the office the day the orange cat came in. It had climbed one of the wooden pillars and found its way along a crossbeam. A dog was after it, barking at the foot of the pillar. Jack gave it water in the candle dish, petted it, and called it Sugarpuss. The dog kept barking and Jack fired stones at it with his slingshot. When it wouldn't leave, Jack shinnied down, clubbed it with a two-by-four, cut its throat, and threw it out by the crossties.

Sugarpuss remained the mascot of the brothers and the select group of friends they allowed up the rope. It lived in the warehouse, and all the gang brought it food. During the winter Jack found Sugarpuss outside, frozen in the ice, its head almost eaten off where another animal had gotten it. He insisted it be given a decent burial and immediately got another cat to replace it. But the second cat ran away, an early lesson in subtraction for Jack.

We came out of the woods onto the highway and walked back toward Jack's house. A car passed us, and a middle-aged man and woman waved and tooted at Jack, who explained they were neighbors and that he'd had an ambulance take their kid to Albany Hospital, some thirty miles away, about six months back when the local sawbones didn't know what ailed the boy. Jack footed the bill for examinations and a week's stay in the hospital, and the kid came out in good shape. An old woman down the road had a problem with her cow after her shed collapsed, and so Jack paid for a new shed. People in Acra and Catskill told these stories when the papers said Jack was a heartless killer.

Jack's Uncle Tim was working on the rosebushes when we reached the house. The lawn had been freshly cut, some grass raked into piles on the front walk. Tamu was watering the flower beds of large and small marigolds, dahlias, snapdragons, on the sunny side of the brown shingled house. The flowers reached up toward a second-story window where, it was authoritatively reported in the press at a later date, Jack had his machine guns mounted. The fortress notion was comic but not entirely without foundation, for Jack did have floodlights on the house to illuminate all approaches, and the maple trees on the lawn were painted white to a point higher than a man, so anyone crossing in front of one was an instant target. Jack installed the lights back in 1928 when he was feuding with Schultz and Rothstein, right after a trio of hirelings tried to kill Eddie in Denver. Eddie went to Denver because the Catskills hadn't solved his lung problems, and Denver must have helped, for when they shot at him he leaped out of his car and outran the killers. One killer, when he saw Eddie'd gotten away, grabbed a bull terrier pup in front of somebody's house and shot off one of its paws, an odd substitute for murder. But then I guess in any realm of life you solve your needs any way you can.

Jack and I stood on the lawn and watched the grooming of the landscape. Domestic felicity. Back to the soil. Country squirearch. It didn't conform to my preconceptions of Jack, but standing alongside him, I had to admit it didn't sit so badly on him either.

'Pretty good life you've got here,' I told him. He wanted to hear that.

'Beats hell out of being at the bottom of the river,' he said.

'A striking truth.'

'But this is nothing, Marcus, nothing. Give me a year, maybe even six months, you'll see something really special.'

'The house, you mean, the purple house?'

'The house, the grounds, this whole goddamn county.'

He squinted at me then and I waited for clarification.

'It's a big place, Marcus, and they pack in the tourists all summer long. You know how many speakeasies in this one county? Two hundred and thirty. I don't even know how many hotels yet, but I'm finding out. And every goddamn one of them can handle beer. Will handle beer.'

'Who's servicing them now?'

'What's the difference?'

'I don't know what the difference is, except competition.'

'We'll solve that,' Jack said. 'Come on, let's have some champagne.'

Pistol, who had followed us out of the woods and along the road, pounced on a mole that made the mistake of coming out of his tunnel. The cat took him to the back steps and played with him alongside the carcass of the squirrel, who had died of wounds. Or perhaps Pistol had finished him off when he decided to take a walk with us. He let the mole run away a little, just as he'd let the squirrel, then he pounced.

We were hardly inside the house when Alice called out to Jack, 'Will you come here please?' She was on the front porch, with Oxie and Fogarty still on the sofa. They were not moving, not speaking, not looking at Alice or at Jack or at me either when we got there. They both stared out toward the road.

Alice opened the canary cage and said to Jack, 'Which one do you call Marion?'

Jack quickly turned to Fogarty and Oxie.

'Don't look at them, they didn't tell me,' Alice said. 'I just heard them talking. Is it the one with the black spot on its head?'

Jack didn't answer, didn't move. Alice grabbed the bird with the black spot and held it in her fist.

'You don't have to tell me – the black spot's for her black hair. Isn't it? Isn't it?'

When Jack said nothing, Alice wrung the bird's neck and threw it back in the cage. 'That's how much I love you,' she said and started past Jack, toward the living room, but he grabbed her and pulled her back. He reached for the second bird and squeezed it to death with one hand, then shoved the twitching, eyebleeding corpse down the crevice of Alice's breasts. 'I love you too,' he said.

That solved everything for the canaries.

We left the house immediately, with a 'Come on, Marcus' the only words Jack said. Fogarty followed him wordlessly, like Pistol. 'Haines Falls,' Jack said in a flat, hostile voice.

Fogarty leaned over the seat to tell Jack, 'We didn't know she was listening or we . . .'

'Shut your fucking mouth.'

We drove a few miles in silence, and then Jack said in a tone that eliminated the canary episode from history, 'I'm going to Europe. Ever been to Europe?'

'I was there with the AEF,' I said. 'But it was a Cook's Tour. I was in a headquarters company in Paris. Army law clerk.'

'I was in Paris. I went AWOL to see it.'

'Smart move.'

'When they caught up with me, they sent me back to the States. But that was a long time ago. I mean lately. You been to Europe lately?'

'No, that was the one and only.'

'Fantastic place, Europe. Fantastic. I'd go all the time if I could. I like Heidelberg. If you go to Heidelberg, you got to eat at the castle. I like London, too. A polite town. Got class. You want to go to Europe with me, Marcus?'

'Me go to Europe? When? For how long?'

'What the hell's the difference? Those are old lady questions. We go and we come back when we feel like it. I do a little business and we have ourselves some fun. Paris is big fun, I mean big fun.'

'What about your business here? All those hotels. All those speakeasies.'

'Yeah, well, somebody'll look after it. And it won't be all that long of a trip. Goddamn it, a man needs change. We get old fast. I'm an old son of a bitch, I feel old, I could die any time. I almost died twice already, really close. So goddamn stupid to die when there's so many other things to do. Jesus, I learned that a long time ago; I learned it in Paris from an old crone – old Algerian chambermaid with her fingers all turned into claws and her back crooked and every goddamn step she took full of needles. Pain. Pain she wanted to scream about but didn't. Tough old baby. I think she was a whore when she was young, and me and Buster Deegan from Cleveland, we went AWOL together to see Paris before they shot us in some muddy fucking trench, and we wind up talking every morning to this old dame who spoke a little English. She wore a terrycloth robe – maybe she didn't even own a dress – and a rag on her head and house slippers because her feet couldn't stand shoes. We double-tipped her every day and she smiled at us, and one day she says to me, "M'sieur, do you have fun in Paris?" I said I was having a pretty good time. "You must, M'sieur," she said to me. "It is necessary." Then she give me a very serious look, like a teacher giving you the word, and she smiled. And I knew she was saying to me, yeah, man, I got pain now, but I had my day long, long ago, and I still remember that, I remember it all the time.'

I'd been watching Jack have fun all day, first with his machine gun and then his champagne and his Rabelais and his dream of a purple mansion; but his fun was nervous, a frenetic motion game that seemed less like fun than like a release of energy that would explode his inner organs if he held it in.

We were climbing a mountain by this time, along a two-lane road that wound upward and seemed really about as wide as a footpath when it snaked along the edges of some very deep and sudden drops. I saw a creek at one point, visible at the bottom of a gorge. When you looked up, you saw mountains to the left, and you climbed and climbed and climbed and then made a hairpin turn and saw a waterfall cascading down the side of a great cliff.

'Get a look at that,' Jack said, pointing. 'Is that some sight?'

And at another sharp turn he told Fogarty to stop, and we both got out and looked back down the mountain to see how far and how steeply we had climbed; and then he pointed upward where you could see more mountains beyond mountains. The stop was clearly a ritual for Jack, as was pointing out the waterfall. It was his mountain range somehow, and he had a proprietor's interest in it. We made a cigarette stop as we entered Haines Falls, a store where Jack knew they carried Rameses, his exotic, Pharaonic brand, and he dragged me to the souvenir counter and urged me to buy something.

'Buy your wife a balsam pillow or an Indian head scarf.'

'My wife and I split up two years ago.'

'Then you got no reason not to go to Europe. How about a cigarette box for yourself or a pinetree ashtray?'

I thought he was kidding, but he was insisting; a souvenir to seal our bargain, a trinket to affirm the working relationship. He fingered the dishes and glassware with their gaudy Catskill vistas, the thermometers framed in pine, toothbrush holders, inkstands, lampstands, photo albums, all with souvenir inscriptions burned into them, commemorating vacation time spent in this never-never land in the clouds. I finally agreed on a glass paperweight with an Indian chief in full war bonnet inside it, and Jack bought it. Forty-nine cents. The action was outrageously sentimental, the equivalent of his attitude toward that Algerian crone or the deceased brother, from whom, I would later come to know, Jack felt all his good luck had come. 'All my troubles happened after Eddie died,' Jack told me in the final summer of his life when he was learning how to die. Thus his replacement of the brother with Fogarty had a talismanic element to it. Talismanic paperweight, talismanic brother-substitute, talismanic memory of the Arthritic Witch of Fun. And here we were in old talismanic Haines Falls, the highest town in the Catskills, Jack said, and of course, of course, the proper place for him to stash the queenly consort of his fantasy life, the most beautiful girl I've ever known.

Jack said he once saw Charlie Northrup belly-bump a man with such force that the man did a back-flip over a table. Charlie was physical power, about six four and two forty. He had a wide, teeth-ridden smile and blond hair the color and straightness of straw, combed sideways like a well-groomed hick in a tintype. He was the first thing we saw when we entered Mike Brady's Top o' the Mountain House at Haines Falls. He was at the middle of the bar, standing in brogans with his ankles crossed, his sportshirt stained with sweat from armpit to armpit, drinking beer, talking with the bartender, and smiling. Charlie's smile went away when he met Jack eyeball to eyeball.

'Missed you the other night, Charlie,' Jack said.

'Yeah. I think you're gonna keep missing me, Jack.'

'That's a wrong attitude.'

'May be. But I'm stuck with it.'

'Don't be stupid, Charlie. You're not stupid.'

'That's right, Jack. I'm not stupid.'

Jack's face had all the expression of an ice cube, Charlie's full of overheated juices. He was telling Jack now about something I had no clue to; but from their tone there were confidences between them. It turned out Charlie was responsible for Jack being in the Masons. They had been young thieves together on Manhattan's West Side in 1914, running with The Gophers, a gang Owney Madden led until he went to jail for murder. They both wound up in the Bronx about 1925, with Charlie gone semi-straight as a numbers writer and Jack a feared figure in the New York underworld because of his insane gang tactics and his association with the powerful Arnold Rothstein. Jack had also opened a place he called The Bronx Theatrical Club, whose main theatrical element was Jack's presence as a performing psychopath. I say performing because I don't think Jack was psychopathic in its extreme sense. He was aberrated, yes, eccentric, but his deeds were willful and logical, part of a career pattern, even those that seemed most spontaneous and most horrendous. He was rising in the world, a celebrated hijacker, and Charlie was a working stiff with money problems. Charlie married Jimmy Biondo's sister and they vacationed in the Catskills. When times got very rough in New York, Charlie and some two-bit Jersey thieves bought a defunct brewery in Kingston and went into shoestring bootlegging. In the years after, Charlie opened his roadhouse and also became the biggest beer distributor in Greene and Ulster counties. He was tough, with a reputation for muscle if you didn't pay promptly for your goods. But he was different from Jack. Just a bootlegger. Just a businessman.

'I'm having a little meeting tomorrow night,' Jack told him, 'for those who couldn't make it to the last one.'

'I'm booked up.'

'Unbook, Charlie. It's at the Aratoga. Eight o'clock. And I'm all business, Charlie. All business.'

'I never knew you to be anything else, Jack.'

'Charlie, old brother, don't have me send for you.'

Jack left it there, turned his back on Charlie and walked down the bar and into the table area where only one table was occupied: by that beauty in a white linen suit and white pumps; and at the table with her a five-foot-five, one-eyed, waterheaded gnome. This was Murray (The Goose) Pucinski who'd worked for Jack for the past five years.

'Oh, God, Jack, oh, God where've you been?' was Kiki's greeting. She stood to hug him.

Jack squeezed her and gave her a quick kiss, then sat alongside her.

'She behaving herself, Goose?' Jack asked the waterhead.

Goose nodded.

'How could anybody misbehave up here?' Kiki said, looking me over. I was struck by the idea of misbehaving with her. That was the first logical thing to consider when you looked at Kiki. The second was the flawless quality of her face, even underneath all that professionally applied makeup; a dense rather than a delicate beauty, large, dark eyes, a mouth of soft, round promise, and an abundance of hair, not black as Alice had said, but auburn, a glorious Titian mop. Her expression, as we visually introduced ourselves, was one of anxious innocence. I use the phrase to describe a moral condition in fragments, anxious to be gone, but with a large segment still intact. The condition was visible in the eyes, which for all their sexual innuendo and expertise, for all their knowledge of how beauty rises in the world, were in awe, I suspect, of her rarefied situation: its prisonerlike quality, its dangers, its potential cruelties, and its exhilarating glimpses of evil. By eye contact alone, and this done in a few seconds, she conveyed to me precisely how uneasy she was with The Goose as her chaperon. A quick glance at him, then at me, then a lift of the eyebrows and twist of the pursed lips, was my clue that The Goose was a guardian of negative entertainment value.

'I wanna dance,' she said to Jack. 'Jackie, I'm dying to dance. Speed, play us something so we can dance.'

'It's too early to dance,' Jack said.

'No, it isn't' – and her entire body did a shimmy in anticipation. 'Come on, Joey, come on, puh-leeeze.'

'My fingers don't wake up till nine o'clock at night,' Fogarty said. 'Or after six beers.'

'Aw, Joey.'

Fogarty hadn't sat down yet. He looked at Jack who smiled and shrugged, and so Fogarty went to the piano on the elevated bandstand and, with what I'd call a semipro's know-how, snapped out a peppy version of 'Twelfth Street Rag.' Kiki was up with the first four bars, pulling Jack to his feet. Jack reluctantly took an armful of Kiki, then whisked her around in a very respectable foxtrot, dancing on the balls of his feet with sureness and lightness. Fogarty segued into the 'Charleston' and then the 'Black Bottom,' and Kiki split from Jack and broke into bouncily professional arm maneuvers and kicks, showing a bit of garter.

Interested as I was in Kiki's star and garter performance, it was Jack who took my attention. Was Legs Diamond really about to perform in public? He stood still when Kiki broke away, watched her for a step or two, then assessed his audience, especially the bar where Charlie Northrup and the barkeep were giving Jack full eyeball.

'C'mon, Jackie,' said Kiki, her breasts in fascinating upheaval. Jack looked at her and his feet began to move, left out, right kick, right back, left back, basic, guarded, small-dimensioned movements, and then 'C'mon, dance,' Kiki urged, and he gave up his consciousness of the crowd and then left out, right kick, right back, left back expanded, vitalized, and he was dancing, arms swinging, dancing, Jack Diamond, who seemed to do everything well, was dancing the Charleston and Black Bottom, dancing them perfectly, the way all America had always wanted to be able to dance them – energetically, controlled, as professionally graceful as his partner who had danced these dances for money in Broadway shows, who had danced them for Ziegfeld; and now she was dancing on the mountaintop with the king of the mountain, and they were king and queen of motion together, fluid with Fogarty's melody and beat.

And then above the music, above the pounding of Fogarty's foot, above the heavy breathing and shuffling of Jack and Kiki and above the concentration that we of the small audience were fixing on the performance, there came the laughter. You resisted acknowledging that it was laughter, for there was nothing funny going on in the room and so it must be something else, you said to yourself. But it grew in strength and strangeness, for once you did acknowledge that yes, that's laughter all right, and you said, somebody's laughing at them, and you remembered where you were and who you were with, you turned (and we all turned) and saw Charlie Northrup at the end of the bar, pounding the bar with the open palm of his right hand, laughing too hard. The bartender told him a joke, was my thought, but then Charlie lifted the palm and pointed to Jack and Kiki and spluttered to the barman and we all heard, because Fogarty had heard the laughing and stopped playing and so there was no music when Charlie said, 'Dancin' . . . the big man's dancin' . . . dancin' the Charleston on Sunday afternoon . . .' and then Jack stopped. And Kiki stopped six beats after the music had and said, 'What happened?'

Jack led her to the table and said, 'We're going to have a drink,' and moved her arm and made sure she sat down before he walked to the bar and spoke to Charlie Northrup in such a low voice that we couldn't hear. Charlie had stopped laughing by then and had taken a mouthful of beer while he listened to whatever it was Jack said. Then he swallowed the beer, and with a mirthless smile he retorted to Jack, who did not wait for the retort but was already walking back toward us.

'I'm trembling, brother,' Charlie called to him. 'Trembling.' He took another mouthful of beer, swished it around in his mouth, and spat it in a long arc after Jack. Not hitting him, or meaning to, but spitting as a child spits when he can think of no words as venomous as his saliva. Then he turned away from the direction of his spit, swallowed the last of his beer, and walked his great hulk out of the bar.

Holy Flying Christ, I said to myself when I understood Charlie's laughter and saw the arc of beer, for I understood much more than what we were all seeing. I was remembering what Jack's stylized terror could do to a man, remembering Joe Vignola, my client in the Hotsy Totsy case, a man visited not by Jack's vengeance but merely by the specter of it. I was remembering Joe on his cot in the Tombs, tracing with his eye a maze a prisoner before him had drawn on the wall, losing the way, tracing with his finger, but the finger too big, then finding a broom straw and tracing with that. And scratching his message above the maze with a spoon: *Joe Vignola never hurt nobody, but they put him in jail anyway.* Joe was dreaming of smuggling a gun in via his wife's brassiere, but he couldn't conceive of how to ask her to do such an embarrassing thing. And the district attorney was explaining almost daily to him, it's just routine, Joe, we hold 'em all the time in cases like this, an outrage, as you know, what happened, and we must have witnesses, must have them. Also a precautionary measure, as I'm sure you're aware, Joe, you're safer here. But I want to go home, Joe said, and the DA said, well, if you insist, but that's twenty thousand. Twenty thou? Twenty thou. I'm not guilty, you've got the wrong man. Oh no, said the DA, you're the right man. You're the one who saw Legs Diamond and his friends being naughty at the Hotsy Totsy. I'm not the only one, Joe said. Right, Joe, you are not the only one. We have other witnesses. We have the bartender. We have Billy Reagan, too, who is coming along nicely. An open-and-shut case, as they say.

Joe Vignola was in jail eight days when his wife got a phone call. Somebody, no name, told her: Look on such and such a page of the *Daily News* about what happened to Walter Rudolph. Walter Rudolph was the DA's corroborating witness, and two kids had found him lying off the Bordentown Turnpike near South Amboy, wearing his blue serge suit, his straw hat alongside him, eleven machine-gun slugs in him.

I was called into the case at this point. Vignola's lawyer was suddenly inaccessible to Vignola's wife, and an old show business friend of mine, Lew Miller, who produced Broadway shows and had patronized the Hotsy and gotten to know Joe Vignola well enough to go to bat for him, called me up and asked me to see what I could do for the poor bird.

Memory of my first interrogation of Joe:

Why did you tell the cops what you saw? Why did you identify photos of Jack Diamond and Charlie Filetti for the grand jury?

Because I wanted people to know I had nothing to do with it. Because I didn't want them to put me in jail for withholding evidence. And a cop slapped me twice.

But why, really, Joe? Did you want your name in the papers, too?

No, because Billy Reagan had talked and would be the main witness and because the cops had at least twenty-five other witnesses who were in the club, and they told the same story I did, the DA said.

But, Joe, knowing what we know about Jack Diamond and people like him, how could you do it? Was it time to die?

Not at all. Basically, I don't approve of murder, or Jack Diamond or Charlie Filetti either. I was brought up a Catholic and I know the value of honesty. I know what a citizen has to do in cases like this. Don't I hear it in church and on the radio and in the papers about being a good citizen? We can't let these bums take over America. If I don't stand up and fight, how can I expect the next guy to stand up? How could I look myself in the mirror?

But why, Joe? Lay off the bullshit and tell me for chrissake, why?

Why? Because it takes big balls. Because Jack Diamond was always cracking wise about the guineas and nobody is going to say that Joe Vignola is a yellow-bellied guinea. Joe Vignola is an Italian-descent American with big balls.

Big balls, Joe? Was that really it?

Right.

You dumb bastard.

I got in touch with the lawyer for Charlie Filetti, who they caught in Chicago and hit with murder one. They hadn't picked up Jack. I told the lawyer poor Joe was of no use to the prosecution because he would not be able to remember anything at the time, and that I wanted to be in touch with somebody in the Diamond gang who I could relay this message to at first hand so that Jack would also know what Joe was up to, which was not much. The lawyer put me on to Jimmy Biondo, who met me at the Silver Slipper on Forty-eighth Street one night. We talked briefly, as follows:

'You guarantee he's no pigeon?'

'I guarantee,' I said.

'How?'

'Every way but in writing.'

'The bum. The fuckin' bum.'

'He's all right. He won't talk. Lay off the telephone threats. He's got three kids and a nice wife. He's a nice Italian boy like yourself. He doesn't want to hurt anybody. He's an altar boy.'

'Funeral for altar boys,' said eloquent Jimmy.

'I guarantee you. What do you want from me? I'm his lawyer. He can't fire me. He hasn't even paid me yet.'

'Fuckin' . . .' said Jimmy.

'Easy does it. He won't talk.'

'Fuck . . .'

'I guarantee.'

'You guarantee?'

'I guarantee.'

'You better fuckin' guarantee.'

'I said I guarantee, and when I say I guarantee, I guarantee.'

'Fuckin' well better . . .'

'Right, Jimmy. You got my word. Joe won't talk.'

'Fuck.'

Joe told me Jack Diamond, disguised as a Boy Scout, came through the bars of his cell one night and stood alongside Joe's bunk as he slept. 'It's time to have your ears pierced,' Jack said to Joe, and he shoved the blade of his Scout knife into Joe's left ear. Joe's brain leaked out through the hole.

'Help me,' Joe yelled. 'My ear is leaking.' From the next cell somebody yelled, 'Shut up, you looney son of a bitch.'

But Joe didn't feel he was looney. He told the Bellevue alienist how it was when they wanted to know why he hid food under the bedclothes.

'That was for Legs Diamond. If he wants a bite to eat and I got nothing, that's trouble.'

'Did it occur to you that the food would rot and give off a stench?'

'Rotten, it doesn't really matter. It's the offer that counts.'

'Why did you cover your head with the blanket?'

'I wanted to be alone.'

'But you were alone.'

'I didn't want visitors.'

'The blanket kept them away?'

'No, I could see them through the blanket. But it was better than nothing.'

'Why did you hide the spoon?'

'So my visitors would have something to eat with.'

'Then why did you scratch at the concrete floor with it?'

'I wanted to dig a place to hide so the visitors couldn't find me.'

'How did you tear up your fingers?'

'When they took my spoon away.'

'You dug at the concrete with your fingers?'

'I knew it'd take a long time; the nails'd have to grow back before I could dig again.'

'Who visited you?'

'Diamond came every night. Herman Zuckman came, cut up the middle and half a dozen iron bars inside him, and wire wrapped around his stomach to keep the bars from falling out. He dripped muck and seaweed all over. "What did you do wrong, Herman?" I said to him.

'"Jew people have a tough life,"' he said.

'And I told him, "You think it's easy being Italian?"'

'Any other visitors?'

'Walter Rudolph came in to cheer me up and I saw daylight through his bullet holes.'

The night the dead fish leaped out of Herman's tuxedo Joe finally won his straitjacket.

The judge ordered the acquittal of Filetti after four days of trial, saying that the state had utterly failed to prove its case. Jack, still a fugitive, was never mentioned during the trial. Of the fifteen witnesses who testified, not one claimed to have seen Filetti actually shoot anybody. Joe Vignola, who was described as the state's most important witness, said he was dozing in another room when the shooting broke out and he saw nothing. His speech was incoherent most of the time.

Billy Reagan testified he was too drunk after drinking twenty shots of gin to remember what happened. Also, Tim Reagan's last words, originally said to have incriminated Diamond and Filetti, were not about them at all, a detective testified, but rather a violent string of curses.

Jack was a fugitive for eight months, and most of his gang, which was an amalgam of old-timers and remnants of Little Augie Orgen's Lower East Side Jews, drifted into other allegiances. The bond had not been strong to begin with. Jack took the gang over after he and Augie were both shot in a labor racketeering feud. Augie died, but you can't kill Legs Diamond.

Eddie Diamond died in January, 1930. Jack was still a fugitive when he met Kiki Roberts in April at the Club Abbey, and he immediately dropped Elaine Walsh. Half a dozen gangland murders were credited to his feud with Dutch Schultz during these months.

He saw the Jack Sharkey – Tommy Loughran fight at Yankee Stadium, as did Al Smith, David Belasco, John McGraw, and half the celebrities of New York. Jack couldn't miss such a show, even if he did have to raise a mustache and sit in an upper deck to avoid recognition. He bet on Loughran, like himself a Philadelphia mick; but Sharkey, the Boston sailor, won.

The crest of his life collapsed with the Hotsy shooting. All he'd been building to for most of a decade – his beer and booze operations, the labor racketeering he built with and inherited in part from Little Augie, his protection of the crooked bucketshops which bilked stock market suckers, an inheritance from Rothstein, his connections with the dope market, and, most ignominiously, his abstract aspiration to the leadership mantle that would somehow simulate Rothstein's – all this was Jack's life-sized sculpture, blown apart by gunpowder.

Dummy, you shoot people in your own club?

Jack got the word from Owney Madden, his old mentor from Gopher days, a quiet, behind-the-scenes fellow who, after doing his murder bit, came out of Sing Sing in 1923 and with a minimum of fanfare became the Duke of New York, the potentate of beer and political power in the city's underworld. Madden brought Jack the consensus sentiment from half a dozen underworld powerhouses: Go someplace else, Jack. Go someplace else and be crazy. For your own good, go. Or we'll have to kill you.

Jack's pistol had punctuated a decade and scribbled a finale to a segment of his own life. He had waged war on Schultz, Rothstein, and half a dozen lesser gang leaders in the Bronx, Jersey, and Manhattan, but he could not war against a consortium of gangs and he moved to the Catskills. I knew some of this, and I was certain Charlie Northrup knew much more, which is why Charlie's spitting beer at Jack and mocking him to his face did not seem, to say the least, to be in Charlie's own best interest.

After Charlie walked out of the Top o' the Mountain House Kiki said she was sick of the place and wanted to go someplace and have fun, and Jack-the-fun-seeker said okay, and we stopped at a hot dog stand, Kiki's choice, and sought out an aerial bowling alley which intrigued her and was a first for me. A genuine bowling ball was suspended on a long cable, and you stood aloof from the pins below and let the ball fly like a cannon shot. It then truly or falsely spun through the air and knocked over all the pins your luck and skill permitted. Kiki scored sixty-eight and almost brained the pinboy with a premature salvo, Jack got one fourteen and I won the day with one sixty-four. Jack was coming to respect my eye at least as much as he respected my legal acuity.

From bowling we went to miniature golf, where we played eighteen holes. Some holes you climbed stairs to and putted downhill. Kiki went first at one of those, and when you stood to the rear of her, as Jack and I did – Fogarty and The Goose were consuming soda pop elsewhere – you had total visibility of the girl's apparatus. She wore rolled silk stockings with frilly black garters about five inches above the knee, the sheerest pair of lace panties I'd theretofore seen, and areas of the most interesting flesh likely to be found on any mountain anywhere, and I also include the valleys.

I see her there yet. I see her also crossing and uncrossing her silkiness, hinting at secret reaches, dark arenas of mystery difficult to reach, full of jewels of improbable value, full of the *promise* of tawdriness, of illicitness, of furtiveness, of wickedness, with possibly blue rouge on the nipples, and arcane exotica revealed when she slips down the elastic waistband of those sheerest of sheers. They infected my imagination, those dark, those sheer, those elasticized arenas of that gorgeous girl's life.

I did not know that the infection would be prophetic of Kiki, prophetic of revelations of flesh, prophetic of panties. Nor did I know that this afternoon, with its sprinkles of rain interrupting our sport, would be the inspiration for Jack to initiate his organized shakedown of hot dog stands and miniature golf courses all over Greene and Ulster counties.

Kiki showed me a clipping once with a coincidence that made her believe in destiny. It was an item out of Winchell, which said,

'Dot and Dash is a mustache. Yaffle is an arrest. Long cut short is a sawed-off shotgun. White is pure alcohol. Simple Simon is a diamond . . .' It appeared the day before Kiki met Jack at a nightclub party, and she was just about to go into rehearsal for a new musical, *Simple Simon*.

I look back to those early days and see Kiki developing in the role of woman as sprite, woman as goddess, woman as imp. Her beauty and her radiance beyond beauty were charms she used on Jack, but used with such indifference that they became subtle, perhaps even secret, weapons. I cite the dance floor episode at the Top o' the Mountain House as as example, for she had small interest in whether it was Jack who danced with her or not. Her need was to exult in her profession, which had not been chosen casually, which reflected a self dancing alone beneath all the glitter of her Broadway life. 'I must practice my steps,' she said numerous times in my presence, and then with a small radio Jack had given her she would find suitable music and, oblivious of others, go into her dance, a tippy-tap-toe routine of cosmic simplicity. She was not a good dancer, just a dancer, just a chorus girl. This is not a pejorative reduction, for it is all but impossible for anyone to be as good a chorus girl as Kiki proved to be, proved it not only on stage – Ziegfeld said she was the purest example of sexual nonchalance he'd ever seen – but also in her photogenicity, her inability to utter a complex sentence, her candor with newspapermen, her willingness to trivialize, monumentalize, exalt, and exploit her love for Jack by selling her memoirs to the tabloids – twice – and herself to a burlesque circuit for the fulfillable professional years of her beauty and the tenacious years of Jack's public name. More abstractly she personified her calling in her walk, in her breathing, in the toss of her head, in her simultaneous eagerness and reluctance to please a lover, in her willingness to court wickedness without approving of it, and in her willingness to conform to the hallowed twentieth-century chorus-girl stereotype that Ziegfeld, George White, Nils T. Granlund, the Minskys, and so many more men, whose business was flesh, had incarnated, and which Walter Winchell, Ed Sullivan, Odd McIntyre, Damon

Runyon, Louis Sobol, and so many others, whose business was to muse and gossip on the ways of this incarnated flesh, had mythicized. And as surely as Jack loved pistols, rifles, machine guns – loved their noise, their weight, their force, the power they passed to him, their sleekness, their mechanical perfections, their oily surfaces as balm for his ulcerated gangster soul – so did he cherish the weaponistic charms of Kiki. And as the guns also became his trouble as well as his beloved, so became Kiki. She did not know such ambivalence was possible when she met Jack, but her time alone with The Goose on the mountaintop was the beginning of her wisdom, painful wisdom which love alone could relieve.

A quick summer storm blew up and it started to rain as Fogarty drove Kiki, Jack, and me back to Haines Falls after the golf. There was talk of dinner, which I declined, explaining I had to get back to Albany. But no, no, Jack wouldn't hear of my leaving. Wasn't I done out of a champagne lunch by the canary scene? We went to the Top o' the Mountain House to freshen up before we ate, and Jack gave me the room The Goose had been using, next to Kiki's. Jack joined Kiki in her room for what I presumed was a little mattress action, and I pursued a catnap. But the walls were thin and I was treated instead to a memorably candid conversation:

'I'm going back to New York,' Kiki said.

'You don't mean it,' Jack said.

'I don't care what you do. I'm not staying in this prison with that goon. He never says a word.'

'He's not good at talking. He's good at other things. Like you.'

'I hate having a bodyguard.'

'But your body deserves guarding.'

'It deserves more than that.'

'You're very irritable tonight.'

'You're damn right I am.'

'You've got a right to be, but don't swear. It's not ladylike.'

'You're not so particular in bed about ladylike.'

'We're not in bed now.'

'Well, I don't know why we're not. I don't see you for two days and you show up with a stranger and don't even try to be alone with me.'

'You want a bed, do you? What do you want to put in it?'

'How's this? How does it look?'

'Looks like it's worth putting money into.'

'I don't want money in it.'

'Then I'll have to think of something else.'

'I love to kiss your scars,' Kiki said after a while.

'Maybe you'll kiss them all away,' Jack said.

'I wouldn't want to do that. I love you the way you are.'

'And you're the most perfect thing I've ever seen. I deserve you. And you don't have any scars.'

'I'm getting one.'

'Where?'

'Inside. You cut me and let me bleed, and then I heal and you leave me to go back to your wife.'

'Someday I'll marry you.'

'Marry me now, Jackie.'

'It's complicated. I can't leave her. She's in a bad way lately, depressed, sick.'

'She goes to the movies. She's old and fat.'

'I've got a lot of money in her name.'

'She could run off with it, wipe you out.'

'Where could she run I couldn't find her?'

'You trust her, but you don't trust me alone.'

'She's never alone.'

'What is she to you? What can she give you I can't?'

'I don't know. She likes animals.'

'I like animals.'

'No, you don't. You never had a pet in your life.'

'But I like them. I'll get a pet. I'll get a cat. Then will you marry me?'

'Later I'll marry you.'

'Am I your real lay?'

'More than that.'

'Not much more.'

'Don't be stupid. I could lay half the town if I wanted to – Catskill, Albany, New York, any town. Unlimited what I could lay. Unlimited.'

'I want a set of those Chinese balls. The metal ones.'

'Where'd you hear about those?'

'I get around. I get left alone a lot now, but I didn't always.'

'What would you do with them?'

'What everybody does. Wear them. Then when nobody's around to take care of me and I get all hot and bothered, I'd just squeeze them and they'd make me feel good. I want them.'

'Will you settle for an Irish set?'

'Can I keep them with me?'

'I'll see they don't get out of range.'

'Well, see to it then.'

'Everything was still incredible with me and Jack back then,' Kiki said to me much later, remembering the sweet time. 'It was thrilling just to see him from a new angle, his back, or his stomach, any part of his bare skin. He had gouges and scars from knife fights when he was a kid, and where he'd been shot and kicked and beaten with clubs and boards and pipes. I got sad up on the mountain one night looking at them all. But he said they didn't hurt him anymore, and the more I looked at them and touched them, the more they made his body special, the way his head was special. It wasn't an all white and smooth and fatty body like some I've seen but the body of a man who'd gone through a whole lot of hell. There was a long red scar on his stomach just above his belly button, where he'd almost died from a cut in a knife fight over a girl when he was fifteen. I ran my tongue over it and it felt hot. I could almost taste how much it hurt when he'd got it and what it meant now. To me it meant he was alive, that he didn't die easy. Some people could cut their little toe and give up and bleed to death. Jack never gave up, not his body, not anything.'

*   *   *

Well, we all did have dinner on the mountain, and then I insisted on leaving. 'It's been a special day,' I told Jack, 'but an odd one.'

'What's so odd about it?'

'Well, how about buying a paperweight for starters?'

'Seems like an ordinary day to me,' he said. I assumed he was kidding. But then he said, 'Come to dinner next week. I'll have Alice cook up another roast. I'll call you during the week to set it up. And think about Europe.'

So I said I would and turned to Kiki, whom I'd spoken about forty words to all day. But I'd smiled her into my goodwill and stared her into my memory indelibly, and I said, 'Maybe I'll see you again, too,' and before she could speak Jack said, 'Oh you'll see her all right. She'll be around.'

'I'll be around he says,' Kiki said to me in a smart-ass tone, like Alice's whippy retort had been earlier in the day. Then she took my hand, a sensuous moment.

Everything seemed quite real as I stood there, but I knew when I got back to Albany the day would seem to have been invented by a mind with a faulty gyroscope. It had the quality of a daydream after eight whiskeys. Even the car I was to ride down in – Jack's second buggy, a snazzy, wire-wheeled, cream-colored Packard roadster The Goose was using to chauffeur Kiki around the mountains – had an unreal resonance.

I know the why of this, but I know it only now as I write these words. It took me forty-three years to make the connection between Jack and Gatsby. It should have been quicker, for he told me he met Fitzgerald on a transatlantic voyage in 1926, on the dope-buying trip that got him into federal trouble. We never talked specifically about Gatsby, only about Fitzgerald, who, Jack said, was like two people, a condescending young drunk the first time they met, an apologetic, decent man the second time. The roadster was long and bright and with double windshields, and exterior toolbox, and a tan leather interior, the tan a substitute, for Gatsby's interior was 'a sort of green leather conservatory.' But otherwise it was a facsimile of the Gatsby machine, and of that I'm as certain as you can be in a case like this. Jack probably read *Gatsby* for the same reason he read every newspaper story and book and saw every movie about gangland. I know he saw Von Sternberg's *Underworld* twice; we did talk about that. It was one way of keeping tabs on his profession, not pretension to culture. He mocked Waxey Gordon to me once for lining his walls with morocco-bound sets of Emerson and Dickens. 'They're just another kind of wallpaper to the bum,' Jack said.

I accept Jack's Gatsby connection because he knew Edward Fuller, Fitzgerald's neighbor on Long Island who was the inspiration for Gatsby. Fuller and Rothstein were thick in stocks, bonds, and bucketshops when Jack was bodyguarding Rothstein. And, of course, Fitzgerald painted a grotesque, comic picture of Rothstein himself in *Gatsby*, wearing human molar cuff buttons and spouting a thick Jewish accent, another reason Jack would have read the book.

I rode with The Goose in Jack's roadster and tried to make a little conversation.

'You known Jack long?'

'Yeah,' said Murray, and then nothing for about three miles.

'Where'd you meet him?'

'Th'army,' said Murray, not spending two words where one would do.

'You've been working with him since then?'

'No, I did time. Jack, too.'

'Ah.'

'I got nine kids.'

Murray looked at me when he said this, and I guess I paused long enough before I said, 'Have you?' to provoke him.

'You don't believe me?'

'Sure I believe you. Why shouldn't I?'

'People don't believe I got nine kids.'

'If you say it, I believe it. That's a lot of kids. Nobody lies about things like that.'

'I don't see them. Once a year. Maybe, maybe not. But I send 'em plenty.'

'Uh-huh.'

'They don't know what I do for a living.'

William Kennedy

'Oh?'

Then we had another mile or so of silence, except for the thunder and lightning and the heavy rain, which kept Murray creeping slowly along the snaky road down the mountain. I judged him to be about forty-five, but he was hard to read. He might've seemed older because of the menace he transmitted, even when he talked about his kids. His mouth curled down into a snarleyow smile, his lone eye like a flat spring, tightly coiled, ready to dilate instantly into violent glare. He was obviously the pro killer in the gang, which I deduced as soon as I saw him. Oxie may have had some deadly innings in his career, but he looked more like a strongarm who would beat you to death by mistake. Murray's clothes were a shade too small for him, giving him a puffy, spaghetti-filled look. I thought I detected tomato sauce stains on his coat and pants and even his eyepatch. I choose to believe he was merely a slob rather than inefficient enough to walk around with bloodstains from his last victim. I doubt Jack would have approved of that sort of coarseness.

'You workin' for Jack now?' Murray asked me.

'Tentatively,' I said, wondering whether he understood the word, so I added, 'for the time being I guess I am.'

'Jack is a pisser.'

'Is he?'

'He's crazy.'

'Is that so?'

'That's why I work for him. You never know what'll happen next.'

'That's a good reason.'

'He was crazy in the Army. I think he was always crazy.'

'Some of us are.'

'I said to myself after he done what he done to me, this is a crazy guy you got to watch out for because he does crazy stuff.'

'What did he do to you?'

'What did he do to me? What did he do to me?'

'Right.'

'I was in the stockade at Fort Jay for raping a colonel's wife, a

556

bum rap. I only did her a favor after she caught me in the house and I rapped her one and she fell down. Her dress goes up and she says, "I suppose you're gonna strip and rape me," and I hadn't figured on it, but you take what comes. So I'm in for that, plus burglary and kickin' an MP when Jack comes in to wait for his court-martial.

'"Whatcha in for?" I asked him.

'"Desertion and carrying a pistol."

'"That's heavy duty."

'"I figure I'll do a little time," he said. "They want my ass."

'"Likewise," I said and told him my story.

'"What'd you do before you got in?" he asks me and I tell him. "I was a burglar." He got a kick out of that because he done a bit for the same thing when he was a kid. So we talk and Jack gets a pint of whiskey from the corporal who made bedcheck. I don't drink that shit, so Jack asks me if I wanna drink some rain instead. It's raining out just like now, and Jack puts a cup out the window. Took about five minutes to fill it up part way, and by that time Jack's whiskey is most gone and he gets the cup of rain and gives it to me.

'"I don't want no rain," I says to him. "It's dirty."

'"Who says it's dirty?"

'"Everybody says."

'"They're wrong," he says. "Best water there is."

'"You drink it," I says, "I don't want no part of any dirty, shitty rain."

'"Goddamn it, I told you rain wasn't dirty. You think I'd drink rain if it was dirty?" And he takes a drink of it.

'"Anybody who'd drink rain'd shit in church," I says to him.

'"Did you say shit in church?"

'"Shit in church and then kick it out in the aisle."

'"That's a goddamn lie. I'd never shit in church."

'"If you'd drink rain, you'd shit in church all right."

'"Not me. I'd never shit in church. You hear that, goddamn it? Never!"

'"All them rain drinkers. They all shit in church."

' "Not me, no sir. Why do you say that?"

' "I never knew an Irishman wouldn't shit in church if he thought he could get away with it."

' "Irishmen don't shit in church. I don't believe that."

' "I seen four Irishmen at the same time, all taking a shit in church."

' "Polacks shit in church."

' "I once seen an Irishman shit right in the holy water fountain."

' "That's a goddamn lie."

' "Then I seen two Irishmen takin' shits in the confessional boxes and about a dozen more takin' shits up on the altar all at once. I seen one Irishman shit during a funeral. Irishmen don't know no better."

'I was layin' on my cot while this was going on. Then Jack got up and punched me in the right eye so hard I lost the sight of it. Jesus, that was a crazy thing to do. I didn't even see it comin'. I had to kick him all over the room, broke ribs and stuff. The guards pulled me off him. I woulda killed him if I knew the eye was gone, but I didn't know it then. When I saw him a week later he got down on his knees and asked me to forgive him what he done. I said, "Fuck you, Jack," and left him on his knees. But we shook hands before I left and I told him "Okay, don't worry about it." But I was still sore about it. I done six years because the MP I kicked died, and when I come out I looked Jack up because I figure he owes me a job. He thought he did a tough thing about the eye, but shit, once you get used to one eye it's just as good as two. And workin' for Jack, you get to do everything you got to do, so I got no complaints.'

We were about halfway down the mountain when Murray hit the brakes, but not soon enough, and we skidded into a rock slide and smashed into a boulder that must've just landed because other little rocks kept bouncing off the car. Both of us hit the windshield, and I got a hell of a bump and a four-day headache out of it. Murray's forehead was cut, a horizontal gash like a split seam.

'We better haul ass before another one falls on top of us,' Murray said, a thought I hadn't had yet since I was preoccupied with my pain. He tried backing up, but the car made a weird noise and was hard to move. He got out in the rain and so I got out after him. There was about one foot between me and about a four-hundred-foot drop, so I got carefully back inside and out Murray's door. He was pulling on the front left fender, which was smashed and rubbing against the wheel. Murray was a small man but a strong one, for the fender came almost straight at this tug. He cut his right hand on the edge of it, and when I offered him my pocket handkerchief, he shook his head and scooped up a handful of earth and grass and patted it on his forehead and then globbed a wad into his sliced right palm.

'Get in,' he said, his face and hand smeared and dripping with bloody mud.

'I'll drive,' I told him.

'No, I'll handle it.'

'You're in no shape to drive.'

'This is not your car, mister,' he said in a tone that was unarguably the last word.

'All right, then, back up and turn around. I'll direct you. You're damn near over the edge right there, and it's one hell of a long way down.'

It was dark now and I was wet to the underwear, standing in the middle of desolation, maybe about to be buried in a landslide, giving traffic directions to a bleeding, one-eyed psychopath who was, with one hand, trying to drive a mythic vehicle backwards up an enchanted mountain.

I'd come a long way from the K. of C. library.

Johnny Raw,
Jack Gentleman

Jack came to Albany to see me four days after my time on the mountain. He was full of Europe and its glories, the spas at Bad Homburg and Wiesbaden, the roulette and baccarat in the casinos where croupiers spoke six languages, the eloquent slenderness of the Parisian whore. He came to my office with Fogarty; he was in town on other business we didn't discuss but which I presume was beer supply for his expanding clientele. He handed me five hundred cash as my initial retainer.

'What do I do for this?'

'Buy a ticket to Europe.'

'Jack, I've got no good reason to go to Europe.'

'You owe it to your body,' he said. 'All that great wine and great food.'

'All right, maybe,' I said. But what, really, did I need with this kind of action? Where was the profit? Jack merely said he'd be in touch within the week and that was that.

Then I got a weird call at three the next morning from him, saying he'd decided to go to New York immediately instead of next week and leave for Europe in the afternoon if he got the booking, and was I ready, did I live in control of the quick decision or was I going to take a week to think it over? It meant being in Manhattan in about nine or ten hours and committing myself to the booking and turning off my practice. He kept saying, 'Well? Well? What do you think?' And so I said, 'All right, yes,' against all sane judgment, and he said, 'You're a winner, Marcus,' and I rolled over and went back for two more hours. Then I closed off my Albany life with four phone calls and caught the ten-thirty train to New York.

A fox terrier leaped overboard, an apparent suicide, the day the news broke aboard ship that Charlie Northrup's bloodstained Buick was found in a Sixty-first Street garage near the Brooklyn Army Base. The garage was owned by Vannie Higgins, a pal of Jack's and the crown prince of Long Island rum-runners. Oxie and a Brooklyn couple, the wife a pal of Alice's, were arrested in their apartment with an arsenal: tear-gas grenades, ammo, flares, fountain-pen pistols, bulletproof vests, and enough explosives to blow up a city block. Brooklyn war with Capone, said the papers. Oxie said only that he was sleeping on Jack's porch at Acra when two men he wouldn't identify woke him and offered him fifty bucks to take the Buick to New York and dump it. Cops saw him and the other man near a Fifty-eighth Street pier acting suspiciously, and Oxie admitted that the blocks in the Buick were to be used to run it over the stringpiece.

We were two days out of New York on the *Belgenland*, bound for Plymouth and Brussels, and suddenly our foursome – Jack, Count Duschene, Classy Willie Green, and myself – was the center of all attention. Jack was traveling under the name of John Nolan, a name of notable nautical import, and he got away with it until the radio brought news bulletins from the New York City police commissioner, a feisty old Irishman named Devane, that Jack was fleeing from a foul murder and was now on the high seas, bound for England to buy dope.

He wasn't wanted by the police, but Devane felt it his duty to alert the nations of Europe that a fiend was approaching. The Northrup car was the subject of daily bulletins in the ship's newspaper, and as the mystery of what happened to Charlie intensified, so did Jack's celebrity. Passengers snapped his picture, asked for his autograph, assured him they didn't believe such a nice person as he was would have anything to do with such terrible goings on.

The fox terrier: He appeared as I stood on the sports deck near the rail, while Jack was shooting skeet. I saw nothing chasing the dog, which came at me in a blur of brown and white, but there must have been something, for he was panicky or perhaps suddenly maddened. He took a corner at high speed, dead-ended into a bulkhead, turned around, and leaped through the rail, flailing like a crazy-legged circus clown falling off a tightrope into a net. I saw him surface once, go into a wave, bob up again, and then vanish. I doubt anyone else saw it.

A man finally came toward me at a brisk pace and asked if I'd seen his dog, and I said, yes, I'd just seen it leap overboard.

'Leap overboard?' the man said, stunned by the concept.

'Yes. He leaped.'

'He wasn't thrown?'

'Nobody threw him, I can tell you that. He jumped.'

'A dog wouldn't leap overboard like that.'

He looked at me, beginning to believe I'd killed his dog. I assured him I'd never seen such a thing either, but that it was true, and just then he looked past me and said, 'That's Legs Diamond,' the dog instantly forgotten, the man already turning to someone to pass along his discovery. In a matter of minutes a dozen people were watching Jack shoot. He had been reloading during my encounter and saw the crowd before he put the shotgun again to his shoulder. He fired, missed, fired, missed. The crowd tittered, but he looked at them and silenced the titters. He fired again, missed again, fired again, missed again, and thrust the gun angrily at the man in charge of lofting the clay pigeons. Then he and I went quickly down to the parlor where Classy Willie and The Count, a dapper pair, were jointly relieving four other passengers of their vacation money in a poker game. I knew neither The Count nor Willie before I boarded the ship with Jack, but it turned out that The Count was Jack's international associate, an expert bottom dealer who spoke French, German, and Spanish and did not lose his head in the presence of too many forks, and that Classy Willie was a card thief, specializing in ocean liners, who had been hired by Jimmy Biondo to represent him in the dope deal. Willie had a certain suavity behind his pencil-line mustache, but he was also known for his erratic violence on behalf of his employer.

I understood these relationships only much later. At this point in the trip I assumed both men worked for Jack.

I asked Jack about Oxie and the car and he said, 'I take no responsibility for mugs like him once they're out of my sight.'

'Goddamn it, Jack, you've got me involved in the biggest murder case in upstate New York in Christ knows how long and you give me this evasive routine?'

'Who said you're involved? I'm not even involved.'

'You're involved. On the radio is involved.'

'Tomorrow there'll be an earthquake in Peru and they'll try to stick me with it.'

'Bullshit.'

'Shove your bullshit up your ass,' he said and walked away.

But he came back an hour later and sat down beside me in a deckchair, where I was brooding on my stupidity and reading Ernest Dimnet on how to think better, and he said, 'How's things now?'

'I'm still involved.'

'You worry a lot, Marcus. That's a bad sign. Gets you into trouble.'

'I'm in trouble now because I didn't worry enough.'

'Listen, you got nothing to be afraid of. Nobody's after your ass, nobody wants to put you on the spot. I never knew a fucking lawyer yet couldn't talk his way out of a sandstorm. You'll do all right if you don't lose your head.'

'There was blood in that car, and Oxie was with it. And Oxie is your man.'

'Somebody could've had a nosebleed. For chrissake, don't fuck me AROUND!' And he walked away from me again.

We didn't speak a direct word to each other, apart from pass the salt, for two days. My plan was to get off at Plymouth and get the next boat home. I observed him from a distance, seeing people go out of their way for a look at him playing cards in his shirtsleeves. I saw a blond librarian ask him to dance and begin a thing with him. He was a bootlegger and, as such, had celebrity status, plus permission from the social order to kill, maim, and befoul the legal system, for wasn't he performing a social mission for the masses? The system would stay healthy by having life both ways: first, relishing Jack's achievement while it served a function, then slavering sensually when his head, no longer necessary, rolled. This insight softened my hard line on Northrup. Maybe it was all a bootleggers' feud, which somehow made the consequent death okay. Let others assess the moral obliquity in this.

Jack went through a tango with the librarian, who was from Minneapolis, a fetchingly rinsed-out blonde who wore school-marmish tweed suits with low-cut blouses beneath. You saw the blouses only when she peeled off the top covering as the dancing went on and on. Jack invited her to eat with us when he started up with her, and he saw to it that none of us lingered over coffee.

Then one day at dinner she wasn't there. Her empty chair went unremarked upon until Jack himself gestured toward it and said, 'She wanted my autograph on her briefs,' which I thought was a quaint euphemism for Jack.

Everyone laughed at the absurdity, even me.

'I gave her a bullet,' Jack said, and I fell into uncertainty until he added, 'She says to me, "It's the right shape but the wrong size." And I told her, "Use it sideways."'

We were swilling duck à l'orange when the librarian came up to the table with her jacket off and put her face inches away from Jack's.

'You turn women into swine,' she said.

Jack nodded and bit the duck.

The morning news was that the search for Charlie Northrup had turned into one of the biggest manhunts in New York State history. He was presumed dead, but where? On top of this came a cable from Jimmy Biondo to Classy Willie, precipitating an impromptu meeting of our small quartet in Jack's cabin. Willie arrived, visibly equipped with a pistol for the first time since we boarded ship.

Sensing tension, I got up to leave. But Jack said stick around, and so I did.

'Jimmy wants to call off the deal,' Willie said to Jack, the first time a deal had been mentioned on the trip.

'Is that so?'

Willie handed the cable to Jack, who read it to us. 'Tell our friend we can't stay with him,' it said.

'I wonder what he's worried about?' Jack said.

Classy Willie didn't say anything.

'Do you know what he means, Willie?'

'He's talking about the money. Wants me to take it back to him.'

'Our money?'

'Jimmy figures it's his money until we make the buy.'

'Until I make the buy,' Jack said.

'You know what I mean, Jack.'

'No, Willie, I can't say that I do. You're a card thief. I never knew a card thief who could talk straight.'

'Jimmy must figure you're too hot. The radio says they won't let you into England.'

'I wasn't going to England.'

'You know what I'm talking about, Jack.'

'I suppose I do, Willie. I suppose I do.' Jack put on his weary tone of voice. 'But I'll tell you the truth, Willie, I'm not even thinking about money. What I'm thinking about is jewels.'

'What jewels?'

'I got eighty grand worth and I don't know how to get them off the boat. They'll go through my luggage with a microscope.'

'Let your friend Marcus carry them,' Willie said. 'He's legitimate.'

'Not interested, thank you,' I said.

'That's not a bad idea, Marcus,' Jack said.

'It's a terrible idea, Jack. I want no part of hot merchandise. No part whatever. Not my line of work.'

'If Marcus says no, it's no,' Jack said. 'We'll have to find another way.'

I believe Jack already knew what he was going to do with the jewels and was merely testing me for a reaction. My reaction was so instantaneous he didn't even press it a second time. I was more attuned to Classy Willie's problem. If Biondo ever had any sense at all, he wouldn't have sent a dapper thief, a man long known as the Beau Brummell of Forty-eighth Street, to play watchdog to a man as devious as Jack.

'Jimmy wants me to get off at England and come back home with the cash,' Willie said. 'That was the plan if there was a hitch. He said he talked to you about it.'

'I do remember something like that,' Jack said. 'But how do I know you won't take the cash and hop a boat for the Fiji Islands? I already told you I don't trust card thieves, Willie. I couldn't jeopardize Jimmy's money that way. No. We'll get to Germany and make the deal, and we'll all be a little fatter when we get home. Am I right, Count?'

'The beer is good in Germany,' said The Count, a diplomat. 'You don't have to needle it.'

The façade of the deal was that Jack was to buy booze and wines, and ship them from Bremen to somewhere off Long Island. That's what I was told, by Jack. But Devane was right that Jack was after dope – heroin, which Jack had been buying in Germany since '26 when Rothstein was financing the imports. A federal charge Jack had been dodging successfully since then had come with the bustup of an elaborate smuggling scheme in which Jack was a key figure. The present destination was Frankfurt and, after the deal was wrapped up, a week's vacation in Paris. I remember when we got back to the States that a federal narcotics nabob told the press that Jack's dope smuggling made his booze and beer business look like penny-candy stuff. But people didn't pay attention to such official guff. Their image of Jack was fixed. He was a bootlegger. Locking him into dope was only a source of confusion.

I have vivid recollections of Jack and the press meeting in the hallways of courthouses, at piers and railroad stations in New

William Kennedy

York, Philadelphia, Albany, Catskill. I remember the aggression the newsmen always showed, persistent in their need to embarrass him with gross questions, but persistent also in their need to show him affection, to laugh harder than necessary at his *bons mots*, to draw ambivalent pleasure from his presence – a man they loved to punish, a man they punished with an odd kind of love. When the British newsmen invaded the *Belgenland* on our arrival in Plymouth, some thirty reporters and cameramen pushed their way into Jack's stateroom to be greeted by the presence himself, clad in black slippers, sky-blue silk pajamas with a white chalk stripe, a navy-blue silk robe, and a Rameses between index and middle fingers. The British behaved no differently from their American brethren, except that Jack's being a foreigner diminished their need to insult him for the sake of the homeland. But their self-righteousness shone through in their questions: Why does America tolerate gangsters? How long have you been a gangster? Was Mr Charles Northrup murdered at your order? Do you think gangsterism will end when Prohibition ends? How many men have you killed in your life? What about Capone and your Brooklyn arsenal?

Jack treated them like children, laughing at their requests for a laundry list of his victims. 'First off, boys, I'm not a gangster, only a bootlegger. There are no gangsters in America. Too easy to get rich other ways. I'm just a civilized citizen. Not a dese, dem, and dose guy. Just a man of the people, trying to make a dollar. Over here getting the cure. Got some stomach trouble and I was advised to go to Vichy and Wiesbaden and take the waters. Brooklyn arsenal? I own nothing in Brooklyn. Capone used to work for me years ago, driving a truck, but I haven't seen him in years. That feud is a lot of nonsense. I get along with people. I'm a legitimate citizen. You newspaper guys scream at the cops to pick me up, and they hold me a few days and find out I'm clean and let me go. I'm not claiming you treat me wrong, but I never see anybody write big headlines when they tell me the charge don't stick. I'm sick of headlines, boys. I came to Europe to get away from it all for a while. Leave that hubbub behind. Make a kind

570

of grand tour on my own, take the waters and cure what ails me. You can understand that, can't you, fellows?'

Sure they could.

Jack's fame at this point was staggering. About four hundred Englishmen had come to the pier by six-thirty just to get a glimpse of him. The press of the whole Western world was following our transatlantic voyage, front-paging it with an intensity not quite up to what they did for Byrd, Peary, and other world travelers, but I'll bet with more reader interest. One English paper was so anxious for a story that it invented a phone interview with Jack two days before our boat reached an English pier. 'I'm here in London on a secret mission,' they quoted him as saying.

So the newsmen, installing Jack in the same hierarchy where they placed royalty, heroes, and movie stars, created him anew as they enshrined him. They invented a version of him with each story they wrote, added to his evil luster by imagining crimes for him to commit, embellishing his history, humanizing him, defining him through their own fantasies and projections. This voyage had the effect of taking Jack Diamond away from himself, of making him a product of the collective imagination. Jack had imagined his fame all his life and now it was imagining him. A year hence he would be saying that 'publicity helps the punk' to another set of newsmen, aware how pernicious a commodity it could be. But now he was an addict, a grotesquely needy man, parched for glory, famished for public love, dying for the chance at last to be everybody's wicked pet.

He called the stateroom press conference to a halt after fifteen minutes and said he had to get dressed. The newsmen waited and he joined them on deck, clad now in his blue pinstriped suit, his wide-brimmed white felt hat, his seven-and-a-half-B black wingtips, his purple tie, and his Knight Templar pin in his lapel.

'Hello, boys,' he said, 'what else do you want from me?'

They talked for another quarter hour and asked, among other things, about that lapel pin; and a story goes with that.

When we talked after the press left, Jack told me that Charlie Northrup was why he was in the Masons. Back in the Bronx in the mid-twenties Jack was playing cards in the back room of his garish Theatrical Club, orange and black decor, and Charlie was sitting in. For no reason he could remember, Jack wondered out loud what a jack was, the picture card. Charlie told him the symbolic meaning of a knave among kings and queens, and Jack liked the whole idea.

Charlie talked about the Masons and their symbols, and it was like the dawn of a new era for Jack. He pumped Charlie for more, then talked him into proposing him as a candidate in the order. He went through in a whoosh and obviously with attention to all the arcane mumbo jumbo he had to memorize. The Masonic books I inherited from him were well marked and annotated in the margins, in his handwriting.

Alongside one section on an old Templar rite of initiation, a Christly pilgrimage through red, blue, black, and then the final white veils of the temple, Jack had noted: 'Good stuff. Sounds like one of my dreams.'

Just after meeting the British press Jack complained to me of itching hands, small red dots which gave up a clear fluid when squeezed. The broken pustules then burned like dots of acid. A passenger shot off three of his toes at skeet and blamed Jack for hexing the weapon. Then the Minneapolis librarian cut her wrists, but chose against death and summoned help. Her condition became common knowledge on the ship.

I saw Jack on deck alone after that, toying with a rosary, the first time I knew he carried one. He was not praying – only staring at it, strung like webbing through his fingers, as if it were a strange, incomprehensible object.

The night we were steaming toward Plymouth, a steward came to Jack's room with a message from the captain that the British authorities had definitely proclaimed Jack *persona non grata*. Stay out, you bum. The message jolted him, for it suddenly put our destination in jeopardy. What would Belgium do? And Germany?

Jack came to my stateroom and said he wanted to go up on deck and talk, that he didn't trust the walls. So we walked in the sea-sweetened night along the main deck where a few night walkers took the air, most memorably a rheumatic old aristocratic woman with a belief in the curative power of voyaging that was so religious she left her deckchair only during storms and meals, and to sleep and, I presume, to pee. She chewed tobacco and had a small pewter spittoon alongside her chair which she would pick up and spit her little bloody gobs into in a most feminine manner, that is, through taut, narrow lips.

She was the only witness to my conversation with Jack, and her presence and periodic spitting were the only intrusions on our conversation, apart from the splash of the sea, as we talked and walked, up and then back, in our desolated section of deck. We talked only of Jack's rejection by England until he decided to get to the point.

'Marcus, I want you to do me a favor.'

'A legal one?'

'No.'

'I thought as much. The jewels. I told you I want no part of it, Jack.'

'Listen to me. This is a lot of money. Do you believe in money?'

'I do.'

'So do I.'

'But I don't want to go to jail to get it.'

'How many lawyers you know ever went to jail?'

'A few, and you'd have a point if we were back in Albany.'

'I told you a long time ago you were a thief in your heart.'

'No, we're still not talking about thievery.'

'Right. This is just a proposition. You don't have to take it.'

Jack then took from his inside coat pocket a long slender box, and we paused under one of the wall lights so I could view its contents: an array of gems, rings, and necklaces. Some jewel thief had stolen them, fenced them, and they'd found their way to Jack, the internationalist, who would refence them in Europe. I knew he hadn't stolen them. He wasn't above such activity, just afield of it. No longer a burglar. He'd failed at that as a teen-ager and graduated to the activity that conformed to his talent, which was not stealth but menace.

'They don't take up much space,' Jack said, and I nodded and made no answer.

'I planned to get rid of them in Brussels, but they're too hot to carry. I mean look at that' – and he held up a ruby for me to admire. 'It's kind of famous, I'm told, and where it came from is even more famous.'

'I don't think I'm interested.'

'My suitcase has special bindings for this stuff. You could get it off the boat and through customs. But not me, not now.'

I toyed with it. NOTED UPSTATE LAWYER CAUGHT WITH MRS ASTOR'S FAVORITE RUBY, Or was it Mrs Carnegie's? Or that tobacco-chewing lady aristocrat behind us, whoever she might be?

'If you don't handle them, I dump them. Now.'

'Dump them?'

'Overboard.'

'Christ, why do that? Why not hide them in a chandelier and come back later for them? Isn't that how it's done?'

'Fuck 'em,' Jack said. 'I don't want anything to do with this goddamn boat again once I get off it. It's a jinx.'

'A jinx? You don't really believe in jinxes.'

'I'd be fucking well dead if I didn't. Are you game? Yes or no.'

'No.'

He walked to the railing and I trailed him, expecting the next ploy in the act. A final appeal to my greed.

'You wanna watch?' he said, and so I moved alongside him in time to see him tip the box and see, yes, jewels falling, a few, and disappearing in shadow long before they hit the water. He tipped the box further and a few more plummeted toward the deep, then he shook it empty, looked at me, and, while looking, let the box flutter toward the water. It flipped a few times, made a silent plop we could see because it was white, and was then glommed by the blackness.

*   *   *

Jack was in shirtsleeves, sitting alone at the card table where Classy Willie fleeced the suckers, when I came up for brunch one day. I ate and then watched Jack playing solitaire and losing. I sat across from him and said, 'I was planning to get off this tub and go home, but I think I'll stay on for the full treatment.'

'Good. What changed your mind?'

'I don't know. Maybe the jewels. But I think I decided to trust you. Is that a mistake?'

'Trust me with anything but women and money.'

'I also want a straight answer on Charlie Northrup. Is that asking too much?'

Jack mused, then with high seriousness said, 'I think he's dead. But I'm not sure. If he's dead, it wasn't murder. That I am sure of.'

'That's straight?'

'That's as straight as I can say it.'

'Then I guess I have to believe it. Deal the cards.'

He picked them up and shuffled. 'Blackjack,' he said and, after burying a card, dealt us both a hand. I had eighteen. He had twenty, which he showed me before I could bet. I looked blank and he said only, 'Watch,' and then dealt six hands, face up. I got between thirteen and seventeen in all six. He got twenty four times and two blackjacks.

'Impressive. Are you always that lucky?'

'They're marked,' he said. 'Never play cards with a thief.' He tossed the deck on the table, leaned back, and looked at me.

'You think I killed Northrup.'

'You say you didn't. I told you I accept that.'

'You don't convince me.'

'Maybe it's the other way around.'

He put his coat on and stood up. 'Let's go out on deck. I'll tell you a couple of stories.' I followed and we found our way back to the desolate spot where he'd dumped the jewels. The old lady was there, and it was still as private as any place on deck.

'How are you today?' Jack said to the old dame, who took the remark first as an intrusion, then looked at Jack as if he were invisible. He shrugged and we walked to the rail and looked down at the waves and at our foamy wake.

'I dumped a guy in the water once over marked cards.'

I nodded, waited. He stared out at the ocean and went on: 'A card game in a hotel. It was the first time I ever met Rothstein. I was working as a strikebreaker with Little Augie, breakin' heads, just out of jail. A bum. I was a bum. Augie says to me, "You wanna work strongarm at a card game?" And I said all right and he sent me to this hotel room and there's Rothstein, the cocksucker, and he says to me, "What happened to your head?" "Nothin' happened to it," I said. "That haircut," he said. "You look like a skinned rabbit, skinned by somebody who don't know how to skin. Get a haircut for pity's sake." Can you imagine that son of a bitch? He's got seventy-six grand in his pocket, he told me so, and he tells me get a haircut. Arrogant bastard. He was right about the haircut. A barber-school job. Awful. I tell you I was a bum on the street and I looked like one. But he made me feel like a zero.

'So the game went on and there's this high roller – let me call him Wilson – who's challenging Rothstein. There's other players, but he wants to beat A. R., who's the king. And he's doing it. Wins eleven thousand one hand, eight the next, in five thousand-dollar freezeout. Rothstein has two men in the bathroom looking over the decks Wilson brought, and they find the marks, little tits on the design in the corner. First-rate work by the designer. Rothstein hears the news and calls a break but doesn't let on, and then tells me to brain Wilson if he gets out of hand, and I say all right because he's paying me. He bottom-deals Wilson a six and Wilson calls him on it. Then A. R. says never mind about bottom dealing, what about a man who brings paper into a legitimate game? And when Wilson stood up, I brained him. Didn't kill him. Just coldcocked him and he went down. When he came to, they told me to take him someplace he wouldn't be a bother. They didn't say kill him. I took him to the river with a driver and walked him to the edge of a dock. He offered me four grand, all he had left from the game, and I took it. Then I shot him three times and dumped him in. It turned out he had three kids. He was a cheater, but he was complicated. He looked at me and said, "Why? I give you the four grand." His life had to be complicated with three kids and I killed him. I wanted the four grand bad and I knew he had it. But I never killed anybody before and I tell you I blame Rothstein. Maybe I wouldn't have killed him if he didn't say that about the haircut, make me feel I was such a bum. I knew I was a bum, but I didn't think it showed so much. With the four grand I wasn't a bum anymore. I bought a new suit and got a haircut at the Waldorf-Astoria.'

The money inspired Jack. He and his brother Eddie met one Ace O'Hagan, who drove for Big Bill Dwyer, the king of Rum Row. Dwyer had the Coast Guard, Jersey City, and part of Long Island on his payroll, and Jack gave Ace fifty to connect him to Dwyer for a job. Ace called Dwyer from the bar where he and the Diamond boys were drinking and found Dwyer was partying and wouldn't be back. Then, in the back of Jack's car, with Eddie driving, Jack had another idea and stuck a pistol in O'Hagan's ear and asked for the location of Dwyer's most vulnerable drop.

'He wouldn't tell me,' Jack said, 'so I smashed his nose with the pistol and he flooded himself. Bled all the way to the Bronx where I knew we could get a truck. I told him I'd burn his toes to cinders if he didn't tell me, and he told and we packed his nose with toilet paper and headed for Dwyer's smallest drop in White Plains. I cooked up a story that we were sent to load up the truck for a millionaire named Riley, a fellow Dwyer was doing business with, and Ace was the convincer. He talked the two guys guarding the drop into loading the truck with Scotch and champagne, and on the way back to the city, he says to me, "Dwyer'll kill you." And I said, "Bill's a nice guy from what I hear. He wouldn't hurt a fellow with a little ambition."

'Then we took Ace to the hospital and I paid to get his nose fixed up. We kept him at our rooms till I figured out what to do next, and during the night he says to Eddie, "He's going to kill me, isn't he?" And Ed told him, "No, I don't think so. If he was going to kill you, why would he pay for your nose?"'

*   *   *

Jack then went to Rothstein with a proposition.

'Listen, I have quite a lot of booze. I mean quite a lot.'

'What are you asking?' Rothstein said, surprised Jack had anything of value besides his pistol.

'The going rate.'

'The rate varies. Quality talks.'

'Taste it yourself.'

'I drink very little. Only at bar mitzvahs and weddings. But I have a friend who drinks nicely and understands what he drinks.'

Jack led Rothstein and friend to the West Side garage where the booze truck was parked. The genuine article, said the taster.

'I take it you imported these goods yourself,' A. R. said.

'Since when does Arnold Rothstein worry about such details?'

'In some ways, I'm particular about whose pockets my friends pick.'

'I'll tell you straight. It's Dwyer's stock.'

Rothstein laughed and laughed and laughed.

'That's quite a daring thing, to do this to Big Bill. And I'm laughing also because Bill owes me for several loads of whiskey for which he borrowed a certain sum, and so it's just possible you're trying to sell me goods with a personal interest to me.'

'Dwyer doesn't have to know you bought the stuff.'

Rothstein laughed again at this devious fellow.

'If I had two more trucks, I could get you this much twice over,' Jack said. 'That's also part of my proposition. Fit me out with two fast trucks and I'll keep you hip-deep in booze.'

'You're moving very fast,' said A. R.

'Just a young fellow trying to get ahead,' said Jack.

Rothstein came to an end of business dealing with Dwyer as a result of Jack Diamond, the underworld *arriviste*, who, the day after Rothstein bought him two trucks, went back to the White Plains drop and, with his new assistants, and their new shotguns, newly sawed off, cleaned the place out down to the last bottle.

Jack was notorious as a hijacker by 1925, Rothstein's crazy – his own man, however – nabob at his Theatrical Club by then, and making enemies like rabbits make rabbits.

'I felt the pellets hit me before I heard the noise, and I saw the cut barrel sticking out of the window as the car passed before I felt the pain. I scrunched sideways below the bottom level of the window so they couldn't fire another one except through the metal door, and while I was down I heard their wheels scream, and I knew I had to come up to steer when I felt the bullet hit my right heel. I didn't run into anything because there was nothing to hit, just traffic way off and no intersection or parked cars. I was around a Hundred and Sixth Street when I looked up and saw them going away. I knew I had to stop. Make them think I was out of it. I veered off to the curb and put my head back on the seat, like a collapse. Wet with blood, and then the pain came. Bloody heel. A woman looked in at me, scared, and ran off. I saw the car away up the block, turning off Fifth, probably coming back to inspect their work. My car was stalled by this time. I started it and saw my hat on the floor, a new straw sailor, the brim half shot off. I lifted my foot, trying not to let the heel touch the floor, put the car in gear, clutch, gas. Goddamn but that pain was heavy. People were out there hiding behind parked cars. I had to get away, so I turned off Fifth then, touched my head. The blood was everywhere and the fucking pain was incredible. I headed for Mount Sinai, the only hospital I knew, a few blocks back on Fifth. "Don't let the toes go dead or I'm through driving. Don't think about the blood. Move the toes." You know what else I thought? I wondered could you buy an artificial heel. They weren't following me. Probably pissed now that they knew they didn't kill me. My vision was going on me, the pain getting to where it counted. "Don't black out now, tough monkey. Here we go." Then, Jesus, a red light. I was afraid if I ran it I'd get hit, and then I'd be dead for sure. Bleed to death. So I waited for the light, if you can believe that, a goddamn lake of blood on the floor and another lake I'm sitting in. My ass floating in blood, ruining the suit, the hat already ruined. I didn't see the face behind the muzzle of the shotgun, but I saw the driver. Ace O'Hagan. He'd be smiling, remembering the night his own blood

579

flowed all over the seat. Ace would pay. And Ace would tell me who the shooter was because Ace couldn't take the pain. I promised I'd make him pick me out a new suit and hat before I did the son of a bitch. Then I was almost to the hospital, and I remembered my pistol and threw it out the window. Didn't want to get caught with that goddamn thing. I opened the car door and I remember thinking to myself, is my underwear clean? Imagine that? I moved the bum leg then, limped toward the door, and I started to spin. I spun through the doorway and began to topple and just inside, mother, here comes the floor.

'It was a guinea mob from the Bronx did it. I'd lifted some of their dope. But I got the bum who led them. He floated up the East River wearing a stolen watch. The boys dressed like cops the day they went to his house to get him. O'Hagan, that prick, I got him good, too. The fish ate his fingers. And he named the shooter like I knew he would. A greaseball from St Louis. I got *him* in a whorehouse.'

It wasn't until after Jack died that I heard the whorehouse story. Flossie told it to me one night at Packy Delaney's Parody Club in Albany, one of Jack's latter-day hangouts. The Floss worked at Packy's as a singer and free-lance source of joy. She and I had no secrets, physical or professional, from each other.

'He was a handsome boy,' she began, 'with hair like Valentino, shiny and straight and with a blue tint to it because it was so black. Maybe that's why they called him Billy Blue. And they always said from St Loo whenever they said his name. Billy Blue from St Loo. I don't think his real name was Blue because he was Italian, like Valentino. He talked and laughed at the bar just like a regular fella, but you know they just ain't no regular fellas anymore, not since I was a kid in school. They all got their specialties. I never would've figured him for what he was. I never even figured him for carryin' a gun. He looked too pretty.

'I was working in Loretta's place on East Thirty-third Street, her own house which she'd lived in alone since her husband was clubbed to death by two fellas he tried to cheat with loaded dice. Loretta had been in the life when she was young and went back to it after that happened. It was a nice place, an old town house with all her old kerosene lamps turned into electric, and nice paintings of New York in the old days, and a whole lineup of teapots she'd collected when she went straight. We were as good as there was in the city and we got a lot of the swells, but we also got a lot of business from hoodlums with big money. Billy was one of those.

'"What's your name?" he says to me when he come in.

'"The Queen of Stars, that's my name."

'"Beautiful Queen of Stars," he says to me. "I'm going to screw love into you."

'Nobody knew my real name and they never would. And it's not Flossie neither. My old man would've died of shame if he knew what I was doin', and I didn't want to hurt him more than I already done. So I picked Queen of Stars when Loretta asked me what my name was. I was thinking of Queen of Diamonds, but I never figured I'd ever get any diamonds, and I was dead right about that. All I ever got was rhinestones. So I said Stars because I had as much right to them as anybody livin'. Then Loretta said okay and we went from there to business, that lousy business. You couldn't get out once you were in because they hooked you. They even charged you for the towels. And the meals? You'd think it was some swanky place the way they priced everything. Then they took half what you made, and by the time you were done payin', what you had left wasn't worth sockin' away. And try and quit. Marlene got it with a blackjack in the alley, and she didn't quit anymore. They even beat up Loretta once after she complained about how much she had to pay the guys up above. The only thing to do was forget it. Just work and don't try to beat 'em out of anything because you couldn't. They were bastards, all of 'em, and a girl had no chance. I saved what I could and figured when I got enough money, I'd make a move. But I never did because I never knew where to move to.

'So Billy Blue, he called me by my full name anyway. Some of them called me Queenie and most everybody that knew me good called me Stars, but he was one of the few called me the whole thing. I liked him. Most of them I didn't like, but most I didn't even look at. Billy was pretty to look at. He got me to sit on the edge of my oak dresser, and then he walked into me. He had his pistol in his hand and stuck it in my mouth and told me to suck it. Jeez, that got me. I was scared as hell. It tasted like sour, oily stuff and I kept thinking, if he gets too excited when he comes, he'll blow a hole in my head. But what could I do?

'"You like my pistol?" he asks me.

'Now what do you say to a goofy question like that? I couldn't say anything anyway with the thing in my mouth, but I tried to smile and I give him a nod and he seemed to like that. You can't understand how a nice-lookin' fella like that could be so bugs. The first bug I ever had stuck a feather duster up his hiney, his own duster he brought with him, and jumped around the room makin' noises like a turkey. All I did was sit on the bed so he could look at me while he did his gobbles.

'So I'm on the table and Billy's doing his stuff and I got the pistol in my mouth when the door opens and in comes Jack Diamond and two other guys, one of them was The Goose with his one eye and the other was fat Jimmy Biondo, and they got guns out, but not Jack, who was just lookin' around with them eyes of his that looked right through doors and walls, and The Goose shoots twice. One bullet hit the mirror of my oak dresser. The other one got Billy in the right shoulder, and he let go the pistol, which fell out of my mouth onto the floor and cut my lip. Billy didn't fall. He just spun around and stared at the men, with nothing on him at all but the safety.

'Jack looked at me and said, "It's all right, Stars, don't worry about anything."

'I was scared as hell, but I felt sorry for Billy because he looked so pretty, even if he was bugs. I started to get off the table, but The Goose says to me "Just stay there," and so I did, because he was the meanest-looking guy I ever saw. Jack was just lookin' at Billy and gettin' red in the face. You could see how mad he was, but he didn't talk. He just stared, and all of a sudden he takes a gun out of his coat pocket and shoots Billy in the stomach three times, and Billy falls sideways on my bed, bleedin' all over the new yellow blanket I had to pay eleven bucks for after a customer peed all over my other one and the pee smell wouldn't wash out.

'Loretta came runnin' then, and was she mad.

'"Why the hell'd you do that here?" she asked Jack. "What'm I supposed to do with him? Goddamn it all, Jack, I can't handle this."

'Billy was moanin' a little bit, so I sat down alongside him, just to be near him. He looked at me like he wanted me to do somethin' for him, get a doctor or somebody, but I couldn't do anything except look at him and nod my head, I was so scared. I thought if they decided to leave maybe I could help him then.

'"We'll take him with us," Jack said. "Wrap him up."

'The Goose and Biondo walked over to the bed and stood over Billy. Billy's eyes were still open and he looked at me.

'"It's sloppy," The Goose said, and he took an ice pick out of his coat and punched it half a dozen times through Billy's temples, first one side then the other. It happened so fast I couldn't not look. Then he and Jimmy Biondo wrapped Billy in my yellow blanket and carried him down the back way to the alley. Billy was still straight up and still had the safety on. I'd told him I was clean, that I got regular checkups, but he wore it anyway. I didn't see The Goose or Biondo again for years, but I saw Jack quite a lot. He was our protector. That's what they called him anyway. Some protector. It was him and his guys beat up Loretta and Marlene – the bastards, the things they could do and then be so nice. But they also took care nobody shook us down and nobody arrested us. I don't know how he did it, but Jack kept the cops away, and my whole life I never been in jail except for being drunk. Jack didn't own us, though. I always heard Arnold Rothstein did, but I never knew for sure. Loretta never told us anything. Jack did own some places later and got me a job in a House of All Nations he was partners in, up in Montreal. I was supposed to be either a Swede or a Dutchie because of my blond hair. Jack brought me back down to Albany a couple of years later and I've been here ever since.

'I really hardly knew him, saw him in Loretta's a few times, that's all, until he gave Billy Blue his. Then one night about a month later he come in and buys me a real drink. None of that circus water Loretta dished us out when the chumps were buying. Jack bought the real stuff for us.

'"I'm sorry about that whole scene, Stars," he said, "but we had to settle a score. Your guinea friend tried to kill me six months ago."

'Jack took my fingers and ran them over the back of his head where he said there were still some shotgun pellets. It was very bumpy behind his left ear.

'"Were you scared, Stars?"

'"Was I! I been sick over it. I can't sleep."

'"Poor kid. I was really sorry to do that to you."

'He was still holding my hand and then he rubbed my hair. The first thing you know we were back up in my room and we really got to know one another, I'll tell the world.'

The Wilson, Rothstein, O'Hagan, and Blue confessions came out of Jack so totally without reservation that I told him, 'I believe you about Northrup now.'

'Sometimes I tell the truth.'

'I don't know as I'm so sure why you've told me all these stories, though.'

'I want you to know who you're working for.'

'You seem to trust me.'

'If you ever said anything, you'd be dead. But you know some people well enough they'd never talk. I know you.'

'I take that as a compliment, but I'm not looking for information. Now or ever.'

'I know that. You wouldn't get a comma out of me if I didn't want to give it. I told you, I want you to know who I am. And who I used to be. I changed. Did you get that? I come a long way. A long fucking way. A man don't have to stay a bum forever.'

'I see what you mean.'

'Yeah, maybe you do. You listen pretty good. People got to have somebody listen to them.'

'I get paid for that.'

'I'm not talking about pay.'

'I am. I'm for sale. It's why I went to law school. I listen for money. I also listen for other reasons that have nothing to do with money. You're talking about the other reasons. I know that.'

'I knew you knew, you son of a bitch. I knew it that night you cut Jolson up that you talked my language. That's why I sent you the Scotch.'

'You're a prescient man.'

'You bet your ass. What does that mean?'

'You don't have to know.'

'Blow it out your whistle, you overeducated prick.'

But he laughed when he said it.

My memories of Jack in Europe during our first stops are like picture postcards. In the first he walks off the *Belgenland* at Antwerp in company of two courteous, nervous Belgian gendarmes in their kicky bucket hats and shoulder straps. He had hoped to sneak off the ship alone and meet us later, but helpful passengers pointed him out to the cops and they nailed him near the gangway.

Down he went but not without verbal battle, assertion of his rights as an American citizen, profession of innocence. In the postcard Jack wears his cocoa-brown suit and white hat and is held by his left arm, slightly aloft. The holder of the arm walks slightly to the rear of him down the gangplank. The second officer walks to their rear entirely, an observer. The pair of ceremonial hats and Jack's oversized white fedora dominate the picture. They led the angry Jack to an auto, guided him into the back seat, and sat on either side of him. A small crowd followed the action. The car turned a corner off the pier into the thick of an army that had been lying in wait for the new invasion of Flanders. Poppies perhaps at the ready, fields of crosses under contract in anticipation of battle with the booze boche from the west. Four armored cars waited, along with six others like the one carrying

Jack, each with four men within and at least fifty foot-patrolmen armed with clubs or rifles.

You can see Jack's strong suit was menace.

We left Belgium the next day, the twerps, as Jack called them, finally deciding Jack must be expelled by train. Jack chose Germany as his destination and we bought tickets. The American embassy involved itself by not involving itself, and so Jack was shunted eastward to Aachen, where the Belgian cops left off and the German *Polizei* took over. A pair of beefy Germans in mufti held his arms as he looked over his shoulder and said to me through a frantic, twisted mouth: 'Goddamn it, Marcus, get me a goddamn lawyer.'

Instead of turning the money over to Classy Willie, Jack gave a hundred and eighty thousand of it to me, some in a money belt, which gave me immediate abdominal tensions, and the rest inside my Ernest Dimnet best seller, *The Art of Thinking*, out of which we cut most of the pages. I carried thirty thousand in thousand-dollar bills in the book and kept the book in the pocket of my hound's-tooth sport jacket until I reached Albany. The money that didn't fit into the book and the money belt we rolled up and slid into the slots in Jack's bag reserved for the jewels. And the bag became mine.

Police were still dragging lakes all over the Catskills. They preferred to do that rather than follow the tip that led to a six-mile stretch of highway near Saugerties that was paved the day after Charlie disappeared.

Jack's home was searched; Alice was nowhere to be found. A shotgun and rifle in a closet were confiscated. Fogarty was seminude with a buxom Catskill waitress of comparable nudity when the raid came.

Life went on.

I noticed that Jack had a luminous quality at certain moments, when he stood in shadow. I suspect a derangement of my vision even now, for I remember that the luminosity intensified when Jack said that I should carry a pistol to protect myself (he meant to protect his money) and then offered me one, which I refused.

'I'll carry the stuff, but I won't defend it,' I said. 'If you want that kind of protection give it to The Count to take home.'

Since that perception of Jack's luminosity, I've read of scientists working to demystify psychic phenomena who claim to have photographed energy emitted by flowers and leaves. They photograph them while they are living, then cut them and photograph them in progressive stages of dying. The scientists say that the intense light in the living flower or leaf is energy, and that the luminous quality fades slowly until desiccation, at which point it vanishes.

I already spoke of Jack's energy as I saw it that memorable Sunday in the Catskills. The luminosity was further evidence of it, and this finally persuaded me of a world run not by a hierarchy of talents but by a hierarchy of shining energetics. In isolation or defeat some men lapse into melancholia, even catatonia, the death of motion a commonplace symptom. But Jack was volatile in his intensifying solitude, reacting with anger to his buffetings, also trying to convince, bribe, sweet-talk, harass his way out. At Aachen he argued with the German cops, saying, yes, he had the same name as the famous gangster, but he wasn't the same man. In protest of their disbelief he did a kind of Indian war dance in the aisle of the first-class coach, a dance at which one could only marvel. Ah, the creative power of the indignant liar.

I remember my own excitement, the surge of energy I felt rising in myself from some arcane storage area of the psyche when I strapped on the money belt. No longer the voyeur at the conspiracy, I was now an accessory, and the consequence was intoxicating. I felt a need to drink, to further loosen my control center, and I did.

At the bar I found a woman I'd flirted with a day or so earlier and coaxed her back to my cabin. I did not wait to strip her, or myself, but raised her dress swiftly, pulled her underclothing off one leg, and entered her as she sat on the bed, ripping her and myself in the process so that we both bled. I never knew her name.

I have no recollection of the color of her hair, the shape of her face, or any word she might have said, but I still have an indelible memory of her pubic region, its color and its shape, at the moment I assaulted it.

No one suspected me of carrying The Great Wad, not even Classy Willie. I passed along the sap question to Willie over drinks on the train out of Belgium. 'Did Jack ever give you back Biondo's bankroll?' He gave me a hangdog look that deflated his dapper façade and reduced him forever in my mind to the status of junior villain.

The Berlin lawyer I contacted when Jack was grabbed at Aachen and held for four days was named Schwarzkopf, his name the gift of a German detective who took a liking to Jack and spoke English to him, calling him 'der Schack,' a mythic nickname the German press had invented. (The French called Jack Monsieur Diamant; the Italians, Giovanni Diamante; and he was 'Cunning Jackie' to the British.)

Schwarzkopf turned out to be one of Berlin's leading criminal lawyers, but he failed to delay Jack's deportation for even a day. He even failed, when it became clear that Germany was not an open door, to get Jack aboard the liner I'd booked us on out of Bremen. The liner said no.

Nevertheless, Jack commissioned Schwarzkopf with a one-grand retainer to sue the German government for mistreatment and expenses, and to grease enough levers to get him back into Germany when the fuss went away. It was typical of Jack not to yield to what other men would consider the inevitable.

When we met Schwarzkopf in the palm garden of the Bremen hotel where Jack was staying, he brought along his nephew, a young, half-drunk playwright named Weissberg, who in turn brought along a gum-chewing, small-breasted, brassiereless, and dirty little whore, dirtier than street whores need to be. She spoke only three words near the end of our conversation, stroking Weissberg's silky black mustache and calling him '*Mein schön Scheizekopf*.'

Weissberg had written a well-received play about burglars, pimps, and pickpockets in Berlin, but he'd never met anybody in the underworld with the exalted status of Jack and so he'd persuaded Schwarzkopf to arrange a meeting. The violinist and accordion player were sending out Straussian strains suitable to palm gardens as we all drank our dunkelbock and schnapps under an open sky. The tables were small, and so Classy Willie and The Count, who both carried weapons now, sat apart from our quartet, just as Fogarty and The Goose had on the mountain. Jack, like the aristocratic Germans around us, had an acute sense of class distinction.

Jack's German mood, after he was refused first-class passage, seemed, finally, glum. That's how I read it, and I was wrong. He was more disturbed than that, but I was unable to perceive it. I excuse myself for this failure of perception, for I think he was concealing it even from himself. It was Weissberg who brought him to explosion. Weissberg began with questions, not unlike the press, only more penetrating.

'Do you know anyone in the underworld who has a conscience, Herr Diamond?'

'I don't know anybody in the underworld. I'm only a bootlegger.'

'What are your feelings about willful murder?'

'I try to avoid it.'

'I have known people who would steal and yet would not maim another person. I know people who would maim and yet stop short of murder. And I know of men who claim that they could murder in anger but never in cold blood. Is this the way the underworld is morally structured?'

Jack seemed to like that question. Possibly he'd thought of its import over the years without ever raising the question quite so precisely. He squinted at the playwright, who talked with a cigarette constantly at the corner of his mouth, never removing it, letting the ashes fall as they would, on his chest or into the schnapps, or snorting them away with nasal winds. He was accomplished at this gesture, which I guessed he'd adopted when he first entered the underworld milieu.

'There's always a guy,' Jack said to him, 'who's ready to do what you won't do.'

'What is your limit? What is it you will not do?'

'I've done everything at least twice,' Jack said with a satiric snicker, 'and I sleep like a baby.'

'*Wunderbar!*' said Weissberg, and he threw his arms in the air and arched his body backward in the chair in a physical demonstration of Eureka! We listened to more waltz music and we drank our legal alcohol and we watched the playwright commune silently, smilingly, with this sudden inflation of meaning. He threw off the half inch of cigarette from his lip and leaned toward Jack.

'I want to write a play about your life,' he said. 'I want to come to America and live with you. I don't care what might happen in your life, and I fully expect you'll kill me if you think I'm informing on you. I want to see you eat and breathe and sleep and work and do your bootleg things and steal and rob and kill. I want to witness everything and write a great play, and I will give it all to you, all my glory, all my money. I want only the opportunity to write what I believe, which is that there are similarities among the great artist, the great whore, and the great criminal. The great artist is the work he does which outlives him. The great whore lives in the memory of ineffable sensual gratification that outlasts the liaison; she is also the beauty of the parts, as is art. And she is the perversion of love, as art is the exquisite perversion of reality. Of course, with both artist and whore, the rewards are ever-greater recompense, ever-greater renown. And I see the great criminal shining through the bold perversion of his deeds, in his willingness to scale the highest moral barriers (and what is morality to the whore, the artist?). In all three professions is the willingness to withhold nothing from one's work. All three, when they achieve greatness, have also an undeniable high style which separates them from the pedestrian mobs. For how could we tell a great criminal from a thug in the alley, or a great whore from a street slut, if it were not for style? Yesssss, Herr Diamond, yesssss! It is abandon, first, which goes without saying, but it is finally style that makes *you* great and will make *me* great, and it is why we are drinking here together in this elegant hotel and listening to this elegant music and drinking this elegant schnapps.

'My little piglet here,' he said, turning to his own whore, who understood no English and whose breasts look like two fried eggs in my memory, 'knows nothing of style and can never be more than a gutter animal. She is a filthy woman and I do enjoy this. I enjoy paying her and stealing back the money. I enjoy infecting her with my diseases and then paying her doctor bills. I enjoy squeezing her nipples until she screams. She is a superb companion, for she is stupid and knows nothing of me. She is not capable of even conceiving of how the great whores of Germany function today. I will have them, too, in time. But now my piglet exalts my young life.

'And you, sir, are a great man and have achieved great things. I can see in your eyes that you have leaped all moral and social barriers, that you are no prisoner of creeds and dogmas. You are intelligent, Herr Diamond. You live in the mind as well as on the street of bullets and blood. I too live in the mind and in the heart. My art is my soul. It is my body. Everything I do contributes to my art. We live, you and I, Herr Diamond, in the higher realms of the superman. We have each overcome our troublesome self. We exist in the world of will. We have created the world before which we can kneel. I speak Nietzsche's words. Do you know him? He says clearly that he who must be a creator in good and evil has first to be a destroyer and break values. We have both destroyed, Herr Diamond. We have both broken old values. We have both gone into the higher planes where the supermen dwell, and we will always triumph over the spirits of defeat that try to pull us down. Will you let me live with you and write your story – our story? Will you do this, Herr Diamond?'

Jack gave it a few seconds, letting it all settle, watching those electric eyes under Weissberg's bushy black brows. Then he went over to The Count's table and came back with The Count's small .25-caliber pistol half-concealed from the two dozen customers who sat in the garden's magical twilight, letting Strauss, the gentle swaying of the potted palms, and the intoxicating mellowness of the afternoon's first drinks lull them into sweet escape. Jack pulled his chair close to Weissberg's until they were knee to knee, and he then showed the playwright the pistol, holding it loosely in his palm. He said nothing at all for perhaps a minute, only held the weapon as a display item. Then suddenly and with eyes turned snakish, with a grimace of hate and viciousness whose like I had never seen before on his face, he nosed the barrel downward and fired one shot into the grass between Weissberg's feet, which were about six inches from each other. The downward course of the firing, the small caliber of the weapon, the shot muffled by pants legs and overwhelmed by music, created a noise that did not disrupt. A few people turned our way, but since we seemed at ease, no disturbance in process, the noise was assumed to be something as trivial as a broken glass. Jack took no notice of any external reaction. He said to Weissberg, 'You're a kid, a fool.'

The pistol was already in his pocket as he stood up and tossed a handful of deutsche marks on the table to pay for the drinks.

'My beautiful shithead,' said the dirty little whore, stroking Weissberg's mustache, which by then was wet with tears, as wet as the front of his pants. Weissberg, the young playwright, had very suddenly liquefied.

Jack was two days out of Hamburg on the freighter *Hannover*, the only passenger, before he heard the strange melodic chaos coming up from below. He went through corridors and down a stairway where he found the forty-five hundred canaries the *Hannover* was bringing to the American bird-cage crowd. The Hartz Mountain birds, yellow and green, stopped singing when Jack entered their prison, and he thought: *They've smelled me.* But canaries are idiots of smell and wizards of hearing and love. The prison was moist and hot and Jack began to sweat. A sailor feeding the birds looked up and said, 'I'm feedin' the birds.'

'So I see.'

'If you don't feed 'em, they drop dead.'

'Is that so?'

'They eat a lot of food.'

'You wouldn't think it to look at them.'

'They do, though.'

'Everybody needs a square meal,' Jack said.

'Canaries especially.'

'Can I help you feed them?'

'Nah. They wouldn't like you.'

'What makes you think they wouldn't like me?'

'They know who you are.'

'The canaries know me?'

'You saw the way they quit singin' when you come in?'

'I figured they were afraid of people.'

'They love people. They're afraid of you.'

'You're full of shit,' Jack said.

'No, I'm not,' said the sailor.

Jack opened a cage to gentle one of the birds. It pecked once at his knuckle. He lifted the bird out and saw it was dead. He put it in his pocket and opened another cage. That bird flew out, silently, and perched on top of the highest stack of cages, beyond Jack's reach unless he used the sailor's ladder. The bird twisted its tail and shat on the floor in front of Jack.

'I told you,' the sailor said. 'They don't want nothin' to do with you.'

'What've they got against me?'

'Ask them. If you know what music is all about, you can figure out what they're sayin'. You know how they learn to sing so good? Listenin' to flutes and fiddles.'

Jack listened, but all he heard was silence. The bird shat at him again. Jack yelled, 'Fuck you, birdies,' to the canaries and went back topside.

Jack heard from the radio operator that he was still steady news across the world, that now everyone knew he was on a ship with forty-five hundred canaries and that the corpse of Charlie Northrup had still not turned up. The sailor who fed the birds came up from below one morning, and Jack detected traces of the Northrup mouth on the man, a semitaut rubber band with the round edges

593

downward turning. No smile, no smile. When the sailor opened the hatch, Jack heard the music of the birds. He inched toward it as it grew more and more glorious. The song heightened his sense of his own insignificance. What song did *he* sing? Yet it unaccountably pleased him to be nothing on the high seas, a just reward somehow; and now the birds were singing of justice. Jack remembered how satisfying it was to be shot and to linger at the edge of genuine nothingness. He remembered touching the Kiki silk and strong Alice's forehead. How rich! How something! And the vibrancy of command. Ah yes, that was *some*thing. Get down, he said to a nigger truck driver one night on the Lake George road; and the nigger showed him a knife, stupid nigger, and Jack fired one shot through his forehead. When Murray opened the door, the nigger fell out. Power! And when they got Augie – the lovely pain under Jack's own heart. Bang! And in the gut. Bang! Bang! Fantastic! Let us, then, be up and doing, with a heart for any fate.

'How's all the birdies?' Jack asked the sailor.

'Very sad,' said the sailor. 'They sing to overcome their sadness.'

'That's not why birds sing,' Jack said.

'Sure it is.'

'Are you positive?'

'I live with birds. I'm part bird myself. You should see my skin up close. Just like feathers.'

'That's very unusual,' Jack said.

The sailor rolled up his sleeve to show Jack his biceps, which were covered with brown feathers.

'Now do you believe me?' the sailor asked.

'I certainly do. It's absolutely amazing.'

'I used to be a barn swallow before I became a sailor.'

'You like it better as a bird or this way?'

'I had more fun as a bird.'

'I would've given nine to five you'd say that,' Jack said.

A sailor told me a story when I boarded the *Hannover* back in the States.

'A strange man, der Schack, und I like him,' the sailor said. 'Good company, many stories, full of the blood that makes a man come to life as thousands around him become dead. A natural man. A man who knows where to find Canis Major. I watch him by the railing, looking out at the waves, not moving. He looks, he trembles. He holds himself as you hold a woman. He is a man of trouble. The captain sends me to his cabin when he does not come to breakfast, und on the table by the bed are three birds, all dead. Der Schack is sick. He says he vill take only soup. For three days he stays in the room und just before Philadelphia he comes to me und says he wants to buy three birds to take home. "They are my friends," he says. When I get the birds for him, he wants to pay me, but I say, "No, Schack, they are a gift." In his cabin I look for the three dead ones, but they are gone.'

I beat Jack home, caught a liner a day and a half after he left Hamburg, and probably passed his floating birdhouse before it was out of the English Channel. The money passed back to America with me without incident, and so, I thought, had I, for I had been a passive adjunct to Jack's notoriety, a shadowy figure in the case, as they say. But my shadow ran ahead of me, and when I returned to Albany and rented a safe-deposit box for the cash, I found I was locally notorious. My picture had been taken in Germany with Jack, and it had smiled all over the local papers. My legal maneuvering on the Continent, however marginal and unpublic, had been ferreted out by German newsmen and duly heralded at home.

I'd told Jack in Hamburg, when we shook hands at the gangplank, that I'd meet him when he docked in the U. S. and I'd bring Fogarty with me. But Fogarty, I discovered, couldn't leave the state, and Jack was coming in to Philadelphia. The federals had Fogarty on three trivial charges while they tried to link him to a rum-boat raid they'd made at Briarcliff Manor, a hundred-and-twenty-five-thousand-dollar haul of booze, the week before we left for Europe. This was the first I'd heard of the raid or of Fogarty's arrest. He'd been waiting in a truck as the boat docked, and when he spotted a cop, he tried to make a run. They charged him with vagrancy, speeding, and failing to give a good account of himself, my favorite misdemeanor.

'They can't tie me to it,' Fogarty said on the phone from Acra. 'I never went near the boat. I was in the truck taking a nap.'

'Excellent alibi. Was it Jack's booze?'

'I wouldn't know.'

'As one Irishman to another, I don't trust you either.'

So I drove to Philadelphia by myself.

The reception for Jack was hardly equal to the hero welcomes America gives its Lindys, but it surpassed anything I'd been involved in personally since the armistice. I talked my way onto the cutter that was to bring a customs inspector out to meet the *Hannover* at quarantine on Marcus Hook. A dozen newsmen were also aboard, the avant-garde eyeballs of the waiting masses.

We saw Jack on the bridge with the captain when we pulled alongside. The captain called out, 'No press, no press,' when the customs inspector began to board, and Jack added his greeting: 'Any reporter comes near me I'll knock his fucking brains out.' The press grumbled and took pictures, and then Jack saw me and I climbed aboard.

'I was just passing by,' I said, 'and thought I might borrow a cup of birdseed.'

Jack grinned and shook hands, looking like an ad for what an ocean voyage can do for the complexion. He was in his favorite suit – the blue double-breasted – with a light gray fedora, a baby blue tie, and a white silk shirt.

'I'm big pals with these birds,' he said. 'Some of them whistle better than Jolson.'

'You're looking fit.'

'Greatest trip of my life,' he said. The captain was a hell of a fellow, the food was great, the sea air did wonders for his stomach and blah blah blah. Marvelous how he could lie. I told him about the reception he was going to get, some evidence of it already in view: tugs, police launches, chartered press boats, that customs cutter, all of them steaming along with us as we glided up the Delaware toward Pier Thirty-four. Jack's navy.

'I'd estimate three thousand people and a hundred cops,' I said.

'Three thousand? They gonna throw confetti or rocks?'

'Palm fronds is my guess.'

I told him about Fogarty's travel restrictions, and asked:

'Was that your booze they got on that boat?'

'Mostly mine,' he said. 'I had a partner.'

'A sizable loss – a hundred and twenty-five thousand dollars.'

'More. Add another twenty-five.'

'Were you on the scene?'

'Not at the dock. I was someplace else, waiting. And nobody showed. My old pal Charlie Northrup worked that one up.'

'He was your partner?'

'He tipped the feds.'

'Ah. So that's what this is all about.'

'No, that's not even half of it. What about Jimmy Biondo?'

'I had a call from him. He wants his money.'

'I don't blame him, but he's not going to get it.'

'He threatened me. He thinks maybe I've got it. I didn't think he was that bright.'

'How did he threaten you?'

'He said he'd make me dead.'

'Don't pay any attention to that bullshit.'

'It's not something I hear every day.'

'I'll fix the son of a bitch.'

'Why don't you just give him back his money?'

'Because I'm going back to Germany.'

'Oh, Christ, Jack. Don't you learn?'

When he talked to Schwarzkopf about greasing the way for a return trip, I took it as the necessary response of an angry reject. I couldn't imagine him really risking a second international fiasco. But I was making a logical assumption and Jack was working out of other file cabinets: his faith in his ability to triumph over hostility, his refusal to recognize failure even after it had kicked him in the crotch, and, of course, his enduring greed. As a disinterested observer I might have accepted all but the greed as admirable behavior, but now with Biondo on my back as well as Jack's, such perseverance struck me as an open invitation to assassination.

'Let's get it straight, Jack. I'm not comfortable.'

'Who the hell is?'

'I used to be. I want to get rid of that money and I want to get rid of Jimmy Biondo. I went along for the ride, but it's turned into something else. You don't know how big this Northrup thing is. In the papers every day. Biggest corpse hunt in years, which raises our old question again. Is he or isn't he? I've got to know this time.'

We were on the forward deck, watching the boats watch us. The captain and his sailors were nowhere near us, but Jack looked behind and then spoke so no breeze would carry the words aft.

'Yeah,' he said.

'Great. Jesus Christ, that's great news.'

'It wasn't my fault.'

'No?'

'It was a mistake.'

'Then that makes everything all right.'

'Don't fuck around with this, Marcus. I said it was a mistake.'

'It's a mistake I'm here.'

'Then get the fuck off.'

'When it's over. I don't quit on my clients.'

I think I knew even as I said it that there would be no quitting. Certainly I sensed the possibility, for just as Jack's life had taken a turning in Europe, so had mine. Our public association had done me in with the Albany crowd. They could do beer business all year long with Jack, but after mass on Sunday they could also tut-tut over the awful gangsterism fouling the city. It followed they could not run a man for the Congress who was seeking justice for an animal like Jack. Forget about Congress, was the word passed to me at the Elks Club bar after I came home from Germany. When I think back now to whether the Congress or the time with Jack would have given me more insight into American life, I always lean to Jack. In the Congress I would have learned how rudimentary hypocrisy is turned into patriotism, into national policy, and into the law, and how hypocrites become heroes of the people. What

I learned from Jack was that politicians imitated his style without comprehending it, without understanding that their venality was *only* hypocritical. Jack failed thoroughly as a hypocrite. He was a liar, of course, a perjurer, all of that, but he was also a venal man of integrity, for he never ceased to renew his vulnerability to punishment, death, and damnation. It is one thing to be corrupt. It is another to behave in a psychologically responsible way toward your own evil.

The police came aboard, just like Belgium, with a warrant for Jack as a suspicious character. Jack was afraid of the mob, afraid he was too much of a target, but the cops formed a wedge around him and moved him through. The crowd pushed and broke the wedge, calling out hellos and welcome backs to Jack; and some even held up autograph books and pencils. When all that failed, the fan club began to reach out to feel him, shake his hand. A woman who couldn't reach him hit his arm with a newspaper and apologized – 'I only wanted to touch you, lover' – and a young man made a flying leap at Jack's coat, got a cop's instead, also got clubbed.

'Murderer,' someone called out.

'Go home. We don't want you here.'

'Don't mind them, Jack.'

'You look great, Legs.'

'He's only a bird in a gilded cage.'

'Give us a smile, Legs,' a photographer said and Jack swung at him, missed.

'Hello, cuz!' came a yell and Jack turned to see his cousin William, an ironworker. Jack asked the cops to let him through, and William, six four with major muscles and the facial blotch of a serious beer drinker, moved in beside the car where Jack was now ringed by police.

'Lookin' snappy, Jack,' William said.

'Wish I could say the same for you, Will.'

'What's that you got there in the lapel?'

'Knight Templar pin, Will.'

'Son of a bitch, Jack, ain't that a Protestant bunch?'

'It's good for business, Will.'

'You even turned on your own religion.'

'Ah shit, Will, have you got anything to tell me? How's Aunt Elly?'

'She's fit.'

'Does she need anything?'

'Nobody needs anything from you.'

'Well, it was nice seeing you, Will. Give my regards to the worms.'

'We know who the worm in this family is, cousin.'

And Jack got into the car.

'What do you think of the killing of the dry agent yesterday at the Rising Sun Brewery in Newark?' a reporter asked through the window.

'First I heard of it, but it's the most foolish thing in the world. It'll cramp business for a month.'

'Can you whistle for us?' another reporter asked.

'Up your whistle, punk,' Jack said, and the reporter faded.

'How did you find Europe?'

'I got off the boat and there it was.'

'Who was the blonde you were with in Hamburg?'

'A Red Cross nurse I hired to take my pulse.'

'How well did you know Charlie Northrup?'

'A personal friend.'

'The police think you killed him.'

'Never trust what a cop or a woman thinks.'

No longer amused, the cops shoved the reporters back and made a path for the car. Jack waved to me as it pulled away, smiling, happy to be vulnerable again. My subconscious works in musical ways at times and as I wrote that last sentence I heard an old melody float up and I couldn't say why. But I trust my music and when I sang it all the way through I could hear a jazz band playing it in raucous ragtime, Jack giving me that going-away smile on the pier forty-two years ago, soothed by the music, which I hear clearly, with a twist all my own:

It goes Na-Da, Na-Da,
Na-Da-Na-Da nil-nil-nil.

Jack was twenty hours in jail. His aunt sent him a box of molasses cookies, and I sent him two corned beefs on rye. Commissioner Devane in New York had asked Philadelphia to hold Jack, but they found nothing to prosecute and by midmorning I'd worked out a release arrangement. We'd announce we were leaving town, assuring the citizenry that no carpetbaggers would invade the territory of the local hoodlums. Jack wanted only two hours to visit relatives and the judge said all right, so we went through a four-minute court ritual. But the judge found it necessary to give Jack a dig: 'This court considers the attention you have received from the press and from the vast numbers of people who gathered at the pier to witness your arrival, to be twin aberrations of the public mind, aberrations which find value in things that are worth nothing at all. I speak for the decent people of this city in saying that Philadelphia doesn't want you any more than Europe did. Get out of this city and stay out.'

In the car, Jack looked like a man trying to see through a rain of cotton balls. The reporters tailed us, so he said, 'Skip the relatives, head for New York.' We lost the last of the press about thirty miles out of the city. It was a decent fall day, a little cloudy, but with a lot of new color in the world. But then it started to drizzle and the road got foggy. The fog seemed to buoy Jack's spirits and he talked about his women. He'd left his canaries on the ship and now wanted to buy something for Alice and Kiki, so we stopped at Newark, which he seemed to know as well as he knew Manhattan.

'Dogs,' he said. 'Alice loves dogs.'

We went to three pet shops before we found a pair of gray Brussels griffons. They appealed to Jack because he could claim he'd bought them in Belgium. There were four in the litter and I suggested another pair for Kiki.

'She'd lose them or let them die,' he said, and so we found a jewelry store and he bought her an eight-hundred-dollar diamond, elaborately set ('A diamond from my Diamond,' she quickly dubbed it).

I'd expected him to emphasize one or the other woman when he arrived, depending on his mood: horny or homey. But he balanced them neatly, emphasizing neither, impatient to see them both, moving neither away from one nor toward the other but rather toting one on each shoulder into some imagined triad of love, a sweet roundelay which would obviate any choice of either/or and would offer instead the more bountiful alternative of both. More power to you, old boy.

But his mood was not bountiful at the moment. We came out of the jewelry store and got in the car, and he looked at me and said, 'Did you ever feel dead?'

'Not entirely. I woke up once and felt my leg was dead. Not pins and needles but genuinely dead. But that's as far as I ever got.'

'I feel like I died last week.'

'You've had a pretty negative experience. It's understandable.'

'I didn't even feel like this when I *was* dying.'

'Go someplace and sleep it off. Always works for me when I hit bottom.'

'Some cocaine would fix my head.'

'I'll stop at the next drugstore.'

'Let's get a drink. Turn right, we'll go to Nannery's' – and we hunted down a small speakeasy where Jack knew the doorman and got the biggest hello of the week from half the people in the place.

'I just heard about you on the radio ten minutes ago,' Tommy Nannery told him, a spiffy little bald-headed Irishman with oversize ears. He kept clapping Jack on the back and he put a bottle of rye in front of us. 'They sure gave you a lot of shit over there, Jack,' Nannery said.

'It wasn't so bad,' Jack said. 'Don't believe all that horseshit you read in the papers. I had a good time. I got healthy on the ocean.'

'I didn't believe any of it,' Nannery said. 'Talkin' here the other night about it I says to a fellow, they don't shove Jack Diamond around like that, I don't care who they are. Jack has got friends a way up. Am I right?'

'You're right, Tommy. Here's to my friends.'

Jack drank about three straight ones while I was getting halfway through my first. He put a twenty on the bar and said he'd take the bottle.

'My treat, Jack, my treat,' Nannery said. 'Glad to see you back in Newark.'

'It's nice to have good friends,' Jack said. 'Tommy, it's nice.'

He had another two fast ones before we left, and in the car he sat with the bottle between his legs, swilling it as we went. When I got into Manhattan, he was out of his depression with a vengeance, also out of control with good old Marcus at the wheel. I'd every intention of dropping him in the city and going straight on to Albany with a demarcating flourish. The end. For the peculiar vanity that had first sent me to Catskill on that odd summer Sunday, the need for feeding the neglected negative elements of my too-white Irish soul, the willful tar-and-feather job on my conscience, all that seemed silly now. Childish man. Eternal boy. Bit of a rascal. Unpredictable Marcus. The wiping away of my political future, however casually I'd considered it in the past, the prospect of assassination, and my excursion into quasi-rape convinced me my life had changed in startling ways I wouldn't yet say I regretted. But what would I do with such developments? Underneath, I knew I was still straight, still balancing the either/or while Jack plunged ahead with diamonds and doggies toward the twin-peaked glory of bothness. I felt suddenly like a child.

I looked at Jack and saw him whiten. Was that a bad bit of barley he was swilling? But the bottle was two-thirds down. He was suddenly quite drunk, and without a sound or a move toward the door, he puked in his lap, onto the seat, onto the gearshift, the floormat, the open ashtray, my shoes, my socks, my trousers, and the Philadelphia *Inquirer* I'd bought before going to court, Jack's face in closeup staring up from it at Jack, receiving mouth-to-mouth vomit.

'Fucking ocean,' Jack said, and he collapsed backward with his eyes closed, lapsing into a ragged flow of mumbles as I looked frantically for a gas station. He rattled on about being offered fifteen hundred a month to perform in a German cabaret, and twenty-five thousand by an English news syndicate for his life story and a blank check by the *Daily News* for the same thing. I'd heard all this in Germany and was now far more interested in any sign of the flying red horse on Eleventh Avenue, steed that would deliver me from puke.

''Magine 'em asking Rothstein?' Jack said, eyes closed, words all tongued. ''Magine him packin' 'em in?'

'No, I can't imagine it,' I said, distracted still. Jack opened his eyes when I spoke.

'Wha'?'

'I said I couldn't imagine it.'

''Magine wha'?'

'Rothstein onstage.'

'Where?'

'Forget it.'

'They wouldn't put that bum onstage,' he said and he closed his eyes. He snapped to when I hosed down his lap and shoes at the gas station, and by the time we got to the Monticello Hotel where Kiki was waiting, he was purged, stinking and still drunk but purged of salt air and European poisons, cured by America's best home remedy. And good old Uncle Marcus was still there, guiding him with as little guidance as possible toward the elevator. Upstairs, Jack could lie down and think about puke and poison. He could discover in quiet what his body already understood: that his fame hadn't answered the basic question he had asked himself all his life, was still asking.

Playing the Jack

Jimmy Biondo visited Kiki three hours before we knocked on her door. The result was still on her face. She'd met him with Jack frequently, and so, when he knocked, she let him in. He then dumped his froggy body into the only easy chair in the room, keeping his hat on and dripping sweat off his chin onto his bow tie.

'Where's your friend Diamond?'

'He hasn't called me yet.'

'Don't lie to me, girlie.'

'I don't lie to people and don't call me girlie, you big lug.'

'Your friend's got trouble.'

'What kind of trouble?'

'He's gunna grow great big holes in his belly.'

'He better not hear you say that.'

'He'll hear it all right. He'll hear it.'

'Listen, I don't want to talk to you and I'll thank you to leave.'

'I'll tank you to leave.'

'So get lost.'

'Shut up, you dumb cunt.'

'Oh! I'm tellin' Jack.'

'Just right. And tell him I want my money and tell him he shouldn'a done what he done to Charlie Northrup.'

'He didn't do anything to Charlie Northrup.'

'You dumb cunt, what do you know? You think he's a nice

guy, wouldn't hurt anybody? I wanna tell you what a nice guy your boyfriend is and what nice guys he's got workin' for him. You ever hear of Joe Rock? Your boyfriend's pals took him up inna woods, and when he said he wooden pay off the ransom, Murray the Goose pulls himself off inna cloth and rubs it in Joe's eyes and ties the rag on the eyes and Joe goes bline because The Goose has got the clap and the syph, both kinds of diseases, and that's your boyfriend Jack Diamond. I tell you this because Joe Rock was a business associate of mine. And after your boyfriend burns up Red Moran inna car over inna Newark dump and finds out Moran's girl knows who done it, he ties her up with sewer grates and dumps her inna river while she's still kickin'. That's your boyfriend Jack Diamond. How you like your boyfriend now, you dumb cunt?'

'Oh, oh, oh!' said Kiki as Joe left the room.

After we heard her story Jack shoved a fifty into my hand with the suggestion: 'How you like to take a pretty girl out to dinner?' He called somebody and went out with word to us that he'd be back in a few hours and was gone before I found the way to tell him we were quits. I can't say the idea of Kiki's company repelled me, but I was intimidated. I've talked about her beauty, and it was never greater than at that moment. She'd been primping for Jack, calling up all her considerable wisdom of sex and vanity, and had created a face I've since thought of as The Broadway Gardenia. It was structured with eyebrow pencil, mascara, an awareness of the shape of the hairline and the fall of the loose curl. It was beauty that was natural and artificial at once, and the blend created this flower child of the Follies. No carefree Atlanta belle, no windblown, wheat-haired Kansas virgin, no Oriental blossom, or long-stemmed Parisian rose could quite match her. Beauty, after all, is regional. I remember the high value the Germans put on their rose-cheeked Fräuleins. And to me the cheeks were just blotchy.

'Are you leaving me alone?' Kiki said as Jack kissed her.

'I'll be back.' He had sobered considerably in less than ten minutes.

'I don't want to be alone anymore. He might come in again.'

'Marcus is here.'

That's when he gave me the fifty and left. Kiki sat on the bed looking at the door, and when she decided he was definitely gone, she said, 'All right, goddamn it,' and went to the mirror and looked at her face and took out some black wax I've since learned is called beading and heated it in a spoon and dabbed it on her eyelids with a toothpick. Her eyes didn't need such excess, but when she looked at me, I saw something new: not excess but heightening. Magic beyond magic. I've never known another woman in the world who used that stuff and only one who even knew what it was. It was an object out of Kiki's mystical beauty kit like all her other creams and powders and soft pencils and lip brushes, and as I looked at the bottles and jars on the dressers, they all illuminated something central to her life: the studied passivity of being beautiful, of being an object to be studied, of being Jack's object. Her radio was on the dresser and exaggerated the passivity for me – lying there waiting for Jack, always waiting for Jack, and letting the music possess her as a substitute; the pink rubber douche equipment on top of the toilet tank – more proof of Kiki as Jack's vulnerable receptacle.

She stood, after she finished her eyebrows, and lifted her dress over her head, a navy-blue satin sheath with silver spangles on the bodice – Jack loved spangles. Her slip went partway up, and there flashed another view of some of the underneath dimension, to which I reacted by saying, memorably, 'Whoops.' She laughed and I stood up and said, 'I'll meet you in the lobby.'

'Why?'

'Give you a little privacy.'

'Listen, I'm all fed up with privacy. Stick around. You won't see half what you'd see if I was in one of my costumes. I'm just changing my dress.'

She moved around in her slip, sat down at the dressing table and combed the hair she had mussed, then turned quickly, faced me, giving me a full central view of upper, gartered thigh, and I thought, oh, oh, if I do what I am being tempted to do, I will end up with very substantial trouble; thinking also: vengeful concubine. But I was wrong there.

'You know,' she said, 'I don't know why I'm here.'

'In this room or on this earth?'

'In this room waiting for that son of a bitch to come and see me whenever he goddamn feels like it, even after I tell him a story like I told him about Jimmy Biondo.'

I sensed she was talking to me this way because she had taken her dress off and felt powerful. She was a sexual figure without the dress and merely a vulnerable beauty with it. Sitting there giving me an ample vision of her hinterlands was a gesture of power. Tenors shatter glassware. Strongmen bend iron bars. Sexual powerhouses show you their powersources. It reassures them in the place where they are strongest, and weakest, that they are significant, that the stares that automatically snap toward that sweet region of shadow are stares of substance and identification. With this stare, I thee covet. Desirable. Yes, yes, folks, see that? I'm desirable and everything is going to be all right. Feeling powerful, she could talk tough.

'Do you work for him all the time now, Mr Gorman?' That 'Mr' destroyed my fantasy of being seduced. A disappointment and a relief.

'I've done some things for him.'

'Do you remember Charlie Northrup from that day up on the mountain?'

'I do indeed.'

'Do you think Jack really did something to him? Hurt him?'

'I have no firsthand information on that.'

'I don't think Jack would kill him like that Biondo man said. And what he said about that man's eyes and that girl in the river. Jack wouldn't do that stuff.'

'I'm sure he wouldn't.'

'I couldn't stay with him if he did that stuff.'

'I understand.'

'I'd leave right now if I thought he did that stuff. You think

610

I could love a man who could do something to somebody's eyes like that?'

'Didn't you say it was Murray who did that?'

'That's what Biondo said, but he said Jack knew about it.'

'Well, you can't believe Biondo.'

'That's just what I think. I know Jack liked Charlie Northrup. When he spit that beer at Jack up on the mountain, Jack told me that night, "If I didn't like that guy, he'd be in a lot of trouble." Everybody thinks Jack is such a tough guy, but he's really sweet and gentle and never hurts nobody. I never even saw him pop the guts on a fly. Jack is a gentleman always and one of the tenderest, sweetest human persons I've ever come across, and I've come across my share of persons and they're not all human, I'll tell you that. I saw him with Charlie Northrup up in the mountains, and they were talking together and walking around the front yard. So I know Jack wouldn't hurt him. It's a bunch of lies what's in the papers because I know what I saw.'

'That happened *after* that day we were all on the mountain?'

'Five days after. I counted the days. I always count the days. At Biondo's farm up there. Jack said staying up on the mountain was too far away for me, and he moved me down to the farm for a few days.'

'What about dinner?'

'Jesse cooked for me. The old nigger man who runs the still.'

'I mean now.'

'Oh, now. All I have to do is put my dress on.'

She closed her gates of power and stood up.

'You know,' she said, 'I like you. I could talk to you. Don't take this the wrong way now.'

'I take it as a statement of friendship.'

'That's just what I mean. Some people you talk to them and ka-zoom, it's a pass, just because you said something nice.'

'You like me because I didn't make a pass?'

'Because you wanted to and didn't and you had such a good chance.'

'You're a perceptive girl.'

'What's that mean?'

'You see inside people.'

'I see how they look at me, that's all.'

'Not many people see that much.'

'You see, I knew I could talk to you. You don't make me feel like a dumb bunny.'

The night I went to dinner with Kiki, Tony (The Boy) Amapola was shot through the head and neck four times and dumped outside Hackensack. The papers said he was a close pal of Jimmy Biondo's and that Biondo was Capone's man in town, which wasn't true. Another victim of another beer war, was the consensus, but I suggest he was a victim of Jimmy's bad manners toward ladies.

I sat talking with Kiki that night until Jack came back around midnight, and then I drove to Albany without telling him I was all through. A call from Jesse Franklin was waiting for me when I got to the office the next day, asking me to come and see him. I don't think I'd have remembered him if Kiki hadn't mentioned him as her cook at the farm the night before. I called him back and got a hotel which turned out to be a flophouse for Negroes in Albany's South End. I told him to come and see me, but he said he couldn't, and would I come to see him? I never met a client in a flophouse before, so I said I would.

It turned out to be the ground floor of an old converted livery stable with a dozen cots, two of which were occupied: one by a man wheezing and ranting in a drunken, mumbly wine coma, and the other by Jesse, who sat on his cot like a bronze sculpture of despair, a weary old man with nubby white hair, wearing ratty overalls and staring downward, watching the roaches play around his muddy shoes. He hadn't been out of the flop in three weeks except to go to a corner store and buy food, then come back and sleep and wait.

'You remember me, Mr Gorman?'

'I was talking about you with Kiki Roberts only last night.'

'Pretty lady.'

'That's her truth all right.'

'She didn't see nothin' what I seen, what I wants to tell you 'bout. Nobody seen what I seen.'

'Why do you want to tell me about it?'

'I got some money. I can pay.'

'I would expect it.'

'I sent my boys away but I don't wanna go myself, don't know where to go. Only one place to go I know of is back to the farm and work for Mr Jack, but I don't wanna go back there. Can't go back to that old place after what I seen. I fear 'bout those men. I know the police lookin' for me too 'cause they askin' Mr Fogarty 'bout me before he go to jail and I don't want no police, so I highfoots it up to Albany 'cause I know they got coloreds up here plenty and nobody know me, and then I know I gonna run out of money and have to be on the road and I gonna get picked up sure as Jesus. So I been sittin' here thinkin' 'bout what I gonna do and I remember Mr Jack got a lawyer friend in Albany. I been sittin' here three weeks tryin' to 'member your name. Then yesterday this old bum he fall right in front of me, right there by them little roaches, and he got a newspaper in his pocket and I seen your picture and Mr Jack's picture and I say, that's my man all right, that's my man. Man who runs this place got me your phone number all right. I gets picked up you goin' help me?'

'I'll help you if I can, but I've got to know what this is all about.'

'Yep. I gonna tell you but nobody else. No how. What I see I don't want no more part of. I see it when I just about finished at the still for about five hours, sun goin' down and I throwed down my head to sleep off the miseries when I heerd this automobile pull up in front of the barn. I sleeps in the back of the house, so I look out and see Mr Fogarty openin' the barn doors and other fellas Mr Jack have around him all the time in the car and they drives right inside. Now I never did see this before. Mr Jack use that barn for storage and he don't want no automobiles drivin' in and out of where he keep his beer and his whiskey 'cept for loadin' and that ain't no loadin' car I see. But Jesse ain't about to tell them

613

fellas they can't use Mr Jack's barn. Bye'em bye, Mr Fogarty he come in the house and then he and Miss Kiki go out with Mr Jack. I spies out the window at the gay-rage and I sees the light on there. I don't see nobody comin' or goin' out of that old place so I figure it ain't none of Jesse's business and I tries to go back and sleep. Bye'em bye, I hear that car again and it's dark now and in a little bit Mr Fogarty comes in and gets some old newspapers and calls up to Jesse, is you up there and I say I is and he say Mr Jack say for me not to go near the still tonight and I say okay by me and I don't ask why because Jesse ain't a man who asks why to Mr Jack and his friends. Mr Fogarty carries them papers back out and about twenty minutes go by and I heerd that car again and I sits right up in the bed and says, well they's done whatever they's done and I look out the window and they's no light in the gay-rage and I call down the stairs to Mr Fogarty, but he don't say nothin' back and nobody else does neither, and I know my boys won't, 'cause they sleep like fishbones on the bottom of a mud pond, and so I think of what they been doin' in the gay-rage and I can't figure it out. But I say to myself, Jesse, you ought to know what's goin' on hereabouts since this is where you livin' and maybe they up to somethin' you don't want yourself fixed up in. So I takes my flashlight and I spokes quiet like down them stairs and out into the backyard and they's no light in the gay-rage so I sprites 'round by the back in case somebody pull up. And inside it's the same old gay-rage, a couple three newspapers on the floor 'longside the wheelbarra. Coolin' room's the same as usual and Mr Jack's tahger's on the back wall's the same as usual and all the tools on the bench. I can't see no difference nowhere. Then I see in the corner of the coolin' room a big piece of somethin' all wrapped up and I knows this wasn't there before and I knows what I think it is soon as I sees it. And I shines the light on it. It look like a rug all rolled up 'cept it ain't no rug. It's canvas we throwed over the beer barrels first time the roof leaked. And I goes over and touches that canvas with my toe and it is solid. It feel just like I 'spect it to feel. And Jesse beginnin' to worry what gonna happen if he caught here with this thing alone. But I got to make sure it's what I think, so I puts my whole foot on it and feel how it feels, and it ain't exactly like what I 'spect, so I touches it with my hand. And that ain't exactly like I 'spect either and so I opens one end of the canvas to peek inside and see what is this thing that ain't like what it ought to be like, and out come this here head. All by itself. It roll out just a little bit, and I tell you if I ain't 'lectrified dead now, I don't know why I ain't. And I highfoots it out of that barn and back into the house and up them stairs and back to my own room and under the covers so's I can think by myself what I ought to do. And I thinks. And I thinks. And I don't hear nobody comin' back. Then I say to myself, Jesse, if somebody do come back, you is in mighty trouble. Because that head ain't where it ought to be and they is goin' to know somebody been out peekin' into that canvas. And first thing, they comin' back in here and say to you, Jesse, why you foolin' around with that head out in that barn? What you say then, old man? So bye'em bye, I sits up, and gets up, and goes downstairs and out to the gay-rage and what scare me now ain't that head, but them lights of the car if they come shootin' back in the road. But I say to myself, Jesse, you got to go put that head back where you got it. So I goes back in the coolin' room and shines the light down and sees the old head lookin' up at me three feet out from the end of the canvas where it rolled. And I gets a good look at that face which I can't reckonize and maybe nobody on this earth gonna reckonize over again, because it been beat so bad it ain't no face at all. It just a head full of beat-up old flesh. I feels sorry for that poor fella 'cause he got his. No doubt 'bout that. But I say, Jesse, feel sorry for this man when you gets back to your bed. Right now, get yourself busy puttin' that head back in with the rest of him. Now I don't like it nohow, but I pick up that old head and opens up the canvas so's I can put it back in and, oh God A'mighty, there's two hands and a foot side by side like the Lord never intended nobody's hands and foot to be put together. And I opens up the canvas wider and oh God A'mighty, they ain't one whole piece of that poor fella no more. He is in ten, fifteen pieces, oh my Jesus, I gonna die. I put that head back where it used to be and fold that canvas up the way it used to be. Then I look around on the floor for any little blood drippin's I might of spilt, but I can't see none. I can't see none they might of left either, so I guess they got it all mopped up with them newspapers Mr Fogarty picked out. Oh, sweet Jesus. And I go back out of the coolin' room then, and back into the house. I ain't worried now whether they gonna find me out there, because they ain't. It just like it was before I seen it the first time. Now I'se worryin' about somethin' else, which is how I gonna get myself and the boys out of this here butcher shop. I sure can't do it right away or they gonna know I knows more'n I s'pose to know. So I lays there thinkin' 'bout how long it'd be before it be right for me to go my own way and take my boys with me. And wonderin' where we gonna go, 'cause we ain't had no job good as this in mighty a year. But I ain't worryin' now 'bout no job. I worryin' 'bout the jailhouse gettin' me, and what my boys gonna do then? I'se still thinkin' 'bout this when I hears the car pull into the yard and I looks out and there comes Mr Murray and somebody I can't see and they pulls in the gay-rage again but with one of Mr Jack's trucks and stays 'bout five minutes and they back out and close the door. Then goodbye. They gone. I know the canvas and the head and the rest of the pieces of that poor ol' boy done gone too, but I don't move, 'cause it's daylight just beginnin', and ain't nobody gonna see Jesse Franklin in that barn today. Not any of those fellas, not Mr Jack, not any stranger, not Jesse hisself. Jesse is gonna stay clear of that ol' gay-rage till somebody come who got business to do in it. And when it all simmer down, Jesse gonna take his boys and he goin' waaaay 'way from here. These is bad people, cut a man up like that. How he gonna make it all back together again come judgment time? Bad people, doin' that to a man.'

It was Fogarty who told me how Charlie Northrup got it, told me later when he was figuring out where his life went, still drunk, still ready to muzzle any pussy that showed itself. He never changed and I always liked him and I knew all along why Jack kept him on – because he was the opposite of Murray. He was Fogarty, the group's nice guy. I liked him in that context, probably because of the contrast. I no longer think it strange that Jack had both kinds – Fogarty kind, Murray kind – working for him. Jack lived a long time, for Jack, and I credit it to his sense of balance, even in violent matters, even in the choice of killers and drivers, his sense that all ranges of the self must be appeased, and yet only appeased, not indulged. I make no case for Jack as a moderate, only as a man in touch with primal needs. He read them, he answered them, until he stopped functioning in balance. That's when the final trouble began.

Charlie Northrup drove his car to the Biondo farm at dusk to keep his appointment with Jack. Fogarty said Murray and Oxie were on the porch, rocking in the squeaky, green rockers while Jack waited inside.

'I don't go inside,' Charlie said at the foot of the steps.

'Then you wait there,' Murray said, and he went for Jack, who came out through the screen door and walked down the stairs and put his hand out to shake Charlie's hand. But it wasn't there.

'Never mind jerking me off,' Charlie said. 'Get to the point.'

'Don't talk nasty, Charlie,' Jack said, 'or I'll forget we're brothers.'

'Brothers. You got some rotten fucking way of being a brother. What you done to me, you're a bum in my book, a bum in spades.'

'Listen, Charlie. I got something to say to you. I ought to blow your face off. Anybody talks to the federals has a right to get their face blown off, isn't that so?'

Fogarty said Charlie shut up at that point, that he obviously didn't think Jack knew.

'I got some good friends who happen to be federals,' Jack said.

Charlie kept quiet.

'But the way I look at it, Charlie, I blow your face off and I lose all that money I'd have had if the federals didn't pick up my cargo. And what I figure is, set up a working relationship with

Charlie and he'll pay me back what I lost. All we do is cooperate and the problem is solved.'

'Cooperate,' said Charlie, 'means I give you my shirt and kiss your ass for taking it.'

'Partners, Charlie. That's what I got in mind. Partners in an expanding business. I produce the business, you provide the product. We split seventy-thirty till you pay off the debt, then we reduce it, fifty-fifty, because we're brothers. Business doubles, triples at higher prices and a locked-up market. It's brilliant, Charlie, brilliant.'

'You know I got partners already. They're nobody's patsies.'

'I take the risk about your partners.'

'I don't want no part of you,' Charlie said. 'I wouldn't hold onto you in an earthquake.'

Charlie stopped walking. They were under the maples, a few feet from the porch, Jack in a tan suit and Charlie in his sweat shirt.

'I said it before, Jack. Stuff it up your ass. You're not talking to a man without power. Play with me you're not playing with some apple-knocker up here, some dummy saloonkeeper. You know my friends. I'm done talking about it.'

He walked away from Jack, toward his car.

'You stupid fucking donkey,' Jack said, and he looked up at Oxie and Murray, who stood up and pointed their pistols at Charlie. Fogarty remembered only his own rocker squeaking at that point. He kept rocking until Murray gave him the gesture and then he got out of the chair and in behind the wheel of Northrup's car and drove it back into the garage with Oxie and Murray inside it holding their pistols against Charlie's belly. Fogarty remembered Jack climbing the porch steps and watching them all get in the car.

'Now, Charlie,' he said, 'you got to get a lesson in manners.'

Murray always wore steel-toed shoes and I never knew that either until Fogarty told me this whole story. He used a gun or the long, pointed, three-cornered file he carried (his improvement on the ice pick Flossie remembered) when necessary, but he used his feet when he could. The story is he took lessons from a French killer he met in jail and who used to box savate style. Murray had the rep of being able to kill you with one kick.

He kicked Charlie in the belly as soon as they got out of the car. Charlie doubled up but charged Murray head down, two hundred and forty pounds of wild bull. Murray sidestepped and kicked Charlie in the leg. Charlie crashed into a wall and bounced off it like a rubber rhino. Murray the shrimp gave a high kick and caught Charlie under the chin, and as Charlie wobbled, Murray kicked him in the kneecap and he went down. Murray kicked him in the groin, creased his face, crunched his nose with the side of his shoe. He danced around Charlie, kicking elbows, ribs, shins, calves, and thighs, kicking ass and back and then kicking Charlie's face lightly, left foot, right foot, lightly but still a kick, drawing blood, rolling the head from side to side like a leaky soccer ball.

Fogarty left the garage and went inside the house. He poured himself a double whiskey and stood looking at a fly on the front screen door. Jack and Kiki came down the stairs, Jack carrying Kiki's suitcase.

'Can I see you, Jack?' he said and they went out on the porch, and Fogarty said, 'I don't need that stuff going on back there. That cocksucker's not going to leave any on the man.'

'All right. The Goose and Oxie can handle it alone.'

'The Goose is a fucking maniac. He oughta be in a cage.'

'The Goose knows what he's doing. He won't hurt him too bad.'

'He's gonna kill him. You said you didn't want to kill him.'

'The Goose won't kill him. He's done this before.'

'He's a sick son of a bitch.'

'Listen, don't get your balls out of joint. Drive us to town. Have a drink in the village while we have dinner. Change your mood.'

So Fogarty drove them in, and Jack checked Kiki in at the Saulpaugh to get her away from the farm. He moved her around like a checker. Fogarty drove Jack back to his own house at midnight and went to sleep himself on the porch sofa where he was awakened at two in the morning by the private buzzer, the one under the second porch step. Jack was at the door almost as soon as Fogarty got himself off the sofa. Jack was wide awake, in his red silk pajamas and red silk robe. It was Oxie at the door.

'Northrup's shot,' Oxie said.

'Who shot him?'

'Murray.'

'What the hell for?'

'He had to. He acted up.'

'Where are they?'

'In Northrup's car, in the driveway.'

'You half-witted cocksucker, you brought him here?'

'We didn't want to leave him no place.'

'Get him over to the farm. I'll meet you there in ten minutes.'

Fogarty pulled up behind the Northrup car which Oxie had parked in shadows on the farm's entrance road.

'He looks dead,' Jack said when he looked at Charlie's crumpled frame in the back seat. The seat was full of blood near his head.

'He ain't peeped,' Murray said. 'I think he's a cold fishy.'

Jack picked up Charlie's hand, felt it, dropped it.

'What happened?'

'I was past Newburgh when he got the rope off,' Murray said.

'Who tied him up?'

'Me,' said Murray.

'He got free and swung a tire iron and hit me in the neck,' Murray said. 'Almost broke my neck.'

'I was followin' in our car and I saw him swerve, almost go in a ditch,' Oxie said.

'Where'd he get a tire iron?'

'It musta been down behind the seat,' Murray said. 'It wasn't on the floor when we put him in.'

Jack kept nodding, then threw up his hands in a small gesture.

'You had to shoot him?'

'It was only one shot, a fluke. What am I supposed to do about a guy with a tire iron?'

'You're a fucking maniac. You know what this could cost me?

Front pages. Not to mention a fucking war.' He hit the roof of the car with his fist.

'What do we do with him?' Oxie asked.

'Get some weights, we'll put him in the river,' said Murray.

'Goddamn this,' Jack said. He kicked Northrup's fender. Then he said, 'No, the river he could float up. Take him in the woods and bury him. No, wait, they could still find the son of a bitch. I want no evidence on this. Burn him.'

'Burn him?' Fogarty said.

'Use the fire out at the still. You can make it as big as you want, nobody pays attention.' And then he said to Fogarty, 'If he's dead, he's dead, right? A lump of mud.'

'What about Jesse and his kids?'

'Go see them. Tell them to stay away from the still tonight.'

'You can't burn a man's body in that pit out there,' Fogarty said. 'It's big but not that big.'

'I'll take care of that,' Murray said. 'I'll trim off the edges.'

'Christ Almighty.'

'Try not to burn down the woods,' Jack said. 'When you're done, let me know. And you won't be done till there's nothing left, even if it takes two days. And then you clean out the pit and sift the ashes and smash the teeth and the bones that don't burn, especially the teeth. And scatter the pieces and the dust someplace else.'

'Gotcha,' said Murray. It was his kind of night.

'Speed, you better give 'em a hand,' Jack said. 'Drive and stand guard. He don't have to touch anything,' Jack told Murray.

'What does he ever touch?' Murray said.

Fogarty's stomach was burbling as he drove Northrup's car inside the barn. Murray said he needed a lot of newspapers, and so Fogarty went into the house and got some and told Jesse to stay clear of the still until he was told he could go back. Fogarty walked slowly back to the barn, feeling like he might puke. When he saw what Murray had already done to Charlie with the hatchet, it shot out of him like a geyser.

'Tough guy,' Murray said.

* * *

'Marcus,' Kiki said from the other end of the phone, and it was the first time she called me that, 'I'm so damn lonely.'

'Where's your friend?'

'I thought you might know.'

'I haven't seen him since the night I took you to dinner.'

'I've seen him twice since then. Twice in seventeen days. He's up in the country with her all the time. Christ, what does he see in that fat old cow? What's the matter with me? I wash my armpits.'

'He's all business these days. He'll turn up.'

'I'm getting bedsores waiting. What he don't know is I'm not waiting anymore. I'm going into a new show. I just couldn't cut it anymore, sitting, waiting. Maybe he sees me dancing again he'll think twice about playing titball with his fat-assed wife. I bet when she takes off her brassiere they bounce off her toes.'

Kiki was tight, another road to power.

'What's the show and when does it open? I wouldn't miss that.'

'*Smiles* is the name of it, and I do one routine by myself, a tap number. It's swell, Marcus, but I'd rather make love.'

'Sure. Had any more visits from Jimmy Biondo?'

'Nobody visits me. Why don't you come down to the city and see me? Just to talk, now. Don't let the little lady give you the wrong impression.'

'Maybe I will,' I said, 'next time I'm down there on business.'

I had no pressing business in New York, but I made it a point to go, and I presume it was for the same reason I'd helped old Jesse frame a new identity for himself and then got him a job in Boston – because I was now addicted to entering the world of Jack Diamond as fully as possible. I was unable not to stick around and see how it all turned out. And yes, I know, even as a spectator, I was condoning the worst sort of behavior. Absolute worst. I know, I know.

I called Jack when I decided to go down, for I had no wish to put myself in the middle of the big romance.

'Great,' he said. 'Take her to a movie. I'll be down Friday and we'll all go out.'

'You know I still have some of your belongings.'

'Hang onto them.'

'I'd rather not.'

'Only for a little while more.'

'A very little while.'

'What's the problem? They taking up too much room?'

'Only in my head.'

'Clean out your head. Go see Marion.'

So I did and we went to dinner and talked and talked, and then I took her to see Garbo in *Flesh and the Devil* in a place that hadn't yet converted to talkies. Kiki was a Garbo fanatic and looked on herself as a *femme fatale* even though she was nothing of the sort. The main thing she had in common with Garbo was beauty. There is a photo of Garbo at fifteen that has something of Kiki about it, but after that the ladies were not playing the same game. 'The spiritually erotic rules over the sensually erotic in her life,' an astrologist once said of Garbo, which was a pretty fair critical summary of her movie self at least.

Kiki was something else: a bread-and-butter sensualist, a let's-put-it-all-on-the-table-folks kind of girl. She actually enjoyed the feeling of being wicked. In the movie Garbo rushes to save her two loves from a duel, repentant that she started it all as a way of simplifying her choice between them. She falls through the ice on the way and it's goodbye Greta. Kiki leaned over to me and whispered, 'That's what you get for being a good girl.'

Kiki started out with the glitter dream, a bathing beauty at fifteen, a Follies' girl at eighteen, a gangster's doll at twenty. She yearned for spangles and got them quickly, then found she didn't really want them except for what they did for her head. They preserved her spangly mood. She was in spangles when she met Jack at the Club Abbey during his fugitive time, and he loved them almost as much as he loved her face.

'I always knew exactly how pretty I was,' she told me, 'and I knew I could write my own ticket in show business, even though

I don't dance or sing so great. I don't kid myself. But whatever you can get out of this business with good looks, I'm going to get. Then when I met Jack it changed. My life started going someplace, someplace weird and good. I wanted to feel that good thing in me, and when I did it with Jack, I knew I didn't care about show business except as a way to stay alive and keep myself out front. I'm Jack's girl, but that's not all I am, and supposing he drops me? But I know he won't do that because what we have is so great. We go out, me and Jack, out to the best places with the best people, rich people, I mean, society people, famous people like politicians and actors and they fall all over us. I know they envy us because of what we've got and what we are. They all want to make sex with us and kiss us and love us. All of them. They look up my dress and down my front and touch me any place they can, stroke my wrist or hair or pat my fanny and say excuse me, or take my hand and say something nice and stupid, but it's all an excuse to touch. And when practically everybody you come across does this to you, women too, then you know you're special, maybe not forever, but for now. Then you go home and he puts it up in you and you wrap around him and you come and he comes, and it mixes up together and it's even greater than what was already great, but it's still the same fantastic thing. You're in love and you're wanted by everybody, and is anything ever better than that? One night, when Jack was in me, I thought, Marion, he's not fucking you, he's fucking himself. Even then I loved him more than I'd ever loved anything on earth. He was stabbing me and I was smothering him. We were killing everything that deserved to die because it wasn't as rich as it could be. We were killing the empty times, and then we'd die with them and wake up and kill them again until there wasn't anything left to kill and we'd be alive in a way that you can never die when you feel like that because you own your life and nothing can ruin you.

'And then he leaves me here for seventeen days and keeps track of everygoddamnbody I buy a paper off or smile at in the lobby, and so I stay in and practice my dance steps and listen to Rudy Vallee and Kate Smith, and I don't even have a view of the park because Jack doesn't want to be a target from the trees. This is a nice little suite and all, and do I mean little. Because you can lose your mind staying in two rooms, and so I fix my hair and pluck my eyebrows. I know when every hair in my eyebrows first pokes its way out. I watch it grow. I take a hot bath and I rub myself off to forget what I want. One day I did that four times and that's not healthy for a young person like me and I'll tell you straight, I'm to the point where I'm not going to be so damn particular who's inside me when I want to feel that good thing. But I never cheated on him yet, and I don't want to. I don't want to leave him, and that's the God's truth. I almost said I can't leave him, but I know I can. I can leave if I want. But I don't want to leave. That's why I took the job in *Smiles*. To show him I can leave him, even when I don't want to.'

At 9:30 P.M. on Saturday, October 11, 1930, three men, later identified as members of the Vincent Coll gang, walked into the Pup Club on West Fifty-first Street in Manhattan. One walked up to the short one-eyed man at the bar and said softly to him, 'Murray?' The one-eyed man turned on his stool and faced two guns.

'You're out, Murray,' the man who had spoken to him said, and the other two fired six bullets into him. Then they left.

An hour and a half later, in an eighth-floor room at the Monticello Hotel, across the hall from the room occupied by Marion Roberts, two men stepped off the elevator at the same time that two others were touching the top step of the stairs leading to the eighth floor. The four fanned out into the cul-de-sacs of the hallways and returned to the elevator with an all clear, and Jimmy Biondo stepped out past a blanched elevator man. The five men, Jimmy at the center, walked down the hall to Room 824 and knocked three times, then twice, then once, and the door opened on Jack Diamond in shirtsleeves, a pistol on the arm of the chair he was sitting in. Count Duschene said he stood to Jack's left, and at other points around the room were the men who had confronted Murray earlier in the evening: Vincent Coll, Edward (Fats McCarthy) Popke, and Hubert Maloy.

'Hey, Jimmy,' Jack said. 'Glad you could come. How you getting along?'

Pear-shaped Jimmy, still mistrusting the room, stared at all faces before settling on Jack's and saying, 'Whatayou got to offer aside from my money?'

'Sit down, Jimmy, chair there for you. Let's talk a little.'

'Nothing to talk about. Where's the money?'

'The money is in good hands. Don't worry about that.'

'Whose good hands?'

'What's the difference if it's safe?'

'Never mind the horseshit, where's the money?'

'What would you say if I told you it's on its way back to Germany?'

'I'd tell you you ain't got very fucking long to live.'

'I'm going back there, Jimmy, and this time I'll get in. Don't you like instant seven-to-one on your money?'

'I like my money.'

'We made a deal. I want to keep my part of the bargain is all.'

'No deal. Tony Amapola knows how you deal. Charlie Northrup knows how you deal.'

'I knew you'd think of me when Tony got it. But I had nothing to do with that. I like Tony. Always did. As for Charlie I do know what happened. It was a freelance job. Charlie made enemies up in the country. But Charlie and I were as close as you and Tony. We were like brothers.'

'Charlie had a different story. He said you were a fuckhead.'

'You don't believe me, ask any of these boys who it was gave it to Charlie.'

Jimmy looked around, settled on Fats McCarthy. Fats nodded at him.

'Murray The Goose,' Fats said. 'He give it to Charlie.'

'You heard yet what happened to Murray The Goose?' Jack asked Jimmy.

'No.'

'Somebody just dealt him out, up in the Pup Club. Walked in

and boom-boom-boom. Cooked The Goose. Somebody got even for Charlie is how I read it. Now how do you like your friends?'

'It's a fact,' The Count said. 'I happened to be in the club at the time.'

'There's a coincidence for you,' Jack said.

'Puttin' it on The Goose don't mean he was even in the same state.'

'Ask around. Don't tell me you didn't hear the rumors.'

'I hear nothin'.'

'You oughta listen a little instead of talking so much about money. There's more to life than money, Jimmy.'

'Fuck life. I been listenin' too long. I been listenin' to your bullshit here five minutes, and I don't see no money onna fuckin' table. I tell you what – you got a telephone I make a call to an old frienda yours. Charlie Lucky.'

'Always glad to say hello to Charlie.'

'He be glad to say hello to you too because half the two hundred come outa his pocket. Whataya think of that, you Irish fuck?'

'I'll tell you what, you guinea fuck, call Charlie. He tells me it's half his I'll have it for him in the morning.'

Jimmy moved his elbow at one of his young gunmen: early twentyish, pencil-line mustache. The gunman dialed, said something in Italian, waited, handed the phone to Jimmy.

'That you, Charlie?' Jimmy said. 'I'm with our friend. He wants to know were you my silent partner. Okay. Sure.' He handed Jack the phone.

'Charlie, how you doin'? You staying thin? Right, Charlie, that's the only way. You were. You did. So. Yeah. Now I get it. You're not saying this just for Jimmy. You wouldn't con me after all these years. Right. I understand. Let's have a drink one of these days, Charlie. Any time. Beautiful.'

Jack hung up and turned to Jimmy. 'He said he loaned you twenty grand at fourteen percent.'

'He don't say that.'

'I just talked to the man. Did you hear me talk to him? What am I, a guy who makes up stories you see with your own eyes?'

William Kennedy

'He's in for half, no interest.'

'I tell you what, Jimmy. I'll have twenty available in the morning. I'll call you and tell you where to pick it up and you can pay Charlie back. Meantime we still got a deal with what's left.'

'Charlie, give me a hundred, you fuckheaded fuck!' Jimmy screamed and stood up, and everybody's pistol came out at the same time. Jack didn't touch his. All the pistols were pointed at all the other pistols. Anybody moved it was ten-way suicide.

'We don't seem to be getting anyplace,' Jack said. He lit a Rameses and sat down and crossed his legs. 'Why don't you go have a drink and think about life, Jimmy? Think about how rich you'll be when I come back with all that beautiful white stuff. A million four. Is that hard to take or is that hard to take?'

'I'm talkin' to a dead man,' Jimmy said.

'Dead men pay no debts, Jimmy.'

'Keep lookin' for me,' Jimmy said.

'Watch yourself crossing the street,' Jack said.

These were atrocious melodramatics, and I would not give them the time of day, despite my trust in Fogarty, except that when Jimmy and his friends left the Monticello and walked down West Sixty-fourth Street, a car came in their direction at low speed and two shotgun blasts from a back window blew apart two of Jimmy's shooters. Jimmy and the other two escaped with only a certain loss of dignity.

Count Duschene later remembered Jack's reaction when he heard the news: 'Mustache cocksuckers. Fast as you knock 'em off they bring in another boatload.' The rest of the news came out in the morning paper: Murray, with six bullets in him, was not yet dead.

Kiki said that the positively worst time of her life was when she was hiding at Madge's apartment and the knock came on the door and Madge turned to her and said, 'Get in the bedroom and hide.' So she went first behind Madge's big Morris chair, but then she said to herself, Gee, they'd look here right away, and so she started to roll under Madge's canopy bed with the beaded curtain, but then she said to herself, Won't they look under here, too? And so she stood in the closet behind Madge's summer and winter dresses and coats until she realized that anybody opening the door would look right through the hangers into her great big beautiful brown eyes, and so she took Madge's dyed muskrat everybody thought was mink off the wooden hanger and covered herself with it and rolled into the smallest ball she could make out of herself and faced the wall with her rounded back to the door so they would think the coat had fallen off the hanger on top of a pile of shoes and little boxes and galoshes. And then they'd go away. Yes. Go away. Let me alone.

Right then, Kiki would have said if anyone had asked her, she ordinarily didn't like to be alone. But now it was quite necessary, for she had to figure out what she was going to do with her life. She never had to hide in a closet before, ever. Jack's fault. Her fault too for staying with him, waiting for him. She had decided to leave him for good, truly leave this time and not just go back into show business or take a train home to Boston with her mad money. No. This was the end. Nothing on earth could make her stay with Jack Diamond for another day because he truly did kill people.

She had read all the news stories when he was in Europe, but she didn't read past the parts where they began to say things about him. She'd just throw the papers in the bottom of her closet for Jack because she knew how he loved to save clippings about himself. And what a big stack it got to be! She didn't even read any of the long series of articles they wrote about him because the first one began by calling him Eggs Diamond. Because eggs are yellow. And though she knew Jack wasn't yellow, she didn't really know what color he was. She didn't know anything really deep about him except what he said and what she wanted him to say and what he said was 'You're gorgeous in my life' and 'You're the most beautiful thing in the world. I deserve you.' And she said to that, 'And I deserve you, too.' And they went into their silk cocoon then. Her warm bed with the pink silk sheets and her white silk nightgown and Jack in his yellow silk pajamas with the green dragon on them, and slowly they took the silk off one another and just smothered themselves in the cocoon and fucked and fucked and fucked. And when they were all through they went to sleep and woke up, and then they fucked and fucked some more and took a shower and went to see Jolson again in *Mammy*, and had dinner and came back to the cocoon, and didn't they fuck even more? They certainly did. Oh, wasn't that the cat's knickers? Vo-de-oh-do! There was never anything like that in her life before Jack, though she knew about fucking all right, all right. But fucking is one thing and fucking with Jack was another thing altogether. It was not the glitter. Sometimes when you fucked it was just to get something or because you thought you ought to or because you liked his looks and he was nice to you and it was expected of you and you wanted to do what was expected. It was your role to fuck men who were nice because you're only young once, isn't that so? Isn't that why you wanted to be in the glitter dream? To glitter by yourself? And what better way to glitter than to fuck whenever you felt like it? Fuck the best people, the most beautiful people. Do you like to fuck? Oh, I love it, don't you?

But then she met Jack and she didn't want anybody but him. Now it wasn't just liking to fuck. It was liking to fuck Jack. And it was feeling wanted and taken and also taking and also wanting, which was the key to the thing that changed in her. She wanted in a new way. Jack taught her that. She wanted not just for the moment or the hour or the day, but she wanted permanently.

'We'll always live in the cocoon, won't we?'

'Sure, kid.'

'We'll make love even when you're seventy-five, won't we?'

'No, kid. I'm not going to live to be seventy-five. I didn't expect to make it to thirty-three.'

And that changed her again. She wanted him and wanted what he gave her forever and ever, but now she had to think about outliving him, of this maybe being that last time she would ever put her arms around him and bite his ear and play with his candy cane because then he might get up and get dressed and go out and die. Well, then she wanted him more than ever. She didn't know why. She just called it love because that's what everybody else called it. But it wasn't only that, because now she wanted not just Jack himself but Jack who was going to die. She wanted to kiss and fuck somebody who was going to die. Because when he died, then you had something nobody else could ever get again.

And then Jimmy Biondo came and talked to her and she said she didn't believe what he said about Jack being so awful. But she went and read all the papers she was saving in the closet and oh, the things they said that Jack did all his life, and she couldn't believe her eyes because they were so awful, so many killings and torturing people and burning prostitutes with cigarettes. Oh, oh, oh! And so she knew then she would leave him. She knew it and she knew it and she knew it all Saturday night even after he came to her room and they went into the cocoon killing the bad things. She forgot while that was happening that she was going to leave him, for how can you leave a person when they're making you forget the bad things? But when it was over she remembered and when she went to sleep alongside him she thought of it and she was still thinking about it when she woke up and saw him drinking the orange juice he'd ordered for them both, with toast and eggs and coffee and a steak for him, and she thought of it while he ate the steak in his blue pajamas with the red racehorses on them. I am seeing you eat your last piece of steak. I am seeing you wear your last pajamas. She would kill him in her mind and that would be the end of Jack Diamond for Marion Roberts. So long, Jackie boy. I loved your candy. Gee it was swell. But you're dead now for me. You're mine forever. Marion Roberts is not going to go on living her life as a gangster's doll, a gangster's moll. Marion Roberts is her own woman and she is not going to live for fucking. She is not going to live for any one man. She is not going to live for killing because she knows better. She knows how good life is and how hard it is to make life good. She's going to move on to something else. She can go on dancing. She will find a way to live out her life without gangster Jackie.

But then she wondered: What is it about a gangster like him? Why did I take up with him? Why didn't I believe what everybody said about him, that I might wind up in the river, that I might get shot in bed with him, that he might ruin my face if he ever caught me cheating? Because gangsters are evil and don't care about anybody but themselves. Why didn't she believe those things? Because she wanted it all out of life, all all all there was to get. The top, the tip, the end, the reach, the most, the greatest, the flashiest, the best, the biggest, the wildest, the craziest, the worst.

Why did Kiki want the worst? Because she was a criminal too? A criminal of love? Birds of a feather, Marion. You knew even as you were saying that you were leaving him that you wouldn't leave. You knew as you read about the torture he did and the killing he did that you wouldn't give him up because you knew about the other side of that glorious man, with his candy up in your sweet place and his mouth on yours. You wouldn't give that up.

Even when those men came to the hotel this morning and Jack went to meet them and said to them while you were lying there in the half-empty cocoon, even when he said: 'Hello, boys, how are you? Be right with you,' and said to you that he'd only be a few minutes, and that he had some business to finish up, and went out in the hallway still in his blue pajamas with the red racehorses and the darker blue robe with the white sash and the white diamond embroidered on the breast pocket, even then you knew.

You got up and went into the shower and you let it smother you like you smothered him and you were standing in that sweet heat after love in the morning when you heard the shots: two, four, six, then none, then three more and another and another and another. And you froze in all that heat because you said to yourself (Oh, God forgive you for saying it), you said: That murdering bastard, he's killed somebody else.

Later, when she started to dance, she remembered looking at her feet and said to herself: These are going to be the most famous legs on Broadway. And she danced on that for five minutes to the piano man's rippling repetition of a tune of four-four tempo whose name she couldn't remember any more than she could remember the piano man's name or the director's name or the name of the musical itself. Black mesh stockings enveloped her most famous legs. White trunks covered her most famous hips. A white blouse tied at the midriff covered her most famous breasts. And black patent leather tap shoes covered her most famous toes, which nobody realized yet were famous. She thought of how people would behave when they found out how famous they were and tried to let that thought crowd out the rest. But she couldn't. Because her mind went back to what it was that was going to make her toes so famous and she stopped dancing, seeing it all again, seeing herself see it this time and knowing she was webbed in something that wasn't even going to be possible to get out of. So she looked at the piano man and then at the director, and while the other girls went on dancing, she decided to fall down.

The next thing she knew she was sitting at her mirror with all her theatrical makeup on the table in front of her, and the calico kitten Jack had won for her at the Coney Island shooting gallery, all cuddly and sleepy in the middle of the table. In the mirror she saw Madge Conroy sitting on a chair beside her, and Bubble, the chorus boy who had helped Madge pick her off the floor. They both stared at her.

'She finally blinked,' Bubble said.

'You all right?' Madge asked.

'Close your eyes, for heaven's sake,' Bubble said, 'before they explode all over us.'

The mirror was outlined by a dozen bare bulbs, all illuminating her face, so famous to be, so unknown to even its own exploding eyes. Why aren't you running away, pretty lady in the brilliant mirror? What brought you to the theater? Is it that you don't know what to be afraid of yet? Do you think the theater will protect you? Do you think the mirror will?

Bubble said, 'Mirror, mirror on the wall, who's got the Kikiest eyes of all?'

'Shut up,' Madge said, 'and get her a drink someplace.' Madge rubbed Kiki's wrists as Bubble went away.

'Oh, Madge, I just got to talk to somebody.'

'I had a hunch you did. I kept watching you dancing out

there. You looked like somebody kidnapped your brain. Like a zombie.'

'Honest to God, Madge, it's something awful. It's so awful.'

Bubble came back with an unlabeled half-pint. Madge grabbed it and looked at it, smelled it and poured Kiki a drink. She capped the bottle, set it on Kiki's table, and told Bubble, 'Will you please, please, please get lost?'

'What's the *matter* with her?'

'I'll find out if you let us be.'

'Yes, nursie.'

'You oughta be rehearsing out there,' Kiki said to Madge.

'They can do without me. I know the routine.'

'It was so awful. Honest to God, this is the worst thing that ever happened to me.'

'What? What the hell happened?'

'I can't tell you here. Can we go someplace? I don't know what to do, Madge. Honest to God I don't.'

'We can go over to my apartment. Change your clothes.'

But it took so much effort for Kiki to take off her trunks that she left on the rest, her mesh stockings and the rehearsal blouse and only put on her skirt and street shoes. She threw her other street clothes and the trunks and tap shoes into her red patent-leather hatbox and saw, as she did, her street makeup and her purse, the only things she took when she ran out of the hotel.

'I'm ready,' she said to Madge.

'You better buy a paper,' Kiki told Madge when they came to a newsstand at Broadway and Forty-seventh. And as Madge did and after Kiki saw her utter a small 'Oh' and throw her face into the paper, Kiki turned to see an old man in a gray bowler, with a yellowing white walrus mustache and pince-nez specs, wearing a frock coat with lapel gardenia and a brocaded yellow vest across which dangled an old watch chain and fob in the design of a mermaid. Blank cards, an ink bottle, and a quill pen lay in front of him on a table that folded into a suitcase. Samples of his script-for-sale, tacked to the table's drop-leaf front, were splendid with antique swirls, curlicues, and elegant hills, valleys, and ovals.

'I hope you're in show business, young lady,' the old gent said to her over his pince-nez.

'As a matter of fact, I am.'

'It's the only safe place for talentless beauty, miss.'

'You've got some crust saying I don't have any talent.'

'Anywhere else you'll be destroyed.'

'As a matter of fact, I'm quitting show business.'

'A disastrous move.'

'But none of *your* business.'

'Forgive me for speaking so freely, but you look to me like a bird wounded in the heart, the brain, and between the legs, and we in the Audubon Society do what we can for the wounded. My card.'

'I'm Jack Diamond's girl. What about that?'

'Ah, then, ah. I had no way of knowing' – and the old man retrieved his card and handed her another. 'Jack Diamond is an entirely safe place. You have nothing to fear, my dear, as long as you have a role in Jack Diamond's hilarious tragedy.'

She looked at the card and saw in the obsolete glory of his pen strokes the biography of her vampy, bondaged, satin-slippered addiction. The card read: 'There is no good and bad in the elfin realm.' When she looked up, the man had packed his table and was halfway down the block.

Kiki looked over Madge's shoulder at the headline which read: JACK DIAMOND SHOT FIVE TIMES BY GUNMEN IN 64TH STREET HOTEL.

'I was there,' Kiki told Madge.

'You didn't shoot him, did you?'

'Oh, Madge, I love him.'

'What's that got to do with it? Come on, we've got to get you off the street.'

And so they took a cab to Madge's place and Kiki had a stiff drink, a very stiff one, and then she started to weep. So Madge held her hand and Kiki knew that even though Madge was her friend that she was touching her because she was a special person. Because Madge never touched her like that before, stroking the back of her hand, patting it with her fingertips; and Kiki felt good because somebody was being nice to her and she finally told Madge then how she heard the shots as she stood in the shower. And she thought somebody would come in and shoot her. And she would die in the bathtub, her blood going down the drain. Maybe Jack would be the one to shoot her. Why did Kiki think that about Jack?

Then she heard the running in the corridor, and she said to herself, why, Jack wouldn't run away and leave me, and so she quickly got into her pink robe and went next door to Jack's own room and saw the door open and Jack on the floor with his eyes open but not moving, looking up at her. And she said, 'Oh, Jackie, you're dead,' but he said, 'No I'm not, help me up,' and they were just the best old words she'd ever heard and she put her arms under him and lifted him and he put one of his hands over his stomach and the other over his chest to hold in the blood where they'd shot him. Blood was coming down his face and all down his blue pajamas so you couldn't even see the red racehorses anymore.

'Get the whiskey,' Jack told her when she had him sitting on the bed, and she looked around the room and couldn't see it, and Jack said, 'In the bathroom,' and when she got it, he said, 'In my mouth,' and she wiped the blood off his lips and poured in the whiskey. Too much. He choked and coughed and new blood spurted out of one of the holes in his chest, and like a little fountain turned on and off by the pumping of his heart, it flowed down over his fingers.

'Get The Count,' he said, 'across the hall,' and she knocked on The Count's door until her knuckles hurt and he came to Jack's room and Jack said to her then: 'Get the hell out of here and don't come back and don't admit you were here or you're all washed up.' And Kiki nodded but didn't understand and said to Madge, 'How would I be washed up, Madge? Did he mean in show business?' And Madge said, 'Go on,' so she said The Count called a doctor as she was leaving and then took Jack to another room in the hotel, down the hall, because Jack said the killers might come back to see if they did the job right. And Kiki, still in her pink robe, backed down the hallway toward her own room, and watched The Count walking and holding Jack, who was bent like a wishbone, and in they went to another room, which was when Kiki decided she would go to the theater and behave like nothing at all had happened. And things went along perfectly well, didn't they? They went along fine, just fine until she saw it all again while she was dancing. What she saw was that little spurt of blood coming out of Jack's chest like a fountain after she gave him too much whiskey. That was when she decided to fall down.

Madge read in the paper that two gunmen came running out of the hotel about the time Jack was shot and got into a car with its motor running and its door open and drove off with their New Jersey license plates. Those men, awful men, had shot Jack two places in the chest and once in the stomach and once in the thigh and once in the forehead, and the doctor said he was certainly not going to be able to go on living with all those holes in himself. The paper made no mention of the pretty little lady who was the first to see it all, but Kiki knew that her time of attention was going to come.

She caught the faintest smell of mothballs in Madge's closet, and she thought of marriage because only married people need mothballs. Kiki would never keep anything long enough to worry about moths unless she happened to be married. Last year's things? She stuck them away and bought new ones and let the moths have their fun. Kiki never thought of herself as married, even though she and Jack talked about it all the time. She talked about it and Jack tried to change the subject, is more like it.

'I'll marry you someday, kid,' he told her once, but she didn't believe that and wasn't even sure she wanted to believe it. Kiki doing the wash. Kiki beating the rugs. Kiki making fudge. It was certainly a laughing matter.

When the second knock on the door came, just seconds after Madge told her to hide in the bedroom (and she was in the closet by then, under the muskrat and smelling the mothballs by then), she heard Madge say to somebody, 'What the hell are you bothering me for? You have no right to come in here.' But they didn't go away. Kiki heard them walking in the rooms and heard them just outside the door, so she breathed so silently that not even a moth would have known she was there.

Who are those men is what Kiki wanted to know. Are they after me? And at that the light flashed into the closet and the muskrat unwrapped itself from her back and a hand grabbed her and two great big faces stared down at her.

'Go away,' she said. 'I don't know you men.' And she pulled one of Madge's dresses over her face. She could hear Madge saying, 'I had no idea she was involved in any shooting. I certainly wouldn't have brought her into my own home if I thought she was mixed up in any sort of nasty shooting business. I don't want this kind of publicity.'

But they put Madge's picture in the papers too. With her legs crossed.

Jack didn't die. He became more famous than ever. Both the *News* and the *Mirror* ran series on him for weeks. The *News* also ran Kiki's memoirs: How I went from bathing beauty to the Ziegfeld chorus to Jack Diamond's lap. She and Jack were Pyramus and Thisbe for the world and no breakfast table was without them for at least a month. Kiki overnight became as famous as most actresses, her greatest photo (that gorgeous pout at the police station) on every page one.

Jack recovered at Polyclinic Hospital, and when he came to and saw where he was, he asked to be moved into the room where Rothstein had died. The similarities to this and A. R.'s shooting, both shot in a hotel, both mysterious about their assailants, money owed being at the center of both cases, and Jack being A. R.'s man of yore, were carefully noted by the press. You'd think it was the governor who'd got it, with all the bulletins on conditions and the endless calls from the public. The hospital disliked the limelight and worried too about the bill until a delivery boy brought in an anonymous thirty-five hundred dollars in crumpled fifties and twenties and a few big ones with a note: 'See Jack Diamond gets the best.' This the work of Owney Madden.

Of course Jack never said who shot him. Strangers he could never possibly identify, he told Devane. Didn't get a good look at them. But the would-be assassins were neutral underworld figures, not Jack's enemies and not in Biondo's or Luciano's circle (nor Dutch Schultz's either, who was generally credited with the work at the time). Their neutrality was why Jack let them in.

Their function was to retrieve Charlie Lucky's money, but Jack refused to give it back, claiming finally that Luciano was lying about his role in the transaction. This was not only Jack's error, but also his willful need to affront peril. The visitors' instructions were simple: Get *all* the money or kill him.

He was sitting on the bed when they took out their guns. He ran at them, swinging the pillow off the bed, swinging in rage and terror, and though both men emptied their pistols, the pillow deflected both their attention and their aim so that only five of twelve bullets hit him.

But five is a lot. And the men ran, leaving him for dead.

The Count called me to say that Jack mentioned me just before he went unconscious from his wounds. 'Have Marcus take care of Alice and see she doesn't get the short end from those shitkickers up in the country,' he told The Count. Then when Alice called me from the hospital and said Jack wanted to see me, I went down, and it turned out he wanted to make his will: a surreptitious ten thousand to Kiki, a token bequest, no more; everything else to Alice. The arrangement seemed to speak for itself: Alice, the true love. But Jack wasn't that easy to read even when he spelled it out himself. Money was only the measure of his guilt and his sense of duty, a pair of admitted formidables, but not his answer to his enduring question.

He was in good spirits when I saw him, his bed near the window so he could hear the city, the roar of the fans spiraling upward from Madison Square Garden during the fights, all the cars on Broadway squealing and tooting, the sirens and bells and yells and shouts of the city wafting Jackward to comfort him, the small comfort being all he would have for two and a half months, for Jack Diamond the organism, was playing tag with adhesions, abscesses and lungs which had the congenital strength of tissue paper.

Jack's mail came in sacks and stacks, hundreds upon hundreds of letters during the first weeks, then dwindling to maybe a steady twenty-five a day for a month. A good many were sob stories, asking for his money when he shuffled off. Get well wishes ran second, and dead last were the handful who wanted him dead: filthy dog, dirty scum. Women were motherly, forgiving, and, on occasion, uninhibited: 'Please come to my home as soon as you are up and around and I will romp you back to good health. First you can take me on the dining room table, and then in the bathroom on our new green seat, and the third time (I know you will be able to dominate me thrice) on my husband's side of the bed.'

'Please when you are feeling better I would like you to please come and drown our six kittens,' another woman wrote. 'My husband lost everything in the crash. We cannot afford to feed six more mouths, and children come before cats. But I am much too chickenhearted to kill them myself and know you are strong enough to oblige.'

'I have a foolproof plan for pass-posting the bookie I bet with,' wrote a horseplayer, 'but, of course, I will need protection from his violence, which is where you come in as my partner.'

'Dear Mr Legs,' a woman wrote, 'all my life I work for my boy. Now he gonna go way and leave his momma. He is no dam good. I hope he die. I hope you shoot him for me. I will pay what you think up to fifty-five dollars, which is all the extra I got. But he deserve it for doing such a thing to his momma who gave him her life. His name is Tommy.'

'Dear Sir,' wrote a man, 'I read in the papers where you have been a professional killer. I would like to hire you to remove me from this life. I suppose a man in your position gets many requests like this from people who find existence unbearable. I have a special way I would prefer to die. This would be in lightly cooked lamb fat in my marble bathtub with my posterior region raised so you may shoot several small-caliber bullets into my anus at no quicker than thirty-second intervals until I am dead.'

A package came which the police traced, thinking someone was trying to make good on the numerous threats that Jack would never leave the hospital alive. An eight-year-old girl from Reading, Pennsylvania, had sent it – an ounce of holy oil from the shrine of Ste Anne de Beaupré.

'I read about Mr Diamond being shot and how his arm is paralyzed, and I have been taught in school to help those who are down and out,' the child told police.

'Punk kid,' Jack said. 'What does she mean down and out?'

On the street in front of Polyclinic little clusters of Jack's fans would gather. A sightseeing bus would pass and the announcer would say, 'On your right, folks, is where the notorious Jewish gangster Legs Diamond is dying,' and all would crane but none would ever see the lip quivering as he slept or the few gray hairs among all the chestnut, or the pouches of experience under his eyes, or the way his ears stuck out, and how his eyes were separated by a vertical furrow of care just above the nose, or that nose: hooked, Grecian, not Jewish, not Barrymore's either, merely a creditable piece of work he'd kept from damage, now snorting air. He was twelve pounds under his normal one fifty-two and still five ten and a half while I sat beside his bed with his last will and testament in my pocket for his signature. And he wheezed just like other Americans in their sleep.

I'd been fumbling through a prayer book on Jack's bedside table while he slept and I had turned up a credo I no more accepted as mere coincidence than I did the congruence of his and my pleasure in Rabelais; which is to say I suspected a pattern hovering over our relationship. The credo read:

> You work much harm in these parts, destroying and slaying
> God's creatures without his leave; and not only have you slain
> and devoured beasts of the field but you have dared to destroy
> and slay men made to the image of God: wherefore you are

worthy of the gallows as a most wicked thief and murderer; all folk cry out and murmur against you. But I would make peace, Brother Wolf, between them and you, and they shall obtain for you so long as you live, a continual sustenance from the men of this city so that you shall no more suffer hunger, for well I know that you have done all this harm to satisfy your hunger . . .

This paraphrased perfectly my private plot to forget Charlie Northrup the way everybody else was forgetting him. He was gone off page one, only a subordinate clause in Jack's delightful story. Charlie, thanks for giving us so much of your time. Such fun having a cadaver in the scenario, especially one we can't locate. But, Charl, please excuse us while we say a little prayer for Jack.

I remember also the passing thought that maybe it would be better if Jack never woke up, and then I remember seeing him wide awake, swathed in hospital-white hygienic purity.

'Hey, Marcus,' he said, 'great to wake up to a friendly face instead of some snooping cop. How's your ballocks?'

'Friendly toward ladies,' I said, and when he laughed he winced with pain.

'I been dreaming,' he said. 'Talking to God. No joke.'

'Uh-oh.'

'Why the hell is it I'm not dead? You figured it out?'

'They were bum shooters? You're not ready to die?'

'No, it's because I'm in God's grace.'

'Is that a fact? God told you that?'

'I'm convinced. I thought I was just lucky back in '25 when they hit me. Then when Augie got it, I thought maybe I was as strong as a man can be, you know, in health. But now I think it's because God wants me to live.'

He was not quite sitting up in bed, his prayer book there all soft and black on the white table and his rosary twined around the corner post of his bed, shiny black beads capturing the white tubing. Did he appreciate the contrast? I'm convinced he created it.

'You've got the disease of sanctity,' I told him.

'No, that's not it.'

'You've got it the way dogs get fleas. It's common after assassination attempts. It accounts for the closeness between the church and aging dictators. It's a kind of infestation. Look at this room.' Alice had hung a crucifix over the bed and set a statue of the virgin on the windowsill. The room had been priest-ridden since Jack moved into it, the first a stranger who came to hear his confession and inquired who shot him. Even through quasi-delirium Jack recognized a Devane stooge. The next, a Baltimore chum of Alice's who dropped in without the press learning his name, comforted Jack, blessed him through opiated haze, then told newsmen: 'Don't ask me to tell you anything about that poor suffering boy in there.' And then came good Father Skelly from Cairo, indebted to Jack for the heavenly music in his church.

'God won't forget that you gave us a new organ,' said the priest to the resurrecting Jack.

'Will God do the same for us when ours gets old?' Jack asked.

The priest heard his confession amid the two bouquets of roses Alice renewed every three days until Jack said the joint smelled like a wake, and so she replaced them with a potted geranium and a single red wax rose in a vase on the bedside table.

'I thought you'd given up the holy smoke,' I said. 'I thought you had something else going for you.'

'What the hell am I supposed to do after people keep shooting me and I don't die? I'm beginning to think I'm being saved.'

'For dessert? Looks classic to me, Jack. Shoot a man full of bullets and he's a candidate for blessedness.'

'What about you and your communion breakfasts? Big-shot Catholic.'

'Don't be misled. That's just part of being an Albany Democrat.'

'So you're a Democrat and I got fleas. But it turns out I don't mind them.'

'I can see that, and it all ties in. Confession, sanctity, priests. Yes, it goes with having yourself shot.'

'Come again?'

'The shooting. I've assumed all along that you rigged it.'

'You're not making sense.'

'Could it have happened without your approval? You saw them alone, you know what they were. I know what such go-betweens can be, and I'm not even in your business. And you never had any intention of turning over that money. You asked for exactly what you got. Am I exaggerating?'

'You got some wild imagination, pal. I see why you score in court.'

But when he looked at me, that furrow of care between his eyes turned into a question mark. He ran his fingertips along the adhesive tape of his chest bandage, pleasurably some might say, as he looked at the author of the bold judgment. Jack Diamond having himself shot? Ridiculous. He fingered the rosary entwined over his right shoulder on the bed, played the beads with his fingertips as if they were keys on an instrument that would deliver the music he wanted to hear. Organ music. A sound like Skelly's new machine. No words to it, just the music they play at benediction after the high mass. Yes, there are words. From a long time ago. The '*Tantum Ergo.*' All Latin words you never forget, but who the hell knows what they mean? '*Tantum ergo sacramentum, veneremur cernui; et antiquum documentum, Novo cedat ritui.*'

A bridge.

A certain light.

Something was happening to him, Jack now knew.

'I want you to talk for me,' he said. He had recovered from my impertinence, was restoring the client–attorney relation, putting me in my place. 'I want you to talk to some people upstate. A few judges and cops, couple of businessmen, and find out what they think of my setup now. Fogarty's handling it, but he can't talk to those birds. He's too much of a kid. I got through to all those bastards personally, sent them whiskey, supported their election campaigns, gave 'em direct grease. All them bums owe me favors, but the noise in the papers about me, I don't know now whether it scares 'em or not.'

'"Pardon me, your honor, but are you still in the market for a little greasy green as a way of encouraging Jack Diamond with his bootlegging, his shakedowns, and his quirky habit of making competitors vanish?" Is that my question?'

'Any fucking way you like to put it, Marcus. You're the talker. They all know my line of work. It'll be simpler if I still got the okay, but I don't really give a goddamn whether they like it or not. Jack Diamond's got a future in the Catskills.'

'Don't you think you ought to get straight first?'

'You don't understand, Marcus. You can carve out a whole goddamn empire up there if you do it right. Capone did it in Cicero. Sure there's a lot of roads to cover, but that's all right. I don't mind the work. But if I slow now, somebody else covers those roads. And it's not like I got all the time in the world. The guineas'll be after me now.'

'You think they won't ride up to the Catskills?'

'Sure, but up there I'll be ready. That's my ball park.'

I've often vacillated about whether Jack's life was tragic, comic, a bit of both, or merely a pathetic muddle. I admit the muddle theory moved me most at this point. Here he was, refocusing his entire history, as if it had just begun, on the dream of boundless empire. It was a formidable readjustment and I considered it desperate, but maybe others would find it only confused and ridiculous. In any case, given the lengths he was willing to go to carry it off, it laid open his genuine obsession.

I might have credited the whole conversation about the Catskills to Jack's extraordinary greed if it hadn't been for one thing he said to me. It took me back to 1928 when Jack was arrested with his mob in a pair of elegant offices on the fourteenth and fifteenth floor of the Paramount Building, right on Times Square. Some address. Some height. Loftiness is my business, said the second-story man.

Now Jack gave me a wink and ran his hand sensuously along the edge of the chest bandage that was giving him such pleasure. 'Marcus,' he said, 'who else do you know collects mountains?'

I've been in Catskill maybe a dozen and a half times, most of those visits brief, on behalf of Jack. I don't really know the place, never needed to. It's a nice enough village, built on the west bank of the Hudson River about a hundred or so miles north of the Hotsy Totsy Club. Henry Hudson docked near this spot to trade with the Indians and then went on up to Albany, just like Jack. The village had some five thousand people in this year of 1931 I'm writing about. It had a main street called Main Street, a Catskill National Bank, a Catskill Savings Bank, a Catskill Hardware and so on. Formal social action happened at the IOOF, the Masonic Temple, the Rebekah Lodge, the American Legion, the PTA, the Women's Progressive Club, the White Shrine, the country club, the Elks. Minstrel shows drew a good audience and visiting theater companies played at the Brooks Opera House. The local weekly serialized a new Curwood novel at the end of 1931, which Jack would have read avidly if he'd not been elsewhere. The local daily serialized what Jack was doing in lieu of reading Curwood.

Catskill was, and still is, the seat of Greene County, and just off Main Street to the north is the four-story county jail, where Oxie Feinstein was the most celebrated resident on this particular day. Before I was done with Jack, there would be a few more stellar inmates.

The Chamber of Commerce billed the village as the gateway to the Catskills. The Day Line boats docked at Catskill Landing, and tourists were made conscious of the old Dutch traditions whenever they were commercially applicable. A Dutch friend of mine from law school, Warren Van Deusen, walked me through the city one day and showed me, among other points of interest, the home of Thomas Cole on Spring Street. Cole was the big dad of the nineteenth-century's Hudson River school of painting, and one of his works 'Prometheus Bound,' a classic landscape, I remember particularly well, for it reminded me of Jack. There was this giant, dwarfed by the landscape, chained to his purple cliff in loincloth and flowing beard (emanating waves of phlogiston, I'll wager) and wondering when the eagle was going to come back and gnaw away a few more of his vitals.

I called Van Deusen, who was involved in Republican county politics, as a way of beginning my assignment for Jack. In the early days of our law practice, his in Catskill, mine in Albany, I recommended him to a client who turned into very decent money for Van, and he'd been trying for years to repay the favor. I decided to give him the chance and told him to take me to lunch, which he did. We dined among men with heavy watch chains and heavier bellies. Warren, still a young man, had acquired a roll of well-to-do burgher girth himself since I'd last seen him, and when we strolled together up Main Street, I felt I was at the very center of America's well-fed, Depression complacency. It was an Indian summer day, which lightened the weight of my heavy question to Warren, that being: 'What does this town think of Jack Diamond?'

'A hero, if you can believe it,' Van said. 'But a hero they fear, a hero they wished lived someplace else.'

'Do you think he's a hero?'

'You asked about the town's feelings. My private theory is he's a punishment inflicted on us for the sins of the old patroons. But maybe that's just my Dutch guilt coming out.'

'You know Jack personally?'

'I've seen him in some of our best speakeasies and roadhouses. And like most of the town, I at least once made it a point to be passing by that little barbershop right across the street there when he and his chums pulled up at eleven o'clock one morning. They always came at eleven for their ritual daily shave, hair trim, shampoo, hot towels, shoe shine, and maybe a treatment by the manicurist from up the street.'

'Every day?'

'Whatever else I say about him, I'll never accuse him of being ill-groomed.'

'I can't imagine this being the extent of your knowledge, a political fellow like yourself.'

Van gave me a long quiet look that told me the subject was taboo, if I wanted to talk about a subsidy from Jack — that he was not in the market and knew no one who was.

'I know all the gossip,' he said, finessing it. 'Everybody does.

He's the biggest name we've had locally since Rip Van Winkle woke up. I know his wife, too; I mean, I've seen her. Alice. Not a bad-looking woman. Saw her awhile back at the Community Theater, as a matter of fact. They change the movie four times a week and she sees them all. People seem to like her, but they don't know why she stays with Diamond. Yet they kind of like him, too – I suppose in the same way you find him acceptable.'

'I accept him as a client.'

'Sure, Marcus, And what about that European jaunt? Your picture even made the Catskill paper, you know.'

'Someday when I understand it all better, I'll tell you about that trip. Right now all I want to know is what this town thinks.'

'What for?'

'Grounding purposes, I suppose. Better my understanding of the little corner of the world where my candle burns from time to time.'

Van looked at me with his flat Dutch face that seemed as blond as his hair. He was smiling, a pleasant way of calling me a liar. Van and I knew each other's facial meanings from days when our faces were less guarded. We both knew the giveaway smirks, the twitches, puckers, and sneers.

'Now I get it,' he said. 'It's him. He wants to know if the town's changed, how we take to his new notoriety. Is he worried?'

'What are you talking about?'

'All right, Marcus, so you won't play straight. Come on, I want to show you something.'

We walked awhile, Van singling out certain landmarks for my education: There stood the garage the Clemente brothers used before Jack terrorized them out of the beer business. Over that way is a soft drink distributor's warehouse, which Diamond also took over. This was news to me. But I suppose when you set out to corner the thirst market, you corner it all.

Then Van turned in at the Elks' Club and led me to the bar. I ordered a glass of spring water and Van a beer, and then he motioned to the bartender, a man who might have been twenty-eight or forty-five, with a muscular neck; large, furlable

648

ears; and a cowlick at the crown of his head. His name was Frank DuBois and Van said he was a straight arrow, a countryman of old Huguenot stock, and a first-class bartender.

'I was just about to tell Marcus here about your visit from the Diamond boys,' Van said to him, 'but I know you tell it better.'

DuBois snuffed a little air, readying his tale for the four-hundredth telling, and said, 'They come in all right, right through that door. Come right behind the bar here, unhitched the beer tap and rolled the barrel right out the door. "Say," I says to 'em, "what'd ya do that for?" And one of them pokes me with a gun and says it's because we wasn't buying the good Canadian beer and they'd deliver us some in the mornin'. "Yeah," I says, "that's just fine, but what about tonight? What do the fellas drink tonight?" "Not this," said one of 'em, and he shoots a couple of holes in the barrels we got. Not a fella I'd seen around before, and don't want to see him again either. Then they went out back, two of 'em, and shot up the barrels out there. Took me and Pete Gressel half a day to get the place mopped up and dried out. Dangdest mess you ever saw.'

'You know the fellow who poked the gun at you?' I asked.

'I knew him all right. Joe Fogarty. Call him Speed, they do. Nervous fella. Been around this town a long time. I seen him plenty with the Diamond bunch.'

'When was all this?'

'Friday week, 'bout eleven at night. Had to close up and go home. No beer to serve. No people neither, once they saw who it was come in.'

'Is that the right kind of beer Van's drinking now?'

'You betcha, brother. Nobody wants no guns pokin' at them they can help it. Membership here likes peace and quiet. Nobody lookin' for trouble with Legs Diamond. He's a member this here club, you know. In good standin' too. Paid up dues and well liked till all this happen. Don't know what the others think now.'

It was tidy. If Jack let his men point a gun at his own club, what other club could be safe? DuBois moved up the bar and Van said quietly, 'A lot of people aren't just accepting this kind of thing, Marcus.'

'I don't know what that means, not accepting.'

'I'll let you use your imagination.'

'Vigilantes?'

'That's not impossible but not likely either, given the people I'm talking about. At least not at the moment.'

'What people *are* you talking about?'

'I have to exercise a little discretion too, Marcus. But I don't mean helpless people like Frank here.'

'Then all you've got for me is a vague, implied resistance, but without any form to it. People thinking how to answer Jack?'

'More than vague. More than thinking about it.'

'Van, you're not telling me much. I thought I could count on your candor. What the hell good are riddles?'

'What the hell good is Jack Diamond?'

Which was the same old question I'd been diddling with since the start. Van's expression conveyed that he knew the answer and I never would. He was wrong.

John Thomson's Man

When the police went through Jack's house in one of their fine-combings near the end, somebody turned up a piece of plaster, one side covered with the old-time mattress ticking wallpaper. The paper was marked with twenty-five odd squiggles, which the police presumed were some more code notations of booze deliveries; and they saved the plaster along with Jack's coded notebooks and file cards on customers and connections all over the United States and in half a dozen foreign countries.

I asked Alice about the plaster before she was killed, for it turned up in the belongings they returned to her, through my intervention, after Jack died. When she saw it she laughed a soft little laugh and told me the squiggle marks were hers; that she'd made them the first weekend she and Jack were married; that they stayed in an Atlantic City hotel and hardly went out except to eat and that they'd made it together twenty-five times. After number five, she said, she knew they'd only just started and she kept the score on the wall next to the bed. And when they checked out, Jack got the tire iron from the car and hacked out the plaster with all the squiggles on it. They kept it in their dresser drawer until the police took it away. Alice made Jack give the hotel clerk twenty-five dollars for the broken wall. A dollar a squiggle. Half the price of professional action.

I thought of Warren Van Deusen telling me people didn't understand why Alice stayed with Jack. She had her reasons. Her memories were like those squiggles. She was profoundly in love with the man, gave him her life at the outset and never wanted anyone else. She was in love with loving him too, and knew it, liked the way it looked. She won a bundle of psychic points sitting at his bedside after the Monticello, cooing into his ear while the reporters listened at the door and the nurses and orderlies carried messages to tabloid snoops. Alice heroine. Sweet Alice. Alice Blue. When the crash comes they always go back to their wives. Faithful spouse. Betrayed, yet staunch. Adversity no match for Alice. The greatest of the underworld women. Paragon of wifely virtue. Never did a wrong thing in her life. The better half of that bum, all right, all right.

Texas Guinan let her have a limousine, with chauffeur, all the time she was in New York, so she wouldn't have to worry about hawking taxis to and from Jack's bedside. The press gave Kiki the play at first, but then they caught up with Alice at the police station (that's where Kiki and Alice first met; they glowered at each other, didn't speak). The press boys tried to make her the second act of the drama, but Alice wouldn't play.

'Did you know the Roberts girl?'

'No.'

'Did you know any of his friends?'

'He had many friends, but I'm not sure I knew them.'

'Did you know his enemies?'

'He didn't have any enemies.'

Alice was no sap, had no need for publicity. Not then. It was all happening in her ball park anyway, whether she talked or not.

'You know,' she said to me after the shooting, 'I hardly even brought up the subject of Marion with him. Only enough to let him know I wasn't going to die over it, that I was bigger than that. I was just as sweet as I could be. Gave him the biggest old smile I could and told him I remembered the squiggles and let him lay there and fry.'

She said she was thinking about her Mormon dream and how it didn't make any sense when she had it, even after she told John about it and they talked about him having another wife. It was in the time of the roses, after he was shot the first time, on Fifth

Avenue, when he was afraid he would die before he had done what
he set out to do. He saw girls at his Theatrical Club. She knew that.
But that was a trivial thing in the life of Alice Diamond because
she had John as a husband, and that superseded any girl. Alice
Diamond was bona fide. The real thing. A wife. And don't you
forget it, John Diamond. A wife. For life.

She sat on the arm of his chair one night in the living room
and told him she dreamed he'd brought home a second wife. He
stood alongside the woman in the dream and said to Alice, 'Well,
we'll all be together from now on.' And Alice said, 'Not on your
Philadelphia tintype.' But even as she said no to him she knew it
was not no. Never a total no to anything John wanted. Then the
other wife came in and started taking over little things Alice used
to do for John. But after Alice told him the dream, he said, 'Alice,
I love you, nobody else.' And Alice said to him, 'No, you've got
another wife.' And they both laughed when he said to her, 'Alice,
we'll be together as long as we live.'

Alice did not think her dream would ever come true. Maybe
he'd see a woman now and then. But to move into a hotel, to
keep a woman permanently, to see her just hours after he'd seen
Alice, and maybe even after he'd *been with* Alice, was terrible.
It was not incomprehensible. How, after all, could *anything* be
incomprehensible to a person like Alice, who knew what everybody
along Broadway thinks, wants, does, and won't do? Alice was as
smart about life as anybody she ever came up against. She knew the
worst often happened, worse than the worst you can imagine, and so
you made provisions. Her prayer book helped her make provision
for the worst: for the sick, the dying, for a happy death, for the
departed, for the faithful departed, for the souls in Purgatory, for
the end of man, for release from Purgatorial fire. Even a special
one for John. She knew she was deceived by John's capacity for
passion, and so she sat by his bed and read the *Prayer to Overcome
Passions and to Acquire Perfection*: 'Through the infinite merits of
Thy painful sufferings, give John strength and courage to destroy
every evil passion which sways his heart, supremely to hate all sin,
and thus to become a saint.'

Saint John of the Bullets.

'Alice, there you are, Alice,' Jack said when he woke up and saw her. The beginning and the end of his first coherent sentence.

She smiled at him, picked up the wax rose she'd brought him, the one rose, the secret nobody else knew, and said, 'It's wax, John. Do you remember?' The corners of his mouth eased upward and he said, 'Sure,' so softly she could barely hear it. Then she ran her fingers ever so softly through his hair. Bittykittymins. Sweet baby. Son of a bitch. Bittykittymins. And when he was really awake for the first time, when he'd even had a little bouillon and she'd combed his hair and they put a new hospital gown on him, she said to him in her silent heart: I wish you had died.

'How are you, kid?' she said out loud, the first time in a long, long while she called him kid, the code word.

'I might make it.'

'I think you might.'

'They got me good this time.'

'They always get you good.'

'This time it hurt more.'

'Everybody got hurt this time.'

Alice was hurt, and she knew why. Because she loved an evil person and always would. She now wondered about her remarkable desire to see Jack dead. She had at times wished death to bad persons. Because Alice was good. Alice would not stay long in Purgatory. Because she was good. But now she wanted to die herself when she wished John dead and saw how deeply evil she herself was. She prayed to Jesus to let her want John to live. Let me not think that he's evil. Or me either. I know he's a good man in certain ways. Don't tell me I should've married somebody pure and holy. They would've bored the ass off me years ago. After all, I didn't marry a priest, Jesus. I married a thief. And landed on the front pages alongside him. My hubbydubbylubbybubby. People asking me questions. Coming for interviews. Forced to hide. Hide my light under the bushel. It will shine brighter for all that hiding. Light polishes itself under the bushel. What an awful thing for Alice to think: polishing up her own private brilliance through the troubles of Johnny-victim-on-the-boat. Oh, Alice. How awful you really are. It is so enormously wrong and wicked and evil and terrible, loving John for the wrong reasons; wanting him dead; profiteering from your marriage. Alice was evil and she truly hated herself.

But listen, kiddo, Alice knew she was married to one of the rottenest sons of bitches to come along in this century. Just the fact that she was able to sit there stroking his fingers and the back of his hand and running her hand through his bittykittymins gave her the evidence of her moral bankruptcy. Yet she was still trying to reform John. She didn't want him to be a Mason on the square. She wanted a genuine four-cornered Catholic. Four corners on my bed. Four angels overhead. Matthew, Mark, Luke, John. Bless the bed we all lie on. She put a rosary around his neck while he lay under the influence of drugs to invoke grace and secret blessings God couldn't possibly deliver publicly to such a person. Hypocrisy for her to do that. Yes, another sin, Alice. But she knew that without being a hypocrite she could never love John.

Knowing this, knowing how evil she was for being married to evil, she therefore knew she must stay married to it, knew she must suffer all the evil that evil brings. For how else could a girl, an Irish Catholic girl brought up to respect grace and transubstantiation, ever get to heaven? How else could a girl hold her head up in her family? How else could a girl ever show her face among her peers, let alone her sneering inferiors, unless she expiated her awfulness, that black terribleness of marrying and loving evil, except by staying married to it?

Suffer the evil to come unto me, said doughty Alice. Perhaps she enjoyed that evil too much. More than she could ever expiate. Perhaps she will merit longer and more excruciating punishment than she can yet imagine. Yes, the very worst may be in store for this little lady.

But she sat there with the villain, stroking, cooing, telling the Good Lord Above: Go ahead and do me, Lord. I can take it.

Sitting beside his hospital bed watching him breathe perhaps the final breaths of his life, she knew he was unquestionably hers now forever. Nothing and nobody could part them. She had withstood the most scandalous time and had not stopped loving him. She was the victim of love: sucker and patsy for her own sloppy heart. But from suckerdom comes wisdom the careful lover never understands.

'I'm sorry what this is doing to you,' John said to Alice.

'Are you, John? Or is that just another apology?'

'It's a bad time for you, Al, I know. But this ain't exactly a great big bed of roses I got myself into.'

'You'll get out of it.'

'We both will. We'll have a special time when I get my ass up out of here.'

'Give your ass a rest.'

'Anything you say.'

'Give everybody's ass a rest.'

'Whose ass you talking about now?'

'Maybe you could figure it out if you live long enough.'

'I'm in no condition to tire anybody out.'

'That's a nice change. I also mean no visitors. I already put up with more than I can stand, but I won't put up with her here.'

'She hasn't shown up yet. And if she does, it won't be my doing. But she won't.'

'The police won't let her out of custody, that's why she won't.'

'She knows better. She knows her place.'

'Oh? And just what the hell *is* her place?'

'No place. Nothing. She knows she's got no hold on me.'

'That's why you kept her in the hotel.'

'I was doing her a favor.'

'How often? Twice a night?'

'I saw her now and then, no more. A friend. A date when I was in town looking for company.'

'The whole world's got it figured out, John. Don't start with the fairy tales.'

She was talking to him as if he had the strength of a healthy man, but he was only an itty-bitty piece of himself, a lump of torn-up flesh. Why did Alice talk so tough to a sick lump? Because she knew the lump was tough. She was tough too. A pair of tough monkeys, is how John always said he saw this husband–wife team. Yes, it's why we get along, was Alice's way of looking at this toughness. She always treated him this way, even when he was most vulnerable, told him exactly what she thought. There now. See? See his hand move off the sheet and onto her knee? See his fingers raise the hem of her skirt? Feel him touch her with his fingertips on the flesh above her stocking? Home territory. Jack is coming home. Jack is not discouraged by her tough line. Tough monkey, my husband.

When Alice felt these fingers on herself she looked at the single wax rose on the bedside table and remembered the early growth of the rose. There will always be a wax rose in our life, Alice now insisted, and in his own way Jack remembered it too. With a tea rose in his lapel when he wore his tux. Never a gardenia. Never a white carnation. Always the red, red rose.

It was after the Fifth Avenue shooting in 1925 and he sat in the living room of their house on 136th Street in the Bronx with the top and back of his head shaved and bandaged, wearing the old blue wool bathrobe with the holes in the elbows, sitting alone on the sofa, looking at the floor and drinking coffee royals because he liked their name and potency; eating saltine crackers with peanut butter but no meals, awake all night for a week but saying almost nothing, just making soft whimpering sounds like a dog dreaming of his enemies. Keeping Alice awake until her ear got used to the rhythms of the whimpers. When the rhythm was right, she could always sleep.

She had tried the rosary, but he wasn't ready for that, and so it only sat on the coffee table alongside the wax roses in the orange and black Japanese vase. She had tried to calm him, too, by reading from the prayer book, but he wouldn't listen. He was as far from religion as he'd ever been. Alice told him he should take the shooting as a warning from God to get out of the rackets or die in the bullet rain.

'I don't want to be like that woman in Brooklyn who lost a husband and two sons in the gang wars,' Alice said to him. But that had no effect. Alice didn't know what would have any effect.

'Come on out, boy,' she had said one day, a little whisper in his ear. 'We all know you're hiding in there.'

But all he ever asked was did you call in my numbers: 356, 880, and 855. Jackie, Jack and John out of the dream book. Jack always played numbers, from the time he ran them as a teen-ager. Now he played five dollars on each number and she never knew whether he hit them or not. Her game was not played with numbers.

She would also turn the radio on for him, but when she'd leave the room, he'd turn it off.

'Jesus, they really almost got me, almost wiped me out,' he said one night and shook his head as if this were an incredible possibility, some wild fancy that had nothing to do with the real life and potential of John Thomas Diamond. That was when Alice knew he was not going to quit the rackets, that he was committed to them with a fervor which matched her own religious faith.

'They can't keep me down forever' had been his phrase from when she first knew him. She hoped he would find another way up, but this thought still was the central meaning of his whimpers.

The bridge lamp was on the night Alice got out of bed, unable to accept the animal noises John was making. They had become more growls than whimpers or the whisperings of troubled sleep. She saw him on the floor where he'd slid off the couch. He was pointing his pistol at the Japanese vase.

'Are you going to shoot the roses, John?'

He let his hand fall, and after a while she took the pistol. She helped him back onto the sofa and then knelt in front of him in her nightgown, not even a robe over it, and herself visible right through the sheer silk. Her amply visible self.

'I can't sleep no more,' he said to her. 'I close my eyes and I see my mother screaming every time she breathes.'

'It's all right, boy. It's going to be all right.'

And then Alice rose half up out of her kneeling position, but without sitting either, stretched herself lengthwise and leaning, a terribly uncomfortable position as she recalls it. But John could see all of her very private self that way, feel her all along his arm and his hip and his good leg that wasn't shot. And without the pistol his hand was free. First she said the Our Father to him just to put the closeness of God into his head again and then she maneuvered herself until her perfect center was against the back of his hand. Then she moved ever so slightly so he could feel where he was, even if he couldn't see it or didn't sense it.

Did this maneuvering work? Alice put an arm around his neck and kissed him lightly on the ear. He turned his hand so the knuckles faced away from her. Then, with a little bit of help, that sheer silk nightgown rose to the demands of the moment. John said she smelled like grass in the morning with dew on it, and she said he smelled like a puppyduppy, and with both their hands where they had every right in the world to be, Mr and Mrs John Diamond fell asleep on the sofa in their very own parlor. And they slept through the night.

When they killed Alice, she was sitting at the kitchen table of her Brooklyn apartment looking at old clippings of herself and Jack. One clip, of which she had seven copies, showed her beside his bed of Polyclinic pain. She sat beneath her cloche hat in that old clip, a few tufts of blond hair (not yet dyed Titian to match that of Kiki, The Titian-Haired Beauty of the tabloids; not yet dyed saffron to glamorize her for her Diamond Widow stage career) sticking out from underneath. She was all trim and tailored in the gray tweed suit Jack had helped her choose. 'My hero!' was what Alice had written on the clipping.

I imagine her in her final kitchen remembering that bedside scene and all that came later up in Acra when Jack left the Polyclinic bed: Alice nursing her John back to health, massaging his back with rubbing alcohol, taking him for walks in the woods with some of the boys fanning out ahead and behind them, making him toddies and cooking him beef stew and dumplings and tapioca pudding. Now he was more handsome than he'd ever been in his life. Oh, brilliant boy of mine! Hero of the strife! From New Year's

Day, 1931, when he left the hospital, on through early April, she possessed him exclusively. Oh, rapturous time! Nothing like it ever before, ever again. What a bitter cup it was for Alice to leave him after that.

She told me she left him the day after Lew Edwards and I paid a curious visit to idyllic Acra. Lew was a Broadway producer, dead now, who grew up next door to me in North Albany, became the impresario of most of Public School 20's undergraduate productions, and went on to produce plays for Jeanne Eagels, Helen Morgan, and Clifton Webb. Lew knew Jack casually, knew also my connection with Jack, and called me with an idea. I told him it was sensational and would probably die at first exposure to Jack. Lew said it was worth the chance and we met at the Hudson train station. I drove down from Albany to pick him up, we had lunch in Catskill, took a short walk to buy the papers, a fateful purchase, and then drove out to Jack's.

The chief change from my summer visit was the set of outside guards at the house, a pair of heavies I'd never seen before who sat in a parked Packard and periodically left the driveway to explore the road down toward Cairo and up toward South Durham for visitors who looked like they might want to blow Jack's head off. When that pair drove off, another pair on duty on the porch took up driveway positions in a second car, and a set from the cottage took up posts on the porch as inside guards.

'Just like Buckingham Palace,' Lew said.

Alice gave me a big hello with a smooch I remember. That tempting appleness. Fullness. Pungent wetness I remember thee well. But she meant nothing by such a lovely kiss except hello, my friend. Then she said to me: 'Marcus, he's wonderful. He looks better than he has in years. I swear he's even handsomer now than when I married him. And it's better other ways too.'

She shook Lew's hand and took my arm and walked me into the living room and whispered: 'He's all through with her, Marcus, he really is. He hasn't seen her since the shooting, only once. She came to the hospital one day when I wasn't there, but I heard about it. Now she's all a part of the past. Oh, Marcus, you can't imagine how glorious it's been these past few months. We've been so damned happy you wouldn't believe we were the same people you saw the last time you were here.'

She said he was upstairs napping now, and while she went up to rouse him, Cordelia, the maid, mixed us a drink. Jack came down groggy – and in shirtsleeves, baggy pants and slippers – and gave us a few vague minutes. Then we were a group – Jack and Alice on the sofa with Alice's pair of long-legged dolls in crinoline between them, his hand in hers across the dolls, Lew and I in the overstuffed chairs as witnesses to this domestic tranquillity.

'So you've got a deal,' Jack said, and Lew immediately went for his cigar case to get a grip on something. Jack had met Lew five years back when Lew butted aggressively into a bar conversation Jack was having, without knowing who Jack was. That's another story, but it turned out Lew gave Jack a pair of theater tickets that introduced him to Helen Morgan, who became one of Jack's abstract passions. He never could understand why Morgan was so good, why she moved him so. It was perverse of him to want to understand the secrets of individual talent, to want secret keys to success. He was still talking about La Morgan the night he died.

'I got a million-dollar idea for you, Jack,' Lew said, stuffing a cigar in his mush but not lighting it.

'My favorite kind.'

'And you don't have to do a thing for a year.'

'It gets better.'

'I like it too,' said Alice.

'You've got to be one of the most famous, pardon the expression, criminals in the East, am I right?'

'I wouldn't admit to any wrongdoing,' Jack said. 'I just make my way the best I can.'

'Sure, Jack, sure,' said Lew. 'But plenty of people take you for a criminal. Am I right?'

'I got a bad press, no doubt about that.'

'Bad press is a good press for this idea,' said Lew. 'The more people think you're a bad-ass bastard, the easier we make you a star.'

'He's already a star,' Alice said. 'Too much of a one.'

'You mean a Broadway star?' Jack asked. 'I carry a tune, but I'm no Morgan.'

'Not Broadway. I mean all of America. I can make you the biggest thing since Billy Sunday and Aimee Semple McPherson. An evangelist. A preacher.'

'A preacher?' Jack said, and he gave it the big ho-de-ho-ho.

'A preacher how?' Alice said, leaning forward.

Lew said, 'If you'll excuse me for saying it, there's about a hundred million people in this country know your name, and they figure you're one mean son of a bitch. Is this more or less true or am I mistaken?'

'Go on,' Jack said. 'What else?'

'So this mean son of a bitch, this Legs Diamond, this bootlegger, this gang leader, he gives it all up. Quits cold. Goes straight. And a year later he hears the voice of the Holy Spirit. He is touched by a whole damn flock of flaming doves or tongues or whatever the hell they send down to touch guys with, and he becomes an apostle for the Big Fellow. He goes barnstorming, first on a shoestring. A spiritual peanut vendor is all he is. A man with a simple commitment to God and against Satan and his works. He talks to anybody who'll sit still for half an hour. The press picks him up immediately and treats him like a crazy. But also it's a hell of a story for them. Whatsisname, on the road to Damascus. You know the routine. Doesn't care about gin, gangs, guns, gals or gelt anymore. All he wants is to send out the word of God to the people. The people! They'll sell their kids for a ticket. Tickets so scarce you've got to hire a manager, and pretty soon you, he, winds up on the vaude circuits, touches every state, SRO all over. A genuine American freak. Then he gets word from God he shouldn't play theaters with those evil actors. Oughta talk in churches. Of course the churches won't have him. Fiend turned inside out is still a fiend. And a fake. A show biz figure. So he has to play stadiums now, and instead of six hundred he draws maybe twenty thousand and winds up in Yankee Stadium with a turnaway crowd, a full orchestra, four hundred converts around him, the best press agent in town, and the first million-dollar gate that isn't a heavyweight fight. More? Sure. He builds his own temple and they come from all over the world to hear him speak. Then, at his peak, he moves off to Paris, London, Berlin. And hey. Rome.'

Lew fell against his chairback and lit the cigar he'd been using as a pointer, a round little man with a low forehead, thick black hair, and a constant faceful of that stogie. He worked at being a Broadway character, structured comic lines to deliver ad lib at the right moment: 'Jack Johnson got the worst deal of any nigger since Othello' is one of his I never forgot.

Lew had bought the New York *Daily Mirror* and read bits of it in the car on the way to Jack's, and now he pulled it out of his right coat pocket in a gesture he said later was caused by discomfort from the bulk, and tossed it onto the coffee table. Jack opened it, almost as a reflex, and skimmed the headlines while all the silence was drumming at us. Jack turned the pages, barely looking at them, then stopped and said to Lew: 'How the hell could I preach anything anybody'd believe? I haven't made a speech since high school when I did something from Lincoln. I'm no speaker, Lew.'

'I'd make you one,' Lew said. 'I'd get you drama coaches, speech coaches, singing teachers. Why, for Christ's sake, you'd be a voice to reckon with in six months. I seen this happen on Broadway.'

'I think it's a fantastic idea,' Alice said. She stood up and paced in front of the couch nervously.

'You know the power you'd have, Jack?' Lew asked. 'Hell, we might even get a new American church going. Sell stock in it. I'd buy some myself. A man like you carrying the word to America what the rackets are all about, giving people the lowdown on the secret life of their country. Jesus, I get the shivers thinking how you'd say it. Snarling, by God. Snarling at those suckers for God Almighty. Your stories don't have to be true but they'll sound true anyway. Jesus, it's so rich I can hear the swoons already. I could put together a team of writers'd give you the goddamnedest supply of hoopla America ever heard. Force-feed 'em their own home-grown bullshit. Tell 'em you've gotten inside their souls and know what they need. They need more truth from you, that's what they need. Can't you see those hicks who read everything they can lay hands on about crooks and killers? Organ music with it. "The Star-Spangled Banner." "Holy, Holy, Holy." You know what Oscar Wilde said, don't you? Americans love heroes, especially crooked ones. Twenty to one you'd get a movie. Maybe they'd even run you for Congress. A star, Jack, I mean a goddamn one hundred percent true-blue American star. How does it grab you?'

Alice exploded before Jack could say anything at all.

'John, it's absolutely perfect. Did you ever believe anybody'd ask you to do anything as marvelous as this? And you can do it. Everything he said was true. You'd be wonderful. I've heard you talk when you're excited about something and I know you can do it. You know you can act, you did it in high school, oh, I know it's right for you.'

Jack closed the newspaper and folded it. He crossed his legs, left foot on right knee and tapped the paper on his shoe.

'You'd like to do a little barnstorming, would you?' he said to her.

'I'd love to go with you.'

Alice's faith. Love alone. She really believed Jack could do anything. Such an idea also had pragmatic appeal: saving herself from damnation. Show business? So what? As to the stardom, well, the truth is, Alice could no longer get along without it. Yet this promised stardom without taint. Oh, it was sweet! The promise of life renewed for Alice. And her John the agent of renewal.

'What's your reaction, Marcus?' Jack said. And when I chuckled, he frowned.

'I can see it all. I really can see you up there on the altar, giving us all a lesson in brimstone. I think Lew is right. I think it'd work. People would pay just to see you sit there, but if you started saving their souls, well, that's an idea that's worth a million without even counting next month's house.' And I laughed again. 'What sort of robes would you wear? Holy Roman or Masonic?'

Maybe that did it, because Jack laughed then too. He tapped Alice lightly on the knee with the newspaper and tossed it on the coffee table in front of her. It's curious that I remember every move that newspaper made, not that Alice would've missed its message without us, although I suppose that's possible. The point is that Lew and I, on our mission for American evangelism, were innocent bearers of the hot news.

Jack stood up. 'It's a joke,' he said.

'No,' said Lew, 'I'm being straight.'

'Make a funny story back in Lindy's if I said yes.'

'Jack,' said Lew, who was suddenly drained of facial blood by the remark, 'this is an honest-to-God idea I had and told nobody but Marcus and now you and your wife. Nobody else.'

Jack gave him a short look and figured out from his new complexion that he wasn't practical-joking.

'Okay, Lew. Okay. Let's say it's a nice try then. But not for me. Maybe it'd make a bundle, but it rubs me wrong. I feel like a stool pigeon just thinking about it.'

'No names, Jack, nobody's asking for names. Tell stories, that's all. It's what you know about how it all works.'

'That's what I mean. You don't tell the suckers how the game is played.'

Alice picked up the *Mirror* and slowly and methodically rolled it into a bat. She tapped it against her palm the way a cop plays with a sap. I thought she was going to let Jack have a fast one across the nose. Goodbye barnstorm. Goodbye private Diamond altar. Goodbye salvation, for now.

Her crestfallen scene reveals to me at this remove that she really didn't understand Jack as well as I thought she did. She knew him better than anyone on earth, but she didn't understand how he could possibly be true to his nature. She really thought he was a crook, all the way through to the dirty underwear of his psyche.

'It'd be fun, Lew,' Jack said, starting to pace now himself, relaxed that it was over and he could talk about it and add it to his bag of offers. 'It'd be a hell of a lot of fun. New kind of take. And I know I got a little ham in me. Yeah, it'd be a good time, but I couldn't take it for long. I couldn't live up to the part.'

Alice left the room and carried the newspaper with her. It looked like a nightstick now. I can see her unrolling it and reading it in the kitchen, although I was not in the kitchen. She turns the pages angrily, not seeing the headlines, the photos, the words. She stops at Winchell because everybody stops there and reads him. She is not really reading. Her eyes have stopped at his block of black and white, and she stares down at it, thinking of getting off the train in Omaha and Denver and Boston and Tallahassee and spreading the word of John and God and standing in the wings holding her John's robe, making him tea, no more whiskey, washing his socks, answering his mail, refusing interviews. Damn, damn, damn, thinks Alice, and she sees his name in Winchell.

In the living room, standing on his purple Turkish rug, framing himself against the blue silk he'd stolen from a Jersey boxcar eight years before, Jack was saying he couldn't be a hypocrite.

'That sound funny coming from me, Lew?'

'Not a bit, Jack. I understand.' But I could see Lew too, watching a million-dollar idea curl up in the smoke of another Broadway pipe dream.

'Hypocrite? What the hell was he talking about?' Lew asked me later when we were on the way back to the Hudson station. 'Does he think I don't know who he is?'

'He had something else in mind, I'm sure,' I said. 'He knows you know who he is. He knows everybody knows. But he obviously doesn't think what he's doing is hypocritical.'

Lew shook his head. 'All the nuts ain't on the sundaes.'

Lew too. Victim of tunnel vision: A man's a thief, he's dishonest. What we didn't know as we listened to Jack was that he was in the midst of a delicate, supremely honest balancing act that would bring his life together if it worked, let it function as a unified whole and not as warring factions. Maybe Jack thought he was being honest in his retreat from page one, in his acquiescence to Alice's implorings that he become a private man, a country man, a home man, a husband. This behavior generated in Lew's head the idea that if Jack could only stay down long enough, he was fodder for American sainthood.

But Lew's conversion plan was false because Jack's behavior

in retreat was false. Jack wasn't a private but a public man, not a country squire but a city slicker, not a home but a hotel room man, not a husband but a cocksmith, not an American saint but an insatiable extortionist. ('Fuck 'em,' he said when I told him about Warren Van Deusen's vigilantes.) And he was not the sum of all these life-styles either, but a fusion beyond them all.

In a small way this was about to be demonstrated. Shirtsleeved, Jack shook our hands, walked us to the front door, apologized for not standing there with us, but said he didn't want to make it too easy for any passing shooters, and thanked us for livening up his afternoon.

The liveliness was just beginning.

The Winchell item in the *Mirror* read: 'Stagehands in the Chicago theater where Kiki Roberts is dancing in "Flying High" under the name of Doris Kane can set their watch by the phone call she gets every night at 7:30. You guessed the caller: Legs Diamond . . .'

'You son of a bitch, you said you weren't talking to her.'
　'Don't believe everything you read.'
　'You're always out of the house at that hour.'
　'Doesn't mean a thing.'
　'You promised me, you bastard. You promised me.'
　'I talked to her once in four months, that's all.'
　'I don't believe that either.'
　'Believe Winchell then.'
　'I thought you were being straight with me.'
　'You were right. I was. I didn't see her, I didn't see nobody.'
　'After all the goddamn nursing and handholding.'
　'I'm fond of the girl. I heard she was having some trouble and I called her. She's all right.'
　'I don't believe that. You're a liar.'
　'What's that on your housedress?'
　'Where?'
　'By the pocket.'
　'A spot.'

'A spot of what?'

'What's the difference what the spot is. It's a spot.'

'I paid to have that housedress cleaned and pressed and starched. The least you could do is keep it clean.'

'I do keep it clean. Shut up about the housedress.'

'I pay for the laundry and you put these things on and dirty them up. Goddamn money going down the goddamn laundry sink.'

'I'm leaving.'

'What's that in your hair?'

'Where?'

'Behind your right ear. There's something white. Is that gray hair?'

'It might be. God knows I've got a right to some.'

'Gray hair. So that's what you've come to. I spend money so you can get your hair bleached half the colors of the goddamn rainbow and you stand there and talk to me with gray hair.'

'I'm going upstairs to pack.'

'What's that on your leg?'

'Where?'

'Right there on the thigh.'

'Don't touch me. I don't want you to touch me.'

'What is it?'

'It's a run in my stocking.'

'Goddamn money for silk stockings and look what happens to them.'

'Get your hand away. I don't want to feel you. Go on, get it away. I don't want your hand there. No. Not there either. No. You won't get it that way anymore. Not after this. No. Don't you dare do that to me with Cordelia in the kitchen and after what I just read. You've lied once too often. I'm packing and nobody on God's earth can do anything to stop me.'

'What if I moved her in with us?'

'Oh.'

'We could work it out.'

'Oh!'

'She's a great girl and she thinks the world of you. Sit down. Let's talk about it.'

Kiki lay naked on the bed that was all hers and which stood where Alice's had stood before Jack had it taken out and bought the new one. She was thinking of the evening being unfinished, of the fudge that hadn't hardened the last time she touched it, and of Jack lying asleep in his own room, his heavy breathing audible to Kiki, who could not sleep and who resented the uselessness of her nakedness.

They had been together in her bed at early evening, hadn't eaten any supper because they were going to have dinner out later. The fudge was already in the fridge then. Jack was naked too, lying on his back, smoking and staring at the wall with the prints of the Michelangelo sketches, the punishment of Tityus and the head of a giant, prints Jack told her he bought because Arnold Rothstein liked them and said Michelangelo was the best artist who ever brushed a stroke. Jack said Kiki should look at the pictures and learn about art and not be so stupid about it. But the giant had an ugly head and she didn't like the one with the bird in it either, so she looked at Jack instead of dopey pictures. She wanted to touch him, not look at him, but she knew it wouldn't be right because there was no spark in him. He was collapsed and he had tried but wasn't in the mood. He started out in the mood, but the mood left him. He needed a rest, maybe.

He wouldn't look at her. She kept looking at him but he wouldn't look back, so she got up and said, 'I'm going downstairs and see if that fudge is hard yet.'

'Put something on.'

'I'll put my apron on.'

'Take a housecoat. There may be somebody on the porch.'

'They're all out in the cottage playing pool or in the car watching the road. I know they are.'

'I don't want you showing off your ass to the hired help.'

She put on one of Alice's aprons, inside out so it wouldn't look too familiar to Jack, and went downstairs. She looked in the mirror and knew anybody could see a little bit of her tail if there was anybody to see it, but there wasn't. She didn't want clothes on. She didn't want to start something and then have to take the clothes off in a hurry and maybe lose the spark, which she would try to reignite when she went back upstairs. She wanted Jack to see as much of her as he could as often as he could, wanted to reach him with all she could reach him with. She had the house now. She had beaten Alice. She had Jack. She did not plan to let go of him.

The fudge was still soft to her touch. She left another fingerprint in it. She had made it for Jack, but it wasn't hardening. It had been in the fridge twenty-eight hours, and it wasn't any harder now than it was after the first hour.

'What do you like – chocolate or penuche?' she had asked him the day before.

'Penuche's the white one with nuts, right?'

'Right.'

'That's the one.'

'That's the one I like too.'

'How come you know so much about fudge?'

'It's the only thing I ever learned how to cook from my mother. I haven't made it in five or six years, but I want to do it for you.'

The kitchen had all the new appliances, Frigidaire, Mixmaster, chrome orange juice squeezer, a machine for toasting two slices of bread. But, for all its qualities, Kiki couldn't find the ingredients she remembered from her mother's recipe. So she used two recipes, her own and one out of Alice's *Fanny Farmer Cook Book*, mixed them up together and cooked them and poured it all into a tin pie plate and set it on the top shelf of the fridge. But it didn't harden. She tasted it and it was sweet and delicious, but it was goo after an hour. Now it was still goo.

'It's all goo,' she told Jack when she went back upstairs. She stood alongside him and took off her apron. He didn't reach for her.

'Let's go out,' he said, and he rolled across the bed, away from her, and stood up. He put on his robe and went into his own room

672

to dress. Even when Alice was there he had had his own room. Even at the hotel he had kept his own room to go to when he and Kiki had finished making love.

'Are you angry because the fudge didn't harden?'

'For crissakes, no. You got other talents.'

'Do you wish I could cook?'

'No. I cook good enough for both of us.'

And he did, too. Why Jack made the best chicken cacciatore Kiki ever ate, and he cooked a roast of lamb with garlic and spices that was fantastic. Jack could do anything in life. Kiki could only do about three things. She could dance a little and she could love a man and she could be pretty. But she could do those things a thousand times better than most women. She knew about men, knew what men told her. They told her she was very good at love and that she was pretty. They also liked to talk about her parts. They all (and Jack too) told her she was lovely everyplace. So Kiki didn't need to learn about cooking. She wasn't going to tie in with anybody as a kitchen slave and a fat mommy. She wore an apron, but she wore it her way, with nothing underneath it. If Jack wanted a cook, he wouldn't have got rid of Alice. Kiki would just go on being Kiki, somebody strange. She didn't know how she was strange. She knew she wasn't smart enough to understand the reasons behind that sort of thing. I mean I know it already, she said to herself. I don't have to figure it out. I know it and I'm living it.

Kiki thought about these things as she was lying naked in her bed wishing the fudge would harden. Earlier in the night, after Jack had rolled out of her bed, they'd gone out, had eaten steaks at the New York Restaurant in Catskill, one of the best, then had drinks at Sweeney's club, a good-time speakeasy. It was on the way home that everything was so beautiful and quiet. She felt strange then. She and Jack were in the back seat and Fogarty was driving. She was holding Jack's hand, and they were just sitting there, a little glassy-eyed from the booze, yes, but that wasn't the reason it was so beautiful. It was beautiful because they were together as they deserved to be and because they didn't have to say anything to each other.

She remembered looking ahead on the road and looking out the window she'd rolled down and feeling the car was moving without a motor. She couldn't hear noise, couldn't see anything but the lights on the road and the darkened farmhouses and the open fields that were all so brightly lighted by the new moon. The stars were out too, on this silent, this special night. It was positively breathtaking, is how Kiki later described the scene and the mood that preceded the vision of the truck.

That damn truck.

Why did it have to be there ahead of them?

Why couldn't Joe have taken another road and not seen it?

Oh, jeez, wouldn't everything in her whole life have been sweet if they just hadn't seen that truck?

When he saw the old man in the truck, got a good look and saw the side of his face with its bumpkin stupid smile, Jack felt his heart leap up. When Fogarty said, 'Streeter from Cairo – he hauls cider, but we never caught him with any,' Jack felt the flush in his neck. He had no pistol with him, but he opened the gun rack in the back of the front seat and unclipped one of the .38s. He rolled down the window on his side, renewed.

'Jack, what's going to happen?' Kiki asked.

'Just a little business. Nothing to get excited about.'

'Jack, don't get, don't get me, don't get . . .'

'Just shut up and stay in the car.'

They were on Jefferson Avenue, heading out of Catskill when the trucker saw Jack's pistol pointing at him. Fogarty cruised at equal speed with the truck until Streeter pulled to the side of the road across from a cemetery. Jack was the first out, his pistol pointed upward. He saw the barrels on the truck and quick-counted more than fifteen. Son of a bitch. He saw the shitkicker's cap, country costume, and he hated the man for wearing it. Country son of a bitch, where Jack had to live.

'Get down out of that truck.'

Streeter slid off the seat and stepped down, and Jack saw the second head, another cap on it, sliding across the seat and stepping down, a baby-faced teen-ager with a wide forehead, a widow's peak, and a pointy chin that gave his face the look of a heart.

'How many more you got in there?' Jack said.

'No more. Just me and the boy.'

'Who is he?'

'Bartlett, Dickie Bartlett.'

'What's he to you?'

'A helper.'

Streeter's moon face was full of rotten teeth and a grin.

'So you're Streeter, the wise guy from Cairo,' Jack said.

Streeter nodded, very slightly, the grin stayed in place and Jack punched it, cutting the flesh of the cheekbone.

'Put your hands up higher or I'll split your fucking head.'

Jack poked Streeter's chest with the pistol barrel. The Bartlett boy's hands shot up higher than Streeter's. Jack saw Fogarty with a pistol in his hand.

'What's in the barrels?'

'Hard cider,' said Streeter through his grin.

'Not beer or white?'

'I don't haul beer, or white either. I ain't in the booze business.'

'You better be telling the truth, old man. You know who I am?'

'Yes, I know.'

'I know you too. You been hauling too many barrels.'

'Haulin's what I do.'

'Hauling barrels is dangerous business when they might have beer or white in them.'

'Nothing but cider in them barrels.'

'We'll see. Now move.'

'Move where?'

'Into the car, goddamn it,' Jack said, and he slapped Streeter on the back of the head with his gun hand. He knocked off the goddamn stinking cap. Streeter bent to pick it up and turned to Jack with his grin. He couldn't really be grinning.

'Where you taking that cider?'

'Up home, and some over to Bartlett's.'

'The kid?'

'His old man.'

'You got a still yourself?'

'No.'

'Bartlett got a still?'

'Not that I know of.'

'What's all the cider for then?'

'Drink some, make vinegar, bottle some, sell some of that to stores up in the hollow, sell what's left to neighbors. Or anybody.'

'Where's the still?'

'Ain't no still I know of.'

'Who do you know's got a still?'

'Never hear of nobody with a still.'

'You heard I run the only stills that run in this county? You heard that?'

'Yes siree, I heard that.'

'So who runs a still takes that much cider?'

'Ain't that much when you cut it up.'

'We'll see how much it is,' Jack said. He told Kiki to sit in front and he put Streeter and Bartlett in the back seat. He pulled their caps down over their eyes and sat in front with Kiki while Fogarty drove the truck inside the cemetery entrance. Fogarty was gone ten minutes, which passed in silence, and when he came back, he said, 'Looks like it's all hard cider. Twenty-four barrels.' And he slipped behind the wheel. Jack rode with his arm over the back seat and his pistol pointed at the roof. No one spoke all the way to Acra, and Streeter and Bartlett barely moved. They sat with their hands in their laps and their caps over their eyes. When they got out of the car inside the garage, Jack made them face the wall and tied their hands behind them. Fogarty backed the car out, closed the door, and took Kiki inside the house. Jack sat Streeter and Bartlett on the floor against a ladder.

Shovels hung over the old man's head like a set of assorted

guillotines. Jack remembered shovels on the wall of the cellar in The Village where the Neary mob took him so long ago when they thought he'd hijacked a load of their beer – and he had. They tied him to a chair with wire around his arms and legs, then worked him over. They got weary and left him, bloody and half conscious, to go to sleep. He was fully awake and moved his arms back and forth against the wire's twist until he ripped his shirt. He sawed steadily with the wire until it ripped the top off his right bicep and let him slip his arm out of the bond. He climbed up a coal chute and out a window, leaving pieces of the bicep on the twist of wire, and on the floor: skin, flesh, plenty of blood. Bled all the way home. Bicep flat now. Long, rough scar there now. Some Nearys paid for that scar.

He looked at the old man and saw the ropes hanging on the wall behind him, can of kerosene in the corner, paintbrushes soaking in turpentine. Rakes, pickax. Old man another object. Another tool. Jack hated all tools that refused to yield their secrets. Jack was humiliated before the inanimate world. He hated it, kicked it when it affronted him. He shot a car once that betrayed him by refusing to start. Blew holes in its radiator.

The point where the hanging rope bellied out on the garage wall looked to Jack like the fixed smile on Streeter's face. Streeter was crazy to keep smiling. He wasn't worth a goddamn to anybody if he was crazy. You can kill crazies. No loss. Jack made ready to kill yet another man. Wilson, the first one he killed. Wilson, the card cheat. Fuck you, cheater, you're dead. I'm sorry for your kids.

In the years after he dumped Wilson in the river Jack used Rothstein's insurance connections to insure family men he was going to remove from life. He made an arrangement with a thieving insurance salesman, sent him around to the family well in advance of the removal date. When the deal was sealed, give Jack a few weeks, then bingo!

'You got any insurance, old man?'

'No.'

'You got any family?'

'Wife.'

'Too bad. She's going to have to bury you best she can. Unless you tell me where that still is you got hid.'

'Ain't got no still hid nowheres, mister. I told you that.'

'Better think again, old man. You know where the still is, kid?' Dickie Bartlett shook his head and turned to the wall. Only a kid. But if Jack killed one, he would have to kill two. Tough break, kid.

'Take off your shoes.'

Streeter slowly untied the rawhide laces of his high shoe-boots without altering his grin. He pulled off one shoe and Jack smelled his foot, his sweaty white wool sock, his long underwear tucked inside the sock. Country leg, country foot, country stink. Jack looked back at the grin, which seemed as fixed as the shape of the nose that hovered above it. But you don't fix a grin permanently. Jack knew. That old son of a bitch is defying me, is what he thought. He hasn't got a chance and yet he's defying Jack Diamond's law, Jack Diamond's threat, Jack Diamond himself. That grinning façade is a fake and Jack will remove it. Jack knows all there is to know about fake façades. He remembered his own grin in one of the newspapers as he went into court in Philadelphia. Tough monkey, smilin' through. They won't get to me. And then in the courtroom he knew how empty that smile was, how profoundly he had failed to create the image he wanted to present to the people of Philadelphia, not only on his return but all his life, all through boyhood, to live down the desertion charge in the Army, and, worse, the charge that he stole from his buddies. Not true. So many of the things they said about Jack were untrue and yet they stuck.

He was a nobody in the Philadelphia court. Humiliated. Arrested coming in, then kicked out. And stay out, you bum. I speak for the decent people of this city in saying that Philadelphia doesn't want you any more than Europe did. Vomit. Puke, puke. Vomit. Country feet smelled like vomit. Jack's family witnessing it all in the courtroom. Jack always loved them in his way. Jack dumped about eight cigarettes out of his Rameses pack and pocketed them. He twisted the pack and lit it with a loose match, showed the burning cellophane and paper to Streeter, who never lost his grin. Jack said, 'Where's the still?'

'Jee-zus, mister, I ain't seen no still. I ain't and that's a positive fact, I tell you.'

Jack touched the fire to the sock and then to the edge of the underwear. Streeter shook it and the fire went out. Jack burned his own hand, dropped the flaming paper and let it burn out. Fogarty came back in then, pistol in hand.

'Kneel on him,' Jack said, and with pistol pointed at Streeter's head, Fogarty knelt on the old man's calf. The pistol wasn't loaded, Fogarty said later. He was taking no chances shooting anybody accidentally. It had been loaded when they stopped Streeter's truck because he felt when he traveled the roads with Jack he was bodyguard as well as chauffeur, and he would stand no chance of coping with a set of killers on wheels if his gun was empty. But now he wasn't a bodyguard anymore.

'He's a tough old buzzard,' Jack said.

'Why don't you tell him what he wants to know?' Fogarty said conspiratorially to Streeter.

'Can't tell what I don't know,' Streeter said. The grin was there. The flame had not changed it. Jack knew now he would remove that grin with flame. Finding the still was receding in importance, but such a grin of defiance is worth punishing. Asks for punishing. Will always get what it asks for. The Alabama sergeant who tormented Jack and other New York types in the platoon because of their defiance. 'New Yoahk mothahfucks.' Restriction. Punishment. KP over and over. Passes denied. And then Jack swung and got the son bitch in the leg with an iron bar. Had to go AWOL after that, couldn't even go back. That was when they got him, in New Yoahk. Did defiance win the day for Jack? It was satisfying, but Jack admits it did not win the day. Should have shot the son bitch in some ditch off-post. Let the rats eat him.

'Where's that still, you old son bitch?'

'Hey, mister, I'd tell you if I knew. You think I'd keep anythin' back if I knew? I dunno, mister, I just plain dunno.'

Jack lit the sock, got it flaming this time, and the old man yelled,

679

shook his whole leg again and rocked Fogarty off it. The flame went out again. Jack looked, saw the grin. The old man is totally insane. Should be bugged. Crazy as they make 'em. Crazy part of a man that takes any kind of punishment, suffers all humiliations. No pride.

'You old son bitch, ain't you got no pride? Tell me the goddamn answer to my question. Ain't you got no sense? I'm gonna hang your ass off a tree you don't tell me what I want to know.'

But you can't really punish a crazy like that, Jack. He loves it. That's why he's sitting there grinning. Some black streak across his brain makes him crazier than a dog with his head where his ass oughta be. He's making *you* crazy now, Jack. Got you talking about hanging. You can't be serious, can you?

'All right, old man, get up. Speed, get that rope.'

'What you got in mind, Jack?'

'I'm gonna hang his Cairo country ass from that maple tree outside.'

'Hey,' said Streeter, 'you ain't really gonna hang me?'

'I'm gonna hang you like a side of beef,' Jack said. 'I'm gonna pop your eyes like busted eggs. I'm gonna make your tongue stretch so far out you'll be lickin' your toes.'

'I ain't done nothin' to nobody, mister. Why you gonna hang me?'

'Because you're lyin' to me, old man.'

'No, sir, I ain't lyin'. I ain't lyin'.'

'How old are you right now?'

'Fifty.'

'You ain't as old as I thought, but you ain't gonna be fifty-one. You're a stubborn buzzard, but you ain't gonna be fifty-one. Bring him out.'

Fogarty led the old man outside with only one shoe, and Jack threw the rope over the limb of the maple. He tied a knot, looped the rope through the opening in the knot – a loop that would work like an animal's choker chain – and slipped it over Streeter's neck. Jack pulled open a button, one down from the collar, to give the rope plenty of room.

'Jack,' Fogarty said, shaking his head. Jack tugged the rope until he took up all the slack and the rope rose straight up from Streeter's neck.

'One more chance,' Jack said. 'Where is that goddamn still you were headed for?'

'Jee-zus Keh-ryst, mister, there just ain't no still, you think I'm kiddin' you? You got a rope around my neck. You think I wouldn't tell you anything I knew if I knew it? Jee-zus, mister, I don't want to die.'

'Listen, Jack. I don't think we ought to do this.' Fogarty was trembling. The poor goddamn trucker. Like watching a movie and knowing how it ends, Fogarty said later.

'Shitkicker!' Jack yelled. 'Where is it? SHITKICKER! SHIT-KICKER!'

Before the old man could answer, Jack tugged at the rope and up went Streeter. But he had worked one hand loose and he made a leap as Jack tugged. He grabbed the rope over his head and held it.

'Retie the son of a bitch,' Jack said, and Fogarty knew then he was party to a murder. Full accomplice now and the tied-up Bartlett kid a witness. There would be a second murder on this night. Fogarty, how far you've come under Jack's leadership. He tied the old man's hands, and Jack then wound the rope around both his own arms and his waist so it wouldn't slip, and he jerked it again and moved backward. The old man's eyes bugged as he rose off the ground. His tongue came out and he went limp. The Bartlett kid yelled and then started to cry, and Jack let go of the rope. The old man crumpled.

'He's all right,' Jack said. 'The old son of a bitch is too miserable to die. Hit him with some water.'

Fogarty half-filled a pail from an outside faucet and threw it on Streeter. The old man opened his eyes.

'You know, just maybe he's telling the truth,' Fogarty said.

'He's lying.'

'He's doing one hell of a good job.'

Jack took Fogarty's pistol and waved it under Streeter's nose. *At least he can't kill him with that*, Fogarty thought.

'It's too much work to hang you,' Jack said to Streeter, 'so I'm gonna blow your head all over the lawn. I'll give you one more chance.'

The old man shook his head and closed his eyes. His grin was gone. I finally got rid of that, is what Jack thought. But then he was suddenly enraged again at the old man. You made me do this to you, was the nature of Jack's accusation. You turned me into a goddamn sadist because of your goddamn stinking country stubbornness. He laid the barrel of the pistol against the old man's head and then he thought: *Fogarty*. And he checked the cylinder. No bullets. He gave Fogarty a look of contempt and handed him back the empty pistol. He took his own .38 from his coat pocket, and Streeter, watching everything, started to tremble, his lip turned down now. Smile not only gone, but that face unable even to remember that it had smiled even once in all its fifty years. Jack fired one shot. It exploded alongside Streeter's right ear. The old man's head jerked and Jack fired again, alongside the other ear.

'You got something to tell me now, shitkicker?' Jack said.

The old man opened his eyes, saucers of terror. He shook his head. Jack put the pistol between his eyes, held it there for seconds of silence. Then he let it fall away with a weariness. He stayed on his haunches in front of Streeter, just staring. Just staring and saying nothing.

'You win, old man,' he finally said. 'You're a tough monkey.'

Jack stood up slowly and pocketed his pistol. Fogarty and one of the porch guards drove Streeter and Bartlett back to their truck. Fogarty ripped out their ignition wires and told them not to call the police. He drove back to Acra and slept the sleep of a confused man.

When Speed had brought her from the car into the house, Kiki had said to him, 'What's going to happen with those men?'

'I don't know. Probably just some talk.'

'Oh, God, Joe, don't let him hurt them. I don't want to be mixed up in that kind of shit again, please, Joe.'

'I'll do what I can do, but you know Jack's got a mind of his own.'

'I'll go and see him. Or maybe you could tell him to come in. Maybe if I asked him not to do anything, for me, don't do it for me, he wouldn't do it.'

'I'll tell him you said it.'

'You're a nice guy, Joe.'

'You go to bed and stay upstairs. Do what I tell you.'

'Yes, Joe.'

Kiki was thinking that Joe really and truly was a nice guy and that maybe she could make it with him if only she wasn't tied up with Jack. Of course, she wouldn't do anything while she was thick with Jack. But it was nice to think about Joe and his red hair and think about how nice he would be to play with. He was nicer than Jack, but then she didn't love Jack because he was nice.

She worried whether Jack had killed the two men when she later heard the two shots and the screaming. But she had thought the worst at the Monticello, thought Jack had killed *those* men when they had really tried to kill him. She didn't want to think bad things about Jack again. But she lived half an hour with uncertainty. Then Jack came into her room and said the men were gone and nobody got hurt.

'Did you get the information you wanted?' she asked.

'Yeah, I don't want to talk about it.'

'Oh, good. Are you done now?'

'All done.'

'Then we can finish the evening the way we intended.'

'It's finished.'

'I mean really finished.'

'And I mean really finished.'

He kissed her on the cheek and went to his bedroom. He didn't come back to see her or ask her to come to him. She tried to sleep, but she kept wanting to finish the evening, continue from where she and Jack had left off in the car in the silence and the chilliness and the brightness of the new moon on the open fields. She wanted to lie alongside Jack and comfort him because she knew from the way he was behaving that he had the blues. If she went in and loved him, he would feel better. Yet she felt he didn't really want that, and she rolled over and tossed and turned, curled and uncurled for another hour before she decided: Maybe he really does want it. So then, yes, she ought to do it. She got up and very quietly tiptoed into Jack's room and stood naked alongside his bed. Jack was deeply asleep. She touched his ear and ran her fingers down his cheek, and all of a sudden she was looking down the barrel of his .38 and he was bending her fingers back so far she was screaming. Nobody came to help her. She thought of that later. Jack could have killed her and nobody would have tried to stop him. Not even Joe.

'You crazy bitch! What were you trying to do?'

'I just wanted to love you.'

'Never, never wake me up that way. Don't ever touch me. Call me and I'll hear it, but don't touch me.'

Kiki was weeping because her hand hurt so much. She couldn't bend her fingers. When she tried to bend them, she fainted. When she came to, she was in a chair and Jack was all white in the face, looking at her. He was slapping her cheek lightly just as she came out of it.

'It hurts an awful lot.'

'We'll go get a doctor. I'm sorry, Marion, I'm really sorry I hurt you.'

'I know you are, Jack.'

'I don't want to hurt you.'

'I know you don't.'

'I love you so much I'm half nuts sometimes.'

'Oh, Jackie, you're not nuts, you're wonderful and I don't care if you hurt me. It was an accident. It was all my fault.'

'We'll go get the doc out of bed.'

'He'll fix me up fine, and then we can come back and finish the evening.'

'Yeah, that's a swell idea.'

The coroner was Jack's doctor, and they got him out of bed. He bandaged her hand and said she'd have to have a cast made at the hospital next day, and he gave her pills for her pain. She told him she'd been rehearsing her dance steps and had fallen down. He didn't seem to believe that, but Jack didn't care what he believed, so she didn't either. After the doctor's they went back home. Jack said he was too tired to make love and that they'd do it in the morning. Kiki tossed and turned for a while and then went down to the kitchen and checked the fudge again, felt it with the fingers of her good hand. It was still goo, so she put it out on the back porch for the cat.

Clem Streeter told his story around Catskill for years. He was a celebrity because of it, stopped often by people and asked for another rendition. I was being shaved in a Catskill barber chair the year beer came back, and Jack was, of course, long gone. But Clem was telling the story yet again for half a dozen locals.

'The jedge in Catskill axed me what I wanted the pistol *per*mit for,' he said, 'and I told him 'bout how that Legs Diamond feller burned my feet and hung me from a sugar maple th'other night up at his garage. "That so?" axed the jedge. "I jes told you it were," I said. People standin' 'round the courthouse heard what we was sayin' and they come over to listen better. "You made a complaint yet against this Diamond person?" the jedge axes me. But I tell him, only complaint I made so far was to the wife. That jedge he don't know what to do with hisself he's so took out by what I'm sayin'. I didn't mean to upset the jedge. But he says, "I guess we better get the sheriff on this one and maybe the DA," and they both of 'em come in after a little bit and I tell 'em my story, how they poked guns outen the winders of their car and we stopped the truck, me and Dickie Bartlett. They made us git down, but I didn't git fast enough for Diamond, so he hit me with his fist and said, "Put up your hands or I'll split your effin' head." Then they hauled us up to Diamond's place with our caps pulled down so we wouldn't know where we was goin', but I see the road anyway out under the side of the cap and I know that place of his with the lights real well. Am I sure it was Diamond, the jedge axes. "Acourse I'm sure. I seen him plenty over at the garage in Cairo.

He had a woman in the car with him, and I recognized the other feller who did the drivin' 'cause he stopped my truck another night I was haulin' empty barrels 'bout a month back." "So this here's Streeter, the wise guy from Cairo," Diamond says to me and he cuffs me on the jaw with his fist, just like that, afore I said a word. Then up in the garage they tried to burn me up. "What'd they do that for?" the jedge axes me, and I says, "'Cause he wants to know where there's a still I'm s'posed to know about. But I told Diamond I don't know nothin' 'bout no still." And the jedge says, "Why'd he think you did?" And I says, "'Cause I'm haulin' twenty-four barrels of hard cider I'd picked up down at Post's Cider Mill." "Who for?" says the jedge. "For me," I says. "I like cider. Drink a bunch of it." 'Cause I ain't about to tell no jedge or nobody else 'bout the still me and old Cy Bartlett got between us. We do right nice business with that old still. Make up to a hundred, hundred and thirty dollars apiece some weeks off the fellers who ain't got no stills and need a little 'jack to keep the blood pumpin'. That Diamond feller, he surely did want to get our still away from us. I knew that right off. Did me a lot of damage, I'll say. But sheeeeee. Them fellers with guns is all talk. Hell, they don't never kill nobody. They just like to throw a scare into folks so's they can get their own way. Son of a bee if I was gonna give up a hundred and thirty dollars a week for some New York feller.'

Jack Among
the Maids

The Streeter incident took place in mid-April, 1931. Eight days later, the following document was released in the Capitol at Albany:

Pursuant to section 62 of the Executive Law, I hereby require that you, the Attorney General of this state, attend in person or by your assistants or deputies, a regular special and trial term of the Supreme Court appointed to be held in and for the County of Greene for the month of April, 1931, and as such term as may hereafter be continued, and that you in person or by said assistants or deputies appear before the grand jury or grand juries which shall be drawn and sit for any later term or terms of said court for the purpose of managing and conducting in said court and before said grand jury and said other grand juries, any and all proceedings, examinations and inquiries, and any and all criminal actions and proceedings which may be taken by or before said grand jury concerning any and all kinds and – or – criminal offences, alleged to have been committed by John Diamond, also known as Jack (Legs) Diamond and – or – any person or persons acting in concert with him, and further to manage, prosecute and conduct the trial of any indictments found by said grand jury or grand juries at said term or terms of said court or of any other court at which any and all such indictments may hereafter be tried, and that in person or by your assistants or deputies you supersede the District Attorney of the County of Greene in all matters herein specified and you exercise all the powers and perform all the duties conferred upon you by Section 62 of the Executive Law and this requirement thereunder; and that in such proceedings and actions the District Attorney of Greene County shall only exercise such powers and perform such duties as are required of him by you or by the assistants or deputies attorney general so attending.

> Franklin Delano Roosevelt
> Governor of the State of New York

Jack thus became the first gangster of the Prohibition Era to have the official weight of an entire state, plus the gobble of its officialese, directed at him. I find this notable.

I did what little I could to throw a counterweight when the time came. I cited the whole affair as a cynical political response to the harsh spotlight that Judge Seabury, his reformers, and the Republican jackals were, at the moment, shining on the gangsterism and corruption so prevalent in New York City's Tammany Hall, with Democratic Gentleman Jimmy Walker the chief illuminated goat. FDR. I argued when I pleaded Jack's case in the press, was making my client the goat in a Republican stronghold. I voiced particular outrage at superseding the Greene County District Attorney.

But my counterweight didn't weigh much. Jack went to jail and I understood the spadework done in Albany by Van Deusen's vigilantes. FDR even sent his personal bodyguard to Catskill as an observer when the swarm of state police and state attorneys moved toward Jack's jugular.

Knute Rockne told his men: 'Don't be a bad loser, but don't lose.'

Fogarty got me out of bed to tell me Jack had been arrested and that he himself was going into hiding. Jack and Kiki were in the parlor at Acra, and Fogarty was playing pool in the cottage when the trooper rang the bell under the second step. Three times. Jack's straight neighbors thought three was the insider's ring, but it was the ring only for straights.

Jack tried to talk the trooper into letting him surrender in the morning by himself, avoid the ignominy of it, but the trooper said nix, and so Jack wound up on a hard cot in a white-washed third-floor cell of the county jail. Tidy and warm, not quite durance vile, as one journalist wrote, but vile enough for the King Cobra of the Catskills, as he was now known in the press.

I worked on the bail, which was a formidable twenty-five thousand dollars: ten each for assaulting Streeter and Bartlett, five for the kidnapping. Uh-oh, I said, when I heard the news, heard especially how young Bartlett was. What we now are dealing with, I told Fogarty, and Jack too, is not a bootleggers' feud, which is what it was in a left-handed way, but the abduction of children in the dead of night. Not a necessary social misdemeanor, as most bootlegging was contemporaneously regarded, but a high crime in any age.

I called Warren Van Deusen to see if I could pry Jack loose by greasing local pols, but found him haughtily supporting the state's heavy anti-Jack thrust. 'Kidnapping kids now, is he? I hear he's holding up bread truck drivers too. What's next? Disemboweling old ladies?' I wrote off Warren as unreliable, a man given to facile outrage, who didn't understand the process he was enmeshed in.

It has long been my contention that Jack was not only a political pawn through Streeter, but a pawn of the entire decade. Politicans used him, and others like him, to carry off any vileness that served their ends, beginning with the manipulation of strikebreakers as the decade began and ending with the manipulation of stockbrokers at the end of the crash, a lovely, full, capitalistic circle. Thereafter the pols rejected Jack as unworthy, and tried to destroy him.

But it was Jack and a handful of others – Madden, Schultz, Capone, Luciano – who reversed the process, who became manipulators of the pols, who left a legacy of money and guns that would dominate the American city on through the 1970s. Jack was too interested in private goals to see the potential that 1931 offered to the bright student of urban life. Yet he was unquestionably an ancestral paradigm for modern urban political gangsters, upon whom his pioneering and his example were obviously not lost.

I hesitate to develop all the analogies I see in this, for I don't want to trivialize Jack's achievement by linking him to lesser latter-day figures such as Richard Nixon, who left significant history in his wake, but no legend; whose corruption, overwhelmingly venal and invariably hypocritical, lacked the admirably white core fantasy that can give evil a mythical dimension. Only boobs and shitheads rooted for Nixon in his troubled time, but heroes and poets followed Jack's tribulations with curiosity, ambivalent benevolence, and a sense of mystery at the meaning of their own response.

Fogarty, sitting at a bar and waiting for a female form to brighten his life, and meanwhile telling a story about a gang-bang, felt alive for the first time in a week, for the first time since they hauled Jack in and he took off up the mountain. A week in a cabin alone, only one day out for groceries and the paper, is enough to grow hair on a wart, shrivel a gonad.

Fogarty found solitude unbearably full of evaporated milk and tuna fish, beans and cheese, stale bread and bad coffee, memories of forced bed-rest, stultifying boredom with one's own thought. And then to run out of candles.

The old shack on stilts was down the mountain from Haines Falls, half a mile in an old dirt road, then a quarter of a mile walk with the groceries. He walked down from the cabin to his old car every morning and every night to make sure it was still there and to start it. Then he walked alone in the woods looking at the same trees, same squirrels, same chipmunks and rabbits, same goddamn birds with all that useless song, and came back and slept and ate and thought about women, and read the only book in the cabin, *The World Almanac*. He related to the ads – no end to life's jokes:

Last Year's Pay Looks Like Small Change to These Men Today; Raised Their Pay 500% When They Discovered

Salesmanship . . . Have YOU Progressed During the Past Three Years? . . . Ask Your Dealer for Crescent Guns, 12–16–20–410 Gauge . . . A Challenge Made Me Popular! . . . This Man Wouldn't Stay Down . . . It Pays to Read Law . . . Success – Will You Pay the Price? . . . Finest of All Cast Bronze Sarcophagi.

Fogarty closed the book, took a walk in the dark. A wild bird call scared him, and he retreated to the cabin to find only half a candle left, not enough to get him through the night. It's time, he said. It was ten o'clock. The Top o' the Mountain House would have some action and he needed a drink, needed people, needed a look at a woman, needed news. His old relic of a Studebaker started all right. Would he ever again see his new Olds, sitting back in the shed behind his house in Catskill? No chance to take it when he left Jack's in such a hurry.

There were four men at the bar, two couples at one table in the back room. He checked them all, knew nobody, but they looked safe. The bartender, a kid named Reilly he'd talked to, but never pressured, was okay. Fogarty ordered applejack on ice. He made it, sold it, liked it. Jack hated it. He had three and was already half an hour into a conversation with Reilly, feeling good again, telling about the night he and eight guys were lined up in a yard on 101st Street for a girl named Maisie who was spread out under a bush, taking on the line.

'I was about fourth and didn't even know who she was. We just heard it was on and got in line. Then when I saw her, I said to myself, "Holy beazastards," because I knew Maisie, and her brother Rick is my pal and he's in line right behind me. So I said to him, "I just got a look, she's a dog, let's beat it," and I grabbed his arm and pulled, but he was ready, you know, and I couldn't talk him out of it. He had to see her for himself. And when he saw her, he pulled off the guy on her and whipped him, and then beat hell out of Maisie. Next day everybody had trouble looking Rick in the eye. Guys he knew were there all said they were behind him in the line and didn't know who she was either.

Maisie was back a couple of nights later, and we all got her without Rick breaking it up.'

Fogarty paused nostalgically. 'I got in line twice.'

The barman liked the story, bought Fogarty a drink, and said, 'You know, was a guy in here last night askin' about your friend Diamond. Guy with a bandage on his eye.'

'A bandage? You don't mean an eyepatch?'

'No, a bandage. Adhesive and gauze stuff.'

'What'd he want?'

'Dunno. Asks has Jack Diamond been in much and when was the last time.'

'You know him?'

'Never seen him before.'

'You remember a guy named Murray? Called him The Goose.'

'No.'

'Nuts.'

'You know this guy with the eye?'

'I don't know. Could be he's a friend of ours. Your phone working?'

'End of the bar.'

Fogarty felt the blood rise in his chest, felt needed. Reilly had told him Jack was out on bail, so it was important for him to know Murray was around, if he was. All week in the woods Fogarty had cursed Jack, vowed to quit him, leave the country; that if this thing straightened out, he'd find a new connection; that he couldn't go on working with a man who wasn't playing with a full deck. Northrup first, then Streeter. Crazy. But now that feeling was gone, and he wanted to talk to Jack, warn him, protect his life.

'Don't touch that phone.'

Fogarty turned to see old man Brady, the owner, standing alongside him with his hand on a pistol in his belt.

'Get out of here,' Brady said.

'I just want to make a call.'

'Make it someplace else. You or none of your bunch are welcome here. We're all through kissing your ass.'

Brady's beer belly and soiled shirt pushed against the pistol.

The spiderweb veins in Brady's cheeks Fogarty would remember when he was dying, for they would look like the crystalline glaze that covered his own eyes in his last days. Brady with the whiskey webs. Old lush. Throwing me out.

'If it wasn't for your father,' Brady said, 'I'd shoot you now. He was a decent man. I don't know how in the hell he ever got you.'

Fogarty would remember that drops of sweat had run off Brady's spiderwebs one day long ago, the day Fogarty stood in front of him at the bar and told him how much of Jack's beer he would handle a week. Told him. Two of Jack's transient gunmen stood behind him to reinforce the message.

'You're lucky I don't call the troopers and turn you in,' old Brady said to him now, 'but I wouldn't do that to a son of your father's. Remember the favor that decent man did for you from his grave, you dirty whelp. You dirty, dirty whelp. Go on, get out of here.'

He moved his fingers around the butt of his pistol, and Fogarty went out into the night to find Jack.

Fogarty stopped the car and loaded his pistol, Eddie Diamond's .32. If he saw Murray, he would shoot first, other things being equal. He wouldn't shoot him in public. Fogarty marveled at his own aggression, but then he knew The Goose, knew Jack's story of how The Goose stalked a man once who went to the same movie house every week. The Goose sat in the lobby until the man arrived, then shoved a gun in his face, and blew half the head off the wrong man. A week later he was in the same lobby when the right man arrived, and he blew off half the correct head. Jack liked to tell Goose stories, how Goose once said of himself: 'I'm mean as a mad hairy.' What would The Goose have done to Streeter? Old man'd be stretched now, and the kid too. Was Fogarty the difference between life and death on that night?

He wanted to buy a paper, find out what was happening. He hadn't asked many questions at the bar, didn't want to seem ignorant. But he knew from a conversation with Marcus after

Jack's arrest, plus something Reilly said, that the state was sitting heavily on Jack. Old man Brady's behavior meant everybody'd be tough now. Jack is down and so is Fogarty, so put on your kicking shoes, folks.

Was it all over? No more money ('The boss needs a loan') coming in from the hotels and boardinghouses? No more still? Yes, there would be beer runs. There would always be beer runs. And there were the stashes of booze, if nobody found them. Reilly said four of Jack's men, all picked up at the cottage, were booked on vagrancy, no visible income. But they couldn't say that about Fogarty with his three bank accounts, fifteen thousand dollars deposited in one during the past six months. But he couldn't go near them until he knew his status.

Yet he knew what that had to be. Fugitive. They'd try to hang him by the balls. Jack's closest associate. Jack's pal. Jack's bodyguard. A laugh. But he did carry a loaded gun, finally, just for Jack. Why did Joe Fogarty feel the need to protect Jack Diamond? Because there was a bond. Friendship. Brothers, in a way. Jack talked about Eddie, gave him Eddie's pistol, and they swapped TB stories. Eddie was a bleeder. Always had the streak in his sputum the last year of his life, almost never out of bed or a wheelchair except when he came to New York to help Jack during the Hotsy. No wonder Jack loved him. Jack cried when he talked about Eddie: 'He used to bleed so bad they put ice on his chest, made him suck ice too, and the poor guy couldn't move.'

Fogarty knew. He'd seen all that, spent five and a half years in sanitariums, twenty-eight months in bed for twenty-four hours a day. Got up only when they made the bed, a bed bath twice a week. Galloping TB is what Fogarty had, and if they hadn't used the pneumo he'd have been dead long ago. Blew air into his lung, collapsed it, pushed up the poison. Hole in the bronchus, and when the air went in, the pus came up and out his mouth. A basinful of greenish-yellow pus. But after five months that didn't work anymore and the pus stayed in, and he had to lie still for those years.

Death?

Joe Fogarty wasn't afraid of death anymore, only bleeding. He died every day for years. What he was afraid of was lying still and not dying.

'Remember your fibrosis,' the nurses would say. 'Don't raise your arms above your head. Don't even move when you do pee-pee.'

The woodpeckers would come around and tap his chest with stethoscopes and fingers, listen to his percussion. 'Cough and say ninety-nine.' It must heal, you know. Give yourself a chance to heal. Terrific advice. Bring your tissue together. Heal. Oh, nice. Fight off the poison. Of course. Then show a streak in the sputum and they don't let you brush your teeth by yourself anymore. A long time ago, all that; and Fogarty finally got well. And met Jack. And did he then make up for those months in bed doing nothing? Ahhhhhh.

'So you think The Goose is back?' Jack said.

'Who else?'

'Maybe you're right. But maybe it was just a one-eyed tourist. Tourists always asking about me.'

'You want to take that chance?'

'Not with The Goose. He'll find a way if he's up here. I should stay away from the window.'

'You been going out?'

'No, just sticking close here. But we'll go out now.'

'Take me with you,' Kiki said. She was alone on the couch, knees visible, no stockings, slippers on. But sweeeet lover, did she look good to the Speeder.

'No,' said Jack. 'You stay home.'

'I don't want to be here alone.'

'I'll call the neighbor.'

'That old cow, I don't want her here.'

'She'll be company. We won't be long.'

'Where you going?'

'Down the road, make some calls, then we'll be back.'

'You'll be out all night.'

'Marion, you're a pain in the ass.'

'I'm going back to Chicago.'

'That show closed.'

'You think that show is the only offer I got out there?'

'You can't come with us. I'll bring home spaghetti.'

'I want to do something.'

'We'll do something when I get back. We'll eat spaghetti.'

'I want to hear some music.'

'Turn on the radio. Put on a record.'

'Oh, shit, Jack. Shit, shit, shit.'

'That's better. Have a sherry.'

Fogarty finished his double rye and Jack swigged the last of his coffee royal, and they went out the back door. Jack stopped, said, 'We'll take your car. Nobody'd look for me in that jalop.'

'Nobody looking for me at all?'

'Not yet, but that don't mean they won't be out with a posse tomorrow. They'll get to you, all right, but tonight you're a free citizen. Take it from me, and Marcus. He's down at the Saulpaugh while this stuff is going on. We talked before you got here. Joe, I'm glad you came down.'

Jack clapped him on the shoulder. The old jalop was wheezing along. Fogarty smiled, remembered his plan to break with Jack. What a crazy idea.

Jack had taken a rifle from the hall closet, loaded it with dum-dums, and thrown it on the back seat. He wouldn't carry a pistol with all the heat on. He'd also put on his gray topcoat, fedora, and maroon tie with a black pearl tie tack. Fogarty, you bum, you wore a linty black sweater and those baggy slacks you slept in all week.

'It's like a dog race,' Jack said.

'What is?' Fogarty asked, thinking immediately of himself as a dog.

'This thing. I'm the rabbit. And who'll get it first?'

'Nobody gets those rabbits. The dogs always come up empty.'

'The feds are coming into it. The state, all the goddamn cops in the East, Biondo and his guinea friends, Charlie Lucky's pals, and now maybe Murray out there, driving around, trying to make a plan. The good thing about Murray is he can never figure out how to get near anybody. Once he gets near you, so long. But unless you figured it out for him, he could think all month without getting the idea to maybe ring the doorbell.'

'Maybe you ought to get away from here.'

'They're all keeping track of me. Let's see what news we come up with. Hey, you're heating up.'

The temperature gauge was near two twenty when they pulled into the parking lot at Jimmy Wynne's Aratoga Inn on the Acra–Catskill Road. Fogarty unscrewed the radiator cap and let it breathe and blow, and then they went inside, Fogarty with his two pistols Jack didn't even know he had. Fogarty was ready for Murray, who was absent from the gathering of twelve at the bar. It was quiet, the musicians on a break. Fogarty asked Dick Fegan, the bartender, bald at twenty-five, if he'd seen Murray. Fegan said he hadn't seen Murray in months, and Jack went for the telephone. Fogarty dumped four quarts of water into the car radiator and went back in to find Jack off the phone with a Vichy water in front of him, talking about heavyweights to the clarinet player. Heavyweights. 'I lost seven grand on Loughran,' Jack was saying. 'I thought he was the best, gave seven to five, and he didn't last three rounds. Sharkey murdered him. He says, "Let me sit down, I don't know where I am," and then he tried to walk through the ropes. Last time I ever bet on anybody from Philadelphia.' Jack will talk to anybody about anything, anytime. Why shouldn't people like him?

'Seven grand,' said the clarinet player.

'Yeah, I was crazy.'

It seemed like a slip, Jack mentioning money. He never got specific about that, so why now? Must be nervous. Jack went back to the phone and made another call.

'He said he lost seven grand on one fight,' the clarinetist said to Fogarty.

'Probably did. He always spent.'

'But no more, eh?'

It sounded to Fogarty like a line at a wake. That man in the coffin is dead. Fogarty didn't like the feeling he got from shifting from that thought to a thought about Murray walking in the door. But Murray would have to come through the inn's glassed-in porch. Plenty of time to see him. What made Fogarty think he'd pick the one spot in the mountains where Jack happened to be at this odd moment? Did he think maybe he followed the car? Or that he'd been waiting near here for Jack to show up?

'He's probably still got a few dollars in his pocket,' Fogarty said to the clarinetist.

'I wouldn't doubt that.'

'You sounded like you did.'

'No, not at all.'

'You sounded like you were saying he's a has-been.'

'You got me wrong. I didn't mean that at all. Listen, that's not what I meant. Dick, give us a drink here. I was just asking a question. Hell, Jesus, it was just a goddamn silly question.'

'I get you now,' Fogarty said.

Wasn't it funny how fast Fogarty could turn somebody's head around? Power in the word. In any word from Fogarty. In the way people looked at him. But it was changing. Maybe you wouldn't think so, sitting here at the Aratoga, and Jack being respected and Fogarty being respected, with maybe that hint of new tension in the air. But it definitely was changing. Little signs: Jack's living room being different, messy, papers on the floor, the chairs not where they used to be. Authority slipping away from Fogarty, authority that he knew Jack well, could talk all about him, talk for him. Dirty dishes on the dining room table. Picture of Eddie on the coffee table never there before, which meant something Fogarty didn't understand. The parties at Jack's; they were over too, at least for now. Even priests used to come. Neighbors, sometimes a cop or a judge from the city, actors and musicians and so many beautiful women. Women liked Jack and the feeling rubbed off to the benefit of Jack's friends. Jack the pivot man at every party. Funny son of a bitch when he gets a few drinks in. Fogarty couldn't remember one funny joke Jack ever told, but all his stories were funny. Just the way he used his voice. Yes. The story about Murray shooting the wrong man. Split your gut listening to Jack tell it. A good singing voice, too. Second tenor. Loves barbershop. 'My Mother's Rosary.' A great swipe in the middle of that. One of Jack's favorites.

'Well, that's some kind of news,' Jack said, sitting back down beside Fogarty. 'Somebody saw him at the Five O'Clock Club last night.'

'Last night? He must've gone back down.'

'If he was ever up here.'

'Don't you think he must've been?'

'After this, maybe not. He's not the only one-eyed bum in the state. The point is, where is he now? Last night is a long time ago. He could be here in a few hours. They're still checking him out. Give me a small whiskey, Dick.'

And he went back to the phone. Everybody was watching him now. Silence at the bar. Whispers. The clarinetist moved away and stayed away. Dick Fegan set up Jack's drink and moved away. They're watching you, too, Joe. Jack's closest associate. Fogarty drank alone while Jack talked on the phone. The whiskey eased his tension, but didn't erase it. Jack came back and sipped his whiskey, all eyes on him again. When he looked up, they looked away. They always watched him, but never with such grim faces. More finality. Man dying alone in an alley. There's Jack Diamond over there, that vanishing species. That pilot fish with him is another endangered item.

'I can't sit still,' Jack said, and he stood up behind the barstool. 'I been like this for two days.'

'Let's go someplace else.'

'They're going to call me. Then we'll move.'

The musicians started up, a decent sound. 'Muskrat Ramble.' Sounds of life. Memories of dancing. Like old times. Memories of holding women. Got to get back to that.

Three-quarters of an hour passed, with Jack moving back and forth between the bar and the phone, then pacing up and down, plenty nervous. If Jack is that nervous, it's worse than Fogarty thought. Pacing. Jack's all alone and he knows it. And you know what that means, Joe? You know who else is alone if Jack is?

On his deathbed, when fibrosis was again relevant to him, Fogarty would recall how aware he was at this moment, not only of being alone, but of being sick again, of being physically weak with that peculiar early weakness in the chest that he recognized so quickly, so intimately. He would recall that he saw Dick Fegan pick up a lemon to squeeze it for a whiskey sour a customer had ordered. The customer was wearing a sport coat with checks so large Fogarty thought of a horse blanket. He would remember he saw these things, also saw Jack move out of his sight, out onto the porch just as the first blast smashed the window.

Fogarty ordered a hot dog and a chocolate milk and watched a fly that had either survived the winter or was getting an early start on the summer. The fly was inspecting the open hot dog roll.

'Get that goddamn fly off my bun,' Fogarty told the Greek.

The Greek was sweaty and hairy. He worked hard. He worked alone in the all-night EAT. Fogarty has a loaded pistol in his pocket, which is something you don't know about Fogarty, Greek. The fly could be a cluster fly. Crazy. Flies into things. Fast, but drunk. Few people realize where the cluster fly comes from. He comes from a goddamn worm. He is an earthworm. A worm that turns into a fly. This is the sort of information you do not come by easily. Not unless you lie on your back for a long, long time and read the only goddamn book or magazine or newspaper in the room. And when you've read it all and there's nobody to talk to you, you read it again and find plenty of things you missed the first time around. All about worms and flies. There is no end to the details of life you can discover when you are flat on your back for a long, long time.

'That goddamn fly is on my bun.'

There is a certain amount of sadness in an earthworm turning into a fly. But then it is one hell of a lot better than staying an earthworm or a maggot.

'You gonna let that goddamn fly eat my bun, or do I have to kill the goddamn thing myself?'

The Greek looked at Fogarty for the first time. What he saw made him turn away and find the flyswatter. Naturally the goddamn fly was nowhere to be found.

Fogarty had parked his 1927 Studebaker in front of the EAT, which was situated on Route 9-W maybe eight or nine miles south of Kingston at a crossroads. The name of the EAT was EAT, and the Greek was apparently the one-man Greek EAT owner who was now looking for the fly while Fogarty's hot dog was being calcified.

'That's enough on the dog,' Fogarty said to the Greek, who was at the other end of the counter and did not see the fly return to the bun. Fogarty saw and he heard his pistol go off at about the same moment the bullet flecked away slivers from the EAT's wooden cutting board. There was a second and then a third and a fourth report from the pistol. The fourth shot pierced the hot dog roll. None of the shots touched the fly. The Greek fled to a back room after the first shot.

Fogarty rejected the entire idea of a hot dog and left the EAT. He climbed into his Studebaker and nosed onto 9-W, destination Yonkers, his sister Peg's, which he knew was a bad idea, but he'd call first and get Peg's advice on where else he might stay. He could stay nowhere in the Catskills. That world exploded with the ten shotgun blasts from a pair of Browning automatic repeaters, fired at Jack as he paced in and out of the porch of the Aratoga. A pair of shooters fired from the parking lot, then stopped and drove away. Somebody snapped out the lights inside at the sound of those shots and everybody hit the floor. Fogarty heard: 'Speed, help me,' and he crawled out to the porch to see Jack on his stomach, blood bubbling out of holes in his back.

'Bum shooting,' Jack said. 'Better luck next time.'

But he was flat amid the millions of bits of glass, and hurting, and Fogarty got on the phone and called Padalino, the undertaker, and told him to send over his hearse because he was not calling the cops in yet.

When it was obvious the shooting was over, the musicians and customers came out to look at Jack on the floor of the porch and

Dick Fegan went for the phone. But Fogarty said, 'No cops until we get out,' and everyone waited for Padalino.

'Find Alice, keep an eye on her,' Jack said to Fogarty.

'Sure, Jack. Sure I will.'

'They're putting me in the meat wagon,' Jack said when Fogarty and Fegan lifted him gently, carefully into the hearse. By then Fogarty had cut Jack's shirt away and tied up the wounds with clean bar towels. He kept bleeding, but not so much.

'I'll follow you,' Fogarty told Padalino, and when they were near Coxsackie, he parked his Studebaker at a closed gas station and got into the hearse alongside Jack. He fed Jack sips of the whiskey he had the presence of mind to take from the bar, tippled two himself, but only two, for he needed to be alert. He kept watching out the window of the rear door. He thought the hearse was being followed, but then it wasn't. Then it was again and then, outside Selkirk, it wasn't anymore. He sat by the rear door of the hearse with a gun in each hand while Jack bled and bled. I know nothing about shooting left-handed, Fogarty thought. But he held both guns, Jack's and Eddie's, a pair. Come on now, you bastards.

'Hurts, Speed. Really hurts. I can't tell where I'm hit.'

They'd hit him with four half-ounce pellets. They'd fired ten double-ought shells with nine pellets to a shell. Somebody counted eighty some holes in the windows, the siding, and the inside porch walls. Ninety pellets out of two shotguns, and they only hit him with four, part of one shell. It really *was* bum shooting, Jack. You ought to be dead, and then some.

But maybe he is by this time, Fogarty thought, for he'd left Jack at the Albany Hospital, checked him into emergency under a fake name, called Marcus and got Padalino to take him back to his car at Coxsackie. Then, with the leftover whiskey in his lap, he headed south, only to have a fly land on his hot dog bun. Bun with a hole in it now.

The temperature gauge on the Studebaker was back in the red, almost to 220 again. He drove toward the first possible water, but saw no houses, no gas station. When the needle reached the top of the gauge and the motor began to steam and clank, he finished the whiskey dregs, shut off the ignition, threw the keys over his shoulder into the weeds and started walking.

Four cars passed him in fifteen minutes. The fifth picked him up when he waved his arms in the middle of the road, and drove him three miles to the roadblock where eight state troopers with shotguns, rifles, and pistols were waiting for him.

Poem from the Albany Times-Union

Long sleeping Rip Van Winkle seems
At last arousing from his dreams,
And reaching for the gun at hand
To drive invaders from his land.
The Catskills peace and quiet deep
Have been too much disturbed for sleep.
The uproars that such shootings make
Have got the sleeper wide awake.

Fogarty called me and asked me to appear for him at the arraignment, which I did. The charges had piled up: Kidnapping, assault, weapons possession, and, in less than two weeks, the federal investigators also charged both him and Jack with multiple Prohibition Law violations. His bail was seventeen thousand five hundred dollars and climbing. He said he knew a wealthy woman, an old flame who still liked him and would help, and I called her. She said she'd guarantee five thousand dollars, all she could get without her husband knowing. Fogarty had more in the bank, enough to cover the bail, but unfortunately his accounts, like Jack's and Alice's, were all sequestered.

Two of Jack's transient henchmen – a strange, flabby young man who wore a black wig that looked like linguine covered with shoe polish, and a furtive little blond rat named Albert – also inquired after my services, but I said I was overloaded.

'What are you going to do about bail?' I asked Fogarty, and he suggested Jack. But Jack was having trouble raising his own, for much of his cash was also impounded.

705

Beyond Jack, the woman, and his own inaccessible account, Fogarty had no idea where to get cash. His new Oldsmobile was repossessed for nonpayment a week after his arrest.

'How do you plan to pay me?' I asked him.

'I can't right now, but that money in the bank is still mine.'

'Not if they prove it was booze profits.'

'You mean they can take it?'

'I'd say they already have.'

I liked Joe well enough – a pleasant, forthright fellow. But my legal career was built on defending not pleasant people, but people who paid my fee. I follow a basic rule of legal practice: Establish the price, get the money, then go to work. Some lawyers dabble in charity cases, which, I suspect, is whitewash for their chicanery more often than not. But I've never needed such washing. It was not one of Jack's problems either. What he did that had a charitable element to it was natural, not compensatory behavior. He liked the woman whose cow needed a shed, and so he had one built. He disliked old Streeter and showed it, which cost him his empire. I've absorbed considerable outrage over Jack's behavior with Streeter, but few people consider that he didn't *really* hurt the old man. A few burns to the feet and ankles are picayune compared to what might have happened. I understand behavior under stress, and I know Streeter lived to an old age and Jack did not, principally because Jack, when tested, was really not the Moloch he was made out to be.

Seeing events from this perspective, I felt and still feel justified in defending Jack. Fogarty took a fall – twelve and a half to fifteen, but served only six because of illness. I feel bad that anyone has to go to prison, but Fogarty was Jack's spiritual brother, not mine, and I am neither Jesus Christ nor any lesser facsimile. I save my clients when I can, but I reserve the right of selective salvation.

Jack took pellets in the right lung, liver, and back, and his left arm was again badly fractured. The pellet in his lung stayed there and seemed to do him little harm. The papers had him near death for three days, but Doc Madison, my own physician, operated on him and said he probably wasn't even close to dying. He beat off an infection, was out of danger in ten days, and out of the hospital in four and a half weeks. One hundred troopers lined the road for forty-seven miles between Albany and Catskill the day he left the hospital for jail, to discourage loyalists from snatching away FDR's prize. New floodlights were installed on the Greene County jail (lit up the world wherever he went, Jack did), and the guard trebled to keep the star boarders inside: Jack, Fogarty, and Oxie, who had gained fifty pounds in the eight months he'd been there.

The feds indicted Jack on fourteen charges: coercion, Sullivan Law and Prohibition Law violations, conspiracy etc., and it was two weeks before we could raise the new bail to put him back on the street. It really wasn't the street, but the luxurious Kenmore Hotel in Albany, a suite of rooms protected by inside and downstairs guards.

The troopers and the revenue men continued their probing of the mountains. They found Jack's books with records of his plane rentals, his commissioning the building of an oceangoing speedboat. They found the empty dovecotes where he kept his carrier pigeons, his way of beating the phone taps. They found his still on the Biondo farm, and, from the records and notations, they also began turning up stashes of whiskey, wine, and cordials of staggering dimension.

The neatly kept files and records showed Jack's tie-in with five other mobs: Madden's, Vannie Higgins', Coll's, and two in Jersey; distribution tie-ins throughout eighteen counties in the state; brewery connections in Troy, Fort Edward, Coney Island, Manhattan, Yonkers, and Jack's (formerly Charlie Northrup's) plant at Kingston; plus dozens of storage dumps and way stations all through the Adirondacks and Catskills, from the Canadian border to just west of Times Square.

The first main haul was evaluated at a mere $10,000 retail, but they kept hauling and hauling. Remember these booze-on-hand statistics the next time anyone tells you Jack ran a two-bit operation. (Source, federal): 350,000 pints and 300,000 quarts of rye whiskey, worth $4 a pint retail, or about $3.8 million;

200,000 quarts of champagne at $10 a bottle, or $2 million; 100,000 half-kegs of wine worth $2.5 million, plus 80,000 fifths of cordials and miscellany for a grand estimated total of $10 million. Not a bad accumulation for a little street kid from Philly.

Catskill was looking forward to Jack's trial, which was going to be great for tourism. The first nationwide radio hookup of any trial in American history was planned, and I think somehow they would've sold tickets to it. A hundred businessmen, many of them hotel and boardinghouse operators, paying up to three hundred dollars in seasonal tribute to the emperor, held a meeting at the Chamber of Commerce, a meeting remarkable for its anonymity. Fifty newsmen were in town covering every development, but none of the hundred attendees at that meeting were identified.

What they did was unanimously ratify a proclamation calling on one another not to be afraid to testify against Jack and the boys. Getting tough with the wolf in the cage. There was even talk around town of burning down Jack's house. And finally, what Warren Van Deusen had been trying and not trying to tell me about Jack was that half a hundred people had written FDR letters over the past two months, detailing Jack's depredations. It was that supply of complaints, capped by the Streeter episode, which fired old Franklin to do what he did. That and politics.

The abandoned getaway car of Jack's would-be killers turned up with a flat tire on Prospect Avenue in Catskill, behind the courthouse. The Browning repeaters were still in it, along with a Luger, a .38 Smith and Wesson, and two heavy Colt automatics with two-inch barrels, all fully loaded. The car had a phony Manhattan registration in the name of Wolfe, a nice touch, and when perspective was gained, nobody blamed Murray for the big do. Too neat. Too well planned. A Biondo job was Jack's guess.

My chief contribution to the history of these events was to snatch the circus away from the Catskill greed mob. They squawked that Jack was robbing them again, taking away their chance to make a big tourist dollar. What I did was win us a change of venue on grounds that a fair trial was impossible in Greene County. The judge agreed and FDR didn't fight us. He hopscotched us up to Rensselaer County. With Troy, the county seat, being my old stamping grounds, I felt like Br'er Rabbit being tossed into the briar patch.

Attorney General Bennett paid homage to Jack at the annual communion breakfast of the Holy Name Society of the Church of St Rose of Lima in Brooklyn. In celebration of Mother's Day he said that if men of Diamond's type had listened to the guidance of their mothers, they would not be what they were today.

'One of the greatest examples of mother's care,' the attorney general said, 'is the result which the lack of it has shown in the life of Legs Diamond. Diamond never had a mother's loving care nor the proper training. Environment has played a large part in making him the notorious character he is today. A mother is the greatest gift a man ever had.'

Alice came out of the elevator, walked softly on the rich, blue carpet toward the suite, and saw a form which stopped all her random thought about past trouble and future anguish. The light let her see the hairdo, and the hair was chestnut, not Titian; and the face was hidden under half a veil on the little clawclutch of a maroon hat. But Alice knew Kiki when she saw her, didn't she? Kiki was locking the door to the room next to Alice's. Then she came toward the elevator, seeming not to recognize Alice. Was it her? Alice had seen her in the flesh only once. She was smaller now than her photos made her out to be. And younger. Her face looked big in the papers. And at the police station. She had sat there at the station and let them take her picture. Crossed her legs for them.

She passed within inches of Alice, explaining herself with the violent fumes of her perfume. It *was* her. But if it truly was, why didn't she give some form of recognition, some gesture, some look? Alice decided that, finally, Kiki didn't have the courage to say hello. Coward type. Brazen street slut. Values of an alleycat. Rut whore. Was it really her? Why was she here? Would Jack know?

Kiki saw Alice coming as soon as she stepped out of the room, and she immediately turned away to lock the door. She recognized the fat calves under the long skirt with the ragged hem. On the long chance Alice wouldn't recognize her, Kiki chose to ignore her, for she feared Alice would turn her in. Kiki the fugitive. But would Alice run that risk? Jack would kill her for that, wouldn't he? Kitchen cow.

Why did life always seem to be saltwater life for Kiki, never life with a sweetness? Violence always taking Jack away. Violence always bringing back the old sow. Meat and potatoes pig. Why was fate so awful to Kiki? And then for people to say she had put the finger on Jack. What an awful thing to think. The cow passed her by and said nothing. Didn't recognize her. Kiki kept on walking to the elevator, then turned to see Alice entering the room next to Kiki's own. But how could that be? Would Alice break into Kiki's room? But for what? Why would she rent a room next to Kiki's? How would she know which one Kiki was in? Kiki would tell Jack about this, all right. But, Fat Mama, why are you here?

The Kenmore had status appeal to Jack: historic haven of gentility from the mauve decade until Prohibition exploded the purple into scarlet splashes. Its reputation was akin to Saratoga's Grand Union in Diamond Jim's and Richard Canfield's day. It was where Matthew Arnold stayed when he came to Albany, and Mark Twain too, on the night he lobbied for osteopathy in the Capitol. It was where Ulysses S. Grant occasionally dined. Al Smith's son lived there when Al was governor, and it was the dining room where any governor was most likely to turn up in the new century. It boasted eventually of Albany's longest bar, always busy with the chatter of legislators, the room where a proper gentleman from Albany's Quality Row could get elegantly swozzled among his peers.

Sure Jack knew this, even if he didn't know the details, for the tradition was visible and tangible, in the old marble, in the polished brass and mahogany, in the curly maple in the lobby, in the stained glass, and the enduring absence of the hoi polloi. Jack was always tuned in to any evidence of other people's refinement.

710

He dominates more memories of the place even now than Vincent Lopez or Rudy Vallee or Phil Romano or Doc Peyton or the Dorsey Brothers or any other of the greater or lesser musicians who held sway in the Rain-Bo room for so long, but whose light is already dim, whose music has faded away, whose mythology has not been handed on.

Jack didn't create the ambience that made the Kenmore so appealing, but he enhanced it in its raffish new age. He danced, he laughed, he wore the best, and moved with the fastest. But I well knew he had conceived that style long ago in desperation and was bearing it along cautiously now, like a fragile golden egg. He was frail, down eighteen pounds again, eyes abulge again, cheekbones prominent again, left arm all but limp, and periodically wincing when he felt that double-ought pellet bobbling about in his liver. But more troubling than this was the diminishing amount of time left for him to carry out the task at hand: the balancing of the forces of his life in a way that would give him ease, let him think well of himself, show him the completion of a pattern that at least would look *something* like the one he had devised as a young man: Young Jack – that desperate fellow he could barely remember and could not drive out.

Empire gone, exchequer sequestered, future wholly imperfect, it occurred to Jack that the remaining values of his life inhered chiefly in his women. Naturally, he decided to collect them, protect them, and install them in the current safe-deposit box of his life, which at the moment was a six-room second-floor suite in the Kenmore.

'Marcus, you won't believe what I'm saying, but it's a true. I'm in the kitchen one day and the boss come in and says, Sal, you busy? I say no, not too much. He says, I gotta friend of mine in such and such a room and his name is Jack Legs Dime. Have you heard him? Well, I say, in the newspape, yes. He says you wanna be his waiter from now on while he stays uppa here? You go upstays every morning eight-thirty breakfast, noon if he's a call, maybe sandwich now and then, don't worry dinner. Take care of him and his friends and he pay you. I say, sure, it's all right with me. So every morning

William Kennedy

I used to knock on the door with the same breakfast – little steak and egg overlight for Jack, coffee, toast, buns, some scramble eggs for everybody, some cornflakes, milk, plenty potsa coffee, all on the wagon, and Hubert, this rough-lookin' bast with a puggy nose, he's got a goddama gun in both hands. I say Hubert, you son um a bitch I won't come up here no more if you don't put them guns away. I talk to him like that more for joke than anything else. So I see Jack Dime and I give him the breakfast and sometime breakfast for two, three extra people they call to tell me about and Jack call to somebody and says, hey, give Sal twenty-five dollar. He says to me, will that be enough? I say Yeah, Legs, plenty. More than what I expect. Just take care a me and my friends and you down for twenty-five a day, how's that? Beautiful. Jesa Christ, them days twenty-five dollar, who the hell ever seen twenty-five dollar like that? Every day was a different five, six new people, I guess they talking about Jack's trial coming up. And one day Jack call the next room and say, hey, Coll, you wanna eat some breakfas? I gotta breakfas here. Hey, Legs, I say, that Vince Coll? He supposed to be you enemy it says in the pape. Jack says no, he's a good friend a mine. And I pour Coll a coffee and some toast. Then three, four weeks later I met another fellow, Schultz. I say, Hey, Legs, you and Schultz, you supposed to be the worst enemies. And he says no, only sometimes. Now we get along pretty nice. So I pour Schultz a coffee and some toast. I say, Hey, Jack, they's a big fight tonight, who you like, we bet a dollar. Nah, he says, them fighters all crooks. Punks, no good. Then how about baseball, I says. Yeah, he says, I bet you a dollar. I take the Yanks. Legs like Babe Ruth and Bill Dickey. Then one day he says to me, Sal, I want you to meet my wife, Mrs Jack Legs Dime. I say it's a pleasure, and then another day I go up and he says, Sal, I want you to meet my friend, Miss Kiki Roberts. And Kiki she says hello and I say it's a pleasure. Jesa Christ, I wonder how the hell Jack Dime got these women together. I see them sit down together, have breakfast, and then go out together and shop down the stores on Pearl Street while Jack stay home. I say to Freddie Robin, the detective sergeant who sits in the lobby looking for punks who don't look right and who

712

ask funny questions about Legs and I say, Freddie, son um a bitch, it's magic. He got the both women up there. Freddie says you think that's something you ought to see them Sunday morn. All in church together. No, I say. Yeah, Freddie say. All in the same pew, seven o'clock mass Saint Mary's. No, I say. Don't tell me no, Freddie says, when I get paid to go watch them. So I says this I got to see for myself and next Sunday seven o'clock mass son um a bitch they don't all come in, first Kiki, then Alice, then Jack, and little ways back in another pew, Freddie. Alice goes a communion and Jack and Kiki sit still. Then later every Friday I see the monsignor come into the hotel and go upstairs. To hear the confessions, Freddie says, and he thinks sometimes they go to communion right in the room. Hey, I says to Freddie, I don't know nobody gets a communion in this hotel. How they get away with that when they all living together in the same rooms? I took a peek one day, the women got a room each, and Legs, he got a room all his own and the bodyguards got a room and they got other rooms for people in and out, transaction business. Course when I was up there, everything was mum. Nobody say anything, and when I go back for the dishes and the wagon Legs is maybe getting a shave and a haircut, every day, saying the rosary beads. They got a candle in every room, burn all day long, and a statue of Saint Anthony and the Blessed Virgin, which, I figure out, maybe is through Alice, who is on the quiet side, maybe because she got too damn much on her mind. She don't smile much at me. Hello, Sal, good morning, Sal, always nice, but not like Kiki, who says, Sal, how are you this morning, pretty good? Howsa weather outside? She liked to talk, some girl, Kiki. Wow! Freddie says to me, Sal, you think they all wind up in bed together? I laugh like hell. Freddie, I say, how the hell anybody going to do anything with a woman when another woman alongside you? No, that's not it. Bad as the guy might be, if I had a swear, put my hands to God and say would the guy do anything like that, I would say no. Maybe he got a desire to stay with his wife, then he call his wife into his room. He gotta desire to stay with his girlfriend, he call his girlfriend. It's the only thing I can see. Nine time out of ten I would say his girlfriend. On the other hand, he had to take care of his wife too. She wasn't so bad-looking, and after all it was a legitimate wife. You ask me was he an animal, a beast – I say no. He was a fanat. If he wasn't a fanat, why the hell he got Saint Anthony up there? He must've had some kind of good in him, I gotta say it. Not for the moneywise he gave me. I wouldn't judge him for that. But I couldn't say nothing bad toward the guy. I never even hear him curse. Very refine. Pardon me, pardon me. If he sneeze sometime, it's pardon me, tank you, see ya tomorra. But, actually speaking, who's a know what the hell really goes on upstays?'

The night I went to dinner with Jack, Alice, and Kiki at the Kenmore, the ménage seemed to be functioning the way Jack wanted it to function. He'd called me to come down and see him, talk about the trial, and, more important, he wanted to pay me. I'd already told him I was fond of him as a friend, even though I disagreed with some of his behavior, and I enjoyed his company. However, I said, all that has nothing to do with business. If I work for you, I expect to get paid, and now that you've got your bank accounts under government lock and key, what are you going to do about my fee, which, I explained, would be ten thousand dollars payable in advance? I knew two aspiring criminal lawyers who waited until after trial for their pay and are waiting yet.

'Jack, let's face it,' I said, 'you're a crook.'

He laughed and said, 'Marcus, you're twice the crook I'll ever be,' which pleased me because it implied prowess in a world alien to me, even if it wasn't true. What he was really doing was admiring my willingness to structure an alibi for his trial, give it a reasonableness that smacked lovingly of truth. I had fifteen witnesses lined up three weeks before we went to trial, and all were ready to testify, in authenticatingly eccentric and voluminous detail, that Jack had been in Albany the night Streeter and the kid were abducted. Waiters saw him, a manicurist, a desk clerk, a physiotherapist, a car salesman, a bootblack, a barber, a garment executive from the Bronx, and more.

I arrived at Jack's Kenmore suite half an hour ahead of schedule and was let in by Hubert Maloy, the plump Irish kid from Troy whom Jack had hired away from Vincent Coll as his inside guard. Hubert knew me and let me sit in the parlor. I immediately caught the odor of exotic incense and saw a wisp of smoke curling upward from an open door to one of the bedrooms. I glimpsed Alice on her hands and knees with a brushbroom, pushing a lemon back and forth on the rug in front of the incense, which burned in a tin dish. The scene was so weird it embarrassed me. It was like intruding on someone's humiliating dream. Alice was in her slip and stocking feet, a long run in the stocking most visible to me. Her hair was uncombed and she was without the protection of makeup. I quietly got up from the chair and moved to another one, where I wouldn't be able to see her room.

Jack arrived with Kiki about ten minutes later, and Alice emerged from the incense room like a new woman, hair combed, lipstick in place, lovely wildflower housecoat covering slip and run. She kissed Jack on the check, kissed me too, and said to Kiki: 'Your black dress came from the cleaners, Marion. It's in the closet.'

'Oh terrific, thanks,' said a smiling, amiable, grateful Kiki.

Such was the nature of the interchanges I observed, and I won't bore you further with the banality of their civility. Jack took me aside, and when we'd finished updating the state of the trial, and of our witnesses (our foreboding reserved not for this but for the federal trial), Jack handed me a white envelope with twenty five-hundred-dollar bills.

'That suit you?'

'Seems to be in order. I'll accept it only if you tell me where it came from.'

'It's not hot, if that's your worry.'

'That's my worry.'

'It's fresh from Madden. All legitimate. My fee for transferring some cash.'

The cash, I would perceive before the week was out, was the ransom paid for Big Frenchy DeMange, Owney Madden's partner in the country's biggest brewery. Vincent Coll, Fats McCarthy, and another fellow whose name I never caught, whisked Big Frenchy off a corner in midtown Manhattan and returned him intact several hours later after the delivery of thirty-five thousand dollars to Jack, who, despite being on bail, left the state and drove to Jersey to pick it up. Madden knew Coll and McCarthy were basically cretins and that Jack was more than the innocent intermediary in such a neat snatch, and so Madden–Diamond relations were sorely, but not permanently, ruptured. I had little interest in any of that. I merely assured Jack he would now have the best defense money could buy.

Kiki had flopped into the chair from which I'd witnessed Alice's lemon brushing, and she said to Jack when he and I broke from conference: 'I wanna go eat, Jackie.' I saw Alice wince at the 'Jackie.' Jack looked at me and said, 'Join us for dinner?' and I said why not and he said, 'All right, ladies, get yourself spiffy,' and twenty minutes and two old-fashioneds later we were all in the elevator, descending to the Rain-Bo room, my own pot of gold tucked away in a breast pocket, Jack's twin receptacles on either side of him, exuding love, need, perfume, promise, and lightly controlled confusion; also present: Hubert, the troll protecting all treasures.

For purposes of polite camouflage, Kiki clutched my arm as we moved toward Jack's corner table in the large room. 'You know,' she said to me softly, 'Jack gave me a gift just before we came down.'

'No, I didn't know.'

'Five hundred dollars.'

'That's a lovely gift.'

'In a single bill.'

'A single bill. Well, you don't see many of them.'

'I never saw one before.'

'I hope you put it in a safe place.'

'Oh, I did, I'm wearing it.'

'Wearing it?'

'In my panties.'

Two days later Kiki would take the bill – well stained by then not only with her most private secretions, but also with Jack's — to Madame Amalia, a Spanish gypsy crone who ran a tearoom on Hudson Avenue, and payd the going fee of twenty-five dollars for the hex of a lover's erstwhile possession, hex that would drive the wedge between man and wife. Knowing whose wife was being hexed and wedged, Madame Amalia was careful not to make the five-hundred-dollar bill disappear.

'Did you see the new picture of me and Jack?' Alice asked me across the table.

'No, not yet.'

'We had it taken this week. We never had a good picture of us together, just the ones the newspapermen snap.'

'You have it there, do you?'

'Sure do.' And she handed it over.

'It's a good picture all right.'

'We never even had one taken on our honeymoon.'

'You're both smiling here.'

'I told Jack I wanted us to be happy together for always, even if it was only in a picture.'

Despite such healthy overtness, the good Alice had pushed the lemon back and forth in front of the incense for three months, a ritual learned from her maid Cordelia, a child of Puerto Rico, where the occult is still as common as the sand and the sea. The lemon embodied Alice's bitter wish that Jack see Kiki as the witch Alice knew her to be, witch of caprice and beauty beyond Alice's understanding; for beauty to Alice was makeshift — nice clothing, properly colored hair, not being fat. And Kiki's beauty, ineffable as the Holy Ghost, was a hateful riddle.

When Jack's lucky blue suit came back from the hotel cleaners, a silver rosary came with it in the key pocket. I always suspected Alice's fine Irish Catholic hand at work in that pocket. The night of our Rain-Bo dinner Jack pulled out a handful of change when he sent Hubert for the *Daily News*, and when I saw the rosary I said, 'New prayer implement there?' which embarrassed him. He nodded and dropped it back into his pocket.

He had examined it carefully when it turned up in that pocket, looked at its cross, which had what seemed to be hieroglyphics on it, and at the tiny sliver of wood inside the cross (which opened like a locket), wood that might well, the monsignor suggested, have been a piece of the true cross. The hieroglyphics and the sliver had no more meaning for Jack than the Hail Marys, the Our Fathers, and the Glory Bes he recited as his fingers breezed along the beads. His scrutiny of the cross was a search for a coded message from his mother, whose rosary, he was beginning to believe, had been providentially returned to him. For he remembered clearly the silver rosary on her dresser and, again, twined in her hands when she lay in her coffin. He studied it until its hieroglyphics yielded their true meaning: scratches. The sliver of wood, he decided, was too new to have been at Calvary. Piece of a toothpick from Lindy's more like it. Yet he fondled those silver beads, recited those holy rote phrases as if he, too, were rolling a lemon or hexing money, and he offered up the cheapjack stuff of his ragged optimism to the only mystical being he truly understood.

Himself.

No one else had the power to change the life at hand.

How does a mythical figure ask a lady to dance? As if Jack didn't have enough problems, now he was faced with this. Moreover, when he has a choice of two ladies, which one does he single out to be the first around whom he will publicly wrap what is left of his arms as he spins through waves of power, private unity, and the love of all eyes? These questions shaped themselves as wordless desires in Jack's head as he read his own spoken words about his own mythic nature.

When Hubert came back with four copies of the *Daily News*, everyone at the table opened to the first of a three-part interview with Jack by John O'Donnell. It was said to be Jack's first since all his trouble, and he corroborated that right there in the *News*' very bold type:

'I haven't been talking out of vanity – the fact that I've never given out my side before would show pretty clearly that I'm not publicity mad.'

Reasonable remark, Jack. Not publicity mad anymore. Too busy using interviews like these to generate sympathy for your cause, for the saving of your one and only ass, to worry about publicity for vanity's sake. Jack could be more pragmatic, now that he's a myth. But was he really a myth? Well, who's to say? But he does note a mythic development in his life in that bold, bold *Daily News* type:

'Here's what I think. This stuff written about me has created a mythical figure in the public mind. Now I'm Jack Diamond and I've got to defend myself against the mythical crimes of the mythical Legs.'

Legs. Who the hell was this Legs anyway? Who here in the Rain-Bo room really knows Legs?
'Hello, Legs.'
'How ya doin', Legs?'
'Good luck on the trial, Legs.'
'Glad to see you up and around, Legs.'
'Have a drink, Legs?'
'We'd like you to join our party if you get a minute, Mr Legs.'
Only a handful in the joint really knew him, and those few called him Jack. The rest clustered 'round the mythic light, retelling stories of origins:
'They call him Legs because he always runs out on his friends.'
'They call him Legs because his legs start up at his chest bone.'
'They call him Legs because he could outrun any cop at all when he was a kid package thief.'
'They call him Legs because he danced so much and so well.'
Shall we dance! Who first?

'This is a good interview, Jack,' said Marcus. 'Good for the trial. Bound to generate some goodwill somewhere.'

'I don't like the picture they put with it,' Alice said. 'You look too thin.'

'I am too thin,' Jack said.

'I like it,' Kiki said.

'I knew you would,' Alice said.

'I like it when your hat is turned up like that,' Kiki said.

'So do I,' Alice said.

'Find your own things to like,' Kiki said.

Who first?

Dance with Alice and have the band play 'Happy Days and Lonely Nights,' your favorite, Jack. Dance with Marion and have them play 'My Extraordinary Gal,' your favorite, Jack.

'Is it true what he says there about Legs and Augie?' Kiki asked.

'All true,' Jack said.

'As a matter of fact I was never called Legs until after that Little Augie affair. Look it up and see for yourself. It don't make much difference, but that's a fact. My friends or my family have never called me Legs. When the name Legs appeared under a picture, people who didn't know me picked it up and I've been called Legs in the newspapers ever since.'

O'Donnell explained that Eddie Diamond was once called Eddie Leggie ('Leggie,' a criminal nickname out of the nineteenth-century slums) and that somehow it got put on Jack. Cop told a newsman about it. Newsman got it wrong. Caption in the paper referred to Jack as Legs. And there was magic forever after.

'I didn't know that,' Kiki said. 'Is it really true, Jackie?'

'All the garbage they ever wrote about me is true to people who don't know me.'

The music started again after a break, and Jack looked anxiously from woman to woman, faced once again with priority. Did his two women think of him as Legs? Absurd. They knew who he was. If anybody *ever* knew he was Jack Diamond and not Legs Diamond, it was those two ladies. They loved him for his own reasons, not other people's. For his body. For the way he talked to them. For the way he loved them. For the way his face was shaped. For the ten thousand spoken and unspoken reasons he was what he was. It wasn't necessary for Jack to dwell on such matters, for he had verified this truth often. What was necessary now was to keep the women together, keep them from repelling each other like a matched pair of magnets. This matched pair would work as a team, draw the carriage of Jack's future. Fugitive Kiki, wanted as a Streeter witness, needed the protection of Jack's friends until the charge against her went away. She would stick, all right. And Alice? Why, she would stick through anything. Who could doubt that at this late date?

A voluptuous woman in a silver sheath with shoulder straps of silver cord paused at the table with her escort.

'This one here is Legs,' she said to the escort. 'I'd know him anywhere, even if he is only a ridiculous bag of bones.'

'Who the hell are you?' Jack asked her.

'I saw your picture in the paper, Legs,' she said.

'That explains it.'

She looked at Alice and Kiki, then rolled down the right strap of her gown and revealed a firm, substantial, well-rounded, unsupported breast.

'How do you like it?' she said to Jack.

'It seems adequate, but I'm not interested.'

'You've had a look anyway, and that counts for something, doesn't it, sweetheart?' she said to her escort.

'It better, by God,' said the escort.

'I can also get milk out of it if you ever feel the need,' she said, squeezing her nipple forward between two fingers and squirting a fine stream into Jack's empty coffee cup.

'I'll save that till later,' Jack said.

'Oh, he's so intelligent,' the woman said, tucking herself back into her dress and moving off.

'I think we should order,' Kiki said. 'I'm ravished.'

'You mean famished,' Jack said.

'Yes, whatever I mean.'

'And no more interruptions,' said Alice.

Jack signaled the waiter and told him, 'A large tomato surprise.'

'One for everybody?'

'One for me,' Jack said. 'I have no power over what other people want.'

The waiter leaned over and spoke into Jack's face so all could hear. 'They tell *me* you've got the power of ten thousand Indians.'

Jack picked up his butter knife and stared at the waiter, prepared to drive the blade through the back of that servile hand. He would take him outside, kick him down the stairs, break his goddamn snotty face.

'The way I get it,' the waiter said, backing away, speaking directly to Jack, 'you know it all. You know who the unknown soldier is and who shot him.'

'Where do they get these people?' Jack asked. But before anyone could respond, the waiter's voice carried across the room from the kitchen, 'A tomato surprise for the lady killer,' and the room's eyes swarmed over Jack in a new way.

Jack straightened his tie, aware his collar was too big for his neck, aware his suit had the ill fit of adolescence because of his lost weight. He felt young, brushed his hair back from his ears with the heels of both hands, thought of the work that lay ahead of him, the physical work adolescents must do. They must grow. They must do the chores of life, must gain in strength and wisdom to cope with the hostile time of manhood. The work of Jack's life lay stretched out ahead of him. On the dance floor, for instance.

He started to get up, but Alice grabbed his arm and whispered in his ear: 'Do you remember, Jack, the time you stole the fox collar coat I wanted so much, but then I took it back and you insisted and went back and stole it all over again? Oh, how I loved you for that.'

'I remember,' he said softly to her. 'I could never forget that coat.'

Kiki watched their intimacy, then leaned toward Jack and whispered, 'I've got my legs open, Jackie.'

'Have you kid?'

'Yes. And now I'm opening my nether lips.'

'You are?'

'Yes. And now I'm closing them. And now I'm opening them again.'

'You know, kid, you're all right. Yes, sir, you're all right.'

He stood up then and said, 'I'm going to dance.'

Alice looked at Kiki, Kiki at Alice, the ultimate decision blooming at long last. They both looked to Jack for his choice, but he made none. He got up from his chair at last and, with his left arm swinging limply, his right shoulder curled in a way to give his movement the quality of a young man in full swagger, he headed for the dance floor where a half dozen couples were twirling about to a waltz. When Jack put a foot on the dance floor, some, then all couples stopped and the band trailed off. But Jack turned to the bandstand, motioned for the music to continue. Then he looked at Kiki and Alice, who stood just off the edge of the floor.

'My arm, Marion,' he said. 'Take my arm.'

And while Alice's eyes instantly filled with tears at the choice, Kiki gripped Jack's all but useless left hand with her own and raised it. As she moved toward him for the dancer's embrace, he said, 'My right arm, Alice,' and Alice's face broke into a roseate smile of tears as she raised Jack's right hand outward.

The women needed no further instruction. They joined their own hands and stepped onto the dance floor with their man. Then, as the orchestra broke into the waltz of now and forever, the waltz that all America, all Europe, was dancing to – 'Two Hearts in Three-Quarter Time,' its arithmetic obviously calculated in heaven – Alice, Marion, and Jack stepped forward into the music, into the dance of their lives.

'One-two-three, one-two-three, one-two-three, one-two-three,' Jack

counted. And they twirled on their own axis and spun around
the room to the waltz like a perfect circle as the slowly growing
applause of the entire room carried them up, up, and up into the
ethereal sphere where people truly know how to be happy.

Jack-in-the-box

I'll spare you the details of the summer's two trials, which produced few surprises beyond my own splendid rhetoric and, in the Troy trial, a perjury indictment for one of our witnesses whose vigorous support of Jack's alibi was, alas, provably untrue. I presume the July verdict must be counted a surprise, being for acquittal of Jack on a charge of assaulting Streeter. The courtroom burst into applause and shouts when the verdict was read. Alice ran down the aisle in her lovely pink frock with the poppy print and her floppy picture hat, leaned over the rail and gave Jack a wet one with gush. 'Oh, my darling boy!' And three hundred people standing outside the Rensselaer County courthouse in Troy, because there were no seats left in the courtroom, sent up a cheer heard 'round the world. Moralists cited that cheer as proof of America's utter decadence and depravity, rooting for a dog-rat like Diamond. How little they understood Jack's appeal to those everyday folk on the sidewalk.

I must admit that the attorney general lined up an impressive supply of witnesses to prove conclusively to any logician that Jack was in Sweeney's speakeasy in Catskill the night Streeter was lifted. But once I identified Streeter as a bootlegger, the issue became a gangster argument about a load of booze, not the torture of innocence. And Jack was home free.

It wasn't so easy to confuse the issue at the federal trial in Manhattan. All that the federal lawyers (young Tom Dewey among them) had to do was connect Jack with the still, which wasn't much of a problem, and *they* were home free. The Catskill burghers, including my friend Warren Van Deusen, spouted for the prosecution, and so did some of Jack's former drivers; but most damning was Fogarty, who called Jack a double-crossing rat who wouldn't put up money for a lawyer, who let this poor, defenseless, tubercular henchman, who had trusted him, take the rap alone and penniless. Alice was in court again, with Eddie's seven-year-old son, a marvelously sympathetic prop, and Jack broke into genuine tears when a newsman asked him in the hallway if the boy really was his nephew. But those feds nailed our boy. My rhetoric had no resonance in that alien courtroom: too many indignant businessmen, too much faceless justice, too far from home, too much Fogarty. In an earlier trial at Catskill, the state had managed to convict Fogarty on the same Streeter charge Jack was acquitted of, which was poetic justice for the turncoat as I see it. Jack drew four years, the maximum, and not really a whole lot, but enough of a prospect to spoil the summer.

Jack had been making plans to merge with Vincent Coll and Fats McCarthy, substitute their mob for his own, refurbish the Catskill scene, and maybe put a toe in the door of the Adirondacks. But Johnny Broderick and a squad of New York dicks followed Coll's crowd up from Manhattan and raided them in Coxsackie, hauling in about a dozen. They missed Coll and McCarthy, who along with a few stragglers holed up in an artist's home in Averill Park, a crossroads summer town east of Troy, where Jack and Coll occasionally met and tried to cook up a future for themselves.

It was a depressing time for Jack. Kiki had to take an apartment away from the Kenmore when the state police began to breathe heavily around the lobby, and Alice was delighted to get rid of the competition. But Jack took Kiki out regularly and brought her back to the hotel for visits after the first trial, and Alice finally said goodbye forever, folks, and went to live in her Manhattan apartment on Seventy-second Street.

The acquittal in Troy came in early July, the federal conviction in early August, and the state announced it would try Jack on a second Streeter charge, kidnapping, in December. It was a very long, very hot summer for all of us, but especially Jack, like the predator wolf pushed ever farther from civilization by angry men, who was learning the hard way how to die.

Jack's federal conviction drove a spike of gloom into everybody. Jack insisted on trying to buy a retrial, his hangover from the days when Rothstein had money in everybody's mouth, all the way up to the Presidential cabinet. That money had bought Jack a delay on a federal charge of smuggling heroin for Rothstein, the noted bowling pin case, and Jack died without ever having to face up to the evidence against him.

'The fuckers are all the same, all the way to the top,' he said to me one night. 'They'll do you any favor you can pay for.'

But times had changed to a certain unpredictable degree in Manhattan, especially for people like Jack. The new federal crowd was young, imbued with Seaburyism, and still unbuyable. Even if we had found somebody to buy, there was the case of the diminishing bankroll. The first thing Jack did after he got out of the Catskill jail on bail was to take the one hundred and eighty thousand dollars I'd held for him in safe deposit. That still seemed like a lot of money to me, but it wasn't for Jack. He owed everybody: me, the hospital, the doc, his barber, his waiter, the hotel, his driver, Hubert the bodyguard, infinite numbers of bartenders who would now and in the future provide him with service. He was keeping apartments in Troy, Watervliet, Albany, East Greenbush, a house in Petersburg, and probably six or eight other cities I don't know about. He was keeping Kiki. He was subsidizing Alice in Manhattan. And, and most costly of all, he was paying off politicians everywhere to keep his freedom, keeping them from infecting him with further trouble. The one hundred and eighty thousand dollars went in a few months, or so Jack said, though I think he must have kept a secret nest egg somewhere, and if he did, of course, he kept it utterly to himself. He didn't leave the egg with me. I also know Vincent Coll offered him a loan of ten thousand dollars after a nifty Coll snatch of a Saratoga gambler, and a handsome ransom of sixty-five thousand dollars; and Jack took it.

He coped with the money problem like the pragmatist he had come to be. He went back to work. I met him at the Albany Elks Club bar on a steamy August evening after a day at Saratoga had given me nothing but the aesthetic boredom of picking losers under the elms of the track's stylish old clubhouse and paddock. I came back to town alone, feeling curiously empty for no reason I could explain. The emptiness was a new development. I decided, after six beers, that I hadn't felt this way since that day I was sitting alone in the K. of C. library. And when this thought registered, I knew the problem was Jack-related. My life was far from empty professionally. Since Jack's acquittal in Troy the calls were flooding in and I could name my price for trial work. Was it, then, the loss of a political career? Like an amputated leg, that particular part of me did pain, even though it wasn't there, and yet I was simultaneously relieved at never having to be a politician. It was such a vapid way to spend your life, and a slavish game, too, slavish to the political clubroom crowd, even to the Elks Club where I was standing, a superb fragment of all I found stagnant, repulsive, and so smugly corrupt in Albany. The Democratic bagman, though it was two months till election, was already in his corner of the card room (two city detectives watching the door), accepting tithes from everybody who fed at the county courthouse or city hall troughs – janitors, lawyers growing fat from the surrogate court, vendors, bankers, cops, firemen, secretaries, clerks, contractors. The pattern was consistent with Jack's notion of how an empire should be run. Everybody pays.

Just as I liked Jack, I also liked the old bagman. He was a dandy and a curmudgeon and a wily and wise old Irishman who had read his Yeats and Wilde as well as his Croker and Tweed. I also liked the men who were next to me at the bar. They were men I'd been raised with, men who knew my father and my uncles: tradesmen and sportswriters and other lawyers and politicians and factory hands who liked pinochle and euchre and salesmen who liked to bowl and drink beer, and, of course, of course, Jack.

Most of the Elks who talked frankly with me were confused by his presence. They knew what his minions had done at the

Elks Club in Catskill, which bothered them far more than the kidnapping of Streeter or making Charlie Northrup disappear. They didn't really want Jack around. But they were also awed when he walked in, flattered when he bought them a drink, and marked forever when he put his arm on their shoulder and talked baseball with them. Hello, Bill! Hello, Jack! Brotherrrrrrrrrrrrr!

'Counselor,' Jack said to me when he moved in alongside me at the bar, 'I'm going to buy you a new hat.'

'So you're at that again,' I said.

'The heat must've got to it, Marcus. It's dead for sure. Take a look.'

I looked at my trusty old Panama, which had aged considerably since I last examined it, I must admit.

'Well, it's getting old, Jack, but then so are we all. And I do feel compassion for things that are deteriorating visibly.'

'Whataya say, you want to take a ride?'

'Sounds sinister, Jack. My father warned me about taking rides with strange gangsters.'

'Little business trip, and what the hell, it's too goddamn hot to stand here smelling armpits. The air'll do you good. Blow the stink off you.'

'You're right, I could stand a change. Who's driving?'

'Hubert.'

'Ah, Hubert. I still find it hard to believe you've got somebody named Hubert in your employ.'

'Good kid, Hubert. Does what he's told.'

We left the bar and walked out to the top of the club's stone stoop, which faced on State Street. It was middle evening, the streetlights on, but the sun still making long shadows. We looked up toward Capitol Park, where Hubert went for the car, where General Philip Sheridan, another Albany Irishman, sat astride his horse, riding into eternity. There were only the two of us on the stoop, which struck me as unnecessarily foolish, given the recurring rumor of gunmen out to get Jack.

'We make nice targets for your friends here,' I said.

'Fuck it. You can't live like a rat in a hole forever.'

731

I could only agree with that, which straightened my back. How little encouragement it takes to place oneself in jeopardy.

'What's this business trip you've got planned?'

'A small delivery to a customer.'

'You don't mean you want me to join you on a booze run.'

'Relax, would I do that to you? We won't be in the same vehicle with the stuff. And it's only beer. We'll follow the truck, well back. Plenty safe. Up to Troy, back down to Packy Delaney's. It's a favor for Packy and I'm glad to do it. I like The Pack.'

'I do myself.'

'I'm glad for the ride, too,' Jack said. 'Jesus, I get bored easy lately.'

'We've got the same affliction.'

Hubert pulled up and we headed for Stell's, a busy Troy brewery run by a gang of beer-savvy Dutchmen Jack had been doing business with for years. But the pickup and delivery of the moment would be a departure for Jack: made in a borrowed truck by the man himself, notable status reduction. His excuse was he was doing Packy a favor. 'He's in a bind with his Albany supplier, hates the beer he has, but he's gotta take it.' It proved to be the other way around, Packy responding to Jack's request for a loan with a pragmatic substitute – a deal. Packy would buy the beer at Jack's price, even though he didn't need it; Jack would show a profit, Packy would avoid making a cash loan that would probably never be repaid, and Packy would have the beer, at least, to show for his investment.

We drove up Broadway and through North Albany, past the streets of my own neighborhood: Emmett, Albany, Mohawk, Genesee, Erie, then the park in front of Sacred Heart Church on Walter and North Second Streets, a view which provided me with a pang of recognition and a sliver of insight which made this trip worth recording. I remembered how my father looked, sitting on a park bench in the years just before his death, teeth too prominent, like a skull's mindless grin, his brain almost as white as his hair, watching the trolleys go to Troy and back. I tried to imagine what that man, who never stole a nickel in his life, would make of his son being on Jack's payroll, a speculation which, I know, reveals more of me than of the old man.

My father was not a religious man in his youth and middle years. He routinely did his Easter duty, kept the Commandments, but often slept through the Sunday slate of masses. Yet he ended his days at daily mass, even serving for the priest when the altar boy of the day overslept. I've long tried to persuade myself that his final conversion to piety was more than simplistic fear of the next, for my father was complex, a teacher, a Latin scholar who named me for his favorite Stoic. Remembering him, then, at that moment by the park when I was also conscious of how Jack was regularly telling his beads, and when I was questioning my own irrational reading of Aquinas long after I'd lost my faith, I knew all three of us were hounded by religious confusion: Jack out of Saint Anne's, both my father and I out of Sacred Heart, products all of the ecclesiastical Irish sweat glands, obeisant before the void, trying to discover something.

And as we passed Sacred Heart, I looked at Jack and said to him, 'My old man used to sit in that park and watch the world go by when he got old.'

Jack craned his neck for a look, smiling at the thought. His own yellowing skin, and his teeth with too much prominence, gave me back the face of my father. And I thought then that I knew what they were both looking for. I thought: They have misplaced tomorrow and are looking for it. And the search is ruining today.

We stopped at a garage on Fourth Street in Troy to pick up the truck Jack was borrowing from a fellow named Curley, who once drove for him. Curley had gone off on his own and now had a fleet of Macks and Reos which did heavy duty on the highways on behalf of public thirst. Hubert got the keys for our truck and drove it from a back lot to the gas pump in front of the garage, where a kid attendant in overalls gassed us up with Socony.

'You want any cupcakes tonight, Legs?' the kid asked.

'Why not?' Jack said and gave him a ten-dollar bill. When the tank was full, the kid ran across the street to an old lady's grocery and came back with three cupcakes in cellophane and an opened bottle of sarsaparilla. Jack ate a cake and sucked at the soda for the kid, who wanted to be near Jack, do things for him.

'You think you can beat that federal rap on an appeal, Legs?'

'A sure thing, kid. Don't bet against me.'

The kid – with his freckles, his large Irish teeth, and a cowlick his barber didn't understand – laughed and said, 'Bet against you? Never do that.'

'Listen, kid,' Jack said, and I can hear Cagney telling Billy Halop almost the same thing years later, 'don't get the wrong idea about me. I'm not going to live much longer. I got more metal in me than I got bones. Stay in school. The rackets are a bum life. There ain't no heroes in the rackets.'

'I heard you were on the spot,' the kid said. 'That true?'

Jack gave him a happy grin. 'I been on the spot all my life.'

'I heard a rumor there's guys around want to get you.'

'The word's even out to the kids,' Jack said to me.

'I wouldn't tell 'em nothing if they come here,' the kid said.

'Attaboy,' Jack said.

'You know I didn't say nothin' about the panel truck.'

'I know that.'

'I heard one of the guys looking for you is called Goose.'

'Yeah? What else do you hear?'

'That they were asking questions up in Foley's last week.'

'Nothing since then?'

'Nothing.'

'I heard about that,' Jack said. 'It's all over with. The Goose flew south.'

'It's okay then,' the kid said. 'Good news.'

'Give your old lady some good news, kid. Don't mess in the rackets.'

'Okay, Legs.'

Jack tipped him five and got behind the wheel of his Lincoln, which he was buying on time. Within a month he'd be too broke to keep it. I got in and we followed Hubert to the brewery, where Jack paid for the beer and saw it loaded. Then we headed for Packy's in downtown Albany. We took a back road from Troy through North Greenbush and into Rensselaer, a town like Albany, where Jack was safe passing through with wet goods, across the Dunn Bridge and up to Packy's on Green Street.

'What was that panel truck the kid mentioned?' I asked when we were rolling again.

'Heavy load of booze. We parked it there one night we were being chased. Oxie sat in it all night with a machine gun.'

'That was nice advice you gave the kid. But I can't believe you don't want disciples in your own image, like the rest of us.'

'Kid's too soft,' Jack said. 'If he was tougher, I'd tell him, "Go ahead kid, see how tough you really are," line him up behind all the other tough guys waiting to die young, let him take his chances. Sure I'd tell him about the easy money, easy pussy, living high. But I like that kid.'

'You liked Fogarty too. Why'd you take him in?'

'He reminded me of Eddie.'

'But you let him sink.'

'Did I? You had more say over that than me.'

'I told you I get paid for what I do. And it was you who said the hell with him, that he was never any good.'

'He wasn't. You saw he turned stool pigeon. He was a weak sister. What'd he expect me to do, mother him? Rothstein not only dumped me, he tried to kill me. But I never blew the whistle on him. Never trust a pussy freak. Fogarty's cock ran ahead of him like a headlight. Made a sucker of a good guy. Why not let him sink? I'd let anybody sink except Eddie. And Alice and Marion. I'd even let you sink, Marcus.'

'I know. And I'd do the same for you, Jack. But the difference is that I'm just a businessman and you're a prick in your heart.'

'Pricks are the only ones got it made in this world.'

'That's a chump's line.'

'Maybe. I look like a chump these days.'

'Chumps never know who their real friends are.'

'Friends,' said Jack. 'I got no friends. You and me, we're just knockin' around, passing the time. You're all right, Marcus, and I always said so, but I only had one friend my whole goddamn life. My brother Eddie. Came down from Saranac when he was dying to help me during the Hotsy thing. Christ, we set up a meeting in the subway, Twenty-eighth Street, and he was all dressed up, coconut straw, brown palm beach, and a new white silk shirt with a lemon tie, looked like a million except you could've got two other guys inside the suit with him. He wanted to make collections for me, wanted to run the operation while I was hiding out. Said he'd do anything and the poor bastard could hardly breathe. We talked an hour, and when we got up to go, I was holding him and he started giving me the Holy Roller malarkey. He got religion up in Saranac and they were calling him. The Saint. Used to go around visiting in his wheelchair, seeing guys who couldn't move a muscle, who were afraid to fucking breathe. Really selling me hard, and so I said to him, forget that guff, Ed, it's not my style. You'll come around, he said, and I say in a pig's whistle, and he keeps at it, so I finally say will you for crissake shut up about it? And we're up in the street by then, so I hailed a taxi to get him back to the Commodore where he had a room. And when I let go of his arm, he fell down and Christ Jesus, he let out a cough I thought his whole insides was liquid. Death rattle is what it was. Fantastic horrible goddamn gurgle. He only lasted a couple of months more. Shortened his life coming down to help me out. Couldn't do a goddamn thing for anybody, but he tried, the son of a bitch tried with all he fucking had. That's what's friends, Marcus. That's what I call friends.'

Jack, the gush, was crying.

Old Joe Delaney opened The Parody Club in 1894 to appease a capricious thirst that took hold of him at odd hours, often after the city's saloons had closed. He ran it until 1919 and dated his retirement to the day a hod carrier swooned at the bar and crumpled like a corpse. Delaney's son Packy (né Patrick), apprenticing as a bartender after a stint with the AEF, looked the hoddy over, kicked his ass, and yelled in his ear, 'Get up and go home, you stewbum.'

'A born saloonkeeper,' the elder Delaney rejoiced, yielding swiftly then to the pull of retirement in his favorite chair, where he died five years later with a bent elbow and foam on his handlebars.

Music greeted us when we walked through the old swinging doors, original doors that led to the Delaney time capsule. We walked under a four-globed chandelier and a four-bladed ceiling fan, past photos on the walls of old railroad men, old politicians, old bare-knuckle fighters, dead Maud Gonne's likeness sketched on a handbill announcing her appearance at Hibernian Hall to raise funds for a free Ireland, defunct Hibernian Society marching down State Street on a sunny Saint Patrick's Day in '95, disbanded private fire companies standing at attention in front of their pumpers, K. of C. beer drinkers, long in their graves, tapping a keg at a McKown's Grove clambake. I went back to Packy's now and again until the place burned down in 1942, when fire dumped all that old history of faces into the powdery ashpit. Nothing ever changed there, till then.

Flossie was making the music when we walked in, the piano being her second talented instrument of pleasure. Flossie was a saucy blond cupcake then, not working directly out of Packy's, where sins of the flesh were traditionally prohibited on premises. But she was advertising from the piano bench and specializing in private sessions to augment her income after her musical workday. Ah, Floss. How well I remember your fingers, so educated to the music of joy.

She was jangling away at the keyboard while Packy and another man delivered up some two-part harmony, not half-bad, of 'Arrah-Go-On, I'm Gonna Go Back to Oregon,' a song from the war years.

'Now this is something like it,' Jack said, and he walked ahead of me past the crowded bar toward an empty back table that gave a view of the door. Hubert, having deposited the truck for unloading inside Packy's garage, followed us; but Jack told him, 'Watch the door and the street.' And without a word Hubert went to the end of the bar and stood there alone while Packy pined for Oregon, where

737

they'd call him Uncle Pat, not Uncle John. He gave Jack a smile on that line and an extended left arm that welcomed and introduced the hero to the customers who hadn't yet recognized him; Jack waved to half a dozen men at the bar looking our way.

'You know those fellows?' he asked me.

'I guess I've seen one or two around town.'

'All thieves or hustlers. This is a good place to buy yourself a new suit or a new radio cheap.'

Jack bought the drinks himself at the bar, then settled into a chair and gave full attention to Flossie's piano and Packy's baritone. Packy came to the table when his harmony ran out.

'Fellow singing with me says he knows you, Jack.'

'I don't place him.'

'Retired railroad cop and not a bad fellow for a cop. Nice tenor too, and he carries a tune. Hey, Milligan.'

The tenor came over and looked at us through cataract lenses. His hair was pure white and standing tall, and his magnified eyes and cryptic smile gave him the look of a man in disguise.

'You don't remember me,' he said to Jack.

'Give me a clue.'

'Silk. New Jersey. 1924.'

'Ah, right. I make you now. You pinched me.'

'You've got it. You were stealing the railroad blind, you and your brother.'

'I remember. You were in the house when I came home. Sure, I remember you now, you son of a bitch. You sapped me.'

'Only after you tried to kick me in the balls.'

'I forgot that.'

'You were out of jail quicker than I put you in.'

'I had some classy political connections in those days.'

'I know all about it. You remember anything else about that night? Remember singing a song coming up the stairs?'

'A song.'

'It was a favorite of mine and I said to myself, now this can't be such a bad fellow if he knows a song like that. Just about then you saw me and tried to kick me in the crotch.'

'I can't remember any song, Milligan, that your name?'

'Milligan's right. You were drunk and howling it out like a banshee. Listen, see if you remember.'

He backstepped and put his hand on his stomach, then gave us:

> There's an old time melody,
> I heard long ago . . .

'I damn well remember that,' Jack said. 'One of my favorites.'

> Mother called it the rosary,
> She sang it soft and low . . .

Jack nodded, grinned, sat back, and listened as most of the customers were also listening now, not merely to Milligan, but to Milligan singing for Legs Diamond.

> Without any rhyme,
> I mean without any prose,
> I even forgot
> How the melody goes . . .

Flossie found Milligan's key and trilled some soft background chords, a flicker of faint melody.

> But ten baby fingers . . .

And then Jack could hold it back no longer and added a spoken line: 'And ten baby toes . . .' And then together he and Milligan finished the song:

> She'd watch them by the setting sun,
> And when her daily work was done,
> She'd count them each and every one,
> That was my Mother's ro-sa-reeeeeeee.

Flossie gave them a re-intro, and with Jack on melody, Milligan on first tenor, and Packy on baritone, the harmonizers sang mournfully, joyously, and profoundly out of the musical realm of their Irish Catholic souls. They sang for all the children who ever had mothers, for all the mothers who ever had children, and when it was over, Jack called out, 'Flossie, love, let's do it again.'

'Anything for you, Jack. Anything you want.'

And the harmonizers moved closer together, their arms on each other's shoulders, and began once more:

> There's an old time melody,
> I heard long ago . . .

We sang songs that way for three hours and drove everybody out of the bar, including the bartender. Packy made our drinks and Flossie stayed and played for us, long after her advertising day had ended without a client. But I think the Floss anticipated things to come, and rejected all Johns who had no hint of transcendence about their requests. I was drinking beer and Jack was not quite reckless, but was at the boilermakers. And so both of us were a little slow on the uptake when Hubert, back in from a reconnaissance walk up the block, quick-stepped over to our table and spoke his first words of the musical evening: 'There's a guy in a car across the street, Jack. Two guys, in fact. One at the wheel looks like he's got that eyepatch you been looking for.'

'Would that be The Goose?' Packy asked. 'I heard he was around asking questions about you.'

'Probably him,' Jack said.

'Then we've got to get you out of here,' said The Pack.

Of our little group of six, only Milligan did not know The Goose. But he asked no questions. The song was over, and Flossie's face showed it. Jack, on the other hand, seemed without tension, which, of course, he was not. Yet his control under the circumstances was almost equal to having none.

'It's tricky with The Goose,' he said. 'He might break in here any minute and start blasting. That's nonprofessional, but he's crazy all the way now. People have to remember that.'

'Sure he's crazy,' said Packy. 'In and out of town all summer asking questions.'

'He's made a game of it,' Jack said. 'He wants me to sweat.'

'But now he's outside,' Hubert said, understandably perplexed by a discussion at such a moment. My own first thoughts were to evacuate the uninvolved from the premises, myself included. Yet it seemed cowardly to think of running away from only the possibility of somebody else's trouble. Yet there *was* the Hotsy to recall, where innocents were nicked by crossfire. So if you didn't run away, you might eventually be obliged to duck. It was the price of being Jack's companion.

'Oh, sweet mother,' Flossie said when the reality of The Goose hit her. Her face collapsed then, perhaps into a vision of Billy Blue. She was having a good time just before Billy got it, too.

'I'll call the dicks, have 'em come down and pick him up,' said Packy, nerve ends flaring, spinning on a proprietor's understandable confusion.

'Pick him up for what?' Jack said. 'Sitting in a car?'

'I can think of half a dozen charges if necessary,' I said. 'Getting them here seems to be the priority.'

Packy was already at the phone. Hubert locked the front door and said the two men were still in the maroon sedan, fifty feet from The Parody, across the street.

'Maybe you should just stay here all night,' I said.

Jack nodded, aware of that possibility. Milligan pushed his chair away from the table, but didn't get up, an ambiguous gesture which suited an ex-cop in such a situation.

'You don't know if they'll come or not,' Packy said after his call. 'I got Conlon on the desk, the prick. You never know what they're gonna do for you. Or to you. He said the lieutenant was at a big fire up in the West Albany railroad shops. He'll try to tear a car loose. The prick, the prick.'

'They want me dead, too,' Jack said.

'I never liked that Conlon,' Milligan said, 'but I never took a backstep from him or any of them up there. I'll call him.'

'It's not your problem, Milligan,' Jack said, amused by the old man's concern.

'I always try to keep down violence in the city,' said Milligan. 'Valuable citizens involved here' – and he gave me a quick eye and a wink and went to the phone. I was left to look at Jack, who'd barely been able to move a shotglass with his left arm all night. He was living mainly by the use of one hand, a liability should he be forced to confront The Goose in any physical way. Hubert was a good shot, which was one reason Jack hired him; but so was The Goose, and who knew about his faceless helper? Jack would be on the short end of any fight, a fact I was just coming to understand.

Milligan came back. 'I called Cap Ronan, but no answer. Maybe he's out at the fire, too. Then I called Conlon again and told him the trouble here personally. He got the message.' Milligan sat down and waited, though he was free to leave. But he would then miss how it all came out, miss the test of cop-to-cop influence.

No police came. Sorry, Milligan.

I've since concluded Jack was right. They would have welcomed his assassination, were perhaps even aware one was impending. The police were called often about Jack during this period: Did Diamond get it yet? . . . He's going to get it tonight. I sensed then, my innocence on such matters at last thinning out, that Jack was not really an enemy of the police as much as he was an object of their envy. I can imagine a roomful of them talking about ways to annihilate his privilege.

Hubert announced from the door: 'They put their headlights on. They're moving.'

'Thank God,' said the Floss.

'They're probably not going anyplace,' Jack said. And he was right again. Within a few minutes they had parked facing the opposite direction, on The Parody side of the street now, still about fifty feet away.

'They just wanted to look in,' Jack said.

The car movement prodded all of us except Jack into standing up and moving around. We turned our attention to each other, and finally, one by one, to Jack for the decision was his alone. Go or stay? Barricade or open season? Packy would probably resent, but maybe not resist a barricade fight. Damage would be minimal, apart from any death, but the legend would be immortal, a shrine of gold established in perpetuity.

Only Hubert lacked doubt about what he was to do. His pistol was already part of our little group because of the way he kept fingering it inside his coat pocket. Jack knew what he was doing when he hired Hubert.

'You have an extra pistol?' Jack asked Packy.

'How many? I got a collection.'

'Two then, and shells.'

Packy unlocked a closet beneath the back bar and brought out a pair of unmatched handguns, one an old Smith and Wesson .32 which I came to know well, its patent dating to 1877, an ugly little bone-handled, hammerless bellygun that was giving in to rust and had its serial number at the base of the butt filed away. No serious gunfighter would have given it room in the cellar. Packy had probably bartered it for beer. Useless, foolhardy, aggravating weapon. It had a broken mechanism behind the firing pin then and still has, but under ideal circumstances it would fire, and it still will. Ugly, deformed little death messenger, like a cobra on a crutch.

'This is insane,' I finally said. 'We sit here watching a man prepare for a gun battle, and we know damn well there are other ways to solve the problem. The whole world hasn't gone nuts. Why not call the *state* police?'

'Call the governor,' Jack said. 'He'll want to keep me healthy.'

'Not a bad idea,' I said.

'Call my relatives in Philadelphia,' Jack said. 'Call your own relatives. Call all your friends and tell them we've got an open house here, free booze. Build up a mob in fifteen minutes.'

'Another brilliant idea,' I said.

'But what do I do tomorrow night?' Jack said.

He loaded one of Packy's pistols while we thought about that one. Flossie decided she was not ready for fatalism.

'If you go upstairs, he'll never find you,' she said.

'Where upstairs?'

'My upstairs. Where I go in a pinch.'

'You got a place upstairs?'

'A place, yeah. But not really a place.'

'He comes in here, don't you figure he'll look upstairs?'

'He'd never find my place, that's the whole point. If you're up there and we go, and the place is dark, he'd never find you in a thousand years. It ain't even in this same building.'

'The Goose is thick, but thorough,' Jack said. 'I wouldn't trust him not to find it.'

'Then let's go meet the Polack son of a bitch on the street,' Hubert said. 'Goddamn fucking sitting ducks here, the hell with it.'

'None of this makes sense,' I said. 'Going, staying, not getting any help, not even trying to get any.'

'One night at a time,' Jack said. 'You work it out slow. I know a lot of dead guys tried to solve a whole thing all at once when they weren't ready. And listen. It's also time you all cleared out.'

'I think I'll have another beer,' I said, and I sat down at the end barstool farthest from the door. Milligan sat alongside me and said, 'I'll have one for the road.'

'I'll be closing up after one drink,' Packy said, going behind the bar. 'I'll put the lights out and leave. I'll get a cop down here if I have to drag him down with a towrope.'

Jack shrugged.

'Upstairs then,' he said to Flossie. 'I guess that's the place.'

'Follow me,' she said.

'Is there a way back down except through here?'

'Two stairways,' Packy said. 'It's an old loft. They used to have a peanut butter factory up there.'

'Jesus, a peanut butter factory?'

'It faces the other side, on Dongan Avenue, and there's no windows. Flossie is right. Nobody'd ever think we were connected to it. Just a quirk of these antique buildings. They made connections you wouldn't believe in these old relics.'

'Nothing'll happen if The Goose *doesn't* come in here,' I said. 'Isn't that right?'

'I don't think he'll come inside anyplace,' Jack said, 'and he don't want to hurt anybody but me. But he's a maniac, so how do you know anything he'll do? You all should wait for Flossie to come back down and then clear the hell out of here. Hubert and I can wait it out.'

That seemed workable. But I said, 'I'll keep you company,' and Jack laughed and laughed. I didn't think it was that funny, but he said, 'All right, let's move,' and I took my bottle of beer and followed him and Hubert to the place where there was no longer any peanut butter.

Flossie led us up an unsafe staircase, through musty corridors, through a rough doorway in the brick wall of another building, and through still more corridors, all in darkness, each of us holding the hand of the other. When she finally lit a kerosene lamp, we were in the loft, a large empty space with a warped floor, a skylight with some of its panes broken and now an access route to a pigeon perch. The pigeons had created a pair of three-inch stalagmites with their droppings, rather brilliant aim, as I remember it. The room held only an old Army cot with an olive-drab blanket and a pillow without a pillowcase. A raw wooden box stood alongside the bed for use as a table, and a straight-back wooden chair stood alongside that. There was nothing else in the room except for the cobwebs, the dust, the rat leavings, and a plentiful scatter of peanut shells.

'You know, Jack,' Flossie said, 'I never use this place except in special emergencies that can't wait. I keep a sheet downstairs. I could go get it.'

'Maybe another time, kid,' Jack said, and squeezed her rump with his good hand.

'You haven't grabbed me in years, Jack.'

'I'd love to think about getting back to that.'

'Well, don't you neglect it. Oh, sweet Jesus, look at that.'

745

She pointed to a wall behind Jack where an enormous rat, bigger than a jackrabbit I'd say, looked out at us, his eyes shining red in the light, white markings under his jaw. He was halfway out of a hole in the wall, about four feet from the floor. He looked like a picture on the wall. As the light reached him, we could see he was gray, brown, and white, the weirdest, handsomest rat I ever saw, and in the weirdest position. A bizarre exhibit, if stuffed, I thought.

'I never saw *him* up here before,' Flossie said.

The rat watched us with brazen calm.

'He was here first tonight,' Jack said, and he sat on the bed and took off his suit coat. Flossie put the lamp on the box table and told us, 'I'll come back and let you know what's going on. I don't know if Delaney's going out, but I'm damn well staying.'

'Lovely, Flossie, lovely,' said Jack.

'He'd never find his way up here, Jack,' she said. 'Just stay put.'

'I want Hubert to check all the stairs. Can he be seen from outside if he walks with the lamp?'

'Not a chance.'

Flossie took the lamp, leaving Jack and me in darkness, the stars and a bright moony sky the only source of our light.

'Some great place to wind up,' Jack said.

'I'm sitting down while I consider it,' I said and groped toward the chair. 'I mean while I consider what the hell I'm doing here.'

'You're crazy. I always knew it. You wear crazy hats.'

Flossie came back with the kerosene lamp and put it back on the box.

'I lit one of my candles and gave it to Hubert,' she said. 'I'll be back.'

Some moths joined us in the new light and Jack sat down on the cot. The rat was still watching us. Jack put the two pistols Packy gave him on the box. He also took a small automatic out of his back pocket. It fit in his palm, the same kind of item he fired between Weissberg's feet in Germany.

'You've been carrying that around?'

'A fella needs a friend,' he said.

'That'd be lovely, picked up with a gun at this point. How many trials do you think you can take?'

'Hey, Marcus, I'm tryin' to stay alive. You understand that?'

'Let Hubert carry the weapons. That's what he's for.'

'Right. Soon as I hear The Goose is gone. Long as he's in town there's liable to be shooting, and I might stay alive if I can shoot back. You on tap for that?'

He picked up the Smith and Wesson and handed it to me.

'The Goose only wants me, but he'd shoot anything that moved or breathed. I don't want to make it tough for you, old pal, but that's where you're livin' right this minute. You're breathing.'

He had a point. I loaded the weapon. In a pinch I could say I pocketed the pistol when we all fled from the maniac.

Jack fell backward on Flossie's dusty cot and said to me, 'Marcus, I decided something. Right now there's nothing in the whole fucking world I want to steal.'

I thought that was a great line and it was my turn to laugh. Jack laughed, too, then said, 'Why is that so funny?'

'Why? Well, here I am, full of beer and holding a gun, joined up with a wild man to hide from a psychopath, watching the stars, staring at a red-eyed rat, and listening to Jack Diamond, a master thief of our day, telling me he's all through stealing. Jesus Christ, this is an insane life, and I don't know the why of any of it.'

'Well, I don't either. I don't say I'm swearing off, because I am what I am. But I say I don't want to steal anything now. I don't want to make another run. I don't want to fight The Goose. I suppose I will, sooner or later, him or some other bum they send.'

'Who is they?'

'Take your pick. They get in line to shoot at me.'

'But you won't shoot back anymore?'

'I don't know. Maybe, maybe not.'

'The papers would eat this up. Jack Diamond's vengeance ends in peanut butter factory.'

'Anybody can get revenge. All it costs is a few dollars. I don't want to touch it anymore, not personally.'

'Are you just tired? Weary?'

'Maybe something like that.'

'You don't believe in God, so it's not your conscience.'

'No.'

'It's caution, but not just caution.'

'No.'

'It's self-preservation, but not just that either.'

'You could say that.'

'Now I've got it. You don't know what's going on either.'

'Right, pal.'

'The mystery of Jack Diamond's new life, or how he found peace among the peanut shells.'

I was too tired, too hot, too drunk to sit up any longer. I slid off the chair onto the floor, clutching the remnants of my beer in my left hand, the snotty little Smith and Wesson in my right, believing with an odd, probably impeachable faith, that if I survived this night I would surely become rich somehow and that I would tell the story of the red-eyed rat to my friends, my clients and my grandchildren. The phrase 'If I survived' gave me a vicious whack across the back of the head. That was a temporary terror, and it eventually left me. But after this night I knew I would never again feel safe under any circumstances. Degeneration of even a marginal sense of security. Kings would die in the bedchambers of their castles. Assassination squads would reach the inner sanctum of the Presidential palace. The lock on the bedroom window would not withstand the crowbar.

Such silly things. Of course, this goes on, Marcus, of course. Mild paranoia is your problem.

Yes. That's it. It goes on and finally I know it. I truly know it and feel it.

No. There is more to it than that. Jack knows more.

Flossie came running. Cops down in the street. Taking Goose away. You can come down. Packy's buying. Milligan got through.

Six detectives, oh, yes. How lovely.

Jack leaped off the bed and was gone before I could sit up.

748

'Are you comin' too, love? Or can't you move?' the Floss asked me. In my alcoholic kerosene light she was the Cleopatra of peanut-butterland. Her blond hair was the gold of an Egyptian sarcophagus, her eyes the Kohinoor diamond times two.

'Don't go, Flossie,' I said and stunned her. I'd known the Floss now and again, sumptuous knowledge, but not in a couple of years. It was past, my interest in professionals. I had a secretary, Frances. But now Flossie's breasts rose and fell beneath her little cotton transparency in a way that had been inviting all of us all night long, and when she had half turned to leave, when my words of invitation stopped her, I caught a vision of her callipygian subtleties, like the ongoing night, never really revealed to these eyes before.

She came toward me as I lay flat on my back, ever so little bounce in the splendid upheaval of her chest, vision too of calf without blemish, without trace of muscular impurity. None like Floss on this earth tonight, not for Marcus.

'Do you want something from me?' she said, bending forward, improving the vision fiftyfold, breathing her sweet, alcoholic whore's breath at me. I loosened my hand from the beer and reached for her, touched her below the elbow, first flesh upon first flesh of the evening. Client at last.

'Come up on the cot, love,' she said, but I shook my head and pulled the blanket to the floor. She doubled it as the moon shone on her. The rat was watching us. I raised the pistol and potshot it, thinking of it dying with a bullet through its head and hanging there on the wall; then thinking of framing it or stuffing it in that position, photographing the totality of the creature in its limp deathperch and titling it 'Night Comes to the Peanut Butter Factory.'

My shot missed and the rat disappeared back into the wall.

'Jesus, Mary, and Holy Saint Joseph,' Flossie said at the shot, which sounded like a cannon. 'What are you doing?'

'Potting the rat.'

'Oh, honeyboy, you're so drunk. Give us that pistol.'

'Of course, Flossie' – and she put it on the table out of my reach. The stars shone on her then as she unbuttoned her blouse, unhooked her skirt, folded the clothes carefully and lay them at the foot of the cot. She wore nothing beneath them, the final glory. She helped prepare me as the men moved in with the peanut butter machine and the women arrived to uncrate the nuts.

'It's been a while, hasn't it?' the Floss said to me.

'Only yesterday, Floss, only yesterday.'

'Sometimes I feel that way, Marcus, but not tonight.'

'It's always yesterday, Floss. That's what's so great.'

'Tonight is something else.'

'What is it?'

'It's better. It's got some passion in it.'

'Lovely passion.'

'I don't get at it very often.'

'None of us do.'

The rat came back to his perch and watched us. The sodden air rose up through the skylight and mated with the nighttime breezes. The machine began to whirr and a gorgeous ribbon of golden peanut butter flowed smoothly out of its jaws. Soon there were jars of it, crates of jars, stacks of crates.

'Isn't it lovely?' said Flossie, flat on her back.

'It's the most ineffable of products,' I said. 'The secret substance of life. If only the alchemists knew of this.'

'Who were the alchemists?' she asked.

'Shhhh,' I said.

And instead of talking, Flossie made me a peanut butter sandwich, and we fortified ourselves against the terror.

Jack o' the Clock

Jack walked up Second Street in Troy, dressed in his double-breasted chinchilla coat and brown velour fedora, walked between his attorney and his wife, a family man today, Kiki discreetly tucked away in the love nest. Jack walked with his hands in his pocket, the press swarming toward him as he was recognized. How do you feel, Legs? Any statement, Mr Gorman? Do you have faith in your husband's innocence, Mrs Diamond?

'You guys are responsible for all this,' Jack said to the newsmen. 'I wouldn't be in trouble if it wasn't for you sonsabitches.'

'Keep out the cuss words, boys,' I said to the press. I smiled my Irish inheritance, easing the boys.

'What'll you make your case on, counselor?' Tipper Kelly said. 'Same as the first trial? An alibi?'

'Our case is based wholly on self-defense,' I said.

Self-defense against a kidnapping charge. Jack laughed. His loyal wife laughed. The newsmen laughed and made notes. A *bon mot* to start the day.

'How do you feel about all this, Mrs Diamond?'

'I'll always be at his side,' said Alice.

'Don't bother her,' said Jack.

'She's just a loyal wife to a man in trouble,' I said. 'That's why she's here.'

'That's right,' said Alice. 'I'm a loyal wife. I'll always be loyal, even after they kill him.'

'We mustn't anticipate events,' I said.

The gray neo-classical Rensselaer County courthouse, with its granite pillars, stood tall over Legs Diamond: legs of Colossus, as this peanut man walked beneath them. Birds roosted on the upper ledges. A stars and stripes snapped in the breeze. As Legs brushed the wall with his shoulder, dust fell from the pillars.

The Pathé News cameraman noted the action and the consequence and asked Legs to come back and do it again. But, of course, Legs could not commit precisely the same act a second time, since every act enhanced or diminished him as well as the world around him. Yet it was that precise moment, that push, that almost imperceptible fall of dust, the cameraman wanted on film.

As the crowd moved into the courtroom the cameraman, exercising a bit of creative enterprise, lifted Legs Diamond's coat and hat from the cloakroom. He dressed his slightly built assistant cameraman in the garments and sent him up the stairs to brush the wall for a repeat performance.

The Pathé News cameraman then filmed it all. Inspecting the floor for a closeup, he discovered that the dust that fell was not dust at all, but pigeon shit.

In the crowded hallway of the courthouse, during a brief moment when no one was holding his arm, a youth Jack did not know separated himself from the mob and whispered, 'You're gonna get it, Diamond, no matter what happens here. Wanna take it now?' Jack looked at the kid – maybe nineteen, maybe twenty-two, with a little fuzz on his lip and a bad haircut – and he laughed. The kid eased himself back into the crowd, and Jack, pulled by me toward the courtroom, lost sight of him.

'Kid was braggin'',' Jack said, telling me about the threat. 'He looked like a hundred-dollar pay killer. Too green to be in the big money.' Jack shook his head in a way I took to be an amused recognition of his own lowly condition. *They send punk kids after me.*

But I also saw a spot of white on his lower lip, a spot of bloodlessness. He bit at the spot, again and again. The bite hardened his face, as if he were sucking the blood out of the point of his own fear, so that when the threat became tangible it would not bleed him into weakness. It struck me as a strange form of courage, but not as I knew it for myself: no intellectual girding, but rather a physiological act: a Jack Diamond of another day, recollected not by the brain but by the body, his back to a cave full of unexplored dangers of its own, staring out beyond a puny fire, waiting for the unspecified enemy who tonight, or tomorrow night, or the next, would throw a shadow across that indefensible hearth.

By eight o'clock on the evening of the first day of Jack's second Troy trial, both the prosecution and the defense attorneys had exhausted their peremptory challenges and the final juror was at last chosen. He was an auto mechanic who joined two farmers, a printer, an engineer, a mason, a lumber dealer, an electrical worker, two laborers, a merchant, and a plant foreman as the peers, the twelve-headed judge, of Legs Diamond. I had sought to relieve the maleness by accepting two female jurors, but Jack's appeal to women had been too widely documented for the prosecution to take such a risk, and both were challenged.

The prosecution's chief trial counsel was a man named Clarence Knought, who wore a gray, hard-finish, three-button herringbone with vest, gray tie, watch chain, and rimless glasses. His thin lips, receding hairline, gaunt figure, and voice, which lacked modulation but gained relentless moral rectitude through its monotony, provided the jury with the living image of New York State integrity, American Puritanism, and the Columbian quest for perfect justice. He spoke for twenty minutes, outlining the case against Legs Diamond, whom he called Diamond. He recapitulated the kidnapping of Streeter and Bartlett in his opening summary, savoring the punching of Streeter, the death threats, the burning and the hanging, details which landed on the jurors' faces like flying cockroaches. The recapitulation set off an uncontrollable twitching in one juror's cheek, dilated just about every eye, wrinkled eyebrows, and dried up lips. Having filled the jurors with terror, Knought congratulated them.

'You are privileged,' he told them. 'You have the chance to rid this nation of one of its worst scourges. You have the chance to put behind bars this man Diamond, this figure of unmitigated evil, this conscienceless devil who has been arrested twenty-five times for every crime from simple assault to foul, vicious murder, whose association with the worst men of our time has been widely reported in the press and whose record of having cheated justice again and again is an appalling blot on our national image. Shall this nation be ruled by the rod? Shall this ogre of bestial behavior paralyze every decent man's heart? You twelve can end this travesty, put him in the penitentiary where he belongs.'

Knought breathed fury, thumped the railing of the jury box with his fist, then walked to his chair and sat down in a cloud of legitimized wrath.

I rose slowly from my chair alongside Jack, this thought in my head as I did: *O priggish stringbean, thank you for befouling my client with your excremental denunciation, with the ordurous funk of your morality, for you now give me the opportunity to wipe this beshitted countenance clean and show the human face beneath the fetid desecration.*

My image before the jury was calculatedly bumpkinish, my clothes workingman's best, aspiring to shabby genteel. I tweaked my bow tie and ran my fingers through my unruly head of hair, which I was told, seemed as gifted with wild statement as the brain it covered. The head was leonine, the mane controlled just this side of bushy frazzle. I wore an apple-red vest, high contrast to my baggy-kneed brown tweed suit. I tucked thumbs in vest and unleashed the major weapon of the defense – my voice – that timbre of significance, that resonant spume of the believer, that majestic chord of a man consecrated to the revelation of boilingly passionate truths. I said:

'I expect low blows from the prosecution's lawyers – all seven of them. Are you aware, my friends, that the state has seven lawyers climbing over one another in a frantic effort to railroad one frail man into jail? Yes, I expected their low blows, but never such base name calling as we have just heard – "figure of unmitigated evil," "conscienceless devil," "ogre of bestial behavior." I would never have dreamed of telling you what I am about to tell if this champion of self-righteousness had not been so vitriolic a few moments ago, so full of acid and poison toward my client. But I will tell you now. I will tell you of the little old lady – no, I won't disguise her vocation, not now. A little old Catholic nun, she was, and she came to this courtroom less than an hour ago to talk with Jack Diamond, only a few steps from where you are seated. She didn't see him, for he was otherwise occupied. She saw me, however, and I will see to it that she gets her wish, for she came here for one reason only – to see the man who was once a boy at her knee. Jackie Diamond was the name she knew him by, a boy she described as one of the most devout Catholic children she has ever known. She sees that boy still in the face of the man you know as Legs Diamond, that mythical figure of unmitigated evil the prosecutor has invented. This woman had heard such cruel insults hurled before at the boy she knew. She had heard them for years. She had read them in the newspapers. But that little old woman, that creature of God Almighty's very own army, sat down in that room with me for five minutes and talked to me about Jackie Diamond's prayers, his prayers for his mother, a woman who died too early, about the Diamond home and family in Philadelphia. And when she was through with her reminiscing she told me precisely what she thought about all those accusations against the boy whose gaunt, troubled face she hardly recognized when she saw it across the room. "They're all lies. Mr Gorman," she said to me, "fiendish lies! Now that I have seen his face for myself I know those were lies, Mr Gorman. I teach children, Mr Gorman, and I have boys and girls in my charge who delight in drowning puppies and stabbing cats and watching them slowly perish, and I know evil when I see it in the eyes of a human being. I came here today to see for myself whether my memory had deceived me, whether I knew good when I saw it, whether I knew evil. I have now seen the eyes of Jack Diamond in this room and I am as certain as I am of God's love that whatever on earth that man may have done, he is not an evil man. I have verified this for myself, Mr Gorman. I have verified it."'

When I finished the rest of my oratory and sat down at the table, Jack leaned over and whispered: 'That nun business was terrific. Where did you dig her up?'

'She wandered in during the recess,' I said, eyes downcast, scribbling a businesslike doodle on a yellow pad. 'She's a regular in the courthouse. Collects nickels for the poor.'

'Does she really know anything about me?'

I looked at my client, astounded.

'How the hell should I know?' I retorted.

The trial proceeded as the first one had in July, with two parades of witnesses for and against Jack. We used fewer for the defense, treading lightly after the perjury indictment from the first trial.

I made two points I remember fondly. The first was a countercharacterization of Streeter, who had been dubbed 'a son of the soil,' by the prosecution. I had not thought to say it in July, but we rise to our challenges, and I said he might better be called a son of the apple tree, which once again reduced the kidnapping to a bootleggers' feud.

I also asked a juror, a wretched little popinjay, whether he thought God loved Legs Diamond. 'God made little green apples,' he said to me crisply, 'but he also put worms in 'em.' He got a laugh at Jack's expense, but I liked his theology and kept him. He wore an orange shirt and I knew my man. He'd have been in line for Jack's autograph if he hadn't been on the jury. He turned out to be a vigorous partisan for acquittal. Jack was, of course, acquitted, December 17, 1931, at 8:03 P.M. The crowd in the street sent up its usual cheer.

I was standing at Keeler's Men's Bar in Albany a week after the trial, talking to the barman about Jack, and I resurrected a story he told me about a day in 1927 when he was walking in Central Park with his brother Eddie and Eddie's baby boy. Jack had the boy in his arms, and they'd paused on a hill which I can picture even now. Jack was tossing the boy and catching him when he saw a car coming with a gun barrel sticking out its window, a vision to which he had been long sensitized. He tossed the baby feet-first into a bushy blue spruce, yelling the news to brother Ed, and both dove in the opposite direction from the baby as the machine gun chopped up the sod where they'd been standing.

Nobody was hit: the baby bounced off the tree and rolled to safety under a lilac bush. And after I'd told this tale, a fellow tippler at the bar asked, 'How many people did he kill?' I said I didn't know, and then, without apparent malice, without actually responding to my baby story, the fellow said, 'Yeah, I remember a lot of otherwise intelligent people used to think he was a nice guy.'

I told the man he was a horse's ass and walked to the other end of the bar to finish my drink. Intelligent people? The man was an insurance salesman. What could he possibly know about intelligent people?

I am bored by people who keep returning life to a moral plane, as if we were reducible, now, to some Biblical concept or its opposite, as if all our history and prehistory had not conditioned us for what we've become. It's enough to make a moral nigger out of a man. The niggers are down there, no doubt about it. But Jack didn't put them there and neither did I. When we get off the moral gold standard, when the man of enormous wealth is of no more importance to anybody than the man in rags, then maybe we'll look back at our own day as a day of justifiable social wrath.

Meantime, the game is rising, not leveling.

Jack taught me that.

Cured me.

(Brother Wolf, are you listening?)

Dove Street runs north and south in Albany through what for years was the rooming house district on the fringe of downtown. Number 67 sits on the west side of the street between Hudson Avenue and Jay Street, a two-story brick building with a six-step wooden stoop, a building not unlike the house on East Albert Street in Philadelphia where Jack lived as a child. The basement shoemaker, the druggist up the block, the grocery and garage at the corner of Hudson Avenue, the nurses and the masseuse next door and across the street and all other life-support systems in the neighborhood were dark at 4:15 A.M. on Friday, December 18, 1931, when Jack pulled up in front of 67 Dove in his hired cab, Frankie Teller at the wheel.

Teller parked and ran around to open the passenger door, took Jack's arm, helped him out. Teller held the arm while Jack stood up, and together they walked raggedly up the stoop. Jack found his key, but it remained for Teller to open the door with it. The two men then walked up the stairs together and into the room at the front of the house, overlooking the street. Jack took off his hat, and then, with Teller's help, his coat, and sat on the side of the bed, which was angled diagonally, foot facing the windows that looked down on the street.

'Frankie,' Jack said. And he smiled at his driver.

'Yeah, Jack.'

'Frankie, I'll duke you tomorrow.'

'Sure, Jack, don't worry about it.'

'Duke you in the morning.'

'Sure, Jack, sure. Anything else I can do for you? You all right here alone?'

'Just get out a here and let me sleep.'

'Right away. Just want you settled in all right.'

'I'm in.'

'Tomorrow, then.'

'Tomorrow,' Jack said.

Frankie Teller went downstairs and got into his car and drove south on Dove Street, back to Packy's to carry the news that Jack was tucked in. A block to the north on the west side of the street a dark red sedan idled with its lights out.

During the eight hours and fifteen minutes that elapsed between his acquittal and the moment when he sat on the bed and looked into the mirror of the scratched and flaking oak dresser in his Dove Street room, Jack had been seeking an antidote to false elation. The jury foreman's saying not guilty created an instant giddiness in him that he recognized. He'd felt it when he saw Streeter's truck in front of him on the road, and he felt it on the ship when he decided not to give Biondo back his money. He could drown in reasons for not yielding the cash and for giving Streeter the heat. But none explained why a man would keep anything that brought on that much trouble, or why a man would jeopardize his entire setup in life for a truckload of cider. And so he feared the giddiness, knew it was to be resisted.

When he'd tossed his forty-dollar brown velour hat onto the bed, it had hit the threadbare spread and rolled off. He folded his brown chinchilla coat (two grand, legitimately acquired) over the footboard, and it too slipped to the floor. When he left the courthouse and saw the newsmen backing away from him in the corridor, saw them on the steps and in the streets with their cameras, he had the impulse to reach into his coat pocket and find the rotten eggs to throw at the bastards. And this was the Jack Diamond who once hired a press agent to get his name around.

He sat on the bed, unable to see the condition of his eyes, which were heavy-lidded with whiskey – too little light in the room and in his brain. He squinted at the mirror, but saw only his squint returned. He felt an irritation of the penis from his lovemaking and adjusted his shorts where they rubbed. He remembered Alice's kiss before he left the party, a wet one. She opened her mouth slightly, as she always did when she had a few whiskeys in. He reached into his pocket, felt a card, and looked at it. Packy's speakeasy card. The Parody Association, members only. Jack had seen it on the bar during the party, never owned one, never needed one, but picked it up and pocketed it out of habit. There was a time when he could enter any speakeasy on his name alone, but now people imitated him, even made collections in his name. I'm Legs Diamond. Oh sure, and I'm Herbert Hoover. He used the cards now because he no longer even looked like his own pictures.

Fifty people were in The Parody when Marcus gave his

victory toast, the words floating now somewhere behind Jack's squint.

'To Jack Diamond's ability to escape from the clutches of righteous official indignation, which would so dearly love to murder him in his bed . . .'

Fifty people with glasses in the air. Would've been more, but Jack said keep it small, it ain't the circus. But it was, in its own way, what with Packy and Marcus and Sal from the Kenmore, and Hubert and Hooker Ryan the old fighter, and Tipper Kelly the newsie, and Flossie, who came with the place.

Jack told me to bring Frances, my secretary, who still thought Jack was the devil, even though he'd been acquitted twice. 'Show her the devil face to face,' Jack said, but when he saw her he mistrusted her face. Lovely Irish face. Reminded Jack of his first wife, Katherine, he married in '17. Army bride. Prettiest Irish kid you ever saw, and she left him because he used coke. Crazy young Jack.

Crazy Jack owes Marcus. Five grand. Coming in the morning from Madden. Where would Jack Diamond be without Uncle Owney? Pay you in the morning, Marcus. Meet you at your office at eleven. Cash on the barrelhead. Jack would be a semifree man, walking Albany's streets, a little less intimidated by the weight of his own future. Maybe his head would clear now that he'd won a second acquittal. They could go on trying him on gun charges, but Marcus said the state boys were whipped, would never try him again with Streeter the adversary witness. The federals were the problem, with four years facing him and no end of other charges pending. No end, even if he reversed the conviction with an appeal. But Jack would worry about the federals when he got well. The immediate future lay in South Carolina. A beachfront spot where he'd holed up when Rothstein and Schultz were both gunning for him in '27. Beautiful old house on a sand dune back from the ocean. Sea air good for the lungs.

Lung talk: Do you know why Jack Diamond can drink so much

whiskey? Because he has TB and the fever burns up the alcohol. Facts. Left lung is congested. But, Jack, really now, you never had TB in your life. What will jail do to your lungs? What will it do to your brain, for that matter? Bore you? You'll have to play a lot of dominoes in jail. Boring dominoes. But you knew that. You were always ready to play dominoes, right? That's part of the game, right?

Wrong. Not part of Jack's game.

Jack took off the coat of his lucky blue suit and hung it on the back of the chair. Suit needs a pressing, Marcus told him, even before the trial began. But Jack told Marcus, told the press boys too: 'This is my lucky suit and I'm not parting with it. If we win, I'll get it pressed to celebrate.' The suit coat fell to the floor in a pile.

Jack took the change out of his pants pockets, his nail file and comb, his white monogrammed handkerchief, and put them on top of the dresser that one of his obituary writers, Meyer Berger, would describe as tawdry. Jack's ethereal mother, starched and bright in a new green frying pan apron, held up Jack's bulletproof vest. 'You didn't wear this,' she said. 'I told you not go out without it, Jackie. Remember what happened to Caesar?' They rendered old Caesar, Jack was about to say when he felt a new surge of giddiness. It was bringing him a breakthrough perception. I am on the verge of getting it all wrapped up, he said to the steam heat that hissed at him from the radiator. I hear it coming. I have been true to everything in life.

'I toast also to his uncanny ability to bloom in hostile seasons and to survive the blasts of doom. Jack, we need only your presence to light us up like Times Square in fervid and electric animation. You are the undercurrent of our lives. You turn on our light . . .'

Freddie Robin, the cop, who stopped in for a quick one, had the glass in his hand when good old Marcus started the toast. And Milligan, the railroad dick alongside him, had a glass in

763

the air, too. Pair of cops toasting Jack's glorious beswogglement of law and order. Hah! And alongside them the priest and the screwball.

'Who the hell is that screwball, anyway?' Jack said to Hubert, who began sniffing. The screwball was talking to everybody, wanted to meet everybody at the party. Looks like a killer to you, does he, Jack? No. But maybe like a cop. Like a federal stooge. They like to crash my parties.

Hubert got his name. He was Mr Biswanger from Buffalo. A lightning rod salesman. What's he doing at your party, Jack? Trying to hustle you a sample to wear behind your ear? He came with the priest, Hubert reported. And the priest came to Albany to see Marcus. Is that true, Marcus? Marcus says yes, but adds, 'He just tagged along, Jack, after a legal chat. I didn't bring the clergy. But they have an affinity for you, like cops. The underside of everybody's life, is what you turn out to be, Jack.'

Jack undid his tie, blue with diagonal white stripes, and hung it on the upright pole of the dresser mirror. It slid off. Priests and cops toasting Jack. It's like those Chinese bandits, Jack. Nobody can tell the good from the bad. China will always have bandits, right? So, fellow Chinks, let's sit back and enjoy them.

'To his talent for making virtue seem unwholesome and for instilling vicarious amorality in the hearts of multitudes . . .'

Alice gave Flossie the fish eye when she kidded Jack about pigeons in the loft and fondled his earlobe. Then Frances gave Flossie the fish eye when the Floss kidded Marcus about pigeons in the loft and fondled his earlobe. The Floss moved alongside the piano, and while the pianoman played 'It's a Sin to Tell a Lie,' she shook her ass to that sweet and gracious waltz, turning, pivoting, shaking. Disgusting. Gorgeous. Oh, Floss, ya look like Mae West. Harpy. Sweetmeat. Goddess of perfume.

'Who is she?' Alice asked.

'Flossie, she works here,' Jack said.

'She knows you pretty well to play with your ear.'

'Nah, she does that with all the boys. Great girl, the Floss.'

'I never knew anybody who liked ears like that.'

'You don't get around, Alice. I keep telling you that.'

'I know you think I'm jealous of all the harpies in the world, but I'm really not, John. Just remember that the truest love is bright green. Avoid substitutes.'

From Buffalo the hunger marchers began their walk toward Washington. John D. Rockefeller, in Ormond, Florida, told newsreel microphones that 'better times are coming,' and he wished the world a Merry Christmas. In Vienna a grand jury unanimously acquitted Dr Walter Pfrimer and seven other Fascist Party leaders of charges of high treason stemming from an attempted putsch. A speedy recovery was predicted for Pola Negri.

Jack took off the signet ring that no longer fit, that had been bothering him all day. He wore it because it was lucky, like his suit, gift from the old man in high school: *D* is also for Dear Daddy. Dead Dad. Defunct Diamond. Sorry, old fellow. Jack listened to the candles burning on the altar of Saint Anne's church. They made the sound of leaves falling into a pond where a calico cat was slowly drowning. In the shadow of the first pillar the old man cried as the candles danced. When the mass was ended, when Jack the small priest had blown out the authenticating candle of his mother's life, the old man stood up and turned to pity, politics, and drink. And, oh, how they laughed back in Cavan. Publicans did not complain when the laughter died and you threw your arms around yourself in a fit of need. 'Nobody knows what it's like until they lose their wife,' old Jack said. 'Then you eat Thanksgiving dinner alone.' Young Jack looked on. 'Just a weak old man. He cried more than I did. I cried only once.'

Jack dropped the signet ring with a clunk into the tawdry dresser alongside two holy pictures (Stephen and Mary) Alice had brought him from New York, alongside the letters, the holy fan mail. Jack kept one letter: 'God bless you, son, from a mother with a large family.' And God bless you too, mother, going away.

The giddiness was turning to smiles. Jack looked at himself in the mirror and smiled at the peeling mercury. His smile was backward. What else was backward? He was. All. All backward in the mirror image. Nobody would ever know which image was the real Jack. Only Jack knows that, and he giggled with the knowledge that he alone was privy to the secret. What a wonderful feeling! A vision of the Jack nobody knows. Fuck that stupid Legs, right Jack? What'd he ever do for you?

One of Marcus' law partners came to the party to meet Legs Diamond – a kid with wide eyes when he shook the hand that shook the Catskills. Hubert brought two poker players from Troy, and they talked to Jack about a little game some night. Love to, boys. Packy had rounded up the musicians, piano, banjoman, drummer. Marcus asked Alice to dance and then Jack took an armful of Frances and foxtrotted around to 'Ain't Misbehavin'.'

'I must say you're a wonderful dancer,' said Frances.

And why, miss, must you say it? Jack dancing with yesterday in his arms. Thank you, young woman out of yesterday.

'You know I never think of you as dancing or doing anything like this.'

'What *do* you think of me doing?'

'Terrible things,' she said. She spoke sternly. Scolded, Jack relaxed, touched her hair with his fingertips, remembering his Army bride.

'Your hair reminds me of Helen Morgan,' he said.

Frances blushed.

Doc Madison pulled his wife to her feet, stepped into a snappy foxtrot with the same certainty he revealed when he removed the filling from Jack, all those double-ought pellets, restoring life to the dying frame. We're all so full of life now, Doc. And ain't it great? So many thanks, Doc.

'. . . perhaps you all noticed the lofty stained-glass windows of the courthouse annex this afternoon as the sun streamed through, as the light fell about our Jack's frail but sturdy shoulder, illuminating in those windows both New York's and Jack's splendid virtues . . . industry, law, peace, learning, prosperity . . .'

The courtroom felt like a church still, old Presbyterian palace desanctified years ago; choir loft over Jack's head, judges sitting where the pulpit used to be, truncated suns over the door, ecclesiastical fenestration and only the faces on the walls different now: clergy and the Jesus crowd replaced with jurists. But retributionists all.

Frankie Teller, of course, came to the party, and so did one of the Falzo boys who ran four houses on The Line in Troy, squiring one of his beauties. Jack asked Johnny Dyke, the Albany bookie, to come by, and Mushy Tarsky too, who ran the grocery on Hudson Avenue where Jack bought ham and cheese sandwiches for three weeks when he and two boys never went off the block because of The Goose. Jack's Uncle Tim, who had hung on at Acra since the roof fell in, waiting for Jack to return to the homestead, came up for the celebration.

Tuohey and Spivak, the bagmen detectives from the gambling squad, dropped in for a look and brought greetings from the Democratic organization.

Marion did not come.

Couldn't do that. Alice would've blown up if she showed. Jack sent Hubert and Frankie Teller up with a pint of whiskey to keep her happy, but she was gone. Note on the door: 'Going to Boston to see Mama.' Frankie brought the note back, and Jack said, 'Go look for her, she's on the street. Try the station, and find her. She wouldn't go without seeing me.' It took Frankie and Hubert an hour, and they found her walking back up Ten Broeck Street toward her apartment house, Number Twenty-one, upstairs. Hubert says he told her, 'Jack is worried about you, Marion,' and then she said, 'You tell him I'm goddamn good and mad. I'll stay till the morning, but then I'm leaving; I'm not putting up with this. One of the biggest nights of his life, and he leaves me alone four hours while he sits around partying with his cow, and I have to go to the talkies to keep myself busy. The talkies on a night like this.'

So Hubert called Jack with the news, and Jack went back to the table and told Alice a fib. Bones McDowell, a newsman, calling with death-threat information. Gotta go see him, Al. But she'd been waiting for this, Jack. She knows you, Jack, you and your fake excuses. Then Jack said, 'Listen, Al, I know you're having a good time, but why don't you come with me? It's business, but Bones is only a newspaperman with some maybe important dope, and it ain't big business or trouble, and I won't be long. Come with me.'

She believed that and gave Jack the wet one with the lips apart, he can see them now, and her tongue just dancing and saying, Come on in, boy, and she smiled too and winked at him, and he let his hand slide down and pat her on the benevolent behind, secretly, so the priest wouldn't be scandalized, so that all the eyes that were never off either of them all night would see something, yes, but not enough to talk dirty about such a sweet, clean woman. And then he let go of her. And she leaned back and gave him a smile, a real smile, crinkling her blue-green eyes and saying, 'No, I'll stay here with Kitty and Johnny,' Ed's wife and the boy alongside her, family lady to the end, the end. He gave her one final peck and looked at her green cloche hat with the little wispy curls of Titian, color of winners, sticking out from underneath.

'Don't be long,' she said. 'It's such a swell party.'

'I'll be back in half an hour,' Jack said, running his fingertips lightly down her cheek. 'You can count on that.'

He stood up then. It was one o'clock and thirty people still at the party when he turned his back on the crowd and walked the length of the bar, past all the enduring dead on the walls, and then out through Packy's swinging doors.

Now Playing in Albany, December 18, 1931
  STRAND: (The clearest picture, the best sound in New York State), George Bancroft in *Rich Man's Folly*.

HARMANUS BLEECKER HALL: (Albany's Palace of Entertainment), Ronald Colman in *The Unholy Garden*.

LELAND: (Where the talkies are better), Billie Dove in *The Age for Love*.

PALACE: (Showplace of The Capital), Leo Carillo in *The Guilty Generation*.

MADISON: Mae Clarke in *Waterloo Bridge*.

COLONIAL: Ann Harding in *Devotion*.

PARAMOUNT: Wheeler and Woolsey in *Hook, Line and Sinker*.

PARAMOUNT: Marian Nixon and Neil Hamilton in *Ex Flame* (a modernized version of *East Lynne*).

ALBANY: Wheeler and Woolsey in *Caught Plastered*.

Jack, sitting on his bed in the rooming house, took off the blue pants, pulled them over the scuffy black shoes, the dark-blue socks with the white clocks. He hung the pants on the open drawer of the tawdry dresser, and they stayed there a few seconds before they fell to the floor. Jack had drunk too much with too many. And yet he was lucid when he left the party, pushed by the whiskey into clarity and anticipation of the sweets of love; that face of perfect worship, the excitement of the body of perfect satisfaction, so wholly Jack's, so fully responsive to his touches, his needs. Climbing the stairs to her apartment, he already relished the look of her, the way she would smile when he greeted her with a kiss, the sweetness of presence alone when they sat and faced each other. This did not change. The power of sweetness had not faded in the almost two years he'd known her.

'They tell me you're going to Boston.'

'I really am.'

'Without even saying goodbye?'

'What's another goodbye? We're always saying that.'

'You're not going anyplace. Tomorrow we'll go down to the mountains, have a drink with old Brady up at Haines Falls. Weather's still pretty good.'

'You say that, but we won't go.'

'Sure. I'll have Frankie pick you up at noon and meet me at Marcus' office, and we'll go from there.'

'What about your darling Alice?'

'I'll send her out shopping.'

'Something'll happen and we won't go.'

'Yes, we'll go. You can count on it. You got my word.'

Jack, euphoric now, opened Marion's robe, gazed on her garden of ecstasy. Always a vision. Now better than ever. Jack had been down. He had hit bottom. But like an astral rubber ball, he was bouncing back toward the stars. When he held Marion in his arms, he felt the giddiness. 'Top of the goddamn world,' he said into her ear. 'I'm on top of the goddamn world.'

'That's nice, Jackie.'

'I'm a winner again.'

'That's really nice.'

Jack knew that winners celebrated with biological food. You found the most beautiful woman on the Eastern Seaboard. You took your body to where she waited. You turned off her radio, then gave her body to your body. Your body would thank you for such a gift. Your body would be a happy body.

Jack laughed out loud, once, in his bed, a resonant 'Haw!'

Moonshine was down to thirty-five cents a pint, and kids were sipping it with two straws. Iced beer was down to five dollars a gallon, and you could get it delivered home. College girls were pledging not to call for drinks costing more than a nickel when their boyfriends took them out for a good time. Dorothy Dix found this a step in the right direction, for matrimony was waning in popularity, a direct result of the high cost of living.

Jack remembered the night he penetrated to the center of Kiki's treasure at Haines Falls and struck something solid.

'What the hell is that?'

'A cork,' she said.

'A cork? How'd it get up there?'

'I took it off a gallon of dago red and put it up there. It's my Italian chastity cork.'

'What the hell's the matter with you?'

'I'm not taking it out till you promise to marry me.'

But she got over that, and when he entered her on this euphoric night in Albany there was no cork, no ultimatum; no climax either. Jack erected, Marion lubricious, they could've danced all night. But Jack wearied of the effort, and Marion ran out of her capacity to groan with pleasure. They rolled away from each other and let the sweat slowly cool, the breathing return to normal, the artifacts dry.

He pulled off one shoe without opening the laces, let it drop. He took off the second shoe, noted its scuffiness and remembered the night he surrendered on the Hotsy charges. He walked into the Forty-seventh Street station house in his navy-blue chesterfield with the velvet lapels, white on white silk scarf, the midnight-blue serge double-breasted, the gray and black dragon tie, and the shoes so highly polished they could pass for patent leather, the derby heightening the tone of his special condition. Jack was on top that night, too, remembering Vinnie Raymond from East Albert Street, who walked by the Diamond house every night in *his* derby and *his* high-polish shoes and spats, on his way to life. The image of that man's perfection was still in the mind that controlled the scuffed shoe, down at the heel. Then he let it, too, drop.

Jack heard the horn blowing in the street outside Marion's Ten Broeck Street apartment. He raised the window.

'It's gettin' late, Jack,' Frankie Teller called up to him. 'You said half an hour. It's going on two hours. You know what Alice told me. You get him back here to this party, back here to me.'

But no partying remained in Jack. He would not return to any festive scene, festive drunks, festive Alice. He closed the window and looked at Marion, who had wrapped herself in a beige floor-length silk robe, gift from Jack six months ago when he had money for anything. The gown had one large brown flower below the knee, same color as the stripe around the small lapel. So gorgeous. Will ever a woman look more gorgeous to Jack than this one?

'You treat women like animals,' Marion said.

'Ah, don't fight me tonight, baby. I'm feelin' good.'

'Like cats. You treat us like damn old cats. Pet us and pussy us up and scratch our neck.'

Jack laughed, fell back on the pillow of his own rooming house bed and laughed and laughed and laughed. She was right. You look a cat in the eye and demand a love song. It sits there, and if it likes you at all, it doesn't run away. It wants its goddamn neck scratched. Wants you to play with its whiskers. Give it what it wants, it turns on its motor. He laughed and raised his feet off the floor and saw his socks, still on.

He sat up and took off one sock, dropped it onto one shoe, missed.

'. . . I toast his defiance, his plan not to seduce the world but to terrify it, to spit in the eye of the public which says no Moloch shall pass . . .'

Jack would not begin life again in the same way. Adirondacks? Vermont? Maybe. But Coll was in jail, his mob busted up after a shoot-out in Averill Park and a roundup in Manhattan. Jack would have to recruit from scratch, and the prospect was wearying. So many dead and gone. Mike Sullivan, Fatty Walsh, Eddie. He reached for the second sock, remembering all the old boys, friends and enemies. Brocco. Babe. Frenchy. Shorty. Pretty. Mattie. Hymie. Fogarty. Dead, gone off, or in jail. And he seemed to himself, for the first time, a curiously perishable item among many such items, a thing of just so many seasons. When does the season end? He has survived again and again to another day, to try yet again to change what he had never been able to change. Would Jack Diamond ever really change? Or would he wake tomorrow out of this euphoria and begin to do what he had done every other day of his senior life? Was there any reason to doubt that recurring pattern? In the morning he would pay Marcus what he owed and take Kiki for a ride and hustle Alice and keep her happy somehow and try to figure out what next. Where was the money coming from? Something would come up.

He would solve it – he, Jack Diamond, who is what was

designed, what was made this morning, yesterday, and the day before out of his own private clay.

Ah. What was designed.

This perception arrived as Jack dropped his second sock to the floor and leaned toward the dresser and saw the rosary in the top drawer. He thought then of saying it again. But no. No rosary. No prayer. No remorse. Jack is so happy with his perception of being what was designed, so released from the struggle to change, that he begins with a low rumble that rises from the sewers of madness; and yet he is not mad, only enlightened, or could they be the same condition? The rumble grows and rises to his throat where it becomes a cackle, and then into his nose where he begins to snort its joy, and into his eyes which cry with this pervasive mirth. Now his whole being – body, mind, and the spirit of nothing that he has at last recognized in the mirror – is convulsed with an ecstasy of recognition.

'. . . Jack, when you finally decide to go, when you are only a fading memory along Broadway, a name in the old police files and yellowing tabloids, then we will not grieve. Yet we will be empty because our friend Jack, the nonpareil, the nonesuch, the grand confusion of our lives, has left us. The outer limit of boldness is what your behavior has been, Jack, and even if Christ came to town, I'm not sure He'd be seen on the same hill with you. Nevertheless, I think I speak for all when I say we're rooting for you. And so here's to your good health, and to ours, and let me add a safe home, Jacko, a safe home.'

Jack heard the cheer go up out in the street in front of the courthouse. But he knew they were cheering for the wrong man.

'I know that son of a bitch,' Jack said as he entered his final dream. 'He was never any good.'

Mrs Laura Woods, the landlady at 67 Dove, said she heard two men climb the carpeted stairs past the potted fern and enter the front room where the noted guest, who had originally rented the room as Mr Kelly, was sleeping. She heard the shots, three into Jack's head, three into the wall, and then heard one man say, 'Let's make sure. I been waiting a long time for this.' And the second man said, 'Oh, hell, that's enough for him.'

Mrs Woods telephoned The Parody Club where she knew Mrs Diamond was partying. It was 6:55 A.M. before the family notified the police and by then Doc Madison had said yes, death seemed to have at last set in for Jack. When the detectives arrived, Alice was holding a bloody handkerchief, with which she had wiped the face of the corpse with the goggle eyes.

'Oh, my beloved boy,' she was saying over and over, 'I didn't do it, I didn't do it.'

'. . . Months ago,' Winchell wrote, 'we called him "On His Last Legs" Diamond . . .'

Jack wore his tuxedo and signet ring and held his rosary at the wake, which was given at the home of Alice's relatives in Maspeth, Long Island. The family sent four floral tributes, and I paid for one-third of the fifth, a pillow of red roses, the other two-thirds kicked in by Packy and Flossie, and signed, 'Your pals.' An eight-foot bleeding heart was dedicated to 'Uncle John,' and Alice sent a five-and-a-half-foot-high floral chair of yellow tea roses and lilies of the valley. On a gauze streamer in two-inch gold letters across the chairback she had inscribed: VACANT CHAIR, TO MY OWN, AFTER ALL, YOUR LOVING WIFE.

Owney Madden paid for the coffin, a dark mahogany box worth eight hundred dollars. Jack had seven hundred dollars' worth of industrial insurance once, but the company canceled it. The plan was to bury Jack in Calvary Cemetery alongside Eddie, but the church wouldn't let him be put in consecrated ground. Wouldn't allow a mass either. And the permission for the final prayer by a priest at the wake house, which I negotiated with Cardinal Hayes, was withdrawn at the last minute, putting the women in tears. A thirteen-year-old cousin of Jack's said the rosary in place of the priest, as a thousand people stood outside the house in the rain.

It rained yellow mud into the grave. A couple of hundred of Jack's fans went to the cemetery with the family and the press. Somebody from the undertakers picked up a shovel and tried to drive the photographers away from the graveside, but none of them gave an inch, and when the man screamed at them, the photographers chased him up a tree. Jack belonged to them.

It was all over quickly. Alice, heavily veiled, said, 'Goodbye, boy, goodbye,' when they began to fill the grave, and then she walked away with a single red rose in her hand. Ten minutes later most of the flowers on the grave were gone. Souvenirs.

When Kiki began her five-a-day stint at the Academy of Music on Fourteenth Street ('See Kiki, the Gangster's Gal'), fifteen hundred people were in line before the theater opened at eleven in the morning, and the manager sold two hundred and fifty SRO tickets. 'She is better box office than Peaches Browning,' the manager said, 'and Peaches was the best I ever had here.' Sidney Skolsky reported Alice was in the balcony at the opening to see the wicked child (she was just twenty-two) tippy-tap-toe to the tune of twin banjos, then take four bows and never mention Jack. But Sidney was wrong. Alice didn't see the show. I called her to offer a bit of consolation after I'd read about Kiki's success.

'Only eighteen days, Marcus,' Alice said. 'He's dead only eighteen days and she's out there with banjos, dancing on his grave. She could at least have waited a month.'

My advice was to stop competing with Kiki for a dead man, but it was an absurd suggestion to a gladiator, and the first time I made the mistake of thinking Jack was totally dead. Alice had already hired a writer and was putting together a skit that would be staged, thirty-five days after Jack's murder, on the boards of the Central Theater in the Bronx. The theme was crime doesn't pay. In one moment of the drama Alice interrupted a holdup, disarmed the gunman, and guarded him with his own gun until the police arrived. Then she said to the audience, 'You can't make a dime with any of them. The straight and narrow is the only way,' which brought to mind the era when she banked eighteen thousand dollars in about six months at Acra. Ambivalence, you're beautiful.

Kiki and Alice both took their acts on the road, in vaudeville and on the Minsky burlesque circuit, outraging any number of actors, the Marx Brothers among them. 'A damn shame and a disgrace,' said Groucho of Kiki's sixteen-week contract, 'especially when so many actors are out of work. For what she is getting they could have hired five good acts, people who know their business. She's nothing but a gangster's moll.'

The girls both played the same big towns, and both scandalized the smaller ones, Alice barred from Paterson, Kiki hustled out of Allentown, Alice presuming to teach a moral lesson with her act, Kiki the successful sinner against holy matrimony. Who drew the crowds? Ah.

By spring Kiki was still traveling, but Alice was no longer a serious road attraction. Alice and I talked a few times because she was having money problems, worried about the mortgage on the Acra house. She said then she was going to open at Coney Island and she chided me for never seeing her perform. So I said I'd come and catch her opener.

There is a photograph of her as she looked on the day her show opened on the boardwalk. I was standing behind the news cameraman as he caught her by surprise, and I remember her face before, during, and after the click: the change from uncertainty to hostility to a smile at me. Her hair is parted and wavy, falling over her forehead and covering her ears. A poster behind her advertises Siamese twins joined at the shoulder blades, and there is a girl outlined by a dozen long-bladed knives. A midget is in the photo, being held aloft by a man with dark, oily hair and a pencil-thin mustache. The sign says SIDE SHOW in large letters and to the right: BEAUTIFUL MRS JACK LEGS DIAMOND IN PERSON.

The weather was unseasonably warm that afternoon, mobs on the boardwalk in shirtsleeves and unnecessary furs, camp chairs on the sand, and young girls blooming in summer dresses as Beautiful Mrs Jack walked onto the simple unpainted board stage.

From the other direction came the tuxedo man with the little mustache. He introduced Alice, then asked if she wanted to say anything at the start.

'Mr Diamond was a loving and devoted husband,' she said. 'Much that was stated and printed about him was untrue.'

'People find it difficult to understand why a woman would stay married to a gangster,' said the tuxedo man.

'Mr Diamond was no gangster. He wouldn't have known how to be a gangster.'

'It's been said he was a sadistic killer.'

'He was a man in love with all of nature, and he celebrated life. I never saw him kill even a fly.'

'How, then, would you say he got the reputation for being a gangster and a killer?'

'He did some very foolish things when he was young, but he regretted them later in life.'

So it went. The sixteen customers paid ten cents each to enter, and after the show Alice also sold four photos of herself and Jack, the one with 'my hero' written on the clipping found in her apartment a year later when they put a bullet in her temple. The photos also sold for a dime, which brought the gross for the first performance to two dollars.

'Not much of a crowd,' she said to me when she came off the stage. Her eyes were heavy and she couldn't manage a smile.

'You'll do better when the hot days come along.'

'The hot days are all over with, Marcus.'

'Hey, that's kind of maudlin.'

'No, just honest. Nothing's like it used to be. Nothing.'

'You look as good as ever. You're not going under, I can see that.'

'No, I don't go under. But I'm all hollow inside. If I went in for a swim I'd float away like an old bottle.'

'Come on, I'll buy you a drink.'

She knew a speakeasy a few blocks off the boardwalk, upstairs over a hot dog stand, and we settled into a corner and talked over her travels, and her fulfilling of her own fragment of Lew Edwards' dream: John the Priest on the boards of America. He was there. The presence within Alice.

'Are you staying alive on this spiel?' I asked her.

'You mean money? No, not anymore. But I've got a little coming in from a dock union John did some favors for. One of his little legacies to me was how and why he did the favors, and who paid off. And when I told them what I had, they kept up the payments.'

'Amazing.'

'What?'

'That he's still taking care of you.'

'But she's living off him, too. That's what galls me.'

'I know. I read the papers. Did you ever catch her act?'

'Are you serious? I wouldn't go within three miles of her footprints.'

'She stopped by to see me when she played a club in Troy. She spoke well of you, I must say. "The old war-horse," she said to me, "they can't beat her."'

Alice laughed, tossed her hair, which was back to its natural color – a deep chestnut – but still a false color, for after Jack died, her roots went white in two days. But it looked right, now. Authentic Alice. She tossed that authentic hair in triumph, then tossed off a shot of straight gin.

'She meant *she* couldn't beat me.'

'Maybe that's what she meant. I only agreed with her.'

'She never knew John, not till near the end. When she moved into Acra she thought she had him. Then, when I walked out of the Kenmore she thought she had him again. But she didn't know him.'

'I thought *she* left the Kenmore.'

'She did. The police came looking and John put her in a rooming house in Watervliet, then one in Troy. He moved her around, but he kept bringing her back to the Rain-Bo room and I refused to take it. I told John that the day I left. I wasn't gone three days when he called me to come back up and set up a house or an apartment. But I didn't want Albany anymore, so he came to New York when he wanted to see me. It must've killed her.'

I remember Jack telling a story twice in my presence about how he met Alice. 'I pulled up to a red light at Fifty-ninth Street and she jumped in and I couldn't get her out.'

In its way it was a true story. Jack couldn't kick her out of his life; Alice couldn't leave. Her wish was to be buried on top of him, but she didn't get that wish either. She had to settle for a spot alongside; and buried, like Jack, without benefit of the religion she loved so well. Her murderers took her future away from her, and that, too, was related to Jack. She was about to open a tearoom on Jones' Walk at Coney, which would have been a speakeasy within hours, and was also lending her name to a sheet to be called *Diamond Widow's Racing Form*. She'd gotten the reputation of being a crack shot from practicing at the Coney shooting galleries and practicing in her backyard with a pistol too, so went the story. And in certain Coney and Brooklyn bars, when she was escorted by gangsters who found her company improved their social status, she would announce with alcoholic belligerence that she could whip any man in the house in a fight. They also said she was threatening to reveal who killed Jack, but I never believed that. I don't think she knew any more than the rest of us. We all had our theories.

I remember her sitting at that Coney table, head back, laughing that triumphant laugh of power. I never saw her again. I talked to her by phone some months later when she was trying to save Acra from foreclosure and she was even talking of getting a few boys together again to hustle some drink among the summer tourists. But she just couldn't put that much money together (sixty-five hundred dollars was due) and she lost the house. I did what I could, which was to delay the finale. She wrote me a thanks-for-everything note, which was our last communication. Here's the last paragraph of that letter:

Jack once told me when he was tipsy that 'If you can't make 'em laugh, don't make 'em cry.' I don't know what in hell he meant by that, do you? It sounds like a sappy line he heard from some sentimental old vaudevillian. But he said it to me and he did mean something by it, and I've been trying to figure it out ever since. The only thing I can come up with is that maybe he thought of himself as some kind of entertainer and, in a way, that's pretty true. He sure gave me a good time. And other people I won't name. God I miss him.

She signed it 'love and a smooch, just one.' She was dead a month later, sixty-four dollars behind in her thirty-two-dollar-a-month rent for the Brooklyn apartment. Her legacy was that trunkful of photographs and clippings, the two Brussels griffons she always thought Jack bought in Europe, and a dinner ring, a wedding ring, and a brooch, all set with diamonds.

She was a diamond, of course.

They never found her killers either.

I saw Marion for the last time in 1936 at the old Howard Theater in Boston, another backstage encounter. But then again why not? Maybe Jack hit the real truth with that line of his. The lives of Kiki and Alice were both theatrical productions; both were superb in their roles as temptress and loyal wife, and as leading ladies of underworld drama. Marion was headlining a burlesque extravaganza called *The Pepper Pot Revue* when I read the item in the *Globe* about her being robbed, and I went downtown and saw her, just before her seven o'clock show.

She was sitting in one of the Howard's large dressing rooms, listening to Bing Crosby on the radio crooning a slow-tempo version of 'Nice Work If You Can Get It.' She wore a fading orchid robe of silk over her costume, wore it loosely, permitting me a glimpse of the flesh-colored patches which made scant effort to cover her attractions. She worked on her toes with two ostrich-feather fans, one of which would fall away by number's end, revealing unclothed expanses of the whitest of white American beauty flesh. She billed herself out front as 'Jack (Legs) Diamond's Lovely Light o'Love,' a phrase first applied to her after the Monticello shooting by a romantic caption writer. Her semipro toe dance, four a day, five on Saturday, was an improvement over her tippy-tap-toe routine, for the flesh was where her talent lay.

'You're still making the headlines,' I told her when the stage doorman showed me where she was.

Her robe flowed open, and she gave me a superb hug, my first full-length, unencumbered encounter with all that sensual resilience, and after the preliminaries were done with, she reached in a drawer, put a finger through an aperture in a pair of yellow silk panties with a border of small white flowers and dangled them in front of me.

'That's the item?'

'That's them. Isn't it ridiculous?'

'The publicity wasn't bad, good for the show.'

'But it's so . . . so cheap and awful.' She broke down, mopped her eyes with the panties that an MIT student had stolen from her as a fraternity initiation prank. He left an ignominious fifty-cent piece in their place, saying, when they nabbed him at the stage door with the hot garment in his pants pocket, 'I would've left more, only I didn't have change.'

I was baffled by her tears, which were flowing not from the cheapness of the deed, for she was beyond that, inured. I then considered that maybe the fifty cents was not enough. But would five or fifty dollars have been enough for the girl who once wore a five-hundred-dollar negotiable hymen inside another such garment? No, she was crying because I was witness to both past and present in this actual moment, and she hadn't been prepared to go over it all again on such short notice. She knew I remembered Ziegfeld and all her promise of greater Broadway glory, plus a Hollywood future. But Ziegfeld turned her down after Jack died, and Will Hays wouldn't let her get a foothold in Hollywood: No molls need apply. And finally, as we talked, she brought it out, tears gone, panties there to haunt both of us (I remembered the vision at the miniature golf course, in her Monticello room, and I thought, Pursue it now; nothing bars the way now; no fear, no betrayal intervening between you and that bound-to-be-lovely by-way), and she said: 'It's so shitty, Marcus. It seems once fate puts the finger on you, you're through.'

'You're still in the paper, kiddo; you're in big letters out front, and you look like seven or eight million dollars. Eight. I know a few young ladies with less to point to.'

'You were always nice, Marcus. But you know I still miss Jack. Miss him. After all these years.'

Would the maudlin time never end?

'You're keeping him alive,' I said. 'Look at it that way. He's on the signs out front, too.'

'He wouldn't like his name there.'

'Sure he would, as long as you were tied to it.'

'No, not Jack. He liked it respectable, the two-faced son of a bitch. He left me that night to go home to bed so Alice wouldn't come find him, so he could be there in bed ahead of her. Imagine a man like him thinking like that?'

'Who said he did that?'

'Frankie Teller told me. Jack mumbled it in the cab when they left my place.'

She let the old memories run by in silence, then she said, 'But I was the last one to see him,' and she meant, to make love to him. 'He always left Old Lady Prune to come to me. I don't think she had a crotch.' And then Kiki laughed and laughed, as triumphantly as Alice had in the Coney speakeasy.

I bought her a sandwich between shows, then took her back to the theater. I kissed her goodbye on the cheek, but she turned and gave me her mouth as I was leaving, a gift. But she didn't linger over it.

'Thanks for coming,' she said, and I didn't know whether to leave or not. Then she said, 'I could've made it with you, Marcus. I think I could've. But he spoiled me, you know.'

'Sometimes friends should just stay friends.'

'He spoiled me for so many men. I never thought any man could do that to me.'

'You'll never be spoiled for me.'

'Come and see me again, Marcus. Next time you see me on a marquee someplace.'

'You can bank on that,' I said.

But I never did. Her name turned up in the papers when she married a couple of times, never with success. About 1941 a patient treated in Bellevue's alcoholic ward gave the name of Kiki Roberts, but the story that it was the real Kiki was denied in the press the next day. She was hurt in a theater fire in Newark somewhere around that time, and a friend of mine from Albany saw her back in Boston in a small club during the middle years of the war, still known professionally as Jack's sweetheart, not stripping any longer, just singing torch songs, like 'Broken Hearted,' a tune from '27, the year they killed Little Augie and shot Jack full of holes, the year he became famous for the first time for not dying. You can't kill Legs Diamond. I've heard Kiki died in Detroit, Jersey, and Boston, that she went crazy, broke her back and had a metal backbone put in, got fat, grew old beautifully, turned lesbian, and that she still turns up in Troy and Catskill and Albany bars whose owners remember Jack. I don't believe any of it. I don't know what happened to her.

That isn't the end of the story, of course. Didn't I, like everybody else who knew him, end up on a barstool telling Jack's tale again, forty-three years later, telling it my own way? And weren't Tipper and The Pack and Flossie there with me, ready, as always with the ear, ready too to dredge up yet another story of their own? The magazines never stopped retelling Jack's story either, and somebody put it out in book form once, a silly work, and somebody else made a bum movie of it. But nobody ever came anywhere near getting it right, and I mean right, not straight, for accuracy about Jack wasn't possible. His history was as crooked as the line between his brain and his heart. I stand on this: that Packy's dog story was closer to the truth about Jack and his world than any other word ever written or spoken about him.

We were all there in the dingy old Kenmore when Packy told it, old folks together, wearying of talk of any kind by now, all of us deep into the drink, anxious to move along to something else, and yet not quite able to let go. I remember I was winding up, telling what happened to The Goose, who at age sixty-eight homosexually assaulted a young boy in a prison shower and was stabbed in his good eye for his efforts. And Oxie, who did seven long ones and then dropped dead of a heart attack on a Bronx street corner after a month of freedom. And Fogarty, who was let out of jail because of his sickness and wasted away with TB in the isolation ward of the Ann Lee Home in Albany, and who called me at the end to handle his legacy, which consisted of Big Frenchy DeMange's diamond wristwatch. Jack gave it to him as a souvenir after the Big Frenchy snatch, and Fogarty kept it in a safe-deposit box and never sold it, even when he didn't have a dime.

My three old friends didn't know either that Jack never paid me for the second trial, nor had he ever paid Doc Madison a nickel for all the doc's attention to his wounds.

'He stole from us all, to the very end,' I said.

'Yes, Marcus,' said Flossie, the loyal crone, misty-eyed over her wine, profoundly in love with all that was and would never be again, 'but he had a right to. He was magic. He had power. Power over people. Power over animals. He had a tan collie could count to fifty-two and do subtraction.'

'I wrote a story about his dog,' said the Tipper. 'It was a black and white bull terrier named Clancy. I went and fed him when they all left Acra and forgot he was there. Smartest dog I ever saw. Jack taught him how to toe dance.'

'It was a white poodle,' said Packy. 'He brought it with him right here where we're sitting one night in the middle of '31. There was a bunch of us and Jack decides he'll take a walk, and we all say, okay, we'll all take a walk. But Jack says he needs his sweater because the night air gets chilly, and we all say, you're right, Jack, it sure gets chilly.'

'Jack could turn on the electric light sometimes, just by snapping his fingers,' Flossie said.

'So Jack says to the white poodle, "Listen here, dog, go up and get my black sweater," and that damn dog got up and went out to the lobby and pushed the elevator button and went up to Jack's suite and barked, and Hubert Maloy let him in.'

'Jack could run right up the wall and halfway across the ceiling when he got a good running start,' Flossie said.

'We all waited, but the poodle didn't come back, and Jack finally says, "Where the hell is that dog of mine?" And somebody says maybe he went to the show to see the new Rin-Tin-Tin, and Jack says, "No, he already saw it." Jack got so fidgety he finally goes upstairs himself and we all follow, and Jack is sayin' when he walks into his room, "Come on, you son of a bitch, where's my goddamn sweater?"'

'Jack could outrun a rabbit,' Flossie said.

'Well, let me tell you, it took the wind right out of Jack when he saw that damn dog sitting on the sofa with the sweater, sewin' on a button that was missin' off the pocket.'

'Jack could tie both his shoes at once,' Flossie said.

Jacked Up

Jack (Legs) Diamond, aged thirty-four years, five months, seven days, and several hours, sat up in bed in his underwear and stared into the mirror at his new condition: incipiently dead.

'Those simple bastards,' he said, 'they finally did it right.'

He moved without being able to move, thought out of his dead brain, smiled with an immobile mouth, his face intact but the back of his head blown away. Already aware he was moving outside time, he saw the yellow fluid coming to his eyes, trickling out his nose, his ears, down the corners of his mouth. He felt tricklings from his rectum, his penis, old friend, and knew those too were the yellow. He turned his head and saw the yellow coming out his wounds, on top of his congealing blood. He had known the yellow would come, for he had been at the edge before. But he always failed to understand the why of it. The wisdom of equality, the Book of the Dead said, but that made no sense. Death did make sense. It was a gift. The dead thanked you with stupid eyes.

'Do you think I worry because I'm dead?' Jack asked aloud.

The yellow oozed its curious answer.

The press of death was deranging. He was fully aware of the pressure, like earth sinking into water. Yet there was time left for certain visitors who were crowding into the room. Rothstein stepped out of the crowd and inspected the crown of Jack's head. He fingered that bloody skull like a father fondling the fontanel of his infant son – and who with a better right? He pulled out two hairs from the center of the scalp.

'What odds that I find the answer, big dad?' Jack said.

Rothstein mulled the question, turned for an estimate to Runyon, who spoke out of a cancerously doomed larynx.

'I've said it before,' said Damon. 'All life is nine to five against.'

'You hear that?' A. R. asked.

'I hear it.'

'I must call against.'

'Then up yours,' said Jack. 'I'll make it my way.'

'Always headstrong,' said A. R.

I took Jack by the arm, guided him back from the mirror to lie on his right side, the lying posture of a lion. I pressed my fingers against the arteries on both sides of his throat.

'It's time, Jack,' I said. 'It's coming.'

'I'm not sure I'll know it when it comes.'

'I'll tell you this. It looks like a thought, like a cloudless sky. It looks like nothing at all.'

'Like nothing?'

'Like nothing.'

'I'll recognize it,' Jack said. 'I know what that looks like.'

'Say a prayer,' I suggested.

'I did.'

'Say another.'

'I knew a guy once had trouble cheating because his wife was always praying for him.'

'Try to be serious. It's your last chance.'

Jack concentrated, whispered, 'Dear God, turn me onto the Great White Way.' He felt the onset of clammy coldness then, as if this body were fully immersed in water. He remembered Rothstein's prayer and said that too, 'O Lord, God of Abraham, keep me alive and smart. The rest I'll figure out for myself.'

'Perfect,' said A. R.

'Dummy,' I said, 'you're dead. What kind of a thing is it, asking to stay alive?'

I eased the pressure on Jack's arteries and pressed his nerve of eternal sleep. Then I knelt beside him, seeing the water of his life sinking into fire, waiting for his final exit from that useless body. But if Jack left his body through the ear instead of the top of the head where Rothstein had pulled out the hairs, he might come back in the next life as a fairy musician.

'Jesus,' Jack said when I told him, 'imagine that?'

'Easy, now,' I said, 'easy. Out through the top.'

Then he was out, just fine, standing in front of the mirror, seeing no more blood, no more yellow.

'Am I completely dead?' he asked, and knew then his last human feeling: his body being blown to atoms, the feeling of fire sinking into air. He looked around the room, but could see no one any longer, though we were all there, watching. He felt his absent pupils dilate to receive the light, which was his own light as well as everyone else's. When the light came, it was not the brilliant whiteness Jack expected, but a yellowish, grayish light that made no one blink. The motion of the light was perceptible. It swirled around Jack's neck like a muffler, rose up past his eyes and hairline like a tornado in crescendo, spun round his entire head with what was obviously a potentially dazzling ferocity, reduced in effect now by the horrendous life-tone of Jack Diamond. It was obvious to everyone that given propitious conditions it could centripetally slurp the entire spirit of Jack into the vortex and make off with it forever; but now it moved only like a bit of fog on a sunny morning, coiled by a frolicsome breeze, then gone, with not enough force to slurp up a toupee.

As Jack's awareness of the light peaked, he was already falling backward. Though he had no arms, he waved them frantically to right himself, and as he fell, twisting and flailing against this ignominious new development, he delivered up one, final, well-modulated sentence before he disappeared into the void, into the darkness where the white was still elusive.

'Honest to God, Marcus,' he said going away, 'I really don't think I'm dead.'